D1337752

'Oddball characters, quirky dialogue and nimble plotting. Wambaugh is
still the best in the business'
Kathy Reichs

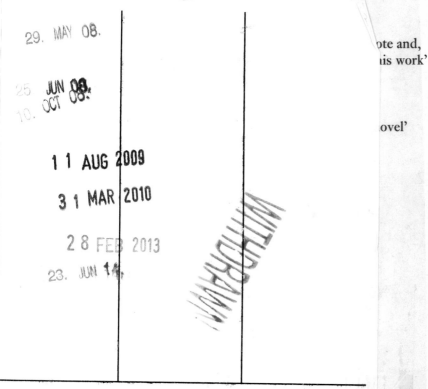

29. MAY 08.

25 JUN 08.

10. OCT 08.

1 1 AUG 2009

3 1 MAR 2010

2 8 FEB 2013

23. JUN 14.

ote and,
is work'

ovel'

WITHDRAWN

ALSO BY JOSEPH WAMBAUGH

FICTION

The Choirboys
The Black Marble
The Glitter Dome
The Delta Star
The Secrets of Harry Bright
The Golden Orange
Fugitive Nights
Finnegan's Week
Floaters

NONFICTION

The Onion Field
Lines and Shadows
Echoes in the Darkness
The Blooding
Fire Lover

THE JOSEPH WAMBAUGH OMNIBUS

HOLLYWOOD STATION
THE NEW CENTURIONS
THE BLUE KNIGHT

Quercus

First published in Great Britain in 2008 by
Quercus
21 Bloomsbury Square
London
WC1A 2NS

A CIP catalogue reference for this book is available
from the British Library

ISBN 978 1 84724 122 1

10 9 8 7 6 5 4 3 2 1

Typeset by Deltatype Ltd, Birkenhead, Merseyside
Printed and bound in Great Britain by Clays Ltd, St Ives plc.

CONTENTS

HOLLYWOOD STATION

Special thanks for the terrific anecdotes and wonderful cop talk goes to officers of the Los Angeles Police Department: Chate Asvanonda, Matt Bennyworth, Michael Berchem, Wendi Berndt, Vicki Bynum, Laura Evens, Heather Gahry, Brett Goodkin, Chuck Henry, Craig Herron, Jack Herron (ret.), Brian Hospodar, Andy Hudlett, Jeff Injalls, Rick Jackson, Dennis Kilcoyne, Al Lopez, Tim Marcia, Kathy McAnany, Roger Murphy, Bill Pack, Mike Porter, Rosie Redshaw, Tom Redshaw, Dave Sigler, Bill Sollie, Olivia Spindola, Joe Witty.

And to officers of the San Diego Police Department: Mark Amancio, Pete Amancio, Andra Brown, Brett Burkett, Laurie Cairncross, Blaine Ferguson, Pete Griffin (ret.), Mike Gutierrez, Gerry Kramer, Vanessa Holland, Charles Lara, Vic Morel, Tony Puente (ret.), Andy Rios, Steve Robinson, Steve Sloan, Elliott Stiasny, Alex Sviridov, Don Watkins, Joe Winney.

And to officers of the Palm Springs Police Department: Dave Costello, Don Dougherty, Steve Douglas, Mitch Spike.

And to special agents of the Federal Bureau of Investigation: Matt Desarno, Jack Kelly (ret.).

And to author James Ellroy for urging this return to LAPD roots.

ONE

'Wanna play pit bull polo, dude?'

'What's that?'

'It's something I learned when I worked Metro Mounted Platoon.'

'It's weird thinking of you as a cowboy cop.'

'All I know about horses is they're assholes, man. But we got the over-time there. You know my little Beemer? I wouldn't have that if I hadn't worked Metro. My last year in Metro I made a hundred grand plus. I don't miss those crazy horses but I miss that OT money. And I miss wearing a Stetson. When we worked the mini-riot at the Democrats convention, a hot little lobbyist with nipples big enough to pack up and leave home said I looked like a young Clint Eastwood in that Stetson. And I didn't carry a Beretta nine then. I carried a six-inch Colt revolver. It looked more appropriate when I was sitting on a horse.'

'A wheel gun? In this day and age?'

'The Oracle still carries a wheel gun.'

'The Oracle's been on the job nearly fifty years. He can wear a codpiece if he wants to. And you don't look like Clint Eastwood, bro. You look like the guy in *King Kong*, except you got even more of a beak and your hair is bleached.'

'My hair is sun-streaked from surfing, dude. And I'm even two inches taller in the saddle than Clint was.'

'Whatever, bro. I'm a whole foot taller on the ground than Tom Cruise. He's about four foot ten.'

'Anyways, those pacifist demonstrators at the convention center were throwing golf balls and ball bearings at our horses, when twenty of us charged. And dude, when you get stepped on by a fifteen-hundred-pound animal, it sucks *bad*. Only one horse went down. He was twenty-eight years old, name of Rufus. That fried him. Had to retire him after that. One of those Jamba Juicers threw a lit trash bag at the one I was riding, name of Big Sam. I beat that bitch with my koa.'

'Your what?'

'It's like a samurai sword made of koa wood. The baton's about as useless

5

as a stalk of celery when you're up there on a horse seventeen hands high. Supposed to strike them in the clavicle, but guess what, she juked and I got her upside the head. Accidentally, wink wink. She did a loop de loop and ended up under a parked car. I saw a horse get stuck with a knitting needle by one of those tree fuckers. The horse was fried after that. Too much stress. They retired him to Horse Rescue. They all get fried sooner or later. Just like us.'

'That sucks. Sticking a horse.'

'That one got a TV interview at least. When cops get hurt, nothing. Who gives a fuck? When a horse gets hurt, you get on TV, maybe with that Debbie D-cup news bunny on channel five.'

'Where'd you learn to ride?'

'Griffith Park. A five-week course at the Ahmanson Training Center. Only horse I ever rode before that was on a merry-go-round, and I don't care if I ever ride another one. Got the job 'cause my sister-in-law went to high school with the platoon lieutenant. Horses're assholes, man. An RTD bus can pass you three inches away at sixty miles an hour and the horse doesn't blink. A little piece of paper blows in his face all of a sudden and he bucks you clear over a pile of tweakers and base heads sleeping on a skid-row sidewalk at Sixth and San Pedro. And you end up in Momma Lucy's shopping cart with her aluminum cans and refundable bottles. That's how I got a hip replacement at the age of thirty. Only thing I wanna ride now is a surfboard and my Beemer.'

'I'm thirty-one. You look a lot older than me.'

'Well I ain't. I just had a lot to worry about. They gave me a doctor that was so old he still believed in bleeding and leeches.'

'Whatever, bro. You might have progeria. Gives you those eyelid and neck wrinkles, like a Galapagos turtle.'

'So you wanna play pit bull polo or not?'

'What the fuck is pit bull polo?'

'Way I learned, they trailered ten of us down to Seventy-seventh Street on a night when they decided to sweep a three-block row of crack houses and gangsta cribs. Whole fucking area is a crime scene. Living next to that is what razor wire was made for. Anyways, all those Bloods and Crips have pit bulls and rotties and they let them run loose half the time, terrorizing the hood and eating any normal dogs they see. And the whole fucking pack of gangsta dogs flew into a blood lust the second they saw us coming in and they attacked like we were riding T-bones and ribeyes.'

'How many did you shoot?'

'Shoot? I need this job. You gotta be richer than Donald Trump and Manny the plumber to fire your piece in today's LAPD, especially at a dog. You shoot a human person and you get maybe two detectives and a team from Force Investigation Division to second-guess you. You shoot a dog and you get three supervisors and four detectives plus FID, all ready to string yellow tape. Especially in the 'hood. We didn't shoot them, we played pit bull polo with the long sticks.'

'Oh, I get it. Pit bull polo.'

'Man, I rode through them, whacking those killer bulls, yelling, "One chukker for my team! Two chukkers for my team!" I only wish I coulda whacked their owners.'

'Bro, a chukker is a period of play. I know 'cause I watched a special on the Royal Family. Horny old Charles was playing a chukker or two for Camilla with big wood in his jodhpurs. That old babe? I don't see it.'

'Whatever. You down with that or not?'

'Yeah, I'm down. But first I wanna know, did anyone beef you for playing polo with the gangsta bulls?'

'Oh yeah, there's always an ABM who'll call IA, his councilman, and maybe long distance to Al Sharpton, who never saw a camera he didn't hug.'

'ABM?'

'You ain't a 'hood rat, are ya? ABM. Angry black male.'

'Spent my nine years in Devonshire, West Valley, and West LA before I transferred here last month. ABMs ain't never been filed on my desk top, bro.'

'Then don't go to a police commission or council meeting. ABMs are in charge. But we don't have hardly any living in Hollywood. In fact, nowadays most of south LA is Latino, even Watts.'

'I been reading that the entire inner city is mostly Latino.'

'Where the fuck have the brothers gone to? I wonder. And why is everybody worrying about the black vote if they're all moving to the suburbs? They better worry about the Latino vote, because they got the mayor's office now and they're about one generation away from reclaiming California and making us do the gardening.'

'You married? And which number is it?'

'Just escaped from number two. She was Druid-like but not as cuddly. One daughter three years old. Lives with Momma, whose lawyer won't be satisfied till I'm homeless on the beach eating seaweed.'

'Is number one still at large?'

'Yeah, but I don't have to pay her nothing. She took my car, though. You?'

'Divorced also. Once. No kids. Met my ex in a cop bar in North Hollywood called The Director's Chair. She wore a felonious amount of pancake. Looked too slutty for the Mustang Ranch and still I married her. Musta been her J Lo booty.'

'Starter marriages never work for cops. You don't have to count the first one, bro. So how do we play pit bull polo without horses? And where do we play?'

'I know just the place. Get the expandable baton outta my war bag.'

7

*

The Salvadoran gang *Mara Salvatrucha*, aka MS-13, began at Los Angeles High School less than twenty years earlier but was now said to have ten thousand members throughout the United States and seven hundred thousand in Central American countries. Many residents of state prison displayed tattoos saying 'MS' or 'MS-13.' It was an MS-13 crew member who was stopped on a street in North Hollywood in 1991 by Officer Tina Kerbrat, a rookie just months out of the LAPD academy, who was in the process of writing him a citation for drinking in public, nothing more than that, when the MS-13 'cruiser' shot her dead. The first LAPD woman officer to be murdered in the line of duty.

Later that evening a besieged Mexican resident living east of Gower Street called Hollywood Station to say that she saw an LAPD black-and-white with lights out driving loops around a dirty pink apartment building that she had reported to the police on several occasions as being full of *Mara Salvatrucha* gang members.

On the other occasions, the officers at the desk kept trying to explain to the Mexican woman about gang injunctions and probable cause, things she did not understand and that did not exist in her country. Things that apparently denied protection to people like her and her children from the criminals in that ugly pink building. She told the officer about how their vicious dogs had mauled and killed a collie belonging to her neighbor Irene, and how all the children were unable to walk safely in the streets. She also said that two of the dogs had been removed by people from the city pound but there were still enough left. More than enough.

The officers told her they were very sorry and that she should contact the Department of Animal Services.

The Mexican woman had been watching a Spanish-language chan-nel and was almost ready for bed when she first heard the howling that drew her to the window. There she saw the police car with lights out, speeding down the alley next to the apartment building, being pursued by four or five barking dogs. On its second pass down the alley, she saw the driver lean out the window and swing something that looked like a snooker stick at one of the brutes, sending it yelping and running back into the pink building. Then the car made another loop and did it to another big dog, and the driver yelled something that her daughter heard from the porch.

Her daughter stumbled sleepily into the tiny living room and said in English, 'Mamá, does chukker mean something very bad, like the F word?'

The Mexican woman called Hollywood Station and spoke to a very senior sergeant whom all the cops called the Oracle. She wanted to say thank you for sending the officers with the snooker stick. She was hope-ful that things might improve around the neighborhood. The Oracle was puzzled but thought it best not to question her further. He simply said that he was glad to be of service.

When 6–X–32's lights were back on and they were cruising Hollywood Boulevard, the driver said, 'Dude, right there's where my career with the Mounted Platoon ended. That's where I decided that overtime pay or not, I was going back to normal patrol.'

His partner looked to his right and said, 'At Grauman's Chinese Theater?'

'Right there in the courtyard. That's where I learned that you never ride a horse on the Hollywood Walk of Fame.'

'Bad juju?'

'Bad footing.'

Sid Grauman's famous theater seemed somehow forlorn these days, dwarfed and sandwiched by the Hollywood & Highland Center, better known as the Kodak Center, containing two blocks of shopping and entertainment. It was home to the Kodak Theatre and the Academy Awards and was overrun by tourists day and night. But the Chinese Theater still held its own when it came to Hollywood weirdness. Even this late, there were a number of costumed creatures posing for photos with tourists who were mainly photographing the shoe- and handprints in the famous forecourt. Among the creatures were Mr. Incredible, Elmo, two Darth Vaders, Batman, and two Goofys, one short, one tall.

'They pose with tourists. Pix for bucks,' the driver said to his partner. 'The tourists think the creatures work for Grauman's, but they don't. Most of them're crackheads and tweakers. Watch little Goofy.'

He braked, making the nighttime traffic go around their black-and-white. They watched the shorter of the two Goofys hassling four Asian tourists who no doubt had refused to pay him for taking his photo or hadn't paid enough. When Goofy grabbed one of the two Asian men by the arm, the cop tooted his horn. When Goofy looked up and saw the black-and-white, he gave up panhandling for the moment and tried to disappear into the throng, even though his huge Goofy head loomed over all but the tallest tourist.

The driver said, 'The subway back there is a good escape route to the 'hood. Dealers hang out by the trains, and the hooks hang around the boulevard.'

'What's a hook?'

'A guy that approaches you and says, "I can hook you up with what you need." These days it's almost always crystal. Everybody's tweaking. Meth is the drug of choice on the Hollywood streets, absolutely.'

And that made him think of his last night at Metro, which was followed by the replacement surgery and a right hip more accurate than a barometer when it came to predicting sudden temperature drops and wind-chill factor.

On that last night in the Mounted Platoon, he and another mounted cop were there for crowd suppression, walking their horses along Hollywood Boulevard all calm and okey-dokey, along the curb past the Friday-night mobs by the subway station, moseying west, when he spotted a hook looking very nervously in their direction.

He'd said to his partner, who was riding a mare named Millie, 'Let's jam this guy.'

He dismounted and dropped his get-down rope. His partner held both horses and he approached the hook on foot. The hook was a sweaty, scrawny white guy, very tall, maybe even taller than he was, though his LAPD Stetson and cowboy boots made him tower. That's when it all went bad.

'I was talking to a hook right about there,' he said to his partner now, pointing to the sidewalk in front of the Kodak Center. 'And the dude just turned and rabbitted. Zip. Like that. And I started after him, but Major freaked.'

'Your partner?'

'My horse. He was fearless, Major was. Dude, I'd seen him chill in training when we were throwing firecrackers and flares at him. I'd seen other horses rear up on their hind legs and do a one-eighty while Major stood his ground. But not that night. That's the thing about horses, they're assholes, man.'

'What'd he do?'

'First, Major reared clear up tall and crazy. Then he bit my partner on the arm. It was like somebody cranked up his voltage. Maybe a tweaker shot him with a BB gun, I don't know. Anyways, I stopped chasing the hook, fuck him, and ran back to help my partner. But Major wouldn't calm down until I made like I was going to climb in the saddle. Then I did something very stupid.'

'What's that?'

'I climbed in the saddle, intending to ride him back to the trailer and call it a night. I did that instead of leading him back, which anybody without brain bubbles woulda done under the circumstances.'

'So?'

'He freaked again. He took off. Up onto the sidewalk.'

The moment would be with him forever. Galloping along the Walk of Fame, kicking up sparks and scattering tourists and panhandlers and purse snatchers and tweakers and pregnant women and costumed nuns and SpongeBob and three Elvises. Clomping over top of Marilyn Monroe's star or James Cagney's or Elizabeth Taylor's or fucking Liberace's or whoever was there on this block of the Walk of Fame because he didn't know who was there and never checked later to find out.

Cursing the big horse and hanging on with one hand and waving the creepy multitudes out of his way with the other. Even though he knew that Major could, and had, run up a flight of concrete steps in his long career, he also knew that neither Major nor any horse belonging to the Mounted Platoon could run on marble, let alone on brass inserts on that marble sidewalk where people spilled their Starbucks and Slurpees with impunity. No horse could trample Hollywood legends like that, so maybe it *was* the bad juju. And very suddenly Major hydroplaned in the Slurpees and just … went … *down*.

His partner interrupted the sweat-popping flashback. 'So what happened, bro? After he took off with you?'

'First of all, nobody got hurt. Except Major and me.'

'Bad?'

'They say I ended up in John Wayne's boot prints right there in Grauman's forecourt. They say the Duke's fist print is there too. I don't remember boots or fists or nothing. I woke up on a gurney in an RA with a paramedic telling me yes I was alive, while we were screaming code three to Hollywood Pres. I had a concussion and three cracked ribs and my bad hip, which was later replaced, and everybody said I was real lucky.'

'How about the nag?'

'They told me Major seemed okay at first. He was limping, of course. But after they trailered him back to Griffith Park and called the vet, he could hardly stand. He was in bad shape and got worse. They had to put him down that night.' And then he added, 'Horses are *such* assholes, man.'

When his partner looked at the driver, he thought he saw his eyes glisten in the mix of light from the boulevard – fluorescence and neon, headlights and taillights, even reflected glow from a floodlight shooting skyward – announcing to all: This is Hollywood! But all that light spilling onto them changed the crispness of their black-and white to a wash of bruised purple and sickly yellow. His partner wasn't sure, but he thought the driver's chin quivered, so he pretended to be seriously studying the costumed freaks in front of Grauman's Chinese Theater.

After a moment the driver said, 'So anyways, I said fuck it. When I healed up I put in for Hollywood Division because from what I'd seen of it from the saddle it seemed like a pretty good place to work, long as you got a few hundred horses under you instead of one. And here I am.'

His partner didn't say anything for a while. Then he said, 'I used to surf a lot when I worked West LA. Lived with my leash attached to a squealy. I had surf bumps all over my knees, bro. Getting too old for that. Thinking about getting me a log and just going out and catching the evening glass.'

'Awesome, dude. Evening glass is way cool. Me, after I transferred to Hollywood I sorta became a rev-head, cruising in my Beemer up to Santa Barbara, down to San Diego, revving that ultimate driving machine. But I got to missing being in the green room, you know? In that tube with the foam breaking over you? Now I go out most every morning I'm off duty. Malibu attracts bunnies. Come along sometime and I'll lend you a log. Maybe you'll have a vision.'

'Maybe I'll get a brain wave out there on evening glass. I need one to figure out how to keep my second ex-wife from making me live under a tree eating eucalyptus like a fucking koala.'

'Of course you're gonna get a surf jacket soon as these hodads around Hollywood Station find out. Everybody calls me Flotsam. So if you surf with me, you *know* they're gonna call you ...'

'Jetsam,' his partner said with a sigh of resignation.

'Dude, this could be the beginning of a choiceamundo friendship.'

'Jetsam? Bro, that is wack, way wack.'

'What's in a name?'

'Whatever. So what happened to the Stetson after you played lawn dart in Grauman's courtyard?'

'No lawn in that courtyard. All concrete. I figure a tweaker picked it up. Probably sold it for a few teeners of crystal. I keep hoping to someday find that crankster. Just to see how fast I can make his body heat drop from ninety-eight point six to room temperature.'

As they were talking, 6-X-32 got a beep on the MDT computer. Jetsam opened and acknowledged the message, then hit the en route key and they were on their way to an address on Cherokee Avenue that appeared on the dashboard screen along with 'See the woman, 415 music.'

'Four-fifteen music,' Flotsam muttered. 'Why the hell can't the woman just go to her neighbor and tell them to turn down the goddamn CD? Probably some juice-head fell asleep to Destiny's Child.'

'Maybe Black Eyed Peas,' Jetsam said. 'Or maybe Fifty Cent. Crank up the decibels on that dude and you provoke homicidal urges. Heard his album called *The Massacre*?'

It wasn't easy to find a parking place near the half block of apartment buildings, causing 6-X-32 to make several moves before the patrol car was able to squeeze in parallel between a late-model Lexus and a twelve-year-old Nova that was parked far enough from the curb to be ticketed.

Jetsam hit the at-scene button on the keyboard, and they grabbed their flashlights and got out, with Flotsam grumbling, 'In all of Hollywood tonight there's probably about thirteen and a half fucking parking places.'

'Thirteen now,' Jetsam said. 'We got the half.' He paused on the sidewalk in front and said, 'Jesus, I can hear it from here and it ain't hip-hop.'

It was the *Schreckensfanfare*, the 'Fanfare of Terror,' from Beethoven's Ninth.

A dissonant shriek of strings and a discordant blast from brass and wood-winds directed them up the outside staircase of a modest but respectable two-story apartment building. Many of the tenants seemed to be out this Friday evening. Porch lights and security lights were on inside some of the units, but it was altogether very quiet except for that music attacking their ears, assaulting their hearing. Those harrowing passages that Beethoven intended as an introduction to induce foreboding did the job on 6-X-32.

They didn't bother to seek out the complainant. They knocked at the apartment from which that music emanated like a scream, like a warning.

'Somebody might be drunk in there,' Jetsam said.

'Or dead,' Flotsam said, half joking.

No answer. They tried again, banging louder. No answer.

Flotsam turned the knob, and the door popped open as the hammering timpani served the master composer by intensifying those fearful sounds. It was dark except for light coming from a room off the hallway.

'Anybody home?' Flotsam called.

No answer. Just the timpani and that sound of brass shrieking at them.

Jetsam stepped inside first. 'Anybody home?'

No answer. Flotsam reflexively drew his nine, held it down beside his right leg and flashed his light around the room.

'The music's coming from back there.' Jetsam pointed down the dark hallway.

'Maybe somebody had a heart attack. Or a stroke,' Flotsam said.

They started walking slowly down the long, narrow hallway toward the light, toward the sound, the timpani beating a tattoo. 'Hey!' Flotsam yelled. 'Anybody here?'

'This is bad juju,' Jetsam said.

'Anybody home?' Flotsam listened for a response, but there was only that crazy fucking music!

The first room off the hall was the bedroom. Jetsam switched on the light. The bed was made. A woman's pink bathrobe and pajamas were lying across the bed. Pink slippers sat on the floor below. The sound system was not elaborate, but it wasn't cheap either. Several classical CDs were scattered on a bookcase shelf beside the speakers. This person lived in her bedroom, it seemed.

Jetsam touched the power button and shut off that raging sound. Both he and his partner drew a breath of relief as though bobbing to the surface from deep water. There was another room at the far end of the hallway, but it was dark. The only other light came from a bathroom that served this two-bedroom unit.

Flotsam stepped to the bathroom doorway first and found her. She was naked, half in half out of the bathtub, long pale legs hanging over the side of the tub. She had no doubt been a pretty girl in life, but now she was staring, eyes open in slits, lips drawn back in that familiar snarl of violent death he'd seen on others: Don't take me away! I'll fight to stay here! Alive! I want to stay alive!

Jetsam drew his rover, keyed it, and prepared to make the call. His partner stayed and stared at the corpse of the young woman. For a few seconds Flotsam had the panicky idea that she might still be alive, that maybe a rescue ambulance would have a chance. Then he moved one step closer to the tub and peeked behind the shower curtain.

There were arterial spurts all over the blue tile of the wall even to the ceiling. The floor of the tub was a blackening vat of viscosity and from here he could see at least three chest wounds and a gaping gash across her throat. At that second but not before, the acrid smell of blood and urine almost overwhelmed him, and he stepped out into the hallway to await the detectives from Hollywood Station and from Scientific Investigation Division.

The second bedroom, apparently belonging to a male roommate, was tidy and unoccupied at the moment, or so they thought. Jetsam had shined his light in there in a cursory check while talking on the rover, and Flotsam had glanced in, but neither had bothered to enter the bedroom and look inside the small closet, its door ajar.

While the two cops were back in the living room making a few notes, careful not to disturb anything, even turning on the wall switch with a pencil, a young man entered from the darkened hallway behind them.

His voice was a piercing rasp. He said, 'I love her.'

Flotsam dropped his notebook, Jetsam the rover. Both cops wheeled and drew their nines.

'Freeze, motherfucker!' Flotsam screamed.

'Freeze!' Jetsam added redundantly.

He was frozen already. As pale and naked as the young woman he'd murdered, the young man stood motionless, palms up, freshly slashed wrists extended like an offering. Of what? Contrition? The gaping wrists were spurting, splashing fountains onto the carpet and onto his bare feet.

'Jesus Christ!' Flotsam screamed.

'Jesus!' Jetsam screamed redundantly.

Then both cops holstered their pistols, but when they lunged toward him the young man turned and ran to the bathroom, leaping into the tub with the woman he loved. And the cops gaped in horror as he curled himself fetally and moaned into her unhearing ear.

Flotsam got one latex glove onto his hand but dropped the other glove. Jetsam yelled into the rover for paramedics and dropped both latex gloves. Then they jumped onto him and tried to drag him up, but all the blood made his thin arms slip through their hands, and both cops cursed and swore while the young man moaned. Twice, three times he pulled free and plopped onto the bloody corpse with a splat.

Jetsam got his handcuff around one wrist, but when he cinched it tight the bracelet sunk into the gaping flesh and he saw a tendon flail around the ratchet and he yelled, 'Son of a bitch! Son of a bitch!' And he felt ice from his tailbone to his brain stem and for a second he felt like bolting.

Flotsam was bigger and stronger than Jetsam, and he muscled the rigid left arm out from under the chest of the moaning young man and forced it up behind his back and got the dangling bracelet around the wrist. And then he got to see it sink into the red maw of tendon and tissue and he almost puked.

They each got him by a handcuffed arm and they lifted him but now all three were dripping and slimy from his spurting blood and her thickening blood and they dropped him, his head hitting the side of the tub. But he was past pain and only moaned more softly. They lifted again and got him out of the tub and dragged him out into the hallway, where Flotsam slipped and fell down, the bleeding man on top of him still moaning.

A neighbor on her balcony screamed when the two panting cops dragged the young man down the outside stairway, his naked bloodslimed body bumping against the plastered steps in a muted plop that made the woman scream louder. The three young men fell in a pile onto the sidewalk under a street lamp, and Flotsam got up and began ransacking the car trunk for the first-aid kit, not knowing for sure what the hell was in it but pretty sure there was no tourniquet. Jetsam knelt by the bleeding man, jerked his Sam Browne free, and was trying to tie off one arm with an improvised tourniquet made from his trouser belt when the rescue ambulance came squealing around the corner onto Cherokee, lights flashing and siren yelping.

The first patrol unit to arrive belonged to the sergeant known as the Oracle, who double-parked half a block away, leaving the immediate area to RA paramedics, Hollywood detectives, evidence collectors from Scientific Investigation Division, and the coroner's team. There was no mistaking the very old patrol sergeant, even in the darkness. As his burly figure approached, they could see those pale service stripes on his left sleeve, rising almost to his elbow. Forty-six years on the Job rated nine hash marks and made him one of the longest-serving cops on the entire police department.

'The Oracle has more hash marks than a football field,' everybody said.

But the Oracle always said, 'I'm only staying because the divorce settlement gives my ex half my pension. I'll be on the Job till that bitch dies or I do, whichever comes first.'

The bleeding man was unmoving and going gray when he was blanketed and belted to the gurney and lifted into the rescue ambulance, both paramedics working to stem the now oozing blood but shaking their heads at the Oracle, indicating that the young man had probably bled out and was beyond saving.

Even though a Santa Ana wind had blown into Los Angeles from the desert on this May evening, both Flotsam and Jetsam were shivering and wearily gathering their equipment which was scattered on the sidewalk next to a concrete planter containing some hopeful pansies and forget-me-nots.

The Oracle looked at the blood-drenched cops and said, 'Are you hurt? Any injuries at all?'

Flotsam shook his head and said, 'Boss, I think we just had a tactical situation they never covered in any class I've taken at the academy. Or if they did, I fucking missed it.'

'Get yourselves to Cedars for medical treatment whether you need it or not,' the Oracle said. 'Then clean up real good. Might as well burn those uniforms from the looks of them.'

'If that guy has hepatitis, we're in trouble, Sarge,' Jetsam said.

'If that guy has AIDS, we're dead,' Flotsam said.

'This doesn't look like that kind of situation,' the Oracle said, his retro gray crewcut seeming to sparkle under the streetlight. Then he noticed Jetsam's handcuffs lying on the sidewalk. He flashed his beam on the cuffs and said to the exhausted cop, 'Drop those cuffs in some bleach, son. I can see chunks of meat jammed in the ratchets.'

'I need to go surfing,' Jetsam said.

'Me too,' Flotsam said.

The Oracle had acquired his sobriquet by virtue of seniority and his penchant for dispensing words of wisdom, but not on this night. He just looked at his bloody, hollow-eyed, shivering young cops and said, 'Now, you boys get right to Cedars ER and let a doc have a look at you.'

It was then that D2 Charlie Gilford arrived on the scene, a gumchewing, lazy night-watch detective with a penchant for bad neckties who was not a case-carrying investigator, his job being only to assist. But with more than twenty years at Hollywood Station, he didn't like to miss anything sensational that was going down and loved to offer pithy commentary on whatever had transpired. For his assessments they called him Compassionate Charlie.

During that evening's events on Cherokee Avenue, after he'd received a quick summary from the Oracle and called a homicide team from home, he took a look at the gruesome scene of murder and suicide, and at the bloody trail marking the grisly struggle that failed to save the killer's life.

Then Compassionate Charlie sucked his teeth for a second or two and said to the Oracle, 'I can't understand young coppers anymore. Why would they put themselves through something like that for a selfsolver? Shoulda just let the guy jump in the tub with her and bleed out the way he wanted to. They coulda sat there listening to music till it was over. All we got here is just another Hollywood love story that went a little bit sideways.'

TWO

It had always seemed to Farley Ramsdale that the blue mailboxes, even the ones on some of the seedier corners of Hollywood, were much more treasure-laden and easier to work than the resident boxes by most of the upmarket condos and apartments. And he especially liked the ones outside the post office because they got really full between closing time and 10 p.m., the hour he found most propitious. People felt so confident about a post office location that they dropped a bonanza in them, sometimes even cash.

The hour of 10 p.m. was midday for Farley, who'd been named by a mother who just loved actor Farley Granger, the old Hitchcock thriller *Strangers on a Train* being one of her favorites. In that movie Farley Granger is a professional tennis player, and even though Farley Ramsdale's mother had signed him up for private lessons when he was in middle school, tennis had bored him silly. It was a drag. School was a drag. Work was a drag. Crystal meth was definitely not a drag.

At the age of seventeen years and two months, Farley Ramsdale had gone from being a beads 'n' seeds pot head to a tweaker. The first time he smoked crystal he fell in love, everlasting love. But even though it was far cheaper than cocaine, it still cost enough to keep Farley hopping well into the night, visiting blue mailboxes on the streets of Hollywood.

The first thing Farley had to do that afternoon was pay a visit to a hardware store and buy some more mousetraps. Not that Farley worried about mice – they were scampering around his rooming house most of the time. Well, it wasn't a rooming house exactly, he'd be the first to admit. It was an old white-stucco bungalow just off Gower Street, the family home deeded to him by his mother before her death fifteen years ago, when Farley was an eighteen-year-old at Hollywood High School discovering the joys of meth.

He'd managed to forge and cash her pension checks for ten months after her death before a county social worker caught up with him, the meddling bitch. Because he was still a teenager and an orphan, he easily plea-bargained down to a probationary sentence with a promise to pay restitution, which he never paid, and he began calling the two-bedroom, one-bath bungalow a rooming house when he started renting space to other tweakers who came and went, usually within a few weeks.

No, he didn't give a shit about mice. Farley needed ice. Nice clear, icy-looking crystal from Hawaii, not the dirty white crap they sold around town. Ice, not mice, that's what he worried about during every waking hour.

While browsing through the hardware store, Farley saw a red-vested employee watching him when he passed the counter where the drill bits, knives, and smaller items were on display. As if he was going to shoplift the shitty merchandise in this place. When he passed a bathroom display and saw his reflection in the mirror, now in the merciless light of afternoon, it startled him. The speed bumps on his face were swollen and angry, a tell-tale sign of a speed freak, as his kind used to be known. Like all tweakers he craved candy and sweets. His teeth were getting dark and two molars were hurting. And his hair! He had forgotten to comb his fucking hair and it was a whirling tangle with that burnt-straw look, hinting at incipient malnutrition, marking him even more as a longtime crystal-smoking tweaker.

He turned toward the employee, an East Asian guy younger than Farley and fit-looking. Probably a fucking martial arts expert, he thought. The way Korea Town was growing, and with a Thai restaurant on every god-damn street and Filipinos emptying bedpans in the free clinics, pretty soon all those canine-eating, dog-breath motherfuckers would be running City Hall too.

But come to think of it, that might be an improvement over the chili-dipping Mexican asshole who was now the mayor, convincing Farley that LA would soon be ninety percent Mexican instead of nearly half. So why not give the slopes and greasers knives and guns and let them waste each other? That's what Farley thought should happen. And if the south end niggers ever started moving to Hollywood, he was selling the house and relocating to the high desert, where there were so many meth labs he didn't think the cops could possibly hassle him very much.

Since he couldn't shake that slit-eyed asshole watching him, Farley decided to stop browsing and headed for the shelf containing the mouse-traps and rat poison, whereupon the Asian employee walked up to him and said, 'Can I help you, sir?'

Farley said, 'Do I look like I need help?'

The Asian looked him over, at his Eminem T-shirt and oily jeans, and said in slightly accented English, 'If you have rats, the springloaded rat traps are what you want. Those glue traps are excellent for mice, but some larger rodents can pull free of the glue pads.'

'Yeah, well, I don't have rats in my house,' Farley said. 'Do you? Or does somebody eat them along with any stray terriers that wander in the yard?'

The unsmiling Asian employee took a deliberate step toward Farley, who yelped, 'Touch me and I'll sue you and this whole fucking hardware chain!' before turning and scuttling away to the shelf display of cleaning solutions, where he grabbed five cans of Easy-Off.

When he got to the checkout counter, he grumbled to a frightened teenage cashier that there weren't enough English-speaking Americans left in all of LA to gang-fuck Courtney Love so that she'd even notice it.

Farley left the store and had to walk back to the house, since his piece-of-shit white Corolla had a flat tire and he needed some quick cash to replace it. When he got to the house, he unlocked the dead bolt on the front door and entered, hoping that his one nonpaying tenant was not at home. She was a shockingly thin woman several years older than Farley, although it was hard to tell, with oily black hair plastered to her scalp and tied in a knot at the nape of her neck. She was a penniless, homeless tweaker whom Farley had christened Olive Oyl after the character in *Popeye*.

He dumped his purchases on the rusty chrome kitchen table, wanting to catch an hour of shut-eye, knowing that an hour was about all he could hope for before his eyes snapped open. Like all tweakers, he was sometimes awake for days, and he'd tinker with that banged-up Jap car or maybe play video games until he crashed right there in the living room, his hand still on the controls that allowed him to shoot down a dozen video cops who were trying to stop his video surrogate from stealing a video Mercedes.

No such luck. Just as he fell across the unmade bed, he heard Olive Oyl clumping into the house from the back door. Jesus, she walked heavy for a stick of a woman. *River Dance* was quieter. He wondered if she had Hep C by now. Or Christ! Maybe AIDS? He'd never shared a needle on the rare occasions when he'd skin-popped ice, but she'd probably done it. He vowed to quit boning her and only let her blow him when he was totally desperate.

Then he heard that tremulous little voice. 'Farley, you home?'

'I'm home,' he said. 'And I need to catch some z's, Olive. Take a walk for a while, okay?'

'We working tonight, Farley?' She entered the bedroom.

'Yeah,' he said.

'Want a knobber?' she asked. 'Help you to sleep.'

Jesus, her speed bumps were worse than his. They looked like she scratched them with a garden tool. And her grille showed three gaps in front. When the hell had she lost the third tooth? How come he hadn't noticed before? Now she was skinnier than Mick Jagger and sort of looked like him except older.

'No, I don't want a knobber,' he said. 'Just go play video games or something.'

'I think I got a shot at some extra work, Farley,' she said. 'I met this guy at Pablo's Tacos. He does casting for extras. He said he was looking for someone my type. He gave me his card and said to call next Monday. Isn't that cool?'

'That's so chill, Olive,' he said. 'What is it, *Night of the Living Dead, Part Two?*'

Unfazed, Olive said, 'Awesome, ain't it? Me, in a movie? Of course it might just be a TV show or something.'

'Totally awesome,' he said, closing his eyes, trying to unwire his circuits.

'Of course he might just be some Hollywood Casanova wanting in my pants,' Olive said with a gap-toothed grin.

'You're perfectly safe with Hollywood Casanovas,' Farley mumbled. 'You got nothing to spank. Now get the fuck outta here.'

When she was gone he actually succeeded in falling asleep, and he dreamed of basketball games in the gym at Hollywood High School and boning that cheerleader who had always dissed and avoided him.

Trombone Teddy had a decent day panhandling on Hollywood Boulevard that afternoon. Nothing like the old days, when he still had a horn, when he'd stand out there on the boulevard and play cool licks like Kai Winding and J.J. Johnson, jamming as good as any of the black jazzmen he'd played with in the nightclub down on Washington and La Brea forty years ago, when cool jazz was king.

In those days the black audiences were always the best and treated him like he was one of them. And in fact he had gotten his share of chocolate cooz in those days, before pot and bennies and alcohol beat him down, before he hocked his trombone a hundred times and finally had to sell it. The horn had gotten him enough money to keep in scotch for oh, maybe a week or so if he remembered right. And no trash booze for Teddy. He drank Jack then, all that liquid gold sliding down his throat and warming his belly.

He remembered those old days like it was this afternoon. It was yesterday he couldn't recall sometimes. Nowadays he drank anything he could get, but oh, how he remembered the Jack and the jazz, and those sweet mommas whispering in his ear and taking him home to feed him gumbo. That's when life was sweet. Forty years and a million drinks ago.

While Trombone Teddy yawned and scratched and knew it was time to leave the sleeping bag that was home in the portico of a derelict office building east of the old Hollywood Cemetery, time to hit the streets for some nighttime panhandling, Farley Ramsdale woke from his fitful hour of sleep after a nightmare he couldn't remember.

Farley yelled, 'Olive!' No response. Was that dumb bitch sleeping again? It burned his ass how she could be such a strung-out crystal fiend and still sleep as much as she did. Maybe she was shooting smack in her twat or someplace else he'd never look and the heroin was smoothing out all the ice she smoked? Could that be it? He'd have to watch her better.

'Olive!' he yelled again. 'Where the fuck are you?'

Then he heard her sleepy voice coming from the living room. 'Farley, I'm right here.' She'd been asleep, all right.

'Well, move your skinny ass and rig some mail traps. We got work to do tonight.'

'Okay, Farley,' she yelled, sounding more alert then.

By the time Farley had taken a leak and splashed water on his face and brushed most of the tangles out of his hair and cursed Olive for not washing the towels in the bathroom, she had finished with the traps.

When he entered the kitchen, she was frying some cheese sandwiches in the skillet and had poured two glasses of orange juice. The mousetraps were now rigged to lengths of string four feet long. He picked up each trap and tested it.

'They okay, Farley?'

'Yeah, they're okay.'

He sat at the table knowing he had to drink the juice and eat the sandwich, though he didn't want either. That was one good thing about letting Olive Oyl stay in his house. When he looked at her, he knew he had to take better care of himself. She looked sixty years old but swore she was forty-one, and he believed her. She had the IQ of a schnauzer or a US congressman and was too scared to lie, even though he hadn't laid a hand on her in anger. Not yet, anyway.

'Did you borrow Sam's Pinto like I told you?' he asked when she put the cheese sandwich in front of him.

'Yes, Farley. It's out front.'

'Gas in it?'

'I don't have no money, Farley.'

He shook his head and forced himself to bite into the sandwich, chew and swallow. Chew and swallow. Dying for a candy bar.

'Did you make a couple auxiliary traps just in case?'

'A couple what?'

'Additional different fucking traps. With duct tape?'

'Oh yes.'

Olive went to the little back porch leading to the yard and got the traps from the top of the washer, where she'd put them. She brought them in and placed them on the drain board. Twelve-inch strips of duct tape, sticky side out with strings threaded through holes cut in the tape.

'Olive, don't put the sticky side down on the fucking wet drain board,' he said, thinking that choking down the rest of the sandwich would take great willpower. 'You'll lose some of the stickiness. Ain't that fucking obvious?'

'Okay, Farley,' she said, looping the strings around knobs on the cupboard doors and hanging them there.

Jesus, he had to dump this broad. She was dumber than any white woman he'd ever met with the exception of his Aunt Agnes, who was a certifiable retard. Too much crystal had turned Olive's brain to coleslaw.

'Eat your sandwich and let's go to work,' he said.

Trombone Teddy had to go to work too. After sundown he was heading west from his sleeping bag, thinking if he could panhandle enough on the boulevard tonight he was definitely going to buy some new socks. He was getting a blister on his left foot.

He was still eight blocks from tall cotton, that part of the boulevard where all those tourists as well as locals flock on balmy nights when the Santa Anas blow in, making people's allergies act up but making some people antsy and hungry for action, when he spotted a man and woman standing by a blue mailbox half a block ahead of him at the corner of Gower Street. The corner was south of the boulevard on a street that was a mix of businesses, apartments, and houses.

It was dark tonight and extra smoggy, so there wasn't any starlight, and the smog-shrouded moon was low, but Teddy could make them out, leaning over the mailbox, the man doing something and the woman acting like a lookout or something. Teddy walked closer, huddling in the shadows of a two-story office building where he could see them better. He may have lost part of his hearing and maybe his chops on the trombone, and he'd lost his sex drive for sure, but he'd always had good vision. He could see what they were doing. Tweakers, he thought. Stealing mail.

Teddy was right, of course. Farley had dropped the mousetrap into the mailbox and was fishing it around by the string, trying to catch some letters on the glue pad. He had something that felt like a thick envelope. He fished it up slowly, very slowly, but it was heavy and he didn't have enough of it stuck to the pad, so it fell free.

'Goddamnit, Olive!'

'What'd I do, Farley?' she asked, running a few steps toward him from her lookout position on the corner.

He couldn't think of what to say she'd done wrong, but he always yelled at her for something when life fucked him over, which was most of the time, so he said, 'You ain't watching the streets. You're standing here talking is what.'

'That's because you said "Goddamnit, Olive,"' she explained. 'So that's why I—'

'Get back to the fucking corner!' he said, dropping the mousetrap into the blue mailbox.

Try as he might, he couldn't hook the glue trap onto the thick envelope, but after giving up on it, he did manage to sweep up several letters and even a fairly heavy ten-by-twelve-inch envelope that was nearly as thick as the one he couldn't catch. He tried the duct tape, but it didn't work any better than the mousetrap.

He squeezed the large envelope and said, 'Looks like a movie script. Like we need a goddamn movie script.'

'What, Farley?' Olive said, running over to him again.

'You can have this one, Olive,' Farley said, handing her the envelope. 'You're the future movie star around here.'

Farley tucked the mail under Olive's baggy shirt and inside her jeans in case the cops stopped them. He knew the cops would bust him right along with her but he figured he'd have a better shot at a plea bargain if they didn't actually find any evidence on his person. He was pretty sure that Olive wouldn't snitch him off and would go ahead and take the rap. Especially if he promised that her bed in the house would be there when she got out. Where else did she have to go?

They walked right past one of the old homeless Hollywood street people when they rounded the corner by the car. He scared the shit out of Farley when he stepped out of the shadows and said, 'Got any spare change, Mister?'

Farley reached into his pocket, took out an empty hand and said to Teddy, 'April Fool, shitbag. Now get the fuck outta my face.'

Teddy watched them walk to an old blue Pinto, open the doors, and get in. He watched the guy turn on the lights and start the engine. He stared at the license plate for a minute and said the number aloud. Then he repeated it. He knew he could remember it long enough to borrow a pencil from somebody and write it down. The next time a cop rousted him for being drunk in public or panhandling or pissing in somebody's storefront, maybe he could use it as a get-out-of-jail-free card.

THREE

There were happier partners than the pair in 6-X-76 on Sunday of that May weekend. Fausto Gamboa, one of the most senior patrol officers at Hollywood Station, had long since surrendered his P3 status, needing a break from being a training officer to rookies still on probation. He had been happily working as a P2 with another Hollywood old-timer named Ron LeCroix, who was at home healing up from painful hemorrhoid surgery that he'd avoided too long and was probably just going to retire.

Fausto was always being mistaken for a Hawaiian or Samoan. Though the Vietnam veteran wasn't tall, only five foot nine, he was very big. The bridge of his nose had been flattened in teenage street fights, and his wrists, hands, and shoulders belonged on a guy tall enough to easily dunk a basketball. His legs were so massive he probably could have dunked one if he'd uncoiled those calf and thigh muscles in a vertical leap. His wavy hair was steel-gray and his face was lined and saddle leather-brown, as though he'd spent years picking cotton and grapes in the Central Valley as his father had done after arriving in California with a truckload of other illegal Mexican immigrants. Fausto had never set eyes on a cotton crop but somehow had inherited his father's weathered face.

Fausto was in a particularly foul mood lately, sick and tired of telling every cop at Hollywood Station how he'd lost in court to Darth Vader. The story of that loss had traveled fast on the concrete jungle wireless.

It wasn't every day that you get to write Darth Vader a ticket, even in Hollywood, and everyone agreed it could only happen there. Fausto Gamboa and his partner Ron LeCroix had been on patrol on an uneventful early evening when they got a call on their MDT computer that Darth Vader was exposing himself near the corner of Hollywood and Highland. They drove to that location and spotted the man in black cycling down Hollywood Boulevard on an old Schwinn three-speed bike. But there was often more than one Darth Vader hanging around Grauman's, Darths of different ethnicity. This one was a diminutive black Darth Vader.

They weren't sure they had the right Darth until they saw what had obviously prompted the call. Darth wasn't wearing his black tights under his black shorts that evening, and his manhood was dangling off the front of the bike saddle. A motorist had spotted the exposed trekkie meat and had called the cops.

Fausto was driving and he pulled the car behind Darth Vader and tooted the horn, which had no effect in slowing down the cyclist. He tooted again. Same result. Then he turned on the siren and blasted him. Twice. No response.

'Fuck this,' Ron LeCroix said. 'Pull beside him.'

When Fausto drew up next to the cyclist, his partner leaned out the window and got Darth's attention by waving him to the curb. Once there, Darth put down the kickstand, got off the bike, and took off his mask and helmet. Then they saw why their attempts to stop him had been ineffective. He was wearing a headset and listening to music.

It was Fausto's turn to write a ticket, so he got out the book and took the trekker's ID.

Darth Vader, aka Henry Louis Mossman, said, 'Wait a minute here. Why you writing me?'

'It's a vehicle code violation to operate a bike on the streets wearing a headset,' Fausto said. 'And in the future, I'd advise you to wear underwear or tights under those short shorts.'

'Ain't this some shit?' Darth Vader said.

'You couldn't even hear our siren,' Fausto said to the littlest Darth.

'Bullshit!' Darth said. 'I'll see you in court, gud-damnit! This is a humbug!'

'Up to you.' Fausto finished writing the ticket.

When the two cops got back in their car that evening and resumed patrol, Fausto said to Ron LeCroix, 'That little panhandler will never take me to court. He'll tear up the ticket, and when it goes to warrant, we'll be throwing his ass in the slam.'

Fausto Gamboa didn't know Darth Vader.

After several weeks had passed, Fausto found himself in traffic court on Hill Street in downtown LA with about a hundred other cops and as many miscreants awaiting their turn before the judge.

Before his case was called, Fausto turned to a cop in uniform next to him and said, 'My guy's a loony-tune panhandler. He'll never show up.'

Fausto Gamboa didn't know Darth Vader.

Not only did he show up, but he showed up in costume, this time wearing black tights under the short shorts. All courtroom business came to a standstill when he entered after his name was called. And the sleepy-eyed judge perked up a bit. In fact, everyone in the courtroom – cops, scofflaws, court clerk, even the bailiff – was watching with interest.

Officer Fausto Gamboa, standing before the bench as is the custom in traffic court, told his story of how he'd gotten the call, spotted Darth Vader, and realized that Darth didn't know his unit was waving in the breeze. And that he couldn't be made to pull over because he was wearing a headset and listening to music, which the cops discovered after they finally stopped the spaceman.

When it was Darth's turn, he removed the helmet and mask, displaying the headset that he said he wore on the day in question. He did a recitation of the vehicle code section that prohibits the wearing of a headset while operating a bike on city streets.

Then he said, 'Your Honor, I would like the court to observe that this headset contains only one earpiece. The vehicle code section clearly refers to both ears being blocked. This officer did not know the vehicle code section then and he don't know it now. The fact is, I did hear the officer's horn and siren but I did not think that it was for me. I wasn't doing nothing illegal, so why should I get all goosey and pull over jist because I hear a siren?'

When he was finished, the judge said to Fausto, 'Officer, did you examine the headset that Mr. Mossman was wearing that day?'

'I saw it, Your Honor,' Fausto said.

'Does this look like the headset?' the judge asked.

'Well ... it looks ... similar.'

'Officer, can you say for sure that the headset you saw that day had two earpieces, or did it have only one, like the headset you are looking at now?'

'Your Honor, I hit the siren twice and he failed to yield to a police vehicle. It was obvious he couldn't hear me.'

'I see,' the judge said. 'In this case I think we should give the benefit of the doubt to Mr. Mossman. We find him not guilty of the offense cited.'

There was applause and chortling in the courtroom until the bailiff silenced it, and when business was concluded, Darth Vader put on his helmet and with every eye still on him said to all, 'May the force be with you.'

Now Ron LeCroix and his hemorrhoids were gone, and Fausto Gamboa, still smarting from having his ass kicked by Darth Vader, gave the Oracle a big argument the moment he learned that he was being teamed with Officer Budgie Polk. When Fausto was a young cop, women didn't work regular patrol assignments at the LAPD, and he sneered when he said to the Oracle, 'Is she one of them who maybe trades badges with a boyfriend copper like they used to do class rings in my day?'

'She's a good officer,' the Oracle said. 'Give her a chance.'

'Or is she the kind who gets to partner with her boyfriend and hooks her pinkie through his belt loop when they walk the boulevard beat?'

'Come on, Fausto,' the Oracle said. 'It's only for the May deployment period.'

Like the Oracle, Fausto still carried an old six-inch Smith & Wesson revolver, and the first night he was paired with this new partner, he'd pissed her off after she asked him why he carried a wheel gun when the magazine of her Beretta 9-millimeter held fifteen rounds, with one in the pipe.

'If you need more than six rounds to win a gunfight, you deserve to lose,' he'd said to her that night, without a hint of a smile.

Fausto never wore body armor, and when she asked him about that too, he had said, 'Fifty-four cops were shot and killed in the United States last year. Thirty-one were wearing a vest. What good did it do them?'

He'd caught her looking at his bulging chest that first night and said, 'It's all me. No vest. I measure more around the chest than you do.' Then he'd looked at her chest and said, 'Way more.'

That really pissed her off because the fact was, Budgie Polk's ordinarily small breasts were swollen at the moment. Very swollen. She had a four-month-old daughter at home being watched by Budgie's mother, and having just returned to duty from maternity leave, Budgie was actually a few pounds lighter than she had been before the pregnancy. She didn't need thinly veiled cracks about her breast size from this old geezer, not when her tits were killing her.

Her former husband, a detective working out of West LA Division, had left home two months before his daughter was born, explaining that their two-year marriage had been a 'regrettable mistake.' And that they were 'two mature people.' She felt like whacking him across the teeth with her baton, as well as half of his cop friends whom she'd run into since she came back to work. How could they still be pals with that dirtbag? She had handed him the keys to her heart, and he had entered and kicked over the furniture and ransacked the drawers like a goddamn crack-smoking burglar.

And why do women officers marry other cops in the first place? She'd asked herself the question a hundred times since that asshole dumped her and his only child, with his shit-eating promise to be prompt with child-support payments and to visit his daughter often 'when she was old enough.' Of course, with five years on the Job, Budgie knew in her heart the answer to the why-do-women-officers-marry-other-cops question.

When she got home at night and needed to talk to somebody about all the crap she'd had to cope with on the streets, who else would understand but another cop? What if she'd married an insurance adjuster? What would he say when she came home as she had one night last September after answering a call in the Hollywood Hills, where the owner of a three-million-dollar hillside home had freaked on ecstasy and crack and strangled his ten-year-old step-daughter, maybe because she'd refused his sexual advances, or so the detectives had deduced. Nobody would ever know for sure, because the son of a bitch blew half his head away with a four-inch Colt magnum while Budgie and her partner were standing on the porch of the home next door with a neighbor who said she was sure she'd heard a child screaming.

After hearing the gunshot, Budgie and her partner had run next door, pistols drawn, she calling for help into the keyed mike at her shoulder. And while help was arriving and cops were leaping out of their black-and-whites with shotguns, Budgie was in the house gaping at the body of the pajama-clad child on the master bedroom floor, ligature marks already darkening, eyes hemorrhaging, pajamas urine-soaked and feces-stained. The step-father was sprawled across the living room sofa, the back cushion soaked with blood and brains and slivers of bone.

And a woman there, the child's crack-smoking mother, was screaming at Budgie, 'Help her! Resuscitate her! Do something!'

Over and over she yelled, until Budgie grabbed her by the shoulder and yelled back, 'Shut the fuck up! She's dead!'

And that's why women officers seemed to always marry other cops. As poor as the marital success rate was, they figured it would be worse married to a civilian. Who would they talk to after seeing a murdered child in the Hollywood Hills? Maybe male cops didn't have to talk about such things when they got home, but women cops did.

Budgie had hoped that when she returned to duty, she might get teamed with a woman, at least until she stopped lactating. But the Oracle had said everything was screwed during this deployment period, with people off IOD from an unexpected rash of on-duty injuries, vacations, and so forth. He had said, she could work with Fausto until the next deployment period, couldn't she? All of LAPD life revolved around deployment periods, and Fausto was a reliable old pro who would never let a partner down, the Oracle said. But shit, twenty-eight days of this?

Fausto longed for the old days at Hollywood Station when, after working the night watch, they used to gather in the upper parking lot of the John Anson Ford Theater, across from the Hollywood Bowl, at a spot they called the Tree and have a few brews and commiserate. Sometimes badge bunnies would show up, and if one of them was sitting in a car, sucking face with some cop, you always could be sure that another copper would sneak up, look in the window, and yell, 'Crime in progress!'

On one of those balmy summer nights under what the Oracle always called a Hollywood moon, Fausto and the Oracle had sat alone at the Tree on the hood of Fausto's VW bug, Fausto, a young cop back from Vietnam, and the Oracle, a seasoned sergeant but less than forty years old.

He'd surprised Fausto by saying, 'Kid, look up there,' referring to the lighted cross on top of the hill behind them. 'That'd be a great place to have your ashes spread when it's your turn. Up there, looking out over the Bowl. But there's even a better place than that.' And then the Oracle told young Fausto Gamboa about the better place, and Fausto never forgot.

Those were the grand old days at Hollywood Station. But after the last chief's 'Reign of Terror,' nobody dared to drive within a mile of the Tree. Nobody gathered to drink good Mexican brew. And in fact, this young generation of granola-crunching coppers probably worried about *E. coli* in their Evian. Fausto had actually seen them drinking organic milk. Through a freaking straw!

So here she was, Budgie thought, riding shotgun on Sunset Boulevard with this cranky geezer, easily older than her father, who would have been fifty-two years old had he lived. By the number of hash marks on Fausto's sleeve, he'd been a cop for more than thirty years, almost all of it in Hollywood.

To break the ice on that first night, she'd said, 'How long you been on the Job, Fausto?'

'Thirty-four years,' he said. 'Came on when cops wore hats and you had to by god wear it when you were outta the car. And sap pockets were for saps, not cell phones.' Then he paused and said, 'Before you were on this planet.'

'I've been on this planet twenty-seven years,' she said. 'I've been on the Job just over five.'

The way he cocked his right eyebrow at her for a second and then looked away, he appeared to be saying, So who gives a shit about your history?

Well, fuck him, she thought, but just as night fell and she was hoping that somehow the pain in her breasts would subside, he decided to make a little small talk. He said, 'Budgie, huh? That's a weird name.'

Trying not to sound defensive, she said, 'My mother was Australian. A budgie is an Australian parakeet. It's a nickname that stuck. She thought it was cute, I guess.'

Fausto, who was driving, stopped at a red light, looked Budgie up and down, from her blond French-braided ponytail, pinned up per LAPD regulations, to her brightly shined shoes, and said, 'You're what? Five eleven, maybe six feet tall in your socks? And weigh what? About as much as my left leg? She shoulda called you "Storkie."'

Budgie felt it right then. Worse breast pain. These days a dog barks, a cat meows, a baby cries, she lactates. This bastard's gruff voice was doing it!

'Take me to the substation on Cherokee,' she said.

'What for?' Fausto said.

'I'm hurting like hell. I got a breast pump in my war bag. I can do it in there and store the milk.'

'Oh, shit!' Fausto said. 'I don't believe it! Twenty-eight days of this?'

When they were halfway to the storefront, Fausto said, 'Why don't we just go back to the station? You can do it in the women's locker room, for chrissake.'

'I don't want anyone to know I'm doing this, Fausto,' she said. 'Not even any of the women. Somebody'll say something, and then I'll have to hear all the wise-ass remarks from the men. I'm trusting you on this.'

'I gotta pull the pin,' Fausto said rhetorically. 'Over a thousand females on the Job? Pretty soon the freaking chief'll have double-X chromosomes. Thirty-four years is long enough. I gotta pull the pin.'

After Fausto parked the black-and-white at the darkened storefront substation by Musso & Frank's restaurant, Budgie grabbed the carryall and breast pump from her war bag in the trunk, unlocked the door with her 999 key, and ran inside. It was a rather empty space with a few tables and chairs where parents could get information about the Police Activity League or sign up the kids for the Police Explorer Program. Sometimes there was LAPD literature lying around, in English, Spanish, Thai, Korean, Farsi, and other languages for the polyglot citizenry of the Los Angeles melting pot.

Budgie opened the fridge, intending to put her blue ice packs in the freezer, and left her little thermal bag beside the fridge, where she could pick it up after going off duty. She turned on the light in the john, deciding to pump in there sitting on the toilet lid instead of in the main room, in case Fausto got tired of waiting in the car and decided to stroll inside. But the smell of mildew was nauseating.

She removed the rover from her Sam Browne, then took off the gun belt itself and her uniform shirt, vest, and T-shirt. She draped everything on a little table in the bathroom and put the key on the sink. The table teetered under the weight, so she removed her pistol from the gun belt and laid it on the floor beside her rover and flashlight. After she'd been pumping for a minute, the pain started subsiding. The pump was noisy, and she hoped that Fausto wouldn't enter the storefront. Without a doubt he'd make some wisecrack when he heard the sucking noise coming from the bathroom.

Fausto had clicked onto the car's keyboard that they were code 6 at the storefront, out for investigation, so that they wouldn't get any calls until this freaking ordeal was over. And he was almost dozing when the hotshot call went out to 6-A-77 of Watch 3.

The PSR's urgent voice said, 'All units in the vicinity and Six-Adam-Seventy-seven, shots fired in the parking lot, Western and Romaine. Possibly an officer involved. Six-A-Seventy seven, handle code three.'

Budgie was buttoning her shirt, just having stored the milk in the freezer beside her blue ice packs. She had slid the rover inside its sheath when Fausto threw open the front door and yelled, 'OIS, Western and Romaine! Are you through?'

'Coming!' she yelled, grabbing the Sam Browne and flashlight while still buttoning her shirt, placing the milk and the freezer bags in the insulated carryall, and running for the door, almost tripping on a chair in the darkened office as she was fastening the Sam Browne around her waspish waist.

There were few things more urgent than an officer-involved shooting, and Fausto was revving the engine when she got to the car and she just had time to close the door before he was ripping out from the curb. She was rattled and sweating and when he slid the patrol car around a corner, she almost toppled and grabbed her seat belt and ... oh, god!

Since the current chief had arrived, he'd decided to curtail traffic collisions involving officers busting through red lights and stop signs minus lights and siren while racing to urgent calls that didn't rate a code 3 status. So henceforth, the calls that in the old days would have rated only a code 2 status were upgraded to code 3. That meant that in Los Angeles today the citizens were always hearing sirens. The street cops figured it reminded the chief of his days as New York's police commissioner, all those sirens howling. The cops didn't mind a bit. It was a blast getting to drive code 3 all the time.

Because the call wasn't assigned to them, Fausto couldn't drive code 3, but neither the transplanted easterner who headed the Department nor the risen Christ could keep LAPD street cops from racing to an OIS call. Fausto would slow at an intersection and then roar through, green light or not, making cars brake and yield for the black-and-white. But by the time they got to Western and Romaine, five units were there ahead of them and all officers were out of their cars, aiming shotguns or nines at the lone car in the parking lot, where they could see someone ducking down on the front seat.

Fausto grabbed the shotgun and advanced to the car closest to the action, seeing it belonged to the surfers, Flotsam and Jetsam. When he looked over at Budgie trailing beside him, he wondered why she wasn't aiming hers.

'Where's your gun?' he said, then added, 'Please don't tell me it's with the milk!'

'No, I have the milk,' Budgie said.

'Just point your finger,' he said and was stunned to see that, with a sick look on her face, she did it! After a pause, he said, 'I have a two-inch Smith in my war bag, wanna borrow it?'

Still pointing her long, slender index finger, Budgie said, 'Two-inch wheel guns can't hit shit. I'm better off this way.'

Fausto came as close to a guffaw as he had in a long time. She had balls. And she was quick, he had to give her that. Then he saw the car door open, and two teenage Latino boys got out with their hands up and were quickly proned-out and cuffed.

The code 4 was broadcast by the PSR, meaning there was sufficient help at the scene. And to keep other eager cops from coming anyway, she added, 'No officer involved.'

Fausto saw one of those surfers, Flotsam, heading their way. Fausto thought about how back when he was a young copper, there was no way in hell bleached hair would be allowed. And what about his partner, Jetsam, swaggering along beside him with his dark blond hair all gelled in little spikes two inches long? What kind of shit was that? It was time to retire, Fausto thought again. Time to pull the pin.

Flotsam approached Fausto and said, 'Security guard at the big building there got hassled by some homies when he caught them jacking up a car to steal the rims. Dumb ass capped one off in the air to scare them away. They jumped in the car and hid, afraid to come out.'

'Sky shooting,' Fausto snorted. 'Guy's seen too many cowboy movies. Shouldn't allow those door shakers to carry anything more than a bag of stones and a slingshot.'

'You should see the ride they were working on,' Jetsam said, joining his partner. 'Nineteen thirty-nine Chevy. Completely restored. Cherry. Bro, it is sweet!'

'Yeah?' Fausto was interested now. 'I used to own an old 'thirty-nine when I was in high school.' Turning to Budgie, he said, 'Let's take a look for a minute.' Then he remembered her empty holster and thought they'd better get away before somebody spotted it.

He said to Flotsam and Jetsam, 'Just remembered something. Gotta go.'

Budgie was thrown back in her seat as they sped away. When she shot him a guilty look, he said, 'Please tell me that you didn't forget your key too.'

'Oh shit,' she said. 'Don't you have your nine-nine-nine key?'

'Where's your freaking keys?'

'On the table in the john.'

'And where is your freaking gun, may I ask?'

'On the floor in the john. By the keys.'

'And what if my nine-nine-nine key's in my locker with the rest of my keys?' he said. 'Figuring I didn't have to bother, since I have an eager young partner.'

'You wouldn't leave your keys in your locker,' Budgie said without looking at him. 'Not you. You wouldn't trust a young partner, an old partner, or your family dog.'

He looked at her then and seeing a tiny upturn at the corner of her lips thought, She really has some balls, this one. And some smart mouth. And of course she was right about him – he would never forget his keys.

Fausto just kept shaking his head as he drove back to the storefront sub-station. Then he grumbled more to himself than to her, 'Freaking surfers. You see that gelled hair? Not in my day.'

'That isn't gel,' Budgie said. 'Their hair is stiff and sticky from all the mai tai mix getting dumped on their heads in the beach bars they frequent. They're always sniffing around like a pair of poodles and getting rejected. And please don't tell me it wouldn't be like that if there weren't so many women officers around. Like in your day.'

Fausto just grunted and they rode without speaking for a while, pretending to be scanning the streets as the moon was rising over Hollywood.

Budgie broke the silence when she said, 'You won't snitch me off to the Oracle, will you? Or for a big laugh to the other guys?'

With his eyes focused on the streets, he said, 'Yeah, I go around ratting out partners all the time. For laughs.'

'Is there a bathroom window in that place?' she asked. 'I didn't notice.'

'I don't think there's any windows,' he said. 'I hardly ever been in there. Why?'

'Well, if I'm wrong about you and you don't have a key, and if there's a window, you could boost me up and I could pry it open and climb in.'

His words laden with sarcasm, Fausto said, 'Oh, well, why not just ask me if I'd climb in the window because you're a new mommy and can't risk hurting yourself?'

'No,' she said, 'you could never get your big ass through any window, but I could if you'd boost me up. Sometimes it pays to look like a stork.'

'I got my keys,' he said.

'I figured,' she said.

For the first time, Budgie saw Fausto nearly smile, and he said, 'It hasn't been a total loss. At least we got the milk.'

At about the same time that Fausto Gamboa and Budgie Polk were gathering her equipment at the substation on Cherokee, Farley Ramsdale and Olive Oyl were home at Farley's bungalow, sitting on the floor, having smoked some of the small amount of crystal they had left. Scattered all around them on the floor were letters they had fished out of seven blue mailboxes on that very busy evening of work.

Olive was wearing the glasses Farley had stolen for her at the drugstore and was laboriously reading through business mail, job applications, notices of unpaid bills, detached portions of paid bills, and various other correspondence. Whenever she came across something they could use, she would pass it to Farley, who was in a better mood now, sorting some checks they could possibly trade and nibbling on a saltine because it was time to put something in his stomach.

The crystal was getting to him, Olive thought. He was blinking more often than usual and getting flushed. Sometimes it worried her when his pulse rate would shoot up to 150 and higher, but if she mentioned it, he just yelled at her, so she didn't say anything.

'This is a lot of work, Farley,' she said when her eyes were getting tired. 'Sometimes I wonder why we don't just make our own meth. Ten years ago I used to go with a guy who had his own meth lab and we always had enough without working so hard. Till the chemicals blew up one day and burned him real bad.'

'Ten years ago you could walk in a drugstore and buy all the goddamn ephedrine you wanted,' Farley said. 'Nowadays a checkout clerk'll send you to a counter where they ask for ID if you try to buy a couple boxes of Sudafed. Life ain't easy anymore. But you're lucky, Olive. You get to live in my house. If you were living in a ratty hotel room, it'd be real dangerous to do the work we do. Like, if you used a hot credit card or a phony name to get your room like you always did before, you'd lose your protection against search and seizure. The law says you have no expectation of privacy when you do that. So the cops could kick your door down without a search warrant. But you're lucky. You live in my house. They need a search warrant to come in here.'

'I'm real lucky,' Olive agreed. 'You know so much about the law and everything.' She grinned at him and he thought, *Kee-rist*, those fucking teeth!

Olive thought it was nice when she and Farley were at home like this, working in front of the TV. Really nice when Farley wasn't all paranoid from the tweak, thinking the FBI and the CIA were coming down the chimney. A couple times when he'd hallucinated, Olive really got scared. They'd had a long talk then about how much to smoke and when they should do it. But lately she thought that Farley was breaking his own rules when she wasn't looking. She thought he was into that ice a whole lot more than she was.

'We got quite a few credit-card numbers,' he said. 'Lots of SS numbers and driver's license info and plenty of checks. We can trade for some serious glass when we take this stuff to Sam.'

'Any cash, Farley?'

'Ten bucks in a card addressed to "my darling grandchild." What kinda cheap asshole only gives ten bucks to a grandchild? Where's the fucking family values?'

'That's all?'

'One other birthday card, "to Linda from Uncle Pete." Twenty bucks.' He looked up at Olive and added, 'Uncle Pete's probably a pedophile, and Linda's probably his neighbor's ten-year-old. Hollywood's full of freaks. Someday I'm getting outta here.'

'I better check on the money,' Olive said.

'Yeah, don't cook it to death,' Farley said, thinking that the saltine was making him sick. Maybe he should try some vegetable soup if there was a can left.

The money was in the tub that Farley had placed on the screened back porch. Eighteen five-dollar bills were soaking in Easy-Off, almost bleached clean. Olive used a wooden spoon to poke a few of them or flip them over to look at the other side. She hoped this would work better than the last time they tried passing bogus money.

That time Olive almost got arrested, and it scared her to even think about that day two months ago when Farley told her to buy a certain light green bonded paper at Office Depot. And then they took it to Sam, the guy who rented them his car from time to time, and Sam worked for two days cutting the paper and printing twenty-dollar bills on his very expensive laser printer. After Sam was satisfied, he told Olive to spray the stack of bogus twenties with laundry starch and let them dry thoroughly. Olive did it, and when she and Farley checked the bills, he thought they were perfect.

They stayed away from the stores like the mini-market chains that have the pen they run over large bills. Farley wasn't sure if they'd bother with twenties, but he was afraid to take a chance. A mini-market clerk had told Farley that if the clerk sees brown under the pen, it's good; black or no color is bad. Or something like that. So they'd gone to a Target store on that day two months ago to try out the bogus money.

In front of the store was a buff young guy with a mullet passing out gay pride leaflets for a parade that was being organized the following weekend. The guy wore a tight yellow T-shirt with purple letters across the front that said 'Queer Pervert.'

He'd offered a handbill to Farley, who pointed at the words on the T-shirt and said to Olive, 'That's redundant.'

The guy flexed his deltoids and pecs, saying to Farley, 'And it could say "Kick Boxer" too. Want a demonstration?'

'Don't come near me!' Farley cried. 'Olive, you're a witness!'

'What's redundant, Farley?' Olive asked, but he said, 'Just get the fuck inside the store.'

Olive could see that Farley was in a bad mood then, and when they were entering, they were partially blocked by six women and girls completely covered in chadors and burkas, two of them talking on cells and two others raising their veils to drink from large Starbucks cups.

Farley brushed past them, saying, 'Why don't you take those Halloween rags back to Western Costume.' Then to Olive, 'Wannabe sand niggers. Or maybe Gypsies boosting merchandise under those fucking mumus.'

One of the women said something angrily in Arabic, and Farley muttered, '*Hasta lasagna* to you too. Bitch.'

There were lots of things that Olive had wanted to buy, but Farley said they were going to maintain control until they tested the money once or twice with small purchases. Farley kept looking at a CD player for $69.50 that he said he could sell in five minutes at Ruby's Donuts on Santa Monica Boulevard, where a lot of tranny streetwalkers hung out.

Olive had always been tenderhearted and she felt sorry for all those transsexuals trapped between two genders. Some of those she'd talked to had had partial gender-changing operations, and a couple of them had endured the complete change, Adam's apple surgery and all. But Olive could still tell they hadn't been born as women. They seemed sad to Olive and they were always nice to her long before she'd met Farley, when she was panhandling and selling ecstasy for a guy named Willard, who was way mean. Many times a tranny who'd just turned a good trick would give Olive five or ten dollars and tell her to go get something to eat.

'You look nervous,' Farley said to Olive as they wandered around the Target store.

'I'm only a little nervous,' Olive said.

'Well, stop it. You gotta look like a normal person, if that's possible.'

Farley eyed a very nice twenty-one-inch TV set but shook his head, saying, 'We gotta start small.'

'Can we just do it now, Farley?' Olive said. 'I just wanna get it over with.'

Farley left the store and Olive took the CD player to the checkout counter, the most crowded one so that she'd encounter a clerk who was too busy to be looking for bogus money. Except that just as the shopper ahead of her was paying for a purchase of blankets and sheets, a manager stepped over and offered to relieve the harried young checkout clerk. He glanced at Olive when he was taking care of the other customer, and Olive had a bad feeling.

She had a real bad feeling when it was her turn and he said suspiciously, 'Will you be paying by check?'

'No, cash,' Olive said innocently, just as a roving store employee walked up to the manager and nodded toward Olive. The roving guy said, 'Where's your friend?'

'Friend?' Olive said.

'Yes, the man who insulted the Muslim ladies,' he said. 'They complained and wanted me to throw him out of the store.'

Olive was so shaken, she didn't notice that she'd dropped the three twenties on the counter until the manager picked them up and held them up to the light and ran them through his fingers. And Olive panicked. She bolted and ran past shoppers with loaded carts, through the doors to the parking lot, and didn't stop until she was on the sidewalk in front.

When Farley found her walking on the sidewalk and picked her up, she didn't tell him about the guy and the complaint from the Muslim women. She knew it would just make him madder and get him in a terrible mood, so she said that the checkout clerk felt the money and said, 'This paper is wrong.' And that's why Farley went back to Sam, who told him to try to get good paper by bleaching real money with Easy-Off.

So today they were trying it again but with real money. She wore her cleanest cotton sweater and some low-rise jeans that were too big, even though Farley had shoplifted them from the juniors' section at Nordstroms. And she wore tennis shoes for running, in case things went bad again.

'This time it won't go bad,' Farley promised Olive while he parked in front of RadioShack, seemingly determined to buy a CD player.

When they were out and standing beside the car, he said, 'This time you got real paper from real money, so don't sweat it. And it wasn't easy to get hold of all those five-dollar bills, so don't blow this.'

'I don't know if they look quite right,' Olive said doubtfully.

'Stop worrying,' Farley said. 'You remember what Sam told you about the strip and the watermark?'

'Sort of,' Olive said.

'The strip on the left side of a five says five, right? But it's small, very hard to see. The president's image on the right-side watermark is bigger but also hard to see. So if they hold the bill up to the light and their eyes start looking left to right or right to left, whadda you do?'

'I run to you.'

'No, you don't run to me, goddamnit!' He yelled it, then looked around, but none of the passing shoppers were paying any attention to them. He continued with as much patience as he could muster. 'These dumb shits won't even notice that the strip ain't for a twenty-dollar bill and that the watermark has a picture of Lincoln instead of Jackson. They just go through the motions and look, but they don't see. So don't panic.'

'Until I'm sure he's onto me. Then I run out to you.'

Farley looked at the low, smog-laden sky and thought: Maintain. Just fucking maintain. This woman is dumb as a clump of dog hair. Slowly he said, 'You do not run to me. You never run to me. You do not know me. I am a fucking stranger. You just walk fast out of the store and head for the street. I'll pick you up there after I make sure nobody's coming after you.'

'Can we do it now, Farley?' Olive said. 'Pretty soon I'll have to go to the bathroom.'

The store was bustling when they entered. As usual, there were a few street people lurking around the parking lot begging for change.

One of the street people recognized Farley and Olive. In fact, he had their license number written down on a card, saving it for a rainy day, so to speak. Farley and Olive never noticed the old homeless guy who was eyeballing them as they entered. Nor did they see him enter the store and approach a man with a 'Manager' tag on his shirt.

The homeless guy whispered something to the manager, who kept his eye on Farley and Olive for the whole ten minutes that they browsed. When Farley walked out of the store, the manager still watched him, until he was sure that Farley wasn't coming back in. Then the manager reentered the store and watched Olive at the checkout counter.

Slick, Olive thought. It's working real slick. The kid at the checkout took the four bogus twenties from Olive's hand and began ringing up the purchase. But then it happened.

'Let me see those bills.'

The manager was talking to the kid, not to Olive. She hadn't seen him standing behind her, and she was too startled by his arrival to do anything but freeze.

He held the bills up to the late-afternoon light pouring through the plate glass, and she saw his eyes moving left to right and right to left, and she didn't care if Farley said they're too dumb to match up strips and watermarks and all that Farley Ramsdale goddamn bullshit! Olive knew exactly what to do and did it right at that instant.

Three minutes later Farley picked her up sprinting across the street against a red light, and he was amazed that Olive Oyl could move that fast, given her emaciated condition. A few minutes after that, Trombone Teddy walked into RadioShack and the manager told him that yes, they were crooks and had tried to pass bogus twenties. He handed Teddy several dollars from his pocket and thanked him for the tip. All in all, Teddy thought that his day was beginning quite fortuitously. He wished he could run into those two tweakers more often.

FOUR

Wondering why in the hell she'd volunteered to read her paper when none of them knew what she did for a living, Andi McCrea decided to sit on the corner of the professor's desk just as though she wasn't nervous about criticism and wasn't scared of Professor Anglund, who'd squawked all during the college term about the putative abuse of civil liberties by law enforcement.

With her forty-fifth birthday right around the corner and her oral exam for lieutenant coming up, it had seemed important to be able to tell a promotion board that she had completed her bachelor's degree at last, even making the Dean's List unless Anglund torpedoed her. She hoped to convince the board that this academic achievement at her time of life – combined with twenty-four years of patrol and detective experience – proved that she was an outstanding candidate for lieutenant's bars. Or something like that.

So why hadn't she just gracefully declined when Anglund asked her to read her paper? And why now, nearly at the end of the term, at the end of her college life, had she decided to write a paper that she knew would provoke this professor and reveal to the others that she, a middle-aged classmate old enough to be their momma, was a cop with the LAPD? Unavoidable and honest answer: Andi was sick and tired of kissing ass in this institution of higher learning.

She hadn't agreed with much of what this professor and others like him had said during all the years she'd struggled here, working for the degree she should have gotten two decades ago, balancing police work with the life of a single mom. Now that it was almost over, she was ashamed that she'd sat silently, relishing those A's and A-pluses, pretending to agree with all the crap in this citadel of political correctness that often made her want to gag. She was looking for self-respect at the end of the academic trail.

For this effort, Andi wore the two-hundred-dollar blue blazer she'd bought at Banana instead of the sixty-dollar one she'd bought at The Gap. Under that blazer was a button-down Oxford in eye-matching blue, also from Banana, and no bling except for tiny diamond studs. Black flats completed the ensemble, and since she had had her collar-length bob highlighted on Thursday, she'd figured to look pretty good for this final performance. Until she got the call-out last night: the bloodbath on Cherokee that kept her from her bed and allowed her just enough time to run home, shower and change, and be here in time for what she now feared would be a debacle. She was bushed and a bit nauseated from a caffeine overload, and she'd had to ladle on the pancake under her eyes to even approach a look of perkiness that her classmates naturally exuded.

'The title of my paper is, "What's Wrong with the Los Angeles Police Department,"' Andi began, looking out at twenty-three faces too young to know Gumby, fourteen of whom shared her gender, only four of whom shared her race. It was to be expected in a university that prided itself on diversity, with only ten percent of the student population being non-Latino white. She had often wanted to say, 'Where's the goddamn diversity for me? I'm the one in the minority.' But never had.

She was surprised that Professor Anglund had remained in his chair directly behind her instead of moving to a position where he could see her face. She'd figured he was getting too old to be interested in her ass. Or are they ever?

She began reading aloud: 'In December of nineteen ninety-seven, Officer David Mack of the LAPD committed a $722,000 bank robbery just two months before eight pounds of cocaine went missing from an LAPD evidence room, stolen by Officer Rafael Perez of Rampart Division, a friend of David Mack's.

'The arrest of Rafael Perez triggered the Rampart Division police scandal, wherein Perez, after one trial, cut a deal with the district attorney's office to avoid another, and implicated several cops through accusations of false arrests, bad shootings, suspect beatings, and perjury, some of which he had apparently invented to improve his plea bargain status.

'The most egregious incident, which he certainly did not invent, involved Perez himself and his partner, Officer Nino Durden, both of whom in nineteen ninety-six mistakenly shot a young Latino man named Javier Ovando, putting him into a wheelchair for life, then falsely testified that he'd threatened them with a rifle that they themselves had planted beside his critically wounded body in order to cover their actions. Ovando served two years in prison before he was released after Perez confessed.'

Andi looked up boldly, then said, 'Mack, Perez, and Durden are black. But to understand what came of all this we must first examine the Rodney King incident five years earlier. That was a bizarre event wherein a white sergeant, having shot Mr. King with a Taser gun after a long auto pursuit, then directed the beating of this drunken, drug-addled African American ex-convict. That peculiar sergeant seemed determined to make King cry uncle, when the ring of a dozen cops should have swarmed and handcuffed the drunken thug and been done with it.'

She gave another pointed look at her audience and then went on: 'That led to the subsequent riot where, according to arrest interviews, most of the rioters had never even heard of Rodney King but thought this was a good chance to act out and do some looting. The riot brought to Los Angeles a commission headed by Warren Christopher, later to become US secretary of state under President Bill Clinton, a commission that determined very quickly, and with very little evidence, that the LAPD had a significant number of overly aggressive, if not downright brutal, officers who needed reining in. The LAPD's white chief, who, like several others before him, had civil service protection, was soon to retire.

'So the LAPD was placed under the leadership of one, then later a second African American chief. The first, an outsider from the Philadelphia Police Department, became the first LAPD chief in decades to serve without civil service protection at the pleasure of the mayor and city council, a throwback to the days when crooked politicians ran the police force. His contract was soon bought back by city fathers dissatisfied with his performance and his widely publicized junkets to Las Vegas.

'The next black chief, an insider whose entire adult life had been spent with the LAPD, was in charge when the Rampart Division scandal exploded, making the race card difficult for anyone to play. This chief, a micromanager, seemingly obsessive about control and cavalier about officer morale, quickly became the enemy of the police union. He came to be known as Lord Voldemort by street cops who'd read *Harry Potter*.

'David Mack, Rafael Perez, and Nino Durden went to prison, where Mack claimed to belong to the Piru Bloods street gang. So, we might ask: Were these cops who became gangsters, or gangsters who became cops?'

Scanning their faces, she saw nothing. She dropped her eyes again and read, 'By two thousand two, that second black chief, serving at the pleasure of City Hall, hadn't pleased the politicians, the cops, or the local media. He retired but later was elected to the city council. His replacement was another cross-country outsider, a white chief this time, who had been New York City's police commissioner. Along with all the changes in leadership, the police department ended up operating under a "civil rights consent decree," an agreement between the City of Los Angeles and the United States Department of Justice wherein the LAPD was forced to accept major oversight by DOJ-approved monitors for a period of five years but which has just been extended for three years by a Federal judge based on technicalities.

'And thus, the beleaguered rank and file of the formerly proud LAPD, lamenting the unjustified loss of reputation as the most competent and corruption-free, and certainly most famous, big-city police department in the country, finds itself faced with the humiliation of performing under outside overseers. Mandated auditors can simply walk into a police station and, figuratively speaking, ransack desks, turn pockets inside out, threaten careers, and generally make cops afraid to do proactive police work that had always been the coin of the realm with the LAPD during the glory days before Rodney King and the Rampart Division scandal.

'And of course, there is the new police commission, led by the former head of the LA Urban League, who uttered the following for the *LA Times* before he took office. Quote: "The LAPD has a longstanding institutionalized culture in which some police officers feel that they have the tacit approval of their leadership ... to brutalize and even kill African American boys and men." End quote. This baseless and crudely racist slander is apparently okay with our new Latino mayor, who appointed him claiming to want harmony in the racial cauldron where the police must do their job.'

Andi looked again at the blank stares as she prepared for her parting shot and said, 'Finally, all of the layers of oversight, based on the crimes of a few cops – costing millions annually, encouraged by cynical politicians and biased reporting and fueled by political correctness gone mad – have at last answered the ancient question posed by the Roman poet Juvenal in the first century AD. He too was worried about law enforcement abuse, for he asked, "But who would guard the guards themselves?" At the Los Angeles Police Department, more than nine thousand officers have learned the answer: Everybody.'

With that, Andi turned to glance at Anglund, who was looking at papers in his lap as though he hadn't heard a word. She said to the class, 'Any questions?'

Nobody answered for a long moment, and then one of the East Asians, a petite young woman about the age of Andi's son, said, 'Are you a cop or something?'

'I am a cop, yes,' Andi said. 'With the LAPD, and have been since I was your age. Any other questions?'

Students were looking from the wall clock to the professor and back to Andi. Finally, Anglund said, 'Thank you, Ms. McCrea. Thank you, ladies and gentlemen, for your diligence and attention. And now that the spring quarter is so close to officially concluding, why don't you all just get the hell out of here.'

That brought smiles and chuckles and some applause for the professor. Andi was about to leave, when Anglund said, 'A moment, Ms. McCrea?'

He waited until the other students were gone, then stood, hands in the pockets of his cords, linen shirt so wrinkled that Andi thought he should either send it out or get his wife an ironing board. His gray hair was wispy, and his pink scalp showed through, flaked with dandruff. He was a man of seventy if he was a day.

Anglund said, 'Why did you keep your other life from us until the end?'

'I don't know,' she said. 'Maybe I only like to don the bat suit when night falls on Gotham City.'

'How long have you been attending classes here?'

'Off and on, eight years,' she said.

'Have you kept your occupation a secret from everybody in all that time?'

'Yep,' she said. 'I'm just a little secret keeper.'

'First of all, Ms. McCrea ... is it Officer McCrea?'

'Detective,' she said.

'First of all, your paper contained opinions and assertions that you may or may not be able to back up and not a few biases of your own, but I don't think you're a racist cop.'

'Well, thank you for that. That's mighty white of you, if that's an acceptable phrase.' Thinking, There goes the Dean's List. She'd be lucky to get a C-plus out of him now.

Anglund smiled and said, 'Sorry. That was very condescending of me.'

'I bored them to death,' Andi said.

'The fact is, they don't really give a damn about civil liberties or police malfeasance or law enforcement in general,' Anglund said. 'More than half of today's university students cannot even understand the positions put forth in newspaper editorials. They care about iPods and cell phones and celluloid fantasy. The majority of this generation of students don't read anything outside of class but magazines and an occasional graphic novel, and barely contemplate anything more serious than video downloading. So, yes, I think you failed to provoke them as you'd obviously intended to do.'

'I guess my son isn't so different after all, then,' she said, seeing her first C-plus morphing into a C-minus.

'Is he a college student?'

'A soldier,' she said. 'Insisted on joining because two of his friends did.'

Anglund studied her for a few seconds and said, 'Iraq?'

'Afghanistan.'

Anglund said, 'Despite the flaws in your thesis, I was impressed by the passion in it. You're part of something larger than yourself, and you feel real pain that uninformed outsiders are harming the thing you love. I don't see much of that passion in classrooms anymore. I wish you'd revealed your other life to us earlier.'

Now she was confused, fatigued and confused, and her nausea was increasing. 'I wouldn't have done it today, Professor,' Andi said, 'except my forty-fifth birthday is coming up in two weeks and I'm into a midlife crisis so real it's like living with a big sister who just wants to dress up in thigh-highs and a miniskirt and dance the funky chicken. No telling what kind of zany thing I'll do these days. And last night I got called out on a murder-suicide that looked like O.J. Simpson was back in town, and I'm exhausted. But I'm not half as tired or stressed as two young cops who had to wallow in a bloodbath doing a job that nobody should ever have to do.

And when it was all over, one of them asked me back at Hollywood Station if I had some moisturizing cream. Because he surfed so much he thought his neck and eyelids looked like they belonged on a Galapagos turtle. I felt like just hugging him.'

Then the catch in her voice made her pause again, and she said, 'I'm sorry. I'm babbling. I've gotta get some sleep. Good-bye, Professor.'

As she gathered her purse and books, he held up his class folder, opened it, and pointed to her name, along with the grade he'd given her presentation when he'd sat there behind her, when she'd thought he wasn't listening. It was an A-plus.

'Good-bye, Detective McCrea,' he said. 'Take care in Gotham City.'

Andi McCrea was driving back to Hollywood Division (she'd never get used to calling it Hollywood Area, as it was supposed to be called these days but which most of the street cops ignored) to assure herself that all the reports from last night's murder-suicide were complete. She was a D2 in one of the three homicide teams, but they were so shorthanded at Hollywood Station that she had nobody else around today who could help with the reports from her current cases, not even the one that had solved itself like the murder-suicide of the night before.

She decided to send an FTD bouquet to Professor Anglund for the A-plus that guaranteed her the Dean's List. That old socialist was okay after all, she thought, scribbling a note saying 'flowers' after she wheeled into the Hollywood Station south parking lot in her Volvo sedan.

The station parking lots were more or less adequate for the time being, considering how many patrol units, plain-wrap detectives units, and private cars had to park there. If they were ever brought up to strength, they'd have to build a parking structure, but she knew that it wasn't likely that the LAPD would ever be brought up to strength. And when would the city pop for money to build a parking structure when street cops citywide were complaining about the shortage of equipment like digital cameras and batteries for rifle lights, shotgun lights, and even flashlights. They never seemed to have pry bars or hooks or rams when it was time to take down a door. They never seemed to have anything when it was needed.

Andi McCrea was bone-weary and not just because she had not slept since yesterday morning. Hollywood Division's workload called for fifty detectives, but half that many were doing the job, or trying to do it, and these days she was always mentally tired. As she trudged toward the back door of Hollywood Station, she couldn't find her ring of keys buried in the clutter of her purse, gave up, and walked to the front door, on Wilcox Avenue.

The building itself was a typical municipal shoe box with a brick facade the sole enhancement, obsolete by the time it was finished. Four hundred souls were crammed inside a rabbit warren of tiny spaces. Even one of the detectives' interview rooms had to be used for storage.

By habit, she walked around the stars on the pavement in front of the station without stepping on them. There was nothing like them at other LAPD stations, and they were exactly like the stars on the Hollywood Walk of Fame except that the names imbedded in the marble were not the names of movie stars. There were seven names, all belonging to officers from Hollywood Station who had been killed on duty. Among them were Robert J. Coté, shot and killed by a robber, Russell L. Kuster, gunned down in a Hungarian restaurant by a deranged customer, Charles D. Heim, shot to death during a drug arrest, and Ian J. Campbell, kidnapped by robbers and murdered in an onion field.

The wall plaque said 'To Those Who Stood Their Ground When in Harm's Way.'

Hollywood Station was also different from any other in the LAPD by virtue of the interior wall hangings. There were one-sheet movie posters hanging in various places in the station, some but not all from cop movies based in Los Angeles. A police station decorated with movie posters let people know exactly where they were.

Andi was passed in the corridor leading to the detective squad room by two young patrol officers on their way out. Although there were several older cops working patrol, Hollywood Division officers tended to be young, as though the brass downtown considered Hollywood a training area, and perhaps they did.

The short Japanese American female officer she knew as Mag something said hi to Andi.

The tall black male officer whose name she didn't know said more formally, 'Afternoon, Detective.'

Six-X-Sixty-six had been asked by the vice sergeant to pop into a few of the adult bookstores to make sure there weren't lewd-conduct violations taking place in the makeshift video rooms. A pair of Hollywood Station blue suits making unscheduled visits went a long way toward convincing the termites to clean up their act, the vice sergeant had told them. Mag Takara, an athletic twenty-six-year-old, and the shortest officer at Hollywood Station, was partnered in 6-X-66 with Benny Brewster, age twenty-five, from southeast LA, who was one of Hollywood's tallest officers.

One morning last month, the Oracle had spotted a clutch of male cops in the parking lot after roll call convulsing in giggles at Mag Takara, who, after putting her overloaded war bag into the trunk, couldn't close the lid because it was sprung and yawned open out of reach.

Mag's war bag was on wheels, jammed with helmet and gear. She had also been carrying a Taser, an extra canister of pepper spray, a beanbag shotgun, a pod (handheld MDT computer), her jacket, a bag of reports, a flashlight, a side-handle baton as well as a retractable steel baton, and the real we-mean-business shotgun loaded with double-aught buck that would be locked in the rack inside the car. She was so short she had to go around to the rear window of the patrol car and close the trunk by walking her hands along the length of the deck lid until it clicked shut.

The Oracle watched her for a moment and heard the loudest of the cops tossing out lines to the others like, 'It's a little nippy, wouldn't you say? A teeny little nippy.'

The Oracle said to the jokester, 'Bonelli, her great-grandparents ran a hotel on First Street in little Tokyo when yours were still eating garlic in Palermo. So spare us the ethnic wisecracks, okay?'

Bonelli said, 'Sorry, Sarge.'

While the cops were all walking to their patrol cars, the Oracle said, 'I gotta balance that kid out.' And he'd assigned Benny Brewster to partner with Mag for the deployment period to see how they got along. And so far, so good, except that Benny Brewster had a cultural hangup about adult bookstores when it came to gay porn.

'Those sissies creep me out,' he said to Mag. 'Some of the gangstas in Compton would cap their ass, they saw the stuff we see all over Hollywood' is how he explained it.

But Mag told him she didn't give a shit if the fuck flicks were gay or straight, it was all revolting. One of her former cop boyfriends had tried to light her fire a couple of times by showing her porn videos in his apartment after dinner, but it seemed to her that act two of all those stories consisted of jizz shots in a girl's face, and how that could excite anybody was way beyond her.

Despite his hangup about gay men, Benny seemed to her like a dedicated officer, never badge-heavy, never manhandling anybody who didn't need it, whether gay or straight, so she had no complaints. And it was very comforting for Mag when Benny was standing behind her, eye-fucking some of those maggots who liked to challenge little cops, especially little female cops.

They met Mr. Potato Head in the first porn shop they checked out. It was on Western Avenue, a dingier place than most, with a few peep rooms where guys could look at video and jerk off with the door locked, but this one had a makeshift theater, a larger room with three rows of plastic chairs posing as theater seats, and a large screen along with a quality projector hanging from the ceiling.

The theater was curtained off by heavy black drapes and there was no lighting inside, except for what came from the screen. The occasional visit from uniformed cops was supposed to discourage the viewers from masturbating in public, whether alone or in tandem, while they watched two or three or five guys porking whatever got in front of them. To background hip-hop lyrics about rape and sodomy.

Benny walked down one aisle, looking like he wanted to get it over with, and Mag started down the other, when she heard him say, 'Do your pants up and come with me!'

The viewer had been so involved in what he was doing that he hadn't seen that very tall black cop in a dark blue uniform until he was standing three feet away. He lost the erection he'd been stroking, as did just about all of the other guys in the room, but Mag figured some of these dudes were so bent that the presence of the law, the danger of it all, probably enhanced the thrill.

She shined her light across the chair to see what was going on but he had already pulled up and belted his pants. He was being led by the elbow toward the black curtain and Benny kept saying, 'Damn!'

When they got him out of the video room, Mag said, 'What? Six-forty-seven-A?' referring to the penal code section for lewd conduct in public.

Benny looked at the guy, at the black elastic straps wound around his wrists, and said, 'What were you doing in there, man? Besides displayin' your willie. What're them straps on your wrists all about?'

He was a fiftyish plump, bespectacled white guy with a pouty mouth and a fringe of brown hair. He said, 'I'd prefer not to explain at this time.'

But when they took him to a glass-windowed holding tank at Hollywood Station, they found out. He gave a short demonstration that caused Benny to exit the scene shortly after the prisoner dropped his pants and unhooked the intricately connected elastic straps that encircled his waist, wound under his crotch from each wrist, and finally threaded through holes in the end of a potato. Which he reached behind and removed from his anal cavity with a magician's flourish and not a little pride of invention.

Performing before five gaping cops who happened by the glass window, the prisoner then demonstrated that if he sat on one buttock and manipulated the straps attached to his wrists, he could adeptly pull the potato halfway out simply by raising his arms, then force it back into its 'magic cave' by sitting on it. He looked like he was conducting an orchestra. Arms raised, potato out, then sit. Arms raised, potato out, then sit. And so forth.

'Probably keeping time with the background music on the video,' Mag suggested. The guy was ingenious, she had to give him that.

'I ain't handling the evidence,' Benny said to Mag. 'No way. In fact, I wanna transfer outta this lunatic asylum. I'll work anywhere but Holly-weird!'

It disappointed her. *Holly-weird*. Why did they all have to say it?

By end-of-watch, Benny would find a gift box tied with a ribbon in front of his locker and a card bearing the name 'Officer Brewster.' Inside the box was a nice fresh Idaho potato to which someone had attached plastic eyes and lips, along with a handwritten note that said, 'Fry me, bake me, mash me. Or bite me, Benny. Love ya. – Mr. Potato Head.'

FIVE

There was always a male cop at LAPD with 'Hollywood' attached to his name, whether or not he worked Hollywood Division. It was usually earned by the cop's outside interest in things cinematic. If he did an occasional job with a TV or movie company as a technical advisor, you could be sure everyone would start calling him 'Hollywood Lou' or 'Hollywood Bill.' Or in the case of aspiring thespian Nate Weiss – who so far had only done some work as an extra on a few TV shows – 'Hollywood Nate.' After he got bitten by the show business bug, he enrolled at a gym and worked out obsessively. With those brown bedroom eyes and dark, wavy hair just starting to gray at the temples, along with his newly buffed physique, Nate figured he had leading-man potential.

Nathan Weiss was thirty-five years old, a late bloomer as far as show business was concerned. He, along with lots of other patrol officers in the division, had done traffic control and provided security when film companies were shooting around town. The pay was excellent for off-duty cops and the work was easy enough but not as exciting as any of them had hoped. Not when all those hot actresses only popped their heads out of their trailers for a few minutes to block out a scene if the director wasn't satisfied with a stand-in doing it. Then they'd disappear again until it was time to shoot it.

Most of the time, the cops weren't up close for the shooting itself, and even when they were, it quickly became boring. After the master shot, they'd do two-shots of the principals, with close-ups and reverse angles, and the actors had to do it over and over. So most of the cops would quickly get bored and hang around the craft services people, who supplied all the great food for the cast and crew.

Hollywood Nate never got bored with any of it. Besides, there were a lot of hot chicks doing below-the-line work and ordinary grunt work on every shoot. Some of them were interns who dreamed of someday being above-the-line talent: directors, actors, writers, and producers. When Nate had a lot of overtime opportunities, he actually made more money than just about all of those cinematic grunts. And unlike them, Nate did not have to suffer the biggest fear in show business: My Next Job.

Nate loved to display his knowledge of the Business when talking to some little hottie, maybe a gofer running errands for the first assistant director. Nate would say things like 'My usual beat is around Beachwood Canyon. That's old Hollywood. A lot of below-the-line people live there.'

And it was one of those gofers who had cost Nate Weiss his less than happy home two years back, when his then-wife, Rosie, got suspicious because every time the phone rang one time and stopped, Nate would disappear for a while. Rosie started making date and time notations whenever one ring occurred, and she compared it with his cell phone bills. Sure enough, Nate would call the same two numbers moments after the one-ring calls she noted. Probably the slut had two cell phones or two home numbers, and it would be just like Nate to think two separate numbers would fool Rosie if she got suspicious.

Rosie Weiss bided her time, and one cold winter morning Nate came home from work at dawn telling her he was just all tuckered out from an overtime hunt for a cat burglar in Laurel Canyon. Rosie thought, Sure, an alley cat, no doubt. And she did a little experiment in Nate's car while he slept, and then managed to just go about her business for the rest of the day and that evening.

The next day, when Nate went to work, he sat in the roll-call room listening to the lieutenant droning on about the US Department of Justice consent decree that the LAPD was under and hinting that the cars that were working the Hispanic neighborhoods on the east side should be turning in Field Data Reports on non-Hispanics, even though there were none around.

Cops did what cops were doing from Highland Park to Watts, those who worked African American 'hoods and Latino barrios. LAPD officers were inventing white male suspects and entering them on FDRs that contained no names or birth dates and were untraceable. Therefore, an abundance of white male field interviews could convince outside monitors that the cops were not racial profiling. In one inner-city division, there was a 290 percent increase in non-Hispanic white male nighttime pedestrian stops, even though nobody had ever seen a white guy walking around the 'hood at night. Even with a flat tire, a white guy would keep riding on the rims rather than risk a stop. Cops said that even a black-and-white had to have a sign in the window saying 'Driver carries no cash.'

This was the federal consent decree's version of 'don't ask, don't tell': We won't ask where you got all those white male names on the FDRs if you don't tell us.

Before the watch commander had arrived at roll call, a cop said aloud, 'This FDR crap is so labor-intensive it makes embryonic cloning look like paint matching.'

Another said, 'We should all just become lawyers. They get paid a lot to lie, even if they have to dress up to do it.'

So it seemed that the Department of Justice, instead of promoting police integrity, had done just the opposite, by making liars out of LAPD street cops who had to live under the consent decree for five years and then had to swallow the demoralizing three-year extension.

During that ponderous roll call, Hollywood Nate was dozing through the consent decree sermon and got surprised when the Oracle popped his head in the door, saying, 'Sorry, Lieutenant, can I borrow Weiss for a minute?'

The Oracle didn't say anything until they were alone on the stairway landing, when he turned to Nate and said, 'Your wife is downstairs demanding to speak to the lieutenant. She wants a one-twenty-eight made on you.'

Nate was mystified. 'A personnel complaint? Rosie?'

'Do you have any kids?'

'Not yet. We've decided to wait.'

'Do you want to save your marriage?'

'Sure. It's my first, so I still give a shit. And her old man's got bucks. What's happened?'

'Then cop out and beg for mercy. Don't try weasel words, it won't work.'

'What's going on, Sarge?'

Hollywood Nate got to see for himself what was going on when he, Rosie, and the Oracle stood in the south parking lot beside Nate's SUV on that damp and gloomy winter night. Still baffled, Nate handed his keys to the Oracle, who handed them to Rosie, who jumped into the SUV, started it up, and turned on the defroster. As the windows were fogging prior to clearing, she stepped out and pointed triumphantly at what her sleuthing had uncovered. There they were, in the mist on the windshield in front of the passenger seat: oily imprints made by bare toes.

'Wears about a size five,' Rosie said. Then she turned to the Oracle and said, 'Nate always did like little spinners. I'm way too zoftig for him.'

When Nate started to speak, the Oracle said, 'Shut up, Nate.' Then he turned to Rosie and said, 'Mrs. Weiss ... '

'Rosie. You can call me Rosie, Sergeant.'

'Rosie. There's no need to drag the lieutenant into this. I'm sure that you and Nate – '

Interrupting, she said, 'I called my dad's lawyer today while this son of a bitch was sleeping it off. It's over. Way over. I'm moving everything out of the apartment on Saturday.'

'Rosie,' the Oracle said. 'I'm positive that Nate will be very fair when he talks with your lawyer. Your idea of making an official complaint for conduct unbecoming an officer would not be helpful to you. I imagine you want him working and earning money rather than suspended from duty, where he and you would lose money, don't you?'

She looked at the Oracle and at her husband, who was pale and silent, and she smiled when she saw beads of sweat on Nate's upper lip. The asshole was sweating on a damp winter night. Rosie Weiss liked that.

'Okay, Sergeant,' she said. 'But I don't want this asshole to set foot in the apartment until I'm all moved out.'

'He'll sleep in the cot room here at the station,' the Oracle said. 'And I'll detail an officer to make an appointment with you to pick up whatever Nate needs to tide him over until you're out of the apartment.'

When Rosie Weiss left them in the parking lot that evening, she had one more piece of information to impart to the Oracle. She said, 'Anyway, since he got all those muscles in the gym, the only time he can ever get an erection is when he's looking in the mirror.'

After she got in her car and drove away, Nate finally spoke. He said, 'A cop should never marry a Jewish woman, Sarge. Take it from me, she's a terrorist. It's code red from the minute the alarm goes off in the morning.'

'She's got good detective instincts,' the Oracle said. 'We could use her on the Job.'

Now, his wife was married to a pediatrician, no longer entitled to alimony, and Nate Weiss was a contented member of the midwatch, taking TV extra work as much as he could, hoping to catch a break that could get him into the Screen Actors Guild. He was sick of saying, 'Well, no, I don't have a SAG card but ...'

Hollywood Nate had hoped that 2006 would be his breakthrough year, but with summer almost here, he wasn't so sure. His reverie ended when he got a painfully vigorous handshake from his new partner, twenty-two-year-old Wesley Drubb, youngest son of a partner in Lawford and Drubb real estate developers, who had enormous holdings in West Hollywood and Century City. Nate got assigned with the former frat boy who'd dropped out of USC in his senior year 'to find himself' and impulsively joined the LAPD, much to the despair of his parents. Wesley had just finished his eighteen months of probation and transferred to Hollywood from West Valley Division.

Nate thought he'd better make the best of this opportunity. It wasn't often he got to partner with someone rich. Maybe he could cement a friendship and become the kid's big brother on the Job, maybe persuade him to chat up his old man, Franklin Drubb, about investing in a little Indie film that Nate had been trying to put together with another failed actor named Harley Wilkes.

The cops often called their patrol car their 'shop' because of the shop number painted on the front doors and roof. This so that each car could be easily identified by an LAPD helicopter, always called an 'airship.' When they were settled in their shop and out cruising the streets that Nate like to cruise no matter which beat he was assigned, the eager kid riding shotgun swiveled his head to the right and said, 'That looks like a fifty-one-fifty,' referring to the Welfare and Institutions Code section that defines a mental case.

The guy was a mental case, all right, one of the boulevard's homeless, the kind that shuffle along Hollywood Boulevard and wander into the many souvenir shops and adult bookstores and tattoo parlors, bothering the vendors at the sidewalk newsstands, refusing to leave until somebody gives them some change or throws them out or calls the cops.

He was known to the police as 'Untouchable Al' because he roamed freely and often got warned by cops but was never arrested. Al had a get-out-of-jail-free card that was better than Trombone Teddy's any old day. This evening he was in a cranky mood, yelling and scaring tourists, causing them to step into the street rather than pass close to him there on the Walk of Fame.

Nate said, 'That's Al. He's untouchable. Just tell him to get off the street. He will unless he's feeling extra grumpy.'

Hollywood Nate pulled the black-and-white around the corner onto Las Palmas Avenue, and Wesley Drubb, wanting to show his older partner that he had moxie, jumped out, confronted Al, and said, 'Get off the street. Go on, now, you're disturbing the peace.'

Untouchable Al, who was drunk and feeling very grumpy indeed, said, 'Fuck you, you young twerp.'

Wesley Drubb was stunned and turned to look at Nate, who was out of the car, leaning on the roof with his elbows, shaking his head, knowing what was coming.

'He's having a bad hair day,' Nate said. 'A dozen or so are hanging out his nose.'

'We don't have to take that,' Wesley said to Nate. Then he turned to Al and said, 'We don't have to take that from you.'

Yes, they did. And Al was about to demonstrate why. As soon as Wesley Drubb pulled on his latex gloves and stepped forward, putting his hand on Al's bony shoulder, the geezer shut his eyes tight and grimaced and groaned and squatted a bit and let it go.

The explosion was so loud and wet that the young cop leaped back three feet. The sulfurous stench struck him at once.

'He's shitting!' Wesley cried in disbelief. 'He's shitting his pants!'

'I don't know how he craps on cue like that,' Nate said. 'It's a rare talent, actually. Kind of the ultimate defense against the forces of truth and justice.'

'Gross!' the young cop cried. 'He's shitting! Gross!'

'Come on, Wesley,' Hollywood Nate said. 'Let's go about our business and let Al finish his.'

'Fucking young twerp,' Untouchable Al said as the black-and-white drove swiftly away.

*

While Untouchable Al was finishing his business, an extraordinary robbery was taking place at a jewelry store on Normandie Avenue owned by a Thai entrepreneur who also owned two restaurants. The little jewelry store that sold mostly watches was this week offering a very special display of diamonds that the proprietor's twenty-nine-year-old nephew, Somchai 'Sammy' Tanampai, planned to take home when he closed that evening.

The robbers, an Armenian named Cosmo Betrossian and his girlfriend, a Russian masseuse and occasional prostitute named Ilya Roskova, had entered the store just before closing, wearing stocking masks. Now Sammy Tanampai sat on the floor in the back room, his wrists duct-taped behind his back, weeping because he believed they would kill him whether or not they got what they wanted.

Sammy forced his eyes from roaming to his son's cartoon-plastered lunch box on a table by the back door. He'd placed the diamonds in little display trays and velvet bags and stacked them inside the lunch box next to a partially consumed container of rice, eggs, and crab meat.

Sammy Tanampai thought they might be after the watches, but they didn't touch any of them. The male robber, who had very thick black eyebrows grown together, raised up the stocking mask to light a cigarette. Sammy could see small broken teeth, a gold incisor, and pale gums.

He walked to where Sammy was sitting on the floor, pulled Sammy's face up by jerking back a handful of hair, and said in heavily accented English, 'Where do you hide diamonds?'

Sammy was so stunned he didn't respond until the large blond woman with the sulky mouth, garishly red under the stocking mask, walked over, bent down, and said in less accented English, 'Tell us and we will not kill you.'

He started to weep then and felt urine soak his crotch, and the man pointed the muzzle of a .25 caliber Raven pistol at his face. Sammy thought, What a cheap-looking gun they are about to shoot me with.

Then his gaze involuntarily moved toward his child's lunch box and the man followed Sammy's gaze and said, 'The box!'

Sammy wept openly when the big blond woman opened the lunch box containing more than a hundred and eighty thousand wholesale dollars' worth of loose diamonds, rings, and ear studs and said, 'Got it!'

The man then ripped off a strip of duct tape and wrapped it around Sammy's mouth.

How did they know? Sammy thought, preparing to die. Who knew about the diamonds?

The woman waited by the front door and the man removed a heavy object from the pocket of his coat. When Sammy saw it he cried more, but the duct tape kept him quiet. It was a hand grenade.

The woman came back in, and for the first time Sammy noticed their latex gloves. Sammy wondered why he hadn't noticed before, and then he was confused and terrified because the man, holding the spoon handle of the grenade, placed it between Sammy's knees while the woman wrapped tape around his ankles. The grenade spoon dug into the flesh of his thighs above the knees and he stared at it.

When the robbers were finished, the woman said, 'You better got strong legs. If you relax too much your legs, you shall lose the handle. And then you die.'

And with that, the man, holding Sammy's knees in place, pulled the pin and dropped it on the floor beside him.

Now Sammy did wail, the muffled sound very audible even with his mouth taped shut.

'Shut up!' the man commanded. 'Keep the knees tight or you be dead man. If the handle flies away, you be dead man.'

The woman said, 'We shall call police in ten minutes and they come to help you. Keep the knees together, honey. My mother always tell me that but I do not listen.'

They left then but didn't call the police. A Mexican dishwasher named Pepe Ramirez did. He was on his way to his job in Thai Town, driving past the boss's jewelry store, and was surprised to see light coming from the main part of the store. It should have been closed. The boss always closed before now so he could get to both his restaurants while they were preparing for the dinner crowd. Why was the boss's store still open? he wondered.

The dishwasher parked his car and entered the jewelry store through the unlocked front door. He spoke very little English and no Thai at all, so all he could think to call out was 'Meester? Meester?'

When he got no answer, he walked cautiously toward the back room and stopped when he heard what sounded like a dog's whimper. He listened and thought, No, it's a cat. He didn't like this, not at all. Then he heard banging, a loud muffled series of thumps. He ran from the store and called 911 on his brand-new cell phone, the first he'd ever owned.

Because of his almost unintelligible English and because he hung up while the operator was trying to transfer the call to a Spanish speaker, his message had been misunderstood. Other undocumented migrants had told him that the city police were not *la migra* and would not call Immigration unless he committed a major crime, but he was uncomfortable around anyone with a uniform and badge and thought he should not be there when they came.

It came out over the air as an 'unknown trouble' call, the kind that makes cops nervous. There was enough known trouble in police work. Usually such a call would draw more than one patrol unit as backup. Mag Takara and Benny Brewster got the call, and Fausto Gamboa and Budgie Polk were the first backup to arrive, followed by Nate Weiss and Wesley Drubb.

When Mag entered the store, she drew her pistol and following her flashlight beam walked cautiously into the back room with Benny Brewster right behind her. What she saw made her let out a gasp.

Sammy Tanampai had hopelessly banged his head against the plasterboard wall, trying to get the attention of the dishwasher. His legs were going numb and the tears were streaming down his face as he tried to think about his children, tried to stay strong. Tried to keep his knees together!

When Mag took two steps toward the jeweler, Benny Brewster shined his light on the grenade and yelled, 'WAIT!'

Mag froze and Fausto and Budgie, who had just entered by the front door, also froze.

Then Mag saw it clearly and yelled, 'GRENADE! CLEAR!' And nobody knew what was going on or what the hell to do except instinctively to draw their guns and crouch.

Fausto did not clear out. Nor did the others. He shouldered past Benny, plunged into the back room, and saw Mag standing two feet from the taped and hysterical Sammy Tanampai. And Fausto saw the grenade.

Sammy's face was bloody where he'd snagged the tape free on a nail head, and he tried to say something with a crumpled wad of tape stuck to the corner of his mouth. He gagged and said, 'I can't ... I can't ...'

Fausto said to Mag, 'GET OUT!'

But the littlest cop ignored him and tiptoed across the room as though motion would set it off. And she reached carefully for it.

Fausto leaped forward after Sammy unleashed the most despairing terrifying wail that Mag had ever heard in her life when his thigh muscles just surrendered. Mag's fingers were inches from the grenade when it dropped to the floor beneath her and the spoon flew across the room.

'CLEAR CLEAR CLEAR!' Fausto yelled to all the cops in the store, but Mag picked up the grenade first and lobbed it into the far corner behind a file cabinet.

Instantly, Fausto grabbed Mag Takara by the back of her Sam Browne and Sammy Tanampai by his shirt collar and lifted them both off the floor, lunging backward until they were out of the little room and into the main store, where all six cops and one shopkeeper pressed to the floor and waited in terror for the explosion.

Which didn't come. The hand grenade was a dummy.

No fewer than thirty-five LAPD employees were to converge on that store and the streets around it that night: detectives, criminalists, explosives experts, patrol supervisors, even the patrol captain. Witnesses were interviewed, lights were set up, and the area for two blocks in all directions was searched by cops with flashlights.

They found nothing of evidentiary value, and a detective from the robbery team who had been called in from home interviewed Sammy Tanampai in the ER at Hollywood Presbyterian Hospital. The victim told the detective that the male robber had briefly smoked a cigarette but none had been found by detectives at the scene.

Sammy grew lethargic because the injection they had given him was making him sleepy, but he said to the detective, 'I don't know how they knew about the diamonds. The diamonds arrived at ten o'clock this morning and we were going to show them tomorrow to a client from Hong Kong who requested certain kinds of pieces.'

'What kind of client is he?' the detective asked.

'My uncle has dealt with him for years. He is very wealthy. He is not a thief.'

'About the blond woman who you think was Russian, tell me more.'

'I think they were both Russians,' Sammy said. 'There are lots of Russians around Hollywood.'

'Yes, but the woman. Was she attractive?'

'Perhaps so. I don't know.'

'Anything out of the ordinary?'

'Big breasts,' Sammy said, opening and closing his aching jaw and touching the wounded flesh around his mouth, his eyelids drooping.

'Have you ever gone to any of the nightclubs around here?' the detective asked. 'Several of them are Russian owned and operated.'

'No. I am married. I have two children.'

'Anything else that you remember about either of them?'

'She made a joke about keeping my knees together. She said that she never did. I was thinking of my children then and how I would never see them again. And she made that joke. I hope you get to shoot them both,' Sammy said, tears welling.

After all the cops who'd been in the jewelry store were interviewed back at the station, Hollywood Nate said to his young partner, 'Some gag, huh, Wesley? Next time I work on a show, I'm gonna tell the prop man about this. A dummy grenade. Only in Hollywood.'

Wesley Drubb had been very quiet for hours since their trauma in the jewelry store. He had answered questions from detectives as well as he could, but there really wasn't anything important to say. He answered Nate with, 'Yeah, the joke was on us.'

What young Wesley Drubb wanted to say was, 'I could have died tonight. I could have ... been ... *killed* tonight! If the grenade had been real.'

It was very strange, very eerie, to contemplate his own violent death. Wesley Drubb had never done that before. He wanted to talk to somebody about it but there was no one. He couldn't talk about it to his older partner, Nate Weiss. Couldn't explain to a veteran officer like Nate that he'd left USC for this, where he'd been on the sailing team and was dating one of the hottest of the famed USC song girls. He'd left it because of those inexplicable emotions he felt after he'd reached his twenty-first birthday.

Wesley had grown sick of college life, sick of being the son of Franklin Drubb, sick of living on Fraternity Row, sick of living in his parents' big house in Pacific Palisades during school holidays. He'd felt like a man in prison and he'd wanted to break out. LAPD was a break-out without question. And he'd completed his eighteen months of probation and was here, a brand-new Hollywood Division officer.

Wesley's parents had been shocked, his fraternity brothers, sailing teammates, and especially his girlfriend, who was now dating a varsity wide receiver – everyone who knew him was shocked. But he hadn't been sorry so far. He'd thought he'd probably do it for a couple of years, not for a career, for the kind of experience that would set him apart from his father and his older brother and every other goddamn broker in the real-estate firm owned by Lawford and Drubb.

He thought it would be like going into the military for a couple of years, but he wouldn't have to leave LA. Like a form of combat that he could talk about to his family and friends years later, when he inevitably became a broker at Lawford and Drubb. He'd be a sort of combat veteran in their eyes, that was it.

Yes, and it had all been going so well. Until tonight. Until that grenade hit the floor and he stared at it and that little officer Mag Takara picked it up with Fausto Gamboa roaring in his ears. That wasn't police work, was it? They never talked about things like that in the academy. A man with a hand grenade between his knees?

He remembered a Bomb Squad expert lecturing them at the police academy about the horrific event of 1986 in North Hollywood when two LAPD officers were called in to defuse an explosive device in a residential garage, rigged by a murder suspect involved in a movie studio/labor union dispute. They defused it but were unaware of a secondary device lying there by a copy of *The Anarchist's Cookbook*. The device went off.

What Wesley remembered most vividly was not the description of the gruesome and terrible carnage and the overwhelming smell of blood, but that one of the surviving officers who had just gotten inside the house before the explosion was having recurring nightmares two decades later. He would waken with his pillow soaked with tears and his wife shaking him and saying, 'This has *got* to stop!'

For a while this evening, after he'd completed his brief statement, after he was sitting in the station quietly drinking coffee, Wesley Drubb could only think about how he'd felt trying to dig with his fingernails into the old wooden floor of that jewelry store. It had been an instinctive reaction. He had been reduced to his elemental animal core.

And Wesley Drubb asked himself the most maddeningly complex, dizzying, profound, and unanswerable question he'd ever asked himself in his young life: How the fuck did I get here?

*

When Fausto Gamboa got changed into civvies, he met Budgie on the way to the parking lot. They walked quietly to their cars, where they saw Mag Takara already getting into her personal car and driving away.

Fausto said, 'It used to drive me crazy seeing that kid doing her nails during roll call. Like she was getting ready to go on a date.'

'I'll bet it won't annoy you anymore, will it?' Budgie said.

'Not as much,' Fausto Gamboa conceded.

SIX

This was supposed to be a routine interview of a missing juvenile, nothing more. Andi McCrea had been sitting in her little cubicle in the detective squad room staring at a computer screen, putting together reports to take to the DA's office in a case where a wife smacked her husband on the head with the side of a roofing hammer when, after drinking a six-pack of Scotch ale, he curled his lip and told her that the meatloaf she'd worked over 'smelled like Gretchen's snatch.'

There were two things wrong with that: First, Gretchen was her twice-divorced, flirtatious younger sister, and second, he had a panicstricken look on his face that denuded the feeble explanation when he quickly said, 'Of course, I wouldn't know what Gretchen's ...' Then he began again and said, 'I was just trying for a Chris Rock kind of line but didn't make it, huh? The meatloaf is fine. It's fine, honey.'

She didn't say a word but walked to the back porch, where the roofer kept his tool belt, and returned with the hammer just as he was taking the first bite of meatloaf that smelled like Gretchen's snatch.

Even though the wife had been booked for attempted murder, the guy only ended up with twenty-three stitches and a concussion. Andi figured that whichever deputy DA the case was taken to would reject it as a felony and refer it to the city attorney's office for a misdemeanor filing, which was fine with her. The hammer victim reminded her of her ex-husband, Jason, now retired from LAPD and living in Idaho near lots of other coppers who had fled to the wilderness locales. Places where local cops only write on their arrest reports under race of suspects either 'white' or 'landscaper.'

Jason had been one of those whom several other women officers had sampled, the kind they called 'Twinkies,' guys who aren't good for you but you have to have one. Andi had been young then, and she paid the price during a five-year marriage that brought her nothing good except Max.

Her only child, Sergeant Max Edward McCrea, was serving with the US Army in Afghanistan, his second deployment, the first having been in Iraq at a time when Andi was hardly ever able to sleep more than a few hours before waking with night sweats. It was better now that he was in Afghanistan. A little better. Eighteen years old, just out of high school, he had gotten the itch, and there was nothing she could do to keep him from signing that enlistment contract. Nothing that her ex-husband could do either, when for once Jason had stepped up and acted like a father. Max had said he was going into the army with two other teammates from his varsity football team, and that was it. Iraq for him, tension headaches for her, lying awake in her two-story house in Van Nuys.

After getting her case file in order, Andi was about to get a cup of coffee, when one of the Watch 2 patrol officers approached her cubicle and said, 'Detective, could you talk to a fourteen-year-old runaway for us? We got a call to the Lucky Strike Lanes, where he was bowling with a forty-year-old guy who started slapping him around. He tells us he was molested by the guy, but the guy won't talk at all. We got him in a holding tank.'

'You need the sex crimes detail,' Andi said.

'I know, but they're not here and I think the kid wants to talk but only to a woman. Says the things he's got to say are too embarrassing to tell a man. I think he needs a mommy.'

'Who doesn't?' Andi sighed. 'Okay, put him in the interview room and I'll be right there.'

Five minutes later, after drinking her coffee, and after getting the boy a soft drink and advising him for the second time of his rights, she nodded to the uniformed officer that he could leave.

Aaron Billings was delicate, almost pretty, with dark ringlets, wide-set expressive eyes, and a mature, lingering gaze that she wouldn't have expected. He looked of mixed race, maybe a quarter African American, but she couldn't be sure. He had a brilliant smile.

'Do you understand why the officers arrested you and your companion?' she asked.

'Oh, sure,' he said. 'Mel was hitting me. Everyone saw him. We were right there in the bowling alley. I'm sick of it, so when they asked for our ID I told them I was a runaway. I'm sure my mom's made a report. Well, I think she would.'

'Where're you from?'

'Reno, Nevada.'

'How long have you been gone?'

'Three weeks.'

'Did you run away with Mel?' Andi asked.

'No, but I met him the next day when I was hitchhiking. I was sick of my mother. She was always bringing men home, and my sister and me would see them having sex. My sister is ten.'

'You told the officer that Mel molested you, is that right?'

'Yes, lots of times.'

'Tell me what happened from when you first met.'

'Okay,' the kid said, and he took a long drink from the soda can. 'First, he took me to a motel and we had sex. I didn't want to but he made me.

Then he gave me ten dollars. Then we went to the movies. Then we had Chinese food at a restaurant. Then we decided to drive to Hollywood and maybe see movie stars. Then Mel bought vodka and orange juice and we got drunk. Then we drove to Fresno and parked at a rest stop and slept. Then we woke up early. Then we killed two people and took their money. Then we went to the movies again. Then we drove to Bakersfield. Then—'

'Wait a minute!' Andi said. 'Let's go back to the rest stop!'

Twenty minutes later Andi was on the phone to the police in Fresno, and after a conversation with a detective, she learned that yes, a middle-aged couple had been shot and killed where they'd obviously been catching a few hours' sleep en route from Kansas to a California vacation. And yes, the case was open with no suspects and no evidence other than the .32 caliber slugs taken from the skulls of both victims at the postmortem.

The detective said, 'We just don't have any leads.'

Andi said, 'You do now.'

When Andi's supervisor, D3 Rhonda Jenkins, came in late that afternoon after a long day in court testifying in a three-year-old murder case, she said, 'My day sucked. How was yours?'

'Tried to keep busy on a typical May afternoon in Hollywood, USA.'

'Yeah? What'd you do?' Rhonda asked, just making conversation as she slipped off her low-heeled pumps and massaged her aching feet.

Deadpan, Andi said, 'First I made calls on two reports from last night. Then I reread the case file on the pizza man shooting. Then I interviewed a banger down at Parker Center. Then I had some coffee. Then I cleared a double homicide in Fresno. Then I wrote a letter to Max. Then—'

'Whoa!' Rhonda said. 'Go back to the double homicide in Fresno!'

'That bitch! You couldn't find her heart with a darkfield microscope,' Jetsam complained to his partner.

Flotsam, who was attending community college during the day, said, 'Dude, you are simply another victim of the incestuous and intertwined and atavistic relationships of the law-enforcement community.'

Jetsam gaped at Flotsam, who was driving up into the Hollywood Hills, and said, 'Just shove those college-boy words, why don't you.'

'Okay, to be honest,' said Flotsam, 'from that photo you showed me, she was spherical, dude. The woman looked to me like a fucking Teletubby. You were blinded by the humongous mammary glands is all. There was no real melding of the hearts and minds.'

'Melding of the ...' Jetsam looked at his partner in disbelief and said, 'Bro, the bitch's lawyer wants everything, including my fucking fish tank! With the only two turtles I got left! And guess what else? The federal consent decree ain't gonna end on schedule because that asshole of a federal judge says we're not ready. It's all political bullshit.'

'Don't tell me that,' Flotsam said. 'I was all ready to yell out at roll call, "Free at last, free at last, Lord God Awmighty, free at last!"'

'I'm outrageously pissed off at our new mayor,' Jetsam said, 'turning the police commission into an ACLU substation. And I'm pissed off at my ex-wife's lawyer, who only wants me to have what I can make recycling aluminum cans. And I'm pissed off living in an apartment with lunging fungus so aggressive it wants to tackle you like a linebacker. And I'm pissed off at my former back-stabbing girlfriend. And I'm pissed off at the Northeast detective who's boning her now. So all in all, I feel like shooting somebody.'

And, as it happened, he would.

The PSR radio voice alerted all units on the frequency to a code 37, meaning a stolen vehicle, as well as a police pursuit in progress of said vehicle.

Ever the pessimist, Jetsam said, 'Devonshire Division. He'll never come this far south.'

The more optimistic Flotsam said, 'You never know. We can dream.'

Jetsam said, 'Since our politician chief won't let us pursue unless the driver's considered reckless, do you suppose this fucking maniac has crossed the reckless-driving threshold yet? Or does he have to run a cop off the road first?'

They listened to the pursuit on simulcast as it crossed freeways and surface streets in the San Fernando Valley, heading in the general direction of North Hollywood. And within a few minutes it was in North Hollywood and heading for the Hollywood Freeway.

'Watch them turn north again,' Jetsam said.

But the pursuit did not. The stolen car, a new Toyota 4Runner, turned south on the Hollywood Freeway, and Jetsam said, 'That one has a pretty hot six under the hood from what I hear. Bet he'll double-back now. Probably some homie. He'll double-back, get near his 'hood, dump the car, and run for it.'

But the pursuit left the Hollywood Freeway and turned east on the Ventura Freeway and then south on Lankershim Boulevard. And now the surfer team looked at each other and Jetsam said, 'Holy shit. Let's go!'

And they did. Flotsam stepped on it and headed north on the Hollywood Freeway past Universal City and turned off in the vicinity of the Lakeside Country Club, where by now a dozen LAPD and CHP units were involved, as well as a television news helicopter, but no LAPD airship.

And it was here that the driver dumped the car on a residential street near the country club, and he was into a yard, over a fence into another yard, onto the golf course, running across fairways, and then back into a North Hollywood residential street where nearly twenty cops were out on foot, half of them armed with shotguns.

Even though a North Hollywood Division sergeant was at the abandoned stolen car, trying to inform the communications operator that there was sufficient help at the scene, cars kept coming, as happens during a long pursuit like this. Soon there were LA Sheriff's Department units as well as more CHP and LAPD cars, with the TV helicopter hovering and lighting up the running cops below.

Flotsam drove two blocks west of the pandemonium and said, 'Wanna get out and go hunting for a while? You never know.'

'Fucking A,' Jetsam said, and they got out of their car with flashlights extinguished and walked through a residential alley behind family homes and apartment buildings.

They could hear voices on the street to their right, where other cops were searching, and Flotsam said, 'Maybe we better turn our flashlights on before somebody caps one off at us.'

Then a voice yelled, 'There he is! Hey, there he is!'

They ran toward the voice and saw a young cop with ginger hair and pink complexion sitting astride an eight-foot block wall dividing an apartment complex from the alley.

He saw them, or rather, he saw two shadow figures in blue uniforms, and said, 'Up there! He's in that tree!'

Flotsam shined his light high into an old olive tree, and sure enough, there was a young Latino up there in an oversize white T-shirt, baggy khakis, and a head bandana.

The young cop yelled, 'Climb down now!' And he pointed his nine at the guy with one hand while with his other hand he shined his light on the treetop.

Flotsam and Jetsam got closer, and the guy in the tree looked down at the young cop straddling the wall and said, 'Fuck you. Come up and get me.'

Flotsam turned to Jetsam and said, 'Tweaked. He's fried on crystal.'

'Ain't everybody?' Jetsam said.

The young cop, who had 'probationer' written all over him, pulled out his rover but before keying it said, 'What's our location? Do you guys know the address here?'

'Naw,' Jetsam said. 'We work Van Nuys Division.'

Now, that was weird, Flotsam thought. Why would his partner tell the boot that they worked Van Nuys instead of telling the truth?

Then the young cop said, 'Watch him, will you? I gotta run out to the street and get the address.'

'Just go out front and start yelling,' Jetsam said. 'There's coppers all over the block.'

Flotsam also found it strange that Jetsam had turned his flashlight off and was standing in deep shadow under a second tree. Almost as though he didn't want the kid to be able to see him clearly. But why? That they had driven a short distance out of their division wasn't a big deal.

After the rookie ran out onto the street in front, Jetsam said, 'Fucking boot doesn't know what to do about a thief in a tree.'

They stood looking up at the guy who squinted down at their light beams, and Flotsam said, 'What would you do besides wait for backup?'

Jetsam looked up and yelled, 'Hey asshole, climb down here.'

The car thief said, 'I'm staying here.'

'How would you like me to blow you outta that tree?' Jetsam shouted, aiming his .40 caliber Glock at him. 'I feel like shooting somebody tonight.'

'You won't shoot,' the kid said. 'I'm a minor. And all I did was joyride.'

Now Jetsam was really torqued. And not for the first time he noticed that the young cop had left his Remington beanbag shotgun with the bright green fore and aft stocks propped against the wall.

'Check this out, partner,' he said to Flotsam. 'That probey grabbed a beanbag gun instead of the real thing. Now he's probably looking for a chain saw to cut the fucking tree down.'

Touching his pepper spray canister, Flotsam said, 'Wish he was closer, dude. A little act-right spray would do wonders for him.' Then Flotsam looked at Jetsam and Jetsam looked at Flotsam and Flotsam said, 'No. I know what you're thinking, but no. Stay real, man!'

But Jetsam said in a quiet voice, 'That boot never saw our faces, bro. There's coppers all over the neighborhood.'

'No,' Flotsam said. 'A beanbag gun is not to be used for compliance purposes. This ain't pit bull polo, dude.'

'I wonder if it would induce some compliance here.'

Flotsam said. 'I don't wanna know.'

But Jetsam, who had never shot anyone with a beanbag or anything else, reached into his pocket, put on a pair of latex gloves so as to not leave latent prints, picked up the shotgun, pointed it up into the tree, and said, 'Hey *vato*, get your ass down here right now or I'll let one go and blow you outta that tree.'

The muzzle of the gun looked big enough to hold a popsicle, but it didn't scare the car thief, who said, 'You and your *puto* partner can just kiss my—'

And the muzzle flash and explosion shocked Flotsam more than the kid, who let out a shriek when the beanbag struck him in the belly.

'Ow ow ow, you pussy!' the kid yelled. 'You shot me, you pussy! Owwwwwww!'

So Jetsam let go with another round, and this time Flotsam ran to the street in front of the apartment complex and saw no less than five shadow figures yelling and running their way while the kid howled even louder and started climbing down.

'Let's get the fuck outta here!' Flotsam said, after running back to Jetsam and grabbing him by the arm.

'He's coming down, bro,' Jetsam said with a dazed expression.

'Toss that tube!' Flotsam said, and Jetsam dropped the shotgun on the grass and scurried after his partner.

Both cops ran back down the alley through the darkness toward their car, and neither spoke until Flotsam said, 'Man, there'll be IA investigators all over this one, you crazy fucker! You ain't even allowed to shoot white guys like that!'

Still running, and gradually realizing that he'd just violated a whole lot of Department regulations, if not the penal code itself, Jetsam said, 'The homie never saw us, bro. The lights were always in his eyes. The little boot copper didn't see our faces neither. Shit, he was so excited he couldn't ID his own dick. Anyways, this is North Hollywood Division. We don't work here.'

'The best-laid plans of mice and rats,' Flotsam said. Then he had a panicky thought. 'Did you go code six?' he said, referring to the safety rule of informing communications of their location when leaving the car. 'I can't remember.'

Jetsam also panicked for a moment, then said, 'No, I'm sure I didn't. Nobody knows we're here in North Hollywood.'

'Let's get the fuck back to our beat!' Flotsam said when they reached their car, unlocked it, and got inside.

He drove with lights out until they were blocks from the scene and heard the PSR voice say 'All units, code four. Suspect in custody. Code four.'

They didn't talk at all until they were safely back cruising Hollywood Boulevard. Then Jetsam said, 'Let's get code seven. Our adventure's made me real hungry all of a sudden. And bro, your shit's kinda weak lately. We gotta jack you up somehow. Why don'tcha get one of those healthy reduced-fat burritos swimming in sour cream and and guacamole.' Then he added, 'It musta been those two shots I gave that homie, but I feel mega-happy now.'

And Flotsam could only gape when Jetsam suddenly began to sing the U2 hit: 'Two shots of happy, one shot of saaaaad. You think I'm no good, well I know I've been baaaaad.'

'You're scary, dude,' Flotsam said. 'You're as scary as a doctor putting on one rubber glove.'

Jetsam kept on singing: 'Took you to a place, now you can't get back. Two shots of happy, one shot of saaaaaad.'

Flotsam kept driving toward Sunset Boulevard and finally said, 'I wanna take you up to the Director's Chair first night we're off together. Have a few beers. Shoot some pool or darts.'

'Okay, I got nothing better to do, but I never been fond of the joint. Don't you wanna go someplace where there ain't so many cops?'

Flotsam said, 'I love a bar with a sign that says "No shirt, no shoes, no badge, no service." Besides, there's always a few badge bunnies around that'll pork any copper, even you.'

Jetsam said, 'Thank you, Dr. Ruth. Why're you so concerned with my sex life all of a sudden?'

Flotsam said, 'It's me I'm thinking about, dude. You gotta take your mind off your ex and her lawyer and that hose monster that dumped you. Either that or in order to protect my career and pension I gotta go find that Northeast detective she's snogging.'

'What for?'

'To cap him. We can't go on like this. You hearing me, dude?'

Cosmo Betrossian had always denied that he was even loosely associated with the so-called Russian Mafia. The federal and local authorities called everybody from the former USSR and eastern Europe 'Russian Mafia.' That is, everyone Cosmo knew, because everyone Cosmo knew was involved in illegal activity of one sort or another. The designations didn't make any sense to Cosmo, who, even though he had grown up in Soviet Armenia and spoke some bastardized Russian, was no more a Russian than George Bush was. He figured that American cops were just full of shit as far as eastern European immigrants were concerned.

But because of their obsession with Russian Mafia, he had to be careful when he had any business dealing with Dmitri, the owner of the Gulag, a nightclub on Western Avenue that wasn't in the best part of town but had a well-lit, well-guarded parking lot. Young people from all over the west side, even Beverly Hills and Brentwood, were not afraid to drive east to Little Siberia, as some called it.

The Gulag's food was good and they poured generous drinks and Dmitri gave them the recorded familiar rock sounds they wanted, which kept the dance floor jammed until closing time. And on the occasional 'Russian Night' Dmitri advertised live entertainment: Russian dancers, balalaikas, violins, and a beautiful singer from Moscow. It brought Dmitri a very wealthy clientele who had emigrated to Los Angeles from all over the former USSR, whether or not they were into legitimate business or smuggling or money laundering. But this night was not going to be one of the Russian nights.

A week had passed since the robbery, and Cosmo felt confident going to Dmitri. The police were even less of a worry. Nobody he knew had even been questioned. Early in the evening, he drove to the Gulag, entered, and went to the bar. He knew the bartender whom the Americans called 'Georgie' because he was from the Republic of Georgia, and asked to see Dmitri. The bartender poured him a shot of ouzo and Cosmo waited for the bartender to deal with two cocktail waitresses at the service bar who were giving the bartender more happy hour drink orders than he could handle.

The nightclub was typical for Hollywood in that there was an area set aside for private parties. In the Gulag the private area was upstairs, with plush green sofas lining walls papered in garish streaks of color – somebody's idea of 'edgy,' that favorite cliché of Hollywood scenesters, the other being 'vibe.' The Gulag was edgy. The Gulag vibed mysterious.

On this evening, the jock was just setting up and he spun some soft-rock standards for the end of the extended happy hour. There were two guys repairing some strobes and spots before the crowd arrived and bodies got writhing in the dance-floor pit. Busboys and waiters were wiping off tables and chairs and dusting the seats in the cuddle-puddle booths on the raised level for those customers who tipped the manager Andrei.

After ten minutes, Cosmo was directed upstairs into Dmitri's surprisingly spartan office where he found the club owner at his desk, slippered feet up, smoking a cigarette in a silver holder, and watching S&M porn on his computer screen. Everybody said that Dmitri indulged in all kinds of exotic sex. He was forty-one years old, not tall, had a slight build, soft hands, and bloodshot blue eyes, and was wearing a chestnut hair weave. He looked unexceptional and harmless in a white linen shirt and chinos, but Cosmo was very scared of him. He had heard things about Dmitri and his friends.

The club owner knew that Cosmo's Russian was extremely poor and Dmitri adored current American slang, so he had always spoken English to Cosmo. Without getting up he said, 'Here comes a happenink guy! A guy who always has it go-ink on! Hello, Cosmo!'

He reached out with one of those soft hands and slapped palms with Cosmo, who said, 'Dmitri, thank you for this talk. Thank you, brother.'

'You got some-think I need?'

'Yes, my brother,' Cosmo said, sitting in the client chair in front of the desk.

'Not credit-card information, I hope. In gen-yural I am not into credit cards no more, Cosmo. I am moving into other directions.'

'No, brother,' Cosmo said. 'I have brought for you something to show.' And with that he produced a single diamond, one of the larger stones from the jewelry store robbery, and put it gingerly on the desk.

Dmitri lowered his feet onto the floor and looked at the stone. He smiled at Cosmo and said, 'I do not know diamonds. But I have a friend who knows. Do you have more?'

'Yes,' Cosmo said. 'Much more. Many rings and earrings too. All very beautiful stones.'

Dmitri looked impressed. 'You are grow-ink in America!' he said. 'No more business with addicts?'

'Addicts do not have diamonds,' Cosmo said. 'I think you shall buy all my diamonds and sell for big profit, my brother.'

'It is possible that I should be een-wolved with you again, Cosmo,' Dmitri said, smiling. 'You are perhaps now a big man in America.'

'I wish to bring every diamond soon. I wish to sell for only thirty-five thousands. The news lady on TV say the diamonds worth maybe two, three hundred thousands.'

'The hand grenade!' Dmitri said with a grin. 'So it was you! But thirty-five thousand? You must bring me high-quality stones for thirty-five thousand.'

'Okay, brother,' Cosmo said. 'I shall bring.'

'I need perhaps one month to make my deal and to get so much cash for you,' Dmitri said. 'And to make sure that police do not arrest you in meantime.'

'I am very sad to hear that,' Cosmo said, sweat popping on his forehead. 'I must get money now.'

Dmitri shrugged and said, 'You may take your treasure to somebody else, Cosmo. No problem.'

Cosmo had nobody else for something like this, and he knew that Dmitri was aware of it.

'Okay,' Cosmo said. 'I wait. Please call me when you have money.'

'Now that you are grow-ink into a businessman,' Dmitri said as Cosmo bowed slightly and prepared to leave, 'you should shave between the eyebrows. Americans like two eyebrows, not one.'

On the night that Jetsam fired two shots of happy with no shot of sad, another shooting would take place, this one in Hollywood Division, that would provoke several shots of sad for two of the officers involved.

The code 3 call was given to 6-A-65 of Watch 3, directing them to a residential street on the west side of Hollywood, an area that seldom was the source of such calls. Half the cars on the midwatch rolled on it when the PSR said the words 'Man with a gun.'

The assigned car, thanks to lights and siren, got there seconds before the others, but two of the midwatch units roared in before the officers of 6-A-65 were out of the car. One of the midwatch units was driven by Mag Takara. Her partner, Benny Brewster, jumped out with a shotgun, and then another car from Watch 3 arrived. Eight cops, four with shotguns, approached the house from which the call had emanated. The porch lights were out, and the street was quite dark. The decision whether to approach the porch did not have to be made. The front door to the house swung open, and the cops at the scene could scarcely believe what they were seeing.

A thirty-eight-year-old man, later identified as Roland Tarkington, owner of the house, stepped out onto the porch. It would be learned that his father had once owned large chunks of commercial property in Hollywood but had lost it all in bad investments, leaving his only child, Roland, the house and sufficient money to exist. Roland was waving a document in one hand and had the other hand behind his back.

In the glare of half a dozen flashlight beams plus a spotlight trained on him by the closest black-and-white, Roland spoke not a word but held up the paper as though it were a white flag of surrender. He struggled down the concrete steps from his porch and advanced toward the cops.

The thing that had the cops amazed was Roland Tarkington's size. He would be measured the next day during a postmortem at five feet six inches. His weight would be listed on the death report as just over 540 pounds. The shadow of Roland Tarkington thrown onto the walk behind him was vast.

After Benny Brewster shouted, 'Let's see the other hand!' there was a cacophony of voices:

'Show us your other hand!'

'Both hands in the air, goddamnit!'

'Get down on the sidewalk!'

'Watch that fucking hand! Watch his hand!'

A probationary cop from Watch 3 left his training officer and crept along the driveway forty feet from the standoff as the obese man stopped, still silently waving the white paper. The probationer was in a position to see behind Roland Tarkington's back and yelled, 'He's got a gun!'

As though on cue, another Hollywood performance ended when Roland Tarkington showed them what he was hiding, suddenly aiming what looked like a .9-millimeter semiautomatic pistol at the closest cop.

And he was hit by two shotgun blasts fired by separate officers from Watch 3 and five rounds from pistols fired by two other Watch 3 officers. Roland Tarkington, despite his great bulk, was lit up by bright orange muzzle blasts, lifted off his feet, and thrown down on his back, where he bled out, dying within seconds, his heart literally shredded. Another five police pistol rounds that missed had riddled the front of the house as Roland Tarkington fell.

Neighbors then poured out of their homes, and voices were yelling, and at least two women across the street were wailing and crying. The Oracle, who arrived just as the rounds exploded in the night, picked up the blood-spattered paper lying on the grass beside the dead man. Roland Tarkington's gun turned out to be a realistically designed water pistol.

The second cop to have fired his shotgun said, 'What's it say, Sarge?'

The Oracle read aloud: '"I offer my humble apologies to the fine officers of the LAPD. This was the only way I could summon the courage to end my life of misery. I ask that my remains be cremated. I would not want anyone to have to carry my body to our family plot at Forest Lawn Cemetery. Thank you. Roland G. Tarkington."'

None of the midwatch units had been in a position to fire, and Mag said to Benny, 'Let's get outta here, partner. This is bad shit.'

When they were back at their car putting the shotgun into the locked rack, Mag heard two cops talking to the Oracle.

One said, 'Goddamnit! Goddamn this bastard! Why didn't he take poison? Goddamn him!'

The Oracle said to the cop, 'Get in your car and get back to the station, son. FID will be arriving soon.'

Another voice said to the Oracle, 'I'm not a fucking executioner! Why did he do this to me? Why?'

The final comment was made by the night-watch detective, Compassionate Charlie Gilford, who showed up as the black-and-whites were driving away. The RA was double-parked, a paramedic standing over the huge mound of bloody flesh that had been Roland Tarkington, glad that the crew from the coroner's would be handling this one.

Compassionate Charlie picked up the water pistol, squeezed the trigger, and when no water squirted out said, 'Shit, it ain't even loaded.' Then he shined his light on the blasted gaping chest of Roland Tarkington and said, 'You would have to call this a heartrending conclusion to another Hollywood melodrama.'

SEVEN

The following Friday evening saw throngs on Hollywood Boulevard at another of the endless red carpet ceremonies, this one at the Kodak Theatre, where show business backslaps and hugs itself before returning to everyday backbiting and seething in never-ending bouts of jealousy over a colleague's getting a job that should have been given to Me! Show business's unmentioned prayer: Please, God, let me succeed and let them ... fail.

The midwatch was in terrible shape as far as deployment was concerned. Fausto was on days off and so was Benny Brewster. Budgie Polk saw the Oracle working at his desk and found it reassuring to see all those hash marks on his left sleeve, all the way up to his elbow. He wore not his heart on his sleeve, but his life. Forty-six years. Nine service stripes. Who could push him around? The Oracle had said he was going to break the record of the detective from Robbery-Homicide Division who'd retired in February with fifty years of service. But sometimes, like now, he looked tired. And old.

The Oracle would be sixty-nine years old in August, and it was all there around his eyes and furrowed brow, all the years with the LAPD. He'd served seven chiefs. He'd seen chiefs and mayors come and go and die. But in those old glory days of LAPD, he couldn't have imagined he'd be serving under a federal consent decree that was choking the life out of the police department he loved. Proactive police work had given way to police paranoia, and he seemed to internalize it more than anyone else. Budgie watched him unscrew a bottle of antacid liquid and swallow a large dose.

Budgie had been hoping to team up with Mag Takara, but after Budgie walked into the watch commander's office and had a look at the lineup, she took the Oracle aside in the corridor, where she said privately, 'Did the lieutenant decide on the assignments tonight, Sarge?'

'No, I did,' he told her, but he stopped talking when Hollywood Nate interrupted by bounding in the back door with three rolls of paper, carrying them like they were treasure maps.

'Wait'll you see these, Sarge,' he said to the Oracle.

He handed two to Budgie while he carefully unrolled the third, revealing a movie one-sheet for Billy Wilder's *Sunset Boulevard*, starring William Holden and Gloria Swanson.

'Don't we have enough movie posters around the station?' the Oracle said.

'But this one's in great shape! It's a copy, but it's a pretty old copy. And in beautiful condition. I'm getting the frames donated tomorrow.'

'All right, put them up in the roll-call room with the others,' the Oracle said, running his hand over his gray crewcut. 'I guess anything's better than looking at all these inmate green walls. Whoever designed our stations must've got his training in Albania during the cold war.'

'Way cool, Sarge,' Nate said. 'We'll decide where to put the others later. One's for *Double Indemnity*, and the other's for *Rebel Without a Cause*, with James Dean's face right under the title. Lots of great shots of Hollywood in those movies.'

'Okay, but pick places where citizens can't see them from the lobby,' the Oracle said. 'Don't turn this station into a casting office.'

After Hollywood Nate had sprinted up the stairs, the Oracle said to Budgie, 'I'm a sucker for young cops who respect old things. And speaking of old things, with Fausto off I thought you wouldn't mind working with Hank Driscoll for a few days.'

Budgie rolled her eyes then. Hank aka 'B.M.' Driscoll was someone nobody liked working with, especially young officers. It wasn't that he was old like Fausto – he had nineteen years on the Job and was only a little over forty – but it was like working with your whiny aunt Martha. The B.M. sobriquet that the other cops hung on him was for Baron Münchhausen, whose invented illnesses resulted in medical treatment and hospitalization, a disorder that came to be known in the psychiatric community as Munchausen syndrome.

B.M. Driscoll probably had more sick days than the rest of the midwatch combined. If they had to arrest a junkie with hepatitis, B.M. Driscoll would go to his doctor with symptoms within forty-eight hours and would listen doubtfully when assured that his claims were medically impossible.

The ten-hour shift of Watch 5 crawled by when you had to work with him. Older cops said that if you felt that life was flying by too quickly, you could bring time almost to a standstill just by working a whole twenty-eight-day deployment period with B.M. Driscoll.

He was tall and wiry, the grandson of Wisconsin farmers who came to California during the Great Depression, which he claimed kept his parents from eating properly, so they passed unhealthy genes down to him. He kept his sparse brown hair clipped almost as close as the Oracle's because he believed it was more hygienic. And he was twice divorced, the mystery being how he found anyone but a psychiatrist to marry him in the first place.

However, there was one event in his career that made him a bit of a police legend. Several years earlier, when he was working patrol in the barrio of Hollenbeck Division, he became involved in a standoff with a drug-crazed, facially tattooed homeboy who was threatening to cut his girlfriend's throat with a Buck knife.

Several cops were there in the middle of the street, pointing shotguns and handguns and cajoling and threatening to no avail. Officer Driscoll was holding a Taser gun, and at one point during the standoff when the homie lowered the blade long enough to wave it during his incoherent rant, B.M. Driscoll fired. The dart struck the homeboy in the left chest area, penetrating the pack of cigarettes in his shirt pocket as well as his butane lighter. Which was ignited by a lit cigarette. Which caused the guy to burst into flames. Which ended the standoff.

They got the shirt off the homeboy before he was seriously burned and threw him into a rescue ambulance, and B.M. Driscoll became something of a celebrity, especially among the Latino cruisers where he was known as 'the dude with the flame thrower.'

But whether he was a legend or not, Budgie Polk was very unhappy about her assignment. She said to the Oracle, 'Just tell me one thing, Sarge. Tell me that you're not keeping me and Mag apart because I'm just back from maternity leave and she's a little munchkin. I can't explain to you how degrading it is when that happens to us women. When male supervisors say stuff like "We're splitting you up for your own safety." After all the shit we women have gone through to get where we are on this Job.'

The Oracle said, 'Budgie, I promise you that's not why I put you with Driscoll instead of Mag. I don't think of you in those terms. You're a cop. Period.'

'And that's not why you put me with Fausto? So the old war horse could look after me?'

'Haven't you caught on by now, Budgie?' the Oracle said. 'Fausto Gamboa has been a bitter and depressed man since he lost his wife to colon cancer two years ago. And both their sons are losers, so they don't help him any. When Ron LeCroix had to get his hemorrhoids zapped, it looked like a perfect time to team up Fausto with somebody young and alive. Preferably a woman, to soften him up a little bit. So I didn't assign him to you for your benefit. I did it for him.'

They didn't call him the Oracle for nothing, Budgie thought. She was painted into a corner now with nowhere to go. 'Hoisted by my own pony-tail' was all she could mutter.

The Oracle said, 'Put some cotton in your ears for a few days. Driscoll's actually a decent copper and he's generous. He'll buy your cappuccino and biscotti every chance he gets. And not because you're a woman. That's the way he is.'

'I hope I don't catch bird flu or mad cow just listening to him,' Budgie said.

73

When they got to their patrol unit, Budgie driving, B.M. Driscoll threw his war bag into the trunk and said, 'Try not to get in my breathing zone if you can help it, Budgie. I know you've got a baby, and I wouldn't want to infect you. I think I could be coming down with something. I'm not sure, but I've got muscle pain and sort of feel chills down my back. I had the flu in October and again in January. This has been a bad year for my health.'

The rest was lost in radio chatter. Budgie tried to concentrate on the PSR's voice and tune his out. She was reminded of an event she'd first heard about when she transferred to Hollywood Division and met Detective Andi McCrea. Other women officers particularly enjoyed the story.

It seemed that several years ago an LAPD officer from a neighboring division was shot by a motorist he'd pulled over for a ticket. Andi McCrea was a uniformed cop in Hollywood Division at that time, and several night-watch units were assigned to patrol their eastern border, where the suspect was last seen abandoning his car after a short pursuit.

It was past end of watch, and cars were working overtime, in communication with one another and checking alleys, storage yards, and vacant buildings, with no sign of the shooter. Then Andi got the word who the officer was: an academy classmate of hers, and he was badly wounded. She'd been relentless that night, shining her spotlight beam onto rooftops, even into trees, and her older male partner, like B.M. Driscoll, was a complainer. Not about imaginary illnesses, but about his need for rest and sleep. He was an unreliable shiftless cop.

Andi McCrea, according to all accounts, endured it for two hours, but after listening to him say, 'We ain't gonna find nobody, let's get the hell outta here and go end of watch – this is bullshit,' she grimly turned north to the Hollywood Freeway, pulled onto the ramp, and stopped.

When her partner said, 'What're we stopping here for?' Andi said, 'Something's wrong. Get out and look at the right front tire.'

He griped about that too, but complied, and when he was out of the car shining his beam onto the tire, he said, 'There's nothing wrong here.'

'There sure as hell is something wrong here, you worthless asshole,' Andi said and drove off, leaving him on the freeway ramp, his rover still on the seat and his cell phone in his locker at the station.

Andi continued searching for another hour and only stopped when the search was called off, after which she drove to the station, still hacked off and ready to take her medicine.

The Oracle was waiting for her, and as she was unloading her war bag from the trunk, he said, 'Your partner arrived about a half hour ago. Flagged down a car. He's torqued. Stay away from him.'

'Sarge, we were hunting a maggot who shot a police officer!' Andi said.

'I understand that,' the Oracle said. 'And knowing him, I can imagine what you had to put up with. But you don't dump a body on the freeway unless it's dead and you're a serial killer.'

'Is he making his complaint official?'

'He wanted to but I talked him out of it. Told him it would be more embarrassing for him than for you. Anyway, he's getting his long-awaited transfer to West LA, so he'll be gone at the end of the deployment period.'

That's how it had ended, except that it was a favorite story of cops at Hollywood Station who knew Andi McCrea. And B.M. Driscoll's whining about his flu symptoms reminded Budgie Polk of the story. It put a little smile on her face, and she thought, How far does he have to push me? Could I get away with it like Andi did? After all, there is precedent here.

And though Budgie was starting to enjoy certain things about working with Fausto now that he'd mellowed a little, wouldn't it be great to be teamed with Mag Takara? Just for girl talk if nothing else. During code 7, when they were eating salads at Soup Plantation, they could kid around about eye candy on the midwatch, saying things like, 'Would you consider doing Hollywood Nate if you thought he could ever keep his big mouth shut about it?' Or, 'How much would it take for you to do either of those two log heads, Flotsam or Jetsam, if you could shoot him afterward?' Girl talk cop-style.

Mag was a cool and gutsy little chick with a quiet sense of humor that Budgie liked. And being of Japanese ethnicity, Mag would no doubt be down for code 7 at the sushi bar on Melrose that Budgie couldn't persuade any of the male officers to set foot in. Of course, two women as short and tall as Mag and Budgie would be butts of stupid male remarks, along with the usual sexist ones that all women officers have to live with unless they want to get a rat jacket by complaining about it. The lamest: What do you call a black-and-white with two females in it? Answer: a tuna boat.

And while Budgie was thinking of ways to trade B.M. Driscoll for Mag Takara without pissing off the Oracle, Mag was thinking of ways to trade Flotsam for anybody at all. With Jetsam on days off, they were teamed for the first time, short and tall, quiet and mouthy. And oh god! He kept sliding his sight line over onto her every time she was looking out at the streets, and if this kept up, he'd be rear-ending a bus or something.

'Where shall we go for code seven?' he asked when they hadn't been on patrol for twenty minutes. 'And don't say the sushi bar on Melrose, where I've seen your shop parked on numerous occasions.'

'I won't, then,' she said, punching in a license plate on a low rider in the number two lane, figuring this surfer probably takes his dates to places with paper napkins and tap water.

Hoping for a smile, he said, 'For me an order of sushi is a dish containing unretouched, recently dead mollusks. Stuff like that lays all over the beach in low tide. You like to surf?'

'No,' Mag said, unamused.

75

'I bet you'd look great shooting a barrel. All that gorgeous dark hair flowing in the wind.'

'A barrel?'

'Yeah, a tube? A pipe? Riding through as the wave breaks over you?'

'Yeah, a barrel.' This loghead's had too many wipeouts, she thought. He's gone surfboard-simple, that's what.

'In one of those bikinis that's just a piece of Lycra the size of a Toll House cookie.'

Just get me through the night and away from this hormone monster, Mag thought. Then she did some serious eye rolling when Flotsam said, 'A surfer might predict that this could be the beginning of a choiceamundo friendship.'

Wesley Drubb got to drive, and he liked that. Hollywood Nate was sitting back doing what he did best, talking show business to his young partner, who didn't give a shit about the movie theater that Nate pointed out there at Fairfax and Melrose, one that showed silent films.

'There was a famous murder there in the nineties,' Nate informed him, 'involving former owners. One got set up by a business partner who hired a hit on him. The hit man is now doing life without. "The Silent Movie Murder," the press called it.'

'Really,' Wesley said, without enthusiasm.

'I can give you a show-business education,' Nate said. 'Never know when it could come in handy working this division. I know you're rich and all, but would you ever consider doing extra work in the movies? I could introduce you to an agent.'

Wesley Drubb hated it when other officers talked about his family wealth and said, 'I'm not rich. My father's rich.'

'I'd like to meet your dad sometime,' Nate said. 'Does he have any interest in movies?'

Wesley shrugged and said, 'He and my mom go to movies sometimes.'

'I mean in filmmaking.'

'His hobby is skeet shooting,' Wesley said. 'And he's done a little pistol shooting with me since I came on the Department.'

'Guns don't have it going on, far as I'm concerned,' Nate said. 'When I talk millimeters, it's not about guns and ammo, it's about celluloid. Thirty-five millimeters. Twenty-four frames per second. I have a thousand-dollar digital video camera. Panavision model. Sweet.'

'Uh-huh,' Wesley said.

'I know a guy, him and me, we're into filmmaking. One of these days when we find the right kind of investor, we're gonna make a little Indie film and show it at the festivals. We have a script and we're very close. All we need is the right investor. We can't accept just anybody.'

They were stopped at a residential intersection in east Hollywood, a street that Wesley remembered hearing about. He looked at a two-story house, home of some Eighteenth Street crew members.

Hollywood Nate was just about to pop the question to Wesley about whether he thought that Franklin Drubb would ever consider including a start-up production company in his investment portfolio, when a head-shaven white guy in faux-leather pants, studded boots, and a leather jacket over a swelling bare chest completely covered by body art walked up to the passenger side of the patrol car and tapped loudly on Nate's window.

It startled both of them, and Nate rolled down the window and said, 'What can I do for you?' keeping it polite but wary.

The man said in a voice soft and low, 'Take me to Santa Monica and La Brea.'

Hollywood Nate glanced quickly at Wesley, then back to the guy, shining his flashlight up under the chin, seeing those dilated cavernous eyes, and said to him, 'Step back away from the car.' Nate got out and Wesley quickly informed communications that 6-X-72 was code 6 at that location. Then he put the car in park, turned off the engine, tucked the keys in the buckle of his Sam Browne and got out on the driver's side, walking quickly around the front of the car, flashlight in one hand, the other on the butt of his Beretta.

The man was a lot older than he looked at first when Nate walked him to the sidewalk and had a good look, but he was wide shouldered, with thick veins on his well-muscled arms, and full-sleeve tatts. It was very dark and the street lamp on the corner was out. An occasional car passed and nobody was walking on the residential street.

Then the guy said, 'I'm a Vietnam vet. You're a public servant. Take me to Santa Monica and La Brea.'

Hollywood Nate looked from the guy to his partner in disbelief and said, 'Yeah, you're a Vietnam vet and you got napalm eyes to prove it, but we're not a taxi. What're you fried on, man? X, maybe?'

The man smiled then, a sly and secretive smile locked in place just this side of madness. He opened his vest, showing his bare torso, and ran his hands over his own waist and buttocks and groin under the tight imitation-leather pants and said, 'See, no weapons. No nothing. Just beautiful tattoos. Let's go to Santa Monica and La Brea.'

Hollywood Nate glanced again at his partner, who looked springloaded, and Nate said, 'Yeah, I see. You got more tatts than Angelina Jolie, but you ain't her. So we're not driving you anywhere.' Then he uttered the Hollywood Station mantra, 'Stay real, dude.'

Those eyes. Nate looked again with his flashlight beam under the guy's chin. Where did he find those eyes? They didn't fit his face somehow. They looked like they belonged to somebody else. Or something else.

Nate looked at Wesley, who didn't know what the hell to do. The man hadn't broken any laws. Wesley didn't know if he should ask the guy for

ID or what. He waited for a cue from Nate. This was getting very spooky. An unhinged 5150 mental case for sure. Still, all he'd done was ask for a ride. Wesley remembered his academy instructor saying as long as they weren't a danger to themselves or others, they couldn't be taken to the USC Medical Center, formerly the old county hospital, for a seventy-two-hour hold.

Nate said to the man, 'The only place this car goes is jail. Why don't you walk home and sleep it off, whatever it is gave you those eyes.'

The man said, 'War gave me these eyes. War.'

Cautiously, Nate said, 'I think we're gonna say good night to you, soldier. Go home. Right now.'

Nate nodded to his partner and backed toward the police car, but when he got in and closed the door and Wesley got in on the driver's side and started the engine, the transmission still in park, the man ran to the car and kicked the right rear door with those studded boots, howling like a wolf.

'Goddamn!' Nate yelled, keying the mike and yelling, 'Six-X-Seventy-two, officers need help!' He gave the location, then threw open his door and jumped out with his baton, which he lost during the first thirty seconds of the fight.

Wesley jumped from the driver's side, not removing the keys, not even turning off the engine, ran around the car, and leaped onto the back of the madman who had Nate's baton with one hand and Nate in a headlock.

All those muscles that Hollywood Nate had found in his gym, that had impressed badge bunnies in the Director's Chair saloon, weren't impressing this lunatic one bit. And even when Wesley hurled his 210-pound body onto the guy, he still kept fighting and kicking and trying to bite like a rabid dog.

Wesley tried the Liquid Jesus on him but the OC can was clogged and it created a pepper-spray mist in front of his own face that almost blinded him. Then he tried again but got more on Hollywood Nate than on the suspect, so he gave up and dropped the canister.

And pretty soon they had tussled, tumbled, and rolled across the lawn of a sagging two-story residence belonging to Honduran immigrants, into the side yard, and then clear into the backyard, where Hollywood Nate was starting to panic as he felt his strength waning. And he thought he might have to shoot this fucking lunatic after he felt the guy trying to grab his sidearm.

And while the battle was raging, some of the Eighteenth Street cruisers from another two-story house looked out the window, and a few of them came out to get a better look and root for the guy to kick some LAPD ass. When their pit bulls tried to follow, they leashed them, knowing that lots of other cops would be coming soon.

The dogs seemed to enjoy the fight even more than the crew did and began snarling and barking, and whenever the leather-clad madman growled and kicked at Wesley Drubb, who was administering LAPD-approved baton strikes, the dogs would bark louder. And then Loco Lennie happened on the scene.

Loco Lennie was not a member of Eighteenth Street but he was oh, such a wannabe. He was too young, too stupid, and too impulsive even for the cruisers to use him as a low-level drug delivery boy. Loco Lennie wasn't watching the fight with the five members of the crew and their crazed dogs. Loco Lennie couldn't take his eyes off the black-and-white that Wesley Drubb had left in gear, engine running, key in the ignition, in his haste to help Hollywood Nate. And Loco Lennie saw a chance to make a name for himself that would live forever in the minds and hearts of these cruisers who had so far rejected him.

Loco Lennie ran to the police car, jumped in, and took off, yelling, 'Viva, Eighteenth Street!'

Hollywood Nate and Wesley Drubb didn't even know that their shop had been stolen. By now they had the guy pinned against the single-car garage of the ramshackle house, and young Wesley was learning that all of the leg and arm strikes he'd been taught at the academy weren't worth a shit when battling a powerful guy who was maybe cooked on PCP or just plain psychotic.

And before the first help came screeching around the corner, siren yelping louder than the homie dogs and even louder than this howling mental case who was trying desperately to bite Hollywood Nate, the cop locked his forearm and biceps in a V around the man's throat. Nate applied all the pressure he could manage to the carotid arteries while Wesley exhausted himself, whacking the guy everywhere from the guy's wingspan on down to his lower legs with little effect.

Flotsam and Mag, Budgie and B.M. Driscoll, and four officers from Watch 3 all came running to the rescue just as the guy was almost choked out, his brain oxygen starved from the infamous choke hold, the carotid restraint that had killed several people over the decades but had saved the lives of more cops than all the Tasers and beanbag guns and side-handle batons and Liquid Jesus and the rest of the nonlethal weapons in their arsenal put together. A form of nonlethal force that, in this era of DOJ oversight and racial politics and political correctness, was treated exactly the same as an officer-involved shooting. And that would require almost as much investigation and as many reports as if Hollywood Nate had shot the guy in defense of his life with a load of double-aught buckshot.

When it looked as though the situation was in hand, one of the dogs belonging to the cruisers did what guard dogs do, after he saw the cops piling out of their black-and-whites and running in the direction of his homeboys. He sprang forward, breaking free of the leash, and raced directly at B.M. Driscoll, who had barely set foot on the sidewalk. When B.M. Driscoll saw those slobbering jaws and those bared fangs and malevolent eyes coming at him, he bellowed, drew his nine, and fired twice, missing once but then killing the dog instantly with a head shot.

The gunfire seemed to stop all action. Hollywood Nate realized that the maniac was choked out, and he let the guy fall to the ground, unconscious. Wesley Drubb looked toward the street for the first time and said, 'Where's our shop?'

Now that the entertainment had ended, the homies and their still-living dogs turned and retreated to their house without complaint about the un-licensed animal they'd lost. And there was lots of talk among them about how Loco Lennie had *pelotas* made of stainless steel. Maybe they should reconsider Loco Lennie as a cruiser, they agreed, if he didn't get himself dusted by some cop who spotted him in the stolen police car.

When Flotsam saw the leather-clad lunatic lying on the ground, he said to Mag, 'Let's do rock-paper-scissors to see who gets the mouth on CPR.'

But as Mag was running to the car to look for her personal CPR mask, the unconscious man started breathing again on his own. He moaned and tried to get up but was quickly handcuffed by Hollywood Nate, who then collapsed beside him, his face bruised and swollen.

It was then that Flotsam noticed something clinging to the guy's bald head. He shined his light on it and saw 'Weiss.' Hollywood Nate's name tag had been pulled off and was sticking to the guy's bare scalp.

'Get me a Polaroid!' Flotsam yelled.

By the time the Oracle had arrived and instructed Flotsam and Mag to ride with him and to give their car to Hollywood Nate and Wesley Drubb, the handcuffed man was alert, and he said to Hollywood Nate, 'You can only hurt me in a physical state.'

And Nate, who was still trying to get his own breathing back to normal, rolled his aching shoulders and answered, 'That's the only state we live in, you psycho motherfucker.'

The Oracle warned that now they might have two FID teams out there: one on the dog shooting and another because Hollywood Nate had applied the dreaded choke hold. Force Investigation Division would have to be convinced that B.M. Driscoll had acted in fear of great bodily injury and that Hollywood Nate had choked out the madman as a last resort in the immediate defense of a life, namely his own.

'Not one but two FID roll-outs on the same freaking incident,' the Oracle moaned.

Flotsam said sympathetically, 'LAPD can't get enough layers of over-sight, Boss. Somebody flipped the pyramid and we're under the pointy tip. We got more layers than a mafia wedding cake.'

When a plain-wrapper detective unit pulled up in front and parked, the Oracle wondered how FID could have gotten there so fast but then saw that it was only the night-watch detective Compassionate Charlie, as usual experiencing morbid curiosity. He was wearing one of his Taiwanese checked sport coats that made people ask if it was flame retardant. Charlie got out, picked some food from his teeth, and surveyed the scene for one of his sage pronouncements.

Flotsam talked for a few minutes to one of the Eighteenth Street crew who had lingered to be sure the dog was dead, and after the short conversation, the surfer jogged up to the Oracle and said, 'Boss, I think we have some extenuating circumstances in this shooting that might help you with those rat bastards from FID.'

'Yeah, what's that?'

Pointing to the deceased pit bull, Flotsam said, 'A homie told me the dog was just ghetto elk when they found him.'

'What?'

'You know, one of those stray dogs that roam around the 'hood? One of the cruisers found the dog down in Watts, brought him here and let him in their pack. But last month the dog came down with terminal cancer and they were just going to put him down any day now.'

'So?'

Compassionate Charlie butted into the conversation, saying to the Oracle, 'Don't you get it? Haven't you read about dogs that can smell malignant tumors?'

'Now, what in hell is your point, Charlie?' the Oracle wanted to know. He didn't have time for this goofy surfer or for one of Charlie's on-scene analyses.

Compassionate Charlie shook his head sadly, sucked his teeth, and said, 'You can call this just another touching drama among the many that occur nightly on the streets of Hollywood. The fucking mutt knew he had cancer, so he decided to do honor to his crew and commit suicide-by-cop.'

Young Wesley Drubb felt sort of dazed for the remainder of the watch. His mind kept wandering away from the issues at hand. For instance, when they drove their prisoner to Central Jail at Parker Center, where medical treatment was available for him, all Wesley could think about when they drove past the parking lot was, Why is the entrance gate blocked with a steel barrier, and the exit gate is wide open with no metal spikes? A terrorist could just drive in the exit. Are we stupid, or what? His mind was wandering like that.

After the prisoner was treated prior to being booked for battery on a police officer, Hollywood Nate and Wesley Drubb decided to go to Cedars for treatment of contusions and abrasions, and in Nate's case muscle spasms. As to the prisoner, Nate told Wesley it would be up to the DA's office to decide if the arrestee was permanently nuts or only temporarily nuts from PCP or whatever a blood test might reveal. Drug-induced craziness would not be a defense in a criminal case, but life-induced craziness like his war experiences might keep him from a jail sentence and put him in a mental ward for a short vacation.

Wesley Drubb's mind remained unfocused for more than an hour. He got alarmed by remarks made by a jail employee who had taken his sweet time returning from the long lunch break that their union had recently won for them.

When their prisoner was strip-searched, the black detention officer studied the darkening welts all over the guy's body and said, 'He looks like a zebra.'

Wesley Drubb had never dreamed a man fifty-seven years old could fight like that and was still trying to sort his feelings about the first act of violence he'd ever committed on another human being in his entire life. And sick from the worry and stress of having lost his police car, he tried to explain the prisoner's bruises by saying, 'We had no choice.'

The jailor chuckled at the shaken young cop and said, 'Boy, lucky for you he's a peckerwood. If this cat was black, you would be facing the wrath of the city council, the United States Department of Justice, and the motherfuckin' ghost of Johnnie Cochran.'

Loco Lennie may or may not have heard the PSR's voice informing all units that 6-X-72's car had been stolen, and he may or may not have opened the text messages sent by other units to 6-X-72 after they'd learned of the incident.

One message said, 'When we see you, you are dead meat.'

Another said, 'We will shoot you and burn your body.'

Another, apparently from a K-9 unit, said, 'Trooper will eat on your sorry ass for as long as he wants. Before you die.'

In any case, Loco Lennie figured he had made his point to the crew, so he abandoned the police car only ten blocks from his house. He found a rock lying beside a chain-link fence, picked it up, and threw it at the windshield, just as a parting shot. Then Loco Lennie sprinted home in glory.

When, at the end of their long and awful duty tour, they were painfully walking to their personal cars, Wesley Drubb, who had been silent most of the night, said to Hollywood Nate, 'I don't care what they taught me in my years at USC. I don't care how unscientific it is. All I know is that since coming on this Job, I no longer believe in evolution. I believe in Creationism.'

'And why is that?' Nate asked.

'For instance, that guy tonight? An evolved form of life could not resemble something like that.'

EIGHT

After stopping at the Gulag for a happy hour drink, Cosmo Betrossian was driving his eighteen-year-old Cadillac east on Sunset to Korea Town, where he was living temporarily, and thinking of how impressed Dmitri had been with him during their meeting last week. This was where he belonged, with people like Dmitri. Cosmo was forty-three years old, too old to be dealing with people addicted to crystal meth. Too old to be buying the paper they'd stolen from mailboxes or from purses left in cars and then shopping the credit-card information to the other freaks at the public libraries and cyber cafés, where they sold stolen information and dealt drugs on the Internet.

Cosmo and Ilya had never committed an armed robbery prior to the jewelry store job. The hand grenade idea came from something he had heard from one of the addicts who had read about it in a San Diego newspaper. The reason the addict had mentioned it to Cosmo at all was that the robbers who did it were Armenians who were supposed to be connected with Russian Mafia. Cosmo had to laugh. He had stolen their idea and their modus operandi, and it had been easy. And it had all come to him because he was an Armenian émigré.

The knowledge about the diamonds arriving on the premises had come to him by way of another of the addicts he had been dealing with for several months. It was information from an invoice receipt acknowledging delivery, sent by the jewelry store to a Hong Kong supplier. Along with that stolen letter had been another one, also bearing the jewelry store's return address, sent to a customer in San Francisco, telling the customer that an 'exciting delivery' of stones had arrived and were just what the customer had in mind when last he'd visited the Los Angeles store. The letters had been stolen from a mailbox by an addict who traded a bag full of credit-card and check information along with the letters in question for four teeners of crystal meth that Cosmo had bought for two hundred fifty dollars and used as trade bait.

He'd been doing business with tweakers for over a year and only on one occasion did he and Ilya smoke some crystal with them, but neither had liked the high, although it did sexually arouse them. They preferred cocaine and vodka. Cosmo had told the addicts that he and Ilya were more normal, old-fashioned people.

The thing that really had him excited now was that the robbery had been easy. It gave him a great thrill to make that jeweler weep and piss all over himself. Cosmo had fucked Ilya all night after they had done the robbery. And she too admitted that it had been sexually stimulating. Though she said that she would not participate in any more armed robberies, he thought that he could persuade her.

Ilya was waiting for him when he got back to their apartment. As soon as they sold the diamonds, they would be moving, maybe to a nicer apartment in Little Armenia. Their two-room hovel over a residential garage had been rented to them by a Korean who never asked questions about the men, both white and Asian, who visited Ilya in that apartment for a 'massage' and left within an hour or so. Ilya had formerly done a lot of out-call work, until she got arrested in a hotel room on a sting by a handsome vice cop who had flash money and nice clothes and rings on his fingers. Ilya wept when he showed his badge that night. She had been naive enough then to think that the handsome stranger had possibilities beyond a quick blow job.

Ilya was thirty-six years old and without a lot of years left for this kind of life, which is how she got teamed up with Cosmo. He'd promised to take care of her, promising that she'd never get arrested again and that he'd make enough money that she'd seldom have to sell her ass. But so far, she was making more money with her ass than he was making with the addicts who brought him things to trade for drugs.

Cosmo saw the outside light on after he'd parked half a block away and walked through the alley to the garage apartment with its termite-eaten stairway leading up. He was puzzled because she did not have a massage scheduled. He had specifically asked her about that. He felt a rush of fear through his bowels because it could mean a warning from her. But no, he could see her moving past the window. If cops were there, she'd be sitting, probably handcuffed. He took the stairs two at a time stealthily and opened the door without announcing his presence.

'Hi, Cosmo!' Olive Oyl said, with a gap-toothed smile, sitting on the small settee.

'Evening, Cosmo,' Farley said with his usual smirk, sitting next to Olive.

'Hello to you, Olive. Hello to you, Farley,' Cosmo said. 'You did not call me. I am not expecting you to come here tonight.'

'They called me,' Ilya said, 'after you went to Dmitri's.'

Cosmo shot her a look. Stupid woman. She mentioned Dmitri in front of these addicts. He turned to Farley and said, 'What is it you bring for me?'

'A business proposition,' Farley said, still smirking.

Puzzled, Cosmo looked at Ilya. Her blond hair was pulled straight back in a tight bun, which she would never do if she was expecting guests, even addict customers like these. And her makeup was haphazardly applied, and there were dark lines under her eyes. He guessed that she had been taking one of her long afternoon naps when the freaks called, and hadn't really pulled herself together before their arrival. Ilya showed Cosmo a very worried face.

'What business?' Cosmo asked.

'Sort of a partnership,' Farley said.

'I do not understand.'

'We figure that the last stuff we brought you was worth more than the few teeners you gave us. A whole lot more.'

'It is very hard thing to sell credit-card information and the banking paper today. Everyone who do crystal can make many deals today. Everybody know about – how they call it?'

'Identity theft,' Farley said.

'Yes,' Cosmo said. 'So I do not make enough money to pay me back for crystal I give to you, Farley.'

'Four lousy teeners,' Farley reminded him. 'That's one-quarter of an ounce. In your country maybe seven grams, right? What'd you pay, sixty bucks a teener?'

Cosmo was getting angry and said, 'We do a deal. It is done. Too late for to complain, Farley. It is done. You go someplace else next time, you don't like us.'

Cosmo's tone disturbed Olive, who said, 'Oh, we like you, Cosmo, and we like Ilya too! Don't we, Farley?'

'Shut up, Olive,' Farley said. 'I'm a smart man, Cosmo. A very smart man.'

Olive was about to verbally agree, but Farley elbowed her into silence. 'Cosmo, I read every fucking thing that I bring to people I deal with. I read those letters from a certain jewelry store. I thought maybe you could do something with it. Like maybe sell the information to some experienced burglar who might tunnel in through the roof when the store was closed and steal the stones. It never occurred to me that somebody might go in with guns and take over the place like Bonnie and Clyde. See, I'm not a violent man and I didn't think you were.'

Now Ilya looked like she was about ready to cry, and Cosmo glowered at her. 'You talk shit, Farley,' he said.

'I watch lots of TV, Cosmo. Smoking glass does that to you. Maybe I don't read the papers much anymore but I watch lots of TV. That hand grenade trick made all the local news shows the night you did it. Shortly after I'd brought the jewelry store's letters to you.'

All Cosmo could say was 'You talk shit, Farley.'

'The description they gave on the news was you.' Then he looked at

Ilya, saying, 'And you, Ilya. I been thinking this over. I can hardly think of anything else.'

Cosmo was now glancing wildly from Farley to Ilya and back again. 'I do not like this talk,' he said.

'There's one more letter you should have,' Farley said. 'But I didn't bring it with me. I left it with a friend.' Farley felt a pang of fear shoot through him when he added, 'If I don't get home safe and sound tonight, he's going to deliver the letter to the Hollywood police station.'

Olive looked quizzically at Farley and said, 'Me too, Farley. Safe and sound, right?'

'Shut up, Olive,' Farley said, smelling his own perspiration now, thinking how the TV news bunny said the guy was waving around a pistol on the night of the robbery.

After a long silence, Cosmo said, 'You want from me what?'

'Oh, about fifteen thousand,' Farley said.

Cosmo jumped to his feet and yelled, 'You crazy! You crazy man!'

'Don't touch me!' Farley cried. 'Don't touch me! I gotta arrive home safe and sound or you're toast!'

Olive put her arms around Farley to calm him down and stop his shaking. Cosmo sat back down, sighed, ran his fingers through his heavy black hair, and said, 'I give you ten. I give you ten thousands sometime next month. Money will come in the month of June. I have nothing today. Nothing.'

Farley figured he'd better settle for the ten, and he was trembling when he and Olive stood. He took her hand. Violence was not his gig. A man like this looking at him with murder in his face? All this was new to Farley Ramsdale.

Farley said, 'Okay, but don't try to sneak outta town. I got somebody watching the house twenty-four-seven.'

Then, before Cosmo could reply and frighten him again, Farley and Olive scuttled down the staircase, Farley yelping out loud when he almost stepped on a half-eaten rat by the bottom step. A black feral cat hissed at him.

By the time they reached the doughnut shop on Santa Monica where the tweakers hung out, Farley had recovered somewhat. In fact, he was feeling downright macho thinking about the ten large that would be theirs next month.

'I hope you don't think that goat eater had me scared,' he said to Olive, even though he'd been so shaky he'd had to pull over and let her take the wheel.

'Of course not, Farley,' Olive said. 'You were very brave.'

'There's nothing to be scared of,' he said. 'Shit, they used a phony hand grenade, didn't they? I'll bet their gun was phony, too. What'd that news reader with the tits call it? A "semiautomatic pistol"? I'll bet it was a fucking toy gun dressed up to look bad.'

'It's hard to believe Cosmo and Ilya would shoot anybody,' Olive agreed.

'Trouble is,' Farley reminded her, 'we ain't got enough glass to last till next month. We gotta get to the cyber café and do some business. Like, right away.'

'Right away, Farley.' She wished they had some money for a good meal. Farley was looking more like a ghost than he ever had.

The cyber café they chose was in a strip mall. It was a large two-story commercial building with at least a hundred computers going day and night. There was lots of business that could be done on the Internet. A tweaker could buy drugs from an on-line bulletin board or maybe do a little whoring on the Internet – male or female, take your choice. Money could be wired from one account to another. Or a tweaker could just sit there phishing for pin numbers and credit-card information. The computers were cheap and could be rented by the hour. Just like the dragons working the corner by the cyber café.

One of the dragons, a six-foot-tall black queen in full drag with a blond wig, short red sheath, three-inch yellow spikes, red plastic bracelets, and yellow ear loops, spotted Farley and Olive and approached them, saying, 'You holding any crystal tonight?' The dragon had scored from Farley on a few occasions when he was dealing crack.

'No, I need some,' Farley said.

The dragon was about to return to the corner to hustle tricks in passing cars, when a very tall teenage crackhead, also African American, with his baseball cap on sideways, wearing a numbered jersey and baggy knee-length jams and high-top black sneakers, looking goofy enough to be shooting hoops for a living in the NBA, approached the dragon and said, 'Hey, Momma, where can I get me some? I needs it bad, know what I'm sayin'?'

'Uh-huh,' the dragon said. 'I know what you're sayin', doodlebug.'

'Well, whatchoo gonna do about it, Momma? I got somethin' to trade, know what I'm sayin'?'

'And what is that?'

He took several rocks wrapped in plastic from his pocket and said, 'This'll take you on a trip to paradise, know what I'm sayin'?'

Pointing to the computer center, the dragon said, 'Go in there and sell it, then. Get some United States legal tender and come back and we'll talk.'

'I come back and show you tender, I make you do more than talk. I make you scream, know what I'm sayin'?'

'Uh-huh,' said the dragon, and when the kid went strutting into the cyber café, the dragon said to Farley and Olive, 'Don't see too many black folk around Hollywood these days 'cept for jive-ass cracked-out niggers like that, come up here from south LA to hustle and steal. Jist havin' them around is bad for my bidness. Fuck things up for everyone.' Then the dragon grinned and added, 'Know what I'm sayin'?'

'If we get any crystal tonight, we'll share with you,' Olive said to the drag queen. 'I remember when you shared with us.'

Farley shot Olive his shut-the-fuck-up look, and the dragon caught it. 'That's okay, honey, your old man needs tweak a lot more than I do, from the looks of him.'

Before Olive, which Farley referred to as BO, he used to do lots of business here. He'd steal a car stereo and sell it at the cyber café on a rented computer. The money was wired on eBay to the Western Union office, where Farley would pick it up and cash it. Then he was back to the cyber café to buy his glass. It was hard for him to imagine life away from this place.

They entered and Farley began looking for someone he could work. He saw a dude he'd been arrested with in a drug sweep a few years back, sitting at one of the computers by the door. Farley stood behind the guy for a minute to see if the guy had it going.

The e-mail message said, 'Need tickets to Tina Turner concert. And want to sit in 8th row. Have teenager with me.'

'That's a fucking cop,' Farley said to the tweaker, who jumped and spun around on his chair. 'Dude, you are doing e-mail with a cop.' He couldn't remember the tweaker's name.

'Yo, Farley,' the tweaker said. 'What makes you think?'

'Every fucking cop on the planet knows Tina Turner is code for tweak. And eighth row? Dude, think about it. What else could it be but an eight ball, right? And teenager means teener, very fucking obviously. So you're either dealing with the stupidest tweaker in cyberspace or a fucking narc. He's using dopey code that nobody uses anymore 'cause anybody can figure it out.'

'Maybe you're right,' the tweaker said. 'Thanks, man.'

'So if I just did you a favor, how about doing me one?'

'I got no ice to share and no cash to loan, Farley. Catch you later.'

'Ungrateful, simpleminded motherfucker,' Farley said to Olive when he rejoined her. 'When we got busted down at Pablo's Tacos two years ago and taken to Hollywood Station in handcuffs, we had to drop our pants and bend over and spread. And crystal went flying out his ass. He told the cop it didn't belong to him. Said he was just holding it for some parolee who pulled a knife and made him put the ice in his ass when the cops surrounded the taco joint.'

'Did you see it happen?' Olive asked.

'What?'

'The parolee with the knife, making him put the crystal up there! God, I'll bet your friend was scared!'

Farley Ramsdale was speechless at times like this and thought that she'd be better off dead. Except that she was so stupendously stupid she actually seemed to enjoy living. Maybe that's the way to cope with life, Farley thought. Get as brain-cooked as Olive and just enjoy the ride as long as it lasts.

When he looked at her, she smiled at him, showing her gums, and a tiny bubble popped out from the left gap in her grille when she said, 'I think there's a little bit of pot left at home. And we could boost you some candy and a bottle of vodka from the liquor store on Melrose. The old Persian man that works nights is almost blind, they say.'

'Persian is a fucking cat, Olive,' Farley said. 'He's an Iranian. They're everywhere, like cockroaches. This is Iran-geles, California, for chrissake!'

'We'll get by, Farley. You should eat something. And you should not get discouraged, and try to always remember that tomorrow's another day.'

'Jesus Christ,' Farley said, staring at her. '*Gone with the Fucking Wind*!'

'What, Farley?'

Farley, who, like most tweakers, stayed up for days watching movie after movie on the tube, said, 'You're what woulda happened to Scarlett O'Hara in later life if she'd smoked a chuck wagon load of Maui ice. She'd have turned into you! "Tomorrow is another fucking day"!'

Olive didn't know what in the world he was raving about. He needed to go to bed whether he could sleep or not. It had been a terrible day for him. 'Come on, Farley,' she said. 'Let's go home and I'll make you a delicious toasted cheese sandwich. With mayonnaise on it!'

Nobody on the beach or in the whole state of California was madder than Jetsam that early morning of June 1. That's what he said to Flotsam when he met him at Malibu and unloaded his log from the Bronco and stopped to stare at the ocean. Both were wearing black wet suits.

The sky was a glare of gold rising up, and smudges of gray scudded low over the horizon. Looking away, Jetsam stared at the smog lying low in wispy veils, and at the bruised, glowering clouds that were curdling down onto all the fucking places where people lived in despair. Jetsam turned and looked out to sea, to the hopeful horizon glistening like an endless ribbon of silver, and for a long moment he didn't speak.

'What's wrong, dude?' Flotsam asked.

'I got stung Thursday night, bro!' Jetsam said.

'Stung?'

'A fucking IA sting! If you'da been on duty, you'da got stung with me. I was working with B.M. Driscoll. Poor fucker might as well set fire to homies and shoot dogs. He's always in trouble.'

'What happened?'

'You know that IA sting they did down in Southeast – when was it, last year? Year before? The one where they put the gun in the fucking phone booth?'

'I sorta remember the gist of it,' Flotsam said while Jetsam waxed the old ten-foot board as he talked.

'On that one, the fucking incompetents working the sting detail at IA leave a gun by a phone booth with one of their undercover guys standing nearby. They put out some kinda phony call to get a patrol unit there. Deal is, a patrol unit they're interested in is gonna come by, see the dude, do an FI, and see the gun there in plain view. The patrol unit's gonna ask what he knows about the gun and the dude's gonna say, "Who, me?" like the brothers always say down there. Then IA, who's watching from ambush, hope the coppers are gonna arrest the brother and claim he was carrying the gun. And if they're real lucky, maybe slap the brother around after he mouths off to them. And if they hit the jackpot, call him a nigger, which of course will get them a death row sentence and a lethal injection. And then maybe they can have a party for a job well done. But not that time. It goes sideways.'

'What happened? A shooting, right?'

'Some homies happen to be cruising by before the black-and-white shows up. These cruisers see a strange brother there who ain't one of their crew and they pop a cap at him. And then the IA cover team comes to the rescue and they fire back but don't really engage. I thought cops're supposed to engage hostile fire, but this is the rat squad. They see life different from regular coppers. So the homies get away, and what does IA do? They grab their sting gun and they get the hell out, and they don't hang around for an FID investigation. So they break every fucking rule the rest of us have to play by during these times. Their excuse was they had to protect the identity of their undercover officer.'

'That is bullshit, dude,' Flotsam said. 'When you apply seven-pound pull on a six-pound trigger, you stay and talk to the Man and make the reports. Undercover is over when the muzzle flashes.'

'Except for those rat bastards.'

'So how did they sting you Thursday night?'

'That's what makes me so mad. They used the same fucking gag, the unimaginative assholes! I thought at first they must be after B.M. Driscoll. He told me he was involved in a shaky shooting before he transferred to Hollywood and was worried about it. One of those deals where he capped a Mexican illegal who drove his car straight at him when the guy was trying to escape after a long car pursuit. The next day, he gets a phone call at the station from an irate citizen who says, 'You gotta come mow my lawn now. You shot my gardener.'

Flotsam said, 'Yeah, our chief says we're supposed to just jump out of the way of cars coming at us, maybe wave a cape like a matador. Then start chasing again, long as we don't endanger anybody but ourselves. Anything but shooting a thief who might be a minor. Or an ethnic. I wish somebody'd make a chart about which ethnics are unshootable nowadays and have Governor Arnold give them a sticker for their license plates. So we'd know.'

Jetsam said, 'Retreat goes against a copper's personality traits. Maybe they want us to just go back to the drive-and-wave policy, like we did under Lord Voldemort.'

'Maybe they should just put trigger locks on all our guns.'

'Anyways, B.M. Driscoll's convinced himself he's targeted by IA,' Jetsam said. 'Checks his house for listening devices every couple weeks. But you know him, he gets a hay fever cough and thinks it's cancer.'

'So how about Thursday night's sting? Are you saying they dropped a gun by a phone booth?'

'Purse,' Jetsam said.

Jetsam said it was a phone booth on Hollywood Boulevard of course, where lots of tourists might do something dumb like that. A phone booth by the subway station. He remembered how it had annoyed him when it popped on their computer screen. No big deal. An unnamed person had called in to say that there was a purse left in the phone booth. And the call was assigned to 6-X-32, on a night when B.M. Driscoll was Flotsam's stand-in.

B.M. Driscoll, who was riding shotgun, said, 'Shit. Found property to book. What a drag. Oh well, it'll give me a chance to get my inhaler outta my locker. I'm getting wheezy.'

'You ain't wheezy,' Jetsam said. The guy's imagined health issues were wearing Jetsam down to the ground. 'My ex was wheezy. Got an asthma attack every time I put a move on her in bed. That was about once every deployment period. Little did I know that her and the plumber down the street were laying pipe twice a week.'

Jetsam parked in a red zone by the intersection of Hollywood and Highland while B.M. Driscoll said, 'I don't like steroid inhalers but there's nothing more fundamental than breathing.'

When Jetsam was getting out of the car, B.M. Driscoll said, 'Be sure to lock it.'

He wasn't worried about their shotgun rack getting pried open or their car getting hot-wired. He was worried about his two uniforms they'd just picked up from the cleaners, which were hanging over the backseat.

After locking the car, Jetsam took his baton and ambled toward the phone booth, letting B.M. Driscoll lag behind and finish his medical monologue on the treatment of asthma with steroid inhalers at a distance where Jetsam could hardly hear him.

It was the kind of early summer evening when the layer of smog burnished the glow from the setting sun and threw a golden light over the Los Angeles basin, and somehow over Hollywood in particular. That light said to people: There are wondrous possibilities here.

Feeling the dry heat on his face, looking at the colorful creatures surrounding him, Jetsam saw tweakers and hooks, panhandlers and ordinary Hollywood crazies, all mingling with tourists. He saw Mickey Mouse and

Barney the dinosaur and Darth Vader (only one tonight) and a couple of King Kongs.

But the guys inside the gorilla costumes weren't tall enough to successfully play the great ape, and he saw a guy he recognized as Untouchable Al walk up to one of them and say, 'King Kong, my ass. You look more like Cheetah.'

Jetsam turned away quickly because if there was a disturbance, he wanted no part of Untouchable Al, especially not here on Hollywood Boulevard where the multitudes would witness the dreadful inevitable outcome.

A team of bike cops, one man and one woman whom Jetsam knew from Watch 3, pedaled by slowly on the sidewalk, over those very famous three-hundred-pound slabs of marble and brass dedicated to Hollywood magic and the glamour of the past.

The bike cops nodded to him but continued on their way when he shook his head, indicating that nothing important had brought him here. He thought they looked very uncool in their bike helmets and those funny blue outfits that the other cops called pajamas.

When B.M. Driscoll caught up with him, he said, 'Don't this look a little bit strange? I mean, a purse is left here by an unknown person-reporting?'

Jetsam said, 'Whaddaya mean?'

B.M. Driscoll said, 'They're out to get me.'

'Who?'

'Internal Affairs Group. In fact, the whole goddamn Professional Standards Bureau. I got grilled like an Al-Qaeda terrorist by a Force Investigation Team when I popped the cap at the goddamn crackhead that tried to run over me. I tell you, IA's out to get me.'

'Man, you gotta go visit the Department shrink,' Jetsam said. 'You're soaring way out there, bro. You're sounding unhinged.'

But B.M. Driscoll said, 'I'll tell you something, if that purse is still there in the midst of this goddamn boulevard carnival, it means one thing. An undercover team has chased away every tweaker that's tried to pick it up during the last ten minutes.'

And now Jetsam started getting paranoid. He began looking hard at every tourist nearby. Could that one be a cop? That one over there looks like he could be. And that babe pretending to be reading the name on one of the marble stars down on the sidewalk. Shit, her purse is bulging like maybe there's a Glock nine and handcuffs in there.

When they were standing at the phone booth and saw a woman's brown leather handbag on the phone booth tray, B.M. Driscoll said, 'The purse is still there. Nobody's picked it up. No tweaker. No dogooder. It's still there. If there's money in it, you can bet your ass this is a sting.'

'If there's money in it, I gotta admit you might have a point here,' Jetsam said, looking behind him for the babe with the bulge in her handbag. And goddamnit, she was looking right at him! Then she gave him a little flirtatious wave and walked away. Shit, just a badge bunny.

B.M. Driscoll picked up the purse and opened it as though he was expecting a trick snake to jump out, removed the thick leather wallet, and handed it to Jetsam, saying, 'Tell me I'm wrong.'

Jetsam opened it and found a driver's license, credit cards, and other ID belonging to a Mary R. Rollins of Seattle, Washington. Along with $367 in currency.

'Bro, I think you ain't paranoid,' Jetsam said. 'Forget what I said about the shrink.'

'Let's take this straight to the station and make a ten-ten,' B.M. Driscoll said, referring to a property report.

'Let's take this to the Oracle,' Jetsam said. 'Let's call information for a phone number on Mary Rollins. Let's check and see if this ID is legit. I don't like to be set up like I'm a fucking thief.'

'It's not you,' B.M. Driscoll said, and now he was twitching and blinking. 'It's me. I'm a marked man!'

When they got to the station, they found the Oracle in the john, reading a paper. Jetsam stood outside the toilet stall and said, 'You in there, Boss?'

Recognizing the voice, the Oracle replied, 'This better be more important than your overwhelming excitement that surf's up tomorrow. At my age, taking a dump is serious business.'

'Can you meet Driscoll and me in the roll-call room?'

'In due time,' the Oracle said. 'There's a time for everything.'

They chose the roll-call room for privacy. The Oracle examined the purse and contents, and as he looked at this angry suntanned surfer cop with his short hair gelled up like a bed of spikes, and at his older partner twitching his nose like a rabbit, he said to them, 'You're right. This has to be a sting. This is unadulterated bullshit!'

Flotsam and Jetsam were lying in the sand next to their boards, by their towels and water, when Jetsam, reaching this part of the story, stopped to take a long pull from his water bottle.

Flotsam said, 'Don't stop, dude. Get to the final reel. What the fuck happened?'

Jetsam said, 'What happened was the Oracle came on like El Niño, and everybody stayed outta his way. The Oracle was hacked off, bro. And I got to see what all those hash marks give you.'

'What besides death before your time?'

'Humongous prunes and no fear, bro. The Oracle jumped their shit till the story came out. It was a sting, but as usual, Ethics Enforcement Section fucked up. It wasn't meant for B.M. Driscoll. He's so straight he won't even remove mattress tags, but they wouldn't say who it was meant for. Maybe somebody on Watch Three. We think communications just gave the call to the wrong unit.'

Flotsam said, 'EES should stick to catching cops who work off-duty jobs when they're supposed to be home with bad backs. That's all they're good for.'

'Being an LAPD cop today is like playing a game of dodgeball, but the balls are coming at us from every-fucking-where,' Jetsam said.

Flotsam looked at his partner's thousand-yard stare, saying, 'Your display is on screen saver, dude. Get the hard drive buzzing and stay real.'

'Okay, but I don't like being treated like a thief,' Jetsam said.

Flotsam said, 'They gotta play their little games so they can say, "Look, Mr. Attorney General, we're enforcing the consent decree against the formerly cocky LAPD." Just forget about it.'

'But we got sideswiped, bro.'

'Whaddaya mean?'

'They burned us.'

'For what?'

'The undercover team saw B.M. Driscoll's uniforms hanging in the car. They had to nail us for something after we didn't fall for their stupid sting, so we're getting an official reprimand for doing personal business on duty.'

'Stopping at the cleaners?'

'You got it, bro.'

'What'd the Oracle say about that?'

'He wasn't there at the time. He'd already headed out for Alfonso's Tex Mex when a rat from PSB showed up. One of those that can't stop scratching all the insect bites on his candy ass. And the watch commander informed us we were getting burned.'

'That is way fucked, dude. You know how many man hours were wasted on that chickenshit sting? And here we are, with half the bodies we need to patrol the streets.'

'That is life in today's LAPD, bro.'

'How's your morale?'

'It sucks.'

'How would it be if I got you laid Thursday night?'

'Improved.'

'There's this badge bunny I heard about at the Director's Chair. Likes midnight swims at the beach, I hear.'

'I thought you said you'd fallen in love with Mag Takara?'

'I am in love, but it ain't working too good.'

'You said it was hopeful.'

'Let's hit it, dude,' Flotsam said to change the subject, grabbing his board and sprinting for the surf. He plunged into a cold morning breaker and came up grinning in the boiling ocean foam.

After Jetsam paddled out to his partner, he looked at Flotsam and said, 'So what happened between you and Mag? Too painful to talk about?'

'She's got it all, dude. The most perfect chick I ever met,' Flotsam said.

'Do you know what the Oracle told me? When he walked a beat in Little Tokyo a hundred years ago, he got to know the Takara family. They own a couple of small hotels, three restaurants, and I don't know how much rental property. That little honey might have some serious assets of her own someday.'

'No wonder you're in love.'

'And she is such a robo-babe. You ever see more beautiful lips? And the way she walks like a little panther? And her skin like ivory and the way her silky hair falls against her gracefully curving neck?'

Sitting astride his surfboard, Jetsam said, '"Gracefully curving" ... bro, you are way goony! Stay real! This could just be false enchantment because she grabbed that dummy hand grenade and tossed it that time.'

Flotsam said, 'Then I got way pumped the last night we worked to-gether. I knew after my days off, you and me would be teamed for the rest of the deployment period, so I took the bit in my teeth and I went for it. I said something like, "Mag, I hope I can persuade you to grab a bikini and surf with me on the twilight ocean with the molten sun setting into the darkling sea."'

'No, bro!' Jetsam said. 'No darkling sea! That is sooo non-bitchin'!' He paused. 'What'd she say to that?'

'Nothing at first. She's a very reserved girl, you know. Finally, she said, "I think I would rather stuff pork chops in my bikini and swim in a tank full of piranhas than go surfing with you at sunset, sunrise, or anytime in between."'

'That is like, way discouraging, bro,' Jetsam said somberly. 'Can't you see that?'

Flotsam and Jetsam weren't the only ones complaining about the LAPD watchers that day. One of the watchers, D2 Brant Hinkle, had been biding his time at Internal Affairs Group. He was on the lieutenant's list but was afraid that the list was going to run out of time before an opening came for him. He was optimistic now that all of the black males and females of any race who'd finished lower on the written and oral exam than he had but got preference had already been selected. Even though he wasn't a D3 supervisor, he'd had enough prior supervisory experience in his package to qualify for the lieutenant's exam, and he'd done pretty well on it. He didn't think anyone else could leapfrog over him before the list expired.

It had been an interesting two-year assignment at IAG, good for his personnel package but not so good for the stomach. He was experiencing acid reflux lately and was staring down the barrel at his fifty-third birthday. With twenty-nine years on the Job this was his last realistic chance to make lieutenant before pulling the pin and retiring to ... well, he wasn't sure where. Somewhere out of LA before the city imploded.

Brantley Hinkle was long divorced, with two married daughters but no grandchildren yet, and he tried for a date maybe twice a month after he heard a colleague his age say, 'Shit, Charles Manson gets a dozen marriage proposals a year, and I can't get a date.'

It made him realize how seldom he had a real date, let alone a sleepover, so he'd been making more of an effort lately. There was a forty-year-old divorced PSR whose honeyed tones over the police radio could trigger an incipient erection. There was an assistant district attorney he'd met at a retirement party for one of the detectives at Robbery-Homicide Division. There was even a court reporter, a Pilates instructor in her spare time, who was forty-six years old but looked ten years younger and had never been married. She'd whipped him into better shape with a diet and as much Pilates as he could stand. His waistband got so loose he couldn't feel his cell phone vibrating.

So he was in decent condition and still had most of his hair, though it was as gray as pewter now, and he didn't need glasses, except for reading. He could usually connect with one of the three women when he was lonely and the need arose, but he hadn't been trying lately. He was more focused on leaving Professional Standards Bureau and getting back to a detective job somewhere to await the promotion to lieutenant. If it came.

At IAG Brant Hinkle had seen complaints obsessively investigated for allegations that would have been subjects of fun and needling at retirement parties back in the days before the Rodney King beating and the Rampart scandal. Back before the federal consent decree.

And they weren't just coming from citizens; they were coming from other cops. He'd had to oversee one where a patrol sergeant his age looked at a woman officer in a halter bra and low-ride shorts who had just come from working out. Staring at her sweaty belly, the sergeant had sighed. That was it, he'd sighed. The woman officer beefed the sergeant, and that very expensive sigh got him a five-day suspension for workplace harassment.

Then there was the wrestling match at arrest-and-control school, where a male officer was assigned to wrestle with a woman officer in order to learn certain holds. The male cop said aloud to his classmates, 'I can't believe I get paid for this.'

She'd beefed him, and he'd gotten five days also.

Yet another involved a brand-new sergeant who, on his way to his first duty assignment as a sergeant, happened to spot one of the patrol units blow a stop sign on their way to a hot call that the unit had not been assigned. The sergeant arrived at his new post, and immediately he wrote a 1.28 personnel complaint.

Within his first month, that sergeant, a man who wore his new stripes with gusto, called one of the officers on his watch a 'dumbbell.' The officer made an official complaint against him. The sergeant got a five-day suspension. The troops cheered.

Under the federal consent decree with the legions of LAPD overseers, the cops were turning on each other and eating their own. It was a different life from the one he'd lived when he'd joined the world-famous LAPD, uncontested leader in big-city law enforcement. In Brant Hinkle's present world, even IAG investigators were subjected to random urine tests conducted by Scientific Investigation Division.

The IAG investigators who had preceded him said that during Lord Voldemort's Reign of Terror, they sometimes had six Boards of Rights – the LAPD equivalent of a military court martial – going on at one time, even though there were only five boardrooms. People had to wait in the corridors for a room to clear. It was an assembly line of fear, and it brought about the phenomenon of cops lawyering up with attorneys hired for them by their union, the Los Angeles Police Protective League.

The more senior investigators told him that at that time, everyone had joked grimly that they expected a cop to walk out of his Board of Rights after losing his career and pension and leap over the wrought-iron railing of the Bradbury Building into the courtyard five stories down.

The Bradbury Building, at 304 South Broadway, was an incongruous place in which to house the dreaded Professional Standards Bureau, with its three hundred sergeants and detectives, including the Internal Affairs Group, all of whom had to handle seven thousand complaints a year, both internally and externally generated against a police force of nine thousand officers. The restored 1893 masterpiece, with its open-cage elevators, marble staircases, and five-story glass roof, was probably the most photographed interior in all of Los Angeles.

Many a film noir classic had been shot inside that Mexican-tile courtyard flooded with natural light. He could easily imagine the ghosts of Robert Mitchum and Bogart exiting any one of the balcony offices in trench coats and fedoras as ferns in planter pots cast ominous shadows across their faces when they lit their inevitable smokes. Brant knew that nobody dared light a cigarette in the Bradbury Building today, this being twenty-first-century Los Angeles, where smoking cigarettes is a PC misdemeanor, if not an actual one.

Brant Hinkle was currently investigating a complaint against a female training officer in a patrol division whose job it had been to bring a checklist every day for a sergeant to sign off. After a year of this bureaucratic widget counting, where half the time she couldn't find a sergeant, she'd just decided to create one with a fictitious name and fictitious serial number.

But then the 'fraud' was discovered, and no check forger had ever been so actively pursued. IAG sent handwriting exemplars downtown to cement the case against the hapless woman whom the brass was determined to fire. But as it turned out, there was a one-year statute on such offenses, and they couldn't fire her. In fact, they couldn't do anything except transfer her to a division that might cause her a long drive and make her miserable, this veteran cop who had had an unblemished record but had finally succumbed to the deluge of audits and paperwork.

Brant Hinkle and his team were secretly happy that she'd kept her job. Like Brant, just about all of them were using IA experience as a stepping stone to promotion and weren't the rats that street cops imagined them to be.

As Brant Hinkle put it, 'We're just scared little mice stuck in a glue trap.'

Once when they were all bemoaning the avalanche of worthless and demoralizing complaints that the oppressive oversight armies had invited, Brant said to his colleagues, 'When I was a kid and *Dragnet* was one of the biggest hits on TV, Jack Webb's opening voice-over used to say, "This is the city. Los Angeles, California. I work here ... I'm a cop." Today all we can say is, "This is the city. Los Angeles, California. I work here ... I'm an auditor."'

Probably the most talked-about investigation handled by Brant Hinkle during these we-investigate-every-complaint years was the one involving a woman who had become obsessed with a certain cop and made an official complaint against him, signed and dated, maintaining, 'He stole my ovaries.'

It had to be investigated in full, including with lengthy interviews. There had to be an on-the-record denial by the police officer in question, who said to Brant, 'Well, I'm glad IA is taking her complaint seriously. There could be something to this ovary theft. After all, you guys are trying real hard to steal my balls, and you've just about done it.'

It was probably at that moment that Brant Hinkle spoke to his boss about a transfer back to a divisional detective squad.

NINE

Watch 5, the ten-hour midwatch, from 5:15 p.m. to 4:00 a.m. with an unpaid lunch break (code 7), had about fifty officers assigned to it. Five of them were women, but three of those women were on light duty for various reasons, and there were only two in the field, Budgie and Mag. And what with days off, sick days, and light duty, on a typical weekend night it was difficult for the Oracle to find enough bodies to field more than six or eight cars. So when one of the vice unit's sergeants asked to borrow both of the midwatch women for a Saturday night mini-version of the Trick Task Force, he got an argument.

'You've got the biggest vice unit in the city,' the Oracle said. 'You've got half a dozen women. Why don't you use them?'

'Only two work as undercover operators and they're both off sick,' the vice sergeant said. 'This isn't going to be a real task force. No motor cops as chase units. No big deal. We only wanna run a couple operators and cover units for a few hours.'

'Why can't you put your uniformed women on it?'

'We have three. One's on vacation, one's on light duty, one's pregnant.'

'Why not use her?' the Oracle said. 'It's a known fact that there's a whole lotta tricks out there who prefer pregnant hookers. Something about a mommy fixation. I guess they want spanked.'

'She's not pregnant enough to notice, but she's throwing up like our office is a trawler in a perfect storm. I ask her to walk the boulevard, she'll start blowing chunks on my shoes.'

'Aw shit,' the Oracle said. 'How're we supposed to police a city when we spend half the time policing ourselves and proving in writing that we did it?'

'I don't answer trick questions,' the vice sergeant said. 'How about it? Just for one night.'

When the Oracle asked Budgie Polk and Mag Takara if they'd like to be boulevard street whores on Saturday night, they said okay. He only got an argument from Budgie's partner, Fausto Gamboa.

Fausto walked into the office, where three supervisors were doing paper-work, and being one of the few patrol officers at Hollywood Station old enough to call the sixty-eight-year-old sergeant by his given name, he said to the Oracle, 'I don't like it, Merv.'

'What don't you like, Fausto?' the Oracle asked, knowing the answer.

'Budgie's got a baby at home.'

'So what's that got to do with it?'

'Sometimes she lactates. And it's painful.'

'She'll deal with it, Fausto. She's a cop,' the Oracle said, while the other sergeants pretended to not be listening.

'What if she gets herself hurt? Who's gonna feed her baby?'

'The cover teams won't let her get hurt. And babies don't have to have mother's milk.'

'Aw shit,' Fausto said, echoing the Oracle's sentiments about the whole deal.

After he'd gone the Oracle said to the other two sergeants, 'Sometimes my ideas work too well. Fausto's not only gotten out of his funk, I think he's about to adopt Budgie Polk. Her kid'll probably be calling him Grandpa Fausto in a couple years.'

Cosmo Betrossian was a whole lot unhappier than Fausto Gamboa. He had diamonds to deliver to Dmitri at the Gulag soon and he had to kill that miserable addict Farley Ramsdale and his stupid girlfriend, Olive, sometime before then. Farley's claim that he had someone watching Cosmo and Ilya's apartment was so ridiculous Cosmo hadn't given it a thought. And as to Farley's other claim, that he had a letter that would be delivered to the police if something happened to him, well, the addict had seen too many movies. Even if there was a letter, let the police try to prove the truth of it without the writer and his girlfriend alive to attest to its veracity.

Cosmo was going to make them disappear, and he would have liked to talk to Dmitri about that. Dmitri would have some good ideas about how to make someone vanish, but if Dmitri learned about the tweakers, he might see them as potential trouble and back out of the arrangement. No, Cosmo would have to deal with them with only Ilya to help. And it would not be easy. Other than a gang rival back in Armenia whom he had shot to death when he was a kid of eighteen, Cosmo had never killed anyone. Here in America he had never even committed violent crime until the jewelry store robbery. His criminal life had been relegated to the smuggling of drugs, which he did not use himself, fencing stolen property, and in recent years, identity theft, which he'd learned from a Gypsy.

He'd met the Gypsy in a Hollywood nightclub on the Sunset Strip. Cosmo had been frequenting the Strip then, doing low-level cocaine sales. But the Gypsy introduced him to a new world. He showed Cosmo how easy it was to walk into the Department of Motor Vehicles, armed with a bit of personal data stolen by common mail thieves like Farley Ramsdale, and tell a DMV employee that he needed a new driver's license because he'd changed his address and misplaced his license. At first the DMV employees would ask for a Social Security Number but seldom if ever bothered to pull up the photo of the legitimate license holder to compare it with the face before them. They'd just take a new photo and change the address to the location where the license would be sent, and business would be concluded.

Cosmo and the Gypsy normally used an address of a house or apartment in their neighborhood where the occupant worked during the day. And either Cosmo or the Gypsy would check their neighbor's mailbox every day until the driver's license arrived. Later, when the DMV started asking for a birth certificate, Cosmo learned that with the information from the stolen mail, it was a simple matter for the Gypsy to make a credible birth certificate that would satisfy most DMV employees.

Cosmo and the Gypsy got so lazy that instead of going to the DMV, they started using a CD template that was making the rounds among all the identity thieves. It showed how to make driver's licenses, Social Security cards, auto insurance certificates, and other documents.

Stealing credit-card numbers became a bonanza. They could buy just about anything. They could even buy automobiles, and since car dealers were all covered by insurance, they were the easiest. By the time the legitimate card owners got their statements, Cosmo and the Gypsy would be off that card and on to another. Sometimes the credit-card statements went to bogus addresses supplied by Cosmo and the Gypsy, so legitimate card owners wouldn't discover the account was delinquent until they tried to buy something of value.

The Gypsy had an interior decorator working with them at that time. She said it was amazing how many people on the affluent west side of town kept their old cards, even ATM cards, thrown into a drawer somewhere. Nobody seemed to care much. The credit-card company only took a hit if the card was presented in person by the thief. If the business was done on the Internet or by phone, the creditcard company was not liable. Banks and credit-card companies had long delays in catching up, and identity thefts were so paper intensive the police were overwhelmed.

For a while Cosmo and the Gypsy had gotten so successful they were hoping to deal with the Russians whose eastern European contacts hacked into US banks and lending institutions for card numbers, then ordered high-quality embossing and encoding strips from China. As it was, they just did their business online in the cyber cafés or by phone and ordered merchandise to be sent to addresses they'd cased. FedEx would drop the parcels on the porch while the resident was at work, and they would be picked up by Cosmo while the Gypsy waited in their car. The resident would be shocked when, after a few months of this, the police showed up at the home with a search warrant for all that stolen property.

Then one day without warning the Gypsy and the interior moved to New

York without notifying Cosmo until they were there. And that was that. Cosmo continued limping through the world that the Gypsy had sailed through, and now Cosmo was dealing with tweaker mail thieves and doing cyber café networking as best he could. He had almost been arrested twice and was losing confidence now that everybody was doing identity theft.

The big break had come in the batch of mail stolen by Farley Ramsdale, when he had found the letter about the diamonds, and Cosmo had committed his first violent crime in America. He was stunned to learn that he liked it. It had thrilled him, that feeling of power over the jewelry store proprietor. Seeing the fear in his eyes. Hearing him weep. Cosmo had had complete control over everything, including that man's life. The feeling was something he could never put into words, but he believed that Ilya felt some of it too. If another chance at a safe and profitable armed robbery came up, he knew he would take it.

But of immediate concern to him was Farley Ramsdale and Olive. And Cosmo was very worried about Ilya as a partner in homicide. Could she do what it took, he wondered. He hadn't spoken with her about the two addicts, not since they had come to the apartment with their blackmail threat. Cosmo sensed that Ilya knew what had to be done but wanted him to deal with it alone. Well, it was not going to work that way. He couldn't do it alone. They wouldn't trust him. Ilya was a very smart Russian, and he needed a plan with her involved.

Hollywood Nate Weiss and Wesley Drubb were having another one of those Hollywood nights, that is, a night of very strange calls. It always happened when there was a full moon over the boulevard and environs.

Actually, the Oracle, who'd read a book or two in his long life, forewarned them all at roll call, saying, 'Full moon. A Hollywood moon. This is a night when our citizens act out their lives of quiet desperation. Share your stories tomorrow night at roll call and we'll give the Quiet Desperation Award to the team with the most memorable story.' Then he added, 'Beware, beware! Their flashing eyes, their floating hair!'

Nate's facial bruises from the fight with the veteran who wanted a ride were healing up well, and though he would never admit it to anyone, he was secretly wishing they'd given the psycho the goddamn ride he'd wanted. His black eye had actually cost him a job as an extra on a low-budget movie being shot in Westwood.

Wesley was driving again, and with the Oracle going to bat for him, he hoped that there wouldn't be disciplinary action for letting their shop get stolen and trashed by the little homie who hadn't been arrested yet but whom detectives had identified. The Oracle had written in his report that Wesley's failure to shut off the engine and take the keys when he'd jumped out of the car was understandable given the extreme urgency of helping his partner subdue the very violent suspect.

Hollywood Nate said that since Wesley had just finished his probation it wouldn't cost him his job, but Nate figured he'd be getting a few unpaid days off. 'Forgiveness is given in church, in temple, and by the Oracle, but it ain't written into the federal consent decree or the philosophy of Internal Affairs,' Nate warned young Wesley Drubb.

Their first very strange call occurred early in the evening on Sycamore several blocks from the traffic on Melrose. It came from a ninety-five-year-old woman in a faded cotton dress, sitting in a rocker on her front porch, stroking a calico cat. She pointed out that the man who lived across the street in a white stucco cottage 'hasn't been around for a few weeks.'

She was so old and shriveled that her parchment skin was nearly transparent and her colorless hair was thinned to wisps. Her frail legs were wrapped in elastic bandages, and though she was obviously a bit addled she could still stand erect, and she walked out onto the sidewalk unaided.

She said, 'He used to have a cup of tea and cookies with me. And now he doesn't come, but his cat does and I feed her every day.'

Hollywood Nate winked at Wesley and patted the old woman on the shoulder and said, 'Well, don't you worry. We'll check it out and make sure he's okay and tell him to drop by and have some tea with you and give you his thanks for feeding his cat the past few weeks.'

'Thank you, Officer,' she said and returned to her rocker.

Hollywood Nate and Wesley strolled across the street and up onto the porch. The few feet of dirt between the house and sidewalk hadn't been tended in a long time but was too patchy and water-starved to have done more than spread a web of crabgrass across its length. There seemed to be several seedy and untended small houses along this block, so there was nothing unusual about this one.

Hollywood Nate tapped on the door and when they received no answer said, 'The guy might have gone out of town for the weekend. The old lady doesn't know a few weeks from a few days.'

Or a few years, as it turned out.

When Wesley Drubb opened the letter slot to take a look, he said, 'Better have a look at this, partner.'

Nate looked inside and saw mail piled up nearly to the mail slot itself. It looked to be mostly junk mail, and it completely covered the small hallway inside.

'Let's try the back door,' Nate said.

It was unlocked. Nate figured to find the guy dead, but there was no telltale stench, none at all. They walked through a tiny kitchen and into the living room, and there he was, sitting in his recliner in an Aloha shirt and khaki pants.

He was twice as shriveled as his former friend across the street. His eyes, or what was left of them, were open. He'd obviously been a bearded man, but the beard had fallen out onto his chest along with most of the hair on his head, and the rest clung in dried patches. Beside his chair was a folding TV tray, and on it was his remote control, a *TV Guide*, and two vials of heart medication.

Wesley checked the jets on the kitchen range and tried light switches and the kitchen faucet, but all utilities had been turned off. On the kitchen table was an unused ticket to Hawaii, explaining the Aloha shirt. He'd been practicing.

Nate bent over the *TV Guide* and checked the date. It was two years and three months old.

Wesley asked Hollywood Nate if this could possibly be a crime scene because the dead man's left leg wasn't there.

Nate looked in the corner behind the small sofa and there it was, lying right near the pet door where his cat could come and go at will. There was almost no dried flesh left on the foot, just tatters from his red sock hanging on bone. The leg had apparently fallen off.

'Good thing he didn't have a dog,' Nate said. 'If grandma across the street had found this on her front porch, she might've had a heart attack of her own.'

'Should we call paramedics?' Wesley said.

'No, just the coroner's crew. I'm pretty sure this man's dead,' said Hollywood Nate.

When they got back to the station at end-of-watch and everyone was comparing full-moon stories, they had to agree that the Quiet Desperation Award went to Mag Takara and Benny Brewster, hands down.

It began when a home owner living just west of Los Feliz Boulevard picked up the phone, dialed 911, gave her address, and said, 'The woman next door is yelling for help! Her door is locked! Hurry!'

Mag and Benny acknowledged the code 3 call, turned on the light bar and siren, and were on their way. When they got to the spooky old two-story house, they could hear her from the street yelling, 'Help me! Help me! Please help me!'

They ran to the front door and found it locked. Mag stepped out of the way and Benny Brewster kicked the door in, splintering the frame and sending the door crashing against the wall.

Once inside the house they heard the cries for help increase in intensity: 'For God's sake, help me! Help me! Help me!'

Mag and Benny ascended the stairs quickly, hearing car doors slam outside as Fausto and Budgie and two other teams arrived. The bedroom door was slightly ajar and Mag stood on one side of it, Benny on the other, and being cops, they instinctively put their hands on their pistol grips.

Mag nudged the door open with her toe. There was silence for a long moment and they could hear the loud tick of a grandfather clock as the pendulum swept back and forth, back and forth.

Then, in the far corner of the large bedroom suite, the voice: 'Help me! Help me! Help me!'

Mag and Benny automatically entered in a combat crouch and found her. She was a fifty-five-year-old invalid, terribly crippled by arthritis, left alone that night by her bachelor son. She was sitting in a wheelchair by a small round table near the window, where she no doubt spent long hours gazing at the street below.

She was holding a .32 semiautomatic in one twisted claw and an empty magazine in the other. The .32 caliber rounds were scattered on the floor where she'd dropped them.

Her surprisingly youthful cheeks were tear-stained, and she cried out to them, 'Help me! Oh, please help me load this thing! And then get out!'

There were two detectives working overtime at Hollywood Station that night. One was Andi McCrea, who had been given the job of finishing what she'd started innocently a few weeks ago as a stand-in for the absent sex crimes detail. But she didn't mind a bit because that was the first time in her career that she had solved a double homicide without knowing a damn thing about it.

The kid from Reno was in Juvenile Hall awaiting his hearing. But more important, his forty-year-old fellow killer, Melvin Simpson, a third-strike ex-con from the San Francisco Bay Area who had been in Reno on a gambling junket, was going to be charged with capital murder.

Now detectives in Las Vegas were also interested in Simpson, since it was discovered through his credit-card receipts that he'd also been in their city for a week. With no means of employment he'd had enough money to gamble in both places, and it turned out that a high-tech engineer from Chicago who was attending a convention had been robbed and murdered at a rest stop outside Las Vegas on the day that Simpson had checked out of his hotel.

The ballistics report hadn't been completed yet, but Andi had high hopes. Wouldn't this be something to talk about to the oral board at the next lieutenant's exam. It might even rate a story in the *LA Times*, except that nobody read the *Times* anymore or any newspaper, so there was no point getting excited about that part of it.

The other detective working late that night was Viktor Chernenko, a forty-three-year-old immigrant from Ukraine, one of two naturalized citizens currently working at Hollywood Station, the other being from Guadalajara, Mexico. Viktor had a mass of wiry, dark hair that he called 'disobedient,' a broad Slavic face, a barrel of a body, and a neck so thick he was always popping buttons.

Once when his robbery team was called to a clinic in east Hollywood to interview the victim of a violent purse snatching, the receptionist saw Viktor enter and said to a woman waiting in the lobby, 'Your cab is here.'

And he was just about the most dedicated, hardworking, and eager-to-please cop that Andi McCrea had ever encountered.

Viktor had emigrated to America in September 1991, a month after the coup that led to the collapse of the Soviet Union, at a time when he was a twenty-eight-year-old captain in the Red Army. His exit from the USSR was unclear and mysterious, leading to gossip that he'd defected with valuable intelligence and was brought to Los Angeles by the CIA. Or maybe not. No one knew for sure, and Viktor seemed to like it that way.

He was the one that LAPD came to when they needed a Russian translator or a Russian-speaking interrogator, and consequently he had become well known to most of the local gangsters from former Iron Curtain countries. And that was why he was working late. He had been assigned to assist the robbery team handling the 'hand grenade heist,' as the jewelry store robbery came to be called. Viktor had been contacting every émigré that he knew personally who was even remotely involved with the so-called Russian Mafia. And that meant any Los Angeles criminal from the Eastern bloc, including the YACS: Yugoslavians, Albanians, Croatians, and Serbs.

Viktor was educated well in Ukraine and later in Russia. His study of English had helped get him promoted to captain in the army before most of his same age colleagues, but the English he'd studied in the USSR had not included idioms, which would probably confound him forever. That evening, when Andi twice offered to get him some coffee, he had politely declined until she asked if she could bring him a cup of tea instead.

Using her proper name as always, he said, 'Thank you, Andrea. That would strike the spot.'

During his years in Los Angeles, Viktor Chernenko had learned that one similarity between life in the old USSR and life in Los Angeles – life under a command economy and a market economy – was that a tremendous amount of business was transacted by people in subcultures, people whom no one ever sees except the police. Viktor was fascinated by the tidal wave of identity theft sweeping over Los Angeles and the nation, and even though Hollywood detectives did not deal directly with these cases – referring them downtown to specialized divisions like Bunco Forgery – almost everybody Viktor contacted in the Hollywood criminal community had something or other to do with forged or stolen identity.

After several conversations with the jewelry store victim, Sammy Tanampai, as well as with Sammy's father, Viktor was convinced that neither of them had had any dealings, legitimate or not, with Russian gangsters or Russian prostitutes. Sammy Tanampai was positive that he had heard a Russian accent from the woman, or something similar to the accents he'd heard from Russian émigrés who'd temporarily settled in cheap lodgings that his father often rented to them in Thai Town.

It was during a follow-up interview that Sammy said to Viktor

Chernenko, 'The man didn't say many words, so I can't be exactly sure, but the woman's accent sounded like yours.'

The more that Viktor thought about how these Russians, if they were Russians, had gotten the information about the diamonds, the more he concluded that it could have come from an ordinary mail theft. Sipping the tea that Andi had brought him, he decided to make another phone call to Sammy Tanampai.

'Did you mail letters to anyone about the diamonds?' he asked Sammy after the jeweler's wife called him to the phone.

'I did not. No.'

'Do you know if your father did so?'

'Why would he do that?'

'Maybe to a client who wanted the kind of diamonds in your shipment? Something like that?'

And that stopped the conversation for a long moment. When Sammy spoke again he said, 'Yes. My father wrote to a client in San Francisco about the diamonds. He mentioned that to me.'

'Do you know where he mailed the letter?' Viktor asked.

'I mailed it,' Sammy said. 'In a mailbox on Gower, several blocks south of Hollywood Boulevard. I was on my way to pick up my kids at the day-care center. Is that important?'

'People steal letters from mailboxes,' Viktor explained.

After he hung up, Andi said, curious, 'Are you getting somewhere on the jewelry store case?'

With a smile, Viktor said, 'Tomorrow I shall be looking through the transient book to see if many homeless people are hanging around Hollywood and Gower.'

'Why?' Andi asked. 'Surely you don't think a homeless person pulled a robbery that sophisticated?'

With a bigger smile, he said, 'No, Andrea, but homeless people can steal from mailboxes. And homeless people see all that happens but nobody sees homeless people, who live even below subculture. My Russian robbers think they are very clever, but I think they may soon find that they have not pulled the fuzz over our eyes.'

One of the reasons given for putting Budgie Polk and Mag Takara out on the boulevard on Saturday night was that Compstat had indicated there were too many tricks getting mugged by opportunist robbers and by the whores themselves. And everyone knew that many of the robberies went unreported because tricks were married men who didn't want mom to know where they went after work.

Compstat was the program of the current chief of police that he'd used when he was police commissioner of the NYPD and that he claimed brought down crime in that city, even though it was during a time when crime was dropping all over America for reasons demographic that had nothing to do with his program. Still, nobody ever expressed doubts aloud and everybody jumped onboard, at least feigning exuberance for the big chief's imported baby, pinching its cheeks and patting its behind when anyone was watching.

Brant Hinkle of Internal Affairs Group thought that Compstat might possibly have helped in New York, with its thirty thousand officers, maybe even in Boston, where the chief had served as a street cop. Perhaps it might be a worthwhile tool in many vertical cities where thousands live and work directly on top of others in structures that rise several stories. But that wasn't the way people lived in the transient, nomadic sprawl of the LA basin. Where nobody knew their neighbors' names. Where people worked and lived close to the ground with access to their cars. Where everyone owned a car, and freeways crisscrossed residential areas as well as business districts. Where only nine thousand cops had to police 467 square miles.

When crime occurred in LA, the perpetrator could be blocks or miles away before the PSR could even assign a car to take a report. If she could find one. And as far as flooding an area with cops to deal with a crime trend, the LAPD didn't have half enough cops to flood anything. They could only leak.

There were a few occasions when Brant Hinkle got to see Compstat in action, during the first couple of years after the new chief arrived. That was when the chief, perhaps a bit insecure on the Left Coast, brought in a journalist crony from New York who had never been a police officer and made a special badge for him saying 'Bureau Chief.' And gave him a gun permit so he'd have a badge and gun like a real cop. That guy seemed to do no harm, and he was gone now and the chief of police was more acclimated and more secure, but Compstat remained.

Back then the chief had also brought several retired cops from New York, as though trying to re-create New York in LA. They would put on a little slide show with two or three patrol captains sitting in the hot seat. On a slide would be a picture of an apartment building, and one of the retired NYPD cops with a loud voice and a Bronx accent would confront the LAPD captains and say, 'Tell us about the crime problems there.'

And of course, none of the captains had the faintest idea about the crime problems there or even where 'there' was. A two-story apartment building? There were hundreds in each division, thousands in some.

And the second-loudest guy, maybe with a Brooklyn accent, would yell in their faces, 'Is the burglary that occurred there on Friday afternoon a single burglary or part of a trend?'

And a captain would stammer and sweat and wonder if he should take a guess or pray for an earthquake.

However, Brant Hinkle learned that there were some LAPD officers who loved the Compstat sessions. They were the street cops who happened to hate their captains. They got a glow just hearing about their bosses melting in puddles while these abrasive New Yorkers sprayed saliva. At least that's how it was described to the cops who wished they could have been there to watch the brass get a taste of the shit they shoveled onto the troops. The street cops would've paid for tickets.

As far as the troops at Hollywood Station were concerned, the East Coast chief was not Lord Voldemort, and that alone was an answered prayer. And he did care about reducing crime and response time to calls. And he did more than talk about troop morale; he allowed detectives to take their city cars home when they were on call instead of using their private cars. And of great importance, he instituted the compressed work schedule that Lord Voldemort hated, which allowed LAPD cops to join other local police departments in working four ten-hour shifts a week or three twelve-hour shifts instead of the old eight-to-five. This allowed LAPD cops, most of whom could not afford to live in LA and had to drive long distances, the luxury of three or four days at home.

As far as Compstat was concerned, the street cops were philosophical and fatalistic, as they always were about the uncontrollable nature of a cop's life. One afternoon at roll call, the Oracle, who was old enough and had enough time on the Job to speak the truth when no one else dared, asked the lieutenant rhetorically, 'Why doesn't the brass quit sweating Compstat? It's just a series of computer-generated pin maps is all it is. Give the chief a little more time to settle down in his new Hollywood digs and go to a few of those Beverly Hills cocktail parties catered by Wolfgang Puck. Wait'll he gets a good look at all those pumped-up weapons of mass seduction. He'll get over his East Coast bullshit and go Hollywood like all the clowns at city hall.'

When his transfer came through, Brant Hinkle was overjoyed. He had hoped he would get Hollywood Detectives and had had an informal interview months earlier with their lieutenant in charge. He had also had an informal interview with the boss of Van Nuys Detectives, the division in which he lived, and did the same at West LA Detectives, pretty sure that he could get one of them.

When he reported, he was told he'd be working with the robbery teams, at least for now, and was introduced around the squad room. He found that he was acquainted with half a dozen of the detectives and wondered where the rest were. He counted twenty-two people working in their little cubicles on computers or phones, sitting at small metal desks divided only by three-foot barriers of wallboard.

Andi McCrea said to him, 'A few of our people are on days off, but this is about it. We're supposed to have fifty bodies, we have half that many. At one time ten detectives worked auto theft, now there're two.'

'It's the same everywhere,' Brant said. 'Nobody wants to be a cop these days.'

'Especially LAPD,' Andi said. 'You should know why. You just left IA.'

'Not so loud,' he said, finger to lips. 'I'd like to keep it from the troops that I did two years on the Burn Squad.'

'Our secret,' Andi said, thinking he had a pretty nice smile and very nice green eyes.

'So where's my team?' he asked Andi, wondering how old she was, noticing there was no wedding ring.

'Right behind you,' she said. He turned and suffered an enthusiastic Ukrainian handshake from Viktor Chernenko.

'I am not usually a detective of the robbery teams,' Viktor said, 'but I am Ukrainian, so now I am a detective of robbery teams because of the hand grenade heist. Please sit and we shall talk about Russian robbers.'

'You'll enjoy this case,' Andi said, liking Brant's smile more and more. 'Viktor has been very thorough in his investigation.'

'Thank you, Andrea,' Viktor said shyly. 'I have tried with all my effort to leave no stone upright.'

The Oracle decided maybe he himself should win honorable mention for the Quiet Desperation Award on that full-moon evening. He had just returned from code 7 and had severe heartburn from two greasy burgers and fries, when the desk officer entered the office and said, 'Sarge, I think you need to take this one. A guy's on the phone and wants to speak to a sergeant.'

'Can't you find out what it's about?' the Oracle said, looking in the desk drawer for his antacid tablets.

'He won't tell me. Says he's a priest.'

'Oh, crap!' the Oracle said. 'Did he say his name is Father William, by any chance?'

'How'd you know?'

'There's a Hollywood moon. He'll keep me on the phone for an hour. Okay, I'll talk to him.'

When the Oracle picked up the phone, he said, 'What's troubling you this time, Father William?'

The caller said, 'Sergeant, please send me two strong young officers right away! I need to be arrested, handcuffed, and utterly humiliated! It's urgent!'

TEN

On Saturday, June 3, Officer Kristine Ripatti of Southwest Division was shot by an ex-con who had just robbed a gas station. Her partner killed the robber but got harassed by homies while he was trying to help the wounded officer, whose spinal wound paralyzed her from the waist down. When Fausto learned that Officer Ripatti, age thirty-three, also had a baby girl, he began to agonize over his partner's upcoming assignment.

When Saturday night arrived, Budgie and Mag got whistles from one end of the station to the other. Budgie grinned and flipped them off and tried not to look too self-conscious. She was wearing a push-up bra that wasn't comfortable given her condition, a lime-green jersey with a plunging neck under a short vest to hide the wire and mike, and the tightest skirt she'd ever worn, which the teenager next door had let her borrow.

The neighbor kid had gotten into the spirit of the masquerade by insisting that Budgie try on a pair of her mother's three-inch stilettos, and they fit, for despite being so tall, Budgie had small feet. A green purse with a shoulder strap completed the ensemble. And she wore plenty of pancake and the brightest creamiest gloss she owned, and she didn't spare the eyeliner. Her braided blond ponytail was combed out and sprinkled with glitter.

Flotsam checked her out and said to Jetsam, 'Man, talk about bling!'

Fausto looked at her with disapproval, then took a five-shot, two-inch Smith & Wesson revolver from his pocket and said, 'Put this in your purse.'

'I don't need it, Fausto,' Budgie said. 'My security team'll be watching me at all times.'

'Do like I say, please,' Fausto said.

Because it was the first time he'd ever said please to her, she took the gun and noticed him looking at her throat and chest. She reached up and unfastened the delicate gold chain and handed the chain and medal to him, saying, 'What kind of whore wears one of these? Hold it for me.'

Fausto took the medal in his hand and said, 'Who is this, anyways?'

'Saint Michael, patron saint of police officers.'

Handing it back to her, he said, 'Keep him in your purse right alongside the hideout gun.'

*

Mag, who wasn't thin like Budgie and was nearly a foot shorter, had all the curves she needed without enhancement, and came off as more of a bondage bitch. She wore a black jersey turtleneck, black shorts, black plastic knee boots that she had bought for this occasion, and dangling plastic earrings. She'd tied back her glossy blunt cut in a severe bun.

Her look said, 'I will hurt you but not too much.'

When the rest of the midwatch gave Mag the same cat calls and whistles, she just struck a pose and slapped her right hip and shot them a steaming look, saying, 'How would you like me to whip you with a licorice rope?'

During the regular roll call, the vice cops escorted their borrowed under-cover operators to their office to get them wired and briefed about the elements of 647b of the penal code, which criminalized an offer of sex for money. The decoys had to remain passive without engaging in an entrap-ment offer, while the cagier of the tricks would try to make them do it, knowing that entrapment would vitiate an arrest if it turned out that the hookers were cops.

After roll call, the Oracle took Fausto Gamboa aside and said privately, 'Stay away from Budgie tonight, Fausto. I mean it. You start hovering around the boulevard in a black-and-white, you'll screw it up for everybody.'

'Nobody should be giving that job to a new mother is all I got to say,' Fausto grumbled and then turned and went to partner with Benny Brewster for the night.

When Budgie and Mag were sitting in the backseat of a vice car being driven out onto east Sunset Boulevard, Mag, who had been loaned to the Trick Task Force on one other occasion, and Budgie, who had never worked as an undercover operator, kept their energy up with a lot of nervous chatter. After all, they were about to step out onto the stage, find their marks, and wait for the vice cop director to say 'Action!' All the time knowing that the part they were playing brought with it an element of danger that higher-paid Hollywood performers never had to face. But both women were eager and wanted to do well. They were smart, ambitious young cops.

Budgie noticed that her hands were trembling, and she hid them under the green plastic purse. She wondered if Mag was as nervous and said to her, 'I wanted to wear a little halter top but I figured if I did, they wouldn't be able to hide the wire.'

'I wanted my belly ring showing,' Mag said. 'But I thought the same thing about concealing the mike. I still like my ring but I'm glad I resisted the impulse to get the little butterfly above the tailbone when it was so popular.'

'Me too,' Budgie said, finding that just doing girl talk calmed her. 'Tramp stamps are out. And I'm even thinking of losing my belly ring. My gun belt rubs on it. Took almost a year to heal.'

'Mine used to rub,' Mag said, 'but now I put a layer of cotton over it and some tape before I go on duty.'

'I got mine right after work one day,' Budgie said. 'I wore my uniform to work in those days to save time for a biology class I was taking at City College. You should've seen the guy when I walked in and took off my Sam Browne. He gawked at me like, I'm putting a belly ring on a cop? His hands were shaking the whole time.'

Both women chuckled, and Simmons, the older vice cop, who was driving, turned to his partner Lane in the passenger seat and said, 'Popular culture has definitely caught up with the LAPD.'

Before they were dropped off at separate busy blocks on Sunset Boulevard, the older vice cop said to Mag, 'The order of desirability is Asian hookers first, followed by white.'

'Sorry, Budgie,' Mag said with a tense grin.

'Bet I'll catch more,' Budgie said also with a tense grin. 'I'll get all the midgets with a tall blonde fantasy.'

'For now I want you just one block apart,' Simmons said. 'There's two chase teams of blue suits to pull over the tricks after you get the offer, and two security teams including us who'll be covering you. One is already there watching both corners. 'You might have some competition who'll walk up to you and ask questions, suspecting you're cops. You're both too healthy looking.'

'I can look very bad very easily,' Budgie said.

'Won't that mess up our play?' Mag asked. 'If we get made by some hooker?'

'No,' he said. 'They'll just catch a ride ten blocks farther east and stay away from you. They know if you're cop decoys, we're close by watching out for you.'

Lane said, 'Most tricks're sick scum, but this early in the evening you might catch some ordinary businessmen driving west from the office buildings downtown. They know that better-class whores work the Sunset track and once in a while they look for a quickie.'

Budgie said, 'I haven't been in Hollywood all that long, but I've been in on some drug busts as transporting officer for trannies and dragons. One of them might recognize me.'

'The trannies mostly work Santa Monica Boulevard,' Simmons explained. 'They do good business with all those parolees-at-large who like that track because they got a taste for dick and ass when they were in the joint. They're disease-ridden. They avoid needles for fear of AIDS, then smoke ice and take it up the toboggan run. Does that make sense? Meth is an erotic drug. Don't even shake hands with trannies or dragons without wearing gloves.'

Knowing it was Budgie's first show, Lane said to her, 'If you should see an Asian hooker on the Sunset track you can figure she might be a transsexual. Sometimes Asian trannies make good money up here because they can fool the straight tricks. Goose bumps from shaving don't show as much on them. They might arrive just before the bars close, when the tricks're too drunk to see straight. But all trannies and dragons should be considered violent felons in dresses. They like to steal a trick's car when they can, and most tricks don't like to admit how the car got stolen, so the tranny or dragon never ends up on the stolen report as a suspect.'

Simmons said, 'Just avoid all the other hookers if possible – straights, dragons, and trannies.'

'*Other* hookers?' said Budgie.

He said, 'Sorry, you're starting to look so convincing I got confused.'

When the women were dropped off half a block from the boulevard, Simmons said, 'If a black trick hits on you, go ahead and talk but look for a too-cool manner and a cool ride. He may be one of the pimps from a Wilshire track checking out the competition, or trying to muscle in. He may talk shit and try to pimp you out and we would love that to happen, but keep both feet on the sidewalk. You never load up. Never get in a car. And remember, sometimes there's interference on the wire and we can't always make out exactly what the tricks're saying to you, so we take our cues from what you say. The wires have been known to fail completely. If you ever get in trouble, the code word is "slick." Use it in a sentence and we'll all come running. If necessary yell it out. Remember: "slick."'

After all that, they were both back to being nervous when they got out. Each spoke in a normal voice into their bras and then heard the cover unit say to Simmons and Lane on their radio band, 'Got them loud and clear.'

The older vice cop seemed clearly more safety conscious, and he said, 'Don't take this wrong. I hope I'm not being sexist, but I always tell new operators, don't take foolish chances for a misdemeanor violation like this. You're competent cops but you're still women.'

'Hear me roar,' Budgie said without conviction.

The younger vice cop said, 'Showtime!'

Both women had some twilight action within the first ten minutes. Budgie traded looks with a blue-collar white guy in a GMC pickup. He circled the block only once, then pulled off Sunset and parked. She walked over to his car, mentally rehearsing the lines she might use to avoid an accusation of entrapment. She needn't have worried.

When she bent down and looked at him through the passenger window, he said, 'I don't have time for anything but a very sweet head job. I don't want to go to a motel. If you're willing to get in and do it in the alley behind the next corner, I'll pay forty bucks. If you're not, see you later.'

It was so fast and so easy that Budgie was stunned. There was no parrying back and forth, no wordplay to see if she might be a cop. Nothing. She didn't quite know how to respond other than to say, 'Okay, stop a block down Sunset by the parking lot and I'll come to you.'

And that was all she had to do, other than signal to her security team by scratching her knee that the deal was done. Within a minute a black-and-white chase unit from Watch 3 squealed in behind the guy, lit him up with their light bar and a horn toot, and in ten minutes it was over. The trick was taken back to the mobile command post, a big RV parked two blocks from the action taking place on Sunset Boulevard.

At the CP were benches for the tricks, some folding party tables for the arrest reports, and a computerized gadget to digitally fingerprint and photograph the shell-shocked trick, after which he might be released. If he failed the attitude test or if there were other factors such as serious priors or drug possession, he would be taken to Hollywood Station for booking.

If it turned out to be a field release, the trick would find his car outside the command post, having been driven there by one of the uniformed cops, but the trick wouldn't be driving it home. The cars were usually impounded, the city attorney's office believing that impound is a big deterrent to prostitution.

Budgie was taken in a vice car to the command post, where she completed a short arrest report after telling the guy who wired her that she didn't need to hear the tape of her conversation with the trick. He was sitting there glaring at her.

He said, 'Thanks a lot.' And mouthed the word 'cunt.'

Budgie said to a vice cop, 'Maybe it's just a hormonal funk I'm in, but I'm starting to hate his guts.'

The vice cop said to Budgie, 'He's the kind of shit kicker that spent his happiest days line dancing and blowing up mailboxes.' Then to the glowering trick he said, 'This is Hollywood, dude. Let's do this cinema vérité.'

The trick scowled and said, 'What the fuck's that?'

The vice cop said, 'You just keep mouthing off, and pretend we're not in your face with a hidden video camera for a scene maybe you can later interpret for momma and the kiddies.'

Mag's first came a few minutes after Budgie's. He was a white guy driving a Lexus, and from the looks of him, one of those downtown businessmen on his way home to the west side. He was more cautious than Budgie's trick and circled the block twice. But Mag was a trick magnet. He pulled around the corner after his second pass and parked.

The vice cops had said that they expected long tall Budgie to get some suspicious questions about being a police decoy, but Mag was so small, so exotic, and so sexy that she should reassure anybody. And indeed, the businessman was not interested in her bona fides.

He said, 'You look like a very clean girl. Are you?'

'Yes, I am,' she said, tempted to try a Japanese accent but changed her mind. 'Very clean.'

'I think you're quite beautiful,' he said. Then he looked around warily and said, 'But I have to know you're clean and safe.'

'I'm a very clean girl,' Mag said.

'I have a family,' he said. 'Three children. I don't want to bring any diseases into my home.'

To calm him down, Mag said, 'No, of course not. Where do you live?'

'Bel Air,' he said. Then he added, 'I've never done anything like this before.'

'No, of course not,' she said. Then came the games.

'How much do you charge?'

'What're you looking for?'

'That depends on how much you charge.'

'That depends on what you're looking for.'

'You're truly lovely,' he said. 'Your legs are so shapely yet strong.'

'Thank you, sir,' she said, figuring that matching his good manners was the way to go.

'You should always wear shorts.'

'I often do.'

'You seem intelligent. So obliging. I'll bet you know how to cater to a man.'

'Yes, sir,' she said, thinking, Jesus, does he want a Geisha or what?

'I'm old enough to be your father,' he said. 'Does that trouble you?'

'Not at all.'

'Excite you?'

'Well ... maybe.'

And with that, he unzipped his fly and withdrew his erect penis and began masturbating as he cried out, 'You're so young and lovely!'

For the benefit of the cover team and because of her genuine surprise, Mag yelled into her bra, 'Holy shit! You're spanking the monkey! Get outta here!'

For a minute she forgot to scratch her knee.

Within two minutes the uniformed chase team lit up and stopped the Lexus, and when her vice cop security team pulled up, Mag said, 'Damn, he just jizzed all over his seventy-five-thousand-dollar car!'

After arriving back at the mobile CP, where the guy was booked for 647a of the penal code, lewd conduct in a public place, Mag was feeling a little bit sorry for the sick bastard.

Until after his digital photographing and fingerprinting, when he turned to Mag and said, 'The truth is, you have fat thighs. And I'll just bet you have father issues.'

'Oh, so you're a psychologist,' Mag said. 'From looking at my thighs you have me all figured out. So long, Daddy dearest.'

Then she turned to leave and noticed a handsome young vice cop named Turner looking at her. She blushed and involuntarily glanced at her thighs.

'They're gorgeous like the rest of you,' Turner said. 'Father issues or not.'

Mag Takara hooked three tricks in two hours, and Budgie Polk got two. When Budgie's third trick, a lowlife in a battered Pontiac, offered her crystal for pussy, Budgie popped him for drug possession.

'How's that? Felony prostitution,' she said, grinning at Simmons when she arrived back at the CP.

'You're doing great, Budgie,' Simmons said. 'Have fun, but stay alert. There's lotsa real weird people out here.'

Mag met one of them ten minutes later. He was a jug-eared guy in his early forties. He drove a late-model Audi and wore clothes that Mag recognized as coming from Banana. He was the kind of guy she'd probably have danced with if he'd asked her at one of the nightclubs on the Strip that she and her girlfriends sometimes visited.

He'd been hanging back when other tricks flitted around her, making nervous small talk for a moment but then driving away in fear. Fear of cops, or fear of robbery, or fear of disease – there was plenty of fear out there mingling with the lust and sometimes enhancing it. There were plenty of neuroses.

When the guy in the Audi took his turn and talked to Mag, broaching the subject of sex for money very tentatively, he became the second guy of the evening to get so excited so fast that he unzipped his pants and exposed himself.

Mag said into her bra, 'Oh my! You're masturbating! How exciting!'

'It's you!' he said. 'It's you! I'd pay you for a blow job, but I'm tapped out. And I can't get old Jonesy stiff, goddamnit!'

And while the chase team was speeding toward the corner, the headlights from a large van lit up the interior of the Audi. Mag looked more closely, and it was true: Jonesy was not stiff. But it was bright crimson!

'Good god!' Mag said. 'Are you bleeding down there?'

He stopped and looked at her. Then he released his flaccid member and said, 'Oh, that. It's just lipstick from the other three whores that sucked it tonight. That's where all my money went.'

A bit later, Budgie violated an order from Simmons by not keeping her feet on the pavement. She couldn't believe it when a big three-axle box truck hauling calves pulled around the corner and parked in the only place he could, in the first alley north.

She couldn't resist this one, approaching the cab of the truck, even though it was very dark in the alley. She climbed up on the step and listened nervously when the scar-faced trucker in a wife beater and cowboy hat said, 'Fifty bucks. Here. Now. Climb on up and suck me off, honey.'

This one was so bizarre that when the second cover team showed up, one of the vice cops said to the guy, 'Wonder what your boss would say if we booked you into jail and impounded your vehicle.'

Budgie said to the cowboy, 'Are they going to be slaughtered?'

The cowboy was so pissed off he didn't answer at first but then said, 'I suppose you don't eat veal? I suppose you shoot your goddamn lobsters before you put them in boiling water? Gimme a break, lady.'

This one presented so many logistical problems that after a field release the cowboy was allowed to continue on his way with his cargo.

When Budgie was finished at the CP and taken back to her corner on Sunset Boulevard, she tried not to remember the doomed calves bawling. It was the first time that evening that she was truly sad.

Budgie wasn't standing on Sunset Boulevard for three minutes when a Hyundai with Arkansas plates pulled up with two teenagers inside. She was still feeling depressed about the calves and about the pathetically reckless husbands and fathers she and Mag had hooked tonight, and she wondered what diseases all these losers would bring home to their wives. Maybe the fatal one. Maybe the Big A.

She could see right away what she was dealing with here: a pair of Marines. Both had tan lines from the middle of their foreheads down, and skinned whitewalls with an inch or two of hair on top. Both were wearing cheap T-shirts with glittery names of rock groups across the front, shirts that they'd probably just bought from a souvenir shop on Hollywood Boulevard. Both had dopey nervous smiles on their dopey young faces, and after being inexplicably sad, Budgie was now inexplicably mad.

The passenger said to her, 'Hey, good-lookin'!'

Budgie walked to the car and said, 'If you say, "Whatchya got cookin'?" I might have to shoot you.'

The word "shoot" changed the dynamic at once. The kid said, 'I hope you're not carrying a gun or something?'

'Why?' Budgie said. 'Can't a girl protect herself out here?'

The kid tried to recover some of his bravado and said, 'Know where we could get some action?'

'Action,' Budgie said. 'And what do you mean by that?'

The passenger glanced at the driver, who was even more nervous, and said, 'Well, we'd like to party. Know what I mean?'

'Yeah,' Budgie said. 'I know what you mean.'

'If it's not too expensive,' he said.

'And what do you mean by that?' Budgie said.

'We can pay seventy bucks,' the kid said. 'But you have to do both of us, okay?'

'Where're you stationed?' Budgie asked, figuring a chase or cover team was getting ready.

'Whadda you mean?' the passenger said.

'I was born at night, but not last night.' They're no more than eighteen, she thought.

'Camp Pendleton,' the kid said, losing his grin.

'When're you leaving for Iraq?'

The kid was really confused now, and he looked at the driver and back to Budgie and trying to retrieve some of the machismo said, 'In three weeks. Why, are you going to give us a free one out of patriotism?'

'No, you dumb little jarhead asshole,' Budgie said. 'I'm gonna give you a pass so you can go to Iraq and get your dumb little ass blown up. I'm a police officer and there's a team of vice cops one minute away, and if you're still here when they arrive you'll have some explaining to do to your CO. Now, get the fuck outta Hollywood and don't ever come back!'

'Yes, ma'am!' the kid said. 'Thank you, ma'am!'

And they were gone before her cover team drove slowly past the corner, and Budgie saw that cute vice cop named Turner shake his head at her, then shrug his shoulders as if to say, It's okay to throw one back, but don't make a habit of it.

The vice cops knew that their operators would need a break about now, so they suggested code 7 at a nearby Burger King, but Mag and Budgie asked to be dropped at a Japanese restaurant farther west on Sunset. They figured that the male officers wouldn't eat raw fish, and they'd had enough of that gender for a while. Thirty minutes to rest their feet and talk about their night's work would be a blessing. The vice cops dropped them and said they'd pick them up for one more hour and then call it a night.

Turner said, all the time looking at Mag, 'Another hour and it's a wrap.'

When Budgie and Mag got inside the restaurant, Budgie said, 'Jesus, in this division *all* the coppers use movie expressions.'

Mag ordered a plate of mixed sashimi, and Budgie a less courageous sushi plate, trying to observe protocol and not blatantly scrape the wooden chopsticks together, as so many round-eyes did at sushi joints. She lowered them to her lap and did it, dislodging a few splinters from the cheap disposable utensils.

Budgie said, 'Do I ever regret borrowing these stilettos.'

'My canines are barking too,' Mag said, looking down.

'How many you hooked so far?'

'Three,' she said.

'Hey, I pulled ahead by one,' Budgie said. 'And I threw a pair back. Jarheads from Camp Pendleton. I was the righteous bitch from hell they'll always remember.'

'I haven't found any worth throwing back,' Mag said. 'Lowest kind of scum is what I've met. Maybe I shouldn't have worn the S&M wardrobe.'

'You still into competitive shooting?' Budgie asked. 'I read about you in the *Blue Line* when I worked Central.'

'Kinda losing interest,' Mag said. 'Guys don't like to shoot with me. Afraid I'll beat them. I even stopped wearing the distinguished expert badge on my uniform.'

'Know what you mean,' Budgie said. 'If we girls even talk about guns, we're gay, right?'

'US Customs had a recent shoot that I was asked to compete in. Until I saw it was called "Ladies Pistol Shoot." Can you believe that? When I got asked, I said, "Oh, goodie. With high tea and cotillion?" The guy from Customs didn't get it.'

Budgie said, 'I had three guys tonight ask me if I was a cop. I was tempted to say, 'Would you like to ask that again with your dick in my mouth?'

Both laughed, and Mag said, 'I got a feeling Simmons would call that entrapment. Did you get a good look at Turner? Mr. Eye Candy?'

'I got a good look at him getting a good look at you,' Budgie said.

'Maybe he's into bondage bitches,' Mag said.

'I got a feeling he'd be interested if you wore overalls and combat boots.'

'Wonder if he's married.'

'God, why do we inbreed with other cops?' Budgie said. 'Why not cross-pollinate with firemen or something?'

'Yeah, there must be other ways to fuck up our lives,' Mag said. 'But he sure is cute.'

'Probably lousy in bed,' Budgie said. 'The cute ones often are.'

Mag said, 'Couldn't be as bad as a twisted detective from Seventy-seventh Street I used to date. The kind that buys you two drinks and expects to mate in his rape room within the hour. He actually stole one of my thongs, the creep.'

Budgie said, 'I hooked a drunk tonight who could hardly drive the car. When the cover team called a shop to take him to jail, he asked me if I was seeing someone. Then he asked me if I could get him out of jail. He asked me a dozen questions. When they took him away I had to tell him, "Yes, I'm seeing someone. No, I can't get you out of jail. No, I can't help it that you have strong feelings for me. And no, this encounter was not caused by fate, it was caused by Compstat." Christ, I just turn on my dumb-blonde switch and they can't let go. The guy tried to hug me when they were writing the citation! He said he forgave me.'

Mag said, 'One trick wanted to really hurt me when they badged him, I could tell. He was eye-fucking me the whole time they were writing him up, and he said, "Maybe I'll see you out on the street sometime, Officer."'

'What'd you say?'

'I said, "Yeah, I know you're bigger than me. I know you can kick my ass. But if I ever run into you and you ever try it, I will shoot you until you are dead. I will shoot you in the face, and you'll have a closed-casket funeral."'

Budgie said, 'When I was a boot I used to say to creepy vermin like that, "You don't get any status points for hitting a girl. But if you try it, my partners will pepper-spray you and kick *your* ass big time."'

'Whadda you tell them these days?'

'I don't. If nobody's looking, I just take out the OC spray and give them a shot of Liquid Jesus. For a while my partners were calling me "OC Polk."'

Mag said, 'The only really scary moment I had tonight was when one trick pulled a little too far off Sunset, and I had to walk past the parking lot. And a big rat ran right across my foot!'

'Oh, my god!' Budgie said. 'What'd you do, girl?'

'I screamed. And then I had to quick tell the cover team that everything was okay. I didn't want to admit it was only a rat.'

Budgie said, 'I'm terrified of rats. Spiders too. I would've cried.'

'I almost did,' Mag said. 'I just had to hang on.'

'How's your sashimi?'

'Not as fresh as I like it. How's your sushi?'

'Healthy,' Budgie said. 'With Fausto I eat burritos and get more fat grams than the whole female population of Laurel Canyon consumes in a week.'

'But they burn calories shopping for plastic surgeons and prepping their meals,' Mag said. 'Imagine laying out a weekly diet of celery stalks and carrot strips according to feng shui.'

Budgie thought about how pleasant and restful it was just to sit there and drink tea and talk to another girl.

During the last hour, Budgie hooked one more trick, and Mag wanted to soar past her with two, but business was slowing. They had only thirty minutes to go when Mag saw a cherry-red Mercedes SUV with chrome wheels drive slowly past. The driver was a young black man in a three-hundred-dollar warm-up suit and pricey Adidas. He made one pass, then another.

Mag didn't return his smile the way she had been doing to other tricks that night, including two who were black. This guy made her think one word: 'pimp.' Then she realized that if she was right, this could be the topper of the evening. A felony bust for pimping. So on his next pass, she returned the smile and he pointed just around the corner and parked the SUV. A hip-hop album was blasting out, and he turned it down to talk.

When she approached cautiously, he said, 'What's a matter, Momma, ain't you into chocolate delight?'

Yeah, he's a pimp, she thought, saying, 'I like all kind of delights.'

'I bet you do,' he said. 'Jump on in here and le's talk bidness.'

'I'm okay out here.'

'What's wrong?' he said. 'You a cop or somethin'?'

He smiled big when he said it, and she knew he didn't believe it. She said, 'I can talk out here.'

'Come on in, baby,' he said, and his pupils looked dilated. 'I might got somethin' for you.'

'What?' she said.

'Somethin'.'

'What something?'

'Get in,' he said, and she didn't like the way he said it this time. He was amped, all right. Maybe crack, maybe crystal.

'I don't think so,' she said and started to walk away. This wasn't going right.

He opened the door of the SUV and jumped out, striding around the back and standing between her and Sunset Boulevard. She was about to use the code word 'slick' but thought about what it would mean if she brought down a pimp. She said, 'You better talk fast because I don't have time for bullshit.'

And he said, 'You think you gonna come and work this corner? You ain't, not without somebody lookin' out for you. And that ain't no bullshit. That is righteous.'

'Whadda you mean?' Mag said.

'I'm gonna be your protector,' he said.

'Like my old man?' she said. 'I don't need one.'

'Yes, you do, bitch,' he said. 'And the protection has started. So how much you made tonight so far? Working on my corner. On my boulevard.'

'I think you better get outta the way, Slick,' Mag said. And now she was definitely scared and could see one of the vice cops running across Sunset Boulevard in her direction.

She was still looking for her mobile cover team when he said, 'I'm gonna show you what is slick.'

And she was shocked when his fist struck. She hadn't seen coming it at all. Her face had been turned toward the boulevard while she waited for her security, thinking, Hurry up. Her head hit the pavement when she fell. Mag felt dizzy and sick to her stomach and tried to get up, but he was sitting on top of her, big hands all over her, looking for her money stash.

'In yo pussy?' he said, and she felt his hands down there. Felt his fingers exploring inside her.

Then she heard car doors slam and voices shouting and the pimp screaming, and she got so sick she vomited all over her bondage bitch costume. And the curtain descended on the last performance of the evening.

Fausto Gamboa was driving when he heard the gut-churning 'Officer down' and that an ambulance was racing code 3 to the Sunset Boulevard whore track. He almost gave Benny Brewster whiplash cranking the steering wheel hard left and blowing a stop sign like it wasn't there. Speeding toward Sunset Boulevard.

'Oh, god!' he said. 'It's one of the girls. I knew it. I knew it.'

Benny Brewster, who had worked with Mag Takara for most of the deployment period, said, 'I hope it's not Mag.'

Fausto glanced sharply at him and felt a rush of anger but then thought, I can't blame Benny for hoping it's Budgie. I'm hoping it's Mag. That was an awful feeling, but there was no time to sort it out. When he made the next left he felt two wheels almost lifting.

The Oracle had been taking code 7 at his favorite taco joint on Hollywood Boulevard when the call came out. He was standing beside his car, working on his second *carne asada* taco and sucking down an enormous cup of *horchata*, Mexican rice water and cinnamon, when he heard 'Officer down.'

He was the first one at the scene other than all the security teams and the paramedics loading Mag into the ambulance. Budgie was sitting in the backseat of a vice car, weeping, and the pimp was handcuffed and lying on the sidewalk near the alley, crying out in pain.

Simmons, the oldest of the vice cops, said to the Oracle, 'We got another ambulance coming.'

'How's Mag?'

'Pretty bad, Sarge,' Simmons said. 'Her left eye was lying out on her cheek. The bones around the eye socket were just about crushed, from what I could see.'

'Oh no,' the Oracle said.

'He hit her once and she fell back and her head bounced off the sidewalk. I think she was awake sort of when we first rolled up, but not now.'

The Oracle pointed to the pimp and said, 'How about him?' And then he saw it in the vice cop's face when Simmons hesitated and said, 'He resisted.'

'Do you know if FID has been notified?'

'Yeah, we called our boss,' Simmons said. 'They'll all be here soon.'

The vice cop's eyes didn't meet the Oracle's when he finally said, 'There's a guy in the liquor store might want to make a complaint about ... how we handled the arrest. He was yammering about it. I told him to wait until Force Investigation Division arrives. I'm hoping he'll change his mind before then.'

'I'll talk to him,' the Oracle said. 'Maybe I can calm him down.'

When the Oracle was walking toward the liquor store, he saw a young vice cop pacing nervously and being spoken to very earnestly by one of the other vice cops. The second ambulance arrived, and the Oracle heard the pimp moan when they put him on the litter.

In the liquor store, the elderly Pakistani proprietor completed a transaction for a customer, then turned to the Oracle and said, 'Are you here for my report?'

'What did you see?' the Oracle asked.

'I hear car doors slam. I hear a man scream. Loud. I hear shouts. Curses. A man screams more. I run out. I see a young white man kicking a black man on the ground. Kick kick kick. Curses and kicks. I see other white men grab the young man and pull him away. The black man continues the screams. Plenty of screams. I see handcuffs. I know these are policemen. I know they come to this block to arrest the women of the street. That is my report.'

'There will be some investigators coming to talk to you,' the Oracle said, leaving the liquor store.

Budgie and one vice car were gone. Four vice cops and two cars were still there. The young cop who had been pacing when the Oracle arrived walked up to him and said, 'I know I'm in trouble here, Sarge. I know there's a civilian witness.'

'Maybe you want to call the Protective League's hotline and get lawyered up before making any statements,' the Oracle said.

'I will,' the vice cop said.

'What's your name, son?' the Oracle asked. 'I can't remember anybody's name anymore.'

'Turner,' he said. 'Rob Turner. I never worked your watch when I was in patrol.'

'Rob,' the Oracle said, 'I don't want you making any statements to me. Call the League. You have rights, so don't be afraid to exercise them.'

It was obvious that Turner trusted the Oracle by reputation, and he said, 'I only want you to know ... everybody to know ... that when I arrived, that fucking pimp was sitting on her with his hands down inside her pants. That beautiful girl, her face was a horrible sight. I want all the coppers to know what I saw when I arrived. And that I'm not sorry for anything except losing my badge. I'm real sorry about that.'

'That's enough talking, son,' the Oracle said. 'Go sit in your car and get your thoughts together. Get lawyered up. You've got a long night ahead of you.'

When the Oracle returned to his car to make his notifications, he saw Fausto and Benny Brewster parked across the street, talking to a vice cop. They looked grim. Fausto crossed the street, coming toward him, and the Oracle hoped this wasn't going to be an I-told-you-so, because he wasn't in the mood, not a bit.

But all Fausto said to him before he and Benny Brewster left the scene was 'This is a crummy job, Merv.'

The Oracle opened a packet of antacid tablets, and said, 'Old dogs like you and me, Fausto? It's all we got. Semper cop.'

ELEVEN

Early that morning Mag Takara underwent surgery at Cedars Sinai to reconstruct facial bones, with more surgeries to follow, the immediate concern being to save the vision in her left eye. After being booked into the prison ward at USCMC, the pimp, Reginald Clinton Walker, also went under the knife, to have his ruptured spleen removed. Walker would be charged with felony assault because of the great bodily injury suffered by Officer Takara, but of course the serious charge of felony assault on a police officer could not be alleged in this case.

There wasn't a cop on the midwatch who didn't think that the felony assault and the pimping allegation wouldn't be the subject of plea bargain negotiations, but both the area captain and the patrol captain vowed that they'd do all they could to keep the DA onboard for a vigorous felony prosecution. However, a caveat was added, because as soon as Walker filed a multimillion-dollar lawsuit against the LAPD and the city for having his spleen destroyed, who could say what the outcome would be?

That afternoon, an hour before midwatch roll call, the floor nurse at Cedars saw a tall man in T-shirt and jeans with a dark suntan and bleached streaky hair enter the ward, carrying an enormous bouquet of red and yellow roses. Sitting outside the room of Officer Mag Takara were her mother, father, and two younger sisters, who were crying.

The nurse said, 'Are those for Officer Takara, by chance?'

'Yeah.'

'I thought so,' she said. 'You're the fourth. But she can't see anybody today except immediate family. They're waiting outside her room for her to have her dressing changed. You can talk to them if you like.'

'I don't wanna bother them,' he said.

'The flowers are beautiful. Do you want me to take them?'

'Sure,' he said. 'Just put them in her room when you get a chance.'

'Is there a card?'

'I forgot,' he said. 'No, no card.'

'Shall I tell her who brought them?'

'Just tell her ... tell her that when she's feeling better, she should have her family take her to the beach.'

'The beach?'

'Yeah. The ocean is a great healer. You can tell her that if you want.'

At midwatch roll call the lieutenant was present, along with three sergeants, including the Oracle. He got the job of explaining what had happened and having it make sense, as though that were possible. The cops were demoralized by the events on Sunset Boulevard the night before, and they were angry, and all the supervisors knew it.

When he was asked to be the one to talk about it, the Oracle said to the lieutenant, 'In his memoir, T. E. Lawrence of Arabia said old and wise means tired and disappointed. He didn't live long enough to know how right he was.'

At 5:30 p.m. the Oracle, sitting next to the lieutenant, popped a couple of antacid tablets and said to the assembly of cops in the roll call room, 'The latest report is that Mag is resting and alert. There doesn't appear to be any brain damage, and the surgeon in charge says that they're optimistic about restoring vision in her eye. At least most of the vision.'

The room was as quiet as the Oracle had ever heard it, until Budgie Polk, her voice quavering, said, 'Will she look ... the same, do they think?'

'She has great surgeons taking care of her. I'm sure she'll look fine. Eventually.'

Fausto, who was sitting next to Budgie, said, 'Is she coming back to work after she's well?'

'It's too soon to say,' the Oracle said. 'That will depend on her. On how she feels after everything.'

'She'll come back,' Fausto said. 'She picked up a grenade, didn't she?'

Budgie started to say something else but couldn't. Fausto patted her hand for a second.

The Oracle said, 'The detectives and our captains have promised that the pimp will go to the joint for this, if they can help it.'

B.M. Driscoll said, 'Maybe they can't help it. I'm sure he's got half a dozen shysters emptying his bedpan right this minute. He'll make more money from a lawsuit than he could make from every whore on Sunset.'

'Yeah, our activist mayor and his handpicked, cop-hating police commissioner will be all over this one,' Jetsam said. 'And we'll hear from the keepers of the consent decree. No doubt.'

Before the Oracle could answer, Flotsam said, 'I suppose the race card will be played here. Dealt from the bottom of the deck, as usual.'

That's what the lieutenant hadn't wanted, the issue of race entering what he knew would be a heated exchange today. But race affected everything in Los Angeles from top to bottom, including the LAPD, and he knew that too.

Looking very uncomfortable, the lieutenant said, 'It's true that the media and the activists and others might have a field day with this. A white cop kicking the guts out of a black arrestee. They'll want Officer Turner not just fired but prosecuted, and maybe he will be. And you'll hear accusations that this proves we're all racists.'

'I got somethin' to say about it, Lieutenant.'

Conversation stopped then. Benny Brewster, the former partner of Mag Takara, the only black cop on the midwatch and in the room except for a night-watch sergeant sitting on the lieutenant's right, had something to say about what? The race card? White on black? The lieutenant was very uncomfortable. He didn't need this snarky shit.

Every eye was on Benny Brewster, who said, 'If it was me that got there first instead of Turner and seen what he seen, I'd be in jail. 'Cause I'da pulled my nine and emptied the magazine into that pimp. So I'd be in jail now. That's all I got to say.'

There was a murmur of approval, and a few cops even clapped. The lieutenant wanted to give them a time-out, wanted to restore order, and was trying to figure out how to do it, when the Oracle took over again.

The Oracle looked at all those faces, wondering how it was possible that they could be so young. And he said to them, 'The shield you're wearing is the most beautiful and most famous badge in the world. Many police departments have copied it and everyone envies it, but you wear the original. And all these critics and politicians and media assholes come and go, but your badge remains unchanged. You can get as mad and outraged as you want over what's going to go down, but don't get cynical. Being cynical will make you old. Doing good police work is the greatest fun there is. The greatest fun you'll ever have in your lives. So go on out tonight and have some fun. And Fausto, try to get by with only two burritos. Speedo weather's coming up.'

After they had handled two calls and written one traffic ticket, Budgie Polk turned to Fausto Gamboa and said, 'I'm okay, Fausto. Honest.'

Fausto, who was riding shotgun, said, 'Whaddaya mean?'

'I mean you gotta quit asking me if I want you to roll up the window or where do I wanna have code seven or do I need my jacket. Last night is over. I'm okay.'

'I don't mean to be a—'

'Nanny. So you can stop now.'

Fausto got quiet then, a bit embarrassed, and she added, 'The Li'l Rascals didn't want Darla in their clubhouse either. But we're in. So you can all just live with it, especially you, you cranky old sexist.'

Budgie glanced sideways at him and he quickly looked out at the boulevard, but she saw a little bit of a smile that he couldn't hide.

Things got back to normal when Budgie went after a silver Saab that pulled out of Paramount Studios heading west a good three seconds late at the first traffic signal. The driver had a cell to his ear.

'Jesus,' she said, 'what's he doing, talking to his agent?'

When they had the Saab pulled over, the driver tried charming Budgie, whose turn it was to write one. He said with an attempt at a flirtatious grin, 'I couldn't have busted the light, Officer. It didn't even turn yellow until I was in the intersection.'

'You were very late on the red signal, sir,' Budgie said, looking at his license, then at the guy, whose grin came off as smarmy and annoying.

'I would never argue with a police officer as attractive as you,' he said, 'but couldn't you be a little mistaken on the light? I'm a very careful driver.'

Budgie started walking back to her car, putting her citation book on the hood to write while Fausto kept his eyes on the driver, who quickly got out and came back to her. Budgie nodded at Fausto that she could handle this schmuck, and Fausto stayed put.

'Before you start writing,' he said, all the charm gone now, 'I'd like to ask for a break here. One more ticket and I'll lose my insurance. I'm in the film business, and I need a driver's license.'

Without looking up, Budgie said, 'Oh, you've had other citations, have you? I thought you said you were a careful driver.'

When she began writing he stormed back to his car, got behind the wheel, and made a call on his cell.

Budgie finished the citation and took it to him, but Fausto stayed glued to the right side of the guy's car, watching his hands like the guy was a gangbanger. She knew that Fausto was still playing guardian angel, but what the hell – it was kind of comforting in a way.

After finishing, she presented the ticket and said, 'This is not an admission of guilt, only a promise to appear.'

The driver snatched the ticket book from her hand, scrawled his signature, and gave it back to her, saying in a low voice that Fausto couldn't hear, 'I'll just bet you get off on fucking over men, don't you? I'll bet you don't even know what a cock looks like that doesn't have batteries included. I'll see you in court.'

Budgie removed his copy, handed it to him, and said, 'I know what a cassette player looks like with batteries included. This.' And she patted the rover on her belt that was the size of a cassette player. 'Let's have a jury trial. I'd love for them to hear what you think of women police officers.'

Without a word he drove away, and Budgie said to the disappearing car, 'Bye-bye, cockroach.'

When Fausto got in the car he said, 'That is an unhappy citizen.'

'But he won't take me to court.'

'How do you know.' She patted the rover.

'He said naughty things and I recorded them on my little tape machine.'

Fausto said, 'Did he fall for that dumb gag?'

'Right on his ass,' she said.

'Sometimes you're not quite as boring as other young coppers,' Fausto said to her, then added, 'How you feeling?'

'Don't start that again.'

'No, I mean the mommy stuff.'

'I may have to stop at the milking station later.'

'I'm gonna keep your gun in the car with me next time,' Fausto said.

Farley Ramsdale was in an awful mood that afternoon. The so-called ice he bought from some thieving lowlife greaser asshole at Pablo's Tacos, where tweakers did business 24/7, had turned out to be shitty. The worst part was having to sit there for an hour waiting for the guy and listening to hip-hop blasting from the car of a pair of basehead smokes who were also waiting for the greaseball. What were they doing in Hollywood?

It turned out to be the worst crystal he'd ever scored. Even Olive complained that they'd been screwed. But it got them tweaked, the proof being that they were both awake all night, pulse rates zooming, trying to fix a VCR that had stopped rewinding. They had parts all over the floor, and they both fell asleep for an hour or so just before noon.

When Farley woke up, he was so disgusted he just kicked the VCR parts under the couch among all the dust balls and yelled, 'Olive! Wake up and get your skinny ass in motion. We got to go to work, for chrissake.'

She was off the couch before he stopped grumbling, and said, 'Okay, Farley. Whatcha want for breakfast?'

Farley pulled himself painfully to his feet. He just had to stop passing out on the couch. He wasn't a kid anymore and his back was killing him. Farley looked at Olive, who was staring at him with that eager, gap-toothed grille, and he stepped closer and looked into her mouth.

'Goddamnit, Olive,' he said. 'Have you lost another tooth lately?'

'I don't think so, Farley,' she said.

He couldn't remember right now either. He had a headache that felt like Nelly or some other nigger was rapping inside his skull. 'You lose another tooth and that's it. I'm kicking your ass outta here,' he said.

'I can get false teeth, Farley!' Olive whined.

'You look enough like George Washington already,' he said. 'Just get the goddamn oatmeal going.'

'Can I first run over to see Mabel for a couple minutes? She's very old, and I'm worried about her.'

'Oh, by all means, take care of the local witch,' he said. 'Maybe next time she makes a stew outta rats and frogs, she'll save a bowl for us.'

Olive ran out of the house, across the street and down three houses to the only home on the block that had weeds taller than those in Farley's yard. Mabel's house was a wood-frame cottage built decades after Farley's stucco bungalow, during the 1950s era of cheap construction. The paint was blistered, chipped, and peeling in many places, and the screen door was so rusted a strong touch would make chunks crumble away.

The inside door was open, so Olive peered through the screen and yelled, 'Mabel, you there?'

'Yes, Olive, come in!' a surprisingly strong voice called back to her.

Olive entered and found Mabel sitting at the kitchen table drinking a cup of tea with lemon slices. She had a few vanilla cookies on a saucer next to a ball of yarn and knitting needles.

Mabel was eighty-eight years old and had owned that cottage for forty-seven years. She wore a bathrobe over a T-shirt and cotton sweatpants. Her face was lined but still held its shape. She weighed less than one hundred pounds but had lots more teeth than Olive. She lived alone and was independent.

'Hello, Olive, dear,' Mabel said. 'Pour yourself a nice cup of tea and have a cookie.'

'I can't stay, Mabel. Farley wants his breakfast.'

'Breakfast? At this time of day?'

'He slept late,' Olive said. 'I just wanted to make sure you're okay and see if you need anything from the market.'

'That's sweet of you, dear,' Mabel said. 'I don't need anything today.'

Olive felt a stab of guilt then because every time she shopped for Mabel, Farley kept at least five dollars from Mabel's change, even though the old woman was surviving on Social Security and her late husband's small pension. Once Farley had kept thirteen dollars, and Olive knew that Mabel knew, but the old woman never said a word.

Mabel had no children or other relatives, and she'd told Olive many times that she dreaded the day when she might have to sell her cottage and move into a county home, where the money from her cottage sale would be used by county bureaucrats to pay for her keep the rest of her life. She hated the thought of it. All Mabel's old friends had died or moved away, and now Olive was the only friend she had in the neighborhood. And Mabel was grateful.

'Take some cookies with you, dear,' Mabel said. 'You're getting so thin I'm worried about you.'

Olive took two of the cookies and said, 'Thanks, Mabel. I'll look in on you later tonight. To make sure you're okay.'

'I wish you could watch TV with me some evening. I don't sleep much at all anymore, and I know you don't sleep much. I see your lights on at all hours.'

'Farley has trouble sleeping,' Olive said.

'I wish he treated you better,' Mabel said. 'I'm sorry to say that, but I really do.'

'He ain't so bad,' Olive said. 'When you get to know him.'

'I'll save some food for you in case you stop in tonight,' Mabel said. 'I

131

can never eat all the stew I cook. That's what happens to old widows like me. We're always cooking the way we did when our husbands were alive.'

'I'll sneak over later,' Olive said. 'I love your stew.'

Pointing at her orange tabby cat, Mabel said, 'And Olive, if Tillie here comes around your house again, please bring her when you come.'

'Oh, I love having her,' Olive said. 'She chases away all the rats.'

Late that afternoon, they were finally on the street, the first day that they'd gotten Farley's car running and Sam's Pinto returned to him.

'Goddamn transmission's slipping on this fucking Jap junker,' Farley said. 'When we collect from the Armenian, I'm thinking of looking around for another ride.'

'We also need a new washing machine, Farley,' Olive said.

'No, I like my T-shirts stiff enough to bust a knife blade,' he said. 'Makes me feel safe around all those greaseballs at Pablo's Tacos.' He was thinking, When Cosmo pays me, bye-bye, Olive. Barnacles are less clingy than this goofy bitch.

He lit a smoke while he drove and, as so often happened since his thirtieth birthday three years ago, he started feeling nostalgic about Hollywood. Remembering how it was when he was a kid, back in those glorious days at Hollywood High School.

He blew smoke rings at the windshield and said, 'Look out the window, Olive, whadda you see?'

Olive hated it when he asked questions like that. She knew if she said the wrong thing, he'd yell at her. But she was obedient and looked at the commercial properties on the boulevard, here on the east side of Hollywood. 'I see ... well ... I see ... stores.'

Farley shook his head and blew more smoke from his nose, but he did it like a snort of disgust that made Olive nervous. He said, 'Do you see one fucking sign in your mother tongue?'

'In my ...'

'In English, goddamnit.'

'Well, a couple.'

'My point is, you might as well live in fucking Bangkok as live near Hollywood Boulevard between Bronson and Normandie. Except here, dope and pussy ain't a bargain like over there. My point is that gooks and spics are everywhere. Not to mention Russkies and Armos, like those fucking thieves Ilya and Cosmo, who wanna take over Hollywood. And I must not forget the fucking Filipinos. The Flips are crawling all over the streets near Santa Monica Boulevard, taking other people's jobs emptying bedpans and jacking up their cars on concrete blocks because no gook in history ever learned to drive like a white man. Do you see what's happening to us Americans?'

'Yes, Farley,' she said.

'What, Olive?' he demanded. 'What's happening to us Americans?'

Olive felt her palms, and they were moist and not just from the crystal. She was on the spot again, having to respond to a question when she had no idea what the answer was. It was like when she was a foster child, a ward of San Bernardino County, living with a family in Cucamonga, going to a new school and never knowing the answer when the teacher called on her.

And then she remembered what to say! 'We'll be the ones needing green cards, Farley,' she said.

'Fucking A,' he said, blowing another cloud through his nose. 'You got that right.'

When they reached the junkyard and he drove through the open gate, which was usually kept chained, he parked near the little office. He was about to get out but suddenly learned why the gate was open. They had other security now.

'Goddamn!' Farley yelled when a Doberman ran at the car, barking and snarling.

The junkyard proprietor, known to Farley as Gregori, came out of his office and shouted 'Odar!' to the dog, who retreated and got locked inside.

When Gregori returned, his face stained with axle grease, he wiped his hands and said, 'Better than chaining my gate. And Odar don't get impressed by police badges.'

He was a lean and wiry man with inky thinning hair, wearing a sweat shirt and grease-caked work pants. Inside the garage a late-model Cadillac Escalade, or most of it, was up on a hydraulic lift. The car lacked two wheels and a front bumper, and two Latino employees were working on the undercarriage.

Olive remained in the car, and when Gregori and Farley were alone, Farley presented a stack of twenty-three key cards to Gregori, who looked them over and said, 'What hotel do these come from?'

'Olive gets them by hanging around certain hotels on the boulevards,' Farley said. 'People leave them at the front desk and in the lobby by the phones. And in the hotel bars.'

Then Farley realized he was making it sound too easy, so he said, 'It's risky and time-consuming, and you need a woman to do it. If you or me tried hanging around a hotel, their security would be all over us in no time. Plus, you gotta know which hotel has the right key cards. Olive has that special knowledge but she ain't sharing it.'

'Five bucks apiece I give you.'

'Come on, Gregori,' Farley said. 'These key cards are in primo condition. The perfect size and color. With a good-looking mag strip. You can buy those bogus driver's licenses from Cosmo and they'll glue to the front of the card just perfect. They'll pass inspection with any cop on the street.'

'I don't talk to Cosmo in a long time,' Gregori said. 'You see him lately?'

'Naw, I ain't seen him in a year,' Farley lied. Then, 'Look, Gregori, for very little money every fucking wetback that works in all your businesses can be a licensed driver tomorrow. Not to mention your friends and relatives from the old country.'

'Friends and relatives from Armenia can get real driver's license,' Gregori said imperiously.

'Of course they can,' Farley said, apologetically. 'I just meant like when they first get here. I been in a couple of Armenian homes in east Hollywood. Look like crap on the outside, but once you get inside, there's a fifty-two-inch TV and a sound system that'd blow out the walls if you cranked it. And maybe a white Bentley in the garage. I know you people are real smart businessmen.'

'You know that, Farley, then you know I ain't paying more than five dollars for cards,' Gregori said, taking out his wallet.

When Farley accepted the deal and was driving back to the boulevard to score some crystal, he said to Olive, 'That cheap communist cocksucker. You see what was up on that lift?'

'A new car?' Olive said.

'A new Escalade. That Armo gets one of his greasers to steal one. Then they strip it right down to the frame and dump the hot frame with its hot numbers. They search every junkyard in the county till they find a wrecked Escalade. They buy the frame, bring it here, and reassemble all the stolen parts right onto their cold frame, then register it at DMV. It's a real Armo trick. They're like fucking Gypsy tribes. Cosmo's one of them. We shoulda nuked all the Soviet puppet states when we had the chance.'

'I'm scared of Cosmo, Farley,' Olive said, but he ignored her, still pissed off at the price he got for the key cards.

'Hear what he called his dog? Odar. That's what Armenians call us non-Armos. Fucking goat eater. If I wasn't a man of property, I'd get outta Hollywood and away from all these immigrant assholes.'

'Farley,' Olive said. 'When your mom left you the house, it was paid for, right?'

'Of course it was paid for. Shit, when my parents bought the house, it only cost about thirty-nine grand.'

'You could sell it for a lot now, Farley,' Olive said. 'We could go somewhere else and not do this thing with Cosmo and Ilya.'

'Pull yourself together,' he said. 'This is the biggest score of my life. I ain't walking away. So just deal with it.'

'We could stop using crystal,' Olive said. 'You could go into rehab, and I really think I could kick if you was in rehab.'

'Oh, I see,' he said. 'I've led you into a life of drugs and crime, is that it? You were a virgin cheerleader before you met me?'

'That ain't what I mean, Farley,' she said. 'I just think I could kick if you did.'

'Be sure to tell that to the casting director when he asks you to tell him all about yourself. You were a good girl seduced into the life by a wicked, wicked man. Who, by the way, provides you with a house and car and food and clothes and every fucking thing that makes life worthwhile!'

Farley parked four blocks from Hollywood Boulevard to keep from getting a ticket, and they walked to one of the boulevard's tattoo parlors, one owned by a member of an outlaw bikers gang. A nervous young man was in a chair being worked on by a bearded tattoo artist with a dirty blond ponytail wearing a red tank top, jeans, and sandals. He was drawing what looked like a unicorn on the guy's left shoulder.

The artist nodded to Farley, dabbed some blood from his customer's arm, and said to him, 'Be right back.' Then he walked to a back room, followed by Farley.

When Farley and the tattoo artist were in the back, Farley said, 'A pair of teens.'

The artist left him, entered a second room and returned in a few minutes with the teeners of crystal in plastic bindles.

Farley gave the guy six twenty-dollar bills and returned to the front, where Olive stood admiring the design on the young man's shoulder, but the guy just looked sick and full of regret.

Olive smiled and said to him, 'That's going to be a beautiful tattoo. Is it a horse or a zebra?'

'Olive, let's go,' Farley said.

Walking to the car, Farley said, 'Fucking bikers're lousy artists. People get bubbles under the skin. All scarred up. Hackers is what they are.'

They were halfway home and stopped at a traffic signal when Olive blurted, 'Know what, Farley? Do you think it might be a little bit big for us? I mean, trying to make Cosmo give us ten thousand dollars? Don't it scare you a little bit?'

'Scare me?' he said. 'I'll tell you what I been thinking. I been thinking about pulling the same gag on that cheap fucking Gregori, that's what I been thinking. Fuck him. I ain't doing business with the cheap bastard no more, so I wonder how he'd like it if I phoned him up and said I was gonna call the cops and tell them what I know about his salvage business. I wonder how he'd like reaching in that fat wallet and pulling out some real green to shut me up.'

Olive's hands were sweating more now. She didn't like the way things were changing so fast. The way Farley was changing. She was very scared of Cosmo and even scared of Ilya. She said, 'I think it will be just awful to meet with Cosmo and collect the money from him. I'm very worried about you, Farley.'

Farley looked surprised and said, 'I'm not stupid, Olive. The fucker robbed the jewelry store with a gun. You think I'm gonna meet him in some lonely place or something? No way. It's gonna happen in a nice safe place with people around.'

'That's good,' Olive said.

'And you're gonna do it, of course. Not me.'

'Me?'

'It's way safe for you,' Farley said. 'It's me he hates. You'll be just fine.'

At 7 p.m. that evening, Gregori phoned his business acquaintance Cosmo Betrossian and had a conversation with him in their language. Gregori told Cosmo that he had had a visitor and had bought some hotel key cards from Farley, the dope fiend that Cosmo had introduced to him last year when identification was needed for employees working in Gregori's salvage yard.

'Farley? I have not seen the little freak in a very long time,' Cosmo lied.

'Well, my friend,' Gregori said, 'I just need to know if the thief can still be trusted.'

'In what way?'

'People like him, they sometimes become police informants. The police trade little fishes for big whales. They might consider me to be a whale.'

Cosmo said, 'You can trust him in that way. He is such a worthless addict that the police would not even want to deal with him. But you cannot lend him money. I was stupid enough to do that.'

'Thank you,' Gregori said. 'Perhaps I could buy you and your lovely Ilya a dinner at the Gulag some evening?'

'I would like that, thank you,' Cosmo said. 'But I have an idea. Perhaps you can do something for me?'

'Of course.'

'I would be very grateful next month on a night I shall designate if you would call Farley and tell him you need more key cards because several new employees have arrived from Mexico with family members. Offer him more than you paid today. Then tell him to deliver the cards to your salvage yard. After dark.'

'My business is closed before dark. Even on Saturday.'

'I know,' Cosmo said, 'but I would like you to give me a duplicate gate key. I will be at the salvage yard when Farley arrives.'

'Wait a moment,' Gregori said. 'What does this mean?'

'It is only about the money he owes me,' Cosmo said reassuringly. 'I want to scare the little dope fiend. Maybe make him give me what money he has in his pocket. I have a right.'

'Cosmo, I do not do violence, you know that.'

'Of course,' Cosmo said. 'The most I will do is to keep his car until he pays me. I will take his keys and drive his car to my place and make him walk home. That is all.'

'That is not a theft? Could he call the police?'

Cosmo laughed and said, 'It is a business dispute. And Farley is the last man in Hollywood to ever call the police. He has never worked an honest day in his life.'

'I am not sure about this,' Gregori said.

'Listen, cousin,' Cosmo said. 'Drop the key at my apartment after work this evening. I cannot be there because of other business, but Ilya will be there. She will make you her special tea. In a glass, Russian-style. What do you say?'

Gregori was silent for a moment, but then he thought of Ilya. That great blond Russian Ilya with her nice plump, long legs and huge tits.

He was silent too long, so Cosmo said, 'Also, I will give you one hundred dollars for your trouble. Gladly.'

'All right, Cosmo,' Gregori said. 'But there must not be violence on my property.'

After Cosmo hung up, he said to Ilya in English, 'You shall not believe our good fortune. In a few hours Gregori of the junkyard shall come here with a key. I promise to him one hundred for the key. Behave nice. Give to him your glass of tea.'

Two hours later when Gregori arrived, he discovered that, true to his word, Cosmo was not there. Ilya invited him in and after he put the salvage yard gate key on the table, he was asked to sit while she put on the tea kettle.

Ilya wore a red cotton dress that hiked up every time she bent over even slightly, and he could see those white plump thighs. And her breasts were spilling from her bra, which Gregori could see was black and lacey.

After putting two glasses and saucers and cookies on the table, Ilya said in English, 'Cosmo is gone all evening. Business.'

'Do you get the lonesomeness?' Gregori asked.

'I do,' she said. 'Gregori, Cosmo promises to pay you one hundred?'

'Yes,' Gregori said, unable to take his eyes from those white ballooning breasts.

'I have it for you, but ...'

'Yes, Ilya?'

'But I must buy shoes and Cosmo is not a generous man, and perhaps I may tell him that I paid money, but ...'

'Yes, Ilya?'

'But perhaps we do like Americans say ...'

'Yes, Ilya?'

'And fuck the brains from outside of our heads?'

The tea was postponed, and within two minutes Gregori was wearing only socks, but he suddenly began to fret about Cosmo and said, 'Ilya, you must promise. Cosmo must never learn we do this.'

Unhooking her bra and removing her black thong, Ilya said, 'Gregori, you have nothing to fear about. Cosmo says that in America someone fuck someone in every business deal. One way or other.'

TWELVE

Hollywood Nate always said that there were two kinds of cops in Hollywood Division: Starbucks and 7-Eleven types. Nate was definitely a Starbucks guy, and lucky for him his protégé Wesley Drubb came from a family that had never set foot in a 7-Eleven store. Nate couldn't work very long without heading for either the Starbucks at Sunset and La Brea or the one at Sunset and Gower. On the other hand, there were Hollywood Division coppers (7-Eleven types) who chose to take code 7 at IHOP. Nate said that eating at IHOP would produce enough bad cholesterol to clog the Red Line subway. He seldom even patronized the ever-popular Hamburger Hamlet, preferring instead one of the eateries in Thai Town around Hollywood Boulevard and Kingsley. Or one of the more health-conscious joints on west Sunset that served great lattés.

The hawkish handsome face of Nate Weiss had now recovered from his battle with the war veteran who insisted on a ride to Santa Monica and La Brea. The last Nate heard about the guy was that he'd plea-bargained down to simple battery and would no doubt soon be returning to drugs and flashbacks and a hankering for another ride to Santa Monica and La Brea.

Nate was back to pumping iron at the gym and jogging three times a week and had an appointment to meet a real agent who might advance his career immeasurably. Being one of the few officers at Hollywood Station who loved to work all the red carpet events at Grauman's or the Kodak Theatre, where sometimes hundreds of officers were needed, he'd met the agent there.

'You know, Wesley,' Nate said, 'about that little Indie film I've been trying to put together? Had a chance to talk to your old man about it yet?'

'Not yet, Nate,' Wesley said. 'Dad's in Tokyo. But I wouldn't get my hopes up. He's a very conservative man when it comes to business.'

'So am I, Wesley, so am I,' Nate said. 'But this is as close to a no-brainer as it gets in the film business. Did I tell you I'm getting my SAG card?'

'I'm not sure if you told me or not,' Wesley said, thinking, Does he ever stop? The guy's thirty-five years old. He'll be a star about the time USC trades its football program for lacrosse.

'Every time I do a union job as a nonunion extra, I get a voucher. One more job and I'll have enough vouchers and pay stubs. Then I'm eligible to join the Screen Actors Guild.'

'Awesome, Nate,' Wesley said.

When Hollywood Nate lay in bed after getting off duty, he had latté dreams and mocha fantasies of life in a high canvas chair, wearing a makeup bib, never dating below-the-line persons, using the word 'energy' at least once in every three sentences, and living in a house so big you'd need a Sherpa to find the guest rooms. Such was the dream of Hollywood Nate Weiss.

As for young Wesley Drubb, his dream was muddled. Lately he'd been spending a lot of time trying to convince himself that he had not made a horrible mistake dropping out of USC, not graduating and going on for an MBA. He often questioned the wisdom of moving away from the Pacific Palisades family home into a so-so apartment in West Hollywood that he couldn't have easily afforded without a roommate. And not without the personal checks he was secretly receiving from his mother's account, checks that he had nobly refused to cash for several months until he'd finally succumbed. What was he proving? And to whom?

After the hand grenade incident and the fight in which Nate got hurt worse than he pretended, Wesley had confided in his brother, Timothy, hoping his older sibling would give him some advice.

Timothy, who had been working for Lawford and Drubb only three years, knocking down more than $175,000 last year (their father's idea of starting at the bottom), said to him, 'What do you get out of it, Wesley? And please don't give me any undergraduate existential bullshit.'

Wesley had said, 'I just ... I don't know. I like what I do most of the time.'

'You are such an asshole,' his brother said, ending the discussion. 'Just try to only get crippled and not killed. It would be the end of Mom if she lost her baby boy.'

Wesley Drubb didn't think that he was terribly afraid of getting crippled or killed. He was young enough to think that those things happened to other guys, or other girls, like Mag Takara. No, the thing that he couldn't explain to his brother or his dad or mom, or any of his fraternity brothers who were now going to grad school, was that the Oracle was right. This work was the most fun he would ever have on any job.

Oh, there were boring nights when not much happened, but not too boring. On the downside, there was the unbelievable oversight that LAPD was presently going through, which created loads of paperwork and media criticism and a level of political correctness that a civilian would never understand or tolerate. But at the end of the day, young Wesley Drubb was having fun. And that's why he was still a cop. And that's why he just might remain one for the foreseeable future. But his thought process went off the rails at that point. At his age, he couldn't begin to fathom what the words 'foreseeable future' truly meant.

After Hollywood Nate had his Starbucks latté and was in a good mood, they got a call to Hollywood and Cahuenga, where a pair of Hollywood's homeless were having a twilight punch-out. Neither geezer was capable of inflicting much damage on the other unless weapons were pulled, but the fight was taking place on Hollywood Boulevard, and that would not be tolerated by the local merchants. Project Restore Hollywood was in full bloom, with everyone dreaming of more and more tourists and of someday making seedy old Hollywood glam up like Westwood or Beverly Hills or Santa Barbara minus the nearby ocean.

The combatants had taken their fight to the alley behind an adult bookstore and had exhausted themselves by throwing half a dozen flailing punches at each other. They were now at the stage of standing ten feet apart and exchanging curses and shaking fists. Wesley parked the shop on Cahuenga north of Hollywood Boulevard, and they approached the two ragbag old street fighters.

Nate said, 'The skinny one is Trombone Teddy. Used to be a hotlicks jazzman a truck load of whiskey ago. The *real* skinny one I've seen around for years, but I don't think I've ever talked to him.'

The *real* skinny one, a stick of a man of indeterminate age but probably younger than Trombone Teddy, wore a filthy black fedora and a filthier green necktie over an even filthier gray shirt and colorless pants. He wore what used to be leather shoes but were now mostly wraps of duct tape, and he spent most evenings shuffling along the boulevard raving at whoever didn't cross his palm with a buck or two.

It was hardly worth worrying about who would be contact and who would be cover with these two derelicts, and Hollywood Nate just wanted to get it over with, so he waded in and said, 'Jesus, Teddy, what the hell're you doing fighting on Hollywood Boulevard?'

'It's him, Officer,' Teddy said, still panting from exertion. 'He started it.'

'Fuck you!' his antagonist said with the addled look these guys get from sucking on those short dogs of cheap port.

'Stay real,' Nate said, looking at the guy and at his shopping cart crammed with odds and ends, bits and bobs. There was no way he wanted to bust this guy and deal with booking all that junk.

Wesley said to the skinniest geezer, 'What's your name?'

'What's it to ya?'

'Don't make us arrest you,' Nate said. 'Just answer the officer.'

'Filmore U. Bracken.'

Trying a positive approach, Wesley smiled and said, 'What's the U for?'

'I'll spell it for you,' Filmore replied. 'U-p-y-u-r-s.'

'Upyurs?' Wesley said. 'That's an unusual name.'

'Up yours,' Nate explained. Then he said, 'That's it, Filmore, you're going to the slam.'

When Nate took latex gloves from his pocket, Filmore said, 'Upton.'

Before putting the gloves on, Nate said, 'Okay, last chance. Will you just agree to move along and leave Teddy here in peace and let bygones be bygones?'

'Sure,' Filmore U. Bracken said, shuffling up to Teddy and putting out his hand.

Teddy hesitated, then looked at Nate and extended his own hand. And Filmore U. Bracken took it in his right hand and suckered Teddy with a left hook that, pathetic as it was, knocked Trombone Teddy on the seat of his pants.

'Hah!' said Filmore, admiring his own clenched fist.

Then the latex gloves went on both cops, and Filmore's bony wrists were handcuffed, but when he was about to be walked to their car, he said, 'How about my goods?'

'That's worthless trash,' Hollywood Nate said.

'My anvil's in there!' Filmore cried.

Wesley Drubb walked over to the junk, gingerly poked around, and underneath the aluminum cans and socks and clean undershorts probably stolen from a Laundromat found an anvil.

'Looks pretty heavy,' Wesley said.

'That anvil's my life!' their prisoner cried.

Nate said, 'You don't need an anvil in Hollywood. How many horses you see around here?'

'That's my property!' their prisoner yelled, and now an asthmatic fat man waddled out the back door of an adult bookstore and said, 'Officer, this guy's been raising hell on the boulevard all day. Hassling my customers and spitting on them when they refuse to give him money.'

'Fuck you too, you fat degenerate!' the prisoner said.

Nate said to the proprietor, 'I gotta ask you a favor. Can he keep his shopping cart inside your storage area here until he gets outta jail?'

'How long will he be in?'

'Depends on whether we just book him for plain drunk or add on the battery we just witnessed.'

'I don't wanna make a complaint,' Trombone Teddy said.

'Shut up, Teddy,' Hollywood Nate said.

'Yes, sir,' said Teddy.

'I ain't as drunk as he is!' the prisoner said, pointing at Teddy.

He was right and everyone knew it. Teddy was reeling, and not from the other geezer's punch.

'Okay, tell you what,' Nate said, deciding to dispense boulevard justice. 'Filmore here is going to detox for a couple hours and then he can come back and pick up his property. How's that?'

Everyone seemed okay with the plan, and the store owner pushed the shopping cart to the storage area at the rear of his business.

While Nate was escorting their prisoner to the car, Trombone Teddy walked over to Wesley Drubb and said, 'Thanks, Officer. He's a bad actor, that bum. A real mean drunk.'

'Okay, anytime,' Wesley said.

But Teddy had a card in his hand and extended it to Wesley, saying, 'This is something you might be able to use.'

It was a business card to a local Chinese restaurant, the House of Chang. 'Thanks, I'll try it sometime,' Wesley said.

'Turn it over,' Teddy said. 'There's a license number.'

Wesley flipped the card and saw what looked like a California license plate number and said, 'So?'

Teddy said, 'It's a blue Pinto. Two tweakers were in it, a man and a woman. She called him Freddy, I think. Or maybe Morley. I can't quite remember. I seen them fishing in a mailbox over on Gower south of the boulevard. They stole mail. That's a federal offense, ain't it?'

Wesley said, 'Just a minute, Teddy.'

When he got back to his partner, who had put Filmore U. Bracken in the backseat of the car, Wesley showed him the card and said, 'Teddy gave me this license number. Belongs to tweakers stealing from mailboxes. The guy's name is Freddy or Morley.'

'All tweakers steal from mailboxes,' Hollywood Nate said, 'or anything else they can steal.'

It seemed to Wesley that he shouldn't just ignore the tip and throw the license number away. But he didn't want to act like he was still a boot, so he went back to Teddy, handed him the card, and said, 'Why don't you take it to a post office. They have people who investigate this sort of thing.'

'I think I'll hang on to it,' Teddy said, clearly disappointed.

Driving to the station, Nate got to thinking about the secretary who worked for the extras casting office he'd visited last Tuesday. She had given him big eyes as well as her phone number. He thought that he and Wesley could pick up some takeout, and he could sit in the station alone somewhere and chat her up on his cell.

'Partner, you up for burgers tonight?' he asked Wesley.

'Sure,' Wesley said. 'You're the health nut who won't eat burgers.'

And then, thinking of the little secretary and what they might do together on his next night off, and how she might even help him with her boss the casting agent, Nate felt a real glow come over him. What he called 'Hollywood happy.'

He said, 'How about you, Filmore, you up for a burger?'

'Hot damn!' the derelict said. 'You bet!'

They stopped at a drive-through, picked up four burgers, two for Wesley, and fries all around, and headed for the station.

When they got there, Nate said to their prisoner, 'Here's the deal. I'm giving you not only a burger and fries, but a get–out–of–jail–free pass. You're gonna sit in the little holding tank for thirty minutes and eat your burger, and I'll even buy you a Coke. Then, after my partner writes an FI card on you for future reference, I'm gonna let you out and you're gonna walk back up to the boulevard and get your shopping cart and go home to your nest, wherever that is.'

'You mean I ain't going to jail or detox?'

'That's right. I got an important phone call to make, so I can't waste time dicking around with you. Deal?'

'Hot damn!' Filmore said.

When their passenger got out of the car in the station parking lot, Wesley looked at the car seat and said to Filmore, 'What's that all over the seat? Beach sand?'

'No, that's psoriasis,' said Filmore U. Bracken.

'Oh, gross!' Wesley cried.

B.M. Driscoll and Benny Brewster caught the call to the apartment building on Stanley north of Fountain. They were half a block from the LA Sheriff's Department jurisdiction of West Hollywood, and later Benny Brewster thought about that and wished it could've occurred just half a block south.

The apartment manager answered their ring and asked them inside. It was by no means a down-market property. In fact, B.M. Driscoll was thinking he wouldn't mind living there if he could afford the rent. The woman wore a blazer and skirt and looked as though she had just come home from work. Her silver-streaked hair was cut like a man's, and she was what is called handsome in women her age.

She said, 'I'm Cora Sheldon, and I called about the new tenant in number fourteen. Her name is Eileen Leffer. She moved in last month from Oxnard and has two young children.' She paused and read from the rental agreement, 'A six–year–old son, Terry, and a seven–year–old daughter, Sylvia. She said she's a model and seemed very respectable and promised to get us references but hasn't done it yet. I think there might be a problem.'

'What kinda problem?' Benny asked.

'I work during the day, but we never see or hear a peep from the kids. The owner of the building used to rent our furnished units to adults only, so this is new to me. I've never been married, but I think normal kids should be heard from sometimes, and these two are not. I don't think they're enrolled in any school. Even on weekends when I'm home, I never hear or see the kids.'

'Have you investigated?' B.M. Driscoll asked. 'You know, knocked on the door with maybe an offer of a friendly cup of coffee?'

'Twice. Neither time was there a response. I'm worried. I have a key, but I'm afraid to just open the door and look.'

'We got no probable cause to enter,' Benny said. 'When was the last time you knocked on the door?'

'Last night at eight o'clock.'

'Gimme the key,' B.M. Driscoll said. 'And you come with us. If there's nobody home, we all just tiptoe away and nobody's the wiser. We wouldn't do this except for the presence of little kids.'

When they got to number fourteen, Benny knocked. No answer. He tapped sharply with the butt of his flashlight. Still no answer.

Benny called out, 'Police officers. Anybody home?' and knocked again.

Cora Sheldon was doing a lot of lip biting then, and B.M. Driscoll put the pass key in the lock and opened the door, turning on the living room light. The room was messy, with magazines strewn around and a couple of vodka bottles lying on the floor. The kitchen smelled of garbage, and when they looked in, they saw the sink stacked with dirty dishes. The gas range was a mess with something white that had boiled over.

B.M. Driscoll switched on a hallway light and looked into the bathroom, which was more of a mess than the kitchen. Benny checked the master bedroom, saw an unmade bed and a bra and panties on the floor, and returned with a shrug.

The other bedroom door was closed. Cora Sheldon said, 'The second bedroom has twin beds. That would be the children's room.'

B.M. Driscoll walked to the door and opened it, turning on the light. It was worse by far than the master bedroom. There were dishes with peanut butter and crackers on the floor and on the dresser top. In front of the TV were empty soda cans, and boxes of breakfast cereal were lying on the floor.

'Well, she's not much of a housekeeper,' he said, 'but other than that?'

'Partner,' Benny said, pointing at the bed, then walking to it and shining his light at wine-dark stains. 'Looks like blood.'

'Oh my god!' Cora Sheldon said as B.M. Driscoll looked under the bed and Benny went to the closet, whose door was partially open.

And there they were. Both children were sitting under hanging garments belonging to their mother. The six-year-old boy began sobbing, and his seven-year-old sister put her arm around him. Both children were blue-eyed, and the boy was a blond and his sister a brunette. Neither had had a decent wash for a few days, and both were terrified. The boy wore shorts and a food-stained T-shirt and no shoes. The girl wore a cotton dress trimmed with lace, also food-stained. On her feet she wore white socks and pink sneakers.

'We won't hurt you, come on out,' Benny said, and Cora Sheldon repeated, 'Oh my god!'

'Where's your mommy?' B.M. Driscoll asked.

'She went with Steve,' the girl said.

'Does Steve live here?' Benny asked, and when Cora Sheldon said, 'I didn't rent to anyone named—' he shushed her by putting up his hand.

The little girl said, 'Sometimes.'

B.M. Driscoll said, 'Have they been gone for a long time?'

The little girl said, 'I think so.'

'For two days? Three days? Longer?'

'I don't know,' she said.

'Okay, come on out and let's get a look at you,' he said.

Benny was inspecting the stain on the bed, and he said to the girl, 'Has somebody hurt you?'

She nodded then and started crying, walking painfully from the closet.

'Who?' Benny asked. 'Who hurt you?'

'Steve,' she said.

'How?' Benny asked. 'How did he hurt you?'

'Here,' she said, and when she lifted her cotton dress slightly, they saw dried blood crusted on both legs from her thighs down, and what looked like dark bloodstains on her lace-trimmed white cotton socks.

'Out, please!' Benny said to Cora Sheldon, taking both children by the hands and walking them into the living room, first closing the bedroom door to protect it as a crime scene.

B.M. Driscoll grabbed his rover to inform detectives that they had some work to do and that they needed transportation to the hospital for the children.

'Wait in your apartment, Ms. Sheldon,' Benny said.

Looking at the children, she said, 'Oh,' and then started to weep and walked out the door.

When she had gone, the girl turned to her younger brother and said, 'Don't cry, Terry. Mommy's coming home soon.'

It was nearly midnight when Flotsam and Jetsam were in the station to get a sergeant's signature on a robbery report. A drag queen claimed to have been walking down the boulevard on a legitimate errand when a car carrying two guys stopped and one of them jumped out and stole the drag queen's purse, which contained fifty dollars as well as a 'gorgeous' new wig that cost three hundred and fifty. Then he'd punched the drag queen before driving away.

Jetsam was in the process of calling to see what kind of record the dragon had, like maybe multiple prostitution arrests, when the desk officer asked Flotsam to watch the desk while he ran upstairs and had a nice hot b.m.

Flotsam said okay and was there when a very angry and outraged Filmore U. Bracken came shuffling into the lobby.

Flotsam took a look at the old derelict and said, 'Dude, you are too hammered to be entering a police station of your own volition.'

'I wanna make a complaint,' the codger said.

'What kinda complaint?'

'Against a policeman.'

'What'd he do?'

'I gotta admit he bought me a hamburger.'

'Yeah, well, I can see why you're mad,' Flotsam said. 'Shoulda been filet mignon, right?'

'He brought me here for the hamburger and left my property with a big fat degenerate at a dirty bookstore on Hollywood Boulevard.'

'Which dirty bookstore?'

'I can point it out to you. Anyways, the degenerate didn't watch my property like he said he would and now it's gone. Everything in my shopping cart.'

'And what, pray tell, was in your cart?'

'My anvil.'

'An anvil?'

'Yeah, it's my life.'

'Damn,' Flotsam said. 'You're a blacksmith? The Mounted Platoon might have a job for you.'

'I wanna see the boss and make a complaint.'

'What's your name?'

'Filmore Upton Bracken.'

'Wait here a minute, Mr. Bracken,' Flotsam said. 'I'm going to talk this over with the sergeant.'

While Jetsam waited for the Oracle to approve and sign the crime report, Flotsam went to the phone books and quickly looked up the law offices of Harold G. Lowenstein, a notorious and hated lawyer in LAPD circles who had made a living suing cops and the city that hired them. Somebody was always saying what they would do to Harold G. Lowenstein if they ever popped him for drunk driving.

Flotsam then dialed the number to the lobby phone. After the eighth ring, as he started to think his idea wasn't going to work, the phone was picked up.

Filmore Upton Bracken said, 'Hello?'

'Mr. Bracken?' Flotsam said, doing his best impression of Anthony Hopkins playing a butler. 'Am I speaking to Mr. Filmore Upton Bracken?'

'Yeah, who's this?'

'This is the emergency hotline for the law offices of Harold G. Lowenstein, Esquire, Mr. Bracken. A Los Angeles police officer just phoned us from Hollywood Station saying that you may need our services.'

'Yeah? You're a lawyer?'

'I'm just a paralegal, Mr. Bracken,' Flotsam said. 'But Mr. Lowenstein is very interested in any case involving malfeasance on the part of LAPD officers. Could you please come to our offices tomorrow at eleven a.m. and discuss the matter?'

'You bet I can. Lemme get a pencil from the desk here.'

He was gone for a moment, and Flotsam could hear him yelling, 'Hey, I need a goddamn pencil!'

When Filmore returned, he said, 'Shoot, brother.'

Flotsam gave him the address of Harold G. Lowenstein's Sunset Strip law office, including the suite number, and then said, 'Mr. Bracken, the officer who just phoned on your behalf said that you are probably without means at present, so do not be intimidated if our somewhat sheltered employees try to discourage you. Mr. Lowenstein will want to see you personally, so don't take no for an answer from some snippy receptionist.'

'I'll kick ass if anybody tries to stop me,' Filmore said.

'That's the spirit, Mr. Bracken,' Flotsam said, his accent shifting closer to the burr of Sean Connery and away from Anthony Hopkins.

'I'll be there at eleven.'

Filmore was waiting in the lobby when Flotsam returned, saying, 'Mr. Bracken? The sergeant will see you now.'

Filmore drew himself up on his tiptoes to lock eyeballs with the tall cop and said, 'Fuck the sergeant. He can talk to my lawyer. I'm suing all you bastards. When I'm through, I'll own this goddamn place, and maybe if you're lucky I'll buy you a hamburger sometime. Asshole.'

And with that, Filmore Upton Bracken shuffled out the door with a grin as wide as Hollywood Boulevard.

When B.M. Driscoll and Benny Brewster went end-of-watch in the early morning hours, they found Flotsam and Jetsam in the locker room, sharing Filmore Upton Bracken adventures with Hollywood Nate and Wesley Drubb.

After the chuckles subsided, Nate said to Flotsam and Jetsam, 'By the way, you guys're invited to a birthday party. My newest little friend is throwing it at her place in Westwood. Might be one or two chicks from the entertainment industry for you to meet.'

'Any of the tribe coming?' Flotsam asked. 'No offense, but I got a two-Jew limit. Three or more Hollywood hebes gather and they start sticking political lapel pins on every animate and inanimate object in sight, which might include my dead ass.'

'Why, you filthy anti-Semitic surfer swine,' Nate said.

'You inviting Budgie?' Flotsam asked.

'Probably,' Nate said.

'Okay, we'll come. My partner admires her from afar.'

They stopped the banter when B.M. Driscoll and Benny Brewster came in looking very grim. Both began quickly and quietly undressing.

'What's wrong with you guys?' Jetsam asked. 'They taking Wrestlemania off the air?'

'You don't wanna know,' B.M. Driscoll said, almost tearing the buttons from his uniform shirt as though he just wanted *out* of it. 'Bad shit. Little kids.'

'So lighten up,' Flotsam said. 'Don't you guys listen to the Oracle? This Job can be fun. Get happy.'

Suddenly, Jetsam did his Bono impersonation, singing, 'Two shots of happy, one shot of saaaaaad.'

Benny Brewster peeled off his body armor and furiously crammed the vest into the locker, saying, 'No shots of happy tonight, man. Just one shot of sad. *Real* sad.'

THIRTEEN

'Excuse me, please, Andrea,' Viktor Chernenko said late in the morning. There were only six detectives in the squad room, the rest being out in the field or in court or, in the case of Hollywood detectives, nonexistent due to the manpower shortage and budget constraints.

'Yes, Viktor?' Andi said, smiling over her coffee cup, fingers still on the computer keyboard.

'I think you are looking very lovely today, Andrea,' Viktor said with his usual diffident smile. 'I believe I recognize your most beautiful yellow sweater from the Bananas Republic, where my wife, Maria, shops.'

'Yeah, I bought it there.'

Then he walked back to his cubicle. This was the way with Viktor. He wanted something, but it might take him half a day to get around to asking. On the other hand, nobody ever paid her the compliments that Viktor did when he needed a woman detective for something or other.

Andi was glad to see that Brant Hinkle was still teamed with Viktor, and because of that she'd probably agree to do whatever Viktor got around to requesting. Ever since Brant had arrived, her belief in his possibilities kept increasing. She'd checked him out by now and found that he'd just turned fifty-three, had only been married and divorced once – a rarity among cops these days – had two adult married daughters, and based on his serial number, had about five more years on the Job than she had. In other words, he was a likely prospect. And she knew he was interested by the way he looked at her, but as yet he hadn't made a move.

Another twenty minutes passed and she was about to go out in the field and call on a couple of witnesses to a so-called attempted murder where a pimp/boyfriend slapped around a whore and fired two shots in her direction when she ran away. Without a doubt, the whore would have changed her mind by now or had it changed for her and all would be forgiven. But Andi needed to go through the motions just in case tomorrow night he murdered her.

'Andrea,' Viktor said when he approached her desk the second time.

'Yes, Viktor.'

'Will you be so kind to help Brant and me? We have a mission for a woman, and as you see, today you are the only woman here.'

'How long will it take?'

'A few hours, and I would be honored to buy your lunch.'

Andi glanced over at Brant Hinkle, who was talking on the phone, wearing little half-glasses as he wrote on a legal pad, and she said, 'Okay, Viktor. My damaged hooker can wait.'

Viktor drove east to Glendale with Andi beside him and Brant in the backseat. Viktor was very solicitous, apologizing because the air conditioner didn't work in their car.

'So okay,' Andi said, 'all I have to do is tail this Russian guy from his job at the auto parts store to wherever he eats lunch?'

Viktor said, 'We have been told that he always walks to a fast-food place, but there are several that are close by.'

Brant said, 'Viktor's informant says this guy Lidorov is very tail conscious, but he probably won't be looking for a woman to be on him.'

'And all we do is get a DNA sample?'

'That is all,' Viktor said. 'My informant is sometimes reliable, sometimes not.'

'Your evidence for a DNA comparison isn't all that reliable either,' she said, turning in her seat to look at Brant, who raised his eyebrows as if to say, Viktor is obsessive.

Viktor said, 'Andrea, when I did my follow-up investigation and found the cigarette butt in that jewelry store far behind the cabinet, I know in my heart it was left there by the suspect.'

'Even though the victim was too terrified to remember for sure if the guy left the butt or took it with him,' Brant said doubtfully.

'It is an intestines feeling,' Viktor said. 'And this Russian in Glendale has two convictions for armed robbery of jewelry stores.'

'I've heard you say you're not sure the man from the jewelry store two-eleven is even a Russian,' Andi said.

Viktor said, 'The accent that the store owner heard from the man was different from the woman's. But everybody is Russian Mafia to people in Hollywood. Actually, Glendale has a very big Armenian population. Many go to the Gulag, where my tip has come from. Criminals from all over former USSR go to the Gulag to drink and dine, including criminals from former Soviet Armenia. But for now, we have this Russian who was a jewel robber in his past life.'

'This isn't much to go on,' Andi said.

'We have nothing else,' Viktor said. 'Except I believe that a theft of mail from a certain mailbox on Gower is where the information about the diamonds was learned about. If only I could get a clue to the mail thief.'

'We can't stake out every mailbox in the area, Viktor,' Brant said.

'No, Brant, we cannot,' Viktor said. 'So that is why I would like to try this thing today. I know it is a far shot.'

They parked on the next block, and Viktor diligently watched the front door of the auto parts store through binoculars while Andi turned in her seat to chat with Brant about how he liked Hollywood so far and where was he on the lieutenant's list.

Brant was surprised to learn that Andi had a son in the army serving in Afghanistan, and said, 'Don't think I say this to all the ladies, but really, you don't look old enough.'

'I'm plenty old enough,' she said, hoping she hadn't blushed. Next thing, she'd be batting her lashes if she didn't get hold of herself.

'I think Afghanistan's fairly quiet these days,' he said.

'Last year he was in Iraq,' she said. 'I don't like to think about how I felt during those months.'

Brant was quiet then, feeling very lucky to have daughters living safe lives. He couldn't imagine how it must feel to have your only child over there in hell. Especially for coppers, whose assertive, in-your-face person-ality is of absolutely no use in such a situation. To just feel helpless and frightened all the time? He believed it must be extra hard for the parents who are police officers.

Viktor lowered the binoculars, picked up a mug shot from his lap, and said, 'It is Lidorov. He is wearing a black shirt and jeans. He has what looks like hair made of patent leather and has a gray mustache and is of medium size. He is walking toward the big mall half a block from the auto parts store.'

Andi was dropped on the east side of the mall and walked inside a minute after Lidorov entered. At first she thought she'd lost him, but heading toward the food court she spotted him.

Lidorov paused before the Greek deli, where two Latino men were making gyros, then moved on to an Italian takeout, where another young Latino was expertly tossing a pizza. Then he settled on Chinese fast food and ordered something in a carton along with a soft drink in a takeout cup. From another Latino.

Andi watched from the Italian side and wondered if chopsticks would be better or worse than forks for the collecting of DNA evidence. But Lidorov shook his head when offered chopsticks and took a plastic fork instead. He sat down at one of three small tables in front of the counter and ate from the carton and sipped his drink and ogled any young women who happened to pass by.

When he got up, she was ready to bus his table for him and scoop up the fork and the drinking straw. But she never got the chance. He took the unfinished carton of food with him along with the cup and strolled back toward the entrance, drinking from the straw. She assumed the fork was in the carton, so now what?

Lidorov went out the door into the sunlight, stretched a little, and strolled right past two perfectly good trash receptacles where he could have dropped the carton and the cup.

Litter, you bastard! Andi thought, following as far as she dared. But since there were few pedestrians on the sidewalk, she crossed over to the other side of the street and waited to be picked up.

When Viktor drove alongside, she got in and said, 'Sorry, Viktor. He's taking his lunch back to the store.'

'Is okay, Andrea,' Viktor said.

'Whoops!' Brant said, looking through the binoculars. 'He's not a litter-bug.'

Two minutes later they were parked just east of the little strip mall that housed the auto parts store. Next to the wall in the parking lot was a very tall trash dumpster sitting on a thick concrete slab. All three detectives were standing in front of it with the lid raised.

Viktor and Brant, who were both more than six feet tall, pulled them-selves up, their feet off the asphalt, and peered down inside the dumpster.

After getting back down, Viktor said to Andi, 'Do you want the news that is good or the news that is not so good?'

'Good,' Andi said.

Brant said, 'Looks like they dumped the trash this morning. There's hardly anything in there. We can see the Chinese takeout carton and the drinking cup and straw.'

'Bad news?'

'We can't reach it without somebody climbing inside,' Brant said.

'Well, I guess one of you fashion plates is going to get your suit dirty,' Andi said.

'Andrea,' said Viktor, 'I am so outside of good shape that I truly do not think I can do it. I am thinking that if I spread my coat over the top here so that you do not mess up the beautiful sweater from Bananas, you could lie down over the top here and reach down and get the fork and the straw?'

'And how do I keep from falling in right on my head?'

'We would each hold you by a leg,' Brant said.

'Oh, you think it's a good idea too?'

'I swear to you, Andi,' Brant said. 'I don't think I could do it without a ladder. And if we mess around here much longer, somebody's gonna see us and the element of surprise will be lost. Even if we do get a match, he'll be long gone, maybe clear back to Russia.'

'My heroes,' Andi said, slipping off her pumps. 'Good thing I'm wear-ing long pants.'

With each man holding a bare foot, Andi was boosted up to the edge of the dumpster, lying across Viktor's suit coat, and very reluctantly she allowed herself to be lowered upside down until she got hold of the carton and the cup.

'Get me outta here. It stinks,' she said.

When they were back in the car, the fork and drinking straw in a large evidence envelope, Viktor said, 'My coat must go to the cleaners. How is your sweater, Andrea?'

'Other than busting a bra strap and bruising my belly and thighs, I'm okay. This lunch better be good, Viktor.'

It was. Viktor took them to a whimsically designed Russian restaurant on Melrose, where they had borscht and black bread and blinis and hot tea in a glass. And even got to hear dreamy Russian violins coming from the sound system, with Viktor acting every inch the host.

'Sometimes they make Ukrainian dishes here,' he told them, as they drank their tea.

'I don't think I'll do Pilates tonight,' Andi said. 'You guys stretched every muscle in my body.'

'Speaking of muscles, yours are way better developed than mine,' Brant said. 'Your legs are buff. I mean, they felt strong when I was holding them.'

That look again. Andi was sure he'd make a move after today's little exercise. Maybe after they got back to the station and Viktor was otherwise occupied.

'I try to stay in shape in case I'm called on for dumpster diving,' she said. 'They should make it an event in the police Olympics.'

When Viktor went to the restroom, Brant said, 'Andi, I was wondering if maybe sometime you might like to join me for dinner at a new trendier-than-trendy-ever-gets restaurant called Jade that I've been reading about.'

Thinking, At last! she said, 'I'd like to have dinner with you, but that's pretty pricey. I read a review.'

He said, 'My daughters're long past child support and my ex remarried ten years ago, so I'm independently comfortable. But on second thought, maybe I'm too old for a place like Jade.'

'You look younger than I do,' she said.

'Bless you, my child,' Brant said. 'So is it a date?'

'Yeah, let's try it on Thursday to avoid the weekend rush. Wonder how I should dress.'

'Anything you wear would look great,' he said, and dropped his eyes in a shy way after he said it.

Andi thought, Those green eyes! This one's going to take me to heaven or bust me down to the ground. Her heart was pounding when Viktor returned to the table.

'There is one thing for sure,' Viktor said to them when he gave his credit card to the waiter, 'even if Lidorov is not our robber, it will be good to have his DNA profile. He is a violent thief. And a leopard cannot change its freckles.'

It was a different thief, newly seduced by the heady excitement of power and control, who that very afternoon was in the process of committing the second armed robbery of his life. But his chain-smoking companion was not the least bit seduced as they sat in a stolen car in a crowded parking lot, waiting. She wished that his Russian wasn't hopeless, and that she didn't have to convey her fears in English.

'I warn you, Cosmo,' Ilya said, looking like a clown to Cosmo in her red wig, wearing big sunglasses. 'This is a foolish thing that we do.'

'Dmitri told me is okay.'

'Fuck Dmitri!' Ilya snapped, and Cosmo impulsively backhanded her across the face, regretting it at once.

He said, 'Dmitri say that this is what he plan for long time. He say he is looking for someone like me and you to do it. We are lucky, Ilya. Lucky!'

'We get killed!' she said, wiping her eyes with tissue and touching up her mascara.

'We get rich,' he said. 'You seen how the man in the jewelry store do when he seen my gun? He piss on his pants. You seen him cry, no? The guards with money do not wish to die. Dmitri say the money is paid back by insurance company. The guards shall see the gun and they shall give the money to me. You going to see.'

Cosmo, now wearing a Dodgers cap and sunglasses, had received the call from Dmitri the afternoon prior. Cosmo had thought it was about the diamonds, and when he showed up at the Gulag just before happy hour, he was sent upstairs to the private office.

Cosmo had not been surprised to see Dmitri sitting feet up, much as he'd seen him last time, again watching porn on his computer screen. But this time it was kiddie porn. When Cosmo entered, Dmitri turned down the sound on the speakers but left the screen on, glancing at it from time to time.

'Did you wish to talk about diamonds?' Cosmo said in English, as always.

'No,' Dmitri said. 'But I been giving much thinking about the happen-ink guy Cosmo, who is my friend. I think about how you get the diamonds and how we going to do the deal for the diamonds very soon. I think maybe you ready for bigger job.'

'Yes?' Cosmo said, and Dmitri knew the look. He had him.

'It feels how? Strong? Sexy? Like fuck-ink when you point the gun in the face of a man. Am I correct, Cosmo?'

'Feels okay,' Cosmo said. 'Yes, I don't mind.'

'So, I have a job where you can get big money. Cash. At least one hundred thousand, maybe lot more.'

'Yes?'

'You know the kiosk in the big mall parking lots? The ATM machine kiosk? I know about one. I know exactly when money will come. Exactly.'

'Big armor car?' Cosmo said. 'I cannot rob the armor car, Dmitri.'

'No, Cosmo,' Dmitri said. 'Only a van. Two guys. They bring money inside a big, how you say, canister? Like soldier in Russia use for ammunition? One man must go behind kiosk, open door with key. Lock self in. Reload machine with nice green bullets from ammunition can.'

'Please, Dmitri, how you know about this?'

'Everyone drink at the Gulag sometime,' Dmitri said, chuckling in that way of his that scared Cosmo. He could imagine Dmitri chuckling like that if he was slitting your eyes.

'These men have guns, Dmitri.'

'Yes, but they be only regular security guard. They are contract out for these deliveries. I know about the two men. They will not die to save money. Insurance will pay anyways. Everybody know that. Nobody lose noth-ink except insurance company. No problem.'

'Two guys, two guns, two keys?'

'Yes, two keys for, how you say, internal security. You must take money before first guy get to kiosk. That is why I think of you. You prove at jewelry store you got lot of guts. And you got woman with big tits.'

'Ilya?'

'Yes. I give you exact day and time. Ilya is there to do business at ATM machine. Ilya know how to distract man who walks from van with money can. Other guy have a habit. Always the same. He wait until partner get to kiosk. Then he get out and come with his key.' Dmitri grinned and said, 'One minute all you need, you happen-ink guy. You rock, Cosmo!'

And now here they were, sitting in a busy Hollywood parking lot, waiting in the fifteen-year-old red Mazda that Dmitri's Georgian bartender had stolen for them with instructions to wipe it clean and abandon it somewhere east of Hollywood.

Ilya had gathered herself now, but every time she turned toward him he saw a hateful glare. He had slapped her around before, but this time it was different. He could smell his stale sweat and the fear on her. He thought she might leave him after this. But if Dmitri was right about how much would be in the can, he would just pay her off and let her go.

He had a passing thought about trying to reduce Dmitri's fifty percent by saying that the amount of money in the can was far less than advertised. It gave him a thrill to think about that, but it was tempered when he thought of Dmitri's sinister chuckle. And for all he knew, one of the security guards might be Dmitri's informer. And might know exactly how much money he was delivering.

Cosmo looked at his Rolex knock-off and said, 'Ilya, go to kiosk now.'

The blue Chevy van looked like anything but an armored car, much to Cosmo's relief. And it sat there a few minutes, just as Dmitri said it would, while the guards looked around but saw nothing out of the ordinary. Just shoppers coming and going to the mall stores. Only one woman, a bosomy redhead was at the ATM machine, looking very frustrated.

Her black purse was beside her on the tray and she took out her cell phone and appeared to be making a call. Then she threw her cell phone into the purse disgustedly and looked around as though she needed ... what? She appeared to be trying her ATM card again but failed to make it work and just walked a short distance away, looking toward the electronics store across the parking lot. Maybe for her husband?

One of the guards glanced at the other. This was their last stop of the day and they couldn't sit there all evening because of one goofy woman. The passenger got out, slid open the door of the van, grabbed the only canister remaining, and slid the door closed. Then he walked from the van to the kiosk, and when he got to the front of it he saw that the red-haired woman was crying.

The six o'clock news would give the security guard's age as twenty-five. He was an 'actor' who had been in Hollywood from Illinois for three years, looking for work and trying to get a SAG card. He had been with the security service for eighteen months. His name was Ethan Munger.

'Are you okay?' Ethan Munger said to Ilya, only pausing for a moment.

She was wiping her cheeks with the tissue and said, 'I cannot make the card work.' And when she put the tissue back inside her purse, she pulled out the Raven .25 caliber pistol, one of the cheap street guns that Cosmo had been given by the bartender. Ilya pointed it at the astonished young guard.

The driver of the van keyed his mike, announced the robbery, and jumped out of the van, his pistol drawn. He ran around the back of the van, where Cosmo Betrossian, crouched below a parked car, said, 'Drop the gun or die!'

The driver dropped the gun and put his hands in the air, lying facedown when ordered to do so. It was just as Dmitri had promised, no problem.

But Ethan Munger was a problem. The young guard began backing toward the van, unaware that his partner had been disarmed. Ethan Munger had his free hand in the air, the other holding the metal container. And he said, 'Lady, you don't want to do this. Please put that little gun away. It will probably blow up in your face. Just put it away.'

'Drop the can!' Ilya screamed it. And it was all she could do not to burst into tears, she was so scared.

'Just don't get excited, lady,' the young guard said, still backing up with Ilya coming toward him.

It seemed to Ilya like minutes had passed, but it was only seconds, and she expected to hear sirens because several passing shoppers were looking and a woman was yelling, 'Help! Somebody call the police!' Another woman was shouting into her cell phone.

Then Cosmo came running up behind the young security guard with a pistol in each hand. Ethan Munger turned, saw Cosmo, and perhaps from having seen too many Hollywood films or played too many action videos tried to draw his pistol. Cosmo shot the young guard with the other guard's pistol. Three times in the chest.

Ilya didn't grab the can. She just put her pistol in her purse and ran screaming back toward the stolen car, the gunfire ringing in her ears. Within a minute, which seemed like ten, Cosmo jerked open the back door of the car and threw the can and two guns inside. And for one terrible moment couldn't get the old Mazda to start. Cosmo turned the key off, then on again three times, and it started and they sped from the parking lot.

Watch 5 was just loading up their war bags and other equipment when the code 3 hotshot call was given to 6-A-65 of Watch 2. And of course all the midwatch officers started throwing gear into their shops, jumping in, and squealing out of the station parking lot. They headed in the general direction of the robbery but really hoped they'd spot the red Mazda containing a dark-haired man wearing a baseball cap and a red-haired woman on the way. It wasn't often that there was a robbery and shooting of a security guard to start off their evening.

Benny Brewster and B.M. Driscoll of 6-X-66 were the last midwatch car out of the parking lot, which didn't surprise Benny. B.M. Driscoll had to run into the station at the last minute to get a bottle of antihistamine tablets from his locker because the early summer Santa Anas were killing him. Benny Brewster just sat and drummed his fingers on the steering wheel and thought about how miserably unlucky he had been in losing a heroic cop like Mag Takara and inheriting a hypochondriac whom nobody wanted.

Benny had visited Mag three times in the hospital and called her every day since she'd been home with her parents. He wasn't sure if her misshapen left cheekbone would ever be rebuilt to look exactly the way it was supposed to look. Mag said that the vision in her left eye was only about sixty percent of what it had been but that it was expected to improve. Mag promised Benny that she was coming back on duty, and he told her sincerely that he longed for the day.

There was still no court date set for the pimp who had assaulted her. Mag had suggested to Benny that with the huge lawsuit filed against the city for internal injuries suffered from the kicks by Officer Turner, maybe some sort of deal was coming down. A deal where the pimp would plea-bargain to county jail time instead of prison hard time, and a settlement would be made with the financially strapped city. Mag said she was very sorry for Turner, who had resigned in lieu of being fired and was awaiting word about whether he would be prosecuted.

'I jist wish I coulda been there, Mag,' Benny said when last they'd talked about it.

Mag had looked at her tall black partner and said, 'I'm glad you weren't, Benny. You've got a good career ahead of you. I predicted that to the Oracle first time you worked with me.'

Benny Brewster was still thinking about all of that when B.M. Driscoll finally got in the car and said, 'Let's not roll down the windows unless we have to.' Then he sniffed and blew his nose, taking another tissue from the box that he put on the floor beside the shotgun rack.

Benny started the car and drove slowly from the parking lot, saying disgustedly, 'Fucking two-eleven suspects that shot the guard're probably outta the county by now.'

B.M. Driscoll didn't respond, only taking off his glasses and cleaning them with a tissue so that he could better read the dosage on the antihistamine bottle.

All that Cosmo Betrossian could think about as he drove away from the scene of the robbery while the young security guard lay dying was the bartender at the Gulag. Cosmo was going to ask Dmitri to torture and kill that Georgian if he and Ilya were not killed themselves in the next few minutes. The stolen Mazda that the bartender assured him was in good working order had stalled at the first traffic light. And as Cosmo sat there grinding and grinding the starter, a police car sped past, light bar flashing and siren screaming, going to the very place from which they had just escaped.

'Let us get out of the car!' Ilya said.

'The money!' Cosmo cried. 'We have money!'

'Fuck money,' Ilya said.

The engine almost started, but he flooded it. He waited and tried again and it kicked over, and the Mazda began lurching south on Gower.

Cosmo decided that she was right, that they must get out and flee on foot. 'Son of bastard!' he screamed. 'I kill fucking Georgian that give me this car!'

'We leave it now?' Ilya said. 'Stop, Cosmo.'

Then the idea came to him. 'Ilya,' he said, 'you know where we be now?'

'Yes, Gower Street,' she said. 'Stop the car!'

'No, Ilya. We be almost at the house of the miserable addict Farley.' Ilya had never been to Farley's house and could not see the significance of this. 'So who gives damn about fucking tweaker? Stop the car! I get out!'

Cosmo realized that he was a block and a half away, that was all. A block and a half. 'Ilya, please do not jump out. Farley has little garage! Farley always park his shit car on the street so is easy to push it.'

'Cosmo!' she screamed again. 'I am going to kill you or me! Stop this car! Let me out!'

'Two minutes,' he said. 'We be at house of Farley. We put this car in garage of Farley. Our money shall be safe. We shall be safe!'

The Mazda bucked and shuddered its way down Gower to the residential street of Farley Ramsdale. Cosmo Betrossian was afraid that the car wouldn't make the final turn, but it did. And as though the Mazda had a mind and a will, it seemed to throw itself in a last lurching effort up the slightly sloping driveway, where it sputtered and died beside the old bungalow.

Cosmo and Ilya got out quickly, and Cosmo opened the garage door and threw some boxes of junk and an old, rusty bike from the garage into the backyard, making room for the Mazda. Cosmo and Ilya both had to push the car into the garage. Cosmo tucked both pistols inside his belt, grabbed the container of money, and closed the termite-riddled door.

They went to the front door of the bungalow and knocked but got no answer. Cosmo tried the door and found it locked. They went to the back door, where Cosmo slipped the wafer lock with a credit card, and they entered to await the return of their new 'partners.'

Cosmo thought that now he had more reason than ever to kill the two tweakers, and that he must do it right after they entered the house. But not with the gun. The neighboring homes were too close. But how? And would Ilya help him?

The canister contained $93,260, all of it in twenty-dollar bills. By the time they had finished counting it, Ilya had smoked half a dozen cigarettes and seemed calm enough, except for her shaking hands. Cosmo began giggling and couldn't stop.

'Is not so much as Dmitri promised, but I am happy!' Cosmo said. 'I am not greedy pig.' That tickled him so much he giggled more. 'I must call Dmitri soon.'

'You kill the guard,' Ilya said soberly. 'They catch us, we go to the house of death.'

'How can you know he is dead?'

'I saw bullets hit him. Three. Right here.' She touched her chest. 'He is dead man.'

'Fucking guy,' Cosmo said, testy now. 'He did not give up money. Dmitri say no problem. The guard shall give up money. Not my fault, Ilya.'

Ilya shook her head and lit yet another cigarette, and Cosmo lit a smoke of his own while he stuffed stacks of money back into the can, leaving out eight hundred, which he divided with Ilya, saying, 'This make you not so much worried about the house of death, no?'

He took the container back out to the car, wanting to lock it in the trunk, but the ignition key did not work the trunk lock. He cursed the Georgian again and put the container in the backseat of the Mazda and locked the door.

When he returned to the house, Ilya was lying on the battered sofa as though she had a terrible headache. He went over to her and knelt, feeling very aroused.

He said to her, 'Ilya, remember how much sex we feel when we rob the diamonds? I feel that much sex now. And you? How would you like to fuck the brains outside my head?'

'If you touch me now, Cosmo,' she said, 'I swear I shall shoot the brains outside your head. I swear this by the Holy Virgin.'

Less than a mile away, Farley and Olive sat in Sam's Pinto, having borrowed it once again, parked by the cyber café. They saw several tweakers entering and then leaving after having done their Internet business, but they saw no one who they thought might have some decent crystal for purchase.

'Let's try the taco stand,' Farley said. 'We gotta get Sam's car back to him before it gets dark and pick up our piece of shit. He musta fixed the carburetor by now. One good thing about tweakers, Sam can sit around his kitchen table with my carburetor in a million pieces and he actually enjoys himself. Like a fucking jigsaw puzzle or something. There's fringe benefits from crystal if you stop and think about it.'

'I'm glad the police cars and ambulances stopped their sirens,' Olive said. 'They were giving me a headache.'

She was like a goddamn dog, Farley thought. Supersensitive hearing even when not tweaked. She could sit in a restaurant and hear conversations on the other side of a crowded room. He thought he should figure out a way to use that, the only talent she possessed.

'Something musta happened at one of the stores in the mall,' Farley said. 'Maybe some fucking Jew actually charged a fair price. That would cause a bunch of greasers to drop dead of shock and tie up some ambulances.'

He was driving out of the parking lot and turning east when a southbound car at the intersection also turned east and drove in front of him, making Farley slam on his brakes.

'Fuck you!' Farley yelled out the window at the elderly woman driver after he flipped her the bird.

He hadn't gone half a block when he heard the horn toot behind him. He looked in the mirror and said, 'Cops! My fucking luck!'

Benny Brewster said to B.M. Driscoll, 'You're up.'

The older cop wiped his runny nose with Kleenex, pushed his drooping glasses back up, sighed, and said, 'I'm really not well enough to be working tonight. I shoulda called in sick.'

Then he got out, approached the car on the driver's side and saw Farley Ramsdale fumbling in his wallet for his driver's license. Olive looked toward the policeman on her right and saw Benny Brewster looking in at her and at the inside of the car.

'Hi, Officer,' Olive said.

'Evening,' Benny said.

As B.M. Driscoll was examining his driver's license, Farley said, 'What's the problem?'

B.M. Driscoll said, 'You pulled out of the lot into the traffic lane, causing a car to brake hard and yield. That's a traffic violation.'

Benny said to Farley, 'Sir, how about showing the officer your registration too.'

Farley said, 'Aw shit, this ain't my car. Belongs to a friend, Sam Culhane. My car's at his house getting fixed by him.'

When he quickly reached over to the glove compartment, Benny's hand went to his sidearm. There was nothing in the glove box except a flashlight and Sam's garage opener.

'Tell the officer, Olive,' he said. 'This is Sam's car.'

'That's right, Officer,' Olive said. 'Our car is getting its carburetor redone. Sam has it all over the table like a jigsaw.'

'That'll do,' Farley said to her. Then turning to B.M. Driscoll, he said, 'I got a cell here. You can use it and call Sam. I'll dial him for you. This ain't a hot car, Officer. Hell, I just live ten blocks from here by the Hollywood Cemetery.'

Benny Brewster looked over the top of the car to his partner and mouthed the word 'tweakers.'

Then, while B.M. Driscoll was returning to their car to run a make on Farley Ramsdale and the car's license number and to write up the traffic citation, Benny decided to screw with the tweakers, saying to Farley, 'And if we followed you to your house just to verify you're who your license says you are, would you invite us inside?'

'Why not?' Farley said.

'Would there be anything in your house that you wouldn't want us to find?'

'Wait a minute,' Farley said. 'Are you talking about searching my house?'

'How many times have you been in jail for drug possession?' Benny asked.

'I been in jail three times,' Olive said. 'Once when this guy I used to know made me shoplift some stuff from Sears.'

'Shut the fuck up, Olive,' Farley said. Then to Benny he said, 'If you don't write me the ticket, you can search me and search this car and you can search Olive here and you can come to my house and I'll prove whatever you want proved, but I ain't letting you do a fishing expedition by looking in my underwear drawer.'

'Underwear floor, you mean,' Olive said. 'Farley always throws his underwear on the floor and I gotta pick them up,' she explained.

'Olive, I'm begging you to shut up,' Farley said.

Benny looked up and saw B.M. Driscoll returning with the citation book and said, 'Too late. Looks like the citation's already written.'

B.M. Driscoll looked over the roof at his tall partner and said, 'Mr. Ramsdale has a number of arrests for drug possession and petty theft, don't you, Mr. Ramsdale?'

'Kid stuff,' Farley mumbled, signing the traffic ticket.

161

'I didn't write you for not having a registration,' B.M. Driscoll said. 'But tell your friend, Samuel Culhane ... where does he live, by the way?'

'On Kingsley,' Olive said. 'I don't know the number.'

B.M. Driscoll nodded at Benny and said, 'That checks.' Then to Farley he said, 'Have a good evening, Mr. Ramsdale.'

When they were once again on their way to the taco stand to score some ice that Farley now needed desperately, he said to Olive, 'You see what happens when you pin a badge on a nigger? That fucking Watusi wanted to go on a fishing expedition in my house.'

'Maybe we shoulda just invited them home to see that you're a property owner and the stuff on your driver's license is correct,' Olive said. 'And it wouldn'ta mattered if they searched. We got nothing but a glass pipe at home, Farley. That's why we're out here. We got no crystal, no nothing at home.'

Farley turned and stared at her until he almost rear-ended a pickup in front of him, then said, 'Invite cops home to search? I suppose you'da made coffee for them?'

'If we had any,' she said, nodding. 'And if they didn't write the traffic ticket. It's always best to be friendly with the police. Being mean will just bring you more trouble.'

'Jesus Christ!' Farley cried. 'And then what? Maybe you woulda told them you were going to fuck them both to be friendly? Well, I hope not, Olive. Because making terroristic threats is a felony!'

FOURTEEN

Budgie and Fausto were the first of the midwatch teams to break away from the hunt for the red Mazda. Virtually every car had driven east toward gang territory and the less affluent neighborhoods where most of Hollywood's street criminals resided, but the suspects' descriptions could have put them anywhere. By now the cars were looking for a male, white or possibly Hispanic, in his midforties, of medium height and weight, with dark hair. He was wearing a Dodgers cap and sunglasses, a blue tee, and jeans. His companion was a female, white, also about forty, tall and full-figured, with red hair that two Latino women said looked like a cheap wig. The woman with the gun wore sunglasses also, a tight, multicolored cotton dress, and white espadrilles. Both witnesses commented on her large 'bosoms.'

A supplemental description was given to the communications operator by Viktor Chernenko during an on-scene interview thirty minutes after the shooting, when the area around the ATM machine was taped off and controlled by uniformed officers. Even though Viktor knew that the Bank Squad from Robbery-Homicide Division would be handling this one, he was confident that these were the suspects from the jewelry store.

When the report call came in on their MDT, Fausto said to Budgie, 'Well, by now they're in their hole. Best we could hope for is to spot the abandoned Mazda. They probably dumped it somewhere.'

The report they were assigned was for attempted murder, which in Hollywood could mean anything. This was, after all, the land of dreams and fantasy. They were sent to a quite expensive, artsy-craftsy, split-level house in Laurel Canyon, certainly not an area where attempted murders occurred frequently. The fact that there was no code assigned to the call made them think that whoever took the call at Communications didn't think it was worthy of urgent response.

The caller was waiting on his redwood balcony under a vaulted roof. He waved after they parked, and they began climbing the outside wooden staircase. It was still nearly an hour before sunset so they didn't need to light their way, but it was dark from shadows cast by all of the ferns and palms and bird of paradise plants on both sides of the staircase.

Fausto, who was getting winded from the steep climb, figured that the gardeners must make a bundle.

The caller held open the door and said, 'Right this way, officers.'

He was seventy-nine years old and dressed in an ivory-white bathrobe with satin lapels, and leather monogrammed slippers. He had dyed-auburn transplants and a gray mustache that used to be called a toothbrush. He introduced himself as James R. Houston but added that his friends called him Jim.

The inside of the house said 1965: shag carpets, lime-green-flowered sofa, Danish modern dining room furniture, and even an elaborate painted clown in a gilded frame resembling the ones that the late actor-comedian Red Skelton had painted.

When Fausto said, 'By any chance is that a Red Skelton?' and got a negative reply, Budgie said, 'Who's Red Skelton?'

'A famous comic actor of yesteryear,' the man said. 'And a fine painter.'

Only after their host insisted did they agree to have a glass of lemonade from a pitcher on the dining room table. Then he said to Fausto, 'Even though I don't have the honor of owning a Red Skelton clown painting, I did work with him in a movie. It was in nineteen fifty-five, I think. But don't hold me to that.'

Of course, he was implying that he was an actor. Budgie Polk had learned by now that in Hollywood Division, when a suspect or victim says he's an actor, a cop's automatic response is 'And what do you do when you're not acting?'

When she said this to him, he said, 'I've dabbled in real estate for years. My wife owns some rental property that I manage. Jackie Lee's my second wife.' Then he corrected himself and said, 'Actually, my third. My first wife died, and my second, well ...' With that he made a dismissive gesture and then said, 'It's about my present wife that I've called you here.'

Budgie opened her report binder and said, 'Is someone trying to murder her?'

'No,' he said, 'she's trying to murder me.'

Suddenly his hand holding the glass of lemonade began to tremble, and the ice cubes tinkled.

With his long experience in Hollywood crime, Fausto took over. 'And where is your wife now?'

'She's gone to San Francisco with her sister-in-law. They'll be back Monday morning, which is why I felt safe to call you here. I thought you might like to look for clues like on ...'

'*CSI*,' Fausto said. These days it was always the *CSI* TV show. Real cops just couldn't measure up.

'Yes,' he said. '*CSI*.'

'How is she trying to kill you?' Fausto asked.

'She's trying to poison me.'

'How do you know that?' Budgie asked.

'I get a stomachache every time she cooks a meal. I've started going out to dinner a lot because I'm so frightened.'

'And you wouldn't have any physical evidence, would you?' Budgie asked. 'Something that you've saved? Like they do on *CSI*?'

'No,' he said. 'But it happens every time. It's a gradual attempt to murder me. She's a very sophisticated and clever woman.'

'Is there any other evidence of her homicidal intent that you can offer?' Fausto asked.

'Yes,' he said. 'She's putting a toxic substance in my shoes.'

'Go on,' Budgie said. 'How do you know?'

'My feet are always tired. And the soles sometime hurt for no reason.'

Fausto glanced at his watch and said, 'Anything else?'

'Yes, I believe she's putting a toxic substance in my hats.'

'Let me guess,' Fausto said. 'You have headaches?'

'How did you know?'

'Here's the problem as I see it, Mr. Houston,' Fausto said. 'If we arrest her, a high-priced shyster like the ones Michael Jackson hires would look at all this evidence and say, your wife's a lousy cook, your shoes're too tight, and so's your hat. You see where I'm coming from?'

'Yes, I take your point, Officer,' he said.

'So I think what you should do is put this aside for now and call us back when you have more evidence. A lot more evidence.'

'Do you think I should risk my life eating her food to collect the evidence?'

'Bland food,' Fausto said. 'It's not easy to disguise poison in bland dishes. Go ahead and enjoy your mashed potatoes and vegetables and a steak or some chicken, but not fried chicken. Just don't go for the spicy stuff and avoid heavy sauces. That's where it could be risky. And buy some shoes that are a half size bigger. Do you drink alcohol with dinner?'

'Three martinis. My wife makes them.'

'Cut back to one martini. It's very hard to put a toxic dose in only one martini. Have it after dinner but not just before bedtime. And only wear hats when you go out in the sun. I think all of this will disrupt a murder plot or flush out the perpetrator.'

'And you'll come back when we have more to go on?'

'Absolutely,' Fausto said. 'It will be a pleasure.'

There was no pleasure to be had in the house of Farley Ramsdale. Three hours had passed since Cosmo and Ilya had pushed the car into the little garage, and still Farley and Olive had not come home. At one point Cosmo thought Ilya was asleep, lying there on the couch with her eyes closed.

But when he got up to look out the window at the darkened street, she said, 'Stay back from the window. Every police in Hollywood looks for a man in a blue shirt and a woman with the hair that they shall know is a wig. We cannot call a taxi here. A driver shall think of us when he hears about the robbery. Then police may come here and talk to Farley and he is going to know it was us and he shall tell them.'

'Shut up, Ilya. I must think!'

'We cannot go to a bus. We may be seen by police. We cannot call any of your friends to come for us unless you wish to share money with them because they shall find out. We are in a trap.'

'Shut up!' Cosmo said. 'We are not in the trap. We have the money. It is dark now.'

'How do we go home, Cosmo? How?'

'Maybe the car will start now.'

'I shall not put myself in that car!' Ilya said. 'Every cop looks for that car. Every cop in Hollywood! Every cop in all Los Angeles!'

'The car must stay here,' he agreed. 'We put the money in shopping bags. There are paper bags in the kitchen.'

'I understand,' Ilya said. 'We walk away from this house because we do not dare to call the taxi to come here? And then we call from my cell phone and taxi is going to meet us out on the street someplace where we hide in shadows? And we get taxi to leave us a few streets from our apartment?'

'Yes. That is exactly correct.'

'And then Farley and Olive come home to find a car in garage and pretty soon when they turn on TV they see about robbery and the death of the guard and how the killer looks like and you don't think they know who done it? And you think they do not call police and say, Is there reward for the name of killers? The car is here. You do not think this shall happen, Cosmo?'

Cosmo sat down then and put his head in his hands. He had been thinking for three hours, and there was no alternative. He had planned to kill Farley and Olive at the junkyard just before getting the money for the diamonds, but now? He had to kill them when they walked in this house. Yet he could not risk gunfire.

He went over to Ilya and knelt on the floor beside her and said, 'Ilya, the two addicts must die when they come home. We got no choice. We got to kill them. Maybe with knife from the kitchen. You must help me, Ilya.'

She sat up and said, 'I will not kill nobody else with you, Cosmo. Nobody.'

'But what must we do?' he pleaded.

'Tell them what we done. Make them partner. Give them half of money. Make them help us to push that goddamn car away from here and leave it or set fire on it. Then they drive us home. And while all this happens, we just got to hope the cops do not see us. That is what we do, Cosmo. We do not kill nobody else.'

'Please, Ilya! Think!'

'If you try to kill Farley and Olive, you shall have to kill me. You cannot stab us all, Cosmo. I shall shoot you if I can.'

And with that, she drew the pistol from her purse, got up, and walked across the room to the sagging TV viewing chair, where she sat down with the gun in her lap.

'Please do not make fool talk,' Cosmo said. I must call Dmitri. But not now. Not today. I do not talk to Dmitri yet. We must see what is what before I call him.'

'We shall get caught,' she said. 'Or killed.'

'Ilya,' he said, looking at her. 'Let us make love, Ilya. You shall feel much better if we make love.'

'Do not come close to me or it shall end here with guns, and you cannot let guns shoot on this quiet street, Cosmo. Or maybe you also wish to stab every neighbor too?'

Budgie and Fausto were back on patrol looking for something to do, when Budgie said, 'Let's go by Pablo's Tacos and jam up a tweaker or two. Maybe we'll shake loose some crystal. We could use an observation arrest on our recap.'

'Okay,' Fausto said, turning east on the boulevard. 'But whatever you do, don't order a taco in that joint. 'You heard about the tweaker at Pablo's that shoved bindles of crystal up his bung and tried to say his partner made him do it? Well, sometimes he cooks there.'

Farley was absolutely livid by now, and Olive was getting an upset stomach from the stress. For the tenth time, he cried out, 'Ain't there a goddamn teener or two left in this fucking town?'

'Please, Farley,' Olive said. 'You'll make yourself sick.'

'I need some ice!' he said. 'Goddamnit, Olive, we been fucking around for hours!'

'Maybe we should try the doughnut shop again.'

'We tried it twice!' Farley said. 'We tried every goddamn place I can think of. Can you think of a place we ain't tried?'

'No, Farley,' she said. 'I can't.'

Farley raised himself up and looked to his right and saw 6-X-76 parking in the lot. A tall blond female cop got out, along with an old rhino who Farley figured must be a Mexican, or these days a Salvadoran, and that was even worse.

Farley turned his face away and said, 'Olive, tell me these two cops ain't gonna jack us up. Not twice in one night, for chrissake!'

'They're looking at us,' Olive said. Then Farley heard her say cheerfully, 'Good evening, officers.'

Farley put both hands on the steering wheel so they wouldn't get goosey and blow his fucking head off, and the female cop said, 'Evening. Waiting for someone?'

Farley pointed to Olive and said, 'Yeah, she's an actress. Waiting to get discovered.'

That did it. Fausto said, 'Step outta the car.'

Since this had happened to Farley dozens of times in his life, he kept his hands in plain view when Fausto pulled open the driver's door. Farley got out, shaking his head and wondering why oh why did everything happen to him?

Fausto patted him down and said, 'Let's see some ID.'

When Olive got out, Budgie looked at Olive's scrawny torso covered only by a short T-shirt, revealing a sunken belly and bony hips. Her jeans were child size, and Budgie perfunctorily patted the pockets to see if she felt any bindles of crystal. Then Budgie shined her flashlight beam on Olive's inner forearms, but since Olive had seldom skin-popped, there weren't any tracks.

Farley said, 'Gimme a break, *amigo*. Some of your *compadres* already rousted us tonight. They ran a make on us and on the car and then gave me a fucking ticket. Can I reach in my glove box and prove it to you?'

'No, stay here, *amigo*,' Fausto said, painting it with sarcasm. To Budgie he said, 'Partner, take a look in the glove compartment. See if there's a citation in there.'

She opened the glove compartment and retrieved the traffic ticket, saying, 'B.M. Driscoll wrote it right after roll call. Near the cyber café.'

'I'll bet it never occurred to you, *amigo*,' Fausto said, 'that maybe the reason you get stopped by so many cops is because you hang out where tweakers score their crystal. Did that ever flash on your computer screen?'

Farley thought he better lose the Spanish words because they didn't work with this fucking greaseball, so he tried a different tack. 'Officer, please help yourself. You don't even have to ask. Search my car.'

And Budgie said, 'Okay,' and she did.

While she was searching, Farley said, 'Yes, I got a minor record for petty theft and possession of crystal meth. No, I don't have drugs on me. If you want, I'll take off my shoes. If we weren't standing out here, I'd take off my fucking pants. I'm too tired to reason with you guys anymore. Just do what you gotta do and let me go home.'

'We even told the other officers they could come home with us,' Olive said helpfully. 'We don't care if you search our house. You can do a fishing exposition, we don't care.'

'Olive,' Farley said, 'I'm begging you. Shut the fuck up.'

'Is that right?' Budgie said. 'You're so clean you'd take us home right now and let us search your house, no problem?' To Fausto, 'Whadda you think of that, partner?'

'Is that what you'd do?' Fausto asked Farley, as he wrote a quick FI card. 'Take us to your crib? You're that clean?'

'Man, at this point I'm just tempted to say yes. If you'd let me go lay in bed, you could turn the fucking place upside down, inside and out. And if you find any dope in that house, it would mean that Olive here must have a secret boyfriend who's supplying her. And if Olive could find a boyfriend, then there really are miracles and maybe I'll win the California lottery. And if I do, I'll move clear outta this fucking town and away from you people, because you're killing me, man, you're killing me!'

Fausto looked at the anguished clammy face of Farley Ramsdale, handed him his driver's license, and said, 'Dude, you better get into rehab ASAP. The trolley you're riding is at the last stop. Nothing left ahead but the end of the line.'

When Fausto and Budgie were back in their car, she said to Fausto, 'I'm tempted to drive by the address on that FI a little later.'

'What for?'

'That guy's gotta score some crystal. They'll be smoking ice and getting all spun out tonight or he'll be in a straitjacket. He's that close to losing it completely.'

Ilya was on her feet, pacing and smoking. Cosmo was the one on the couch now, exhausted from arguing with her.

'How long we sit at this place?' he asked lethargically.

'Almost six hours,' she said. 'We can't wait no more. We got to go.'

'Without our money, Ilya?'

'Did you wipe all evidence from the car, Cosmo?'

'I tell you yes, okay? Now please shut up.'

'Did you empty the cigarette tray in the car? That is evidence.'

'Yes.'

'Get can of money out from the car.'

'You got idea, Ilya? Wonderful. You don't like my ideas. Like we must kill the addicts.'

'Shut up, Cosmo. You will put can of money under this house. Find a little door that go under this house. Put can in there.'

She began emptying ashtrays into a paper bag from the kitchen, and he said, 'Ilya, the car? It cannot travel! What are you thinking about?'

'We are leaving it.'

'Here? Ilya, you are crazy person! Farley and Olive—'

In charge now, she interrupted, 'Did you take things out from garage?'

'Yes, a bike and few boxes. Goddamn garage, full of junk. Almost no room for a goddamn car.'

'As I thought,' she said. 'Put all junk back in.'

'What are you thinking about, Ilya?'

'They are addicts, Cosmo. Look at this house. Trash all around. Junk all around. They do not park car in garage. They do not go in garage almost never. The car must stay for few days. They shall not even know it.'

'And us?'

'Take a shirt from Farley. Look inside bedroom. I am going to remove my wig and we shall walk few blocks from here to phone taxi. It is a little bit safe now. Then we go home.'

'All right, Ilya,' he said. 'But you sleep on top of this idea tonight: The addicts must die. We got no other road to travel. You must soon see that.'

'I must think,' she said. 'Now we go. Hurry.'

When Cosmo came back into the living room from the bedroom, he was wearing a dirty long-sleeved patterned shirt over his T-shirt. 'Hope you happy now, Ilya,' he said. 'Before we get home I shall be bit a hundred times by tiny creatures that crawl inside Farley's clothes.'

After the cops left them in the Pablo's Tacos parking lot, Farley said, 'Olive, I think we gotta go home and white-knuckle it. We ain't gonna score tonight.'

'There's almost a quart of vodka there,' Olive said. 'I'll mix it with some packets of punch and you can just drink as much as you can.'

'Okay,' he said. 'That'll get me through the night. It'll have to.'

'I just hope it won't make you throw up,' Olive said. 'You're so thin and tired-looking.'

'It won't,' he said.

'And I'll make you something delicious to eat.'

'That'll make me throw up,' he said.

When they arrived at Farley's house, he was almost too tired to climb the porch steps, and when he did and they were inside, Olive said, 'Farley, it smells like smoke in here.'

He threw himself on the couch and grabbed the TV remote, saying 'Olive, it should. We smoke crystal in here in case you forgot. Every chance we get, which ain't often enough these days.'

'Yes, but it smells like old cigarette smoke. Don't you notice it?'

'I'm so fucking tired, Olive,' he said, 'I wouldn't smell smoke if you set fire to yourself. Which wouldn't be a bad idea.'

'You'll feel better after a meal,' said Olive. 'How does a toasted cheese sandwich sound?'

The PSR putting out the broadcast decided to have a bit of fun with 6-X-32's call to Grauman's Chinese Theater. She put it out as a hotshot.

Flotsam and Jetsam listened incredulously when, after the electronic beep, she said, 'All units in the vicinity and Six-X-ray-Thirty-two, see the woman on Hollywood Boulevard west of Highland. A battery in progress. Batman versus Spiderman. Batman last seen running into Kodak Center. Person reporting is Marilyn Monroe. Six-X-Thirty-two, handle code three.'

When they got to the scene, Marilyn Monroe was waving at them from the courtyard of Grauman's Chinese Theater and tourists were snapping photos like crazy. B.M. Driscoll and Benny Brewster rolled in right behind them.

Jetsam, who was driving, said, 'Which Marilyn is it, do you think? One of them is hot, bro. Know which one I mean?'

'It ain't the hot one,' Flotsam said.

Their Marilyn was striking the famous over-the-air-vent pose, but there was no air blowing up her dress. She had the Monroe dress and her pricey wig was excellent. Even her coy but sensuous Monroe smile was right on the money. The problem was, she was six feet three inches tall and wasn't a woman.

Flotsam got out first and saw Spiderman sitting on the curb holding his head and rubbing his jaw. Jetsam went over to him and got the details, which of course involved a turf fight between two tourist hustlers.

While Flotsam was talking to Marilyn Monroe, a tourist begged them to move stage left so he could get Grauman's in the background. Marilyn did it gladly. After a moment's hesitation during which several tourists needled him for being a poor sport, Flotsam moved with her and put up with about a hundred photo flashes from every direction.

Finally Marilyn said, 'It was terrible, Officer! Batman struck Spiderman with a flashlight for no reason at all. He's a pig, Batman is. I have always found Spiderman to be a love. I hope you find that cape-wearing rat and toss his fat ass in jail!'

There was quite a bit of applause then, and Marilyn Monroe flashed a smile that could only be called blinding in its whiteness.

As Flotsam was trying to get information from Marilyn Monroe, he was surrounded by all three Elvises. They worked in tandem only on big Friday nights like this one, and seeing the commotion went for the chance at real publicity. And they weren't disappointed. The first TV news van to have heard the police broadcast was dropping a cameraman and reporter at the corner of Hollywood and Highland just as the Elvises gathered.

The Presleys were all talking at once to Flotsam: Skinny Elvis, Fat Elvis, and even Smellvis, he of the yellow sweat stains under the arms of his ice-cream suit, which made tourists hold their breath during his cuddly photo shoots.

'Batman will never eat lunch in this town again!' Skinny Elvis cried.

'Spiderman rules!' Fat Elvis cried.

'I am an eye witness to the caped crusader's vicious attack!' Smellvis announced to the crowd, and he was so rank that Flotsam had to backpedal a few steps.

Flotsam asked B.M. Driscoll to check out the Kodak Center, and when he asked, 'What's the guy look like?' Flotsam said, 'Just hook up any guy you see wearing a cape and hanging upside down somewheres. If it turns out to be Count Dracula, just apologize.'

The midwatch cops didn't know that there was an undercover team at work in the midst of the crowd, posing as tourists with backpacks and cameras. The UC team had Tickle Me Elmo under arrest for manhandling a female tourist after she'd snapped his picture and refused to pay his three-dollar tariff.

Elmo had grabbed her by the arm and said, 'Well you can kiss my ass, bitch!' and next thing he knew, the UC cops had him up against the wall of the Kodak Center and removed his head, inside of which they found more than two hundred dollar bills and a gram of cocaine.

Now the tourists turned on Elmo for photos, but the TV camera crew was still concentrating on Marilyn Monroe, until Benny Brewster said to Flotsam, 'Hey man, Elmo had dope in his head!'

Upon hearing this, the news team swung their cameras toward Elmo, who was yelling that his head was dope-free when he'd put the costume on, implying a police frame-up.

Jetsam decided to help search the Kodak Center, where after a few minutes Batman was spotted. It was a brief chase, since Batman's ample gut was hanging over his utility belt, and he was just slogging along in front of the Kodak Theatre when Jetsam jumped him from behind. For a minute or two Jetsam feared that the exhausted Batman was going into cardiac arrest after he was proned out and cuffed.

Jetsam said to B.M. Driscoll, 'How do you do CPR through a bat mask and breast-plate?'

When Jetsam finally got outside Grauman's forecourt with his hand-cuffed and forlorn prisoner, crowds gathered, camera bulbs flashed, and the news bunny ran up to him, saying, 'Officer, did you have trouble catching up with Batman? Was it an exciting chase?'

The surfer cop struck a semi-heroic pose for the camera and said, 'Weak sauce.' Then he quickly walked Batman to the black-and-white, where he was put into the backseat.

This particular news bunny was a relentless journalist and proud of it. She hurried after Jetsam and stood next to the police car, making a point of handing her mike to one of the guys in her crew so she could appear to confront the cop empty-handed.

'"Weak ... sauce"?' said the news bunny to Jetsam, with arching, perfectly penciled eyebrows, and a lip-licking smile that stopped the surfer cop in his tracks. 'Can you translate that term for us? Off the record?'

Jetsam gaped at her cleavage. And goddamn, she licked her lips again! He looked at her camera crew, who were back on the sidewalk and couldn't even see his face, and he leaned down with his mouth close to her ear and whispered, 'It just means, without his Batmobile he ain't shit.'

Then with a devil-may-care wink, he whirled and hopped into the car behind the wheel. He was tickled to see the news bunny direct the crew to shoot coverage of 6-X-32 as he was driving off.

What Jetsam didn't see, however, was the news bunny fingering the little mike she had wired inside the collar of her jacket. And the triumphant smile she gave to her sound man was even twice as sexy as the one she'd given Jetsam.

On the late news, the producer bleeped out *shit*, but from the context the audience knew what had been said. Then the news bunny appeared on camera, this time directly in front of Grauman's Chinese Theater.

With her Hollywood insider's saucy grin, she said to her audience, 'This is your intrepid reporter coming to you from Hollywood Boulevard, where even superheroes must bow to the forces of LAPD justice – who are anything but ... weak sauce.'

The watch commander told Jetsam that he'd probably get another official reprimand or even a little suspension for the manner of his 'interview.'

Cosmo did not waken until 1 p.m. the next afternoon. The smell of Ilya's tea brought him around, and at first he felt a stab of panic. What if she'd gone back to get the money? But then he heard her and the sound of dishes being washed, so he entered the bathroom and showered.

When he came into the kitchen, she was at the table smoking and drinking a glass of hot tea. Another glass was poured and awaited him. Neither spoke until he drank some and lit a cigarette of his own, and then he said, 'How long you are awake?'

'Three hours,' she said. 'I am thinking many thoughts.'

'And what is the new idea?'

'How much Dmitri is going to give for the diamonds?'

'Twenty thousands,' he lied.

'Okay,' she said. 'Give to him the diamonds. No charge. We keep the money.'

'All the money?'

'No, we share with Farley and Olive. We make the best bargain we can. Then we get out of Los Angeles. Go to San Francisco. Start over. No more guns. No more death.'

'Ilya, Dmitri know how much money we got. Do you not turn on TV and hear about it?'

'No,' she said. 'I have no wish to hear more.'

'The news tell how much we got. Dmitri shall want half.'

'We may leave Los Angeles with almost fifty thousand, even Farley if take away half. We cannot give Dmitri no money. We give him diamonds.'

'Is not enough. He shall kill us, Ilya. I know he is mad now because I did not make a call to him. I know he is very mad.'

'We are leaving Los Angeles.'

'He shall find us and kill us in San Francisco.'

'We take a chance.'

'You think Farley and Olive do not tell police about us after we give them money?'

'No. They must have drugs. They must have money for drugs. After they take half of money, they are, how you say it, partners in the crime. They cannot tell police nothing. We shall wait two, maybe three days. I tell you the addicts will not know the Mazda is in garage. And under the house they never go in all their life. We are okay for two, three days. We hide here.'

'Ilya, we may keep half money and give other half to Dmitri.' Then he almost told the truth about the diamond deal, saying, 'I think I may bargain with Dmitri. I think I say to him I must have thirty-five thousands for diamonds. So, we shall have almost eighty-five thousands and we stay in Los Angeles. All of this if you permit me to kill the addicts. I know how. You shall not need to do nothing.' He was finished now, but he decided to add a postscript. He said, 'Please, Ilya. You love the life here. You very much love the life in Hollywood. Am I correct?'

Ilya's mascara was running when she got up and went to the tea kettle on the stove. She stood there for a long moment before speaking. With her back to him she said, 'All right, Cosmo. Kill them. And do not never talk of it. Never!'

FIFTEEN

The southeastern part of Hollywood Division, near Santa Monica Boulevard and Western Avenue, was the turf of Latino gangs, including Eighteenth Street cruisers and some Salvadorans from the huge MS-13 gang. White Fence, one of the oldest Mexican American gangs was active around Hollywood Boulevard and Western, and Mexican Mafia, aka MM or El Eme, was only here and there but in some ways was the most powerful gang of all and could even operate lethally from inside state prisons. There were no black gangs in the Hollywood area, like the Crips or Bloods of south central and southeast LA, because there were very few blacks living in the Hollywood area.

Wesley Drubb was steeped in this what was to him exciting information, having been permitted to gain new experience by working on loan for two nights with 6-G-1, a Hollywood Division gang unit. But now while driving on Rossmore Avenue, which bordered the Wilshire Country Club, his gang chatter seemed ludicrously inappropriate and especially annoying to Hollywood Nate Weiss.

Wesley said, 'The California Department of Corrections estimates that El Eme has nearly two hundred members in the prison system.'

'You don't say.' Nate was gazing up at the luxurious apartment buildings and condos on both sides of his favorite Los Angeles street.

'They're usually identified by a tattoo of a black hand with an *M* on the palm of it. In the Pelican Bay Maximum Security Prison, an MM gang member had sixty thousand dollars in a trust account before it was frozen by authorities. He was doing deals from inside the strictest prison!'

'Do tell.' Nate imagined Clark Gable in black tie and Carole Lombard in sable, both smiling at the doorman as they went off for a night on the town. At the Coconut Grove, maybe.

Then he tailored the fantasy to fit Tracy and Hepburn, even though he knew that neither of them had ever lived on the street. But what the hell, it was his fantasy.

Wesley said, 'Big homies have been known to order hits from their prison cells. If you're "in the hat" or "green-lighted," it means you're targeted.'

'Weird,' Nate said. 'Green-lighted in the movie business means you got the okay to do the picture. In Hollywood it means you're alive. In prison it means you're dead. Weird.'

Wesley said, 'They told me that sometimes in Hollywood we might encounter southeast Asian gangsters from the Tiny Oriental Crips and the Oriental Boy Soldiers. Ever run into them?'

'I don't think so,' Nate said. 'I've only encountered more law-abiding and sensitive Asians who would bury a cleaver in your neck if you ever referred to them as Orientals.'

Wesley said, 'And the Asian gang whose name I love is the Tiny Magicians Club, aka the TMC.'

'Jesus Christ!' Nate said. 'TMC is The Movie Channel! Isn't anything fucking sacred anymore?'

Wesley said, 'I already knew about the civil injunctions to keep gang members in check, but did you know the homies have to be personally served with humongous legal documents that set forth all terms of the injunction? Two or three gang members congregating can violate the injunction, and even possession and use of cell phones can be a violation. Did you know that?'

Nate said, 'Possession of a cell phone by any person of the female gender who is attempting to operate a motor vehicle should be a felony, you ask me.'

Wesley said, 'I might get to examine the tattoos and talk to some crew members and hear about their gang wars next time.'

'Do I detect a 'hood rat in the making?' Nate said, yawning. 'Are you gonna be putting in a transfer, Wesley? Maybe to Seventy-seventh Street or Southeast, where people keep rocket launchers at home for personal protection?'

'When I got sent to Hollywood I heard it was a good misdemeanor division. I guess I wanna go to a good felony division. I've heard that in the days before the consent decree, Rampart Division CRASH unit used to have a sign that said "We intimidate those who intimidate others." Imagine how it was to work that Gang Squad.'

Nate looked at Wesley the way he'd look at a cuppa joe from Dunkin' Donuts or a Hostess Ding Dong and said, 'Wesley, the days of LAPD rock 'n' rule are over. It's never coming back.'

Wesley said, 'I just thought that someplace like Southeast Division would offer more ... challenges.'

'Go ahead, then,' Nate said. 'You can amuse yourself on long nights down there by going to drug houses and yelling "Police!" then listening to toilets flushing all over the block. Cop entertainment in the 'hood. Watching cruisers throw gang signs beats the hell outta redcarpet events, where the tits extend from Hollywood Boulevard to infinity, right?'

Wesley Drubb was eager indeed to do police work in gang territory, or anyplace where he might encounter real action. He was growing more and more tense and nervous with Nate boring him to death by directing him far from the semi-mean streets of Hollywood for his endless sorties into Hollywood's past. The gang turf was there and he was here. Touring!

Quiet now, Wesley chewed a fingernail as he drove. Nate finally noticed and said, 'Hey pard, you look especially stressed. Got girlfriend troubles maybe? I'm an expert on that subject.'

Wesley wasn't far enough from his probationary period to say, 'I am fucking bored to death, Nate! You are killing me with these trips through movie history!'

Instead, he said, 'Nate, do you think we should be cruising around the country club? This is Wilshire Area. We work in Hollywood Area.'

'Stop saying area,' Nate said. 'Division sounds more coplike. I can't stand these new terms for everything.'

'Okay, Hollywood Division, then. We're out of it right now. This is Wilshire Division.'

'A few blocks, big deal,' Nate said. 'Look around you. This is gorgeous.'

Hollywood Nate was referring to Rossmore Avenue, where the elegant apartment buildings and pricey converted condos had names like the Rossmore, El Royale, the Marlowe, and Country Club Manor, all of them a short walk from the very private golf course. They were built in the French, Spanish, and Beaux Arts styles of Hollywood's Golden Age.

Seeing that Wesley lacked enthusiasm for the architecture, Nate said, 'Maybe you'd like to cruise by the Church of Scientology Celebrity Center? We might spot John Travolta. But we can't hassle any of their so-called parishioners or we'll get beefed by their fascist security force. Do you know they even beefed our airship one time? Said they wanted to make their headquarters an LAPD no-fly zone.'

Wesley said, 'No, I don't have much interest in Scientology or John Travolta, to tell you the truth.'

'This looks like we're in Europe,' Nate said, as the setting sun lit the entry of the El Royale. 'Can't you see Mae West sashaying out that door with a hunky actor on her arm to a limo waiting on the street?'

'Mae West' was how Wesley Drubb's father referred to the life jackets he kept aboard a seventy-five-foot power yacht that he used to own and kept docked at the marina. Wesley didn't know that they were named after a person, but he said, 'Yeah, Mae West.'

'Someday I'll be living in one of those buildings,' Nate said. 'The local country clubs used to restrict Jews. And actors. I've heard it was Randolph Scott who told them, "I'm not an actor and I've got a hundred movies to prove it." But then I heard it was Victor Mature. Even John Wayne, and he didn't hardly play golf. It's a good Hollywood story no matter who said it.'

Wesley had never heard of the first two actor-golfers and was getting a tightness in his neck and jaw muscles. He was even grinding his teeth and only relaxed when Nate sighed and said, 'Okay, let's go find you a bad guy to put in jail.'

And at last, with an enormous sense of relief, Wesley Drubb was permitted to drive away from reel Hollywood and head for the real one.

Darkness fell as they were passing the Gay and Lesbian Center, and Nate said, 'That's where they can go to let their hair down. Or their hair extensions. There's a place for everyone to dream in Hollywood. I don't know why you can't be satisfied.'

A few minutes later, on Santa Monica Boulevard, Wesley said, 'Look how that guy's walking. Let's shake him.'

Nate looked across the street at a pale and gaunt forty-something guy in a crew neck, long-sleeved sweater and jeans, walking along the boulevard with his hands in his pockets.

'Whadda you see that I don't see?'

'He's a parolee-at-large, I bet. He walks like they do in the prison yard.'

'You learned a lot with the gang unit,' Nate said. 'Maybe even something worthwhile, but I haven't noticed it yet.'

Wesley said, 'The parole officers are a few months behind in getting warrants into their computer, but we could check him anyway, okay? Even if there's no warrant, maybe he's holding some dope.'

'Maybe he's cruising for a date,' Nate said. 'This is Santa Monica Boulevard, home of boy love and homo-thugs. He might be looking for somebody like the one he left in prison. A guy with a tattoo of a naked babe on his back and an asshole like the Hollywood subway.'

'Can we check him?'

'Yeah, go ahead, get it outta your system,' Nate said.

Wesley pulled up several yards behind the guy, and both cops got out and lit him with their flashlight beams.

He was used to it. He stopped and took his hands out of his pockets. With a guy like this preliminaries were few, and when Wesley said, 'Got some ID?' the guy shot them a grudging look of surrender and without being asked pulled up the sweater sleeves, showing his forearms, which were covered with jailhouse tatts over old scar tissue.

'I don't use no more,' he said.

Nate moved the beam of his light near the man's face and said, 'Your eyes are down right now, bro.'

'I drink like a Skid Row alky,' the ex-con said, 'but I don't shoot up. I got tired of getting busted for eleven five-fifty. I was always under the influence and I just kept getting busted. Like, I was serving life in prison a few weeks at a time.'

Wesley wrote an FI card on the guy, whose ID said his name was Brian Allen Wilkie, and ran the information on the MDT, coming back with an extensive drug record but no wants or warrants.

Before they let him go, Nate said, 'Where you headed?'

'Pablo's to get a taco.'

'That's tweakerville,' Nate said. 'Don't tell me you're smoking glass now instead of shooting smack?'

'One day at a time, man,' Brian Wilkie said. 'I wouldn't want my PO to know, but I'm down to booze and a little meth now and then. That's an improvement, ain't it?'

'I don't think that's what AA means by one day at a time, man,' Nate said. 'Stay real.'

A few minutes later, when Wesley drove past Pablo's Tacos, they saw an old car parked in front and a pair of skinny tweakers in a dispute with another guy who also had tweaker written all over him. The argument was so animated that the tweakers didn't see the black-and-white when Wesley parked half a block away and turned out the lights to watch.

'Maybe one of them'll stab the other,' Nate said. 'And you can pop him for a felony. Or better yet, maybe one of them'll pull a piece and we can get in a gunfight. Would that relieve your boredom?'

Farley Ramsdale was waving his arms like one of those people with that terrible disease whose name she couldn't remember, and Olive was getting scared. Spit was running down Farley's chin and he was screaming his head off because the tiny tweaker that they knew as Little Bart wouldn't sell one of the two teeners he was holding. Farley refused to meet his excessive price and had tried to bargain him down.

Olive thought it was mean and wrong of Little Bart, because Farley had often sold to him at a decent price. But all this screaming was just going to get them in trouble.

'You are an ungrateful chunk of vomit!' Farley yelled. 'Do you remember how I saved your sorry ass when you needed ice so bad you were ready to blow a nigger for it?'

Little Bart, who was about Farley's age and whose neck bore a tattoo of a dog collar all the way around, said, 'Man, things're bad, real bad these days. This is all I got and all I'm gonna have for a while. I gotta pay the rent.'

'You little cocksucker!' Farley yelled, doubling his fist.

'Hey, dude!' Little Bart said, backing up. 'Take a chill pill! You're freaking!'

Olive stepped forward then and said, 'Farley, please stop. Let's go. Please!'

Suddenly, Farley did something he had never done in all the time they'd been together. He smacked her across the face, and she was so stunned she stared at him for a moment and then burst into tears.

'That's enough,' Wesley said, and got out of the car, followed by Hollywood Nate.

Farley never saw them coming but Little Bart did. The tiny tweaker said, 'Uh-oh, time to go.'

And he started to do just that, until Wesley said, 'Hold it right there.'

A few minutes later, Little Bart and Farley were being patted down by Wesley and Hollywood Nate while Olive wiped her tears on the tail of her jersey.

'What's this all about?' Farley said. 'I ain't done nothing.'

'You committed a battery,' Wesley said. 'I saw it.'

'It was an accident,' Farley said. 'Wasn't it, Olive? I didn't mean to hit her. I was just making a point with this guy.'

'What point is that?' Nate said.

'About whether George W. Bush is really as dumb as he looks. It was a political debate.'

Little Bart wasn't really worried, because the ice was under the rear floor mat of his car, which was half a block down the street. So he just had to chill and not piss off the cops, and then he figured he could skate.

When Nate pulled Farley ten yards away from the other two, Farley yelled back, 'Olive, tell these guys it was an accident!'

'Shut the fuck up,' Nate said. 'Where's your car?'

'I ain't got a car,' Farley lied, and after he did it, he wondered why he had lied. There was no crystal in his car. He hadn't smoked any glass for two and a half days. That's why his nerves were shot. That's why he was on the verge of strangling Little Bart. He was just so sick of being hassled by cops that he lied. Lying was a form of rebellion against all of them. All of the assholes who were fucking with him.

For the next twenty minutes, the shakes were written, and each name was run through CII, with a rap sheet showing for Farley Ramsdale but none for Olive O. Ramsdale. Farley finally stopped bitching and Olive stopped crying.

Little Bart actually began trying to talk politics to Farley to go along with the George Bush crack, but the cops obviously weren't buying it. They knew that some kind of drug deal was going down, and Little Bart just didn't want to give them a good reason to try his car keys in the doors of the eight cars that were parked within half a block of Pablo's. And he especially didn't want them to look under the floor mat.

Farley thought the cops were going to prolong this for as long as possible, but the younger cop ran up to the other one and said, 'Kidnapping in progress, Omar's Lounge on Ivar! Let's go, Nate!'

When Farley and Olive and Little Bart were left standing there outside Pablo's Tacos, Farley said to Little Bart, 'Those cops saved your fucking life.'

Bart said, 'Dude, you need some help. You're way out there. Way, way out there.' And he ran to his car and drove off.

Olive said, 'Farley let's go home now and—'

'Olive,' he said, 'if you say you'll make me a delicious cheese sandwich, I swear I'll knock your fucking tooth out.'

*

Hollywood detectives had been forced to investigate a number of date rapes, called acquaintance rapes by the police. It was usually 'I woke up naked with somebody I didn't know. I was drugged.'

The cases were never prosecuted. Evidentiary requirements necessitated an immediate urine test, but the date rape drugs metabolized in four to six hours. It was always too late for the special analysis that had to be done outside the LAPD crime lab, which did only basic drug screening of controlled substances. In fact, as defense lawyers argued, too much booze produced much the same effect as a date rape drug.

The date rape cases were reported to Hollywood Station by persons of both genders, but only once was there a criminal filing by the District Attorney's Office. The victim had vomited shortly after the encounter, and the drug was able to be recovered and identified.

Six-X-Seventy-six was the unit to receive the code 3 call to Omar's Lounge but Budgie and Fausto were beaten to the call by Wesley Drubb and Hollywood Nate, followed closely by Benny Brewster and B.M. Driscoll, complaining of motion sickness caused by Benny's fast driving.

The first units to arrive gave way to Budgie and Fausto, since they were assigned the call, and Budgie entered the nightclub to interview the victim. Even though Fausto was the report writer on this night and Budgie was driver, she took over with the report because the victim was a woman.

When they were being escorted to a private office inside the nightclub, Fausto whispered to her, 'This joint gets sold to somebody new just about every time they change the tablecloths. It's impossible to keep track of who the owner is, but you can bet your ass it's a Russian.'

Sara Butler was sitting in the office being tended to by a cocktail waitress who wore a starched white shirt, black bow tie and black pants. The waitress was a natural blonde and pretty, but the kidnap victim, who was about Budgie's age, was both prettier and unnaturally more blond. The straps on her black dress were held together with safety pins, and her pantyhose was in shreds around her ankles. Her knees were scraped and bleeding, as were both her palms. Mascara and eye liner were smeared all over her cheeks, and she was wearing most of her lipstick on her chin. She was angry and she was drunk.

The cocktail waitress was applying ice in a napkin to the victim's right knee when the cops walked in. A faux fur coat was draped across the chair behind the young woman.

Budgie sat down and said, 'Tell us what happened.'

'I was kidnapped by four Iranians,' Sara Butler said.

'When?' Budgie asked.

'About an hour ago,' Sara Butler said.

Budgie looked at Fausto, who nodded and went out to broadcast a code 4, meaning sufficient help at the scene, since the suspects were long gone.

'What did you say when you called it in?' Budgie asked. 'We were under the impression that it had just occurred.'

'I don't know what I said, I was so upset.'

'Okay,' Budgie said. 'From the beginning, please.'

After she'd given all of the contact information for the report, and after listing her occupation as actress, Sara Butler said, 'I was supposed to meet my girlfriend here but she called me on my cell and said her husband came home from a trip unexpectedly. And I thought I might as well have a drink since I was here.'

'You had more than one?'

'I don't know how many I had.'

'Go on.'

'I got talking to some guy at the bar and he started buying me martinis. I didn't have that many.'

Worrying about the liquor license, the cocktail waitress looked at Budgie and said, 'We wouldn't serve anyone who's drunk.'

'Continue, please,' Budgie said to Sara Butler.

'So pretty soon I started feeling weird. Dizzy in a weird way. I think the guy slipped me a date rape drug but I didn't drink enough of it to knock me cold.'

'How many martinis did you drink?'

'No more than four. Or possibly five.'

'That could knock a hippo cold,' Budgie said. 'Go on.'

'The guy who bought me the martinis offered to drive me home. Said he had a black Mercedes sedan and a driver parked right in front. Said he'd be in the car. I said okay and went to the ladies room to freshen up.'

'Weren't you worried about the date rape drug?' Budgie asked.

'Not then. I only thought about it after the kidnapping.'

'Okay, continue.'

'Then I left the club, and there was a long black car at the curb and I went to the back door which was open and got in. And goddamn! There were four drunken Iranians in the car and one of them closed the door and they took off with me, just laughing their asses off. And I realized that it was a limo and I was in the wrong car and I yelled at them to stop and let me out.'

'How did you know they were Iranians?'

'I go to acting class with two Iranians and they're always jabbering in Farsi. I know Iranians, believe me. Or Persians, as they prefer to call themselves when they live in a free country, the bastards.'

'Okay, and then?'

'They were groping me and kissing me and I scratched one on the face and he told the driver to stop and they pushed me out of the car right onto the street and I ran back here. I want them arrested and prosecuted for kidnapping.'

'Kidnapping might be very hard to allege in this case,' Budgie said, 'but let's get the report finished and see what the detectives think.'

'I don't care what the detectives think,' Sara Butler said. 'I've done half their job for them already.'

And with that she produced a tissue that was carefully folded, and said, 'These are fingernail scrapings from the Iranian's face. And my coat there can be examined for latent fingerprints.'

'We can't get fingerprints from fur,' Budgie said.

'Officer, don't tell me what you can't do,' Sara Butler said. 'My father's a lawyer and I won't have my report swept under the rug by your detectives. The dirt from my dress will identify where I was lying in the gutter in case someone says I wasn't pushed from the car. And those fingernail scrapings will positively identify one of my assailants after a DNA analysis.' She paused and said, 'And channel seven is on the way.'

'Here?'

'Yes, I called them. So I suggest you take this case very seriously.'

'Tell me, Ms. Butler,' Budgie said. 'Do you watch *CSI*?'

'All the time,' Sara Butler said. 'And I know that some cheap lawyer for the Iranians might say I got into the car by design and not by accident, but I have that covered as well.'

'I'm sure you do,' Budgie said.

'The man who bought me the martinis can testify that he had a car waiting for me, and that will prove I just made a mistake and got into the wrong car.'

'And I suppose you have the man's name and how we can contact him?'

'His name is Andrei. He's a Russian gentleman who said he worked as manager at the Gulag in east Hollywood. And he gave me a business card from there. I think you should check on him and see if he's ever been accused of doctoring a girl's drink either at his nightclub or elsewhere. I still think I was affected too suddenly by the martinis.'

'Anything else you'd like to add?' Budgie said, intending to get the hell out before a news team arrived.

'Only that I intend to have my father call the Gulag or go to the nightclub in person if necessary to make sure someone from the police department properly investigates my crime report. Now, if you'll excuse me, I've got to pull myself together for channel seven.'

When Budgie got back outside, Fausto, who had stepped into the office during part of the interview, said, 'Would you call that a righteous felony or an example of first-stage alcoholism and a slight PMS issue?'

'For once, you sexist old bastard,' Budgie said, 'I think you got it right.'

*

Dmitri would have been even angrier, if that were possible, had he known that Andrei, his night manager, had been out on his night off trying to pick up a woman who subsequently got herself involved with the police. Dmitri did not want the police at his place of business ever, not for any reason. But this night he had cops all over the place, including Andi McCrea, who'd been called in from home by the night-watch detective Compassionate Charlie Gilford.

When Charlie told Andi that he was having trouble reaching other members of the homicide unit, two of whom were sick with the flu that was going around, she suggested he try one of the detectives from Robbery, and gave him Brant Hinkles's cell number.

Charlie rang up Brant Hinkle and told him there was a murder at the Gulag and asked if he'd be willing to help out Andi. Brant said he thought he could manage and that he'd be there ASAP.

Then Brant closed his cell and looked over at Andi, naked in bed beside him, and said, 'That is a very dirty trick.'

She kissed him, jumped out of bed, and said, 'You'd rather investigate a homicide with me than lie here alone all night, wouldn't you?'

'I guess I would at that,' Brant said. 'Is that what you would call a commitment?'

Andi said, 'When two cops are committed, the definition is similar to the one meaning residents of an asylum. Let's go to work.'

There had been a large private party in the VIP section on the upper level of the Gulag, an area roped off and guarded by a bouncer. Dmitri had assigned two waitresses for the party and wished he'd scheduled three when the party grew much larger than had been expected. Soon the sofas along the walls and every chair was occupied in layers, young women sitting on the laps of any guy who would permit it. Everyone else was standing three deep by a railing, watching the mass of dancers writhing in the pit down below on ground level.

They were foreign students from a technical college attending this gathering put together by a party promoter who dealt with various Hollywood nightclubs. Most at the soirée were Arabs, some were Indians, a few were Pakistanis. And there were two uninvited guests from south LA who were members of the Crips gang, out for a night in Hollywood, one of whom claimed to be a cousin of the promoter.

Dmitri had installed a video camera on the patio outside, where customers could go for a smoke, and it was there on the patio that the crime occurred. One of the young Arabs, a twenty-two-year-old student, didn't like something that the taller of the two Crips said to his girlfriend, and a fight started. The taller Crip, who wore a raspberry-colored fedora over a head rag, got knocked down by the Arab with some help from his friends. While several people were separating the combatants, the shorter of the two Crips, the quiet one, walked behind the Arab, reached around, and stabbed him in the belly.

Then both Crips ran from the patio and out through the nightclub's front door as people screamed and an ambulance was called. The young Arab lay thrashing and bled out, displaying no signs of life even before the RA and the first black-and-whites arrived. Still, he was taken straight to Hollywood Presbyterian Hospital while a paramedic worked on him futilely.

It was B.M. Driscoll and Benny Brewster who sealed off the area and kept as many actual eyewitnesses in place as they could, but the nightclub had started emptying fast after word got out about the stabbing. When Andi McCrea and Brant Hinkle arrived (in separate cars so as to stay discreet), Benny Brewster and B.M. Driscoll were writing down information from half a dozen of the Arabs and two of their American girlfriends, who were crying.

Benny Brewster briefed Andi by pointing out the party promoter, Maurice Wooley, a very worried black man who was sitting at the far end of the now-empty bar drinking a tall glass of Jack. He was plump, in his midfifties and wearing a conservative, double-breasted gray suit. He was also bleary-eyed from the booze.

Benny said to him, 'Mr. Wooley, this is Detective McCrea. Tell her about the homie that did the stabbing.'

'I really don't know much about him,' the promoter said to Andi. 'He's jist somebody from Jordan Downs, where I grew up, is all. I don't live down there no more.'

'I understand he's your cousin,' Andi said.

'A much younger cousin to my play cousin,' the promoter said quickly. 'I don't know his real name.'

Benny Brewster abruptly changed tack, glared at him, and said, 'So what's your cousin to your play cousin's street name? Whadda you call him?'

The promoter's jowls waddled slightly and he said, 'Doobie D. That's all I ever did call him, Doobie D. I swear on my momma's grave.'

Benny scowled and said, 'Maybe your momma has room for one more in there.'

Andi said, 'What's his phone number?'

'I dunno,' the promoter said, twisting his zircon ring nervously, glancing every few seconds at the tall black cop, who looked about ready to grab him by the throat.

Andi said, 'This officer tells me you invited him here as your guest tonight.'

'That's 'cause I run into him on the street when I went to visit my momma. He said he wanna go to one of them Hollywood parties I promote. And me, I'm a fool. I say, okay, when I get one, I'm gonna let you know.

So I get this job and I let him know and I comp him in here as my guest. With one of his crew. And look at the grief I get.'

'If you don't have his number, how did you reach him?'

'I jist have his e-mail address,' the promoter said, handing Andi his cell phone. 'His cell company is one of them that you can e-mail or phone.'

When they were finished at the Gulag and ready to go, Andi was approached by a man with an obvious hairpiece and a peculiar smile. He extended his hand to both detectives and said, 'I am Dmitri Sikhonov, proprietor of the Gulag. I am sick to my heart from the terrible think that has een-wolved my club tonight. I shall be of service if you need any-think. Any-think at all.'

He gave them his card and bowed slightly.

'We may have some questions for you tomorrow,' Andi said.

'On the back of the card is my cell number,' he said. 'Anytime you wish to call Dmitri. Please, I shall be at your service.'

After getting back to the station, Andi Googled Doobie D's Internet provider from the text message. Then she left a phone message with the provider, requesting that the customer's name and phone number be pulled up, with the assurance that a search warrant would be faxed to them in the morning before the provider faxed the account information to her.

Andi said to Brant, 'We'll write a three-page search warrant and run it over to the Hollywood court tomorrow. Have you ever done it?'

'I'm real rusty,' he said.

'The provider will triangulate from the cell site towers. If we're real lucky and Doobie D uses his phone, the provider will call us every hour or so to tell us where he is. It's like a GPS on the cell phone. If he disposes of the cell, we're outta luck.'

'Are we gonna finally get home to get the rest of our night's sleep, do you think?'

Looking at those green eyes of his, she said, 'Is that all you're thinking about, sleep?'

'It's *one* of the things I'm thinking about,' he said.

SIXTEEN

The Oracle showed up at roll call that Thursday evening with a detective whom most of them had seen around the station and a few of the older cops knew by name.

The Oracle said, 'Okay, listen up. This is Detective Chernenko. He has a few things to say to you, and it's important.'

Viktor stood before them in his usual rumpled suit with food stains on the lapels and said, 'Good evening to you. I am investigating the jewelry store two-eleven where your Officer Takara was so very brave. And I also have very much interest in the two-eleven of three days ago at the ATM where the guard was killed. I am thinking that the same two people did both of them and now everybody agrees with me.

'What I wish is that you watch out for anybody who might be stealing from a mailbox. It is a crime very typical of addicts, so you might watch for tweakers who are hanging around the blue mailboxes on the corners of the streets. Especially in the area of Gower south of Hollywood Boulevard. If you find a suspect, look for a device like string and tape that they use to fish in a mailbox. If you find nothing, please write a good FI on the suspect and leave it for me at end-of-watch. Any question?'

Wesley Drubb turned and glanced at Hollywood Nate who looked sheepish, obviously thinking what Wesley was thinking.

Fausto Gamboa, the old man of the midwatch, said, 'Why Gower south of the boulevard, Viktor? Can you share it with us?'

'Yes, it is no big secret, Fausto,' Viktor said. 'It is a very small clue. I believe that information about the jewels was learned from a letter stolen from a mailbox there on Gower.'

Wesley Drubb looked at Hollywood Nate again but couldn't wait to see if Nate was going to admit that they might have lost a lead several days ago. Wesley raised his hand.

The Oracle said, 'Yeah, Drubb. Got a question?'

Wesley said, 'Last week we got a call about two homeless guys fighting on Hollywood Boulevard. One of them said that a couple weeks before, he saw a guy and a woman stealing mail from a blue mailbox a few blocks south of Hollywood Boulevard on Gower.'

That didn't elicit too much excitement in itself but Viktor was mildly interested and said, 'Did he provide more details than that?'

Looking at Nate again. 'Yes, he did. He said the guy was driving an old blue Pinto. And his partner was a woman. And he heard the woman call him Freddy or Morley.'

'Thank you, Officer,' Viktor said. 'I will check recent FIs for the name of Freddy and the name of Morley, but of course that will not be easy.'

The Oracle saw Wesley glance at Hollywood Nate again, and he said to Wesley, 'I think you're not through, Drubb. Was there something more?'

'Yes, Sarge,' Wesley said. 'The homeless guy had a card with the mail thief's license number written on it.'

Now Viktor's mouth dropped open. 'Fantastic!' he said. 'Please present me with this card, Officer!'

Wesley looked sheepish, and being loyal to his partner said, 'I'm afraid I gave the card back to him.'

Hollywood Nate spoke up then, saying, 'I told him to give it back. I figured, what the hell, just some tweakers stealing mail, happens all the time. It was my fault, not Drubb's.'

'We're not talking fault here,' said the Oracle. 'What was the name of the homeless guy with the card? Where can Detective Chernenko find him?'

'They call him Trombone Teddy,' Nate said. 'We wrote an FI on him and the other homeless geezer who knocked him on his ass. But neither one of them has a real address. They don't live anywhere, guys like that.'

The Oracle said to Hollywood Nate, 'Weiss, you and Drubb are on a special detail tonight. Don't clear for calls. Just stay off the air and go out there and find Trombone Teddy. Get that license number for Detective Chernenko.'

'I'm sorry, Sarge,' a chastened Hollywood Nate said.

'Do not feel too badly, Officer,' Viktor said. 'These suspects are no doubt lying down low for a few days but soon must act. Our balls are in their court.'

On very busy nights the midwatch units sometimes compared notes for who would get the BHI prize for Bizarre Hollywood Incident of the evening. Six-X-Thirty-two got an honorable mention for a call to east Hollywood, where an Eighteenth Street gang member was loitering by a liquor store with two other homies. A Lebanese store clerk got scared because the guy obviously was hiding something large under his sweatshirt. In the age of terrorism the clerk was afraid that the Eighteenth Street cruisers might be getting ready to bomb his store because he'd once called the cops on one of their crew who had shoplifted a bottle of gin.

Flotsam and Jetsam were the responders, and they had the three cruisers against the wall of the liquor store, assisted by Hollywood Nate and

Wesley Drubb, who were tired of looking for Trombone Teddy. Wesley was thrilled that they'd been close enough to provide cover when gang members were involved.

With flashlights and neon from the store lighting him up, the shortest homie, a head-shaved, tattoo-covered twenty-one-year-old in baggy walking shorts and an enormous cut-off sweatshirt, was looking over his shoulder at them. The cops liked the homie low-slung baggies because they often fell down and tripped them when they ran from cops. But this cruiser had something huge bulging from his chest.

Flotsam drew his nine and holding it down by his leg, said, 'Okay, homes, turn around and raise up your sweatshirt real slow. Let's see what you're hiding.'

When he did, they saw the yellow pages of the Los Angeles telephone directory taped to his chest with elastic wrap.

'What in the hell is that?' Flotsam said.

'It's a phone book,' the cruiser said.

'I know it's a phone book. But why do you have it taped to your chest?'

The gangster looked around and said, 'An old *veterano* from White Fence is after me, man. You think I'm gonna just stand around and take a bullet without some protection?'

'Bro, do you know what you've done here?' Jetsam said to him. 'I think you can take this nationwide. You've just designed an affordable bulletproof vest for the inner city!'

On Saturday, two days after Cosmo and Ilya had hidden the stolen car and the money at the house of Farley Ramsdale, Cosmo decided that they had hidden out as long as they dared. He had phoned Gregori at the junkyard that morning and arranged for one of Gregori's Mexicans to drive the tow truck to Farley's address. Cosmo insisted that timing was important and that the truck should arrive at 7 p.m.

'Why do you buy an old car that will not operate?' Gregori asked him in Armenian.

'For Ilya. We need two cars,' Cosmo said. 'I will give you the repair job and pay three hundred dollars for the tow because it is on Saturday evening. Also, I shall tip your driver another fifty if he arrives at precisely seven p.m.'

'You are generous,' Gregori said. 'And when do you return to me the spare key for my yard that I left with Ilya?'

'On Monday morning,' Cosmo said. 'When I come to see how much repairs the Mazda needs.'

'All right, Cosmo,' Gregori said. 'My driver is named Luís. He speaks pretty good English. He will tow the car to our yard.'

'Thank you, my brother,' Cosmo said. 'I shall see you on Monday.'

When he finished his call to Gregori, Ilya, who was lying on the bed smoking and staring at an old MGM musical on TV, said, 'So today you do what you do?'

'You wish to hear my plan, Ilya?'

'I know I say do not tell me. I have a change of mind about some things. Now I wish you to tell how you get rid of the car and get our money. Do not tell me more than that.'

'Okay, Ilya,' he said. 'I shall be at the house of Farley at seven o'clock to help truck driver to take away the car. I shall give to truck driver fifty dollars to call me when he get the car to junkyard of Gregori. If he do not call me, I shall know that police have him and stolen car he is towing. Then we take our money and our diamonds and fly to San Francisco and never come back.'

She said, 'But maybe yesterday or today Farley has found the car or found our money and made call to police and they are there to wait for you.'

'If I do not phone you at seven-thirty that all is okay, you take taxi to airport and fly to San Francisco with diamonds. And God bless you. Please have good life. I shall never tell the police nothing about you. Never.'

'You take big risk, Cosmo.'

'Yes, but I think is okay. I think Farley and Olive do not look in garage or under house. All they look for is drugs. Nothing else.'

'How you can be sure that Farley and Olive will not be there at the house when you go there at seven o'clock, Cosmo?'

'Now you ask question you say you not wish to know.'

'You are correct. Do not tell me.'

The unanswered question had a simple answer. Cosmo was going to phone Farley to arrange a business meeting and then arrive at Farley's at six p.m., carrying a canvas bag. In the bag he would have his gun, a roll of duct tape and a kitchen knife that he had sharpened when Ilya had gone to the liquor store for cigarettes. If Farley and Olive were at home, he would knock, be admitted on the pretext of paying the blackmail money, take them prisoner at gunpoint and tape their wrists and their mouths. Then cut their throats. Just another addict murder, the police would think. Probably a drug deal gone bad.

If for some reason Farley and Olive could not be home at the appointed hour, there was an alternate plan that involved the spare key to the junkyard. They would be lured there tomorrow by a call from Gregori about buying more key cards. Cosmo would ambush them there and dispose of their bodies somewhere in east Los Angeles. Just another addict murder.

As for the car, if the tow driver phoned his cell, telling him that the towing had been accomplished, Cosmo would go to Gregori's junkyard on Monday morning and tell Gregori he'd changed his mind about repairing the car and ask him to crush the Mazda for scrap. For one thousand dollars cash Cosmo was sure that Gregori would ask no questions and do it.

He could not see a flaw in his plan. It was foolproof. He wished that Ilya would permit him to tell her about all of it. She would be impressed by how much thought he had put into it. The only thing that worried him was that Dmitri might be so angry Cosmo hadn't called him that he would think he was being betrayed and maybe send Russian thugs looking for him.

His hands were shaking at 5:15 p.m. while driving to Farley's house. He decided to make the two crucial calls that would possibly decide his fate. The first was to the cell number that Dmitri said was the only one he should use after the job was done.

It rang five times, and then, 'Yes.'

'Dmitri, it is me.'

'I know who,' Dmitri said. 'I am think-ink that you had run away from me. That will be a stupid think to do.'

'No, no, Dmitri. We are being quiet for two, three days.'

'Do not tell me more. When do I see you for all of our business? You have thinks for me.'

'There is more I must complete, Dmitri. Maybe I come to you to-night.'

'I like that,' Dmitri said.

'Maybe I must wait for Monday morning.'

'I do not like that.'

'There are two peoples—'

'Enough!' Dmitri said, interrupting him. 'I do not want to hear about your business. If you do not call me tonight, I shall be here on Monday. If I do not see you on Monday, you are very stupid person.'

'Thank you, Dmitri,' Cosmo said. 'I shall be correct in my business with you.'

After hanging up, Cosmo made the second crucial call, to Farley Ramsdale's cell number, but got only his voice mail. It was the first time this had ever happened. The addict never slept and was always open for business deals. It staggered him. He would try again in thirty minutes. He still had the alternate plan for Farley and Olive, but this did not bode well. He had all of the killing tools with him and he was ready.

Where in the hell was Olive? She knew they were almost down to their last dollar and had to work the mailboxes or maybe try again to pass some of the bogus money they still had. Or just go to a RadioShack or Best Buy and try to boost a DVD player to sell at the cyber café. Things were that desperate!

But where was the stupid bitch? All Farley knew was she went out searching the goddamn neighborhood for that crazy Mabel's fucking cat! He was about to go out looking for her, when he got a cell call from Little Bart.

When he recognized the voice he said, 'Whadda you want?'

'I felt bad the way things were left between us,' Little Bart said.

'So you're calling to say you wanna send me flowers?'

'I wanna do a deal with you.'

'What kinda deal?'

'I want you to deliver a couple of brand-new computers to a real nice house on the west side of Laurel Canyon.'

'Deliver them how?'

'In your car.'

'Why don't you deliver them?'

'I lost my driver's license on a DUI.'

'That's the only reason?'

'And I hurt my back and can't carry them.'

'They ain't very heavy. Tell you what, how about I deliver in your car?'

'They impounded my car when they popped me.'

'Uh-huh. So how much do I get for this delivery?'

'Fifty bucks.'

'Good-bye, Bart,' Farley said.

'No, wait! A hundred bucks. It'll take you a half hour, tops.'

'One fifty.'

'Farley, I'm not making much on this. They aren't the very best top-of-the-line computers.'

'I don't risk my ass delivering hot computers that you're too chickenshit to deliver for less than one twenty-five.'

'Okay, deal.'

'When?'

'Can you meet me at Hollywood and Fairfax in twenty minutes? I'll be standing on the corner and I'll walk and you follow me to where you pick up and deliver. The merchandise is in a garage there. Then when you got it, I'll ride with you to the drop-off address.'

'Why will you walk to the pickup location instead of riding with me?'

'I can't be anywhere near this pickup. I can't explain.'

'And you'll have the money?'

'Half. I'll give you the other half when the job's done.'

'Can you make it later? I can't find that goddamn bitch of mine.'

'You don't need her.'

'Who the hell you think does the heavy lifting?' Farley said. 'And she goes in first in case there's anything chancy going on.'

'We can't wait for her. Twenty minutes, Farley,' Bart said.

Farley looked all over the street but still no Olive. He made a quick stop at Mabel's and found the old witch reading Tarot cards in which Olive believed with all her heart.

Farley peered through the rusted screen. 'Hey, Mabel, you seen Olive?'

'Yes, she's out looking for Tillie. I think Tillie might be pregnant. She's acting peculiar and roaming around as though she's looking for a nest. She was once a feral cat, you know. I took her in and tamed her.'

Farley said, 'Yeah, I'm sure you got a Humane Society award. If you see Olive, tell her I had to do a quick job and she should wait for me at home.'

'All right, Farley,' Mabel said. 'It might interest you to know that the cards don't look good for you,' she added. 'Maybe you should stay home too.'

She heard him mumble 'Crazy old bitch' when he left her porch.

Olive was in the backyard of a neighbor six houses away, looking for Tillie and chatting with the neighbor about the beautiful white camellias that bordered her property. And Olive just loved the pink and white azaleas that climbed the fence. Olive told her that someday she hoped to have a garden. The woman offered to teach Olive the basics and to get her started with the proper seeds and a few young plants.

Olive thought she heard Farley's Corolla, excused herself, and running to the street saw his taillights at the stop sign. She yelled but he didn't hear her and was gone. Olive then went home, hoping he wasn't mad at her.

There he was on the northeast corner of Hollywood and Fairfax, jumping around like he had to take a leak. Or had to score some tweak, more likely, Farley figured. He didn't like any part of this. Little Bart couldn't drive because he had no license? When did that ever stop a tweaker from driving? He couldn't carry a computer because his back hurt? He couldn't ride in Farley's car to the garage where the computers were? What was this shit all about?

Little Bart walked over to his car and said, 'Just follow me real slow for half a block. When I get to the house, I'll point with my finger behind my back. Then you drive into the driveway and go to the garage. The door will open manually. Get the computers and pick me up two blocks north.'

While he was driving slowly behind Bart, he missed Olive more than he had in the eighteen months they'd been together. This was a very bad deal. Bart was scared to pick up the merchandise, which meant that Bart didn't trust the thief who'd stolen the computers, or the fence who'd hired Bart to deliver them.

If Olive were here, there'd be no problem. He'd drop her off at the pickup address and let her go into the garage and check it out. If the cops were there and grabbed her, he'd just keep on moving down the road. If there was one thing he was sure of, Olive would never rat him out. She'd take the hit and do the time if she had to and come to him when she got out of jail, just as though nothing had happened.

But Olive wasn't here. And that fucking Little Bart was pointing at a

193

house, a modest one for this neighborhood. Then Bart kept walking north. Farley parked across from the house and looked at the garage.

The house wasn't unlike his own. It was in that ubiquitous California style that everyone calls Spanish, which means nothing other than tile roof and stucco walls. The longer he looked at it, the worse he felt about the whole arrangement.

Farley got out of the car and walked across the street to the house. He went to the front door and rang the bell. When he got no answer, he went to the side door, which was only forty feet from the garage, banged on the door, and yelled, 'Olive, you there? Hellooooo? Olive?'

It was then that two Hollywood Division detectives came out of the garage, badged him, put him against the wall, patted him down and then dragged him back into the garage. There was nothing in the garage except a workbench, some tools and tires, and two boxes containing new computers.

'What is this?' he said.

'You tell us,' the older detective said.

'My girlfriend, Olive, went to lunch with a pal of hers and gave me the pal's address. This is it.'

'Right,' the younger detective said. 'What've you been in jail for?'

'Petty kid stuff is all,' Farley said. 'What's this all about?'

'You been busted for burglary?'

'No.'

'Receiving?'

'Receiving what?'

'Don't fuck with us. Receiving stolen property.'

'No, just kid stuff. Drug possession. Petty theft a couple times.'

'Are you going to use the S-O-D-D-I defense?'

'What's that?'

'Some other dude did it.'

'I'm innocent!' Farley cried.

'Well, partner,' the younger detective said to the other. 'Let's take kid stuff here to the station. Looks like our surprise party is blown.'

'Hey, man,' Farley said, 'I musta wrote down the wrong address is all. My girlfriend Olive's gonna be looking for me. If you'll let me call her, she'll tell you.'

'Turn around, kid stuff,' the older detective said. 'Put your hands behind your back.'

After they handcuffed Farley, they led him out to the street, where a detective car drove up from wherever it had been hidden. Then they searched his Corolla, but of course it was clean. There wasn't even a roach in the ashtray.

When they got to the station, Farley saw some movie posters on a wall. What the fuck kind of police station has movie posters on the wall? Farley thought. And how did he get in this horror flick? All he knew was, if he'd had Olive with him, he wouldn't be here. That dumb bitch just got his ass busted!

It was after five o'clock and Farley hadn't come home and hadn't called. Olive was tired and she was very hungry. She remembered what Mabel had said about saving some food for her. She wondered if Mabel might let her help cook the meal. She'd like that, and getting to eat and chat with Mabel.

When she got to Mabel's the old woman was delighted to see her.

'I'm sorry, Mabel,' she said. 'I can't find Tillie.'

'Don't worry, dear,' Mabel said. 'She'll turn up. She always does. She's still a bit of a wild thing. Tillie's got a touch of Gypsy in her soul.'

'Would you like me to help you cook?'

'Oh, yes,' Mabel said. 'If you'll promise to stay and have supper with me.'

'Thank you, Mabel,' Olive said. 'I'll be real happy to join you for supper.'

'Then we'll play gin. If you don't know how, never mind, I'll teach you. I know all about cards. Did I ever tell you I used to make good money telling fortunes with cards? That was sixty-five years ago.'

'Really?'

'Really. There are certain legal technicalities about foretelling the future that I didn't follow. I was arrested twice and taken to Hollywood Station for ignoring those silly technicalities.'

'You, arrested?' Olive couldn't imagine it.

'Oh, yes,' Mabel said. 'I was a bit of a naughty girl in my time. The old police station was a lovely building constructed in nineteen thirteen, the year my parents got married. When I was born, they named me for the silent-screen star Mabel Normand. I never had any siblings. You know, I used to date a policeman from Hollywood Station. He was the one who arrested me the second time and persuaded me to stop telling fortunes for money. He was killed in the war. One week after D-day.'

Loving Mabel's stories and gossip about the old days in Hollywood, Olive hated to interrupt her, but she thought about Farley and said, 'Mabel, let me run home and leave a note for Farley so he'll know where I'm at. Be right back!'

'Hurry, dear,' Mabel said. 'I'll tell you lots of tales about life in the golden age of Hollywood. And we'll play cards. This is going to be such fun!'

SEVENTEEN

Cosmo Betrossian cursed the traffic. He cursed Los Angeles for being the most car-dependent, traffic-choked city in the world. He cursed the Georgian bartender who gave him the stolen car that almost got him captured. But most of all he cursed Farley Ramsdale and his stupid woman. He sat in traffic on East Sunset Boulevard looking at all of the signs around him in the languages of the Far East, and he cursed them too.

Then he heard the siren and for a few seconds it terrified him until he saw an ambulance weaving through traffic on the wrong side of Sunset, obviously trying to get to the traffic accident that had him gridlocked. Glancing repeatedly at his Rolex knockoff, he cursed.

First, they left him in an interrogation room for what seemed like an hour, only letting him go to the bathroom once and then watching him piss, just like the goddamn probation officer who used to make him piss in a bottle twice a month. With no sympathy for the fact that it was hard to piss with someone watching to make sure you piss from your own dick and not from a bottle of clean piss stashed in your underwear.

Then one of the two detectives came in and gave him a bad-cop interrogation about a goddamn warehouse burglary of electronic equipment that he knew nothing about. Then the other detective played good cop and came in and gave him a cup of coffee. Then the bad cop took over and played the game all over again until Farley's hands were shaking and his pulse was vibrating.

Farley knew they didn't buy the wrong-address story, but he stuck with it. And he was pretty sure they were starting to think he hadn't been involved in the warehouse burglary but was just some tweaker with exactly $3.65 in his pocket, hired only to pick up and deliver.

He would have given up Little Bart instantly if he thought it would help him, but something in good cop's tone last time around told him he was going to be released. Except that bad cop came in and walked him to a holding tank with a wooden bench, where they locked him in. And every cop walking by could look through the big glass window and gawk at him like he was a fucking spider monkey at the Griffith Park zoo.

When Watch 5 left roll call at 6 p.m., several of them passed by the holding tank and did gawk at him.

'Hey, Benny,' B.M. Driscoll said to his partner. 'Is that the tweaker we wrote the ticket to?'

'Yeah,' Benny Brewster said. Then he tapped on the glass and said to Farley, 'What happened, man? They catch you selling ice?'

'Fuck you,' Farley mumbled, and when Benny laughed and walked away, Farley growled, 'You're the one oughtta be in a zoo with the rest of the silverbacks, you fucking ape.'

Budgie and Fausto saw Benny talking to someone in the holding tank, and Budgie looked in and said, 'Fausto, that's the guy we FI'd at the taco stand.'

Fausto looked at Farley and said, 'Oh yeah, the tweaker with the skinny girlfriend. Bet they got him doing a deal at Pablo's. They never learn, they never change.'

When Hollywood Nate and Wesley walked past the holding tank, Nate heard Fausto's remark, took a look inside, and said, 'Shit, everyone knows that dude. Hey, Wesley, check this out.'

Wesley looked in and said, 'Oh yeah. That's what's-his-name – Rimsdale? No, Ramsdale.'

'Farley,' Nate said. 'Like the old movie star Farley Granger.'

'Who?' Wesley said.

'Never mind,' Nate said. 'Let's go look for Trombone Teddy. We gotta find him or I'll have stress dreams tonight about chasing an old geezer who keeps holding me off with the slide of his gold trombone.'

'Do you really have dreams like that?'

'No,' Nate said, 'but it would make a good dream sequence in a screenplay, don't you think?'

One of the sergeants on Watch 2 was a forty-year-old black woman, Wilma Collins. She had a good reputation with the troops but had a persistent weight problem that the coppers at Hollywood Station joked about. She wasn't actually obese but they called her a 'leather stretcher.' Her Sam Browne had a lot to hold in place.

Everyone knew that a few hours before end-of-watch, Sergeant Collins liked to sneak into IHOP and load up on buttermilk pancakes swimming in butter, with sausages and fried eggs and butter-drenched biscuits. They made lots of cholesterol and clogged-arteries jokes about Sergeant Collins.

When the surfer team were loading their war bags and getting ready to hit the streets, the entire parking lot and the watch commander's office suddenly erupted. Some of those who heard it had to sit for a moment until they could gain control. It became a Hollywood Station moment.

It seems that Sergeant Collins had left her rover behind on the counter at IHOP, because a message was sent on the Hollywood frequency by a

Mexican busboy who had keyed the mike and talked into the rover.

The busboy said, 'Hello, hello! Chubby black police lady? Hello, hello! You leave radio here! Hello! Chubby black lady? You there, please? Hello, hello!'

Hollywood Nate and Wesley Drubb didn't say much to each other when they left roll call. Nate was driving and Wesley had never seen him so intent on watching the street.

At last Wesley said, 'I had to mention Trombone Teddy at roll call.'

'I know you did,' Nate said. 'The real mistake I made was I shoulda told you to take Teddy's license number and at least write the info on the FI card.'

'I shoulda done that on my own,' Wesley said.

'You're barely off probation,' Nate said. 'You're still in the yessir boot-mode. It was my fault.'

'We'll find Teddy,' Wesley said.

'I hope he still has the card,' Nate said. Then, 'Hey, it was a business card, right? What was the business?'

'A Chinese restaurant. Ching or Chan, something like that.'

'House of Chang?'

'Yeah, that was it!'

'Okay, let's pay them a visit.'

The tow truck was parked in front of Farley Ramsdale's house and the Mexican driver was knocking on the door when Cosmo Betrossian came squealing down the street in his old Cadillac. The traffic had disrupted everything.

He got out and ran toward the porch, saying to the driver, 'I am friend of Gregori. I am the one.'

'Nobody home here,' the Mexican said.

'Is not important,' Cosmo said. 'Come. Let us get the car.'

He ran to the garage, opened the termite-eaten door, and was relieved to see that the garage was just as he'd left it.

'Let us push it out to the street,' Cosmo said. 'We must work fast. I have important business.'

The Mexican and Cosmo easily pushed the car back down the driveway, Cosmo jumping in to steer after they got it going. The driver knew his job and in a few minutes had the Mazda hooked up and winched. It was all that Cosmo could do to keep from running back up the driveway and snatching the big can full of money from under the house.

Before he got in the truck to drive away, the driver said to Cosmo, 'I call you in thirty minute?'

'No, I need more time. Call me in one hour. Traffic very bad tonight. I give you time to get to the yard of Gregori. Then you call, okay?'

'Okay,' the Mexican said, waiting for the promised bonus.

Cosmo opened his wallet and gave the driver fifty dollars and said, 'Put it back where junk cars go. Okay?'

As soon as the truck was halfway down the block, Cosmo went to the trunk of the Cadillac and removed the bag of killing tools. He was going to wait at least an hour for them to show up.

He walked quickly back up the driveway to the rear yard of the house and was shocked to see the little access panel hanging open. He dropped the bag and threw himself onto the dirt, crawling under the house. The can of money was gone!

Cosmo screamed an Armenian curse, got up, took the gun from the bag, and ran to the back porch. He didn't even bother slipping the lock with his credit card like last time. He kicked the flimsy door open and ran inside, prepared to kill anybody in the house after he tortured the truth out of them.

There was no one. He saw a note on the kitchen table in a scrawl. It said, 'Gone to eat with Mabel. Will bring delishus supper for you.'

His alternate plan to lure them to Gregori's junkyard, where they could easily be killed, was finished. They had his money. They would never go near him now except to collect the blackmail money from the diamond robbery. They would ask for even more now that they knew about the ATM robbery and the murder of the guard. They must have discovered the Mazda too. Farley had stolen their money, and he would want more money to keep his mouth shut about everything.

Maybe all he could do was give the diamonds to Farley. Give him every-thing and tell him to do the deal with Dmitri himself. Then beg Dmitri to kill both addicts after they were forced to tell where the money was, and beg Dmitri to be fair with the money split even though so many things had gone wrong. After all, if Dmitri's Georgian bartender hadn't given him a stolen car that could barely run, this would not have happened.

Or maybe he should just go home and get Ilya and the diamonds and head for the airport. It was too much for him to work out. He needed Ilya. She was a very smart Russian and he was far out of his depth. He would do whatever she wanted him to do.

Cosmo took his killing bag and went out to his car. He had never been so demoralized in his life. If the Cadillac failed to start, he would just take the pistol from the bag and shoot himself. But it started and he drove home to Ilya. When he was only two blocks from their apartment his cell rang.

He answered and the driver's voice said, 'Mister, I am at Gregori's with the car. No problem. Everything okay.'

The stolen car was okay, but of course everything else was far from okay.

*

At 7:15 p.m. Farley was released from the holding tank and told that he was free to go.

Bad cop said to him, 'We know you're connected to those computers, but right now we're gonna let you walk. I suspect you'll see us again.'

'Speaking of walk,' Farley said. 'My car's there where you grabbed me. How about a ride back up there?'

'You got a lotta 'tude, dude,' bad cop said. 'We're not running a taxi service.'

'Man, you hassle me, you keep me here for hours when I ain't done nothing wrong. The least you can do is take me back to my car.'

The Oracle heard the bitching and came out of the sergeant's office, saying to Farley, 'Where do you need to go?'

Farley looked at the old sergeant and said, 'Fairfax, just north of Hollywood Boulevard.'

The Oracle said, 'I'm going out now. I'll give you a lift.'

Fifteen minutes later, when the Oracle dropped him at his car, Farley said, 'Thanks a lot, Sergeant. You're okay.'

The Oracle offered the Hollywood mantra: 'Stay real, Farley. Stay real.' But he knew that this tweaker would not. Who in Hollywood ever did?

'Teddy?' Mrs. Chang said when Hollywood Nate had a Latino busboy call her from the kitchen. 'He eat here?'

'He's a bum,' Nate said.

'Bum?' she said, grappling with the English meaning.

'Homeless,' Wesley said. 'Street person.'

'Oh, street person,' she said. 'Him I know. Teddy. Yes.'

'Does he come here?'

'Sometime he come to back door,' Mrs. Chang said. 'Come at maybe seven o'clock, sometime later. And we give him food we got to throw away. Teddy. Yes. He sit in kitchen and eat. Nice man. Quiet. We feel sorry.'

'When did you last see him?' Wesley asked.

'Tuesday night maybe. Hard to remember.'

Nate began writing in his notebook and said, 'When he comes again, I want you to call this number. Ask that Six-X-Seventy-two come right away. I've written it down for you. We don't want to arrest him. We just have to talk to him. Understand?'

'Yes, I call.'

The house was dark when Farley got home, and the garage door was open. Why would Olive go in the garage? There was nothing in there but junk.

He unlocked the front door and entered, yelling, 'Olive! You here?'

She was not, and he went into the kitchen to see if there was any orange juice left and found the back door kicked open!

'Son of a bitch!' he said.

This was the first time that burglars had struck his house, although several houses on the block had been hit by daytime thieves in the past two years. But the TV was still there. He went into the bedroom and saw that the radio–CD player was still there. Nobody had ransacked the bedroom drawers. This wasn't like house breakers. It wasn't the way he worked when he himself was a daytime burglar fifteen years ago.

Then he saw the note on the kitchen table. Mabel. He should have known. The fucking old ghost probably was reading tarot cards for Olive and time had gotten away from the skinny moron. He went into the bedroom to strip down and take a shower and then he saw that something was different. The closet was half empty. All of Olive's clothes were missing, including the jacket he'd shoplifted for her Christmas present. He opened the drawer and saw that her underwear and socks were gone too. She'd bailed on him!

The note. He ran out the front door and across the street to Mabel's. It was such a warm evening that her door was open, and he could see that the TV was on. He put his hands up to the screen door to peer inside and said, 'Mabel!'

The old woman shuffled in from the back bedroom of the cottage, wearing pajamas, a bathrobe, and fuzzy slippers, and said, 'Farley? What're you doing here?'

'Do you know where Olive is?'

'Why, no.'

'She left a note saying she was having supper with you.'

'Yes, she did. And Olive found Tillie under your house where she'd made a nice little den for herself. Tillie's in my bedroom now, the little brat. I never have completely domesticated her.'

'Did Olive say where she was going when she left?'

'Yes, home.'

Farley had to sit down and ponder that when he got back to the house. Everything was going wrong lately. His entire world was upside down. Without a dollar to her name, that toothless fucking scarecrow had abandoned his ass! This was impossible! That imbecile Olive Oyl had actually dumped Farley Ramsdale, who'd given her everything!

This time it was Cosmo who was lying on the bed trying to quell a throbbing headache. He had quickly briefed Ilya on what had happened and then fell on his knees beside her chair and kissed her hands.

He is beaten, Ilya thought. Cosmo is crying for Mommy. He would never strike her again.

Ilya prepared her third glass of hot tea and lit a cigarette with the butt of the last and finally said, 'Cosmo, all is a fuckup.'

'Yes, Ilya,' he murmured painfully.

'I think we must pack the suitcase and make ready to fly away.'

'Yes, Ilya,' Cosmo said. 'What you say, I do.'

'On other hand,' she said, looking from one palm to the other for emphasis, 'we do not know for absolute truth that Farley has our money.'

'Ilya, please!' Cosmo said. 'The money is gone. Farley is gone. I cannot get to Farley with cell. Farley always have cell with him. He is addict. Addict must have cell.'

'One way we find out,' she said. 'Sit up, Cosmo!'

He obeyed instantly.

'Call Farley. Go with plan. Tell him Gregori need key cards. Many more. Will pay top money. Let us hear what he shall say.'

Cosmo's head was aching too much for this but it was impossible not to obey her. He felt as though he was back in Soviet Armenia and the Comrade Chairman himself had spoken. He was afraid of her now. He dialed.

'Hello!' Farley yelled into his cell.

Cosmo was stunned. He couldn't speak for a moment and Farley said, 'Olive? Is that you?'

Looking at Ilya, Cosmo said, 'Is me, Farley.'

'Cosmo?' Farley said. 'I thought it was Olive. That fucking tweaker has up and disappeared!'

'Olive?' Cosmo said. 'Gone?'

He saw the wry smile turn up the corners of Ilya's mouth, and he said, 'You know where she go to?'

'No,' Farley said. 'The cunt. I ain't got a clue.'

Ilya was mouthing the words 'Ask him,' and Cosmo said, 'I very sorry, Farley. You know Gregori? He need more cards right away.'

'Key cards? Cosmo, you forgot that you and me got a little business deal coming up? You think I'm gonna keep waiting? You think I'm gonna fuck around with key cards?'

'Please, Farley,' Cosmo said. 'Do this for me. I owe big favor to Gregori. Just drop off cards at his junkyard tonight. He work to midnight. He will give you fast hundred fifty. You buy crystal.'

The word 'crystal' struck a chord with Farley. He wanted to smoke ice more than he'd ever wanted anything in his life. This was the kind of deal where he desperately needed Olive. If she were here, he'd drive her over there to the junkyard and send her in. If Cosmo had a plan to waste them, he'd have to settle for Olive. Goddamn her!

'I only got about ten of the primo cards left,' Farley said.

'Is enough,' Cosmo said. 'Gregori got a bunch new worker who must have driving license. Gregori so cheap his old worker not stay long. Always new worker.'

'Is that dog in the yard?'

'I tell Gregori to tie up dog. No problem.'

'You tell Gregori to call me. If he says come, I come. He ain't a violent type. He's a businessman. You I ain't so sure about.'

'Okay, I call Gregori now,' Cosmo said. 'And if he say come?'

'Then I'll be there at nine o'clock. Tell Gregori to put the money in a bag and stick the bag between the links of the gate. If the money's there, I'll drive in and give him the cards.'

'Okay, Farley,' Cosmo said. Then he added, 'Call me if Olive come home.'

'Why?'

'I think I got good job for her.'

'You better have my big bucks this weekend, Cosmo,' Farley said. 'Let me worry about Olive if she comes home.'

When Cosmo closed the cell, Ilya took a great puff from her cigarette, sucked it into her lungs, and with her words enveloped in smoke clouds said, 'If he go to junkyard tonight, he don't know nothing about ATM robbery.'

'But I shall kill him anyways. The diamond blackmail shall end.'

'Blackmail still there, Cosmo. Olive has our money and Olive know all about both our jobs. Olive is full of danger for us. Not Farley so much.'

'But I shall kill him anyways?'

'Yes, he must die. Olive may give up the blackmail. She got lot of money now. She buy lot of drugs and die happy in two, three years.'

'Our money,' he said.

'Yes, Cosmo. She got our money, I think so. Call Gregori now. Say again and make him to believe you only scare Farley to pay a debt he owe you. Tell Gregori you will pay money for the Mazda on Monday.'

Before phoning Gregori, Cosmo said, 'Ilya, you tell me. When Gregori come to bring key to junkyard, you fuck him. No?'

'Of course, Cosmo,' she said. 'Why?'

'If he getting scared about Farley, scared about Mazda that I want to crush to scrap, is okay if I tell him you wish to make him glass of tea one more time? To make him calm?'

'Of course, Cosmo,' she said. 'My tea is best in all of Hollywood. Ask Gregori. Ask anybody who taste my tea.'

Six-X-Seventy-two got the call twenty minutes after they'd left the House of Chang. Hollywood Nate spun a U-ee and floored it. He craved redemption.

When they got back to the restaurant, Mrs. Chang tossed her head in the direction of the kitchen. And there they found Trombone Teddy sitting at the chopping block by the back door, happily scarfing down a huge bowl of pan-fried noodles.

'Teddy,' Nate said. 'Remember us?'

'I ain't causing no trouble,' he said. 'They invited me in here.'

'Nobody says you're causing trouble,' Nate said. 'A couple questions and you can sit and enjoy your noodles.'

Wesley said, 'Remember the fight you had on the boulevard? We're the officers that got the call. You gave me a card with a license number on it. Remember?'

'Oh yeah!' Teddy said, a noodle plastered to his beard. 'That son of a bitch sucker-punched me.'

'That's the night,' Nate said. 'Do you still have the card? With the license number?'

'Sure,' Teddy said. 'But nobody wants it.'

'We want it now,' Wesley said. Trombone Teddy put down his fork and searched inside his third layer of shirts, dug into a pocket with grimy fingers, and pulled out the House of Chang business card.

Wesley took it, looked at the license number, and nodded to Nate, who said, 'Teddy, what kind of car was it that the mail thief was driving?'

'An old blue Pinto,' Teddy said. 'Like I wrote down on the card.'

'And what did the guy look like?'

'I can't remember no more,' Teddy said. 'A white guy. Maybe thirty. Maybe forty. Nasty mouth. Insulted me. That's why I wrote down the license number.'

'And his companion?' Wesley said.

'A woman. That's all I can remember.'

'Would you recognize either of them if you saw them again?' Nate said.

'No, they was just dark shadows. He was just a dark shadow with a nasty mouth.'

'Tell us again what she called him,' Wesley said.

'I don't remember,' Teddy said.

'You told me Freddy,' Wesley said.

'Did I?'

'Or Morley?'

'If you say so. But it don't ring a bell now.'

'Have you seen them either before or after that?'

'Yeah, I saw them try to hustle a clerk in a store.'

'When?'

'A few days after he insulted me.'

'What store?'

'Coulda been like a Target store. Or maybe it was RadioShack. Or like a Best Buy store. I can't remember. I get around.'

'At least,' Nate said, 'you got another good look at them, right?'

'Yeah, but I still can't remember what they look like. They're white people. Maybe thirty years old. Or forty. But they could be fifty. I can't tell ages no more. You can check with the guy at the store. He gave me a ten-buck reward for telling him they were crooks. They had a bogus credit card. Or bogus money. Something like that.'

'Jesus,' Nate said, looking at Wesley in frustration.

Wesley said, 'If we can find the store and find the guy who saw them, at least you can say that they're the same two people who stole from the mailbox, isn't that right?'

'He stole from the mailbox,' Teddy said. 'She didn't. I got a feeling she's okay. He's a total asshole.'

Wesley said, 'If the detectives need to talk to you, where can they find you?'

'There's an old empty office building on that street on the east side of Hollywood Cemetery. I'm living there for now. But I come here a few nights a week for supper.'

'Can you remember anything else?' Hollywood Nate said, taking a ten-dollar bill from his wallet and putting it on the chopping block.

'Hell, half the time I can't remember what day it is,' Teddy said. Then he looked at them and said, 'What day is it, anyways?'

Viktor Chernenko was known for working late, especially with his obsession to solve the jewelry store robbery and the ATM robbery-murder, and most of the veteran cops from Hollywood Station were aware of it. Nate knew it and was busting stop signs and speeding to the station faster than he'd driven to the House of Chang.

They ran into the detective squad room and were overjoyed to see Viktor still there, typing on his computer keyboard.

'Viktor,' Nate said. 'Here it is!'

Viktor looked at the business card, at the license number and the words 'blue Pinto' written on it, and he said, 'My mail thief?'

Since he had been on the initial callout, Brant worked all day in southeast LA with Andi on the Gulag homicide. Doobie D, whom they had identified through data received from his cell provider, was Latelle Granville, a twenty-four-year-old member of the Crips with an extensive record for drug sales and weapons violations. He had begun using his cell in the afternoon.

With a team of detectives from Southeast Division assisting, the cell towers eventually triangulated him to the vicinity of a residence on 103rd Street known to be the family home of a Crips cruiser named Delbert Minton. He had a far more extensive record than Latelle Granville and turned out to be the Crip who had been fighting with the slain student. Both were arrested at Minton's without incident and taken back to Hollywood Station for interview and booking. Both Crips refused to speak and demanded to call their lawyers.

It had been a very long day, and the detectives were hungry and tired from working well into an overtime evening. Then Andi returned a phone call from a cocktail waitress, one of the people she'd interviewed at the Gulag on the night of the murder. At that time, the waitress, Angela Hawthorn, had told Andi she was at the service bar fetching drinks when the fight broke out and had seen nothing. So why was she calling now? Andi wondered.

'This is Detective McCrea,' Andi said when the woman answered her cell.

'Hello,' Angela Hawthorn said. 'I'm at home. I don't work at the Gulag anymore. Dmitri fired me because I wouldn't put out for one of his rich Russian customers. I have some information that might help you.'

'I'm listening,' Andi said.

'Up in the corner of the building by the window to Dmitri's office there's a video camera that sees everything on the smoking patio. During the party I'm pretty sure it was there like it always is. But when you showed up it wasn't there. Dmitri probably took it down so you wouldn't see it.'

'Why would he do that?'

'He's paranoid about bad publicity and cops and courtrooms. And he doesn't want trouble with black hoodlums. In fact, he doesn't want black customers. He just wouldn't want to be involved in your murder case. Anyways, if you get that camera from him I'll bet you'll see that black guy sticking the knife in that kid. Just keep my name out of it, okay?'

When Andi hung up, she said to Brant, 'Do you need money?'

'Why?'

'You're going to be getting even more overtime. There might be video at the Gulag with our murder shown right there on it!'

Brant looked around, but all the other detectives had gone home. Only the night-watch detective Compassionate Charlie was there, with his feet up on the desk, sucking his teeth as usual, reading the *LA Times* sports page.

'I'm all you got?' he said.

'Don't be a wuss. This is more fun than being an IA weasel, isn't it?'

'I don't know,' he said. 'I'm starting to miss the Burn Squad. At least I got fed every once in a while.'

'When we're all through tonight, I'm making you a very late supper with a bottle of good Pinot I've been saving. How's that sound?'

'Suddenly I'm renewed,' he said.

'One thing, though,' Andi said. 'I think I should call Viktor. We might find a Russian translator very useful if this nightclub owner starts lyin' and denyin' like he probably will. Viktor is a master at handling those people, a kick-ass skill he learned in the bad old days with the Red Army.'

'He's just getting home by now,' Brant said. 'He won't be pleased.'

'He owes me,' Andi said. 'Didn't I do a dumpster dive for him? Didn't it cost me a busted bra strap?'

Eavesdropping as usual, Compassionate Charlie said, 'Hey, you guys looking for Viktor? He left in a hell of a hurry with Hollywood Nate and that big kid Nate works with. I love to watch Viktor run. Like a bear on roller skates.'

EIGHTEEN

The blue Pinto was registered to a Samuel R. Culhane who lived on Winona Boulevard. Viktor Chernenko was sitting in the backseat of the black-and-white, concerned about whiplash with Hollywood Nate still driving in his high-speed redemption mode.

Wesley said to Viktor, 'You know, Detective, the only problem here is that the first time we talked to Trombone Teddy he said the guy's name sounded like Freddy or Morley.'

'Maybe Samuel sold the car to a Freddy,' Nate said. 'Stay positive.'

'Or lent the car to Morley,' Viktor added.

The house was almost a duplicate of Farley Ramsdale's old Hollywood bungalow except it was in good repair and had a small lawn in front with geraniums along the side of the house and a bed of petunias by the front porch.

Wesley ran to the rear of the house to prevent escape. It was dusk, and he didn't need a flashlight yet. He took cover behind the garage and waited.

Viktor took the lead and knocked, with Nate standing to his left.

Samuel R. Culhane wasn't as thin as Farley but he was in a late stage of methamphetamine addiction. He had pustules on his face and a permanent twitch at the corner of his right eye. He was several years older than Farley and balding, with a bad comb-over. And though he couldn't see Hollywood Nate standing beside the guy at the door, he knew instantly that Viktor was a cop.

'Yeah?' he said cautiously.

Viktor showed his badge and said, 'We need to talk to you.'

'Come back with a warrant,' Samuel Culhane said and started to close the door, but Viktor stopped it with his foot and Nate pushed past and into the room, touching the badge pinned to his shirt, saying, 'This is a brass pass, dude.'

When the back door opened and Nate whistled to him, Wesley entered and saw the tweaker sitting on the couch in the living room looking glum. Viktor was formally reading the guy his rights from a card that every cop, including Viktor, had memorized.

Nate handed Samuel Culhane's driver's license to his partner and said, 'Run him, Wesley.'

After Viktor had finished with the rights advisement, he said to the unhappy homeowner, 'You are not pleased to see us?'

'Look,' Samuel Culhane said, 'you ain't searching my house without a warrant, but I'll talk to you long enough to find out what the hell this is all about.'

'We must find out where you were on a certain night.'

'What night?'

'Three weeks ago. You were driving your Pinto with a lady friend, no?'

'Hah!' Samuel Culhane said. 'Driving with a lady friend? No! I'm gay, dude. Gayer than springtime. You got the wrong guy.'

Persisting, Viktor said, 'You were driving on Gower south of Hollywood Boulevard that evening.'

'And who says so?'

'You were seen.'

'Bullshit. I got no reason to drive down Gower in the evening. In fact, I don't even go out till around midnight. I'm a night person, man.'

'There was a woman in your car,' Viktor said.

'I told you I'm gay! Do I gotta blow you to prove it? Wait a minute, what crime was I supposed to've done?'

'You were seen at a mailbox.'

'A mailbox?' he said. 'Oh, man, now I get it. You're gonna try to fuck me with a mail theft.'

Wesley came in then and handed an FI card to Viktor on which he'd scribbled some of Samuel R. Culhane's rap sheet entries.

Reading, Viktor said, 'You have been arrested for fraud … one, two times. Once for counterfeiting. This is, as they say, consistent with the theft of US mail from a public mailbox.'

'Okay, fuck this,' Samuel Culhane said. 'I ain't spending a night in jail till you guys get your shit together and figure out you got the wrong guy. I'll come right out and tell you what's what if you'll go away and leave me be.'

'Proceed,' Viktor said.

'I rented my Pinto for a week to a guy I know. I got another car. He lives down there off Gower with an idiot tweaker who calls herself his wife but they ain't married. I warned them both, don't fuck around and do any deals in my Pinto. They didn't listen to me, did they? I'll show you where he lives. His name's Farley Ramsdale.'

Hollywood Nate and Wesley Drubb looked at each other and said it simultaneously and with such gusto that it startled not only Samuel Culhane but Viktor Chernenko as well.

'Farley!'

*

That goddamn Olive, she never puts anything in its proper place. Farley was still thinking of Olive in the present tense although he knew in his heart that she was in the past. He had to admit there were things he was going to miss. She was like those Bedouin women who walk through minefields while the old man stays fifty yards behind on the donkey and follows in her footsteps. Never less than obedient. Until now.

Finally he found the key cards in the bottom drawer of the kitchen together with the egg timer she'd never used and a badly burned skillet that she did use. They were the best key cards they'd ever stolen, and they had always fetched a good price. Just the right size and color, with just the right mag code to look exactly like a righteous California driver's license once they slapped the bogus facsimile on the front. He was going to have to find another woman partner to hang around that particular hotel and get more of them. Maybe a halfway classy woman who would never arouse suspicion. He tried to think of a halfway classy woman he might know but gave up trying immediately.

Of course he knew that the junkyard rendezvous was very dangerous and might be a trick of Cosmo's to kill them, but after he'd told Cosmo that Olive had boogied and Cosmo still wanted him to make delivery, he figured it was probably okay. That fucking Armo wouldn't dare try to kill him with Olive out there able to dime him to the cops if Farley went missing. Would he?

He might. Farley had never dealt with anyone as violent as Cosmo, so that's why he'd devised a little plan of his own. Sure, he was going to drive to that lonely junkyard on that lonely fucking road in east LA, where no white man in his right mind would roam around at night. But he wasn't stepping one toe out of his car, no way. He was going to drive up, wrong side of the road to that fence, reach out, and grab the paper bag. And if the money was in there, he'd pull into the yard, spin a sweeping U-turn, blow his horn until Gregori came out, toss him the paper bag with the key cards in it, and zip on out of that yard and back to white man's country – if Hollywood could be called white man's country these days.

And if there wasn't a trap at all and Gregori got insulted by his method of delivery and threatened not to do business with him anymore, too fucking bad. Gregori shouldn't hang with gun-packing Armos like Cosmo. He should stick with thieving, chiseling, bloodsucking Armos like himself. Yeah, Farley thought with waxing confidence as he fantasized about the glass he'd be smoking tonight, where's the glitch in *that* plan?

Suddenly he was hungry from all that thinking, but he couldn't bear the thought of a cheese sandwich. He had a yearning for Ruby's doughnuts, especially for a couple of those big fat cream-filled, chocolate-covered specials. He found the emergency twenty-dollar bill he had stashed in his underwear drawer, where Olive would never look, then propped up the broken back door as best he could and left for Ruby's. Like Pablo's Tacos and the cyber café, Ruby's Donuts was one of the last stops on the Tweaker-ville Line.

He saw a couple of tweakers he knew in the parking lot, looking hungry but not for doughnuts. Come to think of it, this was the first time he'd ever gone to Ruby's looking for something to put in his stomach. The Hollywood nights were growing more and more strange and weird and scary for Farley Ramsdale, and he couldn't seem to stop it from happening.

They didn't really need Samuel R. Culhane to lead them to Farley's house. A call took care of that. The FI file was full of shakes involving Farley Ramsdale and Olive O. Ramsdale, and it also had their correct address as shown on his driver's license. Like other tweakers, they were always getting stopped and FI'd. But Viktor pretended that Culhane's presence was needed just to be sure that if left alone, he wouldn't make a warning call to Farley.

Driving his Pinto, Samuel L. Culhane did as he was told and led 6-X-72 and Viktor Chernenko to Farley's house, where he slowed and indicated the house with his left-turn signal. Then he took off for home while the cops parked and piled out of the black-and-white, approaching the house with their flashlights off.

As before, Wesley went to cover the back door. He found it partially ajar, one hinge hanging loose, and propped in place by a kitchen chair. Nate and Viktor got no response and there were no lights on in the house. Wesley checked the empty garage.

'He's a typical tweaker,' Nate said to Viktor. 'Out hunting for crystal. When he finds it he'll come home.'

'I must arrange for a stakeout,' Viktor said. 'I feel very strong that this Farley Ramsdale stole the letter from the mailbox that led to the jewel robbery. Yet it is only a feeling. But I am positive that the jewel robbers are the ATM killers. This shall be the biggest case of my career if I can prove that I am correct.'

'This could be one for the TV news and the *LA Times*,' Hollywood Nate said.

'It is more than possible,' Viktor said.

Hollywood Nate paused for a moment and only one word came to him: 'publicity.' He thought about walking into a casting office with a *Times* under his arm. Maybe with his picture in it.

'Viktor,' he said, 'since we've been in on this with you so far, how about calling us if the guy shows up? We'd be glad to transport for you or help you search for evidence – whatever. We were there during the grenade trick and we sorta feel like this is our case too.'

'Detective,' Wesley added. 'This could be the biggest thing I've ever accomplished in my whole life. Please call us.'

'You may be sure,' Viktor said, 'that I shall personally call you. I am not going home tonight until I have a talk with Mr. Farley Ramsdale and his friend who calls herself Olive O. Ramsdale. And if you wish, you can go now and look for them at tweaker hangouts. Perhaps we do not have enough to tie them into crimes but we do not have to just sit back and cool our toes.'

Now Ilya was lecturing Cosmo as she would a child, and he sat there with a cigarette in his nicotine-stained fingers, taking it gladly, a man bereft of ideas.

'Understand me, Cosmo, and trust,' she said. 'Olive is gone and Farley will not get out of his car in the junkyard of Gregori. He will not, because of you. Do not think all people are as stupid as ...' She stopped there and said, 'You must kill him in his car. Outside the yard.'

'Ilya, I cannot find no place to hide myself outside. It is open road and no cars parked on the road at night. Where can I hide myself?'

'Think on it,' Ilya said. 'Use the brain. After you kill him you take him away in his car. You park one mile away. You leave. You go back to the yard and get our car.'

Interrupting, 'How must I get back to the yard? Call taxi?'

'No!' she said. 'You do not! You want police to find out that taxi takes somebody from a scene of dead body to the junkyard of Gregori? Goddamn, Cosmo!'

'Okay, Ilya. Sorry. I walk back.'

'Then you and me, we drive to Dmitri. You have some diamonds in your pocket. Not too many. You give diamonds to Dmitri. His man inspect diamonds. You say, please bring money downstairs to the nightclub. Give to Ilya. I shall be sitting at the bar. He give me money, I go to ladies' room and get the remaining diamonds from where I hide them in a safe place. Lots of people around in the nightclub. We shall be safe.'

'But Ilya,' Dmitri said. 'You forget about ATM money.'

'No, I do not forget. You must tell Dmitri mostly truth.'

'Ilya! He shall kill me!'

'No, he wants ATM money. You tell him we know where to find Olive. You tell him we shall find her tomorrow. We shall get money and kill her. We shall bring half of money to Dmitri like our deal say we do.'

'He shall be very angry,' a despairing Cosmo said. 'He shall kill me.'

'Dmitri wish to kill someone? Tell him to kill his goddamn Georgian who give us a goddamn car that don't run!'

'Then, what we do tomorrow? We cannot find Olive. We cannot get money to Dmitri.'

'The Americans have saying, Cosmo. I am not for sure what each word mean but I understand the idea. Tomorrow we get the fuck out of Dodge.'

*

The Oracle was having a bad night. The lieutenant was off and he was watch commander, so he had to deal with the angry phone call from the lawyer, Anthony Butler.

'Mr. Butler,' he said, 'the detectives have gone home, so if you'll just call back tomorrow.'

'I have been waiting all day for your detectives!' the lawyer said. 'Or rather my daughter has. Do you know she was given a date rape drug at a place called Omar's Lounge?'

'Yes, I've pulled the report and looked it over as you requested, but I'm not a detective.'

'I talked to your nighttime detective twenty minutes ago. The man's an idiot.'

The Oracle didn't argue with that one but said, 'I will personally make sure that the detective commander knows about your call, and he will send someone to your office tomorrow.'

'The man Andrei who tried to drug my daughter knows she got in the wrong car. He probably knows the police were called. And how do we know that he's not a friend of the Iranians? Maybe he can identify them. What if this was a filthy little plot involving Andrei and the Iranian pigs? I'm shocked that nobody has been to the Gulag to at least identify this Andrei.'

The Oracle said, 'If he's really the manager of the Gulag, he's got a good job and he's not going anywhere. He'll be there tomorrow. And being an attorney, you must understand how impossible it would be to prove that she'd been given a drug last night.'

The lawyer said, 'I want to know if the man has a history of this sort of thing. Sara is my only child, Sergeant. A security officer from our corporation is going to accompany me and my daughter to the Gulag this evening, and she's going to point him out if he's there, and we're going to get his name and address. I intend to make the bastard's life a misery with or without the help of detectives from Hollywood Station.'

'No, no, Mr. Butler,' the Oracle said. 'Don't go to the Gulag and stir things up. That'll just end up a real mess for everyone. Tell you what, I'll go there myself tonight and talk to the guy and get all the necessary information that the detectives can act on. How's that?'

'You give me your personal guarantee, Sergeant?'

'You have it,' the Oracle said.

After he hung up, the Oracle called 6-X-76 to the station while he read through the report in its entirety. This was the kind of petty crap that wore him down more than anything, that made him feel old.

Whenever anybody asked him how old he was, the Oracle always answered, 'I'm the same age as Robert Redford, Jack Nicholson, Jane Fonda, Warren Beatty, and Dustin Hoffman.'

He'd always figured that ageless images of Hollywood stars would somehow mitigate what the mirror was showing him: jagged furrows running down his cheeks and encircling his neck, a sagging jawline, deepening creases between his hazel eyes.

But the trick didn't work anymore. Many of the young coppers would say, 'Who's Warren Beatty?' Or ask what movie Jane Fonda ever played in. Or say, 'Jack Nicholson's the dumpy old guy that goes to the Laker games, right?' He opened the desk drawer and swallowed a dose of antacid liquid from the bottle.

When 6–X–76 entered the watch commander's office, the Oracle said, 'This so-called kidnapping at Omar's Lounge is a piece of shit, right?'

'A smelly one, Sarge,' Budgie said. 'The woman insisted on a kidnapping report. She threatened lawsuits. She called a TV news crew, but I didn't hear anything more, so I guess they also figured it was a piece of shit. Her old man's some kind of politically connected lawyer, according to her.'

'He just called.'

'She's an actress,' Fausto said, and at Hollywood Station that explained a lot.

The Oracle nodded and said, 'Just to keep the peace I'll run up to the Gulag later tonight and get Andrei's name and address so that when her daddy calls, the detectives can pacify him. We don't need any more personnel complaints around here.'

'What time you going?' Fausto asked.

'In a couple hours.'

'We'll meet you there and take you to Marina's.'

'What's that?'

'New Mexican restaurant on Melrose.'

'I'm not rich enough for Melrose.'

'No, this is a little family joint. I'll buy.'

'Is there a rehab for Tex-Mex addiction? I've got permanent heart-burn.'

'Whatever you say.'

The Oracle hesitated and said, 'Home-made tortillas? And *salsa fresca?*'

'I been hearing good things,' Fausto said.

'Okay, I'll call and let you know when I'm at the Gulag,' the Oracle said.

'Catch you in five, Fausto,' Budgie said, obviously going to the bathroom.

When she was gone, the Oracle said, 'I'm doing car assignments for the next deployment period. How do you feel about Budgie?'

'Whaddaya mean?'

'You didn't want to work with a woman, but you did me a favor. I don't wanna ask for a favor two months in a row if you still feel the same way.'

Fausto didn't speak for a moment. He looked up at the ceiling and sighed as though it were a tough decision and then said, 'Well, Merv, if you're on the spot again and need me to help out ...'

'We're so shorthanded that figuring out deployment is awful hard these days,' the Oracle said. 'It would make things easier for me.'

'She's a good enough young copper,' Fausto said, 'but I think she could benefit from having an old dog like as a shepherd for a while longer.'

'I'm glad you feel that way, Fausto,' the Oracle said. 'Thanks for helping me out.'

'Well, I better go collect her,' Fausto said. 'These split tails take a long time to get unrigged just to take a pee. We oughtta come up with some kind of loincloth uniform for them.'

The Oracle saw Fausto go out the back door to the parking lot to wait, and he caught Budgie coming out of the bathroom.

'Budgie,' he said, 'you got any objections to working another deployment period with the old walrus?'

'No, Sarge,' she said, smiling. 'We have an understanding, Fausto and me. We're actually a pretty good team.'

'Thanks,' he said. 'Working with you has done wonders for him. He looks and acts ten years younger. Sometimes I think I'm a genius.'

'We all know that, Sarge,' Budgie said.

Farley arrived at the junkyard at the appointed time and parked fifty yards away with his lights out. If any shadow figure that even slightly resembled Cosmo Betrossian walked up to that fence, he was going to drive away, money or no money. But in ten minutes nothing moved. He had to get close to see if the gate was open and a paper bag was stuffed through the chain link, so he drove slowly toward the yard, lights still out. He heard dogs barking at another yard closer to his car. It reminded him of Odar, the oversized Doberman guard dog that was named for non-Armenians.

He was on the wrong side of the road now, but there was so little night-time traffic on the junkyard road that it didn't matter. Behind the fences were stripped and wrecked cars on both sides of the road as well as huge cranes. He saw small office buildings, or RVs serving as office buildings, and larger buildings where cars could be dismantled or reassembled. And all was dark except for security lights on some of the buildings and along some of the roadside fences.

When he was drifting close to Gregori's car gate, lights out, he could see by moonlight that it was open. And he could see something white in the chain-link mesh. Apparently the bag containing the money was there.

He lowered his window, snatched the bag from the wire, and drove back up the road a safe distance, where he parked. He opened the bag and turned on the overhead light, and there it was – $150 in tens and twenties. He counted it twice. Then excitement began to replace his fear. He thought about the ice he'd be smoking tonight. That was all he could think about for a moment, but then he realized he had to deliver.

Farley drove back boldly now and wheeled into the junkyard with his lights on and his windows rolled up and the doors locked. Odar, tied to a long wire line that allowed him to run from the gate to the office, was barking and snarling, but there was nobody around the gate at all, nothing except an oil drum up against the fence. Farley felt so safe that he made a leisurely U-turn in the yard, blew his horn three times, lowered the window, and tossed the bag of key cards onto the asphalt and headed back to the gate.

His headlight beams caught just enough of Cosmo Betrossian climbing out of the empty drum! Farley had time to step on the accelerator hard, but by the time he got to the gate, Cosmo had swung it closed!

The Corolla slammed into the gate and stopped, its left headlight broken and its front fender driven into the tire. The engine died, and in utter panic Farley turned the key off and on as Cosmo ran up to the car, a pistol in his hand.

'Stop, Farley!' Cosmo yelled. 'I shall not hurt you!'

Farley was sobbing when the engine finally kicked over, and he slammed the shift into reverse and backed all the way across the yard, bashing into the door of the office, breaking both taillights and jerking his head back.

Odar was going mad! The dog was snapping and snarling and barking hoarsely, his muzzle white with froth. He was lunging at the car that was crashing and smashing things. Lunging at the running man who had showed up two hours after his master leashed him to the wire and left him. Odar wanted to attack! Anybody! Anything!

Farley dropped the shift into low and gunned it, aiming at Cosmo, who leaped aside and fired a shot through the passenger window behind Farley's head. Farley drove for the gate and rammed it a second time. The car shuddered and recoiled again but the gate still stood. He looked in his side-view mirror and saw Cosmo running toward the car, gun in one hand, flashlight in the other.

Farley reversed it again and floored the accelerator. The tires spun and burned and smoked and the car jetted in reverse and Cosmo leaped out of the way again and fired a second shot and a third, the recoil taking both rounds over the top of the Corolla's roof.

The car was hurtling backward with its driver not knowing which way to turn, but turn he did, this time avoiding a rear-end crash into the office building. Then Farley slammed on the brakes and spun to a stop, his head still reeling.

He could see the blur in his headlights and knew it was Cosmo Betrossian coming to kill him, so he dropped it in low and gunned it and jerked the wheel left, uncertain if Cosmo was still there, even though he could hear the gunfire and see muzzle flashes coming at him. Farley's damaged left front fender just clipped Cosmo on the hip and he flew twenty feet across the asphalt, landing on that same hip, losing his pistol in a jumble of scrap metal and grease rags.

Farley knew he'd hit Cosmo and he floored it again, driving right at the gate, but at the last second he mashed on the brakes, got out, and ran to the gate, expecting to be struck in the back of the head by a bullet. Farley threw back the steel bolt and swung the gate almost open but when he turned he saw Cosmo staggering toward him, without a pistol now but carrying a metal bar that he'd picked up from the scrap heap. Cosmo was limping and cursing in his language. And coming at him.

Farley got the gate all the way open and headed for the driver's seat but he was too late. Cosmo was on him and the bar smashed the driver's side window after Farley ducked. Then Farley was running with Cosmo after him, running into the darkness, running toward the rows of stacked cars waiting to be crushed, then toward another row waiting to be stripped and sold for parts.

Odar had had all he could handle. These two intruders running through his yard were too much for him. His canine adrenaline was overflowing and he took a run, a long run at both men, and the leash drew as tight as piano wire and the overhead line that held the leash snapped. And Odar, eyes aflame, fangs bared, his entire face covered in foam, narrowed those demon eyes and came at them.

Farley saw Odar first and scrambled on top of a wrecked Plymouth, pulling himself onto the roof. Cosmo saw Odar too but had no time to swing at him with the bar, and taking a cue from Farley, he leaped onto the deck lid of a wrecked Audi, scuttling up onto the roof with Odar behind him, his black coat glistening in the moonlight.

The dog vaulted up, slipped, fell from the car onto the ground, then tried again and in a few seconds was standing on the Audi roof dragging his leash. But Cosmo had jumped from the roof of the Audi to the hood of a Pontiac and from the Pontiac across to the roof of a nearly stripped Suburban. Suddenly, Odar abandoned the chase of Cosmo and switched his attention to Farley, who was also leapfrogging cars and partially stripped car bodies, until he turned around, horrified to see the goddamn dog doing the same and coming after *him*!

Cosmo's injured hip began to freeze up on him now, and Farley caught his breath on the roof of an old Cadillac while the confused dog crouched on the hood of a Mustang between them, looking from one man to the other, uncertain which he should attack.

Cosmo began speaking to the dog in Armenian then, trying to win him over with the language the animal was used to hearing. He began issuing gentle commands in his mother tongue.

Farley, who was not as badly injured as Cosmo but every bit as exhausted, also tried persuading the dog, but when Farley tried to speak, he was blubbering and hysterical and tears ran down into his mouth as he cried, 'Don't listen to him, Odar! You're like me! I'm an odar, too! Kill him! Kill the fucking Armo!'

Odar started for Farley then and Farley screamed like a woman. The scream of terror triggered something in the attack animal. The dog whirled, hurtled from deck lid to hood to roof, flying at Cosmo like a missile, driving Cosmo off the car onto the ground. The dog's momentum took him with Cosmo and he landed on the ground at a twisting angle, yelped in pain, and came up limping badly. Within seconds he was unable to walk at all on his left rear leg, and hardly at all on his right.

By then Farley was running for his car, and he made it and jumped in but was unable to start it. Weeping, he flooded the engine, then turned off the ignition and locked the door as Cosmo limped to the scrap heap where he'd lost the pistol. But Cosmo's flashlight was gone too, and he could only dig his hands into the twisted metal until he found the gun, cutting a finger to the bone in the process.

Farley tried the ignition again and the car started! He dropped it into low and stomped the accelerator at the same instant that Cosmo appeared at the passenger window and fired five rounds through the glass, missing with the first four. The fifth and last round entered through Farley's right armpit as his hand was cranking the wheel left and the car was digging out and burning rubber.

Out of the fight, the dog sat on his right hip, snarling and howling at Cosmo, who limped to his Cadillac which had been concealed behind the office building, started it up, and tried to drive after Farley. But Cosmo hadn't driven a quarter of a mile before he had to pull off the road, rip off his T-shirt, and use it to stem the blood that was flowing from a nasty head gash and running into his eyes and blinding him.

Farley is a quarter of a mile down that junkyard road before he knows he's been shot. He reaches down with his left hand, feels the warm wetness, and begins bawling. Still, he keeps driving, one headlight lighting the road in front, smashed fenders scraping both front tires.

Farley loses track of time but just follows his instincts onto east Sunset Boulevard, where it begins near downtown Los Angeles. Sometimes Farley stops for traffic lights, sometimes not, and he never sees the police car that spots him cruising through a red light at Alvarado as several motorists slam on brakes and blow horns and yell at him.

He is driving leisurely now through all those ethnic neighborhoods where people speak the languages of Latin America, Southeast Asia, and the Far East as well as Russian and Armenian and Arabic and a dozen other languages he hates. Heading west, heading toward Hollywood, heading home.

Farley Ramsdale does not hear the police siren either and of course has no knowledge that a Rampart Division unit has broadcast a pursuit of a white Corolla along with his license number and his location and direction, causing Hollywood Division cars to start heading for Sunset Boulevard, everyone convinced that this incredibly reckless drunk will blow at least a .25 on the Breathalyser because he's weaving along Sunset at only thirty miles an hour, causing oncoming traffic to veer right and stop, and is apparently oblivious to the sirens and the queue of black-and-whites that have joined in behind the pursuit car.

At Normandie Avenue Farley crosses into Hollywood Division, still heading west. But he's not in a car any longer. Farley Ramsdale is fifteen years younger and is in the gymnasium at Hollywood High School shooting hoops in an intramural game, and they are all threepointers that find only net. *Swoosh!* And that cheerleader who always disses him is now giving him the big eye. He'll be boning her tonight, that's for sure.

At the corner of Gower Street his foot slips from the accelerator and the car drifts slowly into the rear of a parked Land Rover and the engine dies. Farley never sees the officers of Hollywood Division midwatch who know him – Hollywood Nate and Wesley Drubb and B.M. Driscoll and Benny Brewster, and Budgie Polk and Fausto Gamboa – and those who don't.

All out of their cars, guns drawn, the cops run very warily toward the Corolla now that Nate's broadcast has alerted all units that the pursued car is wanted in connection with a robbery investigation. They are yelling things, but Farley doesn't hear that either.

Hollywood Nate was the first to reach the car, and he smashed the rear driver's side window open and unlocked the driver's door. When Nate jerked open the door and saw all the blood, he holstered his nine and yelled for someone to call an RA.

Farley Ramsdale's eyes were rolled back showing white, his eyelids fluttering like wings as he went into shock and died long before the rescue ambulance reached Sunset Boulevard.

NINETEEN

Cosmo could not stop cursing as he drove west toward Hollywood. He kept looking at his watch without knowing why. He kept thinking of Ilya, of what she would say, of what they would do. He kept wondering how long it would take that miserable addict Farley to phone the police and tell them about the jewelry store robbery. At least Farley couldn't tell them about the ATM robbery and the killing of the guard. Ilya was correct. Farley did not know about that or he would not have come to Gregori's tonight. But that was very little consolation now.

His finger was throbbing and so was his head. He had a laceration just inside the hairline and it was still oozing blood. His finger would need suturing and maybe his head would as well. Almost every bone and muscle ached. He wondered if his hip was broken. Should he go home? Would the police be waiting for him there?

Tonight he had used the Beretta 9-millimeter pistol that he'd taken from the guard. He thought it would be much more accurate than the cheap street gun he had used in the robberies. And what good did it do him? But at least he still had rounds left in the magazine. He had no intention of living his life in prison like an animal. Not Cosmo Betrossian.

He opened his cell and phoned Ilya. If she did not answer, it meant that the police were already there.

'Yes?' Ilya said.

'Ilya! You are okay?'

'Yes, I am okay. Are you okay, Cosmo?'

'Not okay, Ilya. Nothing is correct.'

'Shit.'

'I am bleeding on my hand and head. I need bandage on my wounds and I need a new shirt and I need a cap to hide blood. Not the cap from that day.'

'I threw the baseball cap away, Cosmo. I am not so stupid.'

'I shall be home soon. I must be putting gas in my car. I think there is more safety if we drive to San Francisco.'

'Shit.'

'Yes, Farley may be calling police now. Make all things ready to travel. I shall see you soon.'

Before she began packing their clothes Ilya went to the closet shelf and removed the bag of rings and earrings and loose diamonds. She left a sufficient sampling of each for Cosmo to show to Dmitri. Then she put the rest in a very safe place.

The intersection of Sunset Boulevard and Gower Street was a very busy place, completely blocked off by police. Viktor Chernenko was there, having left the stakeout at Farley Ramsdale's house. The house would now be the object of a hastily written search warrant as soon as Viktor got back to the office. After Hollywood Nate told him that the homicide victim was definitely his person of interest, Farley Ramsdale, Viktor began to think of Farley as having been much more ambitious than a petty mail thief. Whatever his connection to the Russian robbers, it had gotten him killed.

And when word got to the detective squad room that the pursuit suspect had ended up dead, shot at some location east of Hollywood Division but wanted by Viktor Chernenko, it stirred a lot of interest from the usually disinterested night-watch detective Compassionate Charlie Gilford.

Andi McCrea and Brant Hinkle were just getting ready to leave for the Gulag to follow up on their own homicide case and try to get their hands on Dmitri's videotape, when Compassionate Charlie looked their way.

Andi said, 'Don't even think about it, Charlie. The guy was shot somewhere outside Hollywood, and I've got all I can handle anyway.'

Compassionate Charlie shrugged and started making calls. When he was through, he put on his checked sport coat and headed for Sunset and Gower so as not to miss a chance to offer commentary on another Hollywood dream gone terribly wrong.

Wesley Drubb was so excited that Hollywood Nate told him to hang on to his seat belt for fear of levitation. Viktor Chernenko had spoken to Robbery-Homicide Division detectives from the Bank Squad who were on the ATM case and had phoned his lieutenant at home. Things were happening so fast it was hard to decide what to do next other than to write a search warrant for the Ramsdale house and hope that they could locate the woman who called herself Olive Ramsdale. Another Hollywood robbery team had the house under surveillance, waiting for her.

There wasn't anything else for 6-X-72 to do at the moment, so Nate and Wesley reluctantly had to go back to the streets and return to ordinary police work.

Viktor said to them, 'I shall write you a commendation for your good performance whether or not we solve this case. And do not forget Olive. You know her. You might see her at the taco stand or the doughnut shop or the cyber café.'

'We'll be looking,' Nate said.

'Keep the eyes skinned,' Viktor said. 'And thank you.'

*

Andi and Brant had decided to have a quick bite before going to the Gulag. One thing about Russian nightclubs, they stayed open until the last minute the law allowed, so Andi figured they had plenty of time left.

They were in Thai Town, Andi working on a green papaya salad and Brant devouring a red curry with chicken, his eyes watering from the chilis. They each drank two Thai iced coffees, both to soothe their burning mouths and because they needed the caffeine jolt, having had such little sleep in the past two days.

Brant said, 'Since I'm the new kid on the block and bouncing from robbery team to helping you, I think I'll talk to the lieutenant about working homicide full-time. You're shorthanded.'

'Everybody's shorthanded,' Andi said, sipping the iced coffee through a straw.

'It's not that anybody would fight over me,' Brant said. 'The boss knows I'll only be around here until the promotion list gets down to me and I'm appointed.'

'Lieutenant Hinkle,' Andi said. 'It has a nice sound. You'll be a good watch commander.'

'Not as good as you,' Brant said. 'I expect you to knock 'em dead and be near the top of the next list. The troops will love working for you.'

'Why is that?'

'You have a good heart.'

'How do you know what's inside? You've only seen the outside of me.'

'Cop instinct.'

'Careful, buddy. I'm at the age where I get all giddy when a man flatters me like that. I might do something stupid. Like taking you seriously.'

'I'm several years older than you. I'm ready to be taken seriously.'

'Let's postpone this conversation until end-of-watch,' Andi said, 'when I can focus on it.'

'Whatever you say, partner.'

'I say, let's go get a videotape and clear a homicide.'

'Is Viktor still gonna meet us there for a little Russian fast talk?'

'He's a very busy guy tonight but he said he would.'

'To the Gulag, comrade,' Brant said with a smile that crinkled his heavily lashed green eyes and made Andi's toes curl under.

Cosmo was a shocking sight to Ilya when he limped up the stairs. She helped him clean up the head wound and stanch the ooze of blood. As to his finger, she did her best to hold the laceration together with butterfly Band-Aids, then wrapped and taped the finger until they could get to a doctor tomorrow and have it sutured. Where they would have that done, where they would be tomorrow, was anybody's guess. Ilya just wanted to concentrate on getting the money from Dmitri tonight.

'We may run away now, Ilya,' Cosmo said. 'We have diamonds. We find somebody in San Francisco.'

'We are very much hot,' Ilya said. 'Too much happening. We got no time no more. The police shall be coming when Farley informs to them about us. No time to fish for diamond people in San Francisco. We need money now. You know, Cosmo, I may run clear back to Russia. I do not know.'

He didn't know either. All he knew was that he was very much afraid to face Dmitri tonight without the ATM money. And to try to sell him a lie. Dmitri was very smart. More smart than Ilya, he thought.

He made the phone call to the cell number Dmitri had given to him.

'Yes,' Dmitri answered.

'Is me, brother,' Cosmo said.

'Do not say your name.'

'I shall like to come in thirty minute.'

'Okay.'

'You ready to finish business?'

'Yes, and you?'

Cosmo swallowed and said, 'Ready, brother.'

'See you in thirty,' Dmitri said, and somehow Cosmo could see that smile of his.

Cosmo put on the black beret to hide his head wound. It was something that Ilya wore with her black sweater and boots when she wanted to look very sexy. He wore a pale white sport coat and blue slacks and his best cordovan shoes. He tucked the Beretta inside his waistband in the small of his back. He cinched the leather belt tight to hold the pistol there.

Ilya was wearing the tightest red skirt she owned, and a shell with a deep V neckline, the one that made her breasts swell out, and a short black jacket over that, one trimmed with sequins. And since they were going to a Russian club she wore her black knee boots with three-inch heels. She was not short on bling, she thought. Ilya liked that American word: 'bling.'

Cosmo forced a brave smile and said, 'We go to get our thirty-five thousands, Ilya. We go to the Gulag.'

The Oracle looked at the clock. He was getting hungry and this had been a very busy night what with the pursuit driven by a dead man, and Viktor Chernenko tying up one of his midwatch cars, along with more ordinary Hollywood madness breaking out here and there as though there was a full moon. He felt a stab of heartburn and popped a couple of antacid tablets.

He said to the Watch 3 sergeant, 'I gotta go do a PR job to keep some dirtbag of a lawyer from making a personnel complaint on everybody in Hollywood Division who met or failed to meet his goofy daughter who's made a bogus crime report. I just gotta get the name and address of the manager of a nightclub, if the guy really is the manager. Maybe he just has business cards made up to impress the chicks he meets in bars.'

'Which nightclub you going to?' the sergeant asked.

'A Russian joint called the Gulag. You know it?'

'No, but I imagine it's a Russian Mafia hangout. They change names more often than they change underwear.'

The Oracle said, 'After that, I'll be taking code seven with Fausto and his partner. They found a hot new mama-and-papa Mexican eatery. Call if you need me.'

When the Oracle drove out of the Hollywood Station parking lot, he sent a message to 6-X-76 telling them he was on his way to the Gulag and shouldn't be there for more than fifteen minutes.

The Gulag parking lot was jammed when Cosmo wheeled his Cadillac in. He had to park in the far corner by the trash containers.

'Dmitri should hire valet boys,' Ilya observed nervously.

'Too cheap,' Cosmo said.

They could hear the place rocking the moment they stepped out of their car. Cosmo snuffed out his cigarette, touched the pistol under his coat, and limped to the entrance with Ilya.

Ilya went to the bar, joined the rows of drinkers trying to get service, and called to the sweaty bartender, 'Excuse me, please.'

A boozy young guy sitting at the bar turned and looked at her face, then at her tits, got up from the bar stool, and said, 'I'll give you my seat if you'll let me buy you a drink.'

Ilya gave him her best professional smile, took his bar stool, and said, 'That is lovely, darling.'

Smiling at her accent, he said, 'Are you Russian?'

'Yes, darling,' she said.

'How about I order you a Black Russian?'

'I prefer a white American,' she said, and the young guy laughed out loud, drunk enough that anything was funny.

Ilya wished that the world had not stopped smoking. She would have given a diamond for a cigarette at this moment.

As busy as he was, Viktor Chernenko had made a promise to Andi McCrea, and a promise was a promise. He looked at his watch and told Compassionate Charlie that he had to quickly run to a Russian nightclub called the Gulag to do a verbal muscle job for Andi in the proprietor's own language. As for the outside detectives who were on their way to the station to help piece together the puzzle of the Ramsdale murder and Hollywood robberies, Viktor planned to stay tonight as long as there was hope of finding Farley Ramsdale's woman. He had a copy of her minor rap sheet for petty theft and drug possession and saw that the name 'Olive Ramsdale' must be a recent alias. She'd given the name 'Mary Sullivan' when she'd been arrested, but who could say if that was her true name?

Then he put in a quick phone call home and got his wife, Maria, on the phone.

'Hello, my darling,' he said. 'This is your most loving husband.'

Compassionate Charlie said, 'What the hell?' and looked at Viktor like he'd just burped pepper spray. Charlie couldn't bear telephone canoodling.

'I am working on the most important matter of my entire career, my little sweetheart,' Viktor said. 'It is possible that I shall be sleeping here in the cot room tonight. I do not know for sure.'

Then Viktor listened with a dopey smile on his broad Slavic face, said, 'Me too!' and actually did kisses into the receiver before he rang off.

'Is this your first marriage, Viktor?' Charlie asked him.

'My first, my last,' Viktor said.

Charlie shook his head and said, 'Must be a Russian thing.'

'I am not Russian,' Viktor said patiently. 'I am Ukrainian.'

Compassionate Charlie said, 'Bring me back some kielbasa if the Gulag looks like a clean joint.'

'That is Polish, not Russian,' Viktor said, heading for the door.

'Polish, Russian, Ukrainian. Gimme a fucking break, Viktor,' Compassionate Charlie whined.

Cosmo knocked at the door to Dmitri's office and heard 'Come.'

When he limped into the office, he saw Dmitri in his high-back chair behind the desk, but not with his feet up this time and not watching exotic porn on the computer screen. An older man in a dark suit and a striped necktie, bald except for a scraggly fringe of gray, was sitting on the leather sofa against the wall.

Standing by the window that looked down on the smoking patio where the murder had occurred was the Georgian bartender, wearing a starched white shirt, a black bow tie, and black pants. His wavy black hair was even thicker than Cosmo's and he had a square, dark jaw that no razor could ever shave clean. He nodded to Cosmo.

Dmitri smiled that unreadable smile and said, 'The happen-ink guy is here! Please to meet Mr. Grushin, Cosmo. And show to him your goods for sale.'

'I have some sample,' Cosmo said, and Dmitri's smile faded and his face seemed to grow pale around the corners of his mouth. So Cosmo quickly added, 'All other diamonds downstairs with Ilya. Not to worry, brother.'

'I do not worry,' Dmitri said, smiling again. 'Why are you so injured?'

'I shall explain after,' Cosmo said. Then he removed a plastic sandwich bag from his jacket pocket and poured out two rings, three sets of earrings, and five loose diamonds onto Dmitri's desk.

Mr. Grushin got up and walked to the desk. The Georgian pulled the client chair close so he could sit. Mr. Grushin took a jeweler's loupe from his pocket and examined each item under the light of the desk lamp and when he was through nodded to Dmitri, got up, and left the office.

'I may see money now, brother?' Cosmo said.

Dmitri opened the top desk drawer and withdrew three large stacks of currency, placing them on the desk in front of him. He did not ask Cosmo to sit.

'Okay, my friend,' Dmitri said. 'Tell me of ATM. And when I shall receive my half of money you got from there.'

Cosmo felt the dampness under his arms, and his palms were wet when he pointed his uninjured hand at the Georgian and said, 'He gave us a no-good car. The car die when we leave ATM!'

The Georgian said something quickly in Russian to Dmitri that Cosmo couldn't understand, then turned a scowl toward Cosmo and said, 'You lie! The car is good car. I drove car. You lie.'

Now Cosmo felt his stomach gurgle and his bowels rumble and he said, 'No, Dmitri. This Georgian, he lie! We have to drive the car away from ATM and park at the house of guy I know. We almost get caught by police!'

'You lie!' the Georgian said, taking a menacing step toward Cosmo until Dmitri held up his hand and stopped him.

'Enough,' Dmitri said to both men.

'I tell you truth, brother,' Cosmo said. 'I swear.'

'Now, Cosmo, where is money from ATM?' Dmitri asked.

'The man where we must take no-good car, his woman steal our money and run away from her man. But not to worry. We shall find her. We get money.'

'This man,' Dmitri said calmly, 'he does not know noth-ink of me? Noth-ink of the Gulag?'

'No, brother!' Cosmo said. 'Never!'

'And what of this man? What is his name?'

'Farley Ramsdale,' Cosmo said. 'He is addict.'

Dmitri looked in disbelief at Cosmo, then at the Georgian and back to Cosmo, and said, 'You leave my money with addict?'

'No choice, brother!' Cosmo said. 'This Georgian give us car that don't run. And Farley not at home so we got to hide car in his garage and hide money under his house. But goddamn addict woman, she find it and run away!'

Cosmo's mouth was dry as sand now and it made a popping sound each time his lips opened. The Georgian was glaring at him dangerously but Cosmo could hardly take his eyes from the thirty-five thousand dollars. It was a bigger pile of money than he'd imagined.

'Go get Ilya,' Dmitri said. 'Brink her up and I buy you drinks and we complete diamond deal and you tell me how you catch addict woman and tell me when you goink to get me my money from ATM.'

This was the moment he dreaded. This is what Ilya said he must do regardless of the outcome. Cosmo swallowed twice and said, 'No, brother. I take money now and your Georgian come with me down to the bar and Ilya go to bathroom and get diamonds from safe place and give to this Georgian. Lot of peoples down there. Safe for everybody.'

Dmitri laughed out loud at that and said, 'Cosmo, is information on TV and in newspaper correct? How much you find in the box?'

'Ninety-three thousands,' Cosmo said.

'TV lady say hundred thousand,' Dmitri said, 'but never mind, I believe you. So this mean you owe to me forty-six thousand and five hundred dollars and I owe to you thirty-five thousand dollars. So we do mathematics and we discover eleven thousand, five hundred dollars you owe to me. And the diamonds, too. Is very simple, no?'

Cosmo was dripping sweat now. His shirt was soaked and he kept wiping his palms on his trousers, standing there like a child, looking down at this Russian pervert and up at the Georgian thug standing beside him. And he wanted badly just to touch the Beretta, cold against the sweat on his back.

Cosmo said, 'Please to give me three minute to explain how the car this Georgian steal for us is reason for every problem!'

The Oracle was very surprised to see the detective car parked in the red zone on the east side of the nightclub, where he too was forced to park, the packed parking lot being an impossibility. He wondered which detective was in there and why. As he was walking toward the door, a black-and-white slowed and stopped and Fausto gave a short toot to get his attention. The Oracle walked over to the curb, bent down, and said, 'I won't be long, Fausto.'

'Want some company?' Budgie said. 'I've never been inside one of these Russian glam palaces.'

'Okay, but we'll scare the crap outta them,' the Oracle said. 'There's already a detective team in there.'

'For what?' Fausto said.

'Maybe the murder the other night,' the Oracle said. 'Five cops? They'll think they're back in the USSR.'

When the Oracle entered, followed by Fausto and Budgie, he spotted Andi and Brant standing back by the restrooms talking to a guy in a tuxedo who the Oracle figured might be the manager Andrei.

The decibel level was astounding and multicolored lights and strobes were playing all over the dance floor pit, where couples, mostly young, were 'get-tink down,' as Dmitri called it. From her seat at the end of the bar, Ilya couldn't see the three uniformed cops who entered and headed toward a narrow corridor by the kitchen. The Oracle, Fausto, and

Budgie attracted some attention but not much, and they surprised the detectives.

Andi had to shout over the music. 'What're you doing here? Don't tell me there's another murder on the patio I haven't heard about?'

The Oracle said to the unhappy-looking guy in the tuxedo, 'Are you Andrei?'

'Yes,' the manager said.

'We'll give you cuts in line with this one,' Andi said to the Oracle. 'We're waiting to see Dmitri, the proprietor.'

The Oracle said to Andrei, 'I need to have a chat with you and get your name and address. I'll explain when we get to a quiet place, if such a thing exists around here.' Then, with a wink at Andi, he indicated Fausto and Budgie and said to Andrei, 'These two're my bodyguards. I take them with me wherever I go.'

Andrei had a what-else-can-go-wrong look on his face then. Just as something else was about to go very wrong.

Dmitri's eyes were half closed as Cosmo glossed over the aftermath of the ATM robbery, leaving out his confrontation tonight with Farley Ramsdale.

And when Cosmo was through, Dmitri said, 'You had to shoot the guard?'

'Yes, Dmitri,' Cosmo said. 'He did not give up money like you say.'

Dmitri shrugged and said, 'Sometimes information on enemy is not correct. Ask President Bush.'

Cosmo was getting his hopes built until Dmitri turned to the Georgian and said, 'Okay, maybe is a little piece of truth about the car. Maybe the car is not so good as you think.'

'Dmitri!' the Georgian said, but he saw the look in Dmitri's eye and stopped his protest.

'So, Cosmo,' Dmitri said, 'you are going to get ATM money tomorrow when you catch addict woman, no?'

'That is exactly correct,' Cosmo said.

'Okay, here is what I do for you, Cosmo,' said Dmitri. 'You owe me eleven thousand, five hundred plus diamonds. I am go-ink to cancel the money what you owe me! You get Ilya up here and give me all diamonds and we are even. Tomorrow when you catch addict woman, you keep all ninety-three thousand dollars. Your share, my share. I could not be more generous with my own brother, Cosmo.'

Then Dmitri looked up at the Georgian for validation and got a nod of agreement that said Dmitri was a very reasonable and very generous man.

It was hopeless. Cosmo was the image of despair. As Cosmo was staring at the money on Dmitri's desk, the Russian opened the top drawer and put the first stack back inside. When he reached for the second stack, Cosmo felt that he was outside his body and watching himself pull his coat back and reach behind him for the Beretta.

'Dmitri!' the Georgian yelled, coming up with a small pistol, from where, Cosmo didn't see.

And Dmitri shouted in Russian and opened a second drawer and reached inside for a gun of his own.

Andi said to the other cops and to Andrei the manager, 'We've waited long enough. I'm going to knock on Dmitri's door.'

She was interrupted by one shot followed by two more followed by five! And the two detectives and three uniformed cops ran upstairs. Andi was getting her pistol out of her purse when Fausto and Budgie passed her and both crouched down on one knee, guns extended in two hands aimed at the door of Dmitri's office. The Oracle ran to the other side of the door, and with his old six-inch revolver extended, he backed up, so that all guns, high and low, were deployed diagonally, pointed at the door.

Inside the office, Cosmo Betrossian had pain in his left arm that far exceeded anything he'd suffered this night either from Farley Ramsdale or the killer dog. Cosmo had a through-and-through wound in the biceps that had chipped the bone before exiting, and it burned like liquid fire.

The Georgian was sprawled across Dmitri's desk, spurting blood from an arterial penetration in the neck. But his chest wounds were even more devastating.

Dmitri was sitting back in his chair with a hole in his forehead that was actually a coup de grâce delivered by Cosmo as Dmitri lay dying, having fired the round that wounded Cosmo.

The thundering sounds from the pit below Dmitri's office had actually muffled the sound from the patron's area, and everyone rocked on. From time to time Ilya gazed across the dance floor, wondering why Cosmo had not returned.

Cosmo hoped he didn't faint before he got down to Ilya with the stacks of money inside his shirt against his skin. The money felt good. He was about to put his gun back into his waistband, but thinking that an employee from the kitchen might have heard the shots, he held the gun in front of him with his one good hand and opened the door.

In such confined space it sounded to Fausto like automatic weapon fire that he'd heard in Nam. Budgie later said that it sounded to her like one huge explosion. She couldn't differentiate the separate weapons firing.

Cosmo Betrossian got off exactly one shot, which hit the wall above their heads. He in turn was shot eighteen times with nine rounds missing him, probably as he was twisting and falling. All five cops shot him at least twice, with Fausto and Budgie scoring the most hits.

This being her first shooting, Andi McCrea later said during the FID investigation that it truly was like a slow-motion sequence. She could see, or thought she could see, hot empty shells ejecting into the air from various pistols and slapping against her face.

The Oracle said that in forty-six years, this was the first time he'd ever fired his weapon outside of the police pistol range.

Budgie had the most interesting commentary. She said that in such close confines, all the muzzle blasts and gun smoke had created a condition that, with her mouth wide open and sucking air, got her chewing gum full of grit.

The pandemonium that followed was worse than occurred on the night of the patio stabbing. The customers did hear the roar of the multiple gun shots from the upstairs hallway. Budgie and Fausto ran down the stairs to grab the manager and anybody else who looked like he might know what the hell had happened upstairs to cause the original gunfire. The Oracle made urgent calls on his rover.

By the time Viktor Chernenko pulled up in front, people were pouring from the front door and running for their cars. The parking lot was in such chaos that the cars in the back of the lot could not move. Headlights were flashing and horns were honking. Viktor bulled his way through emerging hysterical customers and took the stairs two at a time.

When he got to the scene of carnage, he said to the Oracle, 'One of these Russians may be the one I am looking for! Maybe the one who shot Farley Ramsdale!'

The Oracle, who was pale and had the worst heartburn of his life, said, 'A busboy told us the one in the chair is the owner. The one lying across the desk is a bartender. The one we shot ...' – and he pointed to the rag-ged, bloody heap lying in the corner just beyond the door – 'I don't know who he is. He killed the other two.'

Viktor said, 'You have latex gloves?' and when the Oracle shook his head, Viktor said, 'Hell with it!' and pulled Cosmo's wallet from his back pocket and ran back down the stairs, his hands stained by Cosmo's blood.

When he got to the sidewalk in front he could hear sirens wailing as patrol units were arriving from all directions.

'Come with me!' Viktor yelled to Wesley Drubb, who had just leaped from their car as Nate was double-parking it.

Wesley followed Viktor to the parking lot, where Viktor looked inside each and every car with his flashlight as the cars took turns trying to funnel out of the narrow driveway. Most cars had couples in them or single men. Less than ten percent of the cars were driven by single women, but for every one that was, Cosmo's flashlight beamed squarely into the driver's face.

He was starting to think that he'd been wrong when he got to the last row of cars, but then he saw a big blond woman with huge breasts behind the wheel of an older Cadillac. Viktor turned to Wesley, his flashlight on Cosmo's driver's license, showing Wesley the name. Then he shined his light on the Cadillac and said, 'Please get a DMV on this license plate! Very fast!'

Viktor hung his badge on his coat pocket, walked up to the driver's door, and tapped on the window with his flashlight, his pistol in hand concealed just below the window ledge. And he smiled.

The woman rolled down the window, smiled back at him, and said, 'Yes, Officer?'

'Your name, please,' Viktor said.

'Ilya Roskova,' she said. 'There is a problem?' Then she looked to see if the queue of cars was moving, but it was not.

'Maybe,' Viktor said. 'And is this your car?'

'No, I borrow this car from a friend. She is a neighbor. I am so stupid I do not even know her family name.'

'May I see the registration?'

Ilya said, 'Shall I look in glove box?'

'By every means,' Viktor said, shining his light on her right hand as well as the glove compartment. His gun coming up a bit higher.

'No,' she said. 'No papers in there.'

'This car belongs to a woman, then?'

'Yes,' Ilya said. 'But not to this woman who sits before you in traffic.' Her smile broke wider, a bit coquettish.

Hollywood Nate and Wesley came running back, and Wesley whispered, 'Cosmo Betrossian. Same as on that driver's license.'

'So you know the owner of the car, then?' Viktor said to Ilya.

'Yes,' Ilya said cautiously. 'Her name is Nadia.'

'Do you know Cosmo Betrossian?'

'No, I do not think so,' Ilya said.

Viktor raised his pistol to her face and said in Russian, 'You will please step from the car with your hands where we can see them at all times, Madame Roskova.'

As Wesley handcuffed Ilya's hands behind her back, she said, 'I shall be calling my lawyer immediately. I am completely full of outrage!'

When they were transporting her to Hollywood Station, Nate said to his partner, 'Well, Wesley, what do you think of your misdemeanor division now?'

TWENTY

At 3 a.m. Ilya Roskova was sitting in the detective squad room, which was more crowded with people than it ever was during daylight hours. There were Force Investigation Division people, there was the area captain, there was the Detective Division commander – everyone had left their beds for this one. And the Gulag had more LAPD cars and personnel swarming around than they ever had customers during happy hour.

What was known so far was that the diamonds found on the desk at the Gulag under the body of the Georgian bartender matched descriptions given by Sammy Tanampai of his jewelry store inventory. The serial number on the Beretta 9-millimeter pistol used by Cosmo Betrossian to kill Dmitri and the Georgian proved to be the weapon taken from the surviving security guard during the ATM robbery.

Viktor Chernenko, the man who had been instinctively correct from the beginning, was told that, along with the captain, he should be prepared to speak to the media in the late morning after he got some much-needed sleep. Viktor predicted that ballistics would show that the bullet that killed Farley Ramsdale came from the same Beretta, and that Farley Ramsdale must have been an accomplice to the robbery and had a falling out with Cosmo Betrossian.

There was a person in the squad room, being guarded by Budgie Polk, who knew if Viktor was correct in both theories, but she wasn't talking. Ilya's wrist was handcuffed to a chair and she'd said *nyet* to every question asked, including whether she understood her constitutional rights. Everyone was waiting for Viktor to find time to try an interview in her language.

Andi McCrea along with the others who had participated in the officer-involved shooting were being separately interviewed by FID and were scattered among several of the station's offices. Andi was the third one finished, and when she came back into the busy squad room, she played the videotape that had been seized along with the other evidence from the desk of Dmitri.

When she watched the video with Brant Hinkle looking over her shoulder, they nodded, satisfied. The stabbing of the student was caught vividly. The identity of the assailant was unmistakable.

'He'll cop a plea when his lawyer sees this,' Andi said.

After packaging the videotape for booking, she looked at Ilya Roskova, sitting in the chair glaring at her stoic guard, Budgie Polk, who had been interviewed for one hour by FID.

Andi pulled Viktor aside and said, 'Have you gotten any information out of her?'

'Nothing, Andrea,' Viktor said. 'She will not speak at all except to ask for cigarettes. And she keeps wanting to go to the bathroom. I was just going to ask Officer Polk to take her.'

Andi kept eying Ilya, looking particularly at her lower body squeezed into that low-rise red skirt, as tight as Lycra. She said, 'Let me take her. Where's her purse?'

He pointed and said, 'Over there on the desk.'

'Does she have cigarettes in there?'

'Yes.'

Andi went to the desk and picked up the purse, then walked over to Ilya Roskova and said, 'Would you like us to take you to the bathroom?'

'Yes,' Ilya said.

'And after that maybe a cigarette?' Andi said.

'Yes.'

'Take the cuff off her, Budgie,' Andi said.

Budgie unlocked the handcuff and the prisoner stood, massaging her wrist for a second, prepared to accompany the cops.

As they started to walk, Andi opened the purse and said to Ilya, 'Yes, I see you have cigarettes in—' Then the purse dropped from Andi's hand onto the floor.

Ilya looked at Andi, who just smiled and said 'I'm sorry' but made no effort to pick up the purse.

Ilya angrily bent over to pick it up, and Andi stepped forward, put her hand on Ilya's shoulder, and forced her down into a full squat with one hand, reaching down toward the purse with her other, saying, 'Here, let me help you, Ms. Roskova.'

And when Ilya was held in the squatting position for a few seconds, making a fish mouth, a diamond hit the floor. Then another. Then a ring with a four-karat stone plinked against the floor and rolled across the squad room, stopping when it hit Viktor's shoe. Diamonds were shooting from that 'safe place' where she'd promised Cosmo to hide them.

Andi reached under Ilya's arm and raised her up, saying, 'We'll let you pee in a urinal and we'll be watching. And Viktor, I think you better put on gloves before you pick up the evidence.'

'Bitch!' Ilya said, as the two women, one on each arm, led her to the door.

'And you can use our bidet,' Budgie said. 'Like the one I have at home. It's called a sink. You jump up on it, but we'll keep the stopper in.'

Brant Hinkle said to Viktor, 'I think she might talk to you now.'

'How did Andi know?' Viktor marveled.

'She noticed right away and told me. No panty line, no thong line, nothing. She guessed that Roskova might want to get rid of them in a hurry first chance she'd get at privacy.'

'But the trick? To put her down in that position? How did she know that trick?'

'Viktor, there're some things you and I didn't learn at detective school that women just know,' Brant Hinkle said.

When Andi and Budgie returned with the cache of diamonds, Budgie said, 'I'm sure glad I didn't have to remove the evidence. I can't even clean out my rain gutters for fear of spiders and other crawly things.'

Late the next day, after getting five hours' sleep in the cot room along with a wardrobe change driven to the station by his wife, Maria, Viktor Chernenko completed his investigation by supervising a thorough search of the car and apartment of Cosmo Betrossian, as well as the house of Farley Ramsdale.

They found Cosmo's Lorcin .380 pistol and the Raven that Ilya had carried during the ATM robbery. At Farley's house they found some stolen mail, a glass pipe for smoking meth, and the usual litter and detritus that are found in the homes of tweakers. There were a few articles of women's clothing, but it appeared that Farley Ramsdale's companion had disappeared.

Viktor and two other detectives inquired at every house on both sides of the street but learned nothing of value. The next-door neighbor, an elderly Chinese man, said in barely understandable English that he had never spoken to Farley and never noticed a woman. The neighbor on the other side was an eighty-two-year-old Romanian who said that she only saw the man and woman coming in late at night and that her night vision was so bad she'd never recognize them in the daylight.

Interviews of other, mostly elderly, residents on the block were equally fruitless. Even when Olive's old mugshot was shown to them, nobody could say that she looked very familiar. She was the kind of person, it seemed, who would live and die on the streets of Hollywood utterly invisible.

Upon reading the news accounts about Farley Ramsdale and the massacre at the Gulag, a very frightened Gregori Apramian called Hollywood Station early in the afternoon to offer information. And after that call, his junkyard was deemed a crime scene and was sealed and scoured by criminalists and detectives from downtown.

Gregori stood in front of his office next to a leashed Doberman who, despite the cast on his rear leg, was snarling and still ready to fight. And scaring the crap out of every cop who got within ten yards.

What Gregori said for the record and what was transcribed onto a police report was: 'I just promise Cosmo to tow the Mazda that night. I don't know about no robberies. Maybe Cosmo bring this guy Farley to my yard to destroy the Mazda? That is what I think. They are going to burn up the Mazda to do the covering up of robberies. But something happen. They get in fight and hurt my Odar. And Cosmo shoot the man Farley. I do not know Farley. I do not know the Russian woman you arrest. I only know Cosmo because we go to same Armenian church sometimes. I am trying to be a friend to a fellow immigrant and be a, how you say, credit to America.'

At the end of his long day, Viktor Chernenko played a tape of Ilya Roskova's interview for the detective lieutenant and both area and station captains. Ilya had stopped saying *nyet* after the diamonds were excreted onto the squad room floor. She had then voluntarily removed the rest in the Hollywood Station bathroom where they were packaged and booked.

Ilya had been advised of her rights in both English and Russian, and she declared her understanding. The interview about her role in both robberies was long and tedious and self-serving. She kept claiming to have been totally in thrall to Cosmo Betrossian, calling herself a mental captive who lived in fear of him.

When one of the captains looked at his watch, Viktor advanced the tape to the portion dealing with the last pieces of the puzzle that remained missing: Olive and the ATM money.

Ilya's voice said, 'Olive was there when Farley did blackmail on Cosmo. When he gave big threat to tell police about the stolen letter. But Olive is, how you say, imbecile. Her brain is in a destroyed condition from drugs. I am very astounded that she have enough of the brain left to find the money Cosmo steal from ATM. Very astounded that she can take the money and vanish into thin smoke.'

Then Viktor's voice said, 'Do you think it is possible that Cosmo was holding back from you? Is it possible that Cosmo hid the money somewhere because he did not wish to share with you?'

After a long pause on the tape, Ilya's voice said angrily, 'Is not possible!' Then she obviously realized that she was blurring her portrait of enslavement and said, 'But of course I was so much in fear that I may be incorrect about what Cosmo can do. He was very much clever. And had two faces.'

Viktor turned off the machine then and said to his superiors, 'So far as I am concerned, we have hit a stone fence. I believe that Cosmo Betrossian took the ATM money from under the house of Farley Ramsdale on the night that the car was towed to the junkyard. I believe that Cosmo Betrossian has disposed of the ATM money with a friend, probably another woman. The Russian pride of Ilya Roskova does not wish to admit such a possibility – that he could have another secret woman and would be leaving her. I believe that Cosmo then tried to tell to Dmitri Sikhonov a false story of

Olive stealing the money, but Dmitri was too smart to buy it. And that's when the shooting started.'

'You've been right on so far,' the area captain said. 'So what do you think happened to this woman Olive?'

'I think she finally got scared enough of Cosmo Betrossian to run away from Farley Ramsdale. She is probably living now with some other tweaker. Or maybe just living out on the street. We shall find her dead sometime from an overdose. Truly, she is of no further use to this investigation.'

'Do you think we'll ever find the ATM money?' the station captain asked.

Viktor said, 'We have learned that Cosmo Betrossian loved Russian woman. There is probably one of them shopping on Rodeo Drive with the ATM money. Right now as we talk.'

'Okay, it's a wrap,' the area captain said. 'When you do press interviews on this, just try to avoid mention of the missing money. The other pieces fit perfectly.'

'Yes, sir,' Viktor Chernenko said. 'That is the only fly in the jelly.'

TWENTY-ONE

By the time the June deployment period was in full swing at Hollywood Station, things were back to normal. The surfer cops were hitting the beach at Malibu every chance they got. B.M. Driscoll was sure that he had a sinus infection from what to him was a severe allergy season. Benny Brewster had persuaded the Oracle to stick B.M. Driscoll with one of the recent arrivals who didn't know him, and the Oracle complied. Fausto Gamboa and Budgie Polk were an effective team, particularly after Budgie convinced Fausto that he absolutely had to treat her more like one of the guys. Wesley Drubb got his wish and was assigned to a gang unit with a chance to do more hardcore police work. And in a pinch, caused by summer vacations, Hollywood Nate agreed to be a temporary training officer to a brand-new probationer named Marty Shaw, who made Nate nervous by constantly calling him sir.

But best of all for the midwatch, Mag Takara came back to duty. The Oracle thought she should be assigned to the desk until her vision improved a bit more, and she agreed. Mag wore glasses now and would soon be taking sick days for future plastic surgery, but she wanted very much to put on the uniform again, and it was permitted. She learned that she was going to be awarded the Medal of Valor for her actions in the jewelry store on the night of the grenade incident. She said her parents would be very proud.

Mag even thanked Flotsam for the beautiful roses he had brought to the hospital, telling him he was a 'choiceamundo friend.' Flotsam actually blushed.

When Budgie Polk saw Mag, they hugged, and Budgie looked at the cheekbone that showed a slight darkened crater where tissue had not yet fully recovered and said, 'You're still the most gorgeous slut that ever hustled tricks on Sunset Boulevard.'

The deployment period was ending on a night when the homicide team of Andi McCrea and Brant Hinkle was working late after having arrested an aging actor who walked into his agent's office, cold-cocked the guy with an

236

Oscar replica that the actor used as a paperweight, and then threatened to return with a gun.

When Hollywood Nate heard about it he said no jury made up of SAG members would ever convict the actor, and they might even make the agent buy him another fake Oscar.

They were just finishing up that evening when the Oracle entered the detective squad room looking very grim. He said, 'Andi, can you come to the captain's office, please?'

'What's up?' she said, following the Oracle to the captain's office, where she saw a US Army sergeant major holding his hat in both hands.

'Noooo!' Andi cried out, and Brant Hinkle heard and ran to the sound of her voice.

'He's not dead!' the Oracle said quickly. 'He's alive!'

He put his arm around her and led her into the office and closed the door.

The sergeant major said, 'Detective McCrea, we've been informed that your son, Max, has been wounded. I'm really sorry.'

'Wounded,' she said, as though the word were foreign to her.

'It wasn't a roadside bomb, it was an ambush. Automatic weapons and mortars.'

'Oh, my god,' she said and started weeping.

'It's his leg. I'm afraid he's lost his right leg.' Then he quickly added, 'But it's below the knee. That's much better.'

'Much better,' Andi murmured, hardly hearing, hardly comprehending.

'He's been flown to Landstuhl Regional Medical Center in Germany, and from there he'll go to Walter Reed Army Medical Center in Washington.'

The sergeant major expressed his and the army's gratitude, offered to assist her in any way he could, and said a lot of other things. And she didn't understand a word of it.

When he was finished, Andi thanked him and walked out into the corridor, where Brant Hinkle took her in his arms and said to the Oracle, 'I'll drive her home.'

There wasn't a more excited homeowner in that part of Hollywood than Mabel was these days. She had so much to do. There just weren't enough hours in the day.

First of all, she got a new screen door. It was a nice aluminum door that the man said would last a lifetime. Then he looked at Mabel and she knew he was thinking, It will surely last your lifetime.

Then came the painting of the exterior, which was still going on. Mabel had to keep the windows open all the time in this hot weather, even though there was the awful smell of paint from outside. But it all just added to the excitement. They were going to start painting the interior of the house very soon and putting wallpaper in the kitchen and bathroom. Mabel thought she'd buy a couple of air conditioners before the interior painting started. It was a thrilling time to be alive.

When they were having breakfast, Mabel said to Olive, 'Do you think you're up to going to an NA meeting this afternoon, dear?'

'Oh, sure,' Olive said, still looking pale from having to whiteknuckle it.

'I started going to AA when I was sixty-two years old,' Mabel said. 'After my husband died, the booze got the best of me. I've been in recovery ever since. You'll meet some grand people there who will always be just a phone call away. I'm sure that the NA meetings are like AA meetings, just a different drug is all. But I have no doubt you'll prevail. You're a strong girl, Olive. You've never had a chance to prove it.'

'I'll be okay, Mabel,' Olive said, trying to eat some scrambled egg.

Mabel's physician had told Olive that a diet of nutritious food was essential for her, and Mabel hadn't stopped cooking since Olive arrived. Mabel had seen that Olive's attempt at unassisted withdrawal from methamphetamine addiction was very hard on her, so Mabel had taken Olive by bus to a doctor who'd treated Mabel for thirty years.

The doctor had examined Olive and given her medication to ease withdrawal symptoms but said that healthy eating was the best medicine, along with abstaining from all drugs forever.

Mabel was pleased watching Olive eat a forkful of scrambled egg and a bite of toast, washing it all down with orange juice. A week earlier she couldn't have done that.

'Dear,' Mabel said, 'do you feel well enough today to talk about the future?'

'Sure, Mabel,' Olive said, realizing that this was the first time in her life that anyone had ever mentioned her future. Olive never thought that she had a future. Or much of a past. She'd always lived in the present.

'As soon as you're well into recovery I'm going to do a quitclaim deed. Do you know what that is?'

'No.'

'I'm going to deed this house to you with the provision that I can live here for the rest of my life.'

Olive looked at Mabel with a blank expression, then said, 'I don't think I understand what you mean.'

'That's the least I can do for you after what you've given me,' Mabel said. 'I was going to leave the house to the Salvation Army so the state doesn't get it. That's what will happen to Farley's house, you know. He had no heirs and no will, so the state of California will take it. I think Governor Schwarzenegger is rich enough. He doesn't need my house.'

Olive clearly couldn't grasp it. 'Me?' she said. 'You're giving me your house?'

'All that I ask is that you take care of me as best you can for as long as you can. We can hire one of those nice Filipino girls to help with the unpleasant nursing when I get to that point. I would like to die at home. I think my doctor will help me achieve that wish. He's a good and decent man.'

Suddenly tears ran down Olive's cheeks, and she said, 'I don't want you to die, Mabel!'

'There there, dear,' Mabel said, patting Olive's hand. 'My parents both lived until they were nearly one hundred. I expect I've got some years left.'

Olive got up and took a tissue from the box beside Mabel's chair, then came and sat down at the table again, wiping her eyes.

Mabel said, 'I never use that silly sewing room anymore, so that will be your bedroom. We'll decorate it up real pretty for you. And it has a good closet. We'll take you shopping and fill up that closet.'

Olive just kept looking at Mabel with eyes as quiet and devoted as a dog's and said, 'My own bedroom?'

'Certainly, dear,' Mabel said. 'But of course we'll always have to share the bathroom. You wouldn't mind not having your own bathroom, would you?'

Olive started to say that in her whole life she'd never had her own bathroom. Or her own bedroom. But she was so overwhelmed she couldn't speak. She just shook her head.

Mabel said, 'I think we'll buy a reliable car right away. You can drive, can't you?'

'Oh, yes,' Olive said. 'I'm a good driver.'

'I think when we get our car, the first thing we'll do is take a drive to Universal Studios and do the tour. Have you ever been to Universal Studios?'

'No,' Olive said.

'Neither have I,' Mabel said. 'But we'll need to buy one of those fold-up wheelchairs. I don't believe I could manage the long walk. You wouldn't mind pushing me in a wheelchair, would you?'

'I'll do anything for you, Mabel,' Olive said.

'Do you have a driver's license?'

'No,' Olive said. 'When I got arrested for DUI, they took mine away. But I know a real nice guy named Phil who makes them. They're very expensive. Two hundred dollars.'

'All right, dear,' Mabel said. 'We have plenty of money, so we'll buy you one of those for now. But someday you should try to get a proper one.'

Thinking of the driver's license, Mabel said, 'Dear, I know your real name is not Olive Oyl.'

'No, that's the name Farley gave me.'

'Yes, he would,' Mabel said. 'What's your real name?'

'Adeline Scully. But nobody knows it. When I got arrested I used a alias.'

'Adeline!' Mabel said. 'Sweet Adeline. I used to sing that song when I was a girl. That's the name that will go on the driver's license. That's who you are from this day forward. Adeline. What a lovely name.'

Just then Tillie, the striped tabby who was lying on the coffee table – a cat who had never heard a negative word spoken to her since Mabel rescued her – finished a can of tuna and slapped the empty can from the table in disgust.

'Oh, goodness,' Mabel said, 'Tillie's getting cross. We'll have to open another can of tuna. After all, if it wasn't for Tillie, we would never be able to have this new and wonderful life, would we?'

'No,' Adeline said, smiling at Tillie.

'And mum's the word, Tillie,' Mabel said to the cat.

'I'm real happy, Mabel,' Adeline said.

Looking at her smile like that, Mabel said, 'Adeline, you have such nice thick hair I'll bet a stylist could give you a beautiful cut. Let's both go get our hair done and a manicure. And I was wondering, would you like to have some teeth?'

'Oh, yes!' Adeline said. 'I'd love to have some teeth.'

'That's going to be something we tend to first thing,' Mabel said. 'We're going to buy you some nice new teeth!'

By the start of the new deployment period things were getting better insofar as car assignments were concerned. The Oracle liked the way Mag Takara was recovering and her vision was improving. He was thinking about putting her back on patrol.

Andi McCrea had been to Washington for a week, where she'd visited her son in Walter Reed every day. When she came back to Hollywood, she said she'd seen courage beyond words and that she'd never underestimate her son's generation, not ever again.

There are no worse gossips in the world than cops, and few can keep a secret, so the word got around Hollywood Station that Andi McCrea and Brant Hinkle were getting married. Compassionate Charlie Gilford quickly offered his usual brand of commentary.

'Another double-handcuff ceremony,' he said to Viktor Chernenko. 'Right now they're calling each other darling babycakes and little buttercup. In another six months they'll blow each other's brains out. That's the way it is in Hollywood.'

Viktor was especially happy, having learned that he'd been named Hollywood Station's Detective of the Quarter, and paid no attention to Compassionate Charlie's unromantic notions. He loved the sound of those terms of endearment.

That evening before going home, he phoned his wife and said, 'I am so joyful, my darling babycakes. Would it be pleasing if I picked up some Big Macs and strawberry ice cream for my little buttertub?'

TWENTY-TWO

With the July Fourth holiday approaching, the Oracle thought he had midwatch well sorted. When Fausto and Budgie brought in a report for signature, he said, 'Fausto, it's time we took code seven at that other new Mexican restaurant – what's it called?'

'Hidalgo's,' Fausto said.

'I'm buying.'

'You hit the lottery?'

'Time to celebrate. It's summer in Hollywood,' the Oracle said. 'I feel expansive in the summer.'

Fausto looked at the Oracle's ample belly and said, 'I see what you mean.'

'You should talk,' Budgie said to Fausto. Then turning to the Oracle she added, 'I have him on a six-burrito diet. He's already had five this week so he only gets one tonight.'

'Give us a few minutes,' Fausto said. 'I gotta get a DR for a report.'

The Oracle was alone again when he started to feel pain in his upper stomach. That damn heartburn again. He was sweating for no reason and felt he needed some air. He walked out into the lobby, passing below the hanging photos of those slain officers whose names were outside on the Hollywood Station Walk of Fame.

The Oracle looked up at the full moon, a 'Hollywood moon,' he always called it, and sucked in air through his nose, blowing it out his mouth. But he didn't feel better. There was suddenly a dull ache in his shoulder and his back.

A woman was coming to the station to make a report on the theft of her son's bicycle when a loud motorcycle roared by and she saw the Oracle grab his chest and fall to the pavement.

She ran into the station, screaming, 'An officer's been shot!'

Fausto almost knocked her down as he threw open the glass door and ran out, followed by Budgie and Mag Takara, who'd been working at the front desk.

Fausto turned the Oracle over onto his back and said, 'He hasn't been shot.'

Then he knelt beside him and started chest compression. Budgie lifted the Oracle's chin, pinched off his nostrils and started breathing into his mouth as Mag called the rescue ambulance. Several officers ran out of the station and watched.

'Come on, Merv!' Fausto said, counting compressions silently. 'Come back to us!'

The RA arrived quickly, but it didn't matter. Budgie and Mag were both crying when the paramedics loaded the Oracle into the ambulance. Fausto turned and pushed two night-watch cops out of his way and wandered alone into the darkness of the parking lot.

One week later at roll call, the lieutenant said to the midwatch, 'There will not be the usual police funeral for the Oracle. His will was very specific and stated that he'd made other arrangements.'

'He should get a star on the Walk,' Flotsam said.

The lieutenant said, 'Well, that's for our Hollywood Division officers killed on duty.'

'He was killed on duty,' Hollywood Nate said. 'Forty-six years around here? That's what killed him.'

'How about a special star for the Oracle?' Mag Takara said.

The lieutenant said, 'I'll have to talk to the captain about this.'

'If anybody deserves a star,' Benny Brewster said, 'that man does.'

Jetsam said, 'No funeral? We gotta do something, Lieutenant.'

B.M. Driscoll said, 'The Oracle always said he was staying on the job till his ex-wife died so she couldn't get any of his pension. What about her? Did they have kids who might want a funeral?'

Getting rattled, the lieutenant said, 'It's out of my control. He'd made special arrangements, I've been told. He left everything he owned to the LA Police Memorial Foundation for scholarships. That's all I know.'

Fausto Gamboa stood up then, the first time he'd ever done such a thing at roll call in his thirty-four-year career. He said, 'The Oracle didn't want any fuss made over him after he was gone. I know that for a fact. We talked about it one night many years ago when we were having a brew up at the Tree.'

B.M. Driscoll said, 'But what's his ex-wife say about it?'

'There is no ex-wife,' Fausto said. 'That was his excuse for being crazy enough to stay on the Job all this time. And if he'd lived, someday they woulda had to tear the badge off his chest to get rid of him. He wouldn'ta liked that at all. He was nearly sixty-nine years old and enjoyed his life and did some good and now he's gone end-of-watch.'

'Didn't he have ... anybody?' Mag asked.

'Sure he did,' Fausto said. 'He had you. He was married to the Job and you were his kids. You and others before you.'

The room was still then until Hollywood Nate said, 'Isn't there ... one little thing we can do for him? For his memory?'

After a pause, Fausto said with a quivering voice, 'Yeah, there is. Remember how he said the Job is fun? The Oracle always said that doing good police work is more fun than anything you'll ever do in your entire lives. Well, you just go out there tonight and have yourselves some fun.'

As soon as darkness fell on Hollywood, 6-X-76 went on a very special mission. A secret mission known to nobody else at Hollywood Station. They didn't speak as Budgie drove up into the Hollywood Hills to Mount Lee. When they got to their destination, she pulled up to a locked gate and stopped.

Fausto unlocked the gate, saying, 'I had to practically sign in blood to get this key from the park ranger.'

Budgie drove as far as they could on the fire road and then parked. There was no sound but cicadas whirring and a barely audible hum of traffic far below.

Then Budgie and Fausto got out and she opened the trunk. Fausto reached into his war bag and lifted out the urn.

Budgie led the way with her flashlight, but it was hardly needed under the light from a full moon. They walked along the path until they were at the base of the sign. It was four stories high and brilliantly lit.

Budgie looked up at the giant *H* looming and said, 'Be careful, Fausto. Why don't you let me do it?'

'This is my job,' Fausto said. 'We were friends for more than thirty years.'

The ground by the *H* had fallen away, so they walked to the center, to the *Y*, where the ground was intact.

The ladder was in place beside scaffolding, and when he had climbed halfway up, Budgie yelled, 'That's high enough, Fausto!'

But he kept going, puffing and panting, pausing twice until he was all the way to the top. And when he was there, he carefully opened the lid from the urn and turned it upside down, saying, 'Semper cop, Merv. See you soon.'

And the Oracle's ashes blew away into the warm summer night, against the backdrop of HOLLYWOOD, four stories high, under magical white light supplied by an obliging Hollywood moon.

When they were finished with their mission and Budgie had driven them back down to the streets of Hollywood, she broke the silence by saying, 'I've been thinking about cooking a turkey dinner. How about coming over and meeting Katie? I want a photo op of you burping her. I'll buy a small bird for just you and me and my mom.'

'I'll check my schedule,' Fausto said. 'Maybe I can make time.'

Budgie said, 'My dad's been dead for three years but Mom hasn't started dating yet, so it probably won't do you much good to hit on her.'

'Oh, sure,' Fausto said. 'Like I'd hit on an old lady.'

Budgie looked at him and said, 'The old lady is nearly ten years younger than you are, buddy.'

'Yeah?' said Fausto, cocking that right eyebrow. 'So what's she look like?'

'Well, Marty,' Hollywood Nate said to his rookie partner. 'We're going to do some good police work and have some fun tonight. You ready for that?'

'Yes, sir,' the young cop said.

'Goddamnit, Marty,' Nate said, 'save that "sir" crap for your real training officer, who'll probably turn out to be one of those GI junkies who grew up watching TV war movies. Me, I watched Fred Astaire and Gene Kelly musicals. My name's Nate. Remember?'

'Okay, Nate. Sorry.'

'By the way, you like movies?'

'Yes ... Nate,' Marty said.

'Your old man wouldn't be rich by any chance, would he?'

'Lord, no,' Marty said.

'Oh, well,' said Nate. 'My last rich partner didn't help my career anyway.'

There was a good crowd on the boulevard, and the young cop turned to Nate and said, 'Sir – I mean, Nate, there's a fifty-one-fifty raising heck over there in front of Grauman's Chinese Theater.'

Without looking, Nate said, 'What's he doing?'

'Waving his arms around and yelling at people.'

'In Hollywood, that's just called communication,' Nate said. 'Nowadays it's hard to tell ordinary boulevard lunatics from people with headsets talking on cells.' But then he glanced toward the famous theater, saw who it was, and said, 'Uh-oh. That guy's a known troublemaker. Maybe we should talk to him.'

Nate pulled the car into a red zone and said to his partner, 'Marty, on this one, you be contact and I'll be cover. I'm gonna stay by the car here and see how you handle him. Think you can deal with it?'

'For sure, Nate,' Marty said with enthusiasm, getting out of the car, collecting his baton, and putting on latex gloves.

The wild man waving his arms saw the young cop coming his way and stopped yelling. He planted his feet and waited.

Young Marty Shaw remembered from academy training that it's usually better to address mental cases in personal terms, so he turned around for a moment and said to Nate, 'Do you remember his name, by chance?'

'Not his full name,' said Hollywood Nate. 'But they call him Al. Untouchable Al.'

THE NEW CENTURIONS

For Dee
and of course
for all the Centurions

Early Summer 1960

ONE

The Runner

Lying prostrate, Serge Duran gaped at Augustus Plebesly who was racing inexorably around the track. That's a ridiculous name, thought Serge – Augustus Plebesly. It's a ridiculous name for a puny runt who can run like a goddamn antelope.

Plebesly ran abreast of, and was matching strides with, the feared P.T. instructor, Officer Randolph. If Randolph took up the challenge he'd never stop. Twenty laps. Twenty-five. Until there was nothing left but forty-nine sweat suit-covered corpses and forty-nine puddles of puke. Serge had already vomited once and knew another was coming up.

'Get up, Duran!' a voice thundered from above.

Serge's eyes focused on the massive blur standing over him.

'Get up! Get up!' roared Officer Randolph, who had halted the wretched weary group of cadets.

Serge staggered to his feet and limped after his classmates as Officer Randolph ran ahead to catch Plebesly. Porfirio Rodriguez dropped back and patted Serge on the shoulder. 'Don't give up, Sergio,' Rodriguez panted. 'Stay with 'em, man.'

Serge ignored him and lurched forward in anguish. That's just like a Texas Chicano, he thought. Afraid I'll disgrace him in front of the *gabachos*. If I wasn't a Mexican he'd let me lay until the crabgrass was growing out my ears.

If he could only remember how many laps they had run. Twenty was their record before today, and today was hot, ninety-five degrees at least. And sultry. It was only their fourth week in the police academy. They weren't in shape yet. Randolph wouldn't dare run them more than twenty laps today. Serge leaned forward and concentrated on placing one foot in front of the other.

After another half-lap the burning in his chest was no longer bearable. He tasted something strange and choked in panic; he was going to faint. But luckily, Roy Fehler picked that exact moment to fall on his face, causing the collapse of eight other police cadets. Serge gave silent thanks to Fehler who was bleeding from the nose. The class had lost its momentum and a minor mutiny occurred as one cadet after another dropped to his knees and retched. Only Plebesly and a few others remained standing.

'You want to be Los Angeles policemen!' shouted Randolph. 'You aren't fit to *wash* police cars! And I guarantee you one thing, if you aren't on your feet in five seconds, you'll never ride in one!'

One by one the sullen cadets got to their feet and soon all were standing except Fehler who was unsuccessfully trying to stop the nosebleed by lying on his back, his handsome face tilted up to the white sun. Fehler's pale crew cut was streaked with dust and blood. Officer Randolph strode over to him.

'Okay, Fehler, go take a shower and report to the sergeant. We'll get you to Central Receiving Hospital for an X-ray.'

Serge glanced fearfully at Plebesly who was doing some knee bends to keep loose. Oh no, Serge thought; look tired, Plebesly! Be human! You stupid ass, you'll antagonize Randolph!

Serge saw Officer Randolph regarding Plebesly, but the instructor only said, 'Okay, you weaklings. That's enough running for today. Get on your back and we'll do some sit-ups.'

With relief the class began the less painful session of calisthenics and self-defense. Serge wished he wasn't so big. He'd like to get paired up with Plebesly so he could crush the little bastard when they were practicing the police holds.

After several minutes of sit-ups, leg-ups, and push-ups, Randolph shouted, 'Okay, onesies on twosies! Let's go!'

The class formed a circle and Serge was again teamed with Andrews, the man who marched next to him in formation. Andrews was big, even bigger than Serge, and infinitely harder and stronger. Like Plebesly, Andrews seemed bent on doing his very best, and he had almost choked Serge into unconsciousness the day before when they were practicing the bar strangle. When Serge recovered, he blindly grabbed Andrews by the shirt front and whispered a violent threat that he couldn't clearly remember when his rage subsided. To his surprise, Andrews apologized, a frightened look on the broad flat face as he realized that Serge had been hurt. He apologized three times that same day and beamed when Serge finally assured him there were no hard feelings. He's just an overgrown Plebesly, Serge thought. These dedicated types are all alike. They're so damn serious you can't hate them like you should.

'Okay, switch around,' shouted Randolph. 'Twosies on onesies this time.'

Each man changed with his partner. This time Andrews played the role of suspect and it was Serge's job to control him.

'Okay, let's try the come-along again,' shouted Randolph. 'And do it right, this time. Ready? One!'

Serge took Andrews' wide hand at the count of one but realized that the come-along hold had vanished in the intellectual darkness that fifteen or more laps temporarily brought about.

'Two!' shouted Randolph.

'Is this the come-along, Andrews?' whispered Serge, as he saw Randolph helping another cadet who was even more confused.

Andrews responded by twisting his own hand into the come-along position and wincing so that Randolph would think that Serge had him writhing in agony, hence, a 'proper' come-along. When Randolph passed he nodded in satisfaction at the pain Serge was inflicting.

'I'm not hurting you, am I?' Serge whispered.

'No, I'm okay,' smiled Andrews, baring his large gapped teeth.

You just can't hate these serious ones, Serge thought, and looked around the sweating ring of gray-clad cadets for Plebesly. You had to admire the control the squirt had over his slim little body. On their first physical qualification test Plebesly had done twenty-five perfect chins, a hundred sit-ups in eighty-five seconds, and threatened to break the academy record for running the obstacle course. It was that which Serge feared most. The obstacle course with the dreaded wall that defeated him at first glance.

It was inexplicable that he should fear that wall. He was an athlete, at least he had been, six years ago at Chino High School. He had lettered in football three years, a lineman, but quick, and well-coordinated for his size. And his size was inexplicable, six feet three, large-boned, slightly freckled, with light brown hair and eyes – so that it was a family joke that he could not possibly be a Mexican boy, at least not of the Duran family who were especially small and dark – and if his mother had not been from the old country and not disposed to off color *chistes* they might have teased her with remarks about the blond *gabacho* giant who owned the small grocery store where for years she bought *harina* and *maíz* for the tortillas which she made by hand. His mother had never put store-bought tortillas on the family table. And suddenly he wondered why he was thinking about his mother now, and what good it did to ever think of the dead.

'All right, sit down,' shouted Randolph, who didn't have to repeat the command.

The class of forty-eight cadets, minus Roy Fehler, slumped to the grass happy in the knowledge that there was only relaxation ahead, unless you were chosen as Randolph's demonstration victim.

Serge was still tense. Randolph often chose the big men to demonstrate the holds on. The instructor was himself a medium-sized man, but muscular, and hard as a gun barrel. He invariably hurt you when applying the holds. It seemed to be part of the game to toss the cadet a little harder than necessary, or to make him cry out from a hand, arm, or leg hold. The class got a nervous laugh from the torture, but Serge vowed that the next time Randolph used him for a onesies on twosies demonstration, he was not going to stand for any rougher than necessary treatment. However he hadn't decided what to do about it. He wanted this job. Being a cop would be a fairly interesting way to make four hundred and eighty-nine dollars a month. He relaxed as Randolph chose Augustus Plebesly for his victim.

'Okay, you already learned the bar strangle,' said Randolph. 'It's a good hold when you apply it right. When you apply it wrong, it's not worth a damn. Now I'm going to show you a variation of that strangle.'

Randolph took a position behind Plebesly, reached around his throat with a massive forearm, and hooked the small neck in the crook of his arm. 'I'm now applying pressure to the carotid artery,' Randolph announced. 'My forearm and bicep are choking off the oxygen flow to his brain. He would pass out very quickly if I applied pressure.' As he said it, he *did* apply pressure, and Plebesly's large blue eyes fluttered twice and bulged in terror. Randolph relaxed his hold, grinned, and slapped Plebesly on the back to indicate he was through with him.

'Okay, ones on twos,' shouted Randolph. 'We only got a few minutes left. Let's go! I want you to practice this one.'

As each number one man got his arm around the waiting throat of number two, Randolph shouted, 'Lift the elbow. You have to get his chin up. If he keeps his chin down, he'll beat you. Make him lift that chin and then put it on him. Easy, though. And just for a second.'

Serge knew that Andrews would be very careful about hurting him after the outburst the other day. He could see that Andrews was trying not to, the big arm around his neck flexed only a little, and yet the pain was unbelievable. Serge instinctively grabbed Andrews' arm.

'Sorry, Duran,' said Andrews with a worried look.

''s alright,' Serge gasped. 'That's a hell of a hold!'

When it was twos on ones, Serge lifted Andrews' chin. He had never hurt Andrews in any of the prior P.T. sessions. He didn't think Andrews could be hurt He squeezed the throat in the crook, pulling his wrist toward him, and held it several seconds. Andrews' hands did not come up as his had. He must be applying it wrong, he thought.

Serge raised the elbow and increased the pressure.

'Am I doing it right?' asked Serge trying to see Andrews' upturned face.

'Let him go, Duran!' screamed Randolph. Serge jumped back, startled, and released Andrews who thudded to the ground red-faced, eyes half open and glazed.

'For chrissake, Duran,' said Randolph, raising the massive torso of Andrews in his arms.

'I didn't mean to,' Serge sputtered.

'I told you guys, easy!' said Randolph, as Andrews lurched to his feet. 'You can cause brain damage with that hold. You stop the oxygen flow to the brain for too long a period and you're really going to hurt somebody, maybe kill them.'

'I'm sorry, Andrews,' said Serge, vastly relieved when the big man gave him a weak smile. 'Why didn't you tap my arm or kick me or something? I didn't know I was hurting you.'

'I wanted you to get the hold right,' said Andrews, 'and after a few seconds, I just blacked out.'

'You be damn careful with that hold,' shouted Randolph. 'I don't want nobody hurt before you even graduate from the academy. But maybe you'll learn something from this. When you guys leave here, you're going out where there's guys that aren't afraid of that badge and gun. In fact, they might try to stick that badge up your ass to say they did it, and that big oval shield would sure hurt coming out. This particular hold might save you. If you get it on right you can put anybody out, and it just might rescue your ass someday. Okay, ones on twos again!'

'Your turn to get even,' said Serge to Andrews who was massaging the side of his throat and swallowing painfully.

'I'll be careful,' said Andrews, putting his huge arm around Serge's neck. 'Let's just pretend I'm choking you,' said Andrews.

'That's okay by me,' said Serge.

Officer Randolph moved from one pair of cadets to another, adjusting the choke hold, raising elbows, turning wrists, straightening torsos, until he had had enough. 'Okay, sit down, you guys. We're just wasting our time today.'

The class collapsed on the grass like a huge gray many-legged insect and each cadet waited for an outburst from Randolph who was pacing in a tight circle, formidable in his yellow polo shirt, blue shorts, and black high-topped gym shoes.

Serge was bigger than Randolph, Andrews much bigger. Yet they all seemed small beside him. It was the sweat suits, he thought, the ill-fitting baggy pants and gray sweat shirts always sweat-soaked and ugly. And it was the haircuts. The cadets wore short military-style haircuts which made all the young men look smaller and younger.

'It's hard to put everything into the self-defense session,' said Randolph, finally breaking silence, still pacing, arms folded as he watched the grass. 'It's damn hot and I run you hard. Maybe sometimes I run you too hard. Well, I got my own theory on physical training for policemen and it's time I explained it to you.'

That's very thoughtful, you bastard, thought Serge, rubbing his side, which still ached from the twenty laps around the track. He was just beginning to be able to take large breaths without coughing or without his lungs hurting.

'Most of you guys don't know what it's like to fight another guy,' said Randolph. 'I'm sure you all had your scraps in high school, maybe a scuffle or two somewhere else. A couple of you are Korean vets and think you seen it all, and Wilson here has been in the Golden Gloves. But none of you really knows what it's like to fight another man no holds barred and win. You're going to have to be ready to do it anytime. And you have to win. I'm going to show you something. Plebesly, come here!'

Serge smiled as Plebesly sprang to his feet and trotted into the center of the circle. The round blue eyes showed no fatigue and stared patiently at the instructor apparently ready for a painful, elbow-wrenching arm hold or any other punishment Officer Randolph cared to offer.

'Come closer, Plebesly,' said Randolph, gripping the little man by the shoulder and whispering in his ear for several seconds.

Serge leaned back on his elbows, happy in the knowledge that Randolph was evidently going to use the remainder of the P.T. class for his demonstration. Serge's stomach muscles loosened and a sunny wave of relaxation swept over him. It was getting so he was having dreams of running the track. Suddenly he saw Randolph staring at him.

'You, Duran, and you, Andrews, come up here!'

Serge fought a momentary surge of anger, but then dejectedly plodded into the circle, remembering that the last time he had failed to master a complicated hold, he was given three laps around the track. He wanted to be a policeman, but he would not run that track again for anyone. Not this day. Not now.

'I picked Duran and Andrews because they're big,' said Randolph. 'Now, I want you two to put Plebesly's hands behind his back and handcuff him. Just simulate the cuffing, but get him in the cuffing position. He's the suspect, you two are the policemen. Okay, go ahead.'

Serge looked at Andrews for a plan to take the retreating Plebesly, who backed in a circle, hands at his sides, away from the two big men. Just like the Corps, thought Serge. Always the games. First in boot camp, then in I.T.R. at Camp Pendleton. The Korean War had been over a year when he joined, and yet they talked about the gooks like they would be waiting to swarm over their ship the first moment they landed in Pacific waters.

Andrews made a lunge for Plebesly, who almost slithered away but was caught by the sleeve of his sweat shirt. Serge jumped on Plebesly's back and the little man went down under Serge's two hundred and fifteen pounds. But then he wriggled and twisted, and suddenly Serge was under Plebesly and Andrews was on Plebesly's back forcing the combined weight of himself and Plebesly on Serge's aching ribs.

'Pull him away, Andrews,' Serge wheezed. 'Get a wristlock!'

Serge pushed himself up but Plebesly had locked his arms and legs around Serge's body from the rear and hung there leechlike with enough weight to topple Serge over backward on the clinging Plebesly who gasped but would not let go. Andrews managed to pry the little man's fingers loose, but the sinewy legs held on and by now Serge was beaten and sat there with the implacable monkey clinging to his torso.

'Get a choke hold on him, damn it,' Serge muttered.

'I'm trying. I'm too tired,' Andrews whispered, as Plebesly buried his face deeper into Serge's dripping back.

'Okay, that's enough,' Randolph commanded. Plebesly instantly released Serge, bounded to his feet and trotted to his place in the grassy circle.

Serge stood up and for a second the earth tilted. Then he dropped to the ground next to Andrews.

'The reason for all that was to prove a point,' shouted Randolph to the sprawling broken circle of cadets. 'I told Plebesly to resist. That's all. Just to resist and not let them pin his arms. You'll notice he didn't fight back. He just resisted. And Andrews and Duran are both twice his size. They would never have got their man handcuffed. They would have lost him eventually. The point is that they were expending twice the energy to over-come his resistance and they couldn't do it. Now, every one of you guys is going to run into this kind of problem lots of times. Maybe your man is going to decide you aren't going to handcuff him. Or maybe he'll even fight back. You saw the trouble little Plebesly gave the two big guys, and he wasn't even fighting back. What I'm trying to do is tell you that these fights out there in the streets are just endurance contests. The guy who can *endure* usually wins. That's why I'm running your asses off. When you leave here you'll have endurance. Now, if I can teach you an arm-lock and that choke hold, maybe that will be enough. You all saw what the choke can do. The trouble is getting the choke on the guy when he's struggling and fighting back. I can't teach you self-defense in thirteen weeks.

'All that Hollywood crap is just that – crap. You try throwing that haymaker at somebody's chin and you'll probably hit the top of his head and break your hand. Never use your fists. If someone uses his fists you use your stick and try to break a wrist or knee like we teach you. If he uses a knife you use a gun and cancel his ticket then and there. But if you find yourself without a stick and the situation doesn't permit deadly force, well then you better be able to out-endure the son of a bitch. That's why you see these newspaper pictures of six cops subduing one guy. *Any* guy or even any woman can wear out several policemen just by resisting. It's goddamn hard to take a man who doesn't want to be taken. But try explaining it to the jury or the neighbors who read in the papers how an arrestee was hurt by two or three cops twice his size. They'll want to know why you resorted to beating the guy's head in. Why didn't you just put a fancy judo hold on him and flip him on his ass. In the movies it's nothing.

'And while I'm on the subject, there's something else the movies have done for us – they created a legend about winging your man, shooting from the hip and all that bullshit. Well I'm not your shooting instructor but it all ties in with self-defense. You guys have been here long enough to know how hard it is to hit a still target, let alone a moving one. Those of you who make your twenty years will miss that goddamn paper man every time you come up here for your monthly pistol qualification. And he's only a paper man. He don't shoot back. The light's good and the adrenalin hasn't turned your arm into a licorice stick like it does in combat. And yet when you blow some asshole up and were lucky to even hit him you'll hear a member of the coroner's jury say, "Why didn't you shoot to wound him? Did you have to kill him? Why didn't you shoot the gun out of his hand!"'

Randolph's face was crimson and two wide sweat streams ran down either side of his neck. When he was in uniform he wore three service stripes on his sleeve indicating at least fifteen years with the Department. Yet Serge could hardly believe he was more than thirty. He hadn't a gray hair and his physique was flawless.

'What I want you guys to take from my class is this: it's a bitch to subdue a man with a gun or a stick or a sap, let alone with your hands. Just keep yourself in half-assed condition and you'll *out-endure* him. Take the bastard any way you can. If you can use these two or three holds I teach you, then use them. If you can't, hit him with a brick or anything else. Just subdue your man and you'll be in one piece the day your twentieth anniversary rolls around and you sign those retirement papers. That's why I run your asses off.'

TWO
Stress

'I don't know why I'm so nervous,' said Gus Plebesly. 'We've been told about the stress interview. It's just to shake us up.'

'Relax, Gus,' said Wilson, who leaned against the wall, smoking, careful not to drop ashes on the khaki cadet uniform.

Gus admired the luster of Wilson's black shoes. Wilson had been a marine. He knew how to spit-shine shoes, and he could drill troops and call cadence. He was Gus's squad leader and had many of the qualities which Gus believed men could only gain in military service. Gus wished he were a veteran and had been places, then perhaps he would have confidence. He should have. He was the number one man in his class in physical training, but at this moment he wasn't sure he would be able to speak during the stress interview. He had waited in dread so many times in high school when he had to give an oral report. In college he had once consumed almost a half pint of gin diluted with soda pop before he could give a three-minute speech in a public speaking class. And he had gotten away with it. He wished he could do it now. But these men were police officers. Professionals. They would detect the alcohol in his eyes, speech, or gait. He couldn't fool them with so cheap a trick.

'You sure look nervous,' said Wilson, offering Gus a cigarette from the pack he kept in his sock, GI fashion.

'Thanks a lot, Wilson,' Gus mumbled, refusing the cigarette.

'Look, these guys are just going to try to psyche you,' said Wilson. 'I talked to a guy who graduated in April. They just pick on you in these stress interviews. You know, about your P.T. or your shooting, or maybe your academic standing. But hell, Plebesly, you're okay in everything and tops in P.T. What can they say?'

'I don't know. Nothing, I guess.'

'Take me,' said Wilson. 'My shooting is so shitty I might as well throw my gun at the goddamn target. They'll probably rip me apart. Tell me how they're going to wash me out if I don't come to the pistol range during the lunch hour and practice extra. That kind of bullshit. But I'm not worried. You realize how bad they need cops in this town? And in the next five, six years it's going to get lots worse. All those guys that came on right after the war will have their twenty years. I tell you we'll all be captains before we finish our tours with the Department.'

Gus studied Wilson, a short man, even a hair shorter than Gus. He must have stretched to meet the minimum five feet eight inches, Gus thought, but husky, big biceps and a fighter's shoulders, with a broken nose. He had wrestled Wilson in the self-defense classes and had found Wilson surprisingly easy to take down and control. Wilson was much stronger, but Gus was more agile and could persevere.

Gus understood what Officer Randolph had told them, and he believed that if he could outlast his opponents he needn't be afraid. He was surprised at how well it had worked so far in training. But what would a man like Wilson, an ex-fighter, do to him in a real fight? Gus had never hit a man, not with a fist, not with anything. What would happen to his splendid endurance when a man like Wilson buried a heavy fist in his stomach or crashed one to his jaw? He had been a varsity sprinter in high school, but had always avoided contact sports. He had never been an aggressive person. What in the hell had made him think he could be a policeman? Sure the pay was pretty good, what with the security and pension. He could never hope to do as well in the bank. He had hated that dreary low-paying job and had almost laughed when the operations officer had assured him that in five more years he could expect to make what he, the operations officer, was making, which was less than a starting Los Angeles policeman. And so he had come this far. Eight weeks and they hadn't found him out yet. But they might at this stress interview.

'Only one thing worries me,' said Wilson. 'Know what that is?'

'What?' asked Gus, wiping his wet palms on the legs of the khaki uniform.

'Skeletons. I hear they sometimes rattle the bones in the stress interview. You know how they say the background investigation of all cadets goes on for weeks after we enter the academy.'

'Yes?'

'Well, I hear they sometimes use the stress interview to tell a guy he's been washed out. You know, like, "The background investigator discovered you were once a member of the Nazi Bund of Milwaukee. You're washed out, kid." That kind of bullshit.'

'I guess I don't have to worry about my background,' Gus smiled feebly. 'I've lived in Azusa my whole life.'

'Come on, Plebesly, don't tell me there isn't something you've done. Every guy in this class has something in his background. Some little thing that he wouldn't want the Department to find out. I saw the faces that day when the instructor said, "Mosley, report to the lieutenant." And Mosley never came back to class. And then Ratcliffe left the same way. They found out something about them and they were washed out. Just like that, they disappeared. You ever read *Nineteen Eighty-Four?*'

'No, but I know about it,' said Gus.

'It's the same principle here. They know none of us has told them every-thing. We all got a secret. Maybe they can stress it out of us. But just keep cool, and don't tell them anything. You'll be okay.'

Gus's heart sank when the door to the captain's office opened and Cadet Roy Fehler strode out, tall, straight, and as confident as always. Gus envied him his assurance and hardly heard Fehler say, 'Next man.'

Then Wilson was shoving him toward the door and he looked at his reflection in the mirror on the cigarette machine and the milky blue eyes were his, but he hardly recognized the thin white face. The sparse sandy hair seemed familiar but the narrow white lips were not his, and he was through the door and facing the three inquisitors who looked at him from behind a conference table. He recognized Lieutenant Hartley and Sergeant Jacobs. He knew the third man must be the commander, Captain Smithson, who had addressed them the first day in the academy.

'Sit down, Plebesly,' said unsmiling Lieutenant Hartley.

The three men whispered for a moment and reviewed a sheaf of papers before them. The lieutenant, a florid bald man with plum-colored lips, suddenly grinned broadly and said, 'Well, so far you're doing fine here at the academy, Plebesly. You might work on your shooting a bit, but in the classroom you're excellent and on the P.T. field you're tops.'

Gus became aware that the captain and Sergeant Jacobs were also smil-ing, but he suspected trickery when the captain said, 'What shall we talk about? Would you like to tell us about yourself?'

'Yes sir,' said Gus, trying to adjust to the unexpected friendliness.

'Well, go ahead then, Plebesly,' said Sergeant Jacobs with an amused look. 'Tell us all about yourself. We're listening.'

'Tell us about your college training,' said Captain Smithson after several silent seconds. 'Your personnel folder says you attended junior college for two years. Were you an athlete?'

'No sir,' croaked Gus. 'I mean I tried out for track. I didn't have time, though.'

'I'll bet you were a sprinter,' smiled the lieutenant.

'Yes sir, and I tried hurdles,' said Gus, trying to smile back. 'I had to work and carry fifteen units, sir. I had to quit track.'

'What was your major?' asked Captain Smithson.

'Business administration,' said Gus, wishing he had added 'sir', and thinking that a veteran like Wilson would never fail to throw a sir into every sentence, but he was not accustomed to this quasi-military situation.

'What kind of work did you do before coming on the Department?' asked Captain Smithson, leafing through the folder. 'Post Office, wasn't it?'

'No sir. Bank. I worked at a bank. Four years. Ever since high school.'

'What made you want to be a policeman?' asked the captain, touching the gaunt tanned cheek with a pencil.

'The pay and the security,' Gus answered, and then quickly, 'and it's a good career, a profession. And I like it so far.'

'Policemen don't make very good pay,' said Sergeant Jacobs.

'It's the most I ever made, sir,' said Gus, deciding to be truthful. 'I never made anywhere near four eighty-nine a month before, sir. And I have two children and one on the way.'

'You're only twenty-two years old,' Sergeant Jacobs whistled. 'What a family you're making.'

'We were married right after high school.'

'Do you intend to finish college?' asked Lieutenant Hartley.

'Oh, yes sir,' said Gus. 'I'm going to switch my major to police science, sir.'

'Business administration is a good field of study,' said Captain Smithson. 'If you like it, stay with it. The Department can find good use for business administration majors.'

'Yes sir,' said Gus.

'That's all, Plebesly,' said Captain Smithson. 'Keep working on your shooting. It could be better. And send in the next cadet, please.'

THREE
The Scholar

R oy Fehler had to admit it pleased him when he overheard two of his classmates mention his name in a whispered conversation during a smoking break after class. He heard the cadet mutter 'intellectual', reverently, he thought, just after he recorded the highest score in the report writing class conducted by Officer Willis. He found the academic portion of recruit training un-challenging and if it weren't for some difficulties on the pistol range and his lack of endurance on the P.T. field, he would probably be the top cadet in his class and win the Smith & Wesson always awarded to the top cadet at graduation. It would be a tragedy, he thought, if someone like Plebesly won the revolver merely because he could run faster or shoot better than Roy.

He was anxious for Sergeant Harris to come in the classroom for their three hours of criminal law. It was the most stimulating part of recruit training even though Harris was only an adequate teacher. Roy had bought a copy of Fricke's *California Criminal Law*, and had read it twice in the past two weeks. He had challenged Harris on several points of law and believed that Harris had become more alert of late for fear of being embarrassed by a knowledgeable recruit. The classroom quieted abruptly.

Sergeant Harris strode to the front of the class, spread his notes on the lectern and lit the first of the several cigarettes he would smoke during his lecture. He had a face like porous concrete, but Roy thought he wore his uniform well. The tailored blue wool seemed particularly attractive on tall slim men, and Roy wondered how he would look when he had the blue uniform and black Sam Browne.

'We're going to continue with search and seizure of evidence,' said Harris, scratching the bald spot at the crown of his rust-colored hair.

'By the way, Fehler,' said Sergeant Harris, 'you were right yesterday about the uncorroborated testimony of an accomplice being sufficient to prove the corpus delicti. But it isn't enough to convict.'

'No, of course not,' said Roy, nodding his thanks to Harris for the acknowledgment. He wasn't sure whether Harris appreciated the significance of a few well-placed brain-teasing questions. It was the student who brought a class to life. He had learned this from Professor Raymond who had encouraged him to specialize in criminology when he was drifting aimlessly in the social sciences unable to find a specialty which really interested him. And it was Professor Raymond who begged him not to drop out of college, because he had added so much to the three classes he had taken from the kindly round little man with the burning brown eyes. But he was tired of college; even the independent study with Professor Raymond had begun to bore him. It had come to him suddenly one sleepless night when the presence of Dorothy and her pregnancy was oppressing him that he ought to leave college and join the police department for a year, two years, until he learned something of crime and criminals that might not be available to the criminologist.

The next day he applied at City Hall wondering if he should phone his father or wait until he was actually sworn in, as he would be in about three months, if he passed all the tests and survived the character investigation which he knew would pose no problem. His father was terribly disappointed and his older brother Carl had reminded him that his education had already cost the family business in excess of nine thousand dollars, especially since he could not wait until he finished college to marry, and that in any event, a criminologist would be of little use to a restaurant supply business. Roy had told Carl that he would pay back every cent, and he certainly intended to, but it was difficult living on the policeman's beginning salary which was not the advertised four hundred and eighty-nine dollars a month – not when they deducted for your pension, Police Relief, the Police Protective League, the Police Credit Union which loaned the money for the uniforms, income tax, and the medical plan. But he vowed he'd pay Carl and his father every cent. And he'd finish college and be a criminologist eventually, never making the money his brother Carl would make, but being infinitely happier.

'Yesterday we talked about the famous cases like Cahan, Rochin, and others,' said Sergeant Harris. 'And we talked about Mapp versus Ohio which any rookie would know was illegal search and seizure, and I mentioned how it sometimes seems to policemen that the court is lying in wait for bad cases like Mapp versus Ohio so they can restrict police power a little more. Now that you're policemen, or almost policemen, you're going to become very interested in the decisions handed down by the courts in the area of search and seizure. You're going to be upset, confused, and generally pissed off most of the time, and you're going to hear locker room bitching about the fact that most landmark decisions are five to four, and how can a working cop be expected to make a sudden decision in the heat of combat and then be second-guessed by the Vestal Virgins of the Potomac, and all that other crap. But in my opinion, that kind of talk is self-defeating. We're only concerned with the US and California supreme courts and a couple of appellate courts. So don't worry about some of these freakish decisions that an individual judge hands down. Even if it's your case and it's one you wanted to win. Chances are the defendant will be busted again before long and we'll get another crack at him. And the judge's decision ends right there on the bench. It's not going to have a goddamn thing to do with the next case you try.

'Now I know I got you guys pretty confused yesterday with the problems of search incident to a lawful arrest. We know we can search when?' Sergeant Harris waved a burning cigarette vaguely toward the rear of the room.

Roy didn't bother to turn toward the voice which answered, 'When you have a search warrant, or when you have consent, or incident to a lawful arrest.' The voice Roy knew belonged to Samuel Isenberg, the only other cadet whom Roy felt might challenge him scholastically.

'Right,' said Sergeant Harris, blowing a cloud of smoke through his nose. 'Half you people will never get a search warrant in your entire careers. Most of the two hundred thousand arrests we make in a year are made on the basis of reasonable cause to believe a felony has been committed, or because a crime has been committed in the officer's presence. You're going to stumble onto crimes and criminals and bang! You've got to move, not take six hours to get a search warrant. It's for that reason that we're not going to talk about this kind of search. I've saved the other kind of search until today because to me it's the most challenging – that's search incident to a lawful arrest. If the court ever takes this kind of search away from us we'll be nearly out of business.'

Isenberg raised his hand, and Sergeant Harris nodded while taking an incredible puff on the cigarette. What was a fairly good-sized butt was now scorching his fingers. He snuffed it out as Isenberg said, 'Would you repeat, sir, about the search of the premises ninety-five feet from the defendant's house?'

'I was afraid of that.' Harris smiled, shrugged, and lit another cigarette. 'I shouldn't bring up those cases. I did what I criticize other officers for doing, bitching about controversial cases and prophesying doom. Okay, I just said that it hasn't yet been defined what *under the defendant's control* means in terms of search of the premises incident to the arrest. The court has deemed in its infinite wisdom that an arrest ninety-five feet away from the house did not give officers the right to go into the house and search under the theory of the defendant having control of the premises. Also, I mentioned that in another case a person sixty feet away was deemed to have control of a car in question. And then I mentioned a third case in which officers arrested some bookmakers in their car a half block away and the court held the search of the car and premises was reasonable.

'But don't worry about that kind of crap. I shouldn't have mentioned it anyway because I'm basically an optimist. I always see the glass half full not half empty. Some policemen predict that the courts will eventually strip us of all our right to search incident to arrest, but that would cripple us. I don't think it will happen. I feel that one of these days the Chief Sorcerer in Washington and his eight little apprentices will get themselves together and all this will be straightened out.'

The class tittered and Roy felt himself becoming irked. Harris just couldn't resist criticizing the Supreme Court, thought Roy. He hadn't heard any instructor discuss the law without taking a few shots at the Court. Harris seemed reasonable but he probably felt obligated to do it too. So far, all of the cases Roy had read, that were so bitterly opposed by the instructors, seemed to him just and intelligent. They were based on libertarian principles and it seemed to him unfair to say such thoughtful decisions were unrealistic.

'Okay you guys, quit leading me off on tangents. We're supposed to be talking about searches incident to a lawful arrest. How about this one: Two officers observe a cab double-parked in front of a hotel. The fare, a man, gets out of the front seat. A woman comes out of the hotel and gets in the rear seat. Another man not with the woman walks up and gets in the back seat with the woman. Two policemen observe the action and decide to investigate. They approach and order the occupants out of the cab. They observe the man remove his hand from the juncture of the seat and back cushion. The officers remove the rear cushion and find three marijuana cigarettes. The man was convicted. Was the decision affirmed or denied by the appellate court? Anyone want to make a guess?'

'Denied,' said Guminski, a thin, wiry-haired man of about thirty, whom Roy guessed to be the oldest cadet in the class.

'See. You guys are already thinking like cops,' Harris chuckled. 'You're ready to believe the courts are screwing us every time. Well you're wrong. The conviction was affirmed. But there was something I failed to mention that contributed to the decision. What do you think it might be?'

Roy raised his hand and when Harris nodded, Roy asked, 'What time of day was it?'

'Good,' said Sergeant Harris. 'You might've guessed, it was an unusual hour. About 3:00 A.M.. Now on what grounds could they search the cab?'

'Incident to a lawful arrest,' said Roy, without raising his hand or waiting for Harris to nod.

'Who were they arresting?' asked Harris.

Roy was sorry he had responded so quickly. He realized he was being trapped. 'Not the defendant or the woman,' he said slowly, while his mind worked furiously. 'The cabdriver!'

The class burst out laughing but was silenced by a wave of Harris' nicotine-stained left hand. Harris bared his large brownish teeth in a grin and said, 'Go ahead, Fehler, what's your reasoning?'

'They could arrest the cabbie for double-parking,' said Roy. 'That's a violation, and then search incident to the lawful arrest.'

'Not bad,' said Harris. 'I like to see you people thinking even when you're wrong.'

Hugh Franklin, the broad-shouldered recruit who sat next to Roy at the alphabetically arranged tables, chuckled louder than Roy felt was necessary. Franklin did not like him, Roy was certain. Franklin was an all-American jock strapper. A high school letterman according to the conversations they had the first few days in the academy. Then three years in the navy, where he played baseball and toured the Orient, thoroughly enjoying himself, and now to the police department, when he couldn't make it in Class D professional baseball.

'Why is Fehler wrong?' Harris asked the class, and Roy became annoyed that the entire class should be asked to attack his answer. Why didn't Harris just give the reason instead of asking everyone to comment? Could it be that Harris was trying to embarrass him? Perhaps he didn't like having a recruit in the class who took the trouble to do independent study in criminal law and not just blindly accept the legal interpretations which evolve from the police point of view.

'Yes, Isenberg,' said Harris, and this time Roy turned around so that he would not miss Isenberg's annoying manner of answering questions.

'I doubt that the search of the cab could be justified incident to the arrest of the driver for double-parking,' said Isenberg carefully, his dark-lidded black eyes moving from Harris to Roy and back to the instructor. 'It's true the driver committed a traffic violation and could be cited, and a traffic ticket is technically an arrest, but how could you search the cab for contraband? That has nothing to do with a traffic violation, does it?'

'Are you asking me?' said Harris.

'No sir, that's my answer.' Isenberg smiled shyly, and Roy felt disgust for Isenberg's pretense at humility. He felt the same toward Plebesly and the diffidence he showed when someone expressed admiration for his athletic prowess. He believed them both to be conceited men. Isenberg was another one, he knew, who was just discharged from the army. He wondered how many men joined the Department because they were simply looking for a job and how many like himself had more serious motives.

'Was the search incident to the arrest of anyone?' asked Harris.

'No, I don't think so,' said Isenberg, clearing his throat nervously. 'I don't think anyone was under arrest at the time the officer found the contraband. The officer could detain and interrogate people under unusual circumstances at night according to Giske versus Sanders, and I don't think there was anything unreasonable in ordering them out of the cab. The officers had a justifiable suspicion that something unusual was going on. When the defendant reached behind the seat I think that might be construed as a furtive action.' Isenberg's voice trailed off and several recruits including Roy raised their hands.

Harris looked at no one but Roy. 'Go ahead, Fehler,' he said.

'I don't think the officers had the right to order them out of the cab. And when were they arrested, after they found the narcotics? What if they would have got out of the cab and just walked away? Would the officers have the right to stop them?'

'How about that, Isenberg?' asked Harris, lighting a fresh cigarette with a battered silver lighter. 'Could the officers stop them from walking away, before the contraband was found?'

'Uh, yes, I think so,' said Isenberg looking at Roy, who interrupted him.

'Were they under arrest then?' asked Roy. 'They must have been under arrest if the officers could stop them from walking away. And if they were under arrest what was their crime? The marijuana wasn't found for several seconds after they had them already under arrest.'

Roy smiled indulgently to show Isenberg and Harris there were no hard feelings at having proved Isenberg wrong.

'The point is, they were not under arrest, Fehler,' said Isenberg, addressing Roy directly for the first time. 'We have the right to stop and interrogate. The person is obliged to identify himself and explain what's going on. And we can resort to any means to make him submit. Yet we haven't arrested him for any crime. If he explains what's going on and it's reasonable, we release him. I think that's what Giske versus Sanders meant. So in this case, the officers stopped, interrogated, and recovered the marijuana during their investigation. Then and only then were the suspects placed under arrest.'

Roy knew from Harris' pleased expression that Isenberg was correct.

'How could you prove someone else hadn't dumped the marijuana behind the seat?' asked Roy, unable to dull the sharp edge on his voice.

'I should've mentioned that the cabbie testified to cleaning out the back of the cab earlier in the evening because of a sick passenger who threw up back there,' said Harris. 'And no one had been in the back seat until the woman and the defendant got in.'

'That certainly makes a difference,' said Roy, appealing to Harris for some concession to his interpretation.

'Well, that wasn't the issue I was concerned with,' said Harris. 'It was the question of searching prior to an actual arrest that I wanted someone to bring out of this case, and Isenberg did it beautifully. You all understand, don't you?'

'Yes sir,' said Roy, 'but the case would certainly have been reversed if the cabbie hadn't testified to cleaning out the back that same evening. That was certainly an important point, sir.'

'Yes, Fehler,' Sergeant Harris sighed. 'You were partly right. I should've mentioned that, Fehler.'

August 1960

CHAPTER FOUR
Huero

Serge gave his shoes a quick buff, threw the shoe brush in his locker, and slammed the metal door. He was late for roll call. It was two minutes after four o'clock. Damn the traffic, he thought. How can I put up with this traffic and smog for twenty years? He paused before the full-length mirror, alone in the locker room. His brass buttons and Sam Browne needed polish. His blue woolen uniform was so lint-covered it looked hairy. He cursed as he realized there might be an inspection tonight.

Serge picked up his notebook, the packet of traffic citations and a map book of city streets. He shoved his shiny new five-cell flashlight into the deep pocket of his uniform pants, grabbed his baton, and put his hat on, since his hands were too full to carry it. The other night watch officers were talking noisily as he entered the roll call room. The watch commander's desk was unoccupied. Serge was relieved to see that he too was late and by the time he arrived five minutes later, Serge had dabbed most of the lint from his uniform with a piece of two-inch-wide masking tape which he carried in his notebook for such emergencies.

'After those new uniforms are cleaned a few times you won't have so much trouble with lint,' said Perkins, the desk officer, a nineteen-year policeman now on light duty while recovering from a serious heart attack.

'Oh, yeah,' Serge nodded, self-conscious of his brand-new, never-cleaned blue uniform, announcing that he was one of the rookies just graduated last week from the academy. He and two members of his class had been assigned to Hollenbeck. It wasn't hard to see how they had been selected, he thought. The other officers were Chacon and Medina. He had heard in the academy that most officers with Spanish surnames ended up in Hollenbeck Division but he had hoped he might be an exception. Not everyone recognized Duran as a Spanish name. He had been mistaken for German and even Irish, especially by people who couldn't believe a Mexican could be fair, freckled, and speak without a trace of a Spanish accent. The Negro officers were not all assigned to the Negro areas; he was irked that the Chicanos were all stuck here in Hollenbeck. He could see the need for Spanish-speaking officers here, but nobody had even bothered to see if he could speak Spanish. It was just 'Duran to Hollenbeck', another victim of a system.

'Ramirez,' said Lieutenant Jethro, settling his long sagging body in the desk chair and opening the time book.

'Here.'

'Anderson.'

'Here.'

'You're working Four-A-Five.'

'Bradbury.'

'Here.'

'Gonsalvez.'

'Here.'

'Four-A-Eleven.'

Serge answered when his name was called along with his partner for the night, Galloway, whom he had not worked with since arriving in the division. He was scheduled off tomorrow, Sunday, after working six days, and wished he weren't. Every night was a new adventure and he smiled as he realized he would probably be glad for days off soon enough. He tired of everything quickly. Still, this was a more interesting job than most. He couldn't honestly think of one he'd like better. Of course, when he finished college, he might find something better. And then he had to smile again at himself. He had enrolled in two night classes at East Los Angeles Junior College. Six units. Only a hundred and eighteen to go, and here I sit dreaming about finishing college, he thought.

'Okay, here's the crimes,' said the lieutenant, after calling the roll. Perkins took the lineup board downstairs to the teletype machine to be forwarded to Communications, so that Communications downtown would know which cars were working in Hollenbeck. The policemen opened their notebooks to a fresh page, and got ready to write.

Lieutenant Jethro was a loose-skinned, sallow man with a hard mouth and very cold eyes. Serge had learned however that he was the division's best-liked supervisor. The men considered him fair.

'Had a robbery at twenty-nine twenty-two Brooklyn Avenue,' he read mechanically. 'At Big G restaurant. Today, 9:30 A.M. Suspect: male, Mexican, twenty-three to twenty-five years, five-five to five-six, hundred sixty to hundred seventy pounds, black hair, brown eyes, medium complexion, wearing a dark shirt and dark pants, carried a hand gun, got eighty-five dollars from the cash register and took victim's wallet and I.D.... Goddamn it, that's a shitty description!' said Lieutenant Jethro suddenly. 'This is what we were talking about last night at roll call training. What the hell good does a description like that do you?'

'Maybe that's all they could get out of the guy, Lieutenant,' said Milton, the burly baiter of supervisors who always took the last seat of the last table in the roll call room, and whose four service stripes, indicating twenty years' service, entitled him to a constant barrage of sarcasm directed at the sergeants. He was usually pretty quiet around the lieutenant though, Serge thought.

'Bullshit, Milt,' said Jethro. 'This poor bastard Hector Lopez has been hit a half dozen times this year. I'm always seeing his name on robbery, burglary, or till tap reports. He's become a professional victim, and he usually gives an outstanding description of the suspect. It's just that some officer – in this case, it was a day watch officer – was in a big hurry and didn't try to get a decent description. This is a good example of a worthless piece of paper that can't be any use to the detectives. That description could fit twenty percent of the guys on the street right now.

'It only takes a few minutes extra to get a decent description the dicks can work with,' Jethro continued. 'How did the guy comb his hair? Did he have a moustache? Glasses? Tattoos? A distinctive walk? How about his teeth? His clothes? There's dozens of little things about clothes that might be important. How did he talk? Did he have a gravel voice? Did he have a Spanish accent? How about that gun? This report says handgun. What the hell does that tell you? I know goddamn well Lopez knows the difference between an automatic and a revolver. And was it chrome plated or blue steel?' Jethro dropped the papers disgustedly into the folder. 'We had lots of crimes last night, but none of the suspect descriptions are worth a shit so I'm not going to read them.' He closed the folders and sat back in his chair on the ten-inch platform, looking down at the policemen of the night watch. 'Anything you guys want to talk about before we have an inspection?' he asked.

A groan went up at the mention of the word inspection, and Serge rubbed the toes of each shoe on the back of his calves, irritated once more at the Los Angeles traffic which prevented him from arriving at the station early enough to shine them.

Jethro's colorless eyes glinted merrily around the room for a moment. 'If no one can think of something to say, we might as well get started with the inspection. We'll have more time to look a little harder.'

'Wait a minute, Lieutenant,' said Milton, a wet stump of cigar between his little teeth. 'Give me a second, I'll think of something.'

'Yeah, Milt, I don't blame you for wanting to stall me,' said Jethro. 'It looks like you shined those shoes with a Hershey bar.'

The men chuckled and Milton beamed and puffed from the end seat at the last row of tables in the rear of the squad room. On his first night in Hollenbeck, Milton had informed Serge that the last row of tables belonged to *los veteranos* and that rookies generally sat toward the front of the room. Serge hadn't worked with Milton yet, and was looking forward to it. He was loud and overbearing but the men told him he could learn a lot from Milton if Milton felt like teaching him.

'One thing before inspection,' said Jethro. 'Who's working Forty-three tonight? You, Galloway?'

Serge's partner nodded.

'Who's working with you, one of the new men? Duran, right? You two check those pin maps before you go out. They're killing us on Brooklyn Avenue about midnight. We've had three window smashes this week and two last week. All about the same time, and they're grabbing quite a bit of loot.'

Serge looked at the walls which were lined with identical street maps of Hollenbeck Division. Each map bore different colored pins, some to indicate burglaries, the multicolored pins indicating whether they occurred on morning, day, or night watch. Other maps showed where robberies were occurring. Still others showed locations of car thefts and thefts from vehicles.

'Let's fall in for inspection,' said Lieutenant Jethro.

This was Serge's first inspection since leaving the academy. He wondered where fourteen men could line up in the crowded room. He saw quickly that they formed one rank along the side wall in front of the pin maps. The tall men fell in toward the front of the room so Serge headed for the front, standing next to Bressler, who was the only officer taller than himself.

'Okay, you're supposed to be at attention,' said the lieutenant quietly to a policeman in the center of the rank who was muttering about something.

'At close interval, dress right, dress!'

The policemen, hands on right hips, elbows touching the man to the right, dressed the rank perfunctorily and Jethro didn't bother to check the line.

'Ready, front!'

When Jethro inspected him, Serge stared at the top of the lieutenant's head as he had been taught in boot camp six years ago when he was eighteen, just graduated from high school, broken-hearted that the Korean War ended before he could get in it and win several pounds of medals which he could pin to the beautiful Marine Corps dress blue uniform which they didn't issue you and he never got around to buying because he grew up quickly under the stunning realities of Marine Corps boot camp.

Jethro paused a few extra seconds in front of Ruben Gonsalvez, a jovial dark-skinned Mexican who, Serge guessed, was a veteran of at least ten years with the Department.

'You're getting rounder every day, Ruben,' said Jethro in his toneless unsmiling voice.

'Yes, Lieutenant,' answered Gonsalvez and Serge did not yet dare to look down the line.

'You been eating at Manuel's again, I see,' said Jethro, and with peripheral vision Serge could see the lieutenant touching Gonsalvez's necktie.

'Yes, sir,' said Gonsalvez. 'The top stains above the tie bar are *chile verde*. The other ones are *menudo*.'

This time Serge turned a fraction of an inch and detected no expression on Jethro or Gonsalvez.

'How about you, Milt? When you changing the oil on your necktie?' said Jethro, moving down the line to the white-haired veteran who stood so straight he looked like a tall man but standing next to him Serge guessed he wasn't five feet ten.

'Right after inspection, Lieutenant,' said Milton, and Serge sneaked a glance at Jethro, who shook his head sadly and moved to the end of the rank.

'Night watch. One pace forward ... No, as you were,' said Jethro, shuffling to the front of the roll call room. 'I'm afraid to inspect you from the rear. Some of you'll probably have bananas or girlie magazines hanging out of your back pockets. Dismissed!'

So this is how it is, thought Serge, gathering up his equipment, looking for Galloway to whom he had never been introduced. He was afraid the division would be GI and he wasn't sure how long he could take military discipline. This was okay. He could tolerate this much discipline indefinitely, he thought.

Galloway walked up and offered his hand. 'Duran?'

'Yeah,' said Serge, shaking hands with the freckled young man.

'What do your friends call you?' asked Galloway and Serge smiled as he recognized the hackneyed opening line that policemen use on suspects to determine street names which were usually much more valuable to know than true names.

'Serge. How about you?'

'Pete.'

'Okay, Pete, what do you want to do tonight?' asked Serge, hoping that Galloway would let him drive. This was his sixth night and he hadn't driven yet.

'You're just out of the class, aren't you?' asked Galloway.

'Yeah,' said Serge, disappointed.

'You familiar with the city?'

'No, I lived in Chino before coming on the job.'

'Guess you better keep books then. I'll drive, okay?'

'You're the boss,' Serge said cheerfully.

'No, we're equals,' said Galloway. 'Partners.'

It was satisfying to be able to get settled in the radio car without asking a dozen inane questions or fumbling around with your equipment. Serge felt he could handle the passenger officer's routine duties as well as possible by now. Serge put his flashlight and hat in the back seat along with his baton which was thrust under the back cushion for easy access. He was surprised to see Galloway slide the baton under the back cushion in the front seat, lancelike, right next to him.

'I like my stick closer to me,' said Galloway. 'It's my blue blanket.'

'Four-A-Forty-three, night watch, clear,' said Serge into the hand mike as Galloway started the engine of the Plymouth, and backed out of the parking space and onto First Street, the setting sun forcing Serge to put on his sunglasses as he wrote their names on the daily log.

'What did you do before coming on the job?' asked Galloway.

'Marine Corps for four years,' said Serge, writing his serial number on the log.

'How do you like police work so far?' asked Galloway.

'Fine,' Serge answered, writing carefully as the car bounced over a rut in the street.

'It's a good job,' said Galloway. 'I'm starting my fourth year next month. Can't complain so far.'

The sandy hair and freckles made Galloway look like a high school kid, Serge thought. With four years on the job he has to be at least twenty-five.

'This your first Saturday night?'

'Yeah.'

'Quite a difference on weekends. Maybe we'll see a little action.'

'Hope so.'

'Done anything exciting yet?'

'Nothing,' said Serge. 'Took some burglary reports. Wrote a few tickets. Booked a couple drunks and a few traffic warrants. Haven't even made a felony arrest yet.'

'We'll try to get you a felony tonight.' Galloway offered Serge a cigarette and he accepted.

'Thanks. I was going to ask you to stop so I could get some,' said Serge, lighting Galloway's with his Zippo that used to have a brass globe and anchor affixed to it. There was now just a naked metallic ring on the lighter where he had pried the Marine Corps emblem off in Okinawa after a salty pfc with a year and a half in the corps had kidded him about only gung-ho recruits carrying P.X. Zippos with big fat emblems on them.

Serge smiled as he remembered how badly the young marines wanted to be salts. How they had scrubbed and bleached their new dungarees and put sea dips in the caps. He hadn't completely gotten over it, he thought, remembering how his new blue uniform made him uneasy tonight when Perkins mentioned the lint.

The incessant chattering on the police radio was still giving Serge trouble. He knew it would be some time before he was able to pick his car number, Four-A-Forty-three, from the jumble of voices that crowded the police frequencies. He was starting to recognize some of the voices of the Communications operators. One sounded like an old maid schoolmarm, another like a youngish Marilyn Monroe, and a third had a trace of a Southern accent.

'We got a call,' said Galloway.

'What?'

'Tell her to repeat,' said Galloway.

'Four-A-Forty-three, repeat, please,' said Serge, his pencil poised over the pad which was affixed to a metal shelf in front of the hot sheet.

'Four-A-Forty-three,' said the schoolmarm, 'one-two-seven South Chicago, see the woman, four-five-nine report.'

'Four-A-Forty-three, roger,' said Serge. And to Galloway, 'Sorry. I can't pick our calls out of all that noise, yet.'

'Takes a little time,' said Galloway, turning around in a gas station parking lot, heading east toward Chicago Street.

'Where you living?' asked Galloway, as Serge took a deep puff on the cigarette to finish it before they arrived.

'Alhambra. I got an apartment over there.'

'Guess Chino's too far to drive, huh?'

'Yeah.'

'Married?'

'No,' said Serge.

'Got parents in Chino?'

'No, they're both dead. Got an older brother there. And a sister in Pomona.'

'Oh,' said Galloway, looking at him like he was a war orphan.

'I have a nice little apartment, and the apartment house is crawling with broads,' said Serge, so his baby-faced partner would stop being embarrassed at prying.

'Really?' Galloway grinned. 'Must be nice being a bachelor. I got hooked at nineteen, so I wouldn't know.'

After turning north on Chicago Street, Galloway gave Serge a puzzled look as Serge craned his neck to catch the house-numbers on the east side of the street.

'One twenty-seven will be on the west,' said Galloway. 'Even numbers are always on the east and south.'

'All over the city?'

'All over,' Galloway laughed. 'Hasn't anybody told you that yet?'

'Not yet. I've been checking both sides of the street on every call. Pretty dumb.'

'Sometimes the senior officer forgets to mention the obvious. As long as you're willing to admit you know nothing, you'll learn fast enough. Some guys hate to show they don't know anything.'

Serge was out of the car while Galloway was still applying the emergency brake. He removed his stick from the back seat and slid it in through the baton holder on the left side of his Sam Browne. He noticed that Galloway left his baton in the car, but he guessed he should adhere to the rules very closely for a while, and the rule was carry your batons.

The house was a one-story faded pink frame. Most of the houses in East Los Angeles seemed faded. This was an old part of the city. The streets were narrow and Serge noticed many aged people.

'Come in, come in, gentlemen,' said the snuffling puckered old woman in an olive-drab dress and bandaged legs, as they stepped on the tiny porch one at a time, shouldering their way through a forest of potted ferns and flowers.

'Step right in, right in,' she smiled and Serge was surprised to see a mouthful of what he was sure were real teeth. She should have been toothless. A fleshy goiter dropped from her neck.

'It's not so often we see the policemen these days,' she smiled. 'We used to know all the police at the Boyle Heights station. I used to know some officers' names, but already they're retired I guess.'

Serge smiled at the Molly Goldberg accent, but he noticed Galloway was nodding soberly at the old woman as he sat in the ancient creaking rocker in front of a brightly painted unused fireplace. Serge smelled fish and flowers, mustiness and perfume, and bread in the oven. He removed his cap and sat on the lumpy napless sofa with a cheap oriental tapestry thrown over the back to dull the thrust of the broken springs he felt against his back.

'I'm Mrs. Waxman,' said the old woman. 'I been right here in this house for thirty-eight years.'

'Is that a fact?' said Galloway.

'Would you like something? A cup of coffee maybe. Or a cup-cake?'

'No thank you,' said Galloway. Serge shook his head and smiled.

'I used to walk down the police station some summer evenings and chat with the desk officer. There was a Jewish boy worked there named Sergeant Muellstein. You ever know him?'

'No,' said Galloway.

'Brooklyn Avenue was really something then. You should have seen Boyle Heights. Some of the finest families in Los Angeles was living here. Then the Mexicans started moving in and all the people ran out and went to the west side. Just the old Jews like me are left with the Mexicans now. What do you think of the church down the street?'

'Which church?' asked Galloway.

'Hah! You don't have to say. I understand you got a job to do.' The old woman smiled knowingly at Galloway and winked at Serge.

'They dare to call the place a synagogue,' she croaked. 'Could you imagine it?'

Serge glanced through the window at the light-studded Star of David atop the First Hebrew Christian Synagogue at the residential corner of Chicago Street and Michigan Avenue.

'You see what's right across the street?' said the old woman.

'What?' asked Serge.

'The United Mexican Baptist Church,' said the old woman, with a triumphant nod of her chalk-white head. 'I knew it was going to happen. I told them in the forties when they all started moving.'

'Told who?' asked Serge, listening intently.

'We could have lived with the Mexicans. An Orthodox Jew is like a Catholic Mexican. We could have lived. Now look what we got. Reform Jews was bad enough. Now, Christian Jews? Don't make me laugh. And Mexican Baptisters? You see, everything is out of whack now. Now there's just a few of us old ones left. I don't even go out of my yard, no more.'

'I guess you called us because of Mrs. Horwitz,' said Galloway, adding to Serge's confusion.

'Yes, it's the same old story. There ain't nobody can get along with the woman,' said Mrs. Waxman. 'She tells everybody her husband has a better shop than my Morris. Hah! My Morris is a watchmaker. Do you understand? A real watchmaker! A craftsman, not some junk repairman!' The old woman stood up, gesturing angrily at the center of the room as a trickle of saliva ran uncontrolled from the corner of her wrinkled mouth.

'Now, now, Mrs. Waxman,' said Galloway, helping her back to the chair. 'I'm going right over to Mrs. Horwitz and tell her to stop spreading those stories. If she doesn't, why I'll threaten to put her in jail.'

'Would you? Would you do that?' asked the old woman. 'But don't arrest her, mind you. Just give her a pretty good scare.'

'We're going over there right now,' said Galloway, putting on his cap and standing up.

'Serves her right, serves her right,' said Mrs. Waxman, beaming at the two young men.

'Good-bye, Mrs. Waxman,' said Galloway.

'Bye,' Serge mumbled, hoping that Galloway had not noticed how long it took him to catch on to the old woman's senility.

'She's a regular,' Galloway explained, starting the car and lighting a cigarette. 'I guess I been there a dozen times. The old Jews always say "Boyle Heights", never Hollenbeck or East LA. This *was* the Jewish community before the Chicanos moved in.'

'Doesn't she have a family?' asked Serge, marking the call in the log.

'No. Another abandoned old lady,' said Galloway. 'I'd rather some ass-hole shoot me in the street tonight than end up old and alone like her.'

'Where's Mrs. Horwitz live?'

'Who knows? West side probably, where all the Jews with money went. Or maybe she's dead.'

Serge borrowed another of Galloway's cigarettes and relaxed as Galloway patrolled slowly in the late summer dusk. He stopped in front of a liquor store and asked Serge what brand he smoked and entered the store without asking for money. Serge knew that this meant the liquor store was Galloway's cigarette stop, or rather it belonged to the car, Four-A-Forty-three. He had accepted the minor gratuity when each partner he had worked with offered it. Only one, a serious, alert young policeman named Kilton, had stopped at a place where Serge had to pay for cigarettes.

Galloway came back after repaying the liquor store proprietor with a few minutes of small talk and flipped the cigarettes into Serge's lap.

'How about some coffee?' asked Galloway.

'Sounds good.'

Galloway made a U-turn and drove to a small sidewalk restaurant on Fourth Street. He parked in the empty parking lot, turned up the police radio and got out leaving the door to the car open so they could hear the radio.

'Hi, baby face,' said the bleached blonde working the counter, who spoiled her eyes by drawing her eyebrows at a ridiculous angle.

If there was one thing most Mexicans had it was good heads of hair, thought Serge. Why had this one destroyed hers with chemicals?

'Afternoon, Sylvia,' said Galloway. 'Meet my partner, Serge Duran.'

'*Qué tal, huero?*' said Sylvia, pouring two steaming cups of coffee which Galloway did not offer to pay for.

'Hi,' said Serge, sipping the burning coffee and hoping the remark would pass.

'*Huero?*' said Galloway. 'You a Chicano, Serge?'

'What do you think, *pendejo?*' Sylvia laughed raucously, showing a gold-capped eyetooth. 'With a name like Duran?'

'I'll be damned,' said Galloway. 'You sure look like a paddy.'

'He's a real *huero*, baby,' said Sylvia with a flirtatious smile at Serge. 'He's almost as fair as you.'

'Can't we talk about something else?' asked Serge, irritated more at himself for being embarrassed than at these two grinning fools. He told himself he was not ashamed of being Mexican, it was simply less complicated to be an Anglo. And an Anglo he had been for the past five years. He had only returned to Chino a few times after his mother died and one of those times was for a fourteen-day leave with his brother when they buried her. He had tired of the dreary little town in five days and returned to the base, selling his unused leave to the Marine Corps when he was discharged.

'Well, it's good to have a partner who can speak Spanish,' said Galloway. 'We can use you around here.'

'What makes you think I can speak Spanish?' asked Serge, very careful to maintain the narrow cordiality in his voice.

Sylvia looked at Serge strangely, stopped smiling, and returned to the sink where she began washing a small pile of cups and glasses.

'You one of those Chicanos who can't speak Spanish?' Galloway laughed. 'We got another one like that, Montez. They transferred him to Hollenbeck and he can't speak Spanish any better than me.'

'I don't need it. I get along well enough in English,' said Serge.

'Better than me, I hope,' smiled Galloway. 'If you can't *spell* better than me we'll be in lots of trouble when we make our reports.'

Serge gulped down the coffee and waited anxiously as Galloway tried in vain to get Sylvia talking again. She smiled at his jokes but remained at the sink and looked coldly at Serge. 'Bye-bye, baby face,' she said, as they thanked her for the free coffee and left.

'It's too bad you don't speak Spanish real good,' said Galloway as the sun dropped through the smoggy glow in the west. 'With a paddy-looking guy like you we could overhear lots of good information. Our arrestees would never guess you could understand them and we could learn all kind of things.'

'How often you pick up a sitting duck?' asked Serge, to change the subject, checking a license plate against the numbers on the hot sheet.

'Ducks? Oh, I get one a week maybe. There's plenty of hot cars sitting around Hollenbeck.'

'How about rollers?' asked Serge. 'How many hot cars do you get rolling?'

'Hot rollers? Oh, maybe one a month, I average. They're just teenage joyriders usually. Are you just half Mexican?'

Bullshit, thought Serge, taking a large puff on the cigarette, deciding that Galloway would not be denied.

'No, I'm all Mexican. But we just didn't talk Spanish at home.'

'Your parents didn't talk it?'

'My father died when I was young. My mother talked half English and half Spanish. We always answered in English. I left home when I got out of high school and went in the Marine Corps for four years. I just got out eight months ago. I've been away from the language and I've forgotten it. I never knew very much Spanish to begin with.'

'Too bad,' Galloway murmured and seemed satisfied.

Serge slumped in the seat staring blankly at the old houses of Boyle Heights and fought a mild wave of depression. Only two of the other policemen he had worked with had forced him to explain his Spanish name. Damn curious people, he thought. He asked nothing of people, nothing, not even of his brother, Angel, who had tried in every way possible to get him to settle in Chino after leaving the corps, and to go into his gas station with him. Serge told him he didn't plan to work very hard at anything and his brother had to put in thirteen hours every day in the grimy gas station in Chino. He could have done that. Maybe marry some fertile Mexican girl and have nine kids and learn to live on tortillas and beans because that's all you could afford when things were lean in the *barrio*. Well here he was working in another Chicano *barrio*, he thought with a crooked smile. But he'd be out of here as soon as he finished his year's probationary period. Hollywood Division appealed to him, or perhaps West Los Angeles. He could rent an apartment near the ocean. The rent would be high, but maybe he could share the cost with another policeman or two. He had heard stories of the aspiring actresses who languished all over the westside streets.

'You ever worked the west side?' he asked Galloway suddenly.

'No, I just worked Newton Street and here at Hollenbeck,' Galloway answered.

'I hear there're lots of girls in Hollywood and West LA,' said Serge.

'I guess so,' said Galloway and the leer looked ridiculous with the freckles.

'You hear a lot of pussy stories from policemen. I've been wondering how true they are.'

'A lot of them are true,' said Galloway. 'It seems to me that policemen do pretty well because for one thing girls trust you right off. I mean a girl isn't going to be afraid to meet a guy after work when she sees him sitting in a black and white police car in a big blue uniform. She knows you're not a rapist or a nut or something. At least she can be pretty sure. That means something in this town. And she can also be pretty sure you're a fairly clean-cut individual. And then some girls are attracted by the job itself. It's more than the uniform, it's the authority or something. We got a half dozen cop chasers in every division. You'll get to know some of them. All the policemen know them. They try their damnedest to lay every guy at the station. Some are actually pretty good-looking. You met Lupe, yet?'

'Who's she?' asked Serge.

'She's one of Hollenbeck's cop chasers. Drives a Lincoln convertible. You'll run into her before long. Good lay, I heard.' Galloway leered again through the freckles and Serge had to laugh aloud.

'I'm looking forward to meeting her,' said Serge.

'There's probably lots of stuff in Hollywood. I never worked those fancy silk stocking divisions so I wouldn't know. But I'd be willing to bet there's more here on the east side than anywhere.'

'Let's drive around the division, do you mind?' asked Serge.

'No, where do you want to go?'

'Let's tour the streets, all around Boyle Heights.'

'One fifty-cent tour of Hollenbeck Division coming up,' said Galloway.

Serge stopped looking for a traffic violator and he didn't check the hot sheet even once for the sitting duck he craved. He smoked and watched people and houses. All the houses were old, most of the people were Mexican. Most of the streets were too narrow, and Serge guessed they were designed decades before anyone dreamed that Los Angeles would be a city on wheels. And when they did realize it, the east side was too old and too poor and the streets stayed too narrow, and the houses got older. Serge felt his stomach tighten and his face grew unaccountably warm as he saw the secondhand stores. *Ropa usada*, the signs said. And the *panadería* filled with sweet breads, cookies and cakes, usually a bit too oily for him. And the scores of restaurants with painted windows announcing that *menudo* was served on Saturdays and Sundays and Serge wondered how anyone could eat the tripe and hominy and thin red broth. Especially he wondered how he had been able to eat it as a child, but he guessed it was because they had been hungry. He thought of his brother Angel and his sister Aurora and how they would squeeze half a lemon in the *menudo*, sprinkle in oregano and slosh corn tortillas in the broth faster than his mother could make them. His father had been a tubercular whom he barely remembered as a smiling man with bony wrists, lying in bed all the time, coughing and smelling bad from the sickness. He only produced three children and little else in this world and Serge couldn't at the moment think of another family on his street with only three children except the Kulaskis and they were Anglos, at least to the Chicanos they were Anglos, but now he thought how humorous it was to have considered these Polacks as Anglo. He also wondered if it was true that the large quantity of corn the Mexicans consumed by eating tortillas three times a day produced the fine teeth. It was Mexican folklore that this was the case and it was certainly true that he and most of his boyhood friends had teeth like alligators. Serge had been to a dentist for the first time while in the Marine Corps where he had two molars filled.

Night was falling faster now that summer had almost gone and as he watched and listened a strange but oddly familiar feeling swept over him. First it was a tremor in the stomach and then up around the chest and his face felt warm; he was filled with anxious longing, or was it, could it be, nostalgia? It was all he could do to keep from laughing aloud as he thought it must be nostalgia, for this was Chino on a grand scale. He was watching the same people who were doing the same things they had done in Chino, and he thought how strange that part of a man could yearn for the place of his youth even when he despised it, and what produced it, and what it produced. But at least it was the only innocent years he had ever known and there had been his mother. He guessed it was really her that he yearned for and the safety she represented. We all must long for that, he thought.

Serge watched the garish lighted madness on the San Bernardino Freeway as Galloway drove south on Soto back to Boyle Heights. There was a minor accident on the freeway below and a flare pattern had traffic backed up as far as he could see. A man held what looked like a bloody handkerchief to his face and talked to a traffic officer in a white hat who held a flashlight under his arm as he wrote in his notebook. No one really wants to grow up and go out in all this, he thought, looking down at the thousands of crawling headlights and the squatty white tow truck which was removing the debris. That must be what you long for – childhood – not for the people or the place. Those poor stupid Chicanos, he thought. Pitiful bastards.

'Getting hungry, partner?' asked Galloway.

'Anytime,' said Serge, deciding to leave Chino five years in the past where it belonged.

'We don't have many eating spots in Hollenbeck,' said Galloway. 'And the few we do have aren't fit to eat in.'

Serge had already been a policeman long enough to learn that 'eating spot' meant more than restaurant, it meant restaurant that served free food to policemen. He still felt uncomfortable about accepting the free meals especially since they had been warned about gratuities in the police academy. It seemed however that the sergeants looked the other way when it came to free cigarettes, food, newspapers and coffee.

'I don't mind paying for dinner,' said Serge.

'You don't have anything against paying half price, do you? We have a place in our area that pops for half.'

'I don't mind at all,' Serge smiled.

'We actually do have a place that bounces for everything. It's called El Soberano, that means the sovereign. We call it El Sobaco. You know what that means, don't you?'

'No,' Serge lied.

'That means the armpit. It's a real scuzzy joint. A beer joint that serves food. Real ptomaine tavern.'

'Serves greasy tacos, I bet.' Serge smiled wryly, knowing what the place would look like. 'Everybody drinking and dancing I bet, and every night some guy gets jealous of his girl friend and you get a call there to break up a fight.'

'You described it perfect,' said Galloway. 'I don't know about the food though. For all I know, they might drive a sick bull out on the floor at dinner time and everybody slices a steak with their blades.'

'Let's hit the half-price joint,' said Serge.

'Tell her to repeat!' Galloway commanded.

'What?'

'The radio. We just got another call.'

'Son of a bitch. Sorry, partner, I've got to start listening to that jumble of noise.' He pressed the red mike button. 'Four-A-Forty-three, repeat.'

'Four-A-Forty-three, Four-A-Forty-three,' said the shrill voice, who had replaced the schoolmarm. 'Three-three-seven South Mott, see the woman, four-five-nine suspect there now. Code two.'

'Four-A-Forty-three, roger,' said Serge.

Galloway stepped down unexpectedly on the accelerator and Serge bounced off the back cushion. 'Sorry,' Galloway grinned. 'Sometimes I'm a leadfoot. I can't help stomping down on a four-five-nine call. Love to catch those burglars.'

Serge was glad to see his partner's blue eyes shining happily. He hoped the thrills of the job would not wear off too soon on himself. They obviously hadn't on Galloway. It was reassuring. Everything in the world seemed to grow so dull so quickly.

Galloway slowed at a red light, looked both ways carelessly and roared across First Street as a westbound station wagon squealed and blasted its horn.

'Jesus,' Serge whispered aloud.

'Sorry,' said Galloway sheepishly, slowing down but only a little. Two blocks farther, he streaked through a partially blind intersection with a posted stop sign and Serge closed his eyes but heard no squealing tires.

'I don't have to tell you you shouldn't drive like this, do I?' said Galloway. 'At least not while you're on probation. You can't afford to catch any heat from the sergeants while you're on probation.' Galloway made a grinding right turn and another left at the next block.

'If I obeyed all the goddamn rules of the road like they tell us to, we'd never get there quick enough to catch anyone. And I figure it's my ass if we get in an accident, so what the hell.'

How about my ass, you dumb ass, Serge thought, one hand braced on the dashboard, the other gripping the top of the black cushion. He had never envisioned hurtling down busy streets at these speeds. Galloway was a fearless and stupidly lucky driver.

Serge realized that he could not afford to get a quick reputation of troublemaker. New rookies should be all ears and short on mouth, but this was too much. He was going to demand that Galloway slow down. He made the decision just as his sweaty left hand lost its grip on the cushion.

'This is the street,' said Galloway. 'It's about mid-block.' He turned off his headlights and glided noiselessly to the curb, several houses from where the address should have been. 'Don't close your door,' said Galloway, slipping out of the car and padding along the curb while Serge was still unfastening his seat belt.

Serge got out and followed Galloway, who wore ripple-soled shoes and his key ring tucked in his back pocket. Serge now saw the reason as his own new leather-soled shoes skidded and crunched noisily on the pavement. He tucked the jingling key ring in the back pocket and walked as softly as he could.

It was a dark residential street and he lost Galloway in the gloom, cursing as he forgot the address they were sent to. He broke into a slow run when Galloway, standing in the darkness of a driveway, startled him.

'It's okay, he's long gone,' said Galloway.

'Got a description?' asked Serge, noticing the side door of the leaning stucco house was standing open and seeing the tiny dark woman in a straight cotton dress standing near Galloway.

'He's been gone ten minutes,' said Galloway. 'She doesn't have a phone and couldn't find a neighbor at home. She made the call at the drugstore.'

'She saw him?'

'Came home and found the pad ransacked. She must've surprised the burglar, because she heard someone run through the back bedroom and go out the window. A car took off down the alley a second later. She didn't see the suspect, the car or anything.'

Two more radio cars suddenly glided down the street, one from each direction.

'Go broadcast a code four,' said Galloway. 'Just say the four-five-nine occurred ten minutes ago and the suspect left in a vehicle and was not seen. When you're finished come in the house and we'll take a report.'

Serge held up four fingers to the policemen in the other cars indicating a code four, that no assistance was needed. As he returned to the house from making the broadcast, he decided that this payday he would invest in a pair of ripple soles or get these leather soles replaced with rubber.

He heard the sobbing as he approached the open side door and Galloway's voice coming from the front of the small house.

Serge did not go into the living room for a moment. He stood and looked around the kitchen, smelling the cilantro and onion, and seeing jalapeño chili peppers on the tile drainboard. He remembered as he saw the package of corn tortillas that his mother would never have any but homemade tortillas in her house. There was an eight-inch-high madonna on the refrigerator and school pictures of five smiling children, and he knew without examining her closely that the madonna would be Our Lady of Guadalupe in pink gown and blue veil. He wondered where the other favourite saint of the Mexicans was hiding. But Martin de Porres was not in the kitchen, and Serge entered the living room, which was small and scantily furnished with outdated blond furniture.

'We bought that TV set so recently,' said the woman, who had stopped weeping and was staring at the dazzling white wall where the freshly cut two-foot antenna wire lay coiled on the floor.

'Anything else missing?' asked Galloway.

'I'll look,' she sighed. 'We only made six payments on it. I guess we got to pay for it even though it's gone.'

'I wouldn't,' said Galloway. 'Call the store. Tell them it's stolen.'

'We bought it at Frank's Appliance Store. He's not a rich man. He can't afford to take our loss.'

'Do you have theft insurance?' asked Galloway.

'Just fire. We was going to get theft. We was just talking about it because of so many burglaries around here.'

They followed her into the bedroom and Serge saw him – Blessed Martin de Porres, the black holy man in his white robe and black cloak and black hands which said to the Chicano, 'Look at my face, not brown but black and yet even for me Nuestro Señor delivers miracles.' Serge wondered if they still made Mexican movies about Martin de Porres and Pancho Villa and other folk heroes. Mexicans are great believers he thought. Lousy Catholics, really. Not devout churchgoers like Italians and Irish. The Aztec blood diluted the orthodox Spanish Catholicism. He thought of the various signals he had seen Mexicans make to their particular version of the Christian deity as they genuflected on both knees in the crumbling stucco church in Chino. Some made the sign of the Cross in the conventional Mexican fashion, completing the sign with a kiss on the thumb-nail. Others made the sign three times with three kisses, others six times or more. Some made a small cross with the thumb on the forehead, then touched the breast and both shoulders, then returned to the lips for another cross, breast and shoulders again, and another small cross on the lips followed by ten signs on the head, breast and shoulders. He loved to watch them then, particularly during the Forty Hours when the Blessed Sacrament was exposed, and he being an altar boy was obliged to sit or kneel at the foot of the altar for four hours until relieved by Mando Rentería, an emaciated altar boy two years younger than he who was never on time for Mass or anything else. Serge used to watch them and he recalled that no matter what sign they made to whatever strange idol they worshiped who was certainly not the traditional Christ, they touched their knees to the floor when they genuflected and did not fake a genuflection as he had seen so many Anglos do in much finer churches in the short time he still bothered to attend Mass after his mother died. And they had looked at the mute stone figures on the altar with consummate veneration. And whether or not they attended Mass every Sunday, you knew that they were communicating with a spirit when they prayed.

He remembered Father McCarthy, the pastor of the parish, when he had overheard him say to Sister Mary Immaculate, the principal of the school, 'They are not good Catholics, but they are so respectful and they believe so well.' Serge, then a novice altar boy, was in the sacristy to get his white surplice which he had forgotten to bring home. His mother had sent him back to get it because she insisted on washing and starching the surplice every time he served a Mass even though it was completely unnecessary and this would wear it out much too soon and then she would have to make him another one. Serge knew who Father McCarthy meant when he said 'they' to the tall craggy-faced Irish nun who cracked Serge's hands unmercifully with a ruler during the first five years of grammar school when he would talk in class or daydream. Then she had changed abruptly the last three years when he was a gangling altar boy tripping over his cassock that was one of Father McCarthy's cut-down cassocks because he was so tall for a Mexican boy, and she doted over him because he learned his Latin so quickly and pronounced it 'so wondrously well'. But it was easy, because in those days he still spoke a little Spanish and the Latin did not seem really so strange, not nearly so strange as English seemed those first years of grammar school. And now that he had all but forgotten Spanish it was hard to believe that he once spoke no English.

'Ayeeee,' she wailed suddenly, opening the closet in the ransacked bedroom. 'The money, it's gone.'

'You had money?' said Galloway to the angular, dark little woman, who stared in disbelief at Galloway and then at the closet.

'It was more than sixty dollars,' she cried. '*Dios mío!* I put it in there. It was sitting right there.' Suddenly she began rummaging through the already ransacked bedroom. 'Maybe the thief dropped it,' she said, and Serge knew that she might destroy any fingerprints on the chest of drawers and the other smooth-surfaced objects in the bedroom, but he had also learned enough by now to know there were probably no prints anyway as most competent burglars used socks on their hands, or gloves, or wiped their prints. He knew that Galloway knew she might destroy evidence, but Galloway motioned him into the living room.

'Let her blow off steam,' Galloway whispered. 'The only good place for prints is the window ledge anyway. She's not going to touch that.'

Serge nodded, took off his hat and sat down. After a few moments, the furious rustling sounds in the bedroom subsided and the utter silence that followed made Serge wish very much that she would hurry and tell them what was missing so they could make their report and leave.

'You're going to find out before too long that we're the only ones that see the victims,' said Galloway. 'The judges and probation officers and social workers and everybody else think mainly about the suspect and how they can help him stop whatever he specializes in doing to his victims, but you and me are the only ones who see what he does to his victims – right after it's done. And this is only a little burglary.'

She should pray to Our Lady of Guadalupe or Blessed Martin, thought Serge. Or maybe to Pancho Villa. That would be just as useful. Oh, they're great believers, these Chicanos, he thought.

FIVE
The Centurions

'Here comes Lafitte,' said the tall policeman. 'Three minutes till roll call but he'll be on time. Watch him.'

Gus watched Lafitte grin at the tall policeman, and open his locker with one hand, while the other unbuttoned the yellow sport shirt. When Gus looked up again after giving his shoes a last touch with the shine rag, Lafitte was fully dressed in his uniform and was fastening the Sam Browne.

'I'll bet it takes you longer to get into your jammies at night than it does to throw on that blue suit, eh Lafitte?' said the tall policeman.

'Your pay doesn't start till 3:00 P.M.,' Lafitte answered. 'No sense giving the Department any extra minutes. It all adds up in a year.'

Gus stole a glance at Lafitte's brass buttons on his shirt pocket flaps and epaulets and saw the tiny holes in the center of the star on the buttons. This proved the buttons had seen a good deal of polishing, he thought. A hole was worn in the middle. He looked at his own brass buttons and saw they were not a lustrous gold like Lafitte's. If he had been in the service he would have learned a good deal about such things, he thought. On the opposite side of the metal lockers was the roll call room, lockers, rows of benches, tables, and the watch commander's desk at the front, all crammed into one thirty by fifty foot room. Gus was told that the old station would be replaced in a few years by a new station, but it thrilled him just as it was. This was his first night in University Division. He was not a cadet now; the academy was finished and he could not believe it was Gus Plebesly inside this tailored blue woolen shirt which bore the glistening oval shield. He took a place at the second row of tables from the rear of the room. This seemed safe enough. The rear table was almost filled with older officers, and no one sat at the front one. The second row from the rear should be safe enough, he thought.

There were twenty-two policemen at this early night watch roll call and he felt reassured when he saw Griggs and Patzloff, two of his academy classmates, who had also been sent to University Division from the academy.

Griggs and Patzloff were talking quietly and Gus debated about moving across the room to their table but he decided it might attract too much attention, and anyway, it was one minute to roll call. The doors at the rear of the room swung open and a man in civilian clothes entered, and a burly, bald policeman at the rear table shouted, 'Salone, why ain't you suited up?'

'Light duty,' said Salone. 'I'm working the desk tonight. No roll call.'

'Son of a bitch,' said the burly policeman, 'too sick to ride around with me in a radio car? What the hell's wrong with you?'

'Gum infection.'

'You don't sit on your gums, Salone,' said the burly policeman. 'Son of a bitch. Now I guess I'll get stuck with one of these slick-sleeved little RE-cruits.'

Everyone laughed and Gus's face turned hot and he pretended he didn't hear the remark. Then he realized why the burly policeman had said 'slick-sleeved'. He glanced over his shoulder and saw the rows of white service stripes on the lower sleeves of the policemen at the rear table, one stripe for each five years' service, and he understood the epithet. The doors swung open and two sergeants entered carrying manila folders and a large square board from which the car plan would be read.

'Three-A-Five, Hill and Matthews,' said the pipe-smoking sergeant with the receding hairline.

'Here.'

'Here.'

'Three-A-Nine, Carson and Lafitte.'

'Here.'

'Here,' said Lafitte, and Gus recognized the voice.

'Three-A-Eleven, Ball and Gladstone.'

'Here,' said one of the two Negro policemen in the room.

'Here,' said the other Negro.

Gus was afraid he would be put with the burly policeman and was glad to hear him answer 'Here' when he was assigned with someone else.

Finally the sergeant said, 'Three-A-Ninety-nine, Kilvinsky and Plebesly.'

'Here,' said Kilvinsky and Gus turned, smiling nervously at the tall silver-haired policeman in the back row who smiled back at him.

'Here, sir,' said Gus, and then cursed himself for saying 'sir'. He was out of the academy now. 'Sirs' were reserved for lieutenants and higher.

'We have three new officers with us,' said the pipe-smoking sergeant. 'Glad to have you men. I'm Sergeant Bridget and this ruddy Irishman on my right is Sergeant O'Toole. Looks just like the big Irish cop you see in all the old B movies, doesn't he?'

Sergeant O'Toole grinned broadly and nodded to the new officers.

'Before we read the crimes, I want to talk about the supervisor's meeting today,' said Sergeant Bridget as he thumbed through one of the manila folders.

Gus gazed around the room at the several maps of University Division which were covered with multicolored pins that he thought must signify certain crimes or arrests. Soon he would know all the little things and he would be one of them. Or would he be one of them? His forehead and armpits began to perspire and he thought, I will not think that. It's self-defeating and neurotic to think like that. I'm just as good as any of them. I was tops in my class in physical training. What right do I have to degrade myself. I promised myself I'd stop doing that.

'One thing the captain talked about at the supervisor's meeting was the time and mileage check,' said Bridget. 'He wanted us to remind you guys to broadcast your time and mileage *every* time you transport a female in a police car – for any reason. Some bitch in Newton Division beefed a police-man last week. Says he took her in a park and tried to lay her. It was easy to prove she lied because the policeman gave his mileage to Communications at ten minutes past eleven when he left her pad and he gave his mileage again at eleven twenty-three when he arrived at the Main Jail. His mileage and the time check proved he couldn't have driven her up in Elysian Park like she claimed.'

'Hey Sarge,' said a lean swarthy policeman near the front. 'If the Newton Street policeman who she accused is Harry Ferndale, she's probably telling the truth. He's so horny he'd plow a dead alligator or even a live one if somebody'd hold the tail.'

'Damn it, Leoni,' grinned Sergeant Bridget as the others chuckled, 'we got some new men here tonight. You roll call pop-offs ought to be trying to set some kind of example, at least on their first night. This is serious shit I'm reading. The next thing the captain wanted us to bring up is that some Seventy-seventh Street officer in traffic court was asked by the defendant's lawyer what drew his attention to the defendant's vehicle to cite it for an illegal turn, and the officer said because the defendant was driving with his arm around a well-known Negro prostitute.'

The roll call room burst into laughter and Bridget held up a hand to quiet them. 'I know that's funny and all that, but number one, you can prejudice a case by implying that you were trying to suppress prostitution, not enforce traffic laws. And number two, this little remark got back to the guy's old lady and he's beefing the policeman. An investigation started already.'

'Is it true?' asked Matthews.

'Yeah, he was with a whore I guess.'

'Then let the asshole beef,' said Matthews, and Gus realized that they used 'asshole' as much here in the divisions as the instructor did in the academy and he guessed it was the favourite epithet of policemen, at least Los Angeles policemen.

'Anyway, the captain says no more of it,' Bridget continued, 'and an-other thing the old man says is that you guys are not at *any* time to push cars with your police vehicle. Snider on the day watch was giving a poor stranded motorist a push and he jumped the bumper and busted the guy's tail-lights and dented his deck lid and the prick is threatening to sue the city if his car isn't fixed. So no more pushing.'

'How about on the freeway, or when a stalled car has a street bottled up?' asked Leoni.

'Okay, you and I know there are exceptions to everything in this business, but in almost all cases no pushing, okay?'

'Has the captain ever done police work out in the street?' asked Matthews. 'I bet he had some cushy office job since he's been on the Department.'

'Let's not get personal, Mike,' smiled Bridget. 'The next thing is these preliminary investigations in burglary and robbery cases. Now, you guys aren't detectives, but you aren't mere report writers either. You're supposed to conduct a preliminary investigation out there, not just fill in a bunch of blanks on a crime report.' Bridget paused and lit the long-stemmed pipe he had been toying with. 'We all know that we seldom get good latent prints from a gun because of the broken surface, but Jesus Christ, a couple of weeks ago an officer of this division didn't bother worrying about prints on a gun a suspect dropped at the scene of a liquor store robbery! And the dicks had a damned good suspect in custody the next day but the dumb ass liquor store owner was some idiot who claimed he was new in the business in this part of town and he couldn't tell Negroes apart. There wouldn't have been any case at all because the officer handled the suspect's gun and ruined any prints there might have been, except for one thing – it was an automatic. Lucky for the officer, because he might've got a couple days suspension for screwing up the case like that.'

'Were the prints on the clip?' asked Lafitte.

'No, the officer screwed those up when he took the clip out, but there were prints on the cartridges. They got part of the friction ridges on the center portion of the suspect's right thumb on several of the shells where he'd pushed them in the clip. The officer claimed the liquor store owner had handled the gun first so the officer decided all possibility of getting prints was destroyed. I'd like to know how the hell he knew that. It doesn't matter who handles the gun, you should still treat it like it's printable and notify the latent prints specialists.'

'Tell them about the rags,' said Sergeant O'Toole without looking up.

'Oh yeah. In another job recently, an officer had to be reminded by a sergeant at the scene to book the rags the suspect used to bind the victim. And the suspect had brought the rags with him! Christ, they could have laundry marks or they could be matched up with other rags that the dicks might later find in the suspect's pad or on some other job. I know you guys know most of this shit, but some of you are getting awful careless. Okay, that's all the bitching I have for you, I guess. Any questions on the supervisor's meeting?'

'Yeah, you ever talk about the good things we do?' asked Matthews.

'Glad you asked that, Mike,' said Sergeant Bridget, his teeth clenched on the black pipe stem. 'As a matter of fact the lieutenant wrote you a little commendation for the hot roller you got the other night. Come on up and sign it.'

'In eighteen years I guess I got a hundred of these things,' grumbled Matthews, striding heavy-footed to the front of the room, 'but I still get the same goddamn skinny paycheck every two weeks.'

'You're getting almost six bills a month, Mike. Quit your kicking,' said Bridget, then turning to the others said, 'Mike went in pursuit and brought down a hot car driven by a damn good burglar and he likes a little "at-a-boy" once in a while just like the rest of us, despite his bitching. You new men are going to find out that if you have a yen for lots of thanks and praise, you picked the wrong profession. Want to read the crimes, William, me boy?' he said to Sergeant O'Toole.

'Lots of crimes in the division last night, but not too many good descriptions,' said O'Toole with a trace of a New York accent. 'Got one happy moment on the crime sheet though. Cornelius Arps, the Western Avenue pimp, got cut by one of his whores and he EX-pired at 3:00 A.M. in General Hospital.'

A loud cheer went up in the room. It startled Gus.

'Which whore did it?' shouted Leoni.

'One calls herself Tammy Randolph. Anybody know her?'

'She worked usually around Twenty-first and Western,' said Kilvinsky, and Gus turned for another appraisal of his partner who looked more like a doctor than what he imagined a policeman should look like. The older ones, he noticed, looked hard around the mouth and their eyes seemed to watch things, not just look at things, but to watch as though they were waiting for something, but that might be his imagination, he thought.

'How'd she do him?' asked Lafitte.

'You'll never believe this,' said O'Toole, 'but the old canoe maker at the autopsy today claimed that she punctured the aorta with a three and a half inch blade! She hit him so hard in the side with this little pocket knife that it severed a rib and punctured the aorta. Now how could a broad do that?'

'You never saw Tammy Randolph,' said Kilvinsky quietly. 'A hundred and ninety pounds of fighting whore. She's the one that beat hell out of the vice officer last summer, remember?'

'Oh, is that the same bitch?' asked Bridget. 'Well, she atoned for it by juking Cornelius Arps.'

'Why didn't you get the lieutenant to write her an at-a-boy like he did me?' asked Matthews as the men laughed.

'Here's a suspect wanted for attempted murder and two-eleven,' said O'Toole. 'Name is Calvin Tubbs, male, Negro, born 6–12–35, five ten, one eighty-five, black hair, brown eyes, medium complexion, wears his hair marcelled, full moustache, drives a 1959 Ford convertible, white over maroon, license John Victor David one seven three. Hangs out here in University at Normandie and Adams, and at Western and Adams. Robbed a bread truck driver and shot him for the hell of it. They made him on six other jobs – all bread trucks. He's bought and paid for, you can render that asshole.'

'Really raping those bread trucks and buses, ain't they?' said Matthews.

'You know it,' said O'Toole, glancing over the bifocals. 'For the benefit of you new men, we should tell you it's not safe to ride a bus in this part of town. Armed bandits rob a bus almost every day and sometimes rob the passengers too. So if you have a flat tire on your way to work, call a cab. And the bread truck drivers or anybody else that's a street vendor gets hit regular, too. I know one bread truck driver that was held up twenty-one times in one year.'

'That guy's a professional victim,' said Leoni.

'He can probably run a show-up better than the robbery dicks,' said Matthews.

Gus glanced over at the two Negro officers who sat together near the front, but they laughed when the others did and showed no sign of discomfort. Gus knew that all the 'down heres' referred to the Negro divisions and he wondered if all the cracks about the crimes affected them personally. He decided they must be used to it.

'Had kind of an interesting homicide the other night,' O'Toole continued in his monotone. 'Family beef. Some dude told his old lady she was a bum lay and she shot him twice and he fell off the porch and broke his leg and she ran inside, got a kitchen knife and came back and started cutting where the jagged bone stuck out. Almost got the leg all the way off by the time the first radio car got there. They tell me they couldn't even take a regular blood test. There was no blood left in the guy's veins. Had to take it from the spleen.'

'Wonder if she *was* a bum lay,' said Leoni.

'By the way,' said Sergeant Bridget, 'any of you guys know an old lady named Alice Hockington? Lives on Twenty-eighth near Hoover?'

No one answered and Sergeant Bridget said, 'She called last night and said a car came by on a prowler call last week. Who was it?'

'Why do you want to know?' asked a bass voice from the last table.

'Goddamn suspicious cops,' Bridget said, shaking his head. 'Well screw you guys then. I was just going to tell you the old girl died and left ten thousand dollars to the nice policemen who chased a prowler away. Now, who wants to cop out?'

'That was me, Sarge,' said Leoni.

'Bullshit,' said Matthews, 'that was me and Cavanaugh.'

The others laughed and Bridget said, 'Anyway, the old girl called last night. She didn't really die, but she's thinking about it. She said she wanted that handsome tall young policeman with the black moustache (that sounds like you, Lafitte) to come by every afternoon and check for the evening newspaper. If it's still on her porch at five o'clock it means she's dead and she wants you to bust the door in if that happens. Because of her dog, she said.'

'She afraid he'll starve or she afraid he won't starve?' asked Lafitte.

'The sympathy of these guys really is touching,' said Bridget.

'Can I go on with the crimes or am I boring you guys,' said O'Toole. 'Attempt rape, last night, 11:10 P.M., three-six-nine West Thirty-seventh Place. Suspect awoke victim by placing hand over her mouth, said, "Don't move. I love you and I want to prove it." Fondled victim's private parts while he held a two-inch blue steel revolver in the air for her to see. Suspect wore a blue suit ...'

'Blue suit?' asked Lafitte. 'Sounds like a policeman.'

'Suspect wore blue suit and light-colored shirt,' O'Toole continued. 'Was male, Negro, twenty-eight to thirty, six foot two, hundred ninety, black, brown, medium complexion.'

'Sounds exactly like Gladstone. I think we can solve this one,' Lafitte said.

'Victim screamed and suspect jumped out window and was seen getting into a late model yellow vehicle parked on Hoover.'

'What kind of car you got, Gladstone?' asked Lafitte and the big Negro policeman turned and grinned, 'She wouldn't have screamed if it'd been me.'

'The hell she wouldn't,' said Matthews. 'I seen Glad in the academy showers one time. That would be assault with a deadly weapon.'

'Assault with a friendly weapon,' said Gladstone.

'Let's go to work,' said Sergeant Bridget, and Gus was glad there was no inspection because he didn't think his buttons would pass and he wondered how often they had inspections here in the divisions. Not very often, he guessed, from the uniforms he saw around him, which were certainly not up to academy standards. He guessed things would be relaxed out here. Soon, he would be relaxed too. He would be part of it.

Gus stood with his notebook a few steps from Kilvinsky and smiled when Kilvinsky turned around.

'Gus Plebesly,' said Gus, shaking Kilvinsky's wide, smooth hand.

'Andy's the first name,' said Kilvinsky looking down at Gus with an easy grin. Gus guessed he might be six feet four.

'Guess you're stuck with me tonight,' said Gus.

'All month. And I don't mind.'

'Whatever you say is okay with me.'

'That goes without saying.'

'Oh, yes sir.'

'You don't have to sir me,' Kilvinsky laughed. 'My gray hair only means that I've been around a long time. We're partners. You have a notebook?'

'Yes.'

'Okay, you keep books for the first week or so. After you learn to take a report and get to know the streets a little bit, I'll let you drive. All new policemen love to drive.'

'Anything. Anything is okay with me.'

'Guess I'm ready, Gus. Let's go downstairs,' said Kilvinsky, and they walked side by side through the double doors and down the turning stairway of old University station.

'See those pictures, partner?' said Kilvinsky pointing to the glass-covered portraits of University policemen who had been killed on duty. 'These guys aren't heroes. Those guys just screwed up and they're dead. Pretty soon you'll get comfortable and relaxed out there, just like the rest of us. But don't get too comfortable. Remember the guys in the pictures.'

'I don't feel like I'll ever get comfortable,' Gus said.

'You will, partner. You will,' said Kilvinsky. 'Let's find our black and white and go to work.'

The inadequate parking lot was teeming with blue uniforms as the night watch relieved the day watch at 3:45 P.M. The sun was still very hot and ties could remain off until later in the evening. Gus wondered at the heavy long-sleeved blue uniforms. His arms were sweating and the wool was harsh.

'I'm not used to wearing such heavy clothes in the heat,' he smiled to Kilvinsky, as he wiped his forehead with a handkerchief.

'You'll get used to it,' said Kilvinsky, sitting carefully on the sun-heated vinyl seat and releasing the seat lock to slide back and make room for his long legs.

Gus placed the new hot sheet in the holder and wrote 3-A-99 on the notebook pad so that he would not forget who they were. That seemed odd, he thought. He was now 3-A-99. He felt his heart race and he knew he was more excited than he should be. He hoped it was just that – excitement. There was nothing yet to fear.

'The passenger officer handles the radio, Gus.'

'Okay.'

'You won't hear our calls at first. That radio will just be an incoherent mess of conversation for a while. In a week or so you'll start to hear our calls.'

'Okay.'

'Ready for a night of romance, intrigue and adventure on the streets of the asphalt jungle?' asked Kilvinsky dramatically.

'Sure,' Gus smiled.

'Okay, kid,' Kilvinsky laughed. 'You a little thrilled?'

'Yes.'

'Good. That's the way you should be.'

As Kilvinsky drove from the station parking lot he turned west on

Jefferson and Gus flipped down the visor and squinted into the sun. The radio car smelled faintly of vomit.

'Want a tour of the division?' asked Kilvinsky.

'Sure.'

'Almost all the citizens here are Negroes. Some whites. Some Mexicans. Mostly Negroes. Lots of crime when you have lots of Negroes. We work Ninety-nine. Our area is *all* black. Close to Newton. Ours are eastside Negroes. When they got some money they move west of Figueroa and Vermont and maybe west of Western. Then they call themselves westside Negroes and expect to be treated differently. I treat everyone the same, white or black. I'm civil to all people, courteous to none. I think courtesy implies servility. Policemen don't have to be servile or apologize to anyone for doing their job. This is a philosophy lesson I throw in free to every rookie I break in. Old-timers like me love to hear themselves talk. You'll get used to radio car philosophers.'

'How much time do you have on the Department?' asked Gus, looking at the three service stripes on Kilvinsky's sleeve which meant at least fifteen years. But he had a youthful face if it weren't for the silver hair and the glasses. Gus guessed he was in good condition. He had a powerful-looking body.

'Twenty years this December,' said Kilvinsky.

'You retiring?'

'Haven't decided.'

They rode silently for several minutes and Gus looked at the city and realized he knew nothing about Negroes. He enjoyed the names on the churches. On a corner he saw a one-story, white-washed frame building with a handmade sign which said, 'Lion of Judah and Kingdom of Christ Church,' and on the same block was the 'Sacred Defender Baptist Church' and in a moment he saw the 'Hearty Welcome Missionary Baptist Church' and on and on he read the signs on the scores of churches and hoped he could remember them to tell Vickie when he got home tonight. He thought the churches were wonderful.

'Sure is hot,' said Gus, wiping his forehead with the back of his hand.

'You don't have to wear your lid in the car, you know,' said Kilvinsky. 'Only when you get out.'

'Oh,' said Gus, taking off the hat quickly. 'I forgot I had it on.'

Kilvinsky smiled and hummed softly as he patrolled the streets, letting Gus sightsee and Gus watched how slowly he drove and how deliberately. He would remember that. Kilvinsky patrolled at fifteen miles an hour.

'Guess I'll get used to the heavy uniform,' said Gus, pulling the sleeve from his sticky arms.

'Chief Parker doesn't go for short sleeves,' said Kilvinsky.

'Why not?'

'Doesn't like hairy arms and tattoos. Long sleeves are more dignified.'

'He spoke to our graduating class,' said Gus, remembering the eloquence of the chief and the perfect English which had deeply impressed Vickie who sat proudly in the audience that day.

'He's one of a vanishing kind,' said Kilvinsky.

'I've heard he's strict.'

'He a Calvinist. Know what that is?'

'A puritan?'

'He professes to be Roman Catholic, but I say he's a Calvinist. He won't compromise on matters of principle. He's despised by lots of people.'

'He is?' said Gus, reading the signs on the store windows.

'He knows evil when he sees it. He recognizes the weakness of people. He has a passion for order and the rule of law. He can be relentless,' said Kilvinsky.

'You sound as if you kind of admire him.'

'I love him. When he's gone, nothing will be the same.'

What a strange man Kilvinsky is, Gus thought. He talked absently and if it weren't for the boyish grin, Gus would have been uncomfortable with him. Then Gus watched a young Negro strutting across Jefferson Boulevard and he studied the swaying, limber shoulder movement, bent-elbowed free swinging arms, and the rubber-kneed big stepping bounce and as Kilvinsky remarked, 'He's walkin' smart,' Gus realized how profoundly ignorant he was about Negroes and he was anxious to learn about them, and about all people. If he could just learn and grow he would know something about people after a few years in this job. He thought of the squirming muscle in the long brown arms of the young man who was now blocks behind him. He wondered how he would fare if the two of them were face to face in a police-suspect confrontation when he had no partner and he could not use his sidearm and the young Negro was not impressed with his glittering golden shield and suit of blue. He cursed himself again for the insidious fear and he vowed he would master it but he always made this vow and still the fear came or rather the promise of fear, the nervous growling stomach, the clammy hands, the leathery mouth, but enough, enough to make him suspect that when the time came he would not behave like a policeman.

What if a man the size of Kilvinsky resisted arrest? Gus thought. How could I possibly handle him? There were things he wanted to ask, but was ashamed to ask Kilvinsky. Things he might ask a smaller man, after he got to know him, if he ever did get to really know him. He had never had many friends and at this moment he doubted that he could find any among these uniformed men who made him feel like a small boy. Maybe it had all been a mistake, he thought. Maybe he could never be one of them. They seemed so forceful and confident. They had seen things. But maybe it was just bravado. Maybe it was that.

But what would happen if someone's life, maybe Kilvinsky's life, depended on his conquest of fear which he had never been able to conquer?

Those four years of marriage while he worked in a bank had not prepared him to cope with that. And why hadn't he the courage to talk to Vickie about things like this, and then he thought of the times he had lain beside her in the darkness, particularly after lovemaking, and he had thought of these things and prayed to have the courage to talk to Vickie about it, but he hadn't, and no one knew that *he* knew that he was a coward. But what would it ever have mattered that he was a coward if he had stayed in the bank where he belonged? Why could he do well in wrestling and physical training, but turn sick and impotent when the other man was not playing a game? Once in P.T. when he was wrestling with Walmsley he had applied the wristlock too firmly as Officer Randolph had shown them. Walmsley became angry and when Gus saw his eyes, the fear came, his strength deserted him and Walmsley easily took him down. He did it viciously and Gus did not resist even though he knew he was stronger and twice as agile as Walmsley. But that was all part of being a coward, that inability to control your body. Is the hate the thing I fear? Is that it? A face full of hate?

'Come on granny, let the clutch out,' Kilvinsky said as a female driver in front of them crept toward the signal causing them to stop instead of making the yellow light.

'One-seven-three west Fifty-fourth Street,' said Kilvinsky, tapping on the writing pad between them.

'What?' asked Gus.

'We got a call. One-seven-three west Fifty-fourth Street. Write it down.'

'Oh. Sorry, I can't make any sense out of the radio yet.'

'Roger the call,' said Kilvinsky.

'Three-A-Ninety-nine, roger,' said Gus into the hand mike.

'You'll start picking our calls out of all that chatter pretty soon,' said Kilvinsky. 'Takes a while. You'll get it.'

'What kind of call was it?'

'Unknown trouble call. That means the person who called isn't sure what the problem is, or it means he wasn't coherent or the operator couldn't understand him, or it could mean anything. I don't like those calls. You don't know what the hell you have until you get there.'

Gus nervously looked at the storefronts. He saw two Negroes with high shiny pompadours and colorful one-piece jump suits park a red Cadillac convertible in front of a window which said, 'Big Red's Process Parlor', and below it in yellow letters Gus read, 'Process, do-it-yourself process, Quo Vadis, and other styles'.

'What do you call the hairdo on those two men?' asked Gus.

'Those two pimps? That style is just called a process, some call it a marcel. Old-time policemen might refer to it as gassed hair, but for police reports most of us just use the word "process". Costs them a lot of money to keep a nice process like that, but then, pimps have lots of money. And a process is as important to them as a Cadillac. No self-respecting pimp would be caught without both of them.'

Gus wished the sun would drop, then it might cool off. He loved summer nights when the days were hot and paper-dry like this one. He noticed the crescent and star over the white two-story stucco building on the corner. Two men in close-cropped hair and black suits with maroon neckties stood in front of the wide doors with their hands behind their backs and glared at the police car as they continued south.

'That a church?' asked Gus to Kilvinsky, who never looked toward the building or the men.

'That's the Muslim temple. Do you know about Muslims?'

'I've read a little in the papers, that's all.'

'They're a fanatical sect that's sprung up recently all over the country. A lot of them are ex-cons. They're all cop haters.'

'They look so clean-cut,' said Gus, glancing over his shoulder at the two men whose faces were turned in the direction of the police car.

'They're just part of what's happening in the country,' said Kilvinsky. 'Nobody knows what's happening yet, except a few people like the chief. It may take ten years to figure it all out.'

'What *is* happening?' asked Gus.

'It's a long story,' Kilvinsky said. 'And I'm not sure myself. And besides, here's the pad.'

Gus turned and saw the one-seven-three over the mailbox of the green stucco house with a trash-littered front yard.

Gus almost didn't see the trembling old Negro in khaki work clothes huddled on an ancient wicker chair on the dilapidated porch of the house.

'Glad yo'all could come, officahs,' he said, standing, quivering, with sporadic looks toward the door standing ajar.

'What's the problem?' asked Kilvinsky, climbing the three stairs to the porch, his cap placed precisely straight on the silver mane.

'Ah jist came home and ah saw a man in the house. Ah don' know him. He jist was sittin' there starin' at me and ah got scairt and run out heah and ovah nex' do' and ah use mah neighbah's phone and while I was waitin' ah look back inside an' theah he sits jist rockin', an' Lord, ah think he's a crazy man. He don' say nothin' jist sits an' rocks.'

Gus reached involuntarily for the baton and fingered the grooved handle, waiting for Kilvinsky to decide their first move and he was embarrassed by his relief when he understood, when Kilvinsky winked and said, 'Wait here, partner, in case he tries to go out the back door. There's a fence back there so he'd have to come back through the front.'

Gus waited with the old man and in a few minutes he heard Kilvinsky shout, 'Alright you son of a bitch, get out of here and don't come back!' And he heard the back door slam. Then Kilvinsky opened the screen and said, 'Okay, Mister, come on in. He's gone.'

Gus followed the gnarled old man, who removed the crumpled hat when he crossed the threshold.

'He sho' is gone, officahs,' said the old man, but the trembling had not stopped.

'I told him not to come back,' said Kilvinsky. 'I don't think you'll be seeing him again around this neighborhood.'

'God bless yo'all,' said the old man, shuffling toward the back door and locking it.

'How long's it been since you had a drink?' asked Kilvinsky.

'Oh, couple days now,' said the old man, smiling a black-toothed smile. 'Check's due in the mail any day now.'

'Well, just fix yourself a cup of tea and try to get some sleep. You'll feel lots better tomorrow.'

'Ah thanks yo'all,' said the old man as they walked down the cracked concrete sidewalk to the car. Kilvinsky didn't say anything as he drove off and Gus said finally, 'Those d.t.'s must be hell, huh?'

'Must be hell,' Kilvinsky nodded.

'We got a coffee spot down the street,' said Kilvinsky. 'It's so bad you could pour it in your battery when she dies, but it's free and so are the doughnuts.'

'Sounds good to me,' said Gus.

Kilvinsky parked in the littered coffee shop parking lot and Gus went inside to get the coffee. He left his cap in the car and felt like a veteran, hatless, striding into the coffee shop where he watched a wizened, alcoholic-looking man who was listlessly pouring coffee for three Negro counter customers.

'Coffee?' he said to Gus, coming toward him with two paper cups in his hand.

'Please.'

'Cream?'

'Only in one,' said Gus, as the counterman drew the coffee from the urns and placed the cups on the counter as Gus self-consciously tried to decide the most diplomatic way to order doughnuts which were free. You didn't wish to be presumptuous even though you wanted a doughnut. It would be so much simpler if they just paid for the coffee and doughnuts, he thought, but then that would counter the tradition and if you did something like that the word might be passed that you were a troublemaker. The man solved his dilemma by saying, 'Doughnuts?'

'Please,' said Gus, relieved.

'Chocolate or plain? I'm out of glazed.'

'Two plain,' said Gus, realizing that Kilvinsky had not stated his preference.

'Tops for the cups?'

'No, I can manage,' said Gus and a moment later discovered that this chain of coffee shops made the hottest coffee in Los Angeles.

'It's sure hot,' he smiled weakly, in case Kilvinsky had seen him spill coffee on himself. His forehead perspired from the sudden flash of pain.

'Wait till you're on the morning watch,' said Kilvinsky. 'Some chilly winter night about 1:00 A.M. this coffee will light a fire in you and see you through the night.'

The sun was dropping on the horizon but it was still hot and Gus thought a Coke would have been better than a cup of coffee but he had already noticed that policemen were coffee drinkers and he guessed he may as well get used to it because he was going to be one of them, come what may.

Gus sipped the steaming coffee a full three minutes after it sat on the roof of the police car and found that he still could not stand the temperature; he waited and watched Kilvinsky out of the corner of his eye and saw him taking great gulps as he smoked a cigarette and adjusted the radio until it was barely audible, still much too low for Gus, but then, Gus knew he could not pick their calls out of that chaotic garble of voices anyway, so if Kilvinsky could hear it, it was enough.

Gus saw a stooped ragpicker in filthy denim trousers and a torn, grimy checkered shirt several sizes too large, and a GI helmet liner with a hole on the side through which a snarled handful of the ragpicker's gray hair protruded. He pushed a shopping cart stolidly down the sidewalk, ignoring six or seven Negro children who taunted him, and until he was very close Gus could not guess what his race was but guessed he was white because of the long gray hair. Then he saw that he was indeed a white man, but covered with crusty layers of filth. The ragpicker stopped near crevices and crannies between and behind the rows of one-story business buildings. He probed in trash cans and behind clumps of weeds in vacant lots until he discovered his prizes and the shopping cart was already filled with empty bottles which the children grabbed at. They shrieked in delight when the ragpicker made ineffectual swipes at their darting hands with his hairy paws too broad and massive for the emaciated body.

'Maybe he was wearing that helmet on some Pacific island when it got that hole blown in it,' said Gus.

'It'd be nice to think so,' said Kilvinsky. 'Adds a little glamour to the old ragpicker. You should keep an eye on those guys, though. They steal plenty. We watched one pushing his little cart along Vermont on Christmas Eve clouting presents out of cars that were parked at the curb. Had a pile of bottles and other trash on top and a cartload of stolen Christmas presents beneath.'

Kilvinsky started the car and resumed his slow patrol and Gus felt much more at ease after the coffee and doughnut which domesticized the strange feeling he had here in the city. He was so provincial, he thought, even though he grew up in Azusa, and made frequent trips to Los Angeles.

Kilvinsky drove slowly enough for Gus to read the signs in the windows of the drugstores and neighborhood markets, which advertised hair straighteners, skin brighteners, scalp conditioner, pressing oil, waxes and pomades. Kilvinsky pointed to a large crudely lettered whitewashed warning on a board fence which said, 'Bab bog,' and Gus noticed the professional lettering on the pool hall window which said, 'Billiard Parler'. Kilvinsky parked in front of the pool hall, telling Gus he had something to show him.

The pool hall, which Gus supposed would be empty at the dinner hour, was teeming with men and a few women, all Negro except for two of the three women who slouched at a table near the small room at the rear of the building. Gus noticed one of the women, a middle-aged woman with hair like flames, scurried into the back room as soon as she spotted them. The pool players ignored them and continued the nine ball contests.

'Probably a little dice game going in the back,' said Kilvinsky as Gus eagerly studied everything about the place, the floor caked with grime, six threadbare pool tables, two dozen men sitting or standing against the walls, the blaring record player being overseen by a pudgy cigar chewer in a blue silk undershirt, the smell of stale sweat and beer, for which there was no license, cigarette smoke, and through it all a good barbecue smell. Gus knew by the smell that whatever else they were doing in the back room, somebody was cooking, and that seemed very strange somehow. The three women were all fiftyish and very alcoholic-looking, the Negro being the slimmest and cleanest-looking of the three although she too was foul enough, Gus thought.

'A shine parlor or pool hall down here is the last stop for a white whore,' said Kilvinsky following Gus's eyes. 'There's what I brought you in here to see.' Kilvinsky pointed at a sign high on the wall over the door which led to the back room. The sign read, 'No liquor or narcotics allowed'.

Gus was relieved to get back in the air, and he inhaled deeply. Kilvinsky resumed patrol and Gus was already starting to know the voices of the female Communications operators, particularly the one with the deep young voice on frequency thirteen, who would occasionally whisper 'Hi' into the mike or 'roger' in coy response to the policemen's voices he could not hear. It had been a surprise to him that the radios were two-way radios and not three-way, but it was just as well, he thought, because the jumble of women's voices was hard enough to understand without more voices from all the radio cars being thrown in.

'I'll wait till dark to show you Western Avenue,' said Kilvinsky and now Gus could definitely feel the refreshing coolness of approaching night although it was far from dark.

'What's on Western Avenue?'

'Whores. Of course there're whores all over this part of town, but Western is the whore center of the city. They're all over the street.'

'Don't we arrest them?'

'*We* don't. What would we arrest them for? Walking the street? Just *being* whores? No crime in that. Vice officers arrest them when they tail them to their trick pad, or when they operate the girl undercover and get an offer of prostitution.'

'I wonder what working vice would be like?' Gus mused aloud.

'You might get a chance to find out someday,' Kilvinsky said. 'You're kind of small and ... oh, a little more docile than the average pushy cop. I think you'd be a good undercover operator. You don't look like a policeman.'

Gus thought of being here in the streets in plainclothes, perhaps without a partner, and he was glad such assignments were voluntary. He watched a very dark-skinned homosexual mincing across Vernon Avenue when the light turned green.

'Hope we don't lose our masquerading laws,' said Kilvinsky.

'What's that?'

'City ordinance against a man dressing up like a woman or vice versa. Keeps the fruits from going around full drag and causing all sorts of police problems. I got a feeling though that that's another law on the way out. Better write that address down.'

'What address?'

'We just got a call.'

'We did? Where?' asked Gus, turning the radio louder and readying his pencil.

'Three-A-Ninety-nine, repeat,' said Kilvinsky.

'Three-A-Ninety-nine, Three-A-Ninety-nine, a forgery suspect there now, at Forty-one-thirty-two south Broadway, see the man at that location, code two.'

'Three-A-Ninety-nine, roger,' said Gus, rubbing his palms on his thighs impatiently, and wondering why Kilvinsky didn't drive a bit faster. After all, it was a code two call.

They were only three blocks from the call but when they arrived another car was already parked in the front of the market and Kilvinsky double-parked until Leoni walked out of the store and over to their car.

'Suspect's a female wino,' said Leoni, leaning in the window on Gus's side. 'Guy offered her ten bucks to try and pass a hundred and thirty dollar payroll check. Probably a phony, but it looks pretty good. Check writer was used. The bitch said the guy was middle-aged, red shirt, average size. She just met him in a gin mill.'

'Negro?' asked Kilvinsky.

'What else?'

'We'll take a look around,' Kilvinsky said.

Kilvinsky circled the block once, studying people and cars. Gus wondered what they were supposed to be looking for because there were less than ten men in the immediate area who were middle-sized and none of them had on a red shirt, but on his second pass around the block,

Kilvinsky turned sharply into a drugstore parking lot and zoomed across the alley toward a man who was walking toward the sidewalk. Kilvinsky jammed on the brakes and was on his feet before Gus was certain he was stopping.

'Just a minute,' said Kilvinsky to the man who continued walking. 'Hold it, there.'

The man turned and looked quizzically at the two policemen. He wore a brown checkered shirt and a black felt stingy brim with a fat yellow feather. He was neither middle-aged nor of average size, but rather he was in his early thirties, Gus guessed, and was tall and portly.

'What you want?' asked the man and Gus noticed the deep scar which followed the cheek line and was at first not apparent.

'Your identification, please,' said Kilvinsky.

'What for?'

'I'll explain in a minute, but let me see your I.D. first. Something just happened.'

'Oh,' sneered the man, 'and I'm suspicious, huh? I'm black so that makes me suspicious, huh? Black man is just ol' Joe Lunchmeat to you, huh?'

'Look around you,' Kilvinsky said, taking a giant stride forward, 'you see anybody that ain't black except my partner and me? Now I picked you cause I got a motherfuckin' good reason. Break out that I.D. cause we ain't got time for shuckin'.'

'Okay, Officer,' said the man, 'I ain't got nothin' to hide, it just that the PO-lice is always fuckin' over me ever' time I goes outside and I'm a workin' man. I works ever' day.'

Kilvinsky examined the social security card and Gus thought how Kilvinsky had talked to the man. His rage was profound and with his size it had cowed the Negro, and Kilvinsky had talked like a Negro, exactly like a Negro, Gus thought.

'This I.D. ain't shit, man,' said Kilvinsky. 'Got something with your thumb print or a picture on it? Got a driver's license maybe?'

'What I need a drivin' license fo'? I ain't drivin'.'

'What you been busted for?'

'Gamblin', traffic tickets, suspicious, a time or two.'

'Forgery?'

'No, man.'

'Flim flam?'

'No, man. I gambles a little bit. I ain't no criminal, no jive.'

'Yeah, you jivin',' said Kilvinsky. 'Your mouth is dry; you're lickin' your lips.'

'Sheee-it, man, when the bluesuits stops me, I always gets nervous.'

'Your heart is hammerin',' said Kilvinsky, placing a hand on the man's chest. 'What's your real name?'

'Gandy. Woodrow Gandy. Just like it say on that card,' said the man who now was obviously nervous. He shuffled his feet and could not control the darting pink tongue which moistened brown lips every few seconds.

'Hop in the car, Gandy,' said Kilvinsky. 'There's an old drunk across the street. I want her to take a look at you.'

'Ohooo man, this is a roust!' said Gandy as Kilvinsky patted him down. 'This is humbug and a roust!'

Gus noticed that Gandy knew which side of the police car to sit in, and Gus sat behind Kilvinsky and reached across locking the door on Gandy's side.

They drove back to the store and found Leoni sitting in his radio car with a frazzled bleary-eyed Negro woman about forty who peeked out the window of Leoni's car toward Gandy when Kilvinsky pulled alongside.

'That's him. That the nigger that got me in all this trouble!' she shrieked, and then to Gandy she said, 'Yeah, you, you bastard, standin' there finger poppin' and talkin' so smart to ever'one and tell me how easy I could earn ten dollars and how smart you was and all, you black son of a bitch. That's the one, Officer, I done told you I would be yo' witness and I means it, no jive. I tol' you he had a big flappy mouf like Cheetah. He the one all right. If I'm lyin', I'm flyin'.'

Gandy turned away from the drunken woman and Gus was embarrassed by her words, but Gandy seemed completely unconcerned and Gus was astonished at how they degraded one another. He guessed they learned from the white man.

It was after nine o'clock when they finally got Gandy in the booking office of University jail. It was an antiquated jail and looked like a dungeon. Gus wondered what the cells were like. He wondered why they didn't take Gandy's shoelaces like they do in movies, but he remembered hearing a policeman in the academy saying that you can't stop a man from committing suicide who really wants to and then he described the death of a prisoner who tied strips of pillowcase around his neck and then to the barred door. The man did a backflip, breaking his neck, and the officer quipped that deaths in jail caused tons of paper work and were very inconsiderate on the part of the deceased. Of course everybody laughed as policemen always did at grim humor and attempts at humor.

Over the booking officer's desk was a sign which read, 'Support your local police. Be a snitch,' and a toy spear perhaps three feet long decorated with African symbols and colorful feathers. It had a rubber blade and a sign over it said, 'Search your prisoners thoroughly'. Gus wondered if the Negro policemen were offended by this and for the first time in his life he was becoming acutely aware of Negroes in general, and he guessed he would become even more so because he would now spend most of his waking hours here among them. He wasn't sorry, he was interested, but he was also afraid of them. But then, he would probably be almost as fearful of any people no matter where he was stationed, and then he thought, what if

Gandy had resisted arrest and what if Kilvinsky were not with him. Could he have handled a man like Gandy?

As the booking officer typed, Gus thought of Gus, Jr., three years old, and how chesty he was. Gus knew he would be a big husky boy. Already he could throw a man-sized basketball halfway across the living room and this was their favorite toy even though they broke one of Vickie's new decanters with it. Gus clearly remembered his own father's rough and tumble play although he never saw him again after the divorce, and how they had played. He remembered the moustache with wisps of gray among the brown and the big dry hard hands which tossed him confidently and surely into the air until he could hardly breathe for the laughter. He described this to his mother once when he was twelve, and old enough to see how miserably sad it made her. He never mentioned his father again and tried to be more helpful to his mother than ever because he was four years older than John and was his mother's little man she said. Gus guessed he was fiercely proud of the fact that he had worked since he was a small boy to help support the three of them. Now the pride was gone and it was a genuine hardship to set aside fifty dollars a month for her and John, now that he and Vickie were married and he had his own family.

'Ready to go, pard?' asked Kilvinsky.

'Oh, sure.'

'Daydreaming?'

'Yeah.'

'Let's go eat now, and do the arrest report later.'

'Okay,' said Gus, brightening at the thought. 'You aren't too mad to eat, are you?'

'Mad?'

'For a minute I thought you were going to eat that suspect alive.'

'I wasn't mad,' said Kilvinsky, looking at Gus in surprise as they walked to the car. 'That was just my. Change the words once in a while, but I use the same tune. Don't they teach you about interrogation in the academy anymore?'

'I thought you were blowing your top.'

'Hell, no. I just figured he was the type who only respected naked strength, not civility. You can't use that technique on everybody. In fact, if you try it on some guys you might find yourself on your back looking up. But I figured he'd quiet down if I talked his language, so I did. You have to size up each suspect fast and make up your mind how you're going to talk to him.'

'Oh,' said Gus. 'But how did you know he was the suspect? He didn't look like her description. His shirt wasn't even red.'

'How did I know,' Kilvinsky murmured. 'Let's see. You haven't been to court yet, have you?'

'No.'

'Well, you'll have to start answering the questions, "How did you know?" I don't honestly know how I knew. But I knew. At least I was pretty sure. The shirt wasn't red, but it wasn't green either. It was a color that could be called red by a fuzzy-eyed drunk. It was a rusty brown. And Gandy was standing a little too casually there in the parking lot. He was too cool and he gave me too much of an "I got nothing to hide" look when I was driving by and eyeballing everybody that could possibly be the guy. And when I came back around he had moved to the other side of the lot. He was still moving when I turned the corner but when he sees us he stops to show us he's not walking away. He's got nothing to hide. I knew this means nothing by itself, but these are some of the little things. I just *knew*, I tell you.'

'Instinct?'

'I think so. But I wouldn't say that in court.'

'Will you have trouble in court with this case?'

'Oh no. This isn't a search and seizure case. If we had a search and seizure case going, that feeling and those little dungs he did wouldn't be enough. We'd lose. Unless we stretched the truth.'

'Do you stretch the truth sometimes?'

'I don't. I don't care enough about people in general to get emotionally involved. I don't give a shit if I busted Jack the Ripper and lost him on an unreasonable search. As long as the asshole stays off *my* property, I don't worry about it. Some policemen become avenging angels. They have a real animal who's hurt a lot of people and they decide they have to convict him even if it means lying in court, but I say it's not worth it. The public isn't worth your risking a perjury rap. And he'll be back on the street before long anyway. Stay frosty. Relax. That's the way to do this job. You can beat it then. You take forty percent after twenty years, and your family, if you still have one, and you make it. Go to Oregon or Montana.'

'Do you have a family?'

'I'm single now. This job isn't conducive to stable family relationships, the marriage counselors say, I think we're near the top in suicide rate.'

'I hope I can do this job,' Gus blurted, surprised at the desperate tone in his own voice.

'Police work is seventy percent common sense. That's about what makes a policeman, common sense, and the ability to make a quick decision. You've got to cultivate those abilities or get out You'll learn to appreciate this in your fellow policemen. Pretty soon, you won't be able to feel the same way about your friends in the lodge or church or in your neighborhood because they won't measure up to policemen in these ways. You'll be able to come up with a quick solution for *any* kind of strange situation because you have to do it every day, and you'll get mad as hell at your old friends if they can't.'

Gus noticed that now that night had come, the streets were filling with people, black people, and the building fronts shone forth. It seemed that every block had at least one bar or liquor store and all the liquor store proprietors were white men. It seemed to Gus that now you didn't notice the churches, only the bars and liquor stores and places where crowds of people were standing around. He saw boisterous crowds around hamburger stands, liquor stores, certain porches of certain apartment houses, parking lots, shine stands, record stores, and a suspicious place whose windows advertised that this was a 'Social Club'. Gus noticed the peephole in the door and he wished that he could be inside there unnoticed, and his curiosity was stronger than his fear.

'How about some soul food, brother?' asked Kilvinsky with a Negro accent as he parked in front of the neat lunch counter on Normandie.

'I'll try anything,' Gus smiled.

'Fat Jack makes the best gumbo in town. Lots of shrimp and crab meat and chicken and okra, easy on the rice and lots of down home flavor. Real looos-iana gumbo.'

'You from the South?'

'No, I just appreciate the cooking,' Kilvinsky said, and held the door as they entered the restaurant. Soon they were served the huge bowl of gumbo and Gus liked the way Fat Jack said, 'They was full of shrimps tonight.' He poured some hot sauce on the gumbo as Kilvinsky did even though it was tangy enough, but it was delicious, even the chopped-up chicken necks and the crab claws which had to be picked and sucked clean. Kilvinsky poured more ladles of hot sauce over the spicy gruel and ate half a pan of corn bread. But it was spoiled a little because they each left a quarter tip for the waitress and that was all, and Gus felt guilty to accept a gratuity and he wondered how he would explain it to a sergeant. He wondered if Fat Jack and the waitresses called them freeloaders behind their backs.

At 11:00 P.M. while cruising the dark residential streets north of Slauson Avenue, Kilvinsky said, 'You ready to go work the whore wagon?'

'The what?'

'I asked the sergeant if we could take the wagon out tonight to roust the whores and he said it'd be okay if the air was quiet and I haven't heard a radio call in University Division for a half hour, so let's go in and get the wagon. I think you might find it educational.'

'There don't seem to be too many whores around,' said Gus. 'There were those two at Vernon and Broadway you pointed out and one on Fifty-eighth, but ...'

'Wait till you see Western Avenue.'

After arriving at the station Kilvinsky pointed to the blue panel truck in the station parking lot with the white 'Los Angeles Police Department' on the side. The back end was windowless and two benches were attached to each wall of the truck. A heavy steel screen separated the passengers from the front of the cab.

'Let's go tell the boss we're going out in the wagon,' said Kilvinsky, and after another fifteen-minute delay while Kilvinsky joked with Candy the policewoman at the desk, they were in the wagon which rumbled down Jefferson Boulevard like a blue rhino. Gus thought he would hate to be sitting on the wooden bench in the back of this hard-riding wagon.

Kilvinsky turned north on Western Avenue and they had not driven two blocks on Western until he found himself counting the sauntering, wriggling, garishly dressed women who strolled down the sidewalks mostly *with* the traffic so that the cars would pull conveniently to the curb. The bars and restaurants on and near Western were bulging with people and there was a formidable fleet of Cadillac convertibles parked in the lot of 'Blue Dot McAfee's Casbah'.

'Pimping is profitable,' said Kilvinsky, pointing to the Cadillacs. 'There's too much money in pussy. I suspect that's why it's not legalized in many countries. Too much profit and no overhead. The pimps would control the economy in no time.'

'Christ, it looks like it's legal *here*!' said Gus, taking in the colorful figures on both sides of Western who were leaning in the windows of parked cars, standing in groups or sitting on the low walls in front of the residences. Gus noticed that the prostitutes looked with concern at the blue wagon as it rumbled north toward Adams Boulevard.

'I believe in giving them one pass down Western to show the wagon's out. If they stay on the street we pick them up. Sure a lot of money in wigs out there, huh?'

'God, yes,' said Gus, looking at an incredibly buxom prostitute standing alone on the corner of Twenty-seventh. He was astounded at how attractive some of them were and he noticed that they all carried purses.

'They've got purses,' Gus said.

'Oh, yeah,' Kilvinsky smiled. 'Just for show. High skinny heels and purses, short skirts or tight pants. Uniform of the day. But don't worry, they don't carry any bread in those purses. All women in these parts carry their money in their bras.'

When they got to Washington Boulevard, Kilvinsky turned around.

'There were twenty-eight whores on the Avenue,' said Gus. 'And I think I missed counting some right at first!'

'The people around here have got to stop it,' said Kilvinsky, lighting a cigarette and inserting it in a plastic cigarette holder. 'Soon as they bitch loud enough the judges will give the girls some time and they'll go underground again. I know a whore with seventy-three prior arrests. Most time she ever did was six months on two separate occasions. This whore wagon is completely illegal by the way.'

'What do we do with them? Where do we take them? I was wondering about that.'

'For a ride, that's all. We pick them up and ride them around for an hour or so and take them to the station and run a make to see if they have any traffic warrants and let them go from the station. It's illegal as hell. We'll be stopped from doing it one of these days, but right now it works. The girls hate to be picked up in the wagon. Stopgap measure. Let's take those two.'

Gus saw no one at first and then saw a movement in the shadows near the phone booth at the corner of Twenty-first Street and two girls in blue dresses walked west on Twenty-first. They ignored Kilvinsky's, 'Evening ladies,' until both policemen were out of the cab and Kilvinsky was holding the back door of the wagon open.

'Shit, fuck, Kilvinsky, you always picks on me,' said the younger of the two, a yellow girl in an auburn wig who, Gus supposed, was even younger. than himself.

'Who's the baby?' asked the other, pointing at Gus and appearing re-signed to climbing the high step into the back of the wagon. She hiked the flesh-tight blue satin dress up to her hips to make the step. 'Give me a lift, baby,' she said to Gus but didn't hold out her hand. 'Grab a handful of mah big ass and push.'

Kilvinsky chewed on the cigarette holder and eyed Gus with frank amusement, and Gus saw her firm pantiless buttocks like a dark melon with a sliver removed. He held her around the waist and boosted her up as she shrieked with laughter and Kilvinsky chuckled softly as he locked the double doors and they climbed back in the cab.

The next girl they picked up at Adams, and there were not so many now that everyone knew the wagon was out, but they picked up three more at Twenty-seventh, one of whom cursed Kilvinsky viciously because someone had made her ride in the wagon only last night and it wasn't her turn again, she said.

Once the prostitutes were in the wagon, they chattered and laughed pleasantly enough. It seemed to Gus that a few of them might be enjoy-ing the respite from the street and Kilvinsky assured him that there was truth in this when Gus asked him, because their work was very dangerous and demanding, what with robbers and sadists prowling for prostitutes. The pimps provided little protection except from other pimps who were constantly trying to enlarge their own stables.

The tall policeman who had talked to Lafitte in the locker room was standing with his partner at Twenty-eighth beside the open door of the radio car talking to two prostitutes. The tall one motioned them to the curb.

'Got two for you, Andy,' said the tall policeman.

'Yeah, you should make sergeant for this, you blue-eyed devil,' said the umber-colored girl, with a natural hairdo, and a severe short-skirted black dress.

'She doesn't like you, Bethel,' said Kilvinsky to the tall policeman.

'He don't know how to talk to a woman,' said the girl. 'Nobody likes this funky devil.'

'I don't see any women,' said Bethel, 'just two whores.'

'Yo' wife's a whore, bastard,' spat the girl, leaning forward at the waist. 'She fucks fo' peanuts. I gets two hundred dollars every day fo' fuckin' you pitiful paddy motherfuckers. Yo' wife's the real whore.'

'Get in the wagon, bitch,' said Bethel, shoving the girl across the sidewalk and Gus grabbed her to keep her from falling.

'We goin' to fix you whiteys, one day,' said the girl, sobbing. 'You devil! I never feel you blue-eyed devils, do you hear? I feel nothin'! You paddy motherfuckers never make me feel nothin' with yo' needle dicks. You ain't gonna git away wif pushin' me aroun', hear me?'

'Okay, Alice, hop in, will you,' said Kilvinsky, holding the girl's arm as she yielded and climbed into the wagon.

'That there suckah don't evah talk right to nobody,' said a voice inside the blackness of the wagon. 'He think people is dogs or somethin'. We is motherfuckin' ladies.'

'I haven't met you yet,' said Bethel, offering his hand to Gus who shook it, looking up at the large brown eyes of Bethel.

'This is quite an experience,' said Gus haltingly.

'It's a garbage truck,' said Bethel. 'But this ain't too bad, really. You ought to work Newton Division ...'

'We've got to get going, Bethel,' said Kilvinsky.

'One thing, Plebesly,' said Bethel, 'at least working around here you never run into nobody smarter than you.'

'Do I have to get in the wagon, too,' asked the second girl and for the first time Gus noticed she was white. She had a high-styled black wig and her eyes were dark. She had a fine sun tan but she was definitely a white woman and Gus thought she was exceptionally pretty.

'Your old man is Eddie Simms, ain't that right, nigger?' Bethel whispered to the girl, whom he held by the upper arm. 'You give all your money to a nigger, don't you? You'd do just anything for that slick-haired boy, wouldn't you? That makes you a nigger too, don't it, nigger?'

'Get in the wagon, Rose,' said Kilvinsky taking her arm, but Bethel gave her a push and she dropped her purse and fell heavily into Kilvinsky, who cursed and lifted her into the wagon with one large hand while Gus picked up the purse.

'When you get more time on the job you'll learn not to manhandle another officer's prisoner,' said Kilvinsky to Bethel as they got back in the wagon.

Bethel faced Kilvinsky for a moment, but said nothing, turned, got back in his car, and was roaring halfway up Western before Kilvinsky ever started the motor.

'Got lots of problems, that kid,' said Kilvinsky. 'Only two years on the Department and already he's got lots of problems.'

'Hey,' said a voice from the back of the wagon as they bounced and jogged across Jefferson and began an aimless ride to harass the prostitutes. 'Yo'all need some pillas back here. This is terrible bumpy.'

'Your pillow is built in, baby,' said Kilvinsky and several girls laughed.

'Hey silver hair. How 'bout lettin' us out ovah on Ver-mont or some-where,' said another voice. 'I jist got to make me some coin tonight.'

'Kilvinsky got soul,' said another voice. 'He git us some scotch if we ask him pretty. You got soul, don't you, Mr. Kilvinsky?'

'Baby, Ah gots more soul than Ah kin control,' said Kilvinsky and the girls burst into laughter.

'He sho' kin talk that trash,' said a throaty voice that sounded like the girl who had cursed Bethel.

Kilvinsky parked in front of a liquor store and shouted over his shoulder, 'Get your money ready and tell me what you want.' Then to Gus, 'Stay in the wagon. I'll be back.'

Kilvinsky went around to the back and opened the door.

'Dollar each,' said one of the girls and Gus heard the rustle of clothing and paper and the clink of coins.

'Two quarts of milk and a fifth of scotch. That okay?' asked one of the girls and several voices muttered, 'Uh huh.'

'Give me enough for paper cups,' said Kilvinsky, 'I'm not going to use my own money.'

'Baby, if you'd turn in that bluesuit, you wouldn't have to worry 'bout money,' said the one called Alice. 'I'd keep you forever, you beautiful blue-eyed devil.'

The girls laughed loudly as Kilvinsky closed the wagon and entered the liquor store, returning with a shopping bag in a few minutes.

He handed the bag in the door and was back in the cab and moving when Gus heard the liquor being poured.

'Change is in the bag,' said Kilvinsky.

'Gud-dam,' muttered one of the prostitutes. 'Scotch and milk is the best motherfuckin' drink in the world. Want a drink, Kilvinsky?'

'You know we can't drink on duty.'

'I know somethin' we can do on duty,' said another one. 'And yo' ser-geant won't smell it on yo' breath. Less'n you want to get down on yo' knees and French me.'

The girls screamed in laughter and Kilvinsky said, 'I'm too damn old for you young girls.'

'You ever change yo' mind, let me know,' said Alice, 'a foxy little whore like me could make you young again.'

Kilvinsky drove aimlessly for more than a half hour while Gus listened as the prostitutes laughed and talked shop, each girl trying to top the last one with her account of the 'weird tricks' she had encountered.

'Hell,' said one prostitute, 'I had one pick me up right here on Twenty-eighth and Western one night and take me clear to Beverly Heels for a hundred bucks and that bastard had me cut the head of a live chicken right there in some plushy apartment and then squish the chicken aroun' in the sink while the water was runnin' and he stood there and comed like a dog.'

'Lord! Why did you do it, girl?' asked another.

'Shee-it, I didn't know what the suckah wanted till he got me in that place and handed me the butcher knife. Then I was so scared I jist did it so he wouldn' git mad. Ol' funky bastard, he was. Didn' think he could even git a stiff one.'

'How 'bout that freak that lives up there in Van Nuys that likes to French inside a coffin. He sho' is a crazy motherfucker,' said a shrill voice.

'That milk bath guy picked Wilma up one night, didn't he, Wilma?' said another.

'Yeah, but he ain't nothin' too weird. Ah don' mind him, 'cept he lives too far away, way up in North Hollywood in one of them pads on a mountain. He jist gives you a bath in a tub full of milk. He pays damn good.'

'He don' do nothin' else?'

'Oh, he Frenches you a little, but not too much.'

'Shit, they almost all Frenches you anymore. People is gettin' so goddamn weird all they evah wants to do is eat pussy.'

'That right, girl. I was sayin' that the other day (pour me a little scotch, honey) people jist French or git Frenched anymore. I can't remember when a trick wanted to fuck me for his ten dollars.'

'Yeah, but these is all white tricks. Black men still likes to fuck.'

'Shee-it, I wouldn' know 'bout that. You take black tricks, baby?'

'Sometimes, don't you?'

'Nevah. Nevah. My ol' man tol' me any who' dum 'nuff to take black tricks deserves it if she gits her ass robbed or cut. Ah never fucked a niggah in my life fo' money. An' ah never fucked a white man fo' free.'

'Amen. Give me another shot of that scotch, baby, ah wants to tell you 'bout this here rich bitch from Hollywood that picked me up one night an' she wanted to give me a hundred an' fifty dollars to go home an' let her eat mah pussy an' her husband is sittin' right there in the car with her an' she tells me he jist likes to watch.'

Gus listened to tale after tale, each more bizarre than the last and when the voices were slurring, Kilvinsky said, 'Let's head for the station and let them go a few blocks away. They're too drunk to take them in the station. The sergeant would want us to book them for being drunk and then they might tell him where they got the booze.'

As the wagon bounced toward the station, the night drawing to a close, Gus found himself more relaxed than he had been for days. As for a physical confrontation, why, it might never happen and if it did, he would probably do well enough. He was feeling a lot better now. He hoped Vickie would be awake. He had so much to tell her.

'You're going to learn things down here, Gus,' said Kilvinsky. 'Every day down here is like ten days in a white division. It's the intensity down here, not just the high crime rate. You'll be a veteran after a year. It's the thousands of little things. Like the fact that you shouldn't use a pay phone. The coin chutes of all the public phones around here are stuffed so you can't get any coins back. Then once every few days the thief comes along and pulls the stuffing out with a piece of wire and gets the three dollars' worth of coins that've collected there. And other things. Kid's bikes. They're all stolen, or they all have stolen parts on them, so don't ask questions to any kid about his bike or you'll be tied up all night with bike reports. Little things, see, like New Year's Eve down here sounds like the battle of Midway. All these people seem to have guns. New Year's Eve will terrify you when you realize how many of them have guns and what's going to happen someday if this Civil Rights push ever breaks into armed rebellion. But the time passes fast down here, because these people keep us eternally busy and that's important to me. I only have a short time to go for my pension and I'm interested in time.'

'I'm not sorry I'm here,' said Gus.

'It's all happening here, partner. Big things. This Civil Rights business and the Black Muslims and all are just the start of it. Authority is being challenged and the Negroes are at the front, but they're just a small part of it. You're going to have an impossible job in the next five years or I miss my guess.'

Kilvinsky steered around an automobile wheel which was lying in the center of the residential street, but he rolled over another which lay on the other side of the street, unobserved, until they were on it. The exhausted blue van bounced painfully on its axle and a chorus of laughter was interrupted by an explosion of curses.

'Goddamn! Take it easy, Kilvinsky! You ain't drivin' no fuckin' cattle truck,' said Alice.

'It's the great myth,' said Kilvinsky to Gus, ignoring the voices behind them, 'the myth whatever it happens to be that breaks civil authority. I wonder if a couple of centurions might've sat around like you and me one hot dry evening talking about the myth of Christianity that was defeating them. They would've been afraid, I bet, but the new myth was loaded with "don'ts", so one kind of authority was just being substituted for another. Civilization was never in jeopardy. But today the "don'ts" are dying or being murdered in the name of freedom and we policemen can't save them. Once the people become accustomed to the death of a "don't", well then, the other "don'ts" die much easier. Usually all the vice laws die first because people are generally vice-ridden anyway. Then the ordinary misdemeanors and some felonies become unenforceable until freedom prevails. Then later the freed people have to organize an army of their own to find order because they learn that freedom is horrifying and ugly and only small doses of it can be tolerated.' Kilvinsky laughed self-consciously, a laugh that ended when he put the battered cigarette holder in his mouth and chewed on it quietly for several seconds. 'I warned you us old coppers are big bullshitters, didn't I, Gus?'

SIX

The Swamper

'How about driving to a gamewell phone? I got to call the desk about something,' said Whitey Duncan, and Roy sighed, turning the radio car right on Adams toward Hooper where he thought there was a call box.

'Go to Twenty-third and Hooper,' said Duncan. 'That's one of the few call boxes that works in this lousy division. Nothing works. The people don't work, the call boxes don't work, nothing works.'

Some of the policemen don't work, thought Roy, and wondered how they could have possibly assigned him with Duncan five nights in a row. Granted, August was a time when the car plan was short due to vacations, but Roy thought that was a feeble reason and inexcusable supervisory technique to give a rookie officer to a partner like Duncan. After his second night with Whitey he had even subtly suggested to Sergeant Coffin that he would like to work with an aggressive younger officer, but Coffin had cut him off abruptly as though a new officer had no right to ask for a specific car or partner. Roy felt that he was being penalized for speaking up by being inflicted with Duncan for five days.

'I'll be right back, kid,' said Whitey, leaving his hat in the radio car as he strolled to the call box, unsnapped the gamewell key from the ring hanging on his Sam Browne, and opened the box which was attached to the far side of a telephone pole out of Roy's line of sight. Roy could only see some white hair, a round blue stomach and shiny black shoe protruding from the vertical line of the pole.

Roy was told that Whitey had been a foot policeman in Central Division for almost twenty years and that he could never get used to working in a radio car. That was probably why he insisted on calling the station a half dozen times a night to talk to his friend, Sam Tucker, the desk officer.

After a few moments, Whitey swaggered back to the car and settled back, lighting his third cigar of the evening.

'You sure like to use that call box,' said Roy with a forced smile, trying to conceal the anger brought about by the boredom of working with a useless partner like Whitey when he was brand-new and eager to learn.

'Got to ring in. Let the desk know where you're at.'

'Your radio tells them that, Whitey. Policemen have radios in their cars nowadays.'

'I'm not used to it,' said Whitey. 'Like to ring in on the call box. Besides, I like to talk to my old buddy, Sam Tucker. Good man, old Sammy.'

'How come you always call in on the same box?'

'Habit, boy. When you get to be old Whitey's age, you start doing everything the same.'

It was true, Roy thought. Unless an urgent call intervened, they would eat at precisely ten o'clock every night at one of three greasy spoon restaurants that served Whitey free meals. Then, fifteen minutes would be spent at the station for Whitey's bowel movement. Then back out for the remainder of the watch, which would be broken by two or three stops at certain liquor stores for free cigars and of course the recurrent messages to Sam Tucker from the call box at Twenty-third and Hooper.

'How about driving through the produce market?' said Whitey. 'I never took you in there yet, did I?'

'Whatever you say,' Roy sighed.

Whitey directed Roy through bustling narrow streets blocked by a maze of trucks and milling swampers who were just coming to work. 'Over there,' said Whitey. 'That's old Foo Foo's place. He has the best bananas in the market. Park right there, kid. Then we'll get some avocados. They're a quarter apiece, right now. You like avocados? Then maybe a lug of peaches. I know a guy on the other side of the market, he has the best peaches. Never a bruise.' Whitey lumbered out of the car, and put on his hat at a jaunty beat officer's angle, grabbed his baton, probably from force of habit, and began twirling it expertly in his left hand as he approached the gaunt Chinese who was sweating in a pair of khaki shorts and an undershirt as he threw huge bunches of bananas onto a produce truck. The Chinese bared his gold and silver bridgework when Whitey approached and Roy lit a cigarette and watched in revulsion as Whitey put his baton in the ring on his belt and helped Foo Foo toss bananas onto the truck.

Professional policeman, Roy thought viciously, as he remembered the suave, silver-haired captain who had lectured them in the academy about the new professionalism. But it seemed the fat cop stealing apples died hard. Look at the old bastard, thought Roy, throwing bananas in full uniform while all the other swampers are laughing their heads off. Why doesn't he retire from the Department, and then he could swamp bananas full time. I hope a tarantula bites him on his fat ass, Roy thought.

How they could have sent him to Newton Street Station, Roy could not understand. What was the sense of giving them three choices of divisions if they were then ignored and sent arbitrarily from the academy to a station twenty miles from home. He lived almost in the valley. They could have sent him to one of the valley divisions or Highland Park or even Central which was his third choice, but Newton Street he had not counted on. It was the poorest of the Negro divisions and the drabness of the area was depressing. This was the 'east side' and he already had learned that as soon as the newly emigrated Negroes could afford it, they moved to the 'west side', somewhere west of Figueroa Street. But the fact that the majority of the people here were Negro was the one thing that appealed to Roy. When he left the Department to be a criminologist he intended to have a thorough understanding of the ghetto. He hoped to learn all that was necessary in a year or so, and then transfer north, perhaps to Van Nuys or North Hollywood.

When they finally left the produce market, the back seat of the radio car was filled with bananas, avocados and peaches, as well as a basket of tomatoes which Whitey had scrounged as an afterthought.

'You know you got a right to half of these,' said Whitey as they loaded the produce into his private car in the station parking lot.

'I told you I didn't want any.'

'Partners got to share and share alike. You got a right to half of it. How about the avocados? Why don't you take the avocados?'

'Son of a bitch,' Roy blurted, 'I don't want it! Look here, I'm just out of the academy. I've got eight months more to do on my probationary period. They can fire me on a whim anytime between now and then. No civil service protection for a probationer, you know. I can't be taking gratuities. At least not things like this. Free meals – cigarettes – coffee – that stuff seems to be traditional, but what if the sergeant saw us in the produce market tonight? I could lose my job!'

'Sorry, kid,' said Whitey with a hurt expression. 'I didn't know you felt that way. I'd take all the heat if we'd got caught, you should know that.'

'Yeah? What would I use as an excuse, that you put a gun to my head and forced me to go with you on that shopping tour?'

Whitey completed the transfer of fruit without further comment and didn't speak again until they were back patrolling their district, then he said, 'Hey, partner, drive to a call box, I got to ring in again.'

'What the hell for?' said Roy, not caring what Whitey thought anymore. 'What's going on? You got a bunch of broads leaving messages at the desk for you or something?'

'I just talk to old Sam Tucker,' said Whitey with a deep sigh. 'The old bastard gets lonesome there at the desk. We was academy classmates, you know. Twenty-six years this October. It's tough on him being colored and working a nigger division like this. Some nights he feels pretty low when they bring in some black bastard that killed an old lady or some other shitty thing like that, and these policemen shoot off their mouth in the coffee room about niggers and such. Sam hears it and it bothers him, so he gets feeling low. Course, he's too old to be a cop anyway. He was thirty-one when he came on the job. He ought to pull the pin and leave this crappy place.'

'How old were you when you came on, Whitey?'

'Twenty-nine. Hey, drive to the call box on Twenty-third. You know that's my favorite box.'

'I ought to know by now,' said Roy.

Roy parked at the curb and waited hopelessly while Whitey went to the call box and talked to Sam Tucker for ten minutes.

Police professionalism would come only after the old breed was gone, Roy thought. That didn't really trouble him though, because he had no intention of making a career of police work. That reminded him he had better get busy and register for the coming semester if he hoped to keep on schedule and complete his degree as planned. He wondered how anyone could want to do this kind of work for a career. Now that the training phase was over, he was part of a system he would master, learn from, and leave behind.

He glanced in the car mirror. The sun had given him a fine color. Dorothy said she'd never seen him so tan, and whether it was the uniform or his fitness she obviously found him more desirable and wanted him to make love to her often. But it may have been only because she was pregnant with their first baby and she knew that soon there would be none of it for a while. And he did it, though the enormous mound of life almost revolted him and he pretended to enjoy it as much as he did when she was lithe with a satin stomach that would probably bear stretch scars forever now that she was pregnant. That was her fault. They had decided not to have children for five years, but she had made a mistake. The news had staggered him. All his plans had to be changed. She could no longer work as a senior steno at Rhem Electronics, and she had been making an excellent wage. He would have to stay with the Department an extra year or so to save money. He would not ask his father or Carl for assistance, not even for a loan now that they all knew he would never enter the family firm.

Trying to please them was the reason he changed his major three times until he took abnormal psychology with Professor Raymond, and learned from the flabby little scholar who he was. The kindly man, who had been like a father, had almost wept when Roy told him he was leaving college to join the Los Angeles Police Department for a year or two. They had sat in Professor Raymond's office until midnight while the little man coaxed and urged and swore at Roy's stubbornness and at last gave in when Roy convinced him he was tired and probably would fail every class next semester if he remained, that a year or two away from the books but in close touch with life would give him the impetus to return and take his bachelor's and master's degrees. And who knows, if he were the scholar that Professor Raymond believed he could be, he might even keep right on while he had the momentum and get his Ph.D.

'We might be colleagues someday, Roy,' said the professor, fervently shaking Roy's dry hand in both his moist soft ones. 'Keep in touch with me, Roy.'

And he had meant to. He wanted to talk with someone as sensitive as the professor about the things he had learned so far. He talked with Dorothy, of course. But she was so involved in the mysteries of childbirth that he doubted that she listened when he brought home the tales of the bizarre situations he encountered as a policeman and what they meant to a behaviorist.

While waiting for Whitey, Roy tilted the car mirror down and examined his badge and brass buttons. He was tall and slim but his shoulders were broad enough to make the tailored blue shirt becoming. His Sam Browne glistened and his shoes were as good as he could get them without the fanatical spit shine that some of the others employed. He kept the badge lustrous with a treated cloth and some jeweler's rouge. He decided that when his hair grew out he would never cut it short again. He had heard that a butch haircut sometimes grows out wavier than before.

'You're absolutely beautiful,' said Whitey, jerking open the door and flopping into the seat with a fatuous grin at Roy.

'I dropped some cigarette ash on my shirt,' said Roy, tilting the mirror to its former position. 'I was just brushing it off.'

'Let's go do some police work,' said Whitey, rubbing his hands together.

'Why bother? We only have three more hours until end of watch,' said Roy. 'What the hell did Tucker tell you to make you so happy?'

'Nothing. I just feel good. It's a nice summer night. I just feel like working. Let's catch a burglar. Anybody show you yet how to patrol for burglars?'

'Thirteen-A-Forty-three, Thirteen-A-Forty-three,' said the operator and Whitey turned up the volume, 'see the woman, landlord-tenant dispute, forty-nine thirty-nine, south Avalon.'

'Thirteen-A-Forty-three, roger,' said Whitey into the hand mike. Then to Roy, 'Well, instead of catching crooks, let's go pacify the natives.'

Roy parked in front of the house on Avalon which was easy to find because of the porch light and the fragile white-haired Negro woman standing on the porch watching the street. She was perhaps sixty and smiled timidly when Roy and Whitey climbed the ten steps.

'This is it, Mr. PO-lice,' she said, opening the battered screen door. 'Won't you please come in?'

Roy removed his hat upon entering and became annoyed when Whitey failed to remove his also. It seemed that everything Whitey did irritated him.

'Won't you sit down?' she smiled, and Roy admired the tidy house she kept which looked old and clean and orderly like her.

'No, thanks, ma'am,' said Whitey. 'What can we do for you?'

'I got these here people that lives in the back. I don't know what to do. I hopes you can help me. They don't pay the rent on time never. And now they's two months behind and I needs the money terrible bad. I only lives on a little social security, you see, and I just got to have the rent.'

'I appreciate your problem, ma'am, I sure do,' said Whitey. 'I once owned a duplex myself. I had some tenants that wouldn't pay and I had a heck of a time. Mine had five kids that like to've torn the place down. Yours have any kids?'

'They does. Six. And they tears up my property terrible.'

'It's rough,' said Whitey, shaking his head.

'What can I do, sir? Can you help me? I begged them to pay me.'

'Sure wish we could,' said Whitey, 'but you see this is a civil matter and we only deal in criminal matters. You'd have to get the county marshal to serve them with a notice to quit and then you'd have to sue them for unlawful detainer. That's what they call it and that would take time and you'd have to pay a lawyer.'

'I don't have no money for a lawyer, Mr. PO-lice,' said the old woman, her thin hand touching Whitey beseechingly on the arm.

'I appreciate that, ma'am,' said Whitey, 'I sure do. By the way, is that corn bread I smell?'

'It sho' is, sir. Would you like some?'

'Would I?' said Whitey, removing his hat and leading the old woman to the kitchen. 'I'm a country-raised boy. I grew up in Arkansas on corn bread.'

'Would you like some?' she smiled to Roy.

'No, thank you,' he said.

'Some coffee? It's fresh.'

'No ma'am, thank you.'

'I don't know when I had such good corn bread,' said Whitey. 'Soon's I finish, I'm going back and talk to your tenants for you. They in the little cottage in the rear.'

'Yes, sir. That's where they is. I sure would appreciate that and I'm going to tell our councilman what a fine PO-lice force we have. You always so good to me no matter what I calls for. You from Newton Street Station, ain't you?'

'Yes, ma'am, you just tell the councilman that you liked the service of old Whitey from Newton Street. You can even call the station and tell my sergeant if you want to.'

'Why I'll do that, I surely will, Mr. Whitey. Can I get you some more corn bread?'

'No, no thank you,' said Whitey, wiping his entire face with the linen napkin the old woman got for him. 'We'll have a little talk with them and I bet they get your rent to you real quick.'

'Thank you very much,' the old woman called, as Roy followed Whitey and his flashlight beam down the narrow walkway to the rear of the property. Roy's frustration had subsided in his pity for the plight of the old woman and his admiration of her neat little house. There weren't enough like her in the ghetto, he thought.

'It's too damned bad that people would take advantage of a nice old woman like that,' said Roy as they approached the rear cottage.

'How do you know they did?' asked Whitey.

'What do you mean? You heard her.'

'I heard one side of a landlord-tenant dispute,' said Whitey. 'Now I got to hear the other side. You're the judge in all these dispute calls we get. Never make a decision till both sides present their cases.'

This time Roy bit his lip to enforce his silence. The absurdity of this man was beyond belief. A child could see the old woman had a just grievance and he knew before the door opened that the cottage would be a filthy hovel where miserable children lived in squalor with deadbeat parents.

A coffee-colored woman in her late twenties opened the door when Whitey tapped.

'Mrs. Carson said she was going to call the PO-lice,' said the woman with a tired smile. 'Come in, Officers.'

Roy followed Whitey into the little house which had a bedroom in the back, a small kitchen, and a living room filled by the six children who were gathered around an ancient television with a dying picture tube.

'Honey,' she called, and a man padded into the room from the back, wearing frayed khaki trousers and a faded blue short-sleeved shirt which revealed oversized arms and battered hardworking hands.

'I just didn't think she'd really call the law,' he said with an embarrassed smile at the officers, as Roy wondered how the cottage could be kept this clean with so many small children.

'We're two weeks behind in our rent,' he drawled. 'We never been behind befo' 'cept once and that was fo' three days. That ol' lady is mighty hard.'

'She says you're over two months behind,' said Roy.

'Looky here,' said the man, going to the kitchen cupboard and returning with several slips of paper. 'Here's last month's receipt and the month befo' and the one befo' that, clear back to January when we fust came here from Arkansas.'

'You from Arkansas?' said Whitey. 'Whereabouts? I'm from Arkansas too.'

'Wait a minute, Whitey,' said Roy, then turned back to the man. 'Why should Mrs. Carson say you were behind in your rent? She said you never pay her on time and she's told you how she needs the money and that your kids have destroyed her property. Why should she say that?'

'Officer,' said the man, 'Mrs. Carson is a very hard lady. She owns most of this side of Avalon from Fo'ty-ninth Street on down to the co'ner.'

'Have your children ever destroyed her property?' asked Roy weakly.

'Look at my house, Officer,' said the woman. 'Do it look like we the kind of folks that would let a chil' tear up a house? Once James there broke her basement window chucking a rock at a tin can. But she added that on our rent payment and we paid fo' it.'

'How do you like California?' asked Whitey.

'Oh, we likes it fine,' smiled the man. 'Soon's we can save a little we wants to maybe buy a small house and get away from Mrs. Carson.'

'Well, we got to be going now,' said Whitey. 'Sure sorry you're having troubles with your landlady. I want to wish you good luck here in California, and listen, if you ever happen to make any down-home Arkansas meals and have some left over you just call Newton Street Station and let me know, will you?'

'Why, we'll do that, sir,' said the woman. 'Who'll we ask fo'?'

'Just say old Whitey. And you might tell the sergeant old Whitey gave you good service. We need a pat on the back once in a while.'

'Thank you, Officer,' said the man. 'It's surely a comfort to meet such fine *po*-licemen here.'

'So long, kids,' shouted Whitey to the six beaming brown faces which by now were gazing reverently at the policemen. They all waved good-byes as Roy followed the fat blue swaggering figure back down the narrow walkway to the car.

While Whitey was lighting a cigar Roy asked, 'How did you know the old lady was lying? You probably answered calls there before, right?'

'Never did,' said Whitey. 'Goddamn cigars. Wonder if good cigars draw better than cheap ones?'

'Well how did you know then? You must've suspected she was lying.'

'I never said she was lying. I don't say it now. There's two sides to every beef. Experience'll teach you that. You got to listen to the first guy like he's giving you the gospel and then go to the second guy and do the same thing. You just got to be patient, use horse sense and this job is easy.'

Handling a rent dispute doesn't make you a policeman, Roy thought. There's more to police work than that.

'You ready to teach me how to catch a burglar now?' asked Roy, know-ing the satirical edge on his voice was apparent.

'Okay, but first I got to make sure you can handle a simple landlord–tenant beef. First thing you already learned, don't take no sides. Next thing, a landlord-tenant beef or anything else could involve a psycho, or a crook with something in the pad he don't want you to see, or somebody that's so pissed off at his landlord or tenant that he's ready to climb the ass of anybody that comes through the door.'

'So?'

'So be careful. Walk into any pad like a policeman not an insurance man. Stick your flashlight in your back pocket if there's light on in the pad, and keep your lid on your head. Then you got two hands ready to use. You start strolling in these pads with a light in one hand and a hat in the other you might find you need a third hand quick some night and you'll be a real courteous corpse with your hat in your hand.'

'I didn't think the old lady was very dangerous.'

'I had a senile old lady stick a pair of scissors right through the web of my hand one time,' said Whitey. 'You do what you want, I just give the tips for what they're worth. Hey, kid, how about letting me call in. Head for my call box, will you?'

Roy watched Whitey at the call box and fumed. Patronizing stupid bastard, he thought. Roy realized he had a lot to learn, but he wanted to learn it from a real policeman, not from an overweight old windbag who was a caricature of a police officer. The incessant chatter of the police radio subsided for a moment and Roy heard a dull clink of glass.

Then the realization struck him and he smiled. How foolish not to have guessed it before! He couldn't help grinning when Whitey returned to the car.

'Let's go to work, kid,' said Whitey, as he got back in.

'Sure thing, partner,' said Roy. 'But first, I think I'll call in. I want to leave a message with the desk.'

'Wait a minute!' said Whitey. 'Let's drive to the station. You can tell him personally.'

'No, it'll just take a minute, I can use this call box,' said Roy.

'No! Wait a minute! The box is screwed up. Just before I hung up, it started buzzing. Almost busted my eardrum. It ain't working right!'

'Well, I'll just try it,' said Roy, and moved as though to get out of the car.'

'Wait, please!' said Whitey, grabbing Roy's elbow. 'Let's go in right now. I got to take a shit terrible bad. Take me to the station right now and you can give your message to Sam.'

'Why, Whitey,' Roy grinned triumphantly, and with Whitey's perspiring face this close, the fresh whiskey odor was overpowering, 'you always crap fifteen minutes after we eat dinner. You told me your guts start rumbling right after your evening meal. What's the matter?'

'It's my age,' said Whitey, staring sadly at the floorboard as Roy gunned the engine and drove into the traffic lane, 'when you get my age you can't depend on nothing, not even your guts, especially not your guts.'

August 1961

SEVEN
Guerra!

They were told by the Gang Squad detective that the war had actually
started six weeks ago when the Junior Falcons jumped a seventeen-
year-old member of *Los Gavilanes* named Felix Orozco who had made the
consummate and final mistake of running out of gas in Falcon territory in
a striped nineteen forty-eight Chevrolet that the Falcons knew belonged
to a *Gavilán*. Felix was beaten to death with his own tire iron which he
had used to break the wrist of the first Falcon who had come at him with a
sharpened screwdriver. The girl friend of Felix Orozco, thirteen-year-old
Connie Madrid, was not killed by the Junior Falcons but her face was badly
ripped by a whistling slash of the car antenna that was broken off the car
by El Pablo of the Junior Falcons who, it was believed by the detectives,
was the one responsible for flogging Felix Orozco with the limber piece
of steel as he lay, already dead, probably, from countless kicks to the head
and face.

Connie had been a less than cooperative witness and now after two hearing postponements in juvenile court, it was believed by the homicide team
that she would probably deny in court that she saw anything.

Since the death of Felix, there had been seven cases of gang reprisals
involving *Los Gavilanes*, and the Junior Falcons, but on one occasion a
member of the Easystreeters, named Ramon Garcia, was mistaken for a
Junior Falcon and the Easystreeters announced against *Los Gavilanes*.
Then, *Los Rojos*, who had no love for the Junior Falcons but who hated the
Easystreeters, saw the opportunity once and for all to join a powerful ally
and destroy the hated Easystreeters. Hollenbeck Division was plunged into
a war that produced at least one gang incident every night, and made Serge
more than ever want to transfer to Hollywood Division.

He had been getting used to Hollenbeck: It was a small division, and
after a year, he was getting to know people. It helped being familiar with
the regulars and when you saw someone like Marcial Tapia – who had been
a burglar for over twenty years when you saw him driving a pickup truck
in the Flats (when he lived his entire life in Lincoln Heights) and the Flats
was an area of commercial buildings, factories, and businesses, which were
closed on weekends and it was five o'clock Sunday afternoon and all the

businesses were closed – well then, you had better stop Marcial Tapia and check the contents of the truck bed which was covered with three barrels of trash and refuse. Serge had done this just three weeks before and found seven new portable television sets, an adding machine, and two typewriters beneath the pile of rubble. He had received a commendation for the arrest of Tapia, his second commendation since becoming a policeman. He had made an excellent arrest report detailing the probable cause for the arrest and search, telling how Tapia had committed a traffic violation which had caused him to stop the truck, and how he had observed the rabbit ear antenna protruding from the pile of trash. He also told how Tapia had appeared exceptionally nervous and evasive when questioned about the telltale antenna, and how when it was all added up he, being a reasonable and prudent man, with a year's experience as a police officer, believed there was something being concealed in the truck and this was how he told it in court, and it was, of course, all bullshit. He had stopped Tapia only because he recognized him and knew his background and suspected what he was doing in the commercial area of the Flats on a Sunday afternoon.

It infuriated him that he had to lie, at least it used to infuriate him, but it soon came easy enough to him when he saw that if he stuck strictly to the truth he would probably lose more than half of his arrests which involved probable cause to stop and search, because the courts were not reasonable and prudent in their assessment of what was reasonable and prudent. So Serge had decided irrevocably several months ago that he would never lose another case that hinged on a word, innuendo, or interpretation of an action by a black-robed idealist who had never done police work. It wasn't that he was trying to protect the victims, he believed that if you did not enjoy taking an asshole off the street, even if it's only for a little while, then you are in the wrong business.

'Why so quiet?' asked Milton, as he propped his elbow on the seat cushion and puffed his foul cigar, looking utterly content because they had just finished an enormous plate of chile verde, rice, and frijoles at a Mexican restaurant where Milton had been eating for eighteen years. He could eat his chile as hot as any Mexican after working Hollenbeck so long, and Raul Muñioz, the owner, challenged Milton by serving them his special chile 'not for gringo tastes'. Milton had consumed the chile with a bland expression saying it was tasty but not hot enough. Serge however had drunk three strawberry sodas with his meal and had his water refilled twice. That had not quenched the fire and he had ordered a large glass of milk finally. His stomach was just now becoming normal.

'What the hell. You never ate real Mexican food before?' asked Milton as Serge drove slowly through the dark summer night, enjoying the cool breeze which made the long-sleeved blue woolen uniform shirt bearable.

'I never ate that kind of green chile,' said Serge, 'you think it's safe to light a cigarette?'

'I think if I ever get married again, I'll marry a *Mexicana* who can make that kind of chile verde that bites back,' Milton sighed, blowing cigar smoke out the window.

Serge was Milton's regular partner this month and so far he could tolerate the overweight blustering old policeman. He thought that Milton liked him, even though he always called him a 'damn rookie' and sometimes treated him as though he had been on the Department fifteen days rather than fifteen months. But then, he once heard Milton call Simon a damn rookie and Simon had eight years on the Department.

'Four-A-Eleven,' said the Communications operator, 'at eighteen-thirteen Brooklyn, see the woman, A.D.W. report.'

Serge waited for Milton to roger the call, which of course was his job as passenger officer, but the old glutton was too comfortable, with one fat leg crossed over the other, a hand on his belly and a pleading look at Serge.

'Four-A-Eleven, roger,' said Serge and Milton nodded his gratitude at not having to move just yet.

'I think I'll trade you in for a police dog,' said Serge, seeing by his watch that it was 9:45. Only three hours to go. It had been a quick evening, though uneventful for a Saturday night.

'At least you can catch a number for me,' said Serge to Milton, who had closed his eyes and leaned his head against the door post.

'Okay, Sergio, my boy, if you're going to nag me,' said Milton, pronouncing it Ser-jee-oh instead of with a soft throaty g in two syllables as it was meant to be pronounced.

Milton shined the spotlight at the housefronts trying to read a number. Serge did not like to be called Sergio no matter how it was said. It was a name from his childhood and childhood was so far in the past that he could hardly remember. He had not seen his brother Angel nor his sister Aurora since Aurora's birthday dinner at Angel's house when he had brought presents to Aurora and all his nephews and nieces. He had been scolded by Aurora and Angel's wife Yolanda for coming by so seldom. But since his mother was gone he had little reason to return to Chino and he realized that when the memory of his mother would begin to fade, his visits would probably be no more than twice a year. But so far, his memories of her were still very vivid and it was difficult to understand because he had never thought of her so frequently when she lived. In fact, when he left her at eighteen to join the Marine Corps, he had intended never to live at home again, but to leave the bleak little neighborhood and go perhaps to Los Angeles. He had not at that time considered being a policeman. Then he thought of how she, like all Mexican mothers, called her sons *mi hijo* and said it like one word which made it more intimate than 'my son' in English.

'Must be the gray house,' said Milton. 'That one. The one with the balcony, Jesus Christ, those timbers are rotten. I wouldn't walk on that balcony.'

'With your weight I wouldn't walk on the First Street bridge,' said Serge.

'Goddamn rookies, no respect for senior partners anymore,' said Milton as Serge parked the radio car.

The house sat on the edge of an alley and north of the alley was a commercial building, windowless on the south wall. The builder of the edifice had made the error of plastering the building with a coat of soft irresistible yellow paint. Serge guessed that the wall had not remained inviolate for two days after it was completed. This was a gang neighborhood, a Mexican gang neighborhood, and Mexican gang members were obsessed with a compulsion to make their mark on the world. Serge stopped for a moment, taking the last puff on his cigarette while Milton got his notebook and flashlight. Serge read the writing on the wall in black and red paint from spray cans which all gang members carried in their cars in case they would spot a windfall like this creamy yellow irresistible blank wall. There was a heart in red, three feet in diameter, which bore the names of 'Ruben and Isabel' followed by *'mia vida'* and there was the huge declaration of an Easystreeter which said *'El Wimpy de los Easystreeters'*, and another one which said 'Ruben *de los Easystreeters'*, but Ruben would not be outdone by Wimpy and the legend below his name said *'de los Easystreeters y del mundo,'* and Serge smiled wryly as he thought of Ruben who claimed the world as his domain because Serge had yet to meet a gang member who had ever been outside Los Angeles County. There were other names of Junior Easystreeters and Peewee Easystreeters, dozens of them, and declarations of love and ferocity and the claims that this was the land of the Easystreeters. Of course at the bottom of the wall was the inevitable *'CON SAFOS'*, the crucial gang incantation not to be found in any Spanish dictionary, which declared that none of the writing on this wall can ever be altered or despoiled by anything later written by the enemy.

As Serge read, the disgust welled in him but it was interrupted by a blast of horns and a caravan of cars moving down State Street decorated with strings of pink and white paper carnations announcing a Mexican wedding. The men in the cars wore white dinner jackets and the girls chiffon dresses of blue. The bride of course wore white and a white veil which she wore pulled back as she kissed her new husband who Serge guessed could not be more than eighteen. The car directly behind the bride and groom's blasted the horn louder than the rest to sound approval at the prolonged kiss.

'In a few months we'll be called in to handle their family disputes,' said Serge, grinding the cigarette out on the sidewalk.

'Think it'll take that long before he starts kicking the hell out of her?' asked Milton.

'No, probably not,' said Serge as they walked to the house.

'That's why I told the lieutenant if he had to stick me with a rookie, to give me that half-breed Mexican Sergio Duran,' said Milton slapping

Serge on the shoulder. 'You may be short on experience, Sergio my boy, but you're as cynical as any twenty-year cop on the Department.'

Serge did not correct Milton who had referred to him on another occasion as his half-caste partner. He had never claimed to be only half-Mexican, but the idea had spread somehow and Serge merely acquiesced by his silence when some overly inquisitive partner asked him if it were true his mother had been an Anglo which would certainly explain why he didn't speak Spanish and why he was such a big man and so fair. At first it had bothered him for someone to think his mother was other than what she had been, but damn it, it was better this way he told himself. Otherwise, he would have been constantly plagued like Ruben Gonsalvez and the other Chicano cops with hundreds of duties involving translation. And it was true, it was utterly true that he no longer spoke the language. Certainly he understood things that were said, but he had to concentrate fully to understand a conversation and it was not worth the effort to him. And he forgot the words. He could not answer even if he did understand a little. So it was better this way. Even with a name like Sergio Duran you could not be expected to speak Spanish if your mother was not Mexican.

'Hope this goddamn balcony doesn't cave in while we're in the pad,' said Milton, flipping the remains of his wet cigar in the alley as they knocked on the screen door.

Two little boys came to the door and held it open silently.

'Is Mama home?' asked Milton, tapping the shorter one under the chin.

'Our father is a policeman too,' said the taller one, who was very thin and dirty. His eyes were as black as his hair and he was obviously excited at having the policemen in his house.

'He is?' said Serge, wondering if it were true. 'You mean he's a guard of some kind?'

'He's a policeman,' said the boy, nodding for emphasis. 'He's a *capitán de policía*. I swear it.'

'Where?' asked Serge. 'Not here in Los Angeles?'

'In Juárez, Mexico,' answered the boy. 'Where we come from.'

Milton chuckled, and when Serge turned he reddened as he saw Milton was laughing at him, not at the boy.

That was something he hadn't yet mastered completely, the capacity to mentally challenge anything, *anything* that people told you because it was usually erroneous, exaggerated, rationalized or downright deceptive.

'Go get Mama,' said Milton, and the shorter child obeyed immediately. The taller one stood staring at Serge in wonder.

The boy reminded Serge of someone, he couldn't remember who. The same hollow eyes of opaque blackness, bony arms, and a buttonless shirt that had never been completely clean. A boy in the old life perhaps, or one of the Korean children who shined their shoes and swept the barracks.

No, it was one from the old life, a childhood friend had eyes like that, but he couldn't remember which one. Why should he try? The memory failure was further proof the cord was irreparably severed, the operation a success.

The child stared at the shiny black Sam Browne belt, the key ring with the huge brass key which unlocked police call boxes, and the chrome-plated whistle which Serge had bought to replace the plastic one the Department supplied. While Serge glanced up the stairs toward the woman who was answering the child they had sent, he felt a light touch on the key ring. When he looked down the child was still staring, but his hands were at his sides.

'Here kid,' said Milton, removing the whistle from his key ring. 'Take it outside and blow your brains out. But I want it back when I leave, hear me?'

The boy smiled and took the whistle from Milton. Before he stepped from the house, the shrill screams of the whistle pierced the summer night.

'Christ, he'll have the whole neighborhood complaining,' said Serge, moving toward the door to call the boy.

'Let him,' said Milton, grabbing Serge's arm.

'You gave it to him,' Serge shrugged. 'It's your whistle.'

'Yep,' said Milton.

'He'll probably steal the goddamn thing,' said Serge, disgustedly.

'You're probably right. That's what I like about you, kid, you're a realist.'

It was an old two-story house and Serge guessed it housed a family on each floor. They were standing in a living room which had two twin beds shoved into a far corner. The kitchen was in the rear of the house and another room which he could not see into. It was probably another bedroom. It was a very large old house, very large for one family. At least it was very large for one family on welfare, as he guessed this one was, for there were no man signs around the house, only children's and women's things.

'Up here, please,' said the woman, who stood at the top of the staircase in the darkness. She was pregnant and carried a baby in her arms who was not more than a year old.

'The light over the steps is out. I'm sorry,' she said, as they used their flashlights to light the creaking, precarious steps.

'In here, please,' she said entering the room to the left of the landing.

It looked very much like the room downstairs, a combination living room and bedroom where at least two children slept. There was a half-dead portable television on a low end table and three girls and the boy they had sent upstairs were sitting in front of it watching a grotesque cowboy whose elongated head sat atop an enormous avocado body.

'That TV needs repair,' said Milton.

336

'Oh yes,' she smiled. 'I'm going to get it fixed soon.'

'You know Jesse's TV Shop on First Street?' asked Milton.

'I think so,' she nodded, 'near the bank?'

'Yeah. Take it to him. He's honest. He's been around here at least twenty years that I know of.'

'I will, thank you,' she said, giving the fat baby to the oldest girl, a child of about ten, who was sitting on the end of the blanket-covered couch.

'What's the problem?' asked Serge.

'My oldest boy got beat up today,' said the woman. 'He's in the bedroom. When I told him I called the cops, he went in there and won't come out. His head is bleeding and he won't let me take him to General Hospital or nothing. Could you please talk to him or something?'

'We can't talk if he won't open the door,' said Serge.

'He'll open it,' said the woman. Her huge stomach was tearing the shapeless black dress at the seams. She shuffled barefoot to the closed door at the rear of a cluttered hallway.

'Nacho,' she called. 'Nacho! Open the door! He's stubborn,' she said turning to the two policemen. 'Ignacio, you open it!'

Serge wondered when was the last time Nacho had been kicked in the ass by his mother. Never, probably. If there had ever been a real father living in the pad, he probably didn't care enough to do the job. He would never have dared to defy his own mother like this, Serge thought. And she had raised them without a father. And the house was always spotless, not like this filth. And she had worked and he was glad because if they had given away welfare in those days like they did today, they probably would have accepted it because who could refuse money.

'Come on, Nacho, open the door and let's stop playing around,' said Milton. 'And hurry up! We're not going to stand around all night.'

The lock turned and a chunky shirtless boy of about sixteen opened the door, turned his back, and walked across the room to a wicker chair where he had apparently been sitting. He held a grimy washcloth to his head, the webs of his fingers crusty with blood and car grease.

'What happened to you?' asked Milton, entering the room and turning up a table lamp to examine the boy's head.

'I fell,' he said, with a surly look at Milton and another at Serge. The look he gave his mother infuriated Serge who shook a cigarette from his pack and lit it.

'Look, we don't care whether your head gets infected or not,' said Milton. 'And we don't care if you want to be stupid and get in gang beefs and die like a stupid *vato* in the street. That's your business. But you think about it, because we're only going to give you about two minutes to decide whether you want to let us take you to the hospital and get your head sewed up and tell us what happened, or whether you want to go to bed like that and wake up with gangrene of the superego which usually only takes three hours to kill you. I can see that wound is already getting green flakes all over it. That's a sure sign.'

The boy looked at Milton's expressionless beefy face for a moment. 'All right, you might as well take me to the hospital,' he said, snatching a soiled T-shirt from the bedpost.

'What happened? *Los Rojos* get you?' asked Milton, turning sideways to get down the narrow creaking stairway with Nacho.

'Will you bring him home?' asked the woman.

'We'll take him to Lincoln Heights Receiving Hospital,' said Serge. 'You'll have to bring him home.'

'I don't got a car,' said the woman. 'And I got the kids here. Maybe I can get Ralph next door to take me. Can you wait a minute?'

'We'll bring him home after he's fixed up,' said Milton.

It was that kind of thing that made Serge damn mad at Milton at least once every working night. It was not their responsibility to bring people home from the hospital, or jail, or anywhere else they took them. Police cars made one-way trips. It was Saturday night and there were lots more interesting things to do than nursemaid this kid. It would never have occurred to Milton to ask him what *he* wanted to do, thought Serge. Serge would need ten more years as a cop before he rated simple consideration from Milton. Besides, that was the trouble with people like these, someone was always doing for them what they should do for themselves.

'We'll have him back in less than an hour,' said Milton to the panting woman who rested her big belly against the precarious banister and apparently decided not to descend the entire stairway.

When Serge turned to go he noticed that above the doorway in the living room of the downstairs family were two eight-by-four-inch holy cards. One was Our Lady of Guadalupe and the other Blessed Martin de Porres. In the center was another card, a bit larger, which contained a green and gold horseshoe covered with glitter and a border of four-leaf clovers.

Nacho had mastered the stride of the Mexican gang member and Serge was looking at him as they crossed the front yard. He didn't see the car cruising slowly down the street, lights out, until it was close. At first he thought it was another radio car on early prowler patrol and then he saw it was a green metal-flaked Chevrolet. Four or five heads barely showed above the window ledges which told Serge automatically that the seats were dropped and that it was probably a gang car.

'Who are those low riders?' Serge asked, turning to Nacho, who was gaping in terror at the car. The car stopped near Nacho's alley and for the first time the low riders seemed to notice the radio car which was partially hidden from view behind a junk-laden van parked in front.

Nacho bolted for the house at the same moment that Serge realized these were *Los Rojos* who had attacked the boy and were probably returning to be more thorough.

Nacho's little brother gave a happy blast on the police whistle.

'*La jura!*' said a voice from the car, apparently seeing the policemen step from the shadows into the light from the open doorway. The driver turned on the lights and the car lurched forward and stalled as Serge ran toward it, ignoring Milton who shouted, 'Duran, get your ass back here!'

Serge had a half-formed thought of jerking the cursing driver out of the car as he ground the starter desperately, but when Serge was ten feet from the car he heard a pop, and an orange fiery blossom flashed from the interior of the car. Serge froze as he instinctively knew what it was before his mind fully comprehended, and the Chevy started, faltered, and roared east on Brooklyn Avenue.

'The keys!' Milton roared, standing beside the open driver's door of the radio car. 'Throw the keys!'

Serge obeyed immediately although still stunned by the realization that they had fired at him point-blank. He had barely jumped in the passenger seat when Milton squealed from the curb and the flashing red light and siren brought Serge back to reality.

'Four-A-Eleven in pursuit!' Serge yelled into the open microphone, and began shouting the streets they were passing as the Communications operator cleared the frequency of conversation so that all units could be informed that Four-A-Eleven was pursuing a 1948 Chevrolet eastbound on Marengo.

'Four-A-Eleven, your location!' shouted the Communications operator.

Serge turned the radio as loud as it would go and rolled up the window but could still hardly hear Milton and the operator over the din of the siren and the roaring engine as Milton gained on the careening low riders who narrowly missed a head-on collision with a left turner.

'Four-A-Eleven approaching Soto Street, still eastbound on Marengo,' Serge shouted, and then realized his seat belt was not fastened.

'Four-A-Eleven your location! Come in Four-A-Eleven!' shouted the Communications operator as Serge fumbled with the seat belt, cursed, and dropped the mike.

'They're bailing out!' Milton shouted and Serge looked up to see the Chevrolet skidding to a stop in the middle of Soto Street as all four doors were flung open.

'The one in the right rear fired the shot. Get him!' Milton yelled as Serge was running in the street before the radio car finished the jolting sliding stop.

Several passing cars slammed on brakes as Serge chased the *Rojo* in the brown hat and yellow Pendleton shirt down Soto and east on Wabash. Serge was utterly unaware that he had run two blocks at top speed when suddenly the air scorched his lungs and his legs turned weak, but they were still running through the darkness. He had lost his baton and his hat, and the flashlight fluttering in his swinging left hand lighted nothing but empty sidewalk in front of him. Then his man was gone. Serge stopped and scanned the street frantically. The street was quiet and badly lit. He heard nothing but his outraged thudding heart and the sawing breaths that frightened him. He heard a barking dog close to his left, and another, and a crash in the rear yard of a run-down yellow frame house behind him. He turned off the flashlight, picked a yard farther west and crept between two houses. When he reached the rear of the house he stopped, listened, and crouched down. The first dog, two doors away, had stopped barking, but the other in the next yard was snarling and yelping as though he was bumping against a taut chain. The lights were going on and Serge waited. He jerked his gun out as the figure appeared from the yard gracefully with a light leap over the wooden fence. He was there in the driveway silhouetted against the whitewashed background of the two-car garage like the paper man on the pistol range, and Serge was struck with the thought that he was no doubt a juvenile and should not be shot under any circumstances but defense of your life. Yet he decided quite calmly that this *Rojo* was not getting another shot at Serge Duran, and he cocked the gun which did not startle the dark figure who was twelve feet away, but the flashlight did, and there he was in the intense beam of the five cell. Serge had already taken up the slack of the fleshy padding of the right index finger and this *Rojo* would never know that only a microscopic layer of human flesh over unyielding finger bone kept the hammer from falling as Serge exerted perhaps a pound of pull on the trigger of the cocked revolver which was pointed at the stomach of the boy.

'Freeze,' Serge breathed, watching the hands of the boy and deciding that if they moved, if they moved at all ...

'Don't! Don't,' said the boy, who stared at the beam, but stood motionless, one foot turned to the side, as in a clumsy stop-action camera shot. 'Oh, don't,' he said and Serge realized he was creeping forward in a duck walk, the gun extended in front of him. He also realized how much pressure he was exerting on the trigger and he always wondered why the hammer had not fallen.

'Just move,' Serge whispered, as he circled the quivering boy and moved in behind him, the flashlight under his arm as he patted the *Rojo* down for the gun that had made the orange flash.

'I don't got a weapon,' said the boy.

'Shut your mouth,' said Serge, teeth clenched, and as he found no gun his stomach began to loosen a bit and the breathing evened.

Serge handcuffed the boy carefully behind his back, tightening the iron until the boy winced. He uncocked and holstered the gun and his hand shook so badly that for a second he almost considered holstering the gun still cocked because he was afraid the hammer might slip while he uncocked it.

'Let's go,' he said, finally, shoving the boy ahead of him.

When they got to the front street, Serge saw several people on the porches, and two police cars were driving slowly from opposite directions, spotlights flashing, undoubtedly looking for him.

Serge shoved the boy into the street and when the beam of the first spotlight hit them the radio car accelerated and jerked to a stop in front of them.

Ruben Gonsalvez was the passenger officer, and he ran around the car throwing open the door on the near side.

'This the one who fired at you?' he asked.

'You prove it, *puto*,' the boy said, grinning now in the presence of the other officers and the three or four onlookers who were standing on porches, as dogs for three blocks howled and barked at the siren of the help car which had raced code three to their aid.

Serge grasped the boy by the neck, bent his head and shoved him in the back seat, crawling in beside him and forcing him to the right side of the car.

'Tough now that you got your friends, ain't you, *pinchi jura*,' said the boy and Serge tightened the iron again until the boy sobbed, 'You dirty motherfucking cop.'

'Shut your mouth,' said Serge.

'*Chinga tu madre!*' said the boy.

'I should have killed you.'

'*Tu madre!*'

And then Serge realized he was squeezing the hard rubber grips of the Smith & Wesson. He was pressing the trigger guard and he remembered the way he felt when he had the boy in his sights, the black shadow who had almost ended him at age twenty-four when his entire life was ahead, for reasons not he nor this little *vato* could understand. He had not known he was capable of this kind of terrifying rage. But to be almost murdered. It was utterly absurd.

'*Tu madre,*' the boy repeated, and the fury crept over Serge again. It wasn't the same in Spanish, he thought. It was so much filthier, almost unbearable, that this gutter animal would dare to mention her like that ...

'You don't like that, do you, gringo?' said the boy, baring his white teeth in the darkness. 'You understand some Spanish, huh? You don't like me talking about your moth ...'

And Serge was choking him, down, down, to the floor he took him, screaming silently, staring into the exposed whites of swollen horrified eyes, and Serge through the irresistible shroud of smothering fury probed for the little bones in front of the throat, which if broken ... and then Gonsalvez was holding Serge across the forehead and bending him backward in a bow. Then he was lying flat on his back in the street and Gonsalvez was kneeling beside him, panting and babbling incoherently in Spanish and English, patting him on the shoulder but keeping a firm grip on one arm.

'Easy, easy easy,' said Gonsalvez. *'Hombre*, Jesus Christ! Sergio, *no es nada*, man. You're okay, now. Relax, *hombre. Hijo la* ...'

Serge turned his back to the radio car and supported himself against it. He had never wept, he thought, never in his life, not when she died, not ever. And he did not weep now, as he shakily accepted the cigarette which Gonsalvez had lit for him.

'Nobody saw nothing, Sergio,' said Gonsalvez, as Serge sucked dully on the cigarette, filled with a hopeless sickness which he did not want to analyze now, hoping he could maintain control of himself because he was more afraid than he had ever been in his life, and he knew vaguely it was things in himself he feared.

'Good thing those people on the porch went in the pad,' Gonsalvez whispered. 'Nobody saw nothing.'

'I'm going to sue you, motherfucker,' said the raspy sobbing voice inside the car. 'I'm going to get you.'

Gonsalvez tightened his grip on Serge's arm. 'Don't listen to that *cabrone*. I think he's going to have bruises on his neck. If he does, he got them when you arrested him in the backyard. He fought with you and you grabbed him by the neck during the fight, got it?'

Serge nodded, not caring about anything but the slight pleasure the cigarette was giving him as he breathed only smoke, exhaling a cloud through his nose as he sucked in another fiery puff.

When Serge sat in the detective squad room at two o'clock that morning, he appreciated Milton as he never had before. He came now to understand how little he had known about the blustering, red-faced old policeman who, after a whispered conversation with Gonsalvez, took charge of the young prisoner, reported verbally to the sergeant and the detectives, and generally left Serge to sit in the detective squad room, smoke, and go through the motions of participating in the writing of reports. The night watch detectives and juvenile officers were all kept overtime interrogating suspects and witnesses. Four radio cars were assigned to search the streets, yards, sidewalks and sewers in the route of the pursuit from the point of inception to the dark driveway where Serge made his arrest. But as of two o'clock the boy's gun had not been found.

'Want some more coffee?' asked Milton, placing a mug of black coffee on the table where Serge sat listlessly penciling out a statement on the shooting that would be retyped on the arrest report.

'They find the gun yet?' asked Serge.

Milton shook his head, taking a sip from his own cup. 'The way I figure it, the kid you chased had the gun with him and dumped it when he was in those yards. You realize the thousands of places a gun could be concealed in one junky little yard? And he was probably in several yards jumping fences. He could've thrown it on the roof of one of the houses. He could've pulled up a little grass and buried it. He could've thrown it as far as he could over to the next street. He could've got rid of it during the pursuit, too. The guys couldn't possibly check every inch of every yard, every ivy path, every roof of every building, and every parked car along the route where he could've thrown it.'

'Sounds like you think they won't find it?'

'You should be ready for the possibility,' Milton shrugged. 'Without the gun, we've got no case. These con wise little mothers are sticking together pretty damn good on their stories. There was no gun, they say.'

'You saw the muzzle flash,' said Serge.

'Sure, I did. But we got to prove it was a gun.'

'How about that kid Ignacio? He saw it.'

'He saw nothing. At least he says he saw nothing. He claims he was running for the house when he heard the loud crack. Sounded like a backfire, he says.'

'How about his mother? She was on the porch.'

'Says she saw nothing. She don't want to get involved with these gang wars. You can understand her position.'

'I can only understand that little killer has to be taken off the street.'

'I know how you feel, kid,' said Milton, putting his hand on Serge's shoulder and pulling a chair close. 'And listen, that kid didn't mention anything that happened later, you know what I mean. At least not yet, he didn't. I noticed some marks on his neck, but he's pretty dark-complected. They don't show up.'

Serge looked into the blackness of the cup and swallowed a gulp of the bitter burning coffee.

'Once a guy swung a blade at me,' said Milton quietly. 'It wasn't too many years ago. Almost opened up this big pile of guts.' Milton patted the bulging belly. 'He had a honed, eight-inch blade and he really tried to hit me. Something made me move. I never saw it coming. I was just making a pinch on this guy for holding a little weed, that's all. Something made me move. Maybe I heard it, I don't know. When he missed me, I jumped back, fell on my ass and pulled my gun just as he was getting ready to try again. He dropped the knife and kind of smiled, you know, like, "This time you win, copper". I put the gun away, took out the baton and broke two of his ribs and they had to put thirteen stitches in his head. I know I'd have killed him if my partner didn't stop me. I never done that before or since. I mean I never let go before. But I was having personal problems at the time, a divorce and all, and this bastard had tried to render me, and I just let go, that's all. I never had no regrets at what I did to him, understand? I was sick at what I did to myself. I mean, he dragged me down to the jungle floor and made me an animal too, that's what I hated. But I thought about it for a few days and I decided that I had just acted like a regular man and not like a cop. A policeman isn't supposed to be afraid or shocked or mad when some bastard tries to make a canoe out of him with a switchblade. So I just did what any guy might've. But that don't mean I couldn't handle it a little better if it ever happened again. And I'll tell you one thing, he only got a hundred and twenty days for almost murdering me, and that didn't bother him, but I'll bet he learned something from what I did to him and he might think twice before trying to knife another cop. This is a brutal business you're in, kid. So don't stew over things. And if you learn something about yourself that you'd be better off not knowing, well, just slide along, it'll work out.'

Serge nodded at Milton to acknowledge what his partner was trying to do. He drained the coffee cup and lit another cigarette as one of the detectives came in the squad room carrying a flashlight and a yellow legal tablet. The detective took off his coat and crossed the room to Milton and Serge.

'We're going to sack up these four dudes now,' said the detective, a youthful curly-haired sergeant, whose name Serge couldn't remember. 'Three of them are seventeen and they're going to Georgia Street, but I'll tell you for sure they'll be out Monday. We got no case.'

'How old is the one that shot at my partner?' asked Milton.

'Primitivo Chavez? He's an adult. Eighteen years old. He'll go to Central jail, but we'll have to kick him out in forty-eight hours unless we can turn up that gun.'

'How about the bullet?' asked Serge.

'From where you were standing and from where those guys were sitting in that low rider Chevy, I'm guessing that the trajectory of the bullet would be at least forty-five degrees out the window of the car. It would've hit you in the face if it'd been aimed right, but since it didn't I'm thinking it went approximately between the house you guys were in and the next one west. That's separated from the other one by about a half acre of vacant lot. In other words, I think the goddamn bullet didn't hit a thing and probably right now is sitting on the freeway out near General Hospital. Sorry, guys, you don't want to nail these four assholes any more than I do. We figure the one cat, Jesus Martinez, is involved in an unsolved gang killing in Highland Park where a kid got blown up. We can't prove that one either.'

'How about the paraffin test, Sam,' said Milton. 'Can't that show if a guy's fired a gun?'

'Not worth a shit, Milton,' said the detective. 'Only in the movie who-dunits. A guy can have nitrates on his hands from a thousand other ways. The paraffin test is no good.'

'Maybe a witness or maybe the gun will turn up tomorrow,' said Milton.

'Maybe it will,' said the detective doubtfully. 'I'm glad I'm not a juvenile officer. They only call us in when these assholes start shooting each other. I'd hate to handle them every day for all their ordinary burglaries and robberies and stuff. I'll stick to adult investigation. At least they get a *little* time when I convict them.'

'What kind of records they got?' asked Milton.

'About what you'd expect: lots of burglaries, A.D.W.'s, joy riding galore, robberies, narco and a scattered rape here and there. The Chavez kid's been sent to Youth Authority camp once. The others never have been sent to camp. This is Chavez' first bust as an adult. He only turned eighteen last month. At least he'll get a taste of the men's jail for a few days.'

'That'll just give him something to talk about when he goes back to the neighborhood,' said Milton.

'I guess so,' sighed the detective. 'He'll already have all the status in the world for getting away with shooting at Duran. I've been trying to learn something from all these little gang hoods you guys bring in. Want to hear something? Follow me.' The detective led the way to a locked door which when opened revealed a small closet filled with sound and recording equipment. The detective turned on the switch to the recorder and Serge recognized the insolent thin voice of Primitivo Chavez.

'I never shot nobody, man. Why should I?'

'Why not?' said the detective's voice.

'That's a better question,' said the boy.

'It would be smart to tell the truth, Primo. The truth always makes you feel better and clears the way for a new start.'

'New start? I like my old start. How about a smoke?'

The tape spun silently for a moment and Serge heard the flicker and spurt of a match and then the detective's steady voice again.

'We'll find the gun, Primo, it's only a matter of time.'

The boy laughed a thin snuffling laugh and Serge felt his heart thump as he remembered how he felt when he had the skinny throat.

'You ain't never going to find no gun,' said the boy. 'I ain't worried about that.'

'You hid it pretty good, I bet,' said the detective. 'You got some brains, I imagine.'

'I didn't say I had a gun. I just said you ain't never going to find no gun.'

'Read that,' the detective suddenly commanded.

'What's that?' asked the boy, suspiciously.

'Just a news magazine. Just something I found laying around. Read it for me, *ese*.'

'What for, man? What kind of games you playing?'

'Just my own little experiment. Something I do with all gang members.'

'You trying to prove something?'

'Maybe.'

'Well prove it with somebody else.'

'How far you go in school, Primo?'

'Twelfth grade. I quit in twelfth grade.'

'Yeah? Well you can read pretty good, then. Just open the magazine and read anything.'

Serge heard the rustle of pages and then a moment of silence followed by, 'Look man, I don't got time for kid games. *Véte a la chingada.*'

'You can't read can you, Primo? And they passed you clear through to the twelfth grade hoping that being in the twelfth grade would make you a twelfth grader and then they made it tough when they realized they couldn't give an illiterate a diploma. These do-gooders really fucked you up, didn't they Primo?'

'What're you talking about, man? I'd rather talk about this shooting you say I did than all this other shit.'

'How far you been in your life, Primo?'

'How far?'

'Yeah, how far. You live in the housing projects down by the animal shelter, right?'

'Dogtown, man. You can call it Dogtown, we ain't ashamed of that.'

'Okay, Dogtown. What's the farthest you ever been from Dogtown? Ever been to Lincoln Heights?'

'Lincoln Heights? Sure, I been there.'

'How many times? Three?'

'Three, four, I don't know. Hey, I had enough of this kind of talk. I don't know what the hell you want, *Ya estuvo.*'

'Have another cigarette,' said the detective. 'And take a few for later.'

'Okay, for cigarettes I can put up with this bullshit.'

'Lincoln Heights is maybe two miles from Dogtown. You ever been farther?'

The tape was silent once again and then the boy said, 'I been to El Serreno. How far is that?'

'About a mile farther.'

'So I seen enough.'

'Ever seen the ocean?'

'No.'

'How about a lake or river?'

'I seen a river, the goddamn LA River runs right by Dogtown, don't it?'

'Yeah, sometimes there's eight inches of water in the channel.'

'Who cares about that shit anyway. I got everything I want in Dogtown. I don't want to go nowhere.'

The tape was silent once more and the boy said, 'Wait a minute. I been somewhere far. A hundred miles, maybe.'

'Where was that?'

'In camp. The last time I got busted for burglary they sent me away to camp for four months. I was fucking glad to get back to Dogtown.'

The detective smiled and turned off the recorder. 'Primitivo Chavez is a typical teen-age gang member, I'd say.'

'What're you trying to prove, Sam?' asked Milton. 'You going to re-habilitate him?'

'Not me,' the detective smiled. 'Nobody could do it now. You could give Primo two million bucks and he'd never leave Dogtown and the gang and the fun of cutting down one of the Easystreeters – or a cop, maybe. Primo is too old. He's molded. He's lost.'

'He deserves to be,' said Milton bitterly. 'That little son of a bitch'll die by the sword.'

EIGHT
Classrooms

'I've already explained to you twice that your signature on this traffic citation is merely a promise to appear. You are not admitting guilt. Understand?' said Rantlee, with a glance at the group of onlookers that suddenly formed.

'Well, I still ain't signin' nothin',' said the tow truck driver, slouched back against his white truck, brown muscular arms folded across his chest. He raised his face to the setting sun at the conclusion of a sentence and cast triumphant looks at the bystanders who now numbered about twenty, and Gus wondered if now were the time to saunter to the radio car and put in a call for assistance.

Why wait until it started? They could be killed quickly by a mob. But should he wait a few more minutes? Would it seem cowardly to put in a call for backup units at this moment, because the truck driver was merely arguing, putting up a bluff for the onlookers? He would probably sign the ticket in a moment or so.

'If you refuse to sign, we have no choice but to arrest you,' said Rantlee. 'If you sign, it's like putting up a bond. Your word is the bond and we can let you go. You have the right to a trial, a jury trial if you want one.'

'That's what I'm going to ask for, too. A jury trial.'

'Fine. Now, please sign the ticket.'

'I'm goin' to make you spend all day in court on your day off.'

'Fine!'

'You jist like to drive around givin' tickets to Negroes, don't you?'

'Look around, Mister,' said Rantlee, his face crimson now. 'There ain't nobody on the streets around here, *but* Negroes. Now why do you suppose I picked on you and not somebody else?'

'Any nigger would do, wouldn't it? I jist happened to be the one you picked.'

'You just happened to be the one that ran the red light. Now, are you going to sign this ticket?'

'You specially likes to pick on wildcat tow truckers, don't you? Always chasin' us away from accident scenes so the truckers that contract with the PO-lice Department can git the tow.'

'Lock up your truck if you're not going to sign. Let's get going to the station.'

'You don't even got my real name on that ticket. My name ain't Wilfred Sentley.'

'That's what your license says.'

'My real name is Wilfred 3X, whitey. Gave to me by the prophet himself.'

'That's fine. But for our purposes, you can sign your slave name to this ticket. Just sign Wilfred Sentley.'

'You jist love workin' down here, don't you? You jist soil your shorts I bet, when you think about comin' here every day and fuckin' all the black people you can.'

'Yeah, get it up in there real tight, whitey,' said a voice at the rear of the crowd of teen-agers, 'so it feels real good when you come.'

This brought peals of laughter from the high school crowd who had run across from the hot-dog stand on the opposite corner.

'Yes, I just love working down here,' said Rantlee in a toneless voice, but his red face betrayed him and he stopped. 'Lock your truck,' he said finally.

'See how they treats black people, brothers and sisters,' the man shouted, turning to the crowd on the sidewalk which had doubled in the last minute and now blocked access to the police car, and Gus's jaw was trembling so that he clamped his teeth shut tight. It's gone too far, thought Gus.

'See how they is?' shouted the man, and several children in the front of the crowd joined a tall belligerent drunk in his early twenties who lurched into the street from the Easy Time Shine Parlor and announced that he could kill any motherfuckin' white cop that ever lived with his two black hands, which brought a whoop and cheer from the younger children who urged him on.

Rantlee pushed through the crowd suddenly and Gus knew he was going to the radio, and for an agonizing moment Gus was alone in the center of the ring of faces, some of which he told himself, would surely help him. If anything happened someone would help him. He told himself it was not hate he saw in every face because his imagination was rampant now and the fear subsided only slightly when Rantlee pushed his way back through the crowd.

'Okay, there're five cars on the way,' Rantlee said to Gus and turned to the truck driver. 'Now, you sign or if you want to start something, we got enough help that'll be here in two minutes to take care of you and anybody else that decides to be froggy and leap.'

'You got your quota to write, don't you?' the man sneered.

'No, we used to have a quota, now I can write every goddamn ticket I want to,' Rantlee said, and held the pencil up to the driver's face. 'And this is your last chance to sign, 'cause when the first police car gets here, you go to jail, whether you sign or not.'

The man took a step forward and stared in the young policeman's gray eyes for a long moment. Gus saw that he was as tall as Rantlee and just as well built. Then Gus looked at the three young men in black Russian peasant hats and white tunics who whispered together on the curb, watching Gus. He knew it would be them that he would have to contend with if anything happened.

'Your day is comin',' said the driver, ripping the pencil from Rantlee's hand and scrawling his name across the face of the citation. 'You ain't goin' to be top dog much longer.'

While Rantlee tore the white violator's copy from the ticket book, the driver let Rantlee's pencil fall to the ground and Rantlee pretended not to notice. He gave the ticket to the driver who snatched it from the policeman's hand and was still talking to the dispersing crowd when Gus and Rantlee were back in the car, pulling slowly from the curb while several young Negroes grudgingly stepped from their path. They both ignored a loud thump and knew that one of the ones in the peasant caps had kicked their fender, to the delight of the children.

They stopped for a few seconds and Gus locked his door while a boy in a yellow shirt in a last show of bravado sauntered out of the path of the bumper. Gus recoiled when he turned to the right and saw a brown face only a few inches from his, but it was only a boy of about nine years and he studied Gus while Rantlee impatiently revved the engine. Gus saw only childlike curiosity in the face and all but the three in the peasant caps were now walking away. Gus smiled at the little face and the black eyes which never left his.

'Hello, young man,' said Gus, but his voice was weak.

'Why do you like to shoot black people?' asked the boy.

'Who told you that? That's not ...' The lurching police car threw him back in his seat and Rantlee was roaring south on Broadway and west on Fifty-fourth Street back to their area. Gus turned and saw the little boy still standing in the street looking after the speeding radio car.

'They never used to gather like that,' said Rantlee lighting a cigarette. 'Three years ago when I first came on the job, I used to like working down here because Negroes understood our job almost as well as we did and crowds never used to gather like that. Not nowadays. They gather for any excuse. They're getting ready for something. I shouldn't let them bait me. I shouldn't argue at all. But the pressure is starting to get to me. Were you very scared?'

'Yeah,' said Gus, wondering how obvious it was that he was paralyzed out there, like he had been on only a few other occasions in the past year. One of these days, he was going to have to take direct forceful action when he was paralyzed like that. Then he'd know about himself. So far, something always intervened. He had escaped his fate, but one of these days, he'd know.

'I wasn't a bit scared,' said Rantlee.

'You weren't?'

'No, but somebody shit on my seat,' he grinned, smoking the cigarette and they both laughed the hearty laugh of tension relieved.

'Crowd like that could do you in two minutes,' said Rantlee, blowing a plume of smoke out the window, and Gus thought that he hadn't shown the slightest fear to the onlookers. Rantlee was only twenty-four years old and looked younger with his auburn hair and rosy complexion.

'Think we ought to cancel the assistance you called for?' asked Gus. 'We don't need them now.'

'Sure, go ahead,' said Rantlee and eyed Gus curiously as Gus said, 'Three-A-Ninety-one, cancel the assistance to Fifty-first and south Broadway, crowd has dispersed.' Gus received no reply and Rantlee grinned wider and Gus for the first time noticed that the radio was dead. Then he saw the mike cord dangling impotently and he realized that someone had jerked the wire out while they had been surrounded.

'You were bluffing them when you told him help was coming.'

'Was I ever!' said Rantlee, and Gus was very glad to be driving toward the radio shop and after that to the Crenshaw area which was the 'silk stocking' part of University Division, where large numbers of whites still resided. The Negroes there were 'west-side Negroes' and the sixty-thousand-dollar homes in Baldwin Hills overlooked the large department stores, where you would not be surrounded by a hostile ring of black faces.

On the side of a stucco apartment building facing the Harbor Freeway, Gus saw sprayed in letters four feet high 'Oncle Remus is an Oncle Tom', and then Rantlee was on the freeway speeding north. In a few moments the tall palms which line the freeway in south central Los Angeles were replaced by the civic center buildings and they were downtown driving leisurely toward the police building radio shop to have the mike replaced.

Gus admired the beautiful women who always seemed to be plentiful on the downtown streets and he felt a faint rumble of heat and hoped Vickie would still be awake tonight. Despite the precautions, Vickie was not the same lover she had been, but he guessed it was only natural. Then he felt the creeping guilt which he had been experiencing periodically since Billy was born and he knew it was ridiculous to blame himself, but yet any intelligent man would have seen to it that a twenty-three-year-old girl did not give birth to three children in less than five years of marriage, especially when the girl was not really mature, depending on her man for all but the most basic decisions, when she believed her man was a strong man, and oh, what a laugh that was.

Since he had admitted to himself that marriage had been a mistake, it had somehow become easier. Once you face something you can live with it, he thought. How could he have known at age eighteen what things were all about? He still didn't know but at least he now knew life was more than a ceaseless yearning for sex and romantic love. Vickie had been a pretty girl with a fine body and he had had to settle for plain girls all his life, even in his senior year in high school when he could not find a date for the Christmas formal, ending up with Mildred Greer, his next-door neighbor, who was only sixteen and built like a shot-putter. She had embarrassed him by wearing a pink chiffon that would have been old-fashioned ten years before. So it was not his fault entirely that he had married Vickie when they were much too young and knew nothing except each other's bodies. What else mattered at age eighteen?

'You see that guy with the mop of blond hair?' asked Rantlee.

'Which guy?'

'The one in the green T-shirt. You see him make us and run through the parking lot?'

'No.'

'Funny, how many people get black and white fever and start moving fast in the opposite direction. You can't go after them all. You think about them though. They make you hinky. What's their secret? You always wonder.'

'I know what you mean,' said Gus and then wondered how a pretty girl like Vickie could be so dependent and weak. He had always thought that attractive people should naturally have a certain amount of confidence. He always thought that if he had been a big man that he would not have been so afraid of people, so unable to converse freely with anyone but intimate friends. The intimate friends were few in number, and at this moment other than his boyhood friend, Bill Halleran, he could think of no one he really wanted to be with. Except Kilvinsky. But Kilvinsky was so much older and he had no family now that his ex-wife was remarried. Every time Kilvinsky came to his house for dinner he played with Gus's children and then became morose, so that even Vickie noticed it. As much as he liked Kilvinsky, whom he felt was a teacher and more than a friend, he didn't really see him much after Kilvinsky had decided to transfer to Communications Division which he said was out to pasture for old cops. Last month he had retired suddenly and was gone to Oregon where Gus pictured him in an extra-large khaki shirt and khaki trousers, his silver hair matted down from the baseball cap he always wore when he fished.

The fishing trip to the Colorado River that he had taken with Kilvinsky and three other policemen had been a wonderful trip and now he could think of Kilvinsky like he had been at the river, chewing on the battered cigarette holder while he all but ignored the burning cigarette it held, casting and reeling in the line with ease, showing that the wide hard hands were nimble and quick, not merely strong. Once when Kilvinsky had been to their house for dinner, right after they bought the three-bedroom house and were still short on furniture, Kilvinsky had taken little John into the almost bare living room and tossed him in the air with his big sure hands until John and even Gus who watched were laughing so hard they could hardly breathe. And, inevitably, Kilvinsky became gloomy after the children went to bed. Once when Gus asked him about his family he said they were now living in New Jersey and Gus realized he must not question him further. All of the other policemen friends were 'on duty' friends. Why couldn't he like anyone else the way he liked Kilvinsky, he wondered.

'I gotta transfer out of University,' said Rantlee.

'Why?'

'Niggers are driving me crazy. Sometimes I think I'll kill one someday when he does what that bastard in the tow truck did. If someone would've made the first move those savages would've cut off our heads and shrunk them. Before I came on this job I wouldn't even use the word nigger. It embarrassed me. Now it's the most used word in my vocabulary. It says everything I feel. I've never used it in front of one yet but I probably will sooner or later and he'll beef me and I'll get suspended.'

'Remember Kilvinsky?' asked Gus. 'He always used to say that the black people were only the spearhead of a bigger attack on authority and law that was surely coming in the next ten years. He always said not to make the mistake of thinking your enemy was the Negro. It wasn't that simple, he said.'

'It's strange as hell what happens to you,' said Rantlee. 'I'm finding myself agreeing with every right wing son of a bitch I ever read about. I wasn't brought up that way. My father's a flaming liberal and we're getting so we hate to see each other anymore because a big argument starts. I'm even getting to become sympathetic with some of these rabid anticommunist causes. Yet at the same time I admire the Reds for their efficiency. They can keep order, for chrissake. They know just how far you can let people go before you pull the chain. It's all mixed up, Plebesly. I haven't figured things out yet.' Rantlee ran his hand through his wavy hair and tapped on the window ledge as he talked and then turned right on First Street. Gus thought he wouldn't mind working Central Division because downtown Los Angeles seemed exciting with the lights and the rush of people, but it was also sordid if you looked closely at the people who inhabited the downtown streets. At least most of them were white and you didn't have the feeling of being in an enemy camp.

'Maybe I'm wrong in blaming it all on the Negroes,' said Rantlee. 'Maybe it's a combination of causes, but by God the Negroes are a big part of it.'

Gus hadn't yet finished his coffee when their radio was repaired and he hurried to the radio shop bathroom and on the way out noticed in the mirror that his always thin straw-colored hair was now falling out badly. He guessed he'd be bald at thirty, but what did it matter anyway he thought wryly. He noticed also that his uniform was becoming shiny which was the mark of a veteran but it was also fraying at the collar and the cuffs. He dreaded the thought of buying another because they were outrageously expensive. The uniform dealers kept the price up all over Los Angeles and you had to pay it.

Rantlee seemed in better spirits as they drove back down the Harbor Freeway to their beat.

'Hear about the shooting in Newton Street?'

'No,' said Gus.

'They got a policeman on the fire for shooting a guy that works in a liquor store on Olympic. Officer rolls up to the store answering a silent alarm, and just as he's getting ready to peek in the window to see if it's for real or phony, the proprietor comes running out and starts screaming and pointing toward the alley across the street. One officer runs in the alley and the other circles the block and picks a spot where he thinks anybody back there would come out, and in a few minutes he hears running footsteps and hides behind the corner of an apartment house with his gun out and ready, and in a few seconds a guy comes busting around the corner with a Mauser in his hand and the officer yells freeze and the guy whirls around and the officer naturally lets go and puts five right in the ten ring.' Rantlee placed his clenched fist against his chest to indicate the tight pattern of the bullets.

'So what's wrong with the shooting?' asked Gus.

'The guy was an employee in the store who was chasing the suspect with his boss's gun.'

'The officer couldn't have known. I don't see any real problem. It's unfortunate, but ...'

'The guy was black and some of the black newspapers are playing it up, you know, how innocent people are killed every day by the storm troops in occupied south central Los Angeles. And how the Jew proprietor in the ghetto sends his black lackeys to do the jobs he hasn't got the guts to do. Odd how the Jews can support the blacks who hate them so much.'

'I guess they haven't forgotten how they suffered themselves,' said Gus.

'That's a kind thought,' said Rantlee. 'But I think it's because they make so goddamn much money off these poor ignorant black people from their stores and rents. They sure as hell don't live among them. Jesus Christ, now I'm a Jew hater. I tell you, Plebesly, I'm transferring to the valley or West LA or somewhere. These niggers are driving me crazy.'

They were barely back to their area when Gus logged the family dispute call on Main Street.

'Oh, no,' Rantlee groaned. 'Back on the goddamn east side.' And Gus noticed that Rantlee, who was not a particularly slow driver, headed for the call at a snail's pace. In a few minutes they were parked in front of an ancient two-story house which was tall and narrow and gray. It seemed to be used by four families and they knew which door to knock on by the shouts which could be heard from the street. Rantlee kicked three times against the base of the door to be heard over the din of voices inside.

A sagging square-shouldered woman of about forty opened the door. She held a plump brown baby in one arm and in the other hand she held a bowl of gray baby food and a spoon. The baby food was all over the infant's face and his diaper was as gray as the siding of the house.

'Come in, Officers,' she nodded. 'I'm the one who called.'

'Yeah, that's right, you punk ass bitch, call the law,' said a watery-eyed man in a dirty undershirt. 'But while they're here, tell them how you drinks away the welfare check and how I has to support these here kids and three of them ain't even mine. Tell them.'

'Okay, okay,' said Rantlee, holding up his hands for silence and Gus noticed that the four children sprawled on the sagging couch watched the TV set with little or no interest in the fight or the officers' arrival.

'You some husban',' she spat. 'You know, when he drunk, Officer, he jist climbs on me and starts ruttin'. Don't make no diff'ence if the chirrun' is here or not. That the kind of man he is.'

'That is a gud-dam lie,' said the man, and Gus saw they were both half drunk. The man must have been fifty but his shoulders were blocklike and his biceps heavily veined. 'I'm goin' tell you like it is,' he said to Rantlee. 'You a man and I'm a man and I works ever' day.'

Rantlee turned to Gus and winked and Gus wondered how many black men he had heard preface a remark to him with, 'You a man and I'm a man,' fearful that the white law did not truly believe it. They knew how policemen could be impressed by the fact that they worked and did not draw welfare. He wondered how many black men he had heard saying, 'I works ever' day,' to the white law, and well they might, Gus thought, because he had seen how it *did* work, how a policeman could be talked out of issuing a traffic ticket to a black man with a workman's helmet, or a lunch basket, or a floor polisher, or some other proof of toil. Gus realized that policemen expected so little of Negroes that a job alone and clean children were unalterable proof that this was a decent man as opposed to the ones with dirty children, who were probably the enemy.

'We didn't come to referee a brawl,' said Rantlee. 'Why don't we quiet down and talk. You come in here, sir, and talk to me. You talk to my partner, ma'am,' Rantlee walked the man into the kitchen to separate them which was of course what Gus knew he would do.

Gus listened to the woman, hardly hearing her, because he had heard similar stories so many times and after they had told the officers their problems, the problems would diminish. Then they could probably talk the man into taking a walk for a while and coming home when things had cooled off and that was the whole secret of handling disputes.

'That man is a righteous dog, Officer,' said the woman, shoving a spoonful of food into the pink little mouth of the greedy baby who would only be silenced by the spoon. 'That man is terrible jealous and he drink all the time and he don't really work. He live on my county check and he jist lay up here and don't never give nothin' to me 'cept chirrun'. I jist wants you to take him out of here.'

'You legally married?' asked Gus.

'No, we's common law.'

'How long you been together?'

'Ten years and that is too long. Last week, when I cashed my check and bought some groc'ries and came home, why that man snatched the change right outten my hand and went out and laid up wif some woman fo' two days and come back here wif not a cent and I takes him back and then tonight that nigger hits me wif his fist 'cause I ain't go' no mo' money fo' him to drink up. An' that's as true as this baby here.'

'Well, we'll try to talk him into leaving for a while.'

'I wants him outten this house fo' good!'

'We'll talk to him.'

'I'm tryin' to raise my chirruns right 'cause I sees all these chirruns nowadays jist jumpin' rope and smokin' dope.'

A loud burst of staccato raps startled Gus and the woman stepped to the door and opened it for a furious, very dark, middle-aged man in a tattered flannel bathrobe.

'H'lo Harvey,' she said.

'I'm gittin gud-dam sick of the noise in this apartment,' said the man.

'He hit me agin, Harvey.'

'You goin' to have to git out if you can't git along. I got other tenants in this house.'

'What do you want?' shouted the woman's husband who crossed the living room in three angry strides. 'We got our rent paid up. You got no right in here.'

'This is my house. I got all the right I need,' said the man in the bathrobe.

'You git yo' raggedy ass outa my apartment before I throws you out,' said the man in the undershirt and Gus saw that the landlord was not as fierce as he seemed and he took a step backward even though Rantlee stepped between them.

'That's enough,' said Rantlee.

'Why don't you take him out, Officers,' said the landlord, wilting before the glare of the smaller man in the undershirt.

'Yeah, so you kin come sniffin' roun' here after my woman. That would tickle you wouldn' it?'

'Why don't you go back to your apartment, sir,' said Rantlee to the landlord, 'until we get things settled.'

'Don't worry, Officers,' said the man in the undershirt, drilling the landlord with his watery black eyes, the blue black lips forming a deliberate sneer, 'I wouldn't hurt that. That's pussy.'

Nobody can manage an insult like them, Gus thought. And he looked with awe at the rough black face, and how the nostrils had flared, and the eyes and mouth and nostrils had joined to create the quintessence of contempt. 'I wouldn' even touch that wif a angry hand. That ain't no man. That's jist pussy!'

They can teach me, thought Gus. There is no other people like them. There was fear, but he could learn things here. And where could he go where there would not be fear?

NINE
Spade Bit

It was Wednesday and Roy Fehler hurried to the station because he was sure he would be on the transfer list. Most of his academy classmates had their transfers by now and he had been requesting North Hollywood or Highland Park for five months. When he did not find his name on the transfer he was bitterly disappointed and now he knew he must intensify his efforts in college to complete his degree so he could quit this thankless job. And it was thankless, they all knew it. They all talked about it often enough. If you want gratitude for your work, be a fireman they always said.

He had done his best for the past year. He had brought compassion to all his dealings with the Negro. He had learned from them, and hoped he had taught them something. It was time to move on now. He had wanted to work on the other side of town. There was still so much to learn about people yet they left him here at Newton Street. They had forgotten him. He'd increase his unit load next semester, and to hell with concentrating his efforts on being a good police officer. What had it gotten him? He had earned only six units in the past two semesters and had gotten only C's because he read law and police science textbooks when he should have been working on course assignments. At this rate it would take years to finish his degree. Even Professor Raymond seldom wrote anymore. Everyone had forgotten him.

Roy examined his lean body in the full-length mirror and thought the uniform still fit as well as the day he left the academy. He hadn't been exercising but he watched what he ate and thought he still wore the blue suit well.

He was a few minutes late for roll call and muttered 'Here' when Lieutenant Bilkins called his name, but he didn't hear Bilkins read the daily crimes and wanted suspects even though he mechanically wrote the information in his notebook just as all the others did. Sam Tucker came straggling in ten minutes after roll call, still adjusting his tie clip with his heavily veined blue-black hands as he sat down at the bench in front of the first row of tables.

'If we could get old Sam to quit counting his money, we could get him here on time,' said Bilkins, glancing down at the grizzled Negro officer with his blank narrow eyes.

'Today's rent day, Lieutenant,' said Tucker. 'Got to stop by my tenants' and collect my share of their welfare checks before they blow it on booze.'

'Just like you Jew landlords,' sniffed Bilkins, 'bleed the ghetto black man, keep him down in the east side.'

'You don't think I'd let them live in West LA with me, do you?' said Tucker with a perfectly sober expression which brought a burst of laughter from the already sleepy morning watch officers.

'For you guys who don't know, Sam owns half of Newton Division,' said Bilkins. 'Police work is a hobby with him. That's why Sam's always late the first Wednesday of every month. If we could stop him from counting his money we could get him here on time. And if we could break all the mirrors in the joint, we could get Fehler here on time.'

Roy cursed himself for flushing deeply as the roll call boomed with the chuckles of his fellow officers. That was unfair as hell, he thought. And it wasn't that funny. He knew he was a bit vain, but so was everyone.

'By the way, Fehler, you and Light keep an eyeball out for the hot prowl suspect in your district. The prick hit again last night and I think it's only a matter of time till he hurts somebody.'

'Did he leave his calling card again?' asked Light, Roy's partner this month, a round-shouldered, two-year Negro policeman, slightly taller than Roy and a difficult man for Roy to understand. He couldn't seem to develop rapport with Light even though he went out of his way as he always did with Negroes.

'He dropped his calling card right on the fucking kitchen table this time,' said Bilkins dryly, running a big hand over his bald head and puffing on a badly scarred pipe. 'For you new guys that don't know what we're talking about, this cat burglar has hit about fifteen times in the past two months in Ninety-nine's district. He never woke nobody in any of his jobs except one when he woke a guy who had just got home and wasn't sleeping too sound yet. He slugged the guy in the chops with a metal ashtray and bailed out the window, glass and all. His calling card is a pile of shit, his shit, which he dumps in some conspicuous place.'

'Why would he do that?' asked Blanden, a curly-haired young policeman with large round eyes, who was new and aggressive, too aggressive for a rookie, Roy thought. And then Roy thought the act of defecation was clearly what Konrad Lorenz called 'a triumph reaction', the swelling and flapping of the geese. It was utterly explainable, thought Roy, simply a biological response. He could tell them about it.

'Who knows?' Bilkins shrugged. 'Lots of burglars do it. It's a fairly common M.O. Probably to show their contempt for the squares and the law and everything, I guess. Anyway, he's a shitter and wouldn't it be nice if somebody would wake up some night and grab a shotgun and catch the bastard squatting on their kitchen table just squeezing out a big one, and baloooey, he'd be shitting out a new hole.'

'Is there any description on this guy yet?' asked Roy, still smarting from Bilkins' gratuitous remark about the mirror, but man enough he thought, to overlook immaturity in a superior.

'Nothing new. Male, Negro, thirty to thirty-five, medium-sized, processed hair, that's it.'

'He sounds like a real sweetheart,' said Tucker.

'His mother should've washed him out with a douche bag,' said Bilkins. 'Okay, I been inspecting you for the last three minutes and you all look good except Whitey Duncan who's got dried barbecue sauce all over his tie.'

'Do I?' said Whitey, looking toward the tie which was ridiculously short hanging over a belly which Roy thought had swelled three inches in the past year. Thank heavens he didn't have to work with Whitey anymore.

'I saw Whitey this afternoon down at Sister Maybelle's Barbeque Junction on Central Avenue,' said Sam Tucker, grinning at Whitey affectionately. 'He comes to work two hours early on pay-day and runs down to Sister Maybelle's for an early supper.'

'Why the hell would Whitey need money to eat?' shouted a voice in the back of the room and the men chuckled.

'Who said that?' said Bilkins. 'We don't accept gratuities or free meals. Who the hell said that?' Then to Tucker, 'What do you think Whitey's up to, Sam? Think he's got the hots for Maybelle?'

'I think he's trying to pass, Lieutenant,' Tucker answered. 'He was sitting there amongst ten or fifteen black faces and he had barbecue sauce from his eyebrows to his chin. Shit, you couldn't even see that pudgy pink face. I think he's trying to pass. Everybody wants to be black, nowadays.'

Bilkins puffed and blew gray clouds and the fathomless eyes roved the roll call room. He seemed satisfied that they were all in good spirits and Roy knew he would never send them out in the morning watch until they were laughing or otherwise cheerful. He had overheard Bilkins telling a young sergeant that no man who did police work from midnight to 9:00 A.M. should be subject to any kind of GI discipline. Roy wondered if Bilkins wasn't too soft on the men because Bilkins' watch was never the high producer in arrests or traffic citations or anything else, except perhaps in good cheer which was a commodity of doubtful value in police work. Police work is serious business, Roy thought. Clowns should join a circus.

'Want to drive or keep score?' asked Light after roll call and Roy realized Light must want to drive because he had driven last night and knew it was Roy's turn to drive tonight. He asked, therefore he must be hoping for another night at the wheel. Roy knew that Light was self-conscious because Roy was such an excellent report writer and that when working with Roy,

Light hated to keep the log and make the reports as the passenger officer must do.

'I'll keep books if you want to drive,' said Roy.

'Suit yourself,' said Light, holding a cigarette between his teeth and Roy often thought he was one of the darkest Negroes he had ever seen. It was hard to see where his hairline began, he was so dark.

'You want to drive, don't you?'

'Up to you.'

'You want to or don't you?'

'Okay I'll drive,' said Light and Roy was starting the night out annoyed. If a man had a deficiency why in the hell didn't he admit the deficiency instead of running away from it? He hoped he had helped Light recognize some of his defense mechanisms with his blunt frankness. Light would be a much happier young man if he could come to know himself just a little better, thought Roy. He always thought of Light as his junior even though he was twenty-five, two years older than Roy. It was probably his college training, he thought, which brought him of age sooner than most.

As Roy was crossing the parking lot to the radio car, he saw a new Buick stop in the green parking zone in front of the station. A large-busted young woman jumped from the car and hurried into the station. Probably a policeman's girl friend he thought. She was not particularly attractive, but down here any white girl attracted attention, and several other policemen turned to watch. Roy felt a sudden longing for his freedom, for the carefree liberty of his early college days before he met Dorothy. How could he ever have thought they could be compatible? Dorothy, a receptionist in an insurance office, barely a high school graduate, having got her diploma only after a math class was waived by an understanding principal. He had known her too long. Childhood sweethearts are the stuff of movie mags. Romantic nonsense, he thought bitterly, and it had never been anything but bickering and misery since Dorothy became pregnant with Becky. But, God, how he loved Becky. She had flaxen hair and pale blue eyes like his side of the family, and she was incredibly intelligent. Even their pediatrician had admitted she was an extraordinary child. It was ironic, he thought, that her conception had shown him irrevocably the mistake he had made in marrying Dorothy, in marrying anyone so young, when he still had the promise of a splendid life to come. Yet, almost from the moment of birth Becky had shown him still another life, and he felt something utterly unique which he recognized as love. For the first time in his life he loved without question or reason, and when he held his daughter in his arms and saw himself in her violet irises, he wondered if he could ever leave Dorothy because he worshiped this soft creature. He was drawn to the tranquility she could produce in him instantly, at almost any moment, when he pressed the tiny white cheek to his own.

'Want some coffee?' asked Light as they cleared from the station, but

361

at that moment the Communications operator gave them a call to Seventh Street and Central. Roy heard the call and heard Light and wrote the address of the call as well as the time the call was received. He did all this mechanically now and never for a moment stopped thinking of Becky. It was becoming too easy, this job, he thought. He could make the necessary moves while only ten percent of his mind was functioning as a policeman.

'There he is,' said Light as he made a U-turn in the intersection at Seventh Street. 'Looks like a ragpicker.'

'He is,' said Roy in disgust as he shined his spotlight on the supine figure, sleeping on the sidewalk. The front of his trousers was soaked with urine and a sinuous trickle flowed down the sidewalk. Roy could smell the vomit and the excrement while still twenty feet away. The drunk had lost one torn and dismal shoe in his travels and a ragged felt hat, three sizes too big, lay crushed beneath his face. His hands clawed at the concrete and his bare foot dug in when Light struck him on the sole of the other foot with his baton, but then he became absolutely still as though he had grabbed for the softness and security of his bed, and having found it relaxed and returned to the slumber of the consummate alcoholic.

'Goddamn winos,' said Light, striking the man more sharply on the sole of the shoe. 'He's got piss, puke, and lord knows what, all over him. I ain't about to carry him.'

'Neither am I,' said Roy.

'Come on, wino. Goddamn,' said Light, stooping down and placing the knuckles of his thick brown index fingers into the hollow behind the ears of the wino. Roy knew how strong Light was, and cringed when his partner applied the painful pressure to the mastoids. The wino screamed and grabbed Light's wrists and came up vertically from the ground clinging to the powerful forearms of the policeman. Roy was surprised to see the man was a light-skinned Negro. The race of the ragpicker was almost indistinguishable.

'Don't hurt me,' said the wino. 'Don't, don't, don't, don't.'

'We don't want to hurt you, man,' said Light, 'but we ain't carrying your smelly ass. Let's walk.' Light released the man who collapsed softly to the sidewalk and then tumbled back lightly on a fragile elbow and Roy thought when they're this far gone with malnutrition, when they bear the wounds of rats and even alley cats that have nibbled at the pungent flesh as they lay for hours in ghastly places, when they're like this, it's impossible to estimate how close to death they are.

'You got gloves on?' asked Light, bending down and touching the wino's hand. Roy shined the flashlight beam in the lap of the man and Light recoiled in horror.

'His hand. Damn, I touched it.'

'What is it?'

'Look at that hand!'

Roy thought at first that the wino was wearing a glove which had been turned inside out and was hanging inside out by the fingertips. Then he saw it was the flesh of the right hand which was hanging from all five fingers. The pink muscle and tendon of the hand were exposed and Roy thought for a minute that some terrible accident had torn his flesh off, but he saw the other hand was beginning to shed the flesh so he concluded the man was deteriorating like a corpse. He was long dead and didn't know it. Roy walked to the radio car and opened the door.

'I hate like hell to go to all the trouble of absentee booking a drunk at the General Hospital prison ward,' said Roy, 'but I'm afraid this guy's about dead.'

'No choice,' Light shrugged. 'I imagine the police been keeping him alive for twenty years now, though. Think we're doing him a favor each time? It would've been over long ago if some policeman would just've let him lay.'

'Yeah, but we got a radio call,' said Roy. 'Somebody reported him lying here. We couldn't ride off and leave him.'

'I know. We got to protect our own asses.'

'You wouldn't leave him anyway, would you?'

'They'll dry him out and give him ninety days and he'll be right back here, come Thanksgiving. Eventually he'll die right here in the street. Does it matter when?'

'You wouldn't leave him,' Roy smiled uneasily. 'You're not that cold, Light. He's a human being. He's not a dog.'

'That right?' said Light to the wino who stared dumbly at Roy, his blue-lidded eyes crusty yellow at the corners.

'You really a man?' asked Light, tapping the wino gently on the sole of his shoe with the baton. 'You sure you ain't a dog?'

'Yeah, I'm a dog,' croaked the wino and the policemen looked at each other in amazement that he could speak. 'I'm a dog. I'm a dog. Bow wow, you motherfuckers.'

'I'll be damned,' grinned Light, 'maybe you're worth saving after all.'

Roy found the absentee booking of a prisoner at General Hospital to be a complicated procedure which necessitated a stop at Central Receiving Hospital and then a trip to Lincoln Heights Jail with the prisoner's property which in this case was the handful of rags that would be burned, and the presentation of the jail clinic with the treatment slips and finally the completion of paper work at the prison ward of the General Hospital. He was exhausted at three-thirty when Light was driving back to their division and they stopped at the doughnut shop at Slauson and Broadway for some bad but very hot coffee and free doughnuts. The Communications operator gave them a family dispute call. Light cursed and threw his empty paper cup in the trash can at the rear of the doughnut shop.

'A family dispute at four in the morning. Son of a bitch.'

'I felt like taking it easy for a while too,' Roy nodded. 'I'm getting hungry, and not for these goddamn doughnuts. I feel like some real food.'

'We usually wait till seven o'clock,' said Light, starting the car while Roy gulped down the last of his coffee.

'I know we do,' said Roy. 'That's the trouble with this goddamn morning watch. I eat breakfast at seven o'clock in the morning. Then I go home and go to bed and when I get up in the late afternoon, I can't stand anything heavy so I eat breakfast again, and then maybe around eleven just before I come to work I grab a couple eggs. Jesus, I'm eating breakfast three times a day!'

Light settled the family dispute the easiest way by taking the husband's identification and calling into R and I where he found there were two traffic warrants out for his arrest. As they were taking him out of the house, his wife, who had called them to complain of his beating her, begged them not to arrest her man. When they put him in the radio car she cursed the policemen and said, 'I'll get bail money somehow. I'll get you out, baby.'

It was almost five o'clock when they got their prisoner booked and drove back to their beat.

'Want some coffee?' asked Light.

'I've got indigestion.'

'Me too. I get it every morning about this time. Too damned late to go to the hole.'

Roy was glad. He hated 'going to the hole' which meant hiding your car in some bleak alley or concealed parking lot, sleeping the fitful frantic half-awake sleep of the morning watch policeman, more nerve-racking than restful. He never objected when Light did it though. He just sat there awake, dozing, mostly awake, and thought about his future and his daughter Becky who was inextricably tied to any dream of the future.

It was 8:30 A.M. and Roy was sleepy. The morning sun was scorching his raw eyeballs when they got the silent robbery alarm call to the telephone company just as they were heading for the station to go home.

'Thirteen-A-Forty-one, roger,' said Roy and rolled up his window so that the siren would not drown out the radio broadcasting, but they were close and Light did not turn on the siren.

'Think it's a false alarm?' asked Roy nervously as Light made a sweeping right turn through a narrow gap in the busy early morning commuter traffic. Suddenly Roy was wide awake.

'Probably is,' Light muttered. 'Some new cashier probably set off the silent alarm and didn't know she did it. But that place has been knocked over two or three times and it's usually early in the morning. Last time the bandit fired a shot at a clerk.'

'Can't get too much money early in the morning,' said Roy. 'Not many people come in this early to pay bills.'

'Hoods around here will burn you down for ten bucks,' said Light, and he turned sharply toward the curb and Roy saw that they had arrived. Light parked fifty feet from the entrance to the building where the lobby was already filling with people paying their utility bills. All of the customers were Negro as were many of the employees.

Roy saw the two men at the cashier's counter turn and look toward him as he came through the front door. Light had gone to cover the side door and now Roy took a step toward the men. They turned before he got very far into the lobby and were almost to the door when he realized they were the only two in the place who could possibly be robbery suspects. The other customers were either women or couples, some with children.

He thought of the embarrassment it would cause them if it was a false alarm, how there was so much talk these days that black men could not proceed about their business in the ghetto without being molested by white policemen, and he had seen what he considered overly aggressive police tactics. Yet he knew he must challenge them and for his own protection should be ready because they had after all received a silent robbery alarm call. He decided to let them reach the sidewalk and then talk to them. Nobody behind the cashier's windows had signaled him. It was undoubtedly a false alarm, but he must talk to them.

'Freeze!' said Light, who had approached from behind him noiselessly and was standing with his gun leveled at the middle of the back of the man in the black leather jacket and green stingy brim who was preparing to shove the swinging door. 'Don't touch that door, brother,' said Light.

'What is this?' said the man closest to Roy, who started to place his left hand in his trouser pocket.

'You freeze, man, or your ass is gone,' Light whispered and the man raised the mobile hand sharply.

'What the fuck is this?' the man in the brown sweater said and Roy thought he was almost as dark as Light but not nearly as hard looking. At the present moment Light looked deadly.

Roy heard four car doors slam and three uniformed officers responding to the hot shot call came running toward the front door while another came in the side door Light had entered.

'Search them,' said Light as the men were pushed outside, and Light walked across the floor to the cashier's cage with Roy.

'Who pushed the button?' Light called to the gathering circle of employees, most of whom were unaware that something unusual was happening until the policemen rushed through the door.

'I did,' said a tiny blond woman who stood three windows away from where the two men had been doing business.

'Were they trying to rob the place or not?' asked Light impatiently.

'Well, no,' said the woman. 'But I recognized the one in the hat. He's the one who robbed us with a gun last June. He robbed my window. I'd know him anywhere. When I saw him this morning, I just pushed the button to get you here quick. Maybe I just should have phoned.'

'No, I guess it's okay to use the silent button in cases like that,' Light grinned. 'Just don't push the button when you want us here to arrest a drunk out front.'

'Oh no, Officer. I know that button is for emergencies.'

'What were they doing?' asked Light to the pretty Mexican girl who worked the counter where the men were standing.

'Just paying a bill,' said the girl. 'Nothing else.'

'You sure about that guy?' Light asked the timorous blond.

'I'm positive, sir,' said the woman.

'Good work, then,' said Light. 'What's your name? The robbery detectives will probably be calling you in a little while.'

'Phyllis Trent.'

'Thanks, ma'am,' said Light and he walked long-legged across the lobby while Roy followed.

'Want us to take them?' asked the day watch officer who had the two men handcuffed and standing next to his radio car.

'Damn right,' said Light. 'We're morning watch. Man, we want to go home. That guy have anything in that left front pocket? He sure wanted to get in there.'

'Yeah, a couple joints, wrapped in a rubber band, and a little loose pot in his shirt pocket in a sandwich bag.'

'Yeah? How about that. I thought it was a gun. If that asshole had decided to go for it quick, I'd have figured it was a gun for sure. He'd be crossing the river Jordan about now.'

'The river Styx,' smiled the day watch officer, opening the door for the man in the black leather jacket, handcuffed now.

As they were driving to the station, Roy thought several times he should let the whole incident pass, but he sensed Light was unhappy with the way he had handled the situation in the lobby. Finally Roy said, 'How did you tumble to them being suspects, Light? Did one of the employees give you a sign?'

'No,' said Light, chewing on the filter of a cigarette, as they sped north on Central Avenue. 'They were the only likely-looking pair in the place, didn't you think?'

'Yes, but for all we knew it was a false alarm.'

'Why didn't you stop them before I came up, Fehler? They were almost out the door. And why didn't you have your gun ready?'

'We didn't know for sure they were suspects,' Roy repeated, feeling the anger well up.

'Fehler, they were, in fact, suspects, and if old stingy brim had brought his iron with him this trip, you'd be laying back there on that floor, you know that?'

'Goddamn it, I'm not a rookie, Light. I didn't think the situation warranted me drawing a gun, so I didn't.'

'Let's clear the air, Fehler, we got a whole month to work together. Tell me something truthfully, if they'd been white would you've been quicker to take positive action?'

'What do you mean?'

'I mean that you're so goddamn careful not to offend black people in any way that I think you risk your goddamn life and *mine* so's not to look like a big blond storm trooper standing there frisking a black man in a public place in front of all those black people. What do you think of that?'

'You know what's wrong with you, Light? You're ashamed of your people,' blurted Roy, and it was out before he could retract it.

'What the hell do you mean?' asked Light and Roy cursed himself but it was too late now and the words he was repressing had to be released.

'Alright Light, I know your problem and I'm going to tell you what it is. You're too damned tough on your people. You don't have to be cruel to them. Don't you see, Light? You feel guilty because you're trying so hard to pull yourself from that kind of degrading ghetto environment. You feel shame and guilt for them.'

'I'll be damned,' said Light, looking at Roy as if for the first time. 'I always knew you were a little strange, Fehler, but I didn't know you were a social worker.'

'I'm your friend, Light,' said Roy. 'That's why I'm telling you.'

'Yeah, well listen, friend, I don't look at a lot of these people as black or white or even as people. They're assholes. And when some of these kids grow up they'll probably be assholes too, even though I feel sorry as hell for them right now.'

'Yes, I understand,' said Roy, nodding tolerantly, 'there's a tendency of the oppressed to embrace the ideals of the oppressor. Don't you see that's what happened to you?'

'I'm not oppressed, Fehler. Why do white liberals have to look at every Negro as an oppressed black man?'

'I don't consider myself a liberal.'

'People like you are worse than the Klan. Your paternalism makes you worse than the other kind. Quit looking at these people as Negroes or problems. I worked a silk stocking division out on the west side when I first came out of the academy and I never thought of a Caucasian asshole in terms of race. An asshole is an asshole, they're just a little darker here. But not to you. He's a Negro and needs a special kind of protective handling.'

'Wait a minute,' said Roy. 'You don't understand.'

'The hell I don't,' snapped Light, who had now pulled to the curb at Washington and Central and turned in the seat to face Roy squarely. 'You been here over a year now, haven't you? You know the amount of crime in the Negro divisions. Yet the D.A. won't hardly file a felony assault if it's a Negro victim and suspect involved. You know what the detectives say, "Forty stitches or a gunshot is a felony. Anything less is a misdemeanor". Negroes are expected to act that way. White liberals have said, "That's alright, Mister Black man," and they're always careful to say *Mister*. "That's alright, you have been oppressed and therefore you are not entirely responsible for your actions. We guilty whites are responsible," and what does the black man do then? Why, he takes full advantage of his tolerant white brother's misplaced kindness, just like the white would do if the positions were reversed because people in general are just plain assholes unless they got a spade bit in their mouths. Remember, Fehler, people need spades, not spurs.'

Roy felt the blood rush to his face and he cursed his stammer as he struggled to master the situation. Light's outburst had been so unwarranted, so sudden ... 'Light, don't get excited, we're not communicating. We're not ...'

'I'm not excited,' said Light, deliberately now. 'It's just that sometimes I've been close to busting since I started working with you. Remember the kid at Jefferson High School last week? The robbery report, remember?'

'Yes, what about it?'

'I wanted to tell you this then. I was choking on my frustration the way you patronized that little bastard. I went to high school right here in southeast LA I saw that same kind of shakedown every day. The blacks were the majority and the white kids were terrorized. "Gimme a dime, motherfucker. Gimme a dime or I'll cut yo' ass." Then we gave whitey a punch in the mouth whether or not we got the dime. And these were *poor* white kids. Poor as us, sometimes from mixed marriages and shack jobs. You didn't want to book that kid. You wanted to apply your double standard because he was a downtrodden black boy and the victim was white.'

'You don't understand,' said Roy bleakly. 'Negroes hate the whites because they know they're faceless nonhuman creatures in the eyes of the whites.'

'Yeah, yeah, I know that's what intellectuals say. You know, Fehler, you're not the only cop that's read a book or two.'

'I never said I was, goddamn it,' said Roy.

'I tell you, Fehler, those white boys in my school were without faces to *us*. What do you think of that? And we terrorized those poor bastards. The few I ever got to know didn't hate us, they were afraid of us, because of our numerical superiority. Get off your knees when you're talking to Negroes, Fehler. We're just like whites. Assholes, most of us. Just like whites. Make the Negro answer to the law for his crimes just like a white man. Don't take away his manhood by coddling him. Don't make him a domestic animal. All men are the same. Just keep him on a mean spade bit with a long shank. When he gets too spirited, jerk those reins, man!'

August 1962

TEN

The Lotus Eaters

Serge listened to the dreary monotone of Sergeant Burke who was conducting roll call training. He looked around the roll call room at Milton and Gonsalvez and the new faces, all of whom he knew by now since his return to Hollenbeck. He remembered how Burke's roll call training used to bore him and still did. But he was no longer annoyed by it.

The five months from January to June which he had spent in Hollywood Division was by now a grotesque candy-striped memory which seemed to have never happened. Though he had to admit it had been educational. Everyone in Hollywood is a phony, a fruit, or a flim-flam man, a partner had warned him. At first the glamour and hilarity fascinated him and he slept with some of the most beautiful girls he would ever see, satin blondes, silky redheads, dark ones he avoided, for those were all he had in Hollenbeck Division. They were not all aspiring actresses, these lovely girls who are drawn to Hollywood from everywhere, but they all yearned for something. He never bothered to find out what. As long as they yearned for him for a few hours, or pretended to, that was all he asked of them.

And then it all began to depress him, especially the intense look of the revelers when he got to know them. He shared an apartment with two other policemen and he could never go to bed before three o'clock because the blue light would be burning, indicating that one of them had been lucky and please give them some more time. They were very lucky, his roommates, who were equally handsome, wholesome-looking, and accomplished handlers of women. He had learned from them, and by being a roommate had been satisfied with the chaff when the chaff was a pale trembling creature who was all lips and breasts and eyes. It didn't even matter if she ate bennies frantically and babbled of the prospective modeling job which would thrust her into the centerfold of *Playboy*. And there was another who, in the middle of the heated preliminaries of lovemaking, said, 'Serge, baby, I realize you're a cop and all, but I know you're no square and you wouldn't mind if I smoked a little pot first, would you? It makes it all so much better. You should try it. We'll be so much better lovers.' He thought about letting her do it, but the bennies were only a misdemeanor and marijuana was a felony, and he was afraid to be here while she did it, and besides, she had annihilated his ego and desire with her need for euphoria. When she disappeared into the bedroom for the marijuana, he put on his shoes and coat and crept out the door, an ache in his loins.

There were lots of other girls, waitresses and office girls, some of whom were ordinary, but then there was Esther, who was the most beautiful girl he had ever met. Esther who had called the police to complain about the peepers who were a constant annoyance to her, but her apartment was on the ground floor and she dressed with her drapes open because she 'just loved the cooling breezes'. She seemed genuinely surprised when Serge suggested she draw her drapes at night or move to an upstairs apartment. It had started out passionately between them but she was totally unique, with her moist lips and face and hands. Her eyes too were moist as was most of her torso, particularly the ample breasts. A fine layer of not unpleasant perspiration covered her during the lovemaking so that sleeping with Esther was like a steam and rub, except it was not as therapeutic – because even though a night-long bout with Esther left him exhausted, he did not feel cleansed from the inside out as he did when he left the steam room at the police academy. Perhaps Esther could not open his pores. Her heat was not purgative.

Her style of love had begun strangely enough, but then a few of her more bizarre improvisations began to repel him slightly. One bawdy Saturday, he had become drunk in her apartment, and she had become drunk too except she drank only a fourth as much as he did. She made frequent trips to the bedroom which he did not question. Then that evening when he was preparing to take her and she was more than ready, they had tumbled and clawed their way to the bed and suddenly the things she was whispering through the drunken mist became coherent. It wasn't her usual string of obscenities and he listened stunned to what she suggested. Then it was not passion but frenzy he saw in the moist eyes and she stepped half naked to the closet and dragged out various accoutrements, some of which he understood and others he did not. She told him that the young couple next door, Phil and Nora, whom he had decided were a pleasant pair, were ready for a 'fabulously exciting evening'. If he would only say the word they would be there in a minute and it could begin.

When he left Esther's apartment a moment later she was uttering a stream of grotesque curses that made him shiver with nausea.

A few nights later Serge was asked by his partner, Harry Edmonds, why he was so quiet and although he answered that there was nothing wrong, he was deeply aware that he was unhappy in Hollywood where life was ethereal and complicated. The most routine call became impossible in this place. Burglary reports would often turn into therapy sessions with unhappy neurotics who had to be subjected to a crude psychoanalysis to determine the true deflated value of a wristwatch or fur coat stolen by a Hollywood burglar who often as not turned out to be as neurotic as his victim.

At ten minutes past nine, that night, Serge and Edmonds received a call to an apartment on Wilcox not far from Hollywood station.

'This is a pretty swinging apartment house,' said Edmonds, a young policeman with sideburns a bit too long and a moustache that Serge thought ridiculous on him.

'You got calls here before?' asked Serge.

'Yeah, the manager's a woman. A dyke, I think. She only rents to broads far as I can see. There's always some beef here. Usually between the manager and some boyfriend of one of the female tenants. If the girls want to have girl parties, she never bitches.'

Serge carried his eight by eleven notebook under his arm and tapped on the manager's door with his flashlight.

'You call?' he asked the lean, sweater-clad woman who held a bloody towel in one hand and a cigarette in the other.

'Come in,' she said. 'The girl you want to talk to is in here.'

Serge and Edmonds followed the woman through a colorful green-gold and blue living room into the kitchen. Serge thought the black sweater and close-fitting pants very becoming. Although her hair was short it was silver-tipped and styled attractively. He guessed her age at thirty-five and wondered if Edmonds was right that she was a lesbian. Nothing in Hollywood could surprise him anymore, he thought.

The quivering brunette was seated at the kitchen table holding a second towel, ice-filled, to the left side of her face. Her right eye was swollen shut and her lower lip was turning blue but was not badly cut. Serge guessed the blood must have been from her nose which was not bleeding now and didn't look broken. It wasn't a particularly good-looking nose at best, he thought, and he looked at her crossed legs which were nicely shaped, but both knees were scraped. The torn hose hung from her left leg and had fallen down around the shoe, but she seemed too miserable to care.

'Her boyfriend did it,' said the manager, who waved them to the wrought-iron leather-padded chairs which surrounded the oval table.

Serge opened his notebook, leafing past the burglary and robbery reports and removed a miscellaneous crime report.

'Lovers' quarrel?' he asked.

The brunette swallowed and the tear-filled eyes overflowed into the blood-stained towel.

Serge lit a cigarette, leaned back and waited for her to stop, realizing vaguely that this might not be *complete* melodrama since the injuries were real and probably quite painful.

'What's your name?' he asked, finally, as he realized it was ten o'clock and their favorite restaurant preferred that they eat before ten-thirty when the paying customers needed most of the counter space.

'Lola St. John,' she sobbed.

'This is the second time that bastard beat you, isn't it, honey?' asked the manager. 'Give the officers the same name you were using when you made the last report.'

'Rachel Sebastian,' she said, dabbing at the tender lip and examining the towel.

Serge erased the Lola St. John and wrote the other name across the top.

'You prosecute him last time he beat you?' Serge asked. 'Or did you drop the charges?'

'I had him arrested.'

'Then you dropped the charges and refused to prosecute?'

'I love him,' she muttered, touching the lip with a pink tongue tip. An exquisite jewel formed at the corner of each eye, gumming with mascara.

'Before we go to a lot of trouble, are you going to go through with the prosecution this time?'

'This time I had it. I will. I swear by all that's holy.'

Serge glanced at Edmonds and began filling in the boxes on the crime report. 'How old are you?'

'Twenty-eight.'

That was the third lie. Or was it the fourth? Sometime he meant to count the lies at the completion of a report.

'Occupation?'

'Actress.'

'What else you do? When you're between acting jobs, I mean.'

'I'm sometimes night manager and hostess at Frederick's Restaurant in Culver City.'

Serge knew the place. He wrote 'carhop' in the space for victim's occupation.

The manager uncoiled and crossed the kitchen to the refrigerator. She refilled a clean towel with ice cubes and returned to the battered woman.

'That son of a bitch is no good. I won't have him back here, honey. I want you for a tenant and all, but that man cannot come in this building.'

'Don't worry, Terry, he won't,' she said, accepting the towel, which was pressed to her jaw.

'Has he beat you on only one prior occasion?' asked Serge, beginning the narrative of the report, wishing he had sharpened the pencil at the station.

'Well, actually, I had him arrested another time,' she said. 'I'm just a sucker for a big good-looking guy, I guess.' She smiled and fluttered the unclosed eye at Serge and he guessed she was signaling that he was big enough to suit her.

'What name were you using that time?' asked Serge, thinking she was probably blousy at best, but the legs were good and the stomach was still pretty flat.

'That time I was using Constance Deville, I believe. I was under contract to Universal under that name. Wait a minute, that was in sixty-one. I don't think ... Christ, it's hard to think. That man of mine knocked something loose. Let's see.'

'Were you drinking tonight?' asked Edmonds.

'It started in a bar,' she nodded. 'I think I was using my real name, then,' she added thoughtfully.

'What's your real name?' asked Serge.

'God, my head hurts,' she moaned. 'Felicia Randall.'

'You want to see your own doctor?' asked Serge, not mentioning that free emergency care was available to crime victims because he did not want to take this woman to the hospital and bring her back.

'I don't think I need a doct ... Wait a minute, did I say Felicia Randall? Christ almighty! That's not my *real* name. I was born and raised Dolores Miller. Until I was sixteen, I was Dolores Miller. Christ almighty! I almost forgot my real name! I almost forgot who I was,' she said, looking at each of them in wonder.

Later that month, while patrolling Hollywood Boulevard at about 3:00 A.M. with a sleepy-eyed partner named Reeves, Serge had taken a good look at the people who walk the streets of the glamour capital at this hour. Mostly homosexuals of course, and he was getting to recognize some of them after seeing them night after night as they preyed on the servicemen. There were lots of other hustlers who in turn preyed on the homosexuals, not for lust but for money which they got one way or the other. This accounted for a good number of beatings, robberies, and killings and until the hour of sunrise when his watch ended, Serge was forced to arbitrate the affairs of these wretched men and he was still revolted with all of it a week later when he returned to Alhambra and rented his old apartment. He talked with Captain Sanders of Hollenbeck Division who agreed to arrange a transfer back to Hollenbeck because he said he remembered Serge as an excellent young officer.

Burke was winding up the roll call training which nobody ever listened to and Serge did not at this moment even know the subject of the lesson. He decided he would drive tonight. He didn't feel like making reports so he'd do the driving. Milton always let him do exactly as he wished. He liked working with Milton and he even liked Burke's slow deliberate ways. There were worse supervisors. It was good to be back in the old station.

Serge was even beginning to lose his dislike for the area. It was not Hollywood, rather it was the opposite of glamorous. It was dull and old and poor with tall narrow houses like gravestones and the smell of the Vernon slaughterhouses remained. It was the place where the immigrants came upon their arrival from Mexico. It was the place where the second and third generations remained, who could not afford to improve their lot. He knew now of the many Russian Molokan families, the men with beards and tunics and the women with covered heads, who lived between Lorena and

Indiana Streets after Russian flats had been changed to a low-priced housing project. There was a sizable number of Chinese here in Boyle Heights
and Chinese restaurants had Spanish menus. There were many Japanese,
and the older women still carried sun parasols. There were the old Jews
of course, few now, and sometimes nine old Jews had to scour Brooklyn
Avenue and finally hire a drunken Mexican for a minyan of ten to start
prayers in temple. These old ones would soon all be dead, the synagogues
closed, and Boyle Heights would be changed without them. There were
Arab street hawkers selling clothing and rugs. There were even gypsies
who lived near North Broadway where many Italians still lived, and there
was the Indian church on Hancock Street, the congregation being mostly
Pima and Navajo. There were many Negroes in the housing projects of
Ramona Gardens and Aliso Village whom the Mexicans only tolerated,
and there were the Mexican-Americans themselves who made up eighty
percent of the population of Hollenbeck Division. There were few white
Anglo-Protestant families here unless they were very poor.

There were few phonies in the Hollenbeck area, Serge thought as he
slowed on Brooklyn Avenue to park in front of Milton's favorite restaurant.
Almost everyone is exactly as he seems. It was very comforting to work in a
place where almost everyone is exactly as he seems.

ELEVEN
The Veteran

'Two years ago tonight I came to University,' said Gus. 'Fresh out of the academy. It doesn't seem possible. Time has passed.'

'You're about due for a transfer, aren't you?' asked Craig.

'Overdue. I'm expecting to be on the next transfer.'

'Where you want to go?'

'I don't care.'

'Another black division?'

'No, I'd like a change. Little further north, maybe.'

'I'm glad I came here. I can learn fast down here,' said Craig.

'Be careful you don't learn too fast,' said Gus and dropped the Plymouth into low as he slowed for the red light because he was getting tired driving. It had been a very quiet evening and policemen toyed with the cars out of boredom after several hours of slow monotonous patrol. It was only nine-thirty. They shouldn't have eaten so early, Gus thought. The rest of the night would drag.

'Have you ever been in a shooting?' asked Craig.

'No.'

'How about a real knockdown fight?'

'I haven't,' said Gus. 'Not a real fight. A few belligerent bastards, but not a real fight.'

'You've been lucky.'

'I have,' said Gus, and for a second it started coming over him again, but he had learned how to subdue it. He was seldom afraid for no reason anymore. The times when he was afraid he had good reason to be. He had worked with an old-time policeman one night who had told him that in twenty-three years he had never had a real fight or fired his gun in the line of duty, or even been close to death except in a few traffic chases and he didn't think a policeman had to become involved in such things unless he went out of his way to become involved. The thought was comforting except that this policeman had spent his career in West Valley and Van Nuys Division which was the next thing to being retired, and he had only been in University for a few months, a disciplinary transfer. Still, Gus thought, after two years he had escaped the confrontation he feared. But did he really fear so much now, he wondered? The blue suit and badge, and the endless decisions and arbitration of other people's problems (when he didn't really know the answers but on the street at midnight there was no one else to find an answer except him and therefore he had made the choices for others and on a few occasions lives had depended on his decisions), yes, these decisions, and the blue suit and the badge had given him confidence he never dreamed he might possess. Though there were still agonizing self-doubts, his life had been deeply touched by this and he was as happy as he ever expected to be.

If he could transfer to a quiet white division, he would probably be happier if he were not troubled by guilt at being there. But if he could be satisfied that he had the necessary courage and had nothing further to prove to himself, why then he could transfer to Highland Park, and be closer to home and finally content. But that of course was bullshit because if police work had taught him anything it had taught him that happiness is for fools and children to dream of. Reasonable contentment was a more likely goal.

He began thinking of Vickie's widening hips and how twenty pounds even on a pretty girl like Vickie could make such a difference so that sometimes he was unsure whether their infrequent lovemaking was because she was so terribly frightened of another pregnancy, for which he couldn't blame her, or was it because she was growing less and less attractive. It wasn't just the bulkiness which had transformed a sleek body that was made for a bed, it wasn't just that, it was the breakdown of personality which he could only blame on a youthful hasty marriage and three children which were too much for a weak-willed girl of less than average intelligence who had always depended upon others, who now leaned so heavily on him.

He guessed he would be up all night with the baby if her cold weren't any better, and he felt a tiny surge of purgative anger but he knew he had no right to be angry with Vickie who was the prettiest girl who had ever shown an interest in him. After all, he was certainly not a trophy to cherish. He glanced in the rearview mirror and saw that his sandy hair was very thin now and he had been forced to reassess his guess; he knew he would be bald long before he was thirty and he already had tiny wrinkles at the corners of his eyes. He laughed at himself for his disappointment in Vickie for getting fat. But that wasn't it, he thought. That wasn't it at all. It was her.

'Gus, do you think policemen are in a better position to understand criminality than, say, penologists or parole officers or other behavioral scientists?'

'My God,' Gus laughed. 'What kind of question is that? Is that a test question?'

'As a matter of fact it is,' said Craig. 'I'm taking psych at Long Beach

State and my professor has quite a background in criminology. He thinks policemen are arrogant and clannish and distrust other experts, and believe they're the only ones who really understand crime.'

'That's a fair assessment,' said Gus. He reminded himself that this would be the last semester he could afford to rest because he would get out of the habit of going to school. If he ever wanted the degree he would have to get back in classes next semester without fail.

'Do you agree with that?' asked Craig.

'I think so.'

'Well I've only been out of the academy a few months but I don't think policemen are clannish. I've still got all my old friends.'

'I still have mine,' said Gus. 'But you'll see after a year or so that you feel a little different about them. They don't know, you see. And criminologists don't know. Police see a hundred percent of criminality. We see noncriminals and real criminals who're involved in crime. We see witnesses to crimes and victims of crimes and we see them during and immediately after crimes occur. We see the perpetrators during and right after and we see victims sometimes before the crimes occur and we know they're going to be victims, and we see perpetrators before and we know they're going to be perpetrators. We can't do a damned thing about it even though we know through our experience. We *know*. Tell that to your professor and he'll think you need a psychologist. Your professor sees them in a test tube and in an institution and he thinks these are criminals, these unfortunate unloved losers he's studying, but what he doesn't realize is that so many thousands of the winners out here are involved in crime just as deeply as his unloved losers. If he really knew how much crime occurs he wouldn't be so damned smug. Policemen are snobs, but we're not smug because this kind of knowledge doesn't make you self-satisfied, it just scares you.'

'I never heard you talk so much, Gus,' said Craig, looking at Gus with new interest, and Gus felt an urge to talk about these things because he never talked about them very much except to Kilvinsky when he was here. He had learned all these things from Kilvinsky anyway, and then his experience had shown Kilvinsky was right.

'You can't exaggerate the closeness of our dealings with people,' said Gus. 'We see them when nobody else sees them, when they're being born and dying and fornicating and drunk.' Now Gus knew it was Kilvinsky talking and he was using Kilvinsky's very words; it made him feel a little like Kilvinsky was still here when he used the big man's words and that was a good feeling. 'We see people when they're taking anything of value from other people and when they're without shame or very much ashamed and we learn secrets that their husbands and wives don't even know, secrets that they even try to keep from themselves, and what the hell, when you learn these things about people who aren't institutionalized, people who're out here where you can see them function every day, well then, you really *know*. Of course you get clannish and associate with others who know. It's only natural.'

'I like to hear you talk, Gus,' said Craig. 'You're usually so quiet I thought maybe you didn't like me. You know, us rookies worry about everything.'

'I know,' said Gus, moved by Craig's frank boyishness.

'It's valuable to hear an experienced officer talk about things,' said Craig, and it was very hard for Gus to control a smile when he thought of Craig thinking of him as a veteran.

'While I'm philosophizing, you want a definition of police brutality?' asked Gus.

'Okay.'

'Police brutality means to act as an ordinary prudent person, without a policeman's self-discipline, would surely act under the stresses of police work.'

'Is that one of the Chief's quotes?'

'No, Kilvinsky said that.'

'Is he the guy who wrote the book on police supervision?'

'No, Kilvinsky was a great philosopher.'

'Never heard of him.'

'On punishment Kilvinsky said, "We don't want to punish offenders by putting them in institutions, we only want to separate ourselves from them when their pattern of deviation becomes immutably written in pain and blood." Kilvinsky was drinking a little when he said that. He was usually much more earthy.'

'You knew him?'

'I studied under him. He also said, "I don't care if you supply the asshole with dames and dope for the rest of his life as long as we keep him in the joint." In fact, Kilvinsky would have out-liberaled the most ardent liberal when it came to prison reforms. He thought they should be very agreeable places. He thought it was stupid and useless and cruel to try to punish *or* to try to rehabilitate most people with "the pattern" as he called it. He had it pretty well doped out to where his penal institutions would save society untold money and grief.'

'Three-A-Thirteen, Three-A-Thirteen,' said the operator. 'See the man, family dispute, twenty-six thirty-five, south Hobart.'

'Well, it's fun to talk on a quiet night,' said Gus, 'but duty calls.'

Craig rogered the call as Gus turned the car north and then east toward Hobart.

'I wish I had had this Kilvinsky for a professor,' said Craig. 'I think I'd have liked him.'

'You'd have loved him,' said Gus.

When Gus stepped out of the radio car he realized how unusually quiet a night it had been for a Thursday. He listened for a moment but the street lined on both sides with one-story private residences was absolutely still.

Thursday, in preparation for weekend activity, was usually a fairly busy night and then he realized that welfare checks would arrive in the next few days. With no money the people were quiet this Thursday.

'I think it's the house in the rear,' said Craig, shining his flashlight to the right of the darkened pink stucco front house. Gus saw the lighted porch and followed Craig down the walk to the rear house where a shirtless Negro stepped out of the shadows with a baseball bat in his hand and Gus had his revolver unsnapped, in his hand, crouching instinctively before he realized why. The man threw the ball bat to the ground.

'Don't shoot I called you. I'm the one that called. Don't shoot.'

'Jesus Christ,' said Gus, seeing the Negro lurch drunkenly to his left, waving his big hands to the officers as he held them high overhead.'

'You could get killed like that, jumping out with a club,' said Craig, snapping his holster.

Gus could not find the pocket in the holster and had to use both shaking hands to put the gun away, and could not speak, did not dare to speak because Craig would see, anyone would see how unreasonably frightened he had been. He was humiliated to see that Craig was merely startled and was already asking questions of the drunken Negro while his own heart was hammering blood into his ears so that he couldn't make out the conversation until the Negro said, 'I hit the motherfucker with the bat. He layin' back there. I think I done killed him and I wants to pay the price.'

'Show us,' Craig commanded, and Gus followed the two of them to the rear of the cottage which was pink like the front house, but a frame building not stucco, and Gus sucked deeply at the air to still his beating heart. In the rear yard they found the lanky Negro with a head like a bloody bullet lying on his face and beating the ground with a bony fist as he moaned softly.

'Guess I didn't kill him,' said the drunken Negro. 'Sho' thought he was dead.'

'Can you get up?' asked Craig, already obviously accustomed to bloody scenes, knowing that most people can shed a great deal of blood and unless wounds are of certain types, people can usually function quite well with them.

'Hurts,' said the man on the ground and rolled over on one elbow. Gus saw that he too was drunk and he grinned foolishly at the officers and said, 'Take me to the hospital and git me sewed up will you, Officer?'

'Shall I call an ambulance?' asked Craig.

'Doesn't really need one,' said Gus, his voice steady now, 'but you may as well. He'd get blood all over the radio car.'

'Don't want to press no cha'ges, Officer,' said the bloody man. 'Jist want sewed up.'

What if I'd shot him, thought Gus while Craig's voice echoed through the narrow walkway and was followed by a static explosion. A female voice blared out and Craig adjusted the volume and repeated his request for an ambulance. Someday I'll become scared like that and I *will* kill someone and I'll cover it up neatly just as I could have covered up this one because a man leaped out of the darkness with an upraised club. But Craig was only startled; he didn't even clear the holster and there I was crouched with three pounds of pressure on the trigger and thank God, I didn't cock the gun unconsciously or I'd have killed him sure. As it was, the hammer was moving back double action, moving, and God, what if Craig hadn't been in front of me, I know I'd have killed him. His body had reacted independent of his mind. He'd have to think about that later. This could be the thing that might save him if *real* danger came. If it ever comes I hope it comes suddenly, he thought, without warning like a man leaping out of darkness. Then my body might save me, he thought.

As his heart pounded more slowly, Gus remembered that he had put off his running program for a week and he must not do that, because if you lose momentum you'll stop. He decided to go to the academy and run tonight after he got off duty. It would be a beautiful night and of course there would be no one else on the track except possibly Seymour, the leathery old motor officer who was a hulking man with a huge stomach, wide hips, and a face like eroded clay from riding the motorcycle more than twenty years. Sometimes Gus would find Seymour out there lumbering around the police academy track at 3:00 A.M. blowing and steaming. After his shower, when he was dressed in the blue uniform, riding breeches, black boots and white helmet, why then Seymour looked formidable again and not nearly as fat. He rode the motor lightly and could do wonders with the heavy machine. He had been a friend of Kilvinsky and how Gus had enjoyed the nocturnal runs when Kilvinsky was with him, and how they would rest on the turf. He had loved listening to Kilvinsky and Seymour discussing the old times on the police department when things were simple, when good and evil were definitive. He remembered how he would pretend to be as tired as Kilvinsky when they had covered their fifteen laps, gone to the steam room and then the showers, but actually he could have run fifteen more without exhausting himself. It was a beautiful night tonight. It would be good to get on the cool grass and run and run. He would try to run five miles tonight, five hard fast miles, and then he would not need a steam bath. He would shower, go home, and sleep into the afternoon tomorrow if it were not too hot to sleep, if the children would let him sleep, and if Vickie would not need him to help her replace a light bulb that was simply too high to reach after she became dizzy standing on a chair. Or to help her shop because it was impossible to shop nowadays alone even if you could leave the children with your neighbor because the markets were horribly confusing and you couldn't find anything, and sometimes you just wanted to scream, especially when you thought of returning to a house with three children and oh, God, Gus, what if I'm pregnant again? I'm five days overdue. Yes I'm sure, I'm sure.

'Ambulance on the way,' said Craig, clicking back down the walkway and Gus made a mental note to suggest to Craig that he get rubber-soled shoes or at least to remove the cleat from his heels because even working uniformed patrol, it paid to walk quietly a good part of the time. It was hard enough to do with a jingling key ring and creaking Sam Browne and jostling baton.

'Why did you hit him?' asked Craig, and by now the bloody man was sitting up and wailing as the pain was apparently penetrating the drunken euphoria.

'Ah tol' him I was goin' to do it nex' time he messed wif Tillie. Las' time I came home early I catched them in bed sleepin' an' drunk on mah whiskey an' there they was comf'table wif Tillie's bare ass right up there nex' to him and that thing still there inside her an' I reached ovah an' pulled it out and I woke him up an' tol' him if he evah did that again why I would whop him up side the head and I came home early tonight and I catched them agin an' I did it.'

'I had it comin', Charlie,' said the bloody man. 'You right. You right.'

Gus heard the wail of the ambulance siren in the distance and looked at his watch. By the time they finished the arrest report it would be end-of-watch and he could go to the academy and run and run.

'Don' you worry, Charlie, I won't have you arrested,' said the bloody man. 'You the bes' friend I evah had.'

'I'm afraid Charlie has to go to jail, friend,' said Craig helping the bloody man to his feet.

'I won' sign no complaint,' warned the bloody man and then winced as he stood erect and touched his head tenderly.

'Doesn't matter if you do or not,' said Gus. 'This is a felony and we're going to put him in jail just in case you up and die on us in the next few days.'

'Don' you worry, Charlie,' said the bloody man. 'I ain't goin' to die on you.'

'You can talk to the detectives tomorrow about refusing to prosecute,' said Gus as they all walked to the front. 'But tonight, your friend is going to jail.'

The winking piercing red siren light announced the arrival of the ambulance even though the driver had killed the siren. Gus flashed his light to show the driver the house and the ambulance slid in at the curb and the attendant jumped out. He took the arm of the bloody man as the driver opened the door.

'Don' you worry now, Charlie, I won' persecute you,' said the bloody man. 'An' Ah'll take good care of Tillie too while you in jail. Don' you worry none 'bout her neither. Hear?'

TWELVE
Enema

Roy's heart thumped as the telephone rang in the receiver which he held pressed to his ear. The door to the vice squad office was locked and he knew the rest of the night watch teams would not be straggling into the office for at least a half hour. He decided to call Dorothy from a police department phone to save the long distance charge. It was hard enough trying to make rent payments in two places and support himself after he sent his monthly payment to Dorothy. Then there was his car payment and it was becoming apparent he would soon have to sell the Thunderbird and settle for a lower priced car when this was one of the few luxuries he had left.

He was almost glad she wasn't home and was about to hang up when he heard the unmistakable pitch of Dorothy's unmistakable voice which so often made a simple greeting sound like a question.

'Hello?'

'Hello, Dorothy, hope I didn't disturb you.'

'Roy? I was in the shower.'

'Oh, I'm sorry, I'll call back.'

'No, it's alright. I'm in my bathrobe. What is it?'

'Is it the gold robe I got you for your last birthday?'

'We were already separated on my last birthday, Roy. It was the year before you got me a gold robe and this isn't it.'

'Oh. How's Becky?'

'You just saw her last week, Roy. She's still the same.'

'Goddamnit, Dorothy, can't you even spare me an occasional kind word.'

'Yes, Roy, but please don't let's get started again on the same old thing. The divorce will be final in just eighty-nine days and that's it. We're not coming back to you.'

Roy swallowed hard and the tears rushed to his eyes. He didn't speak for several seconds until he was sure he had control.

'Roy?'

'Yes, Dorothy.'

'Roy, this is useless.'

'God, I'll do anything you say, Dorothy. Please come home. Don't go through with it.'

'We're been over this again and again.'

'I'm terribly lonely.'

'A handsome man like you? A golden-haired, blue-eyed Apollo like Roy Fehler? You didn't have any trouble finding companionship while we were together.'

'Christ, Dorothy, it only happened once or twice. I've told you all about it.'

'I know, Roy. It wasn't that. You weren't particularly unfaithful as far as men go. But I just stopped caring. I just don't care for you anymore, can't you understand that?'

'Please give her to me, Dorothy,' Roy sobbed brokenly, and then the dam burst and he began crying in the mouthpiece, turning toward the door fearful that one of the other vice officers would come in early, and humiliated that he was doing this and letting Dorothy hear it.

'Roy, Roy, don't do that. I know how you're suffering without Becky.'

'Give her to me, Dorothy,' Roy sniffed, wiping his face on the sleeve of his orange checkered sport shirt which he wore hanging out of his belt to cover the gun and handcuffs.

'Roy, I'm her mother.'

'I'll pay you anything, Dorothy. My father has some money set aside for me in his will. Carl once hinted to me that if I ever changed my mind about going in the family store, I could maybe get my hands on it. I'll get it. I'll give it to you. Anything, Dorothy.'

'I'm not selling my baby, Roy! When the hell are you going to grow up?'

'I'll move back with Mom and Dad. Mom could take care of Becky while I work. I've already talked to Mom. Please, Dorothy, you don't know how I love her. I love her so much more than you do.'

The line was dead for a moment and Roy was coldly afraid she had hung up, then she said, 'Maybe you do, Roy. Maybe in your own way you do. But I don't think you love her for herself. It's something else you see in her. But it doesn't matter who loves her more. The point is that a child, especially a little girl, needs a mother.'

'There's *my* mother ...'

'Goddamnit Roy, will you shut up and stop thinking about yourself for just once in your life? I'm trying to tell you Becky needs a mother, a real mother, and I happen to be that mother. Now my lawyer's told you and I've told you that you can have more than adequate visitation rights. You can have whatever is reasonable. I'll be very liberal in that regard. I don't think I've been unfair in my child support demands. And surely, the dollar a year alimony isn't too difficult to manage.'

Roy heaved three deep breaths and the sting of his humiliation swept over him. He was thankful he had finally decided to make his final plea by telephone because he feared this might happen. He had been so distraught through the divorce that he could hardly control simple emotions anymore.

'You're very generous, Dorothy,' he said, finally.

'I wish you everything good, so help me God I do.'

'Thank you.'

'Can I give you some advice, Roy? I think I know you better than anyone.'

'Why not? I'm vulnerable to anything right now. Tell me to drop dead, I'll probably do it.'

'No you won't, Roy. You'll be all right. Listen, get on course and go somewhere. You studied criminology after switching your major two or three times. You said you'd only be a policeman for a year or so and it's already more than two years and you're nowhere near your degree. But that's okay if being a policeman is what you want. But I don't think it is. You've never really liked it.'

'It's better than working for a living.'

'Please don't joke now, Roy. This is the last free advice I'll ever be giving you. Get on course. Even if it's going back to your dad's store. You could do a lot worse. I don't think you'll be a successful policeman. You always seemed unhappy with some aspect of the job or other.'

'Maybe I'd be miserable at anything.'

'Maybe so, Roy. Maybe so. Anyway, do what you think is best, and I'm sure I'll be seeing you often when you come to get Becky.'

'You can bet on that.'

'Good-bye, Roy.'

Roy sat at the cluttered table in the vice office and smoked, even though he had a severe case of indigestion and suspected an incipient ulcer. He finished the first cigarette and used the smoldering coal to light another. He knew the fire in his stomach would worsen and that was alright too. He thought for an instant about the new untested Smith & Wesson two-inch which rested lightly on his hip and had made him so acutely aware that for the first time in his police career he was working a plainclothes assignment. For the first time he realized how badly he wanted that assignment, and how, when the watch commander had asked him if he would care for a loan to the vice squad for thirty days, he had jumped at it. He began feeling a little better and decided it was foolish and melodramatic to think of the Smith & Wesson as he had for that moment. Things were not that bad yet. He still had hope.

The lock turned and the door swung open in one motion and Roy did not recognize the balding loudly dressed man who came in with a gun belt slung over his shoulder and a paper sack in his hand.

'Hello,' said Roy, standing up and hoping the evidence of tears was no longer in his face.

'Hi,' said the man, extending his hand. 'You must be a new man.'

'I'm Roy Fehler. I'm on loan to vice for the month. This is only my third night here.'

'Oh? I'm Frank Gant. I been on days off since Monday. I heard we were borrowing someone from patrol.' He had a massive hand and shook hands violently. 'I didn't think anyone was here. Usually the first night watch guy that arrives unlocks the door.'

'Sorry,' said Roy. 'I'll unlock the door next time.'

'Oh that's okay. You met the rest of the crew?'

'Yeah. You were the only one I didn't meet.'

'Saved the best till last,' Gant smiled, putting the paper sack on top of a metal file cabinet.

'My lunch,' he said, pointing to the sack. 'You brown bagging it?'

'No, I've bought my lunch the last two nights.'

'Might as well brown bag it,' said Gant. 'You'll find there are lots of disadvantages to working vice. When you take off that blue suit you lose your eating spots. We have to pay for our meals or else brown bag it. I brown bag it. Working vice is expensive enough.'

'Guess I'll do the same. I can't stand to spend too much money these days.'

'You'll be expected to spend some,' said Gant, sitting down at the table and opening the log to make the entry for August third. 'They give us a few bucks a week to operate on, and we usually blow that the first night. From then on, you use your own dough if you want to operate. Me, I try not to spend too much. I got five kids.'

'I'm with you,' said Roy.

'They give you any money yet?'

'We operated a bar last night for liquor law violations,' said Roy. 'I chitted for two dollars, but really I spent five. I lost three on the deal.'

'That's the way vice is,' Gant sighed. 'It's a damn good job and if you like to work you'll love it here, but the bastards won't give us enough money to work on.'

'I'd like to work vice as a regular assignment. Maybe this is a good chance to show what I can do.'

'It is,' said Gant, opening a bulging manila folder and removing some forms which Roy had already come to recognize as vice complaints. 'How long you been in Central, Roy? I don't believe I ever saw you before.'

'Just a few months. I came from Newton.'

'Down in the jungle, huh? Bet you're glad to get away from there.'

'I wanted a change.'

'Any change is for the better when you get away from there. I used to work Newton, but that was before the Civil Rights push. Now that they been promised nigger heaven it's not the same working down there. I'll never go back.'

'It's a very complicated problem,' said Roy, lighting another cigarette as he rubbed his burning stomach and blew a gray plume of smoke through his nose.

'We got some splibs in Central too, but not too many. Just over on the east side and in the projects mostly, and a few others scattered around. Too much business and industry in the downtown area for them to swarm in.'

'I'd like to help you with the paper work,' said Roy, becoming irritated and uncomfortable as he always did when anyone talked about Negroes like this.

'No, that's okay. These are old vice complaints that there's a follow-up due on. You wouldn't know what to write. Why don't you look through the whore book. It's good to get to know the regulars. Or read over some of the arrest reports to see how vice pinches are made. You made a whore pinch yet?'

'No, we tailed a couple last night but we lost them. We've been mostly operating the bars. We got a bartender for serving a drunk, but that's the only pinch we made in two nights.'

'Well Gant's back so we'll go to work now.'

'You're not a sergeant are you?' asked Roy, realizing that he still wasn't sure who were working vice officers and who were supervisors. The whole atmosphere was very informal and different from patrol.

'Hell no,' Gant laughed. 'I should be, but I can't pass the damned exam. Been failing that son of a bitch for fourteen years. I'm just a policeman like you.'

'Not too sure of the chain of command around here,' Roy smiled.

'How much time you got on?'

'Almost three years,' said Roy and then was afraid Gant would pin him down to months because two years and three months was certainly not 'almost three years'.

'Different on vice, isn't it? Calling your sergeant by his first name and all that. Far cry from patrol, huh? This is a close group. Vice work has to be. It's intimate work. You'll be in close and up tight with all kinds of people. You'll see every kind of depravity you ever imagined and some you can't even imagine when you see it. They only let a guy work eighteen months of this shit. Too goddamned sordid, that and the kind of life you lead. Hanging around in bars all night, boozing and playing around with broads. You married?'

'No,' said Roy, and was struck with a spasm of indigestion that made him rub his stomach again.

'The whores don't tempt nobody, at least they shouldn't after you been around them awhile and get to know them. But there's a lot of pretty sexy toadies that hang around in some of these bars, lonely broads on the make, you know, just amateurs, freebies, and we're always hanging around too. It gets kind of tempting. Only thing Sergeant Jacovitch demands of us troops is that we don't play around on company time. If we meet something nice, we should make a date for our night off. Jake says if he catches us fooling around in some gin mill with a babe, she better be a professional whore or he'll bounce us off the squad.'

'I'm going through a divorce right now. I'm not really thinking too much about women.' Roy said it, and hoped Gant would ask him when the divorce was final or make some other comment about Roy's problem because he had a sudden urge to talk to someone, anyone, about it, and perhaps Gant had also been through it. So many policemen had.

'You know the division pretty well, Roy?' asked Gant, disappointing him.

'Pretty well.'

'Well, you can study that pin map on the wall,' said Gant, waving aimlessly at the wall as he made an entry on a work sheet which Roy knew would later be typed onto the vice complaint.

'What will we work tonight, whores?'

'Whores, yeah. We got to get some pinches. Haven't been doing too much lately. Maybe some fruits. We work fruits when we need some bookings. They're the easiest.'

Roy heard voices and Phillips, a swarthy young man with unruly hair and a bristling moustache, walked through the door.

'Hello everybody,' he announced, throwing a binocular case on the table, and carrying a set of walkie-talkies under his arm.

'What're the CC units for?' asked Gant. 'Some kind of big deal tonight?'

'Maybe,' said Phillips nodding to Roy. 'Just before we went home last night we got a call from Ziggy's bull dagger informant that The Cave was going to have some lewd movies going tonight. We might try to operate the place.'

'Hell, Mickey the bartender knows every goddamn one of us. How we going to operate it? I made so damn many pinches in there, they'd know me if I came in a gorilla suit.'

'A gorilla suit would be normal dress in that ding-a-ling joint,' said Phillips.

'You know The Cave?' asked Gant to Roy.

'That fruit joint on Main?' asked Roy, remembering a fight call he had received there on his first night in Central Division.

'Yeah, but it's not just fruits. There's lesbians, sadists, masochists, hypes, whores, flim flammers, paddy hustlers, hugger muggers, ex-cons of all descriptions, and anybody else with a kink of some kind or other. Who in the hell's going to operate for us, Phillips?'

'Guess?' said Phillips, grinning at Roy.

'Oh yeah,' said Gant. 'Nobody around the streets knows you yet.'

'I was there in uniform once,' said Roy, not relishing the idea of going alone into The Cave.

'In uniform you're just a faceless blue man,' said Gant. 'Nobody will recognize you now that you're in plainclothes. You know, Phillips, I think old Roy here will do alright in there.'

'Yeah, those fruits'll go for that blond hair,' said Phillips with a chuckle.

The other night watch team came in. Simeone and Ranatti were neighbors as well as partners and drove to work together. Sergeant Jacovitch came in last and Roy, still an outsider not accustomed to the vice squad routine, read arrest reports while the others sat around the long table in the cluttered office doing their paper work. They were all young men, not much older than himself except for Gant and Sergeant Jacovitch, who were approaching middle age. They all dressed nearly alike with bright-colored cotton shirts hanging outside their pants, and comfortable cotton trousers which it didn't matter if they soiled or tore while climbing a tree or crawling along a darkened hedge as Roy had done the night before when they had followed a whore and a trick to the trick pad, but had lost them when they entered the dingy apartment house because they were spotted by a tall Negro with processed hair who was undoubtedly a lookout. Roy noticed they all wore soft-soled shoes, crepe or ripple soles, so they could creep and peek and pry and Roy was not completely certain that he would like to receive an eighteen-month assignment to vice because he respected the privacy of others. He believed that this undercover surveillance smacked of fascism and he believed that people, damn it, were trustworthy and there were very few bad ones despite what cynical policemen said. Then he remembered Dorothy's admonition that he had never really liked this job, but what the hell, he thought, vice work should be fascinating. At least for a month.

'Bring your arrest reports in here, Roy,' called Jacovitch, who slid his chair to the side. 'Might as well sit in here and listen to all the bullshit while you're reading the lies on those arrest reports.'

'What lies?' asked Ranatti, a handsome, liquid-eyed young man who wore an upside-down shoulder holster over a T-shirt. His outer shirt, a long-sleeved navy-blue cotton was hung carefully over the back of his chair and he checked it often to make sure the tail was not dragging the floor.

'The Sarge thinks we exaggerate sometimes on our arrest reports,' said Simeone to Roy. He was younger-looking than Ranatti, rosy cheeked, and had slightly protruding ears.

'I wouldn't say that,' said Jacovitch. 'But I've tried a dozen operators on Ruby Shannon and you guys are the only ones ever did any good.'

'What're you beefing about, Jake, we got a case on her didn't we?' Ranatti beamed.

'Yeah,' said Jacovitch, with a wary glance first at Ranatti, then at Simeone. 'But she told me you zoomed her. You know the lieutenant doesn't want any hummer pinches.'

'Aw, it was no hummer, Jake,' said Simeone, 'she just went for old Rosso here.' He jerked a finger toward the grinning Ranatti.

'Sure seems funny,' said Jacovitch. 'She can usually smell a cop a block away, and Ranatti fooled her. Shit, he looks like he's fresh off the beat.'

'No, look, Jake,' said Ranatti. 'We really hooked her legal, honest we did. I operated her in my own inimitable style. You know, played a slick young pool room dago, and she went for it. Never dreamt I was the heat.'

'Another thing, it's unusual for Ruby to go on a six-forty-seven A,' said Jacovitch. 'She groped you, huh, Rosso?'

'Honest to God, she honked my horn,' said Ranatti, raising a rather stubby right hand heavenward. 'Gave it two toots with a thumb and fore-finger before I laid the iron on her wrists.'

'I don't trust either of you bastards,' said Jacovitch to the grinning young men. 'Lieutenant Francis and me were cruising the whore spots last week and we stopped and talked to Ruby at Fifth and Stanford. She mentioned the cute little Eye-talian cop that booked her on a hummer. She claims she laid a hand on your knee and you pinched her for lewd conduct right then.'

'Look, boss, I'm lewd from the knee on up. Don't you believe those Latin lover stories?'

They all chuckled and Jacovitch turned to Roy. 'What I'm trying to tell these guys is to lay off the hummers. We got a lieutenant that's very explicit about nice legal pinches. If the whore doesn't say the right words to you for a violation or if she doesn't grope you lewdly, there's no basis for a legal bust.'

'What if she shakes you down for a gun, Jake?' asked Simeone, lighting a fat cigar that looked comical in the puffy young lips. 'If she does that, I say she ought to get busted for lewd conduct. You can embellish your report a bit.'

'Goddamn, Sim, no embellishment. That's what I'm trying to get through to you. Look, I'm not the whole show, I'm just one of the clowns. The boss says we do police work straight arrow.'

'Okay, Jake, but vice is a different kind of police work,' said Gant, join-ing in the conversation for the first time.

'Look,' said Jacovitch in exasperation. 'Do you really want to roust these whores? If you do, you got to make what amounts to a false arrest report and then perjure yourself to convict her. It's not worth it. There'll always be whores. Why risk your job for a lousy misdemeanor? And, while I'm on the subject, the boss is a little hinky about some of these tails you been pulling where you tail the whore to the trick pad and hear her offer the guy a French for ten bucks.'

'So?' said Simeone, not smiling now. 'We made one like that last week. Something wrong with it?'

'The lieutenant told me he drove by one of the apartment houses where a team made a bust like that. He didn't say it was you, Sim, but he did say that the goddamn place had a windowless concrete wall on the side where the offer was supposed to be heard by the officers.'

'Goddamn it,' said Gant, standing up suddenly, and striding across the room to his lunch sack, where he removed another cigar. 'What does that fucking boy-lieutenant think this is, a college debating class with all the fucking rules laid down. I never bitched about him before, Jake, but do you know one night he asked me if I'd been drinking? Can you beat it? Ask a vice officer if he's been drinking. I said fuck, yes, Lieutenant, what the hell do you think I should do when I'm operating a bar. Then he asked me if we always pay for our booze and whether we accept sandwiches from bar owners who know we're heat. He wants a bunch of goody goody teetotalers with their lunch money pinned to their underwear. I'm quitting the squad if this prick gets any worse.'

'Take it easy. Jesus,' said Jacovitch, looking fearfully toward the door. 'He's our boss. We got to have a little loyalty.'

'That guy's blossoming out, Jake,' said Simeone. 'He's trying to be the youngest captain on the job. You got to watch the blossomers, they'll use their troops for manure.'

Jacovitch looked helplessly at Roy and Roy was certain he would be admonished later by Jacovitch to keep silent about the bitching in the vice squad. He was a poor example of a supervisor if he let it die like this, thought Roy. He should never have let it go this far, but now that it had, he should set them straight. The lieutenant was the officer in charge, and if Roy were in charge, by God, he would hope his sergeant did not permit the men to insult him.

'Let's talk about something else, you mutineers,' Jacovitch announced nervously, jerking his glasses off and wiping them although they seemed to Roy perfectly clean.

'Did you guys hear how many marines Hollywood vice busted last weekend?' asked Simeone, and Roy thought Jacovitch looked obviously relieved that the conversation had shifted.

'What's happening in Hollywood?' asked Gant.

'What always happens?' said Simeone. 'The joint is lousy with faggots. I hear they got twenty marines in fruit pinches last weekend. They're going to notify the general at Camp Pendleton.'

'That pisses me off,' said Gant. 'I was in the corps, but things were different in those days. Even marines are different now.'

'Yeah, I hear there're so many fruit marines being busted, the jarheads at Camp Pendleton are afraid to be seen eating a banana,' said Ranatti. 'They eat it sideways now like an ear of corn.'

'Anybody had a chance to work on the vice complaint at the Regent Arms?' asked Jacovitch.

'Maybe we could use our loaner here for that one,' said Ranatti, nodding at Roy. 'I think operating that joint is the only way. We prowled it. I got a ladder up to the balcony on the second floor and saw the room where those two whores are tricking, but I couldn't get close enough to the window.'

'Trouble is, they're damn particular who they take,' said Simeone. 'I think one or maybe two bellboys are working with them and sending up the tricks. Maybe Roy here could check in and we could set something up.'

'Roy's too young,' said Gant. 'We need an old guy like me, but I been around so long one of those whores would probably recognize me. How about you, Jake? You're old enough and prosperous looking. We'll make you an out of town sport and set something up.'

'Might be alright,' said Jacovitch, running his fingers through his thinning black hair. 'But the boss doesn't like the sergeants to operate too much. I'll see what he thinks.'

'The Clarke Apartments is expanding their operations too,' said Ranatti. 'Apartments six, seven, and eight all have hot beds in them now. Sim and me were staked out there last night for less than an hour and we must've seen these three whores take twelve or thirteen tricks in there one after another. The trick checks in at the desk each time too, so the place is making a fortune.'

'One hot bed can make you plenty,' Jacovitch nodded.

'These three are really busy. They don't even bother changing sheets,' said Ranatti.

'That used to be a square place,' said Gant. 'I used to take a date there after work whenever I'd get lucky. Too bad they had to get involved in prostitution. Nice old guy runs the joint.'

'Too much money in vice,' said Jacovitch looking at each of them. 'It can corrupt anybody.'

'Hey, you guys hear what Harwell did in the restroom at the Garthwaite Theater?' asked Simeone.

'Harwell's a day watch vice officer,' said Jacovitch to Roy. 'He's about as psycho as Simeone and Ranatti. We all got our crosses to bear.'

'What did he do this time?' asked Gant, completing his scribbled notes on a page of yellow legal-size paper.

'He was working the restroom on the vice complaint from the manager, and he spots a brand-new glory hole between the walls of the toilets, so he plops his big ass down on the last stool without dropping his pants and he just sits there smoking his big cigar and pretty soon some fruit comes in and goes straight to the glory hole and sticks his joint through at old Harwell. Lopez was watching from the trap behind the air conditioning on the east wall and he could see real good since we had the manager take the doors off all the johns to discourage the fruits. He said when the guy's joint came poking through the hole, why old Harwell tapped the ashes off that big cigar and blew on the coal till it was glowing red then ground it right into the head of the guy's dick. Says the fruit was screaming on the floor when they left.'

'That bastard's psycho,' Jacovitch murmured. 'This is his second tour on vice. I had my doubts about him. Bastard's psycho.'

'You ever hear about the glory hole in Bloomfield's Department Store in the ladies' dressing room?' asked Ranatti. 'Where the wienie wagger shoved it through at the old babe changing clothes and she stuck a hatpin clear through it and the son of a bitch was pinned right there when the cops arrived.'

'I heard that one for years,' said Phillips. 'I think some cop dreamed that one up for a good locker room story.'

'Well, the one about Harwell is true,' said Simeone. 'Lopez told me. Said they got the hell out right away. Harwell wanted to book the fruit. Can you imagine, after he damn near burned his dick off, he wants to put him in jail? Lopez told him, "Let's get the hell out of here and the fruit'll never know it was a cop that did it".'

'Bastard's going to get fired someday,' Jacovitch grumbled.

'Look, you got to keep your sense of humor working this job,' Ranatti grinned. 'You'd go nuts if you didn't.'

'I'd like to've seen that,' said Gant. 'Was the fruit a white guy?'

'Pretty close,' said Simeone. 'He was Italian.'

'You asshole,' said Ranatti.

'You guys remember this is trash night,' said Jacovitch.

'What a pain in the ass,' said Simeone. 'I forgot. Jesus Christ, I wore decent clothes tonight.'

'Trash night is the night we help the day watch,' said Jacovitch to Roy. 'We've agreed to rummage through the garbage cans real late at night on the night before the weekly trash pickup. The day watch gives us the addresses of the places they suspect are bookie joints and we check their trash cans.'

'I can tell all my friends I'm a G-man,' Ranatti muttered. 'G for garbage.'

'It worked pretty good so far,' said Jacovitch to Roy. 'We've found betting markers in garbage cans in three places. That gave day watch something to work on.'

'And I go home smelling like a garbage dump,' said Ranatti.

'One night we were rummaging in the cans back of Red Cat Sam's restaurant,' said Simeone, grinning at Jacovitch, 'and we find a big hog's head. Goddamn hog had a head like a lion. Old Red Cat's a splib, specializes in soul food. Anyway, we brought the head back for Jake, here. We stuck it in his wall locker and went home. Next night we come to work early to make sure we see him open it and that's the goddamn night this new lieutenant gets transferred in, unbeknownst to us. And they gave Jake's locker to him. He opened that door and didn't say a goddamn thing. Nothing! Nobody said nothing. We just all pretended like we were doing our paper work or something, and didn't say nothing!'

'He told me later that he thought this was an initiation for the new commander,' said Jacovitch, lighting a cigarette and coughing hoarsely. 'Maybe that's why he's made it so tough on us.'

'Let's not talk about him anymore. I get depressed,' said Gant. 'You guys ready to go to work?'

'Wait a minute before you go,' said Jacovitch. 'We got something pretty big cooking tonight. We're going to take The Cave at 1:00 A.M. I know you guys've probably heard rumors because it's impossible to keep a secret in this outfit. Anyway, we got some good scam from a reliable snitch that The Cave is having a lewd movie show tonight. I can't understand it unless Frippo the owner is just plain desperate for business. Anyway, the word is out and the goddamn place is going to be packed tonight. Do you know anything about The Cave, Roy?'

'A little,' Roy nodded.

'We been hitting them pretty hard lately,' said Jacovitch. 'One more good bust and I think we can get his liquor license. Tonight should be it. You guys drop whatever you're doing and meet me here at about midnight. We're borrowing about a dozen uniformed policemen from patrol and two teams from Administrative Vice are going to assist. The movie show is supposed to start about one and we're going to have Roy inside. As soon as the movie starts, Roy, you casually walk to the restroom. We already heard from the snitch that nobody's going to get in or out the front door after it starts. Stick a cigarette out the window and wave it around. We'll be sitting outside where we can see that window. Then we'll use the key and come in the front door.'

'You have a key to the place?' asked Roy.

'Yeah,' Ranatti grinned. 'That's it in the corner.' He pointed to a four-foot metal post with a heavy steel plate welded on the end and handles affixed to each side so that four men could swing it.

'It should come off with no problems,' Jacovitch said. 'I don't think you'll have any trouble, but if you should, like if something screwy should happen – if you're made as a vice officer, if you're in any danger at all – you just pick up a barstool or a beer mug or anything and toss it through the front window. Then we'll be right in. But you won't have any trouble.'

'Do I just sit there and have a drink?' asked Roy.

'Yeah. Order beer and drink out of the bottle,' said Ranatti. 'You don't dare drink out of a glass in the slimy place. Hey, Sim, is Dawn LaVere still hustling out of The Cave?'

'I saw her out front last week,' Simeone nodded. 'Watch for that bitch, Roy. She's the smartest whore I ever saw. She can spot a cop quick. If she suspects you're vice she'll start her act. Sit next to you, put a hand around your waist and pat you down for a gun and handcuffs while she's tucking a big tit under your armpit to keep you busy. She'll feel your key ring or get her hands on it if she can to see if you got call box keys or handcuff keys. And she'll feel for two wallets because she knows most policemen carry one wallet with their money and another one for their badge. I'd advise you to leave your badge and gun and everything with Gant before you go in.'

'I don't know about that,' said Jacovitch. 'He'd better be armed. I don't want him getting hurt.'

'A gun can screw up the deal, Jake,' Ranatti protested. 'He might as well get used to taking a few chances. We all got to if we want to work vice.'

'I don't know. I'll think about it,' said Jacovitch.

'Another thing, don't let old Dawn kiss you,' giggled Ranatti. 'She loves to snuggle around with guys she's hustling. Real affectionate whore, but she's got VD and TB.'

'Runny at both ends,' Simeone nodded. 'All the time.'

'She gobbles about twenty joints a night,' said Ranatti. 'Dawn once told me she don't even screw anymore. Most guys would rather have head jobs and that's a lot easier for her. She don't even have to undress.'

'She a dyke?' asked Gant.

'Oh yeah,' said Ranatti. 'She lives over on Alvarado with some big fat bull dagger. Told me one time she can't stand to lay a man anymore.'

'A vice officer hears all the girls' problems,' said Phillips to Roy. 'We get to know all these assholes so well.'

'Want Roy to work with me?' asked Gant to Jacovitch.

'I want the four of you to work together tonight,' said Jacovitch. 'I don't want you guys getting hung up on something and not be ready to go on The Cave when it's time. You four go out together. You can take two cars, but decide what you're going to do till midnight and do it together. Phillips'll work with me.'

'Let's go down on Sixth and see if Roy can operate a street-walker,' said Gant to Ranatti and Simeone who were already taking their small flashlights out of the drawer of a filing cabinet.

'Trash night and I'm wearing a brand-new shirt,' Ranatti grumbled, buttoning the shirt gingerly. Roy noticed it fitted well and the shoulder holster was completely concealed. He wondered if he should invest in a shoulder holster. He decided to wait. He was only working vice this month and it might be a long time before he was given a permanent plainclothes assignment. Surely though, someone would want him soon. Felony car, vice, someone would want him. He was sure it was evident to everyone that he was an exceptionally good policeman but police work was temporary and he knew he should be thinking about what courses he would be taking this semester. He seemed to have lost his drive in that direction. Maybe, he thought, I'll take a vacation this semester.

They took two cars. Gant was driving a two-tone green Chevrolet which the vice officers had done their best to camouflage by putting oversized tires on the back. Someone had hung a fuzzy object from the mirror and Gant told Roy that Simeone was responsible for the college decals plastered all over the rear window. Still, Roy thought, it looked like a stripped-down, low-priced, plainclothes police car. The Department, according to Gant, was very tight with expenditures of funds for undercover operation.

Gant drove Roy to the parking lot where he had his private car.

'Listen Roy,' said Gant. 'We'll be in the vacant lot behind the yellow apartment building north of Sixth just off Towne Avenue. You make a pass by there and see where we are. Then you cruise a few blocks down on Sixth and you should see a hustler or two even this early in the evening. If you get her, bring her back to the meeting place.'

'Okay,' said Roy.

'You sure you learned last night what you need for a whore pinch?' asked Gant.

'Offer of sex for money,' said Roy. 'Seems simple enough.'

'Okay, Roy, go ahead,' said Gant. 'If you see a whore you suspect is a man dressed up as a woman, don't hit on him. Pass him by and try another one. We don't operate fruits alone. They're the most dangerous unpredictable bastards in the world. You just hit on women – *real* women.'

'Okay,' Roy said, getting anxious to start. It was a dark night, and being out here on the city streets in plainclothes was like being out here for the very first time. It was eerie and exciting. His heart began thudding.

'Go ahead, kid,' said Gant. 'Take it easy though.'

Roy noticed that his hands became extremely clammy and the steering wheel slippery as he turned east on Sixth Street. It wasn't that he was alone, because he was not really alone with Gant and Ranatti and Simeone staked out just a few blocks away. But he was for the first time out in the streets minus the security of the badge and blue suit, and though he knew this street fairly well, it seemed altogether strange. A vice officer loses the comfort of the big brass shield, he thought. He acquires an identity. Without the blue suit he becomes a mere man who must function as a street dweller. His confidence was waning. Was it more than nervousness? He put a hand on his chest and measured the thuds. Was it fear?

Roy saw a streetwalker at Fifth and Stanford. She was an emaciated Negro with straight legs and Roy guessed she was an addict with her look of yearning. She smiled as he drove slowly by.

'Hello blondie,' she said, walking up to Roy's car on the passenger side and peering in.

'Hello there,' Roy said, forced a smile, and cursed silently at his quivering voice.

'Haven't I seen you around?' she asked, still smiling an uninviting bad-toothed smile as she glanced around the car, probing, and Roy guessed that she suspected immediately.

'I've never been here before,' Roy answered. 'A friend told me about this place. Said I could have a good time.'

'What do you do for a living, baby?' she smiled.

'Insurance man.'

'That's funny, you look just like a cop to me,' she said, drilling him with her eyes.

'A cop?' he laughed brokenly. 'Not me.'

'You look exactly like a young cop,' she said unblinkingly while he withered.

'Look, you're making me nervous with this cop talk,' said Roy. 'Can I get a good time around here, or not?'

'Maybe you could,' she said. 'What do you have in mind?'

Roy remembered last night's admonishment by Jacovitch about entrapment and he knew she was trying to lead him into making the offer himself.

'Don't you know?' he said, trying a coy smile but uncertain how it looked.

'Give me a card, baby, I might want to buy some insurance sometime.'

'Card?'

'A business card. Give me a business card.'

'Look, I'm a married man. I don't want you to know my name. What're you trying to do, blackmail me?' said Roy, congratulating himself on his quick thinking and making a note to borrow some cards from an insurance office for any future operations.

'Okay,' she smiled easily. 'Tear your name off the card or scratch it out with that pen in your shirt pocket. Just let me see that you have a card.'

'I don't have any with me,' said Roy. 'Come on, let's get down to business.'

'Uh huh,' she said, 'let's do that. And my business is minding my own business. Any insurance man that ain't got a million cards in his wallet is a mighty poor insurance man.'

'So I'm a poor insurance man. What the hell,' said Roy hopelessly as she turned to walk away.

'You ain't even a good vice cop,' she sneered over her shoulder.

'Bitch,' said Roy.

'Paddy, blue-eyed motherfucker,' said the prostitute.

Roy turned right on the next street, drove south to Seventh then back up to Sixth where he parked his car a half block away with the lights out and watched the prostitute talking to a tall Negro in a gray felt hat who nodded and walked quickly down the block to a fat prostitute in a green satin dress whom Roy hadn't seen before. She ran inside the building and talked with two women in the doorway who were just coming out. Roy drove to the meeting place where he found Gant sitting in the back seat of Ranatti's and Simeone's car.

'Might as well go somewhere else,' said Roy. 'I'm burned.'

'What happened?' asked Gant.

'A skinny whore in a brown dress recognized me from working uniform in this area,' Roy lied. 'I saw her look at me and run and tell all the whores on the block. It's no use, I'm burned here.'

'Let's go over to the park and bust a quick fruit or two,' said Ranatti. 'We haven't made a fruit pinch for a few days.'

After leaving his private car in the station parking lot Roy rejoined Gant in the vice car and they drove toward the park. Roy was disappointed that he had so far been unable to make a vice arrest, but he decided he'd operate successfully in The Cave later tonight and it now occurred to him that he had no idea how to arrest a homosexual.

'What're the elements of a fruit pinch?' asked Roy.

'That's easier than a whore bust,' said Gant, driving casually through the early evening traffic. 'If he makes a lewd offer in a public place, that's it. Or if he gropes you. But as far as I'm concerned you don't have to let a man grab your joint. If it looks like he's making a move to honk you, just grab his hand and he's busted. We'll say on the arrest report he touched your privates. I don't give a shit what Jacovitch says about legal arrests and embellishing arrest reports, I don't let nobody touch my tool unless she's wearing a dress and I know for sure there's a female body under the dress.'

'Seems like you could just settle for the verbal offer,' said Roy.

'Yeah, you could. But some faggots are real aggressive. You say hello and bang, they got you by the dork. I don't expect you to submit to that crap. Just operating fruits is bad enough. But maybe we won't have to operate them. Maybe we can catch them in the trap.'

'I heard lots of talk about *the trap*. What is it?' asked Roy, feeling a bit uncomfortable about the prospect of working fruits.

'That's what we call a vantage point,' said Gant, accelerating up the hill on Sixth Street past Central Receiving Hospital. 'There's lots of places where fruits hang out, like public restrooms. Well, some of these places install vents covered with heavy mesh screen or something like that, where we can peek through into the restroom area. Most of the places take the doors off the shithouses for us too. Then we sit in *the trap*, as we call it, and peek through into the restroom. Of course there's legal technicalities like probable cause and exploratory searches involved here, but I'll tell you about that when we make the arrest report – if we catch any. Sometimes we use the CC units and let one guy sit in the trap with a radio and if he sees some fruit action in the john, he whispers to us over the radio and in we come. Let me warn you about fruits. I don't know what you're expecting, but I can tell you that a fruit can look like anything. He can be a big manly guy with a wife and kids and a good job, he can be a professional man, or a priest, or even a cop. We've caught people from every walk of life in these traps. All kinds of people got kinks, and in my opinion, any guy with this particular kind of kink that has to indulge it occasionally will sooner or later look for a public restroom or some other sleazy fruit hangout. It's part of the cruddy thrill I guess. I talked to a million fruits in my time and lots of them cop out to needing a little action in a place like this once in a while even when they can have their kicks in private with a discreet boyfriend. I don't know why, I just know they do it. So the thing is, you might run into a pretty square kind of fruit in here. Like I said, a respectable married guy or something, and when he finds out you're the law, that son of a bitch might come uncorked. Suddenly he pictures a big scandal where Mama and the kiddies and all his friends read on the front page of the *Times* that old Herbie is really a cock-sucker. That's what's going on in his sweaty brain. And you be careful, because if you was taking him for murder he wouldn't be near as panicky or dangerous. This prick might literally try to kill you to get away. I say don't get yourself hurt for a lousy misdemeanor pinch that ain't worth a goddamn in court anyway. You know what the average fruit gets? About a fifty-dollar fine and that's it. He'd have to have a bunch of priors to draw any jail time. But these fruits don't know all this and if they don't know it they don't think of it when you're arresting them. All they're thinking about is getting away from you. And they're fucked up in the head anyway or they wouldn't be there in the first place, so you just be careful working fruits.'

'I will,' said Roy, feeling his heart race again. He hadn't bargained for the dangers of vice work. When he first learned he was going to vice he vaguely pictured girls and drinking. He thought of how he had never actually been in a fight in the two years he had been a policeman. He had to assist a partner wrestle a man to the ground a few times where the handcuffs were applied without too much trouble. But he had never actually struck a man, nor had anyone ever struck him. And a vice officer carried no baton. 'Do you carry a sap?' Roy asked.

'You bet,' said Gant, lifting his shirt and showing Roy the huge black beaver-tail sap he carried inside his waistband.

'Maybe I ought to buy one,' said Roy.

'I think you ought to have one,' Gant nodded. 'Vice officers get in some good ones and that onesies on twosies wristlock they teach you in the academy never seems to work when you're squirming around on some piss-covered restroom floor with some bloody sweaty fruit, or maybe battling some hugger mugger's pimp in some dark hotel lobby when your partner doesn't know where the hell you are.'

'This job doesn't sound too good after all,' Roy smiled weakly.

'I'm just telling the worst that can happen,' said Gant. 'They're the things that happen to young hot dogs like Ranatti and Simeone. But you stick with the old salts like me and nothing's going to happen. We won't make as many pinches as those guys but we'll go home in one piece every night.'

Gant parked the vice car half a block from the park and walked to the hedgerow on the south side of the duck pond where they found Ranatti and Simeone sprawled on the grass smoking and throwing pieces of popcorn to a hissing black gander who accepted the tribute but scorned them for their charity.

'Nobody appreciates something for nothing,' said Ranatti, pointing his cigarette at the ferocious gander who tired of the popcorn and waddled to the water's edge.

'We going to operate, or work the trap?' asked Gant.

'Whatever you want,' Simeone shrugged.

'What do you want to do, Roy?' asked Gant.

'Hell, I'm too new to know,' said Roy. 'If we operate that means we walk around and pose as fruits?'

'Just be available,' said Simeone. 'You don't have to swish around or play with your coins in your pants pocket or anything. Just hang around and talk to the fruits that hit on you. Usually one or two of us operate out around the trees and the other two wait somewhere. If you get an offer you bring the fruit to the waiting place. Tell him you got a car nearby or a pad, or tell him anything. Just get him to us, then we all take him. One man never takes a fruit alone.'

'I already told him that,' said Gant.

'Or, if you're squeamish about playing fruit, and I don't blame you if you are,' said Ranatti, ''cause I never could stand to operate them – well, then we can go to the trap. Then you only watch them in a lewd act. You don't have to actually mingle with them like when you operate.'

'Let's do that,' said Roy.

'You two want inside or outside?' asked Simeone to Gant.

'Outside. What do you think?'

'What did you ask him for?' said Ranatti.

'He respects his elders,' said Gant as they began strolling through the park. It was a warm summer evening, and a slight breeze cooled Roy's face as it came off the pond. Many of the ducks were asleep, and aside from the steady flow of nearby traffic it was quiet and restful here.

'It's a beautiful place,' said Roy.

'The park?' said Ranatti. 'Oh, yeah. But it's full of faggots and thieves and assholes in general. No decent people dare hang around here after dark.'

'Except us vice officers,' said Simeone.

'He said decent people,' Gant reminded him.

'Once in a while some squares that're new in town might come around here after dark with the family, but they soon see what's happening. They used to lock up the johns at night, but some brainy park administrator decided to leave them open. The open restrooms draw fruits like flies.'

'Fruit flies,' said Simeone.

'We used to only have a hundred fruits a night around here. Now we got a thousand. Maybe we can get the restrooms closed again.'

'That's it over there,' said Gant to Roy, pointing at the large stucco outbuilding squatting near a clump of elms that rustled in the wind which had grown stronger.

'Roy, you and me'll wait behind those trees over there,' said Gant. 'When they come out of the trap we'll see them and run over and help them.'

'One time,' said Simeone, 'there were only two of us here and we caught eight fruits in there. One was gobbling another's joint, and the other six were standing around fondling anything they could find.'

'A real circle jerk,' said Ranatti. 'We snuck out of the trap and didn't know what the hell to do with eight of them. Finally Sim spots a pile of roofing tiles at the corner of the tool shed and he sticks his head in and yells, "All you fruits are under arrest". Then he slams the door shut and backs off to the pile of tiles and starts heaving them at the door every time one of them tries to get out. He was really enjoying it, I think. I ran to the call box on the corner and put out a help call and when the black and whites got here we still had all eight fruits trapped in the crapper. But the wall of the building looked like a machine gun squad had strafed it.'

'See what I told you about sticking with me and staying out of trouble,' said Gant, walking toward the clump of trees where they would wait. 'Why don't you go in with them for a while, Roy? You might as well see what it's all about.'

Ranatti removed his key ring from his pocket and unlocked the padlock on a massive tool shed which was attached to the side of the building. Roy entered the shed and was followed by Ranatti who held the door for him and closed it behind them. It was deep and black in the shed except for a patch of light six feet up on the wall near the roof of the shed. Ranatti took Roy's elbow and guided him through the darkness and pointed to a step and a three-foot platform leading up to the patch of light. Roy stepped up and looked through the heavy gauge sheets of wire mesh into the interior of the restroom. The room was about thirty by twenty feet, Roy thought. He envisioned the dimension might be a question by the defense if he ever had to go to court on an arrest he made here. There were four urinals and four stools behind them separated by metal walls. Roy noticed there were no doors on the front of the stalls and several peepholes were drilled in the metal walls which separated the toilets.

They waited silently for several minutes and then Roy heard feet shuffling on the concrete walk leading toward the front door. An old stooped tramp slouched in toting a bundle which he opened when he got inside. The tramp took four wine bottles from the dirty sack and drained the half mouthful of wine which remained in each of them. Then he put the bottles back into the bundle and Roy wondered what value they could have. The old man wobbled over to the last stool where he removed his filthy coat, lunged sideways against the wall, righted himself, and took the floppy hat from his tremendous shaggy head. The tramp dropped his pants and sat down in one motion and a tremendous gaseous explosion echoed through the restroom.

'Oh Christ,' Simeone whispered. 'Just our luck.'

The stench filled the room instantly.

'Jesus Christ,' said Ranatti, 'this place smells like a shithouse.'

'Were you expecting a flower shop?' asked Simeone.

'This is a degrading job,' Roy muttered and went to the door for some fresh air.

'Well, the old thief's got enough asswipe stashed to last a week,' said Simeone in a loud voice.

Roy looked back into the restroom and saw the tramp still sitting on the toilet, slumped against the side wall snoring loudly. A huge wad of toilet paper protruded from the top of his ragged undershirt.

'Hey!' Simeone called. 'Wake up, you old ragpicker. Wake up!'

The tramp stirred; blinked twice and closed his eyes again.

'Hey, he's not sleeping real sound yet,' said Ranatti. 'Hey! Old man! Wake up! Get your ass up and out of here!'

This time the tramp stirred, grunted and opened his eyes with a snap of his head.

'Get the hell out of here, you old crud!' said Simeone.

'Who said that?' asked the tramp, leaning forward on the toilet, trying to peek around the wall of the toilet stall.

'It's me. God!' said Ranatti. 'Get the hell out of here.'

'Wise son of a bitch, huh?' said the tramp. 'Jus' wait a minute.'

As the tramp was struggling back into his pants, Roy heard footsteps and a pale, nervous-looking man with a receding hairline and green-tinted glasses entered the restroom.

'A fruit,' Ranatti whispered in Roy's ear.

The man looked in each toilet stall and seeing only the uninteresting tramp in the last stall, walked to the urinal on the far side of the room.'

The tramp did not buckle his belt but merely tied the leather around his waist. He slammed the floppy hat back on his head and picked up the bundle. Then he saw the man standing at the last urinal. The tramp put down the bundle.

'Hello God,' said the tramp.

'Beg your pardon?' said the man, still standing at the urinal.

'Ain't you God?' asked the tramp. 'Didn't you tell me to get the hell out of here? Well I might not look like much, but no son of a bitch tells me to get my ass out of a public shithouse, you son of a bitch.' The tramp put down his bundle deliberately while the terrified man re-zipped his trousers. As the man skidded toward the door across the slippery floor of the restroom the tramp threw a wine bottle that crashed on the doorjamb and showered the man with glass fragments. The tramp hobbled to the door and looked after his fleeing enemy, then returned to his bundle and hefted it to his shoulder. With a toothless triumphant grin he staggered from the restroom.

'Sometimes you get a chance to do good things for people in this job,' said Simeone lighting a cigarette, making Roy wish he would not smoke in the stifling dark enclosure of the shed.

It was perhaps five minutes when another step was heard. A tall, muscular man of about thirty entered, walked to the sink and ran a comb deliberately through his wavy brown hair without glancing to his left. Then he examined the wide collar of a green sport shirt worn beneath a lightweight well-fitting lime sweater. Then he walked to each toilet stall and looked inside. He then walked to the urinal which had been occupied by the pale man, unzipped his trousers and stood there not urinating. Ranatti nodded in the darkness to Roy but Roy did not believe he could be a fruit. The man stood at the urinal for almost five minutes craning his neck occasionally toward the door when a sound was heard outside. Twice Roy thought someone would enter and he now knew of course what the man was waiting for, and he shivered in the back of his neck and decided when another one came in he did not want to watch, was not curious enough to watch because already he felt slightly nauseated. He always had the idea that fruits were all swishes, hence identifiable, and it sickened him to see this average-looking man in here, and he did not want to watch. Then an old man entered, Roy didn't see him until he was through the door and stepping lightly to the urinal at the opposite end of the line. The old man was perhaps seventy, dressed nattily in a blue pinstripe with natural shoulders and matching vest, and a blue silk tie over a pale blue shirt. His hair was pearl white and styled. His hands were lightly veined and he picked nervously at invisible lint on the impeccable suit. He looked at the tall man at the other urinal and smiled and the light glinted off his silver collar pin and Roy was struck with a wave of revulsion not imperceptible like before, but gut-wrenching as the old man, still holding his hands near his groin out of Roy's line of sight, hopped along the urinals until he was standing next to the tall man. He laughed softly and so did the tall man who said, 'You're too old.' Roy whispered incredulously to Ranatti, 'He's an old man! My God, he's an old man!'

'What the hell,' Ranatti whispered dryly, 'fruits grow old too.'

The old man left after being repulsed another time. He stopped in the doorway but finally left in dejection.

'He didn't really do anything lewd,' Simeone whispered to Roy. 'He just stood next to him at the urinal. No touching or anything. He didn't even jerk off. No good for an arrest.'

Roy thought the hell with it he had seen enough and decided to join Gant on the cool clean grass in the invigorating air when he heard voices and feet scraping and decided to see who or what would enter. He heard a man say something in rapid Spanish and a child answered. The only thing Roy understood was '*Sí Papa.*' Then Roy heard the man walking away from the doorway and he heard other children's voices talking Spanish. A boy of about six skipped into the restroom not looking at the tall man and ran to a toilet where he turned his back to the watchers, dropped his short pants to the floor revealing his plump brown behind, and urinated in the toilet while he hummed a child's song. Roy smiled for a moment, but then he remembered the tall man. He saw the tall man's hand moving frantically in the area of his crotch and then he stepped away from the urinal and masturbated as he faced the boy but hurriedly returned to the urinal when a child's shrill laugh pierced the silence from the outside. The boy adjusted his pants and ran from the restroom still humming, and Roy heard him shout, 'Carlos! Carlos!' to a child who answered from a long way across the park. The child never saw the tall man who now grunted while he stood at the old place and his hand moved more frantically than before.

'See? Our job *is* worth doing,' Simeone grinned viciously. 'Let's take that bastard.'

As the three men broke from the shed door, Simeone whistled and Gant came running from the clump of swaying elms. Roy saw a man and three children across the expanse of darkness strolling across the grass carrying shopping bags. They were almost out of the park.

Simeone led the way into the restroom with his badge in his hand. The man looked at the four vice officers and fumbled with the zipper of his trousers.

'You like kids?' Simeone grinned. 'I'll bet you got some little bubble-gummers of your own. Want to bet, Rosso?' he said and turned to Ranatti.

'What is this?' asked the man, his face white, jaw twitching. 'Answer me!' Simeone commanded. 'You got kids? And a wife?'

'I'm getting out of here,' said the man, walking toward Simeone who shoved him back against the wall of the restroom.

'No need for that,' said Gant, standing on the threshold.

'I'm not getting rough,' said Simeone. 'I just want to know if he's got a wife and kids. They almost always do. Do you, man?'

'Yes, of course. But why are you arresting me? Lord, I didn't do any-thing,' he said as Simeone handcuffed his hands behind his back.

'Always handcuff fruits,' Simeone smiled to Roy. 'Always. No excep-tions.'

As they were leaving the park, Roy walked behind with Gant.

'How do you like working fruits, kid?' asked Gant.

'Not too good,' Roy answered.

'Look over there,' said Gant, pointing toward the pond where a slender young man in tight coffee-colored pants and a lacy orange shirt was minc-ing along the edge of the water.

'That's what I thought all fruits looked like,' said Roy.

The young man stopped every thirty feet or so, genuflected, crossed himself, and prayed silently. Roy counted six genuflections before he reached the street where he disappeared in the pedestrian traffic.

'Some of them are pretty pitiful. That one's trying to resist,' Gant shrugged, offering Roy a cigarette which he accepted. 'They're the most promiscuous creatures that ever walked the earth. They're so goddamned unsatisfied they're always seeking. Now you see why we try to work whores, and gambling, and bars as much as possible. And remember, you can get the shit kicked out of you working fruits. On top of all the rest of the crap you got to put up with, it's dangerous as hell.'

Roy's mind drifted back then, back to college. He had been reminded of someone. Of course! he thought suddenly, as he remembered the mannerisms of Professor Raymond. It had never occurred to him before! Professor Raymond was a fruit!

'Can we work whores tomorrow night?' asked Roy.

'Sure, kid,' Gant laughed.

At midnight, Roy was getting tired of sitting in the vice office watching Gant do his paper work as he talked baseball with Phillips and Sergeant Jacovitch. Ranatti and Simeone had not returned since taking the fruit to jail, but Roy heard Jacovitch mention their names during a phone conversation and he cursed when he hung up and muttered something to Gant while Roy glanced over vice reports in the other room.

Ranatti and Simeone rushed in just after midnight. 'Ready to raid The Cave?' Ranatti grinned.

'I got a call, Rosso,' said Jacovitch quietly. 'Some whore called and asked for the sergeant. Said her name was Rosie Redfield and that you guys tore the wiring out of her car and flattened her tires.'

'Us?' said Ranatti.

'She named you,' said Jacovitch soberly to the young men who did not seem overly surprised.

'That's the whore that thinks she owns Sixth and Alvarado,' said Simeone. 'We told you about her, Jake. We busted her three times last month and she got her cases consolidated and got summary probation. We've done everything to try to get her to hustle someplace else. Hell, we got two vice complaints about her hustling on that corner.'

'Did you know where she parked her car?' asked Jacovitch.

'Yeah, we know,' Ranatti admitted. 'Did she say she saw us fucking up her car?'

'No, if she did, I'd have to take a personnel complaint against you. You realize that, don't you? There'd be an investigation. She just suspects it was you.'

'This ain't no game we're playing out there,' said Simeone. 'We've done our best to get rid of that bitch. She's not just a whore, she's a booster and a hugger mugger and everything else. She's a rotten bitch and works for Silver Shapiro and he's a rotten pimp and extortionist and God knows what all.'

'I'm not even going to ask you if you did it,' said Jacovitch, 'but I'm warning you guys for the last time about this kind of stuff. You got to stay strictly within the law and Department regulations.'

'You know what, Jake?' asked Ranatti, sitting heavily in a chair, and propping a crepe-soled shoe on a typewriter table. 'If we did just that, we wouldn't convict one asshole a week. The goddamn streets wouldn't be safe even for us.'

It was five minutes till one when Roy parked his private car at Fourth and Broadway and walked toward Main in the direction of The Cave. It was a warm evening, but he shivered as he stood waiting for a green light. He knew the rest of the squad was ready and already in position and he knew there was no particular danger in this, but he was unarmed and felt terribly alone and vulnerable. He walked timorously through the oval doorway of The Cave and stood for a moment adjusting his eyes to the blackness, bumping his head on a plaster stalactite which hung down next to the second entryway. The spacious interior was jammed with people and he shouldered his way to the bar, already beginning to perspire, and found a space to stand between a leering red-haired homosexual and a Negro prostitute who looked him over and apparently did not find him as interesting as the balding man to her left who nervously rubbed his shoulder against her large loose breasts.

Roy started to order a whiskey and soda, remembered Ranatti, and asked for a bottle of beer instead. He ignored the glass, wiped the mouth of the bottle with his hand and drank from the bottle.

Roy saw several booths and tables occupied by lesbians, the butches fondling the femmes, kissing shoulders and arms. Homosexual male couples filled a good part of the room but when one couple tried to dance, mannish female waitresses ordered them to sit, pointing at the 'No Dancing' sign. There were prostitutes of all descriptions, some of whom were plainly men masquerading as women, but the Negro next to him was certainly a woman, he thought, as she shook a shoulder strap free so the bald man could see more of the vast brown orbs.

Roy saw a group of leather jackets behind a latticework partition which seemed to be drawing groups of onlookers and he squeezed past several people milling in the aisles and beating the tables with glasses to the strident sounds of an outrageous red jukebox. When he got to the latticework he peered through and saw two young men, long sideburned twins with chain belts, arm wrestling on a swaying table with a burning candle at each side of the table to scorch the back of the loser's hand. Two men watched fascinated from a booth to Roy's right. One was collegiate-looking and blond. The other was equally clean-cut, with thick dark hair. They looked as out of place as Roy felt he *must* look, but when the curling hair on one wrestler's hand began sizzling in the flame of the candle, the young blond man squeezed the thigh of the other, who responded with an excited gasp, and as the candle burned flesh, he held the ear of his blond friend and twisted it violently. No one but Roy seemed to notice, as the onlookers worshiped the searing flame.

Roy returned to the bar and ordered a second beer and a third. It was almost one-thirty and he thought the information had been false when suddenly the jukebox was unplugged and the crowd became silent.

'Lock the door,' shouted the bartender, a hairy giant, who announced to the crowd, 'The show starts now. Nobody leaves till it's over.'

Roy watched the butch waitress switch on the movie projector which was placed on a table near the latticework that divided the two sections of the room. The white wall was the projection screen and the crowd burst into laughter as a silent Woody Woodpecker cartoon flashed on the wall.

Roy was trying to figure it all out when Woody Woodpecker was suddenly replaced by two oiled naked men who were wrestling on a filthy mat in a ramshackle gymnasium. A cheer went up from the leather jackets across the floor, but after a few moments the scene shifted abruptly to two naked women, one young and reasonably attractive, the other puffy and middle-aged. They nibbled and kissed and fondled on an unmade bed for a few moments while the lesbian tables whistled, but the scene shifted another time to a backyard where a woman in a puckered bathing suit orally copulated a fat man in khaki shorts and most of the crowd laughed but no one cheered. Then it was back to the naked male wrestlers which brought some more groans and catcalls from the leather jackets. When the film slipped off the sprocket and the picture jumped out of focus in a crucial scene in the lewd wrestling match, Roy was surprised to see the bald man, who had previously been interested in the Negro prostitute, jerk off his brown loafer and begin banging on the bar shouting, 'Fix it! Hurry up, fix the goddamn thing!' After that, he left the prostitute and joined the leather jackets in the other room.

They were still working on the film when Roy sidled along the bar toward the men's restroom. He walked unnoticed through a doorway and found himself in a dimly lit corridor and saw a sign marked 'Women?' on the left and 'Men?' on the right. He entered the men's restroom, smelled marijuana unmistakably, and found a leather jacket just coming from the toilet by the open window.

Roy pretended to wash his hands while the young man, in Levis, cleated boots, and leather jacket, fumbled drunkenly with the chain around his waist. He had an enormous head with unkempt hair and a ragged light brown moustache.

Roy stalled for a moment and fidgeted with a paper towel but could not get to the window for the signal.

Finally the leather jacket looked at him. 'I'm not interested right now, blondie,' he leered. 'See me later. Give me your phone number.'

'Go to hell,' Roy said, infuriated, forgetting the window for a moment.

'Oh, you got a little spunk? I like that,' said the leather jacket and he put his fists on his hips and looked even thicker through the chest and back. 'Maybe you could interest me after all,' he grinned lasciviously.

'Stay right there,' warned Roy to the advancing barrel-chested sadist, who began uncoiling the chain around his waist.

Roy then, at that moment, for the first time in his life knew real fear, hopeless fear, which debilitated, overwhelmed, flashed and froze him. He was panic-stricken and never clearly knew how he had done it, but he knew later he kicked the assailant once, just as the chain writhed and slid around his fist. The leather jacket screamed and fell to the floor holding his groin with one hand but grabbed Roy's leg with the other and as Roy pulled frantically the whiskered face pressed on his leg and Roy felt the teeth, but jerked free as the teeth closed on his calf. He heard a tearing noise and saw a patch of his trousers hanging from the whiskered mouth, and then Roy leaped over him into the toilet area and thought wildly that the other leather jackets had heard the scream. Roy hurled a metal wastebasket through the glass and scrambled out the window, dropping five feet to a concrete walk where he was struck by the beam of a flashlight in the hand of a uniformed policeman.

'You the vice officer we're waiting for?' the officer whispered.

'Yeah, let's go,' Roy said and ran for the front of The Cave where he saw a dozen blue uniforms already approaching. The vice car zoomed up in front of the bar and Gant and Ranatti alighted carrying 'the key' and they slammed it into the double doors of The Cave as Roy shuffled across the sidewalk and sat on the fender of the vice car and felt like he would vomit.

Roy stepped back away from the entrance and decided he was too sick to go back into that foul steamy place and he watched the door finally fall from the hinges and the wagon pulled up in front. Now there were at least fifteen bluesuits and they formed a sweeping V and Roy was panting from his heart-cracking effort, thinking now he would vomit, and he watched the vast blue wedge of bodies insert itself into the opening of The Cave. Soon the blue line disappeared inside and the others came squirming, running, tumbling out. The drunks were thrown into the wagon expertly by two big policemen wearing black gloves. The others were shoved into various directions, and Roy, holding a handkerchief over his mouth, watched them as they spilled into the street, all gray and brown and faceless now as the lights over the entrance were turned off and the garish colors and frivolity were extinguished. Roy wondered when they would stop coming but after five minutes they still flowed out into the street, noisy and perspiring. Roy thought he could smell them, and they flowed swiftly up and down the street when they hit the sidewalk, those who were not being booked. Soon Roy saw two policemen helping the leather-covered bear out the door and he was still holding his groin. Roy was about to tell them to book that one, but he saw he was being put in the wagon anyway so he remained silent and continued watching in sickened fascination until the street was quiet and the cathartic blue wedge of policemen withdrew from the mouth of The Cave. The wagon drove off as Ranatti and Simeone and Gant had the owner and two barmaids in custody and were nailing the broken front door closed and padlocking it.

'What's the matter, kid?' asked Gant walking up to Roy who still had the handkerchief held to his mouth.

'I had a little scuffle in there.'

'You did?' said Gant, putting a hand on each of Roy's shoulders.

'I'm sick,' said Roy.

'Did you get hurt?' asked Gant, his eyes wide as he examined Roy's face.

'I'm just sick,' said Roy, shaking his head. 'I just saw the asshole of the world get a blue enema.'

'Yeah? Well get used to it, kid,' said Gant. 'Everything you seen in there will be legal before long.'

'Let's get out of here,' Simeone called from behind the wheel of the vice car. He pointed at a crawling yellow street cleaner which was inching down Main Street. Roy and Gant squeezed in the car with the arrestees and Simeone and Ranatti.

Roy leaned out the window as they drove away and saw the street cleaner squirt a stream of water over the street and curb around The Cave. The machine hissed and roared and Roy watched the filth being washed away.

August 1963

THIRTEEN
The Madonna

Serge wondered if any of his academy classmates had plainclothes assignments yet. Probably Fehler or Isenberg and a few of the others had made it to vice or to a felony squad. But not many of them, he guessed. He had been astonished when Sergeant Farrell asked him if he would like to work felony cars this month and then if he worked out it might be a permanent assignment.

This was his second week in F-Cars. He had never realized how much more comfortable it could be to do police work in a business suit rather than the heavy woolen uniforms and unwieldy Sam Browne belt. He wore a four-inch lightweight Colt which he had just bought last payday after seeing how heavy the six-inch Smith rides on your hip in a plainclothes holster.

He suspected that Milton had recommended him to Sergeant Farrell for the F-Car. Milton and Farrell were friends and Farrell seemed to like and respect the old man. However he got here, it was fine to get out of the black and white car for a while. Not that the street people did not know them, two men in business suits, in a low-priced, four-door Plymouth – two men who drove slowly and watched streets and people. But at least they were inconspicuous enough to avoid being troubled by the endless numbers of people who need a policeman to solve an endless number of problems that a policeman is not qualified to solve, but must make an attempt to solve, because he is an easily accessible member of the establishment and traditionally vulnerable to criticism. Serge happily blew three smoke rings which would have been perfect except that the breeze took them, the breeze which was pleasant because it had been a very hot summer and the nights were not as cool as Los Angeles nights usually are.

Serge's partner, Harry Ralston, seemed to sense his contentment.

'Think you're going to like F-Cars?' he grinned, turning toward Serge who was slumped in the seat, admiring an exceptionally voluptuous girl in a clinging white cotton dress.

'I'm going to like it,' Serge smiled.

'I know how you feel. It's great to get out of uniform, ain't it?'

'Great.'

'I was in uniform eight years,' said Ralston. 'I was really ready. Got five years in felony cars now, and I still like it. Beats uniform patrol.'

'I've got a lot to learn,' said Serge.

'You'll learn. It's different from patrol. You're already learning that, I think.'

Serge nodded, dropping the cigarette out the window, a luxury he never could have allowed himself in a black and white car where some citizen with an ax to grind might take his car number and report him to his sergeant for the vehicle code violation of dropping the lighted substance from a car.

'Ready for code seven,' asked Ralston, looking at his watch. 'It's not nine o'clock yet, but I'm hungry as hell.'

'I can eat,' said Serge, picking up the mike. 'Four-Frank-One requesting code seven at Brooklyn and Mott.'

'Four-Frank-One, okay seven,' said the Communications operator and Serge checked his watch to be sure and clear over the radio when their forty-five minutes were up. It irritated him that the Department made them work an eight hour and forty-five minute shift. Since the forty-five minutes was his own time, he made sure he used every minute of it.

'Hello, Mr. Rosales,' said Ralston, as they took the booth on the far wall nearest the kitchen. It was noisy and hot from the stoves in this particular booth, but Ralston loved to be near the kitchen smells. He was a man who lived to eat, Serge thought, and his incredible appetite belied his lankiness.

'Good evening, señores,' smiled the old man, coming from behind the counter where three customers sat. He wiped the table which needed no wiping. He poured two glasses of water for them after swiping at the inside of Ralston's already sparkling glass with a dazzling white towel he carried over a sloping shoulder. The old man wore a full moustache which exactly suited him, Serge thought.

'What will you have, señores?' asked Mr. Rosales, giving them each a hand-printed menu that misspelled the dishes in Spanish on the right side as well as in English on the left side. They can live here all their lives and never learn English, thought Serge. They never learn Spanish either. Just a strange anglicized version, of both, which the educated, old country Mexicans scoff at.

'I'll have *huevos rancheros*,' said Ralston, with an accent that made Serge wince in spite of himself.

The old man seemed to love it however, when Ralston tried Spanish. 'And you, señor?'

'I guess I'll have *chile relleno*,' said Serge with a pronunciation that was every bit as anglicized as Ralston's. All of the officers knew by now that he spoke no Spanish and understood only a few words.

'Smell the onions and green chile,' said Ralston while Mr. Rosales' pudgy little wife was preparing the food in the back room which had been converted into an inadequately ventilated kitchen.

'How can you tell it's green chile?' asked Serge, feeling jovial tonight. 'Maybe it's red chile or maybe it's not chile at all.'

'My nose never fails,' said Ralston, touching the side of his nostril. 'You should quit smoking and your sense of smell would become acute like mine.'

Serge thought that a beer would do good with the *chile relleno* and he wondered if Ralston knew Serge better, would he order a beer with his dinner? They were working plainclothes now, and a beer with dinner wouldn't hurt. Vice officers of course drank freely, and detectives were legendary lushes, so why not F-Car officers? he thought. But he realized that he was drinking too much beer lately and was going to have to trim off ten pounds before his next physical or the doctor would surely send his captain 'a fat man letter'. He hadn't had much beer in Hollywood where martinis were his drink. It had been very easy to get to enjoy martinis. He had been drunk a good deal of his off-duty time. But that was all part of his education, he thought. The body should not be mistreated, at least not badly. He was considering cutting down his smoking to a pack a day and had again begun playing handball at the academy. There was something about being back in Hollenbeck that restored his health.

He looked more than casually at the girl who brought their dinners, holding the burning dishes with two colorful pot holders, the drops of perspiration shining on her bronze cheekbones and on the too long upper lip. She wore her hair braided, close to the head like an Indian, and Serge guessed she was not more than seventeen. Her hands were ghostly white from the flour and they reminded him of his mother's hands. He wondered how long she had been this side of the border.

'Thank you,' he said, smiling as she set the plate in front of him. She smiled back, a clean smile, and Serge noticed she wore only a little lipstick. The heavy eyelashes and perfect brows were not man-made.

'*Gracias, señorita,*' said Ralston, leering at the plate of *huevos rancheros* and ignoring the girl who placed it in front of him.

'*De nada, señor,*' she smiled again.

'Cute kid,' said Serge, toying with the rice and refried beans which were still too hot to eat.

Ralston nodded with enthusiasm, and dumped another ladle of home-made chile sauce on the eggs, the rice, everything. Then he sloshed his large flour tortilla around through all of it and took an enormous bite.

Mr. Rosales whispered to the girl and she returned to the table just as Serge's food was becoming cool enough to eat and Ralston's was half gone.

'Joo wan',' she said. 'Joo weesh ...' She stopped and turned to Mr. Rosales who nodded his approval.

'Coffee,' he urged her. 'Coff – ee.'

'I don' talk *inglés* good,' she laughed to Serge who was thinking how smooth and slim she looked, yet how strong. Her breasts were round and the extra weight womanhood brings could only improve her.

'I'll have some coffee,' Serge smiled.

'*Sí, café, por favor*,' said Ralston, a forkful of frijoles poised at his mobile lip.

When the girl disappeared into the kitchen Mr. Rosales came over to the table. 'Everything is alright?' he smiled through the great moustache.

'Dee-licious,' Ralston murmured.

'Who's the little girl?' asked Serge, sipping at the last of his water which Mr. Rosales hurried to refill.

'She is the daughter of my *compadre*. She just got here from Guadalajara last Monday. I swore to my *compadre* many years ago that if I ever made good in this country I would send for his oldest girl, my godchild, and educate her like an American. He said it would be better to educate a boy and I agreed, but he never had a boy. Not to this day. Eleven girls.'

Serge laughed and said, 'She looks like she'll do.'

'Yes, Mariana is very smart,' he nodded enthusiastically. 'And she was just eighteen. I am sending her to night school next month to learn English and then we shall see what she wants to do.'

'She'll probably find some young guy and get married before you have anything to say about it,' said Ralston, punctuating his pronouncement with a repressed belch.

'Maybe so,' Mr. Rosales sighed. 'You know, it is so much better here than in Mexico that the people do not care to make themselves a great success. Just to be here is so much more than they ever dreamed, that it is enough. They become content to work in a car wash or a sewing factory. But I think that she is a smart girl and will do better.'

The girl made three trips to their table during the remainder of the meal, but didn't try English again.

Ralston caught Serge watching her because he said, 'She's legal, you know. Eighteen.'

'You're kidding. I wouldn't raid a nursery.'

'Some baby,' said Ralston and Serge hoped he wouldn't light one of his cheap cigars. When they were in the car with the windows open they weren't so bad. 'She looks like a young Dolores Del Rio to me,' said Ralston, blowing two heavy palls of smoke over the table.

She did not resemble Dolores Del Rio, Serge thought. But she had the thing that made Del Rio the beloved woman of Mexico, an object of veneration by millions of Mexicans who had seldom if ever seen her in a movie – she too had the madonna look.

'What's your last name?' asked Serge, as she made her last trip to the table with a coffee refill. He knew it was customary for policemen who had received a free meal to tip a quarter, but he slipped seventy-five cents under a plate.

'*Mande, señor?*' she said turning to Mr. Rosales who was busy with a counter customer.

'Your last name,' said Ralston carefully. 'Mariana *qué?*'

'Ah,' she smiled. 'Mariana Paloma,' and then she turned from Serge's steady gaze and took some of the plates to the kitchen.

'Paloma,' said Serge. 'A dove. It fits.'

'I eat here once a week,' said Ralston eyeing Serge curiously. 'We don't want to burn the place up with too many free meals.'

'Don't worry,' said Serge quickly, getting the implication. 'This is your eating spot. I'll never come here unless I'm working with you.'

'The girl is your business,' said Ralston. 'You can come off duty if you want, but I'd hate for someone to burn up the eating spot I cultivated for years. He used to charge me half price and now it's free.'

'Don't worry,' Serge repeated. 'And that girl doesn't interest me like that, for God's sake. I've got enough female problems without a kid that can't speak English.'

'You single guys,' Ralston sighed. 'I should have those problems. You got one lined up tonight after work?'

'I got one,' Serge answered without enthusiasm.

'She got a friend?'

'Not that I know of,' Serge smiled.

'What's she look like?' Ralston leered, now that the hunger drive was apparently slaked.

'A honey blonde. All ass,' Serge answered, and that about described Margie who lived in the upstairs rear of his apartment building. The landlady had already warned him about being more discreet when he left Margie's apartment in the morning.

'A real honey blonde, huh?' Ralston murmured.

'What's real?' asked Serge, and then thought, she's real enough in her own way, and it doesn't matter if the glistening honey is the fruit of the hairdresser's art because everything of beauty in the world has been tinted or somehow transformed by a clever artisan. You can always discover how it's done if you look closely enough. But who wants to look? During those times when he needed her, Margie was plenty real, he thought.

'What's a bachelor do besides lay everything in sight?' asked Ralston. 'You happy being alone?'

'I don't even want a roommate to share expenses. I like being alone.' Serge was the first to get up and turned to look for the girl who was out of sight in the kitchen.

'*Buenas noches*, Señor Rosales,' Ralston called.

'*Ándale pues,*' shouted Mr. Rosales, over the din of a too loud mariachi record which someone had played on the jukebox.

'You watch TV a lot?' asked Ralston when they were back in the car. 'I'm asking about single life because me and the old lady aren't getting along very good at all right now and who knows what might happen.'

'Oh?' said Serge hoping Ralston would not bore him with a long account of his marital problems which so many other partners had done during the long hours on patrol when the night was quiet because it was a week night, when the people were between paydays and welfare checks, and were not drinking. 'Well, I read a lot, novels mostly. I play handball at least three or four times a week at the academy. I go to movies and watch a little TV. I go to a lot of Dodger games. There isn't all the carousing you think.' And then he remembered Hollywood again. 'At least not anymore. That can get old, too.'

'Maybe I'll be finding out,' said Ralston, driving toward Hollenbeck Park.

Serge took the flashlight from under the seat and placed it on the seat beside him. He turned the volume of the radio up slightly, hoping it would dissuade Ralston from trying to compete with it, but Serge felt certain he was going to hear a domestic tirade.

'Four-Frank-One, clear,' said Serge into the mike.

'Maybe you can entice little Dolores Del Rio to your pad if you play your cards right,' said Ralston as the Communications operator acknowledged they were clear. Ralston began a slow half-hearted residential burglar patrol in the area east of the park which had been hard hit by a cat burglar the past few weeks. They had already decided that after midnight, they would prowl the streets on foot which seemed to be the only effective way to catch the cat.

'I told you that babies don't interest me,' said Serge.

'Maybe she's got a cousin or a fat aunt or something. I'm ready for some action. My old lady shut me off. I could grow a long moustache for her like that actor that plays in all the Mexican movies, what's his name?'

'Pedro Armendariz,' said Serge without thinking.

'Yeah, that guy. It seems like he's on every marquee around here, him and Dolores.'

'They were even the big stars when I was a kid,' said Serge gazing at the cloudless sky which was only slightly smoggy tonight.

'Yeah? You went to Mexican movies? I thought you don't speak Spanish.'

'I understood a little when I was a kid,' Serge answered, sitting up in the seat. 'Anybody could understand those simple pictures. All guns and guitars.'

Ralston quieted down and the radio droned on and he relaxed again. He found himself thinking of the little dove and he wondered if she would be as satisfying as Elenita who was the first girl he ever had, the dusky fifteen-year-old daughter of a bracero who was well worn by the time she seduced Serge when he himself was fifteen. He had returned to her every Friday night for a year and sometimes she would have him, but sometimes

418

there would be older boys already there and he would go away to avoid trouble. Elenita was everybody's girl but he liked to pretend she was his girl until one June afternoon when the gossip blazed through the school that Elenita had been taken from school because she was pregnant. Several boys, mostly the members of the football squad, began to talk in frightened whispers. Then came the rumor a few days later that Elenita was also found to have been syphilitic and the frightened whispers became frantic. Serge had terrible fantasies of elephantine pus-filled genitals and he prayed and lit three candles every other day until he felt the danger period had passed even though he never knew for sure if it had, or even whether poor Elenita was really so afflicted. He could ill afford thirty cents for candles in those days when the part-time gas pumping job only netted nine dollars a week which he had to give to his mother.

Then he felt guilty for thinking about the girl Mariana like this because eighteen years, despite what the law said, did not make you an adult. He was twenty-six now and wondered if another ten years would do the job for him. If he could continue to profit from all the lies and cruelty and violence this job had shown him, maybe he could grow up sooner. If he could quit seeing a saint in the tawny face of a perfectly healthy little animal like Mariana he would be so much closer to maturity. Maybe that's the part of being a Chicano I can't shake off, Serge thought, the superstitious longing – brown magic – The Sorceress of Guadelup – or Guadalajara – a simple bastard yearning for the Madonna in a miserable Mexican restaurant.

FOURTEEN
The Operator

'No wonder Plebesly gets more whore offers than anybody else on the squad. Look at him. Does this boy look like a cop?' roared Bonelli, stocky, middle-aged and balding, with dark whiskers which when they were two days old were dirty gray. They always seemed at least two days old, and whenever Sergeant Anderson objected, Bonelli just reminded him that this was Wilshire vice squad and not a goddamned military academy and he was only trying to look like the rest of the assholes out on the street so he could fit in better as an undercover operator. He always addressed Anderson by his first name which was Mike and so did the others because it was customary in a vice squad to be more intimate with your supervisors, but Gus did not like or trust Anderson and neither did the others. He was on the lieutenant's list and would probably someday be a captain at least, but the lanky young man with the blond sparse moustache was a natural disciplinarian and would be better, they all concluded, in a patrol function which was more GI than a vice squad.

'One whore Gus got last week never did believe he was a cop,' laughed Bonelli, throwing his feet up on the table in the vice office and spilling some cigar ashes on a report which Sergeant Anderson was writing. Anderson's lips tightened under the pale moustache, but he said nothing, got up and went to his own desk to work.

'I remember that one, Sal,' said Petrie to Bonelli. 'Old Salvatore had to save Gus from that whore. She thought he was a PO-lice impersonator when he finally badged her.'

They all laughed at Petrie's affected Negro dialect, even Hunter, the slim Negro officer who was the only Negro on the night watch. He laughed heartily, but Gus laughed nervously partly because they were roasting him but partly because he could never get used to Negro jokes in front of a Negro even though he had been a vice officer for three months now and should be accustomed to the merciless chiding which went on ritually every night before they went out to the streets. Each of them subjected the others to cracks which stopped at neither race, religion, nor physical defects.

Yet the six policemen and Sergeant Handle, who was one of *them*, went to Bonelli's apartment at least once a week after work and played pool and drank a case of beer at least. Or sometimes they went to Sergeant Handle's house and played poker all night. Once when they had gone to Hunter's apartment which was here in Wilshire Division in the racially mixed neighborhood near Pico and La Brea, Bonelli had made a whispered remark to Hunter that he had been kicked in the shoulder by a whore while making a lewd conduct arrest and that at his age arthritis might set in. Bonelli couldn't pull the sleeve of his outrageous Hawaiian shirt over the hairy shoulder to show Hunter because the shoulder was too large, and finally, Bonelli said, 'Anyway, the bruise is the color of your ass.' When Hunter's lithe mahogany-colored wife Marie, who had entered the room unnoticed, said, 'What, red?' with a perfectly sober expression, Gus began to enjoy the camaraderie which was not affected or strained and did not pretend that being policemen made them brothers or more than brothers.

But they did have a secret which seemed to unite them more closely than normal friendship and that was the knowledge that they *knew* things, basic things about strength and weakness, courage and fear, good and evil, especially good and evil. Even though arguments would rage especially when Bonelli was drunk, they all agreed on very fundamental things and usually did not discuss these things because any policeman who had common sense and had been a policeman long enough would surely learn the truth and it was useless to talk about it. They mostly talked about their work and women, and either fishing, golf, or baseball, depending upon whether Farrell or Schulmann or Hunter was controlling the conversation. But when Petrie was working they talked about movies, since Petrie had an uncle who was a director, and Petrie was starstruck even though he had been a policeman five years.

There were a few more cracks made about Gus's meek appearance and how none of the whores could believe he was a policeman which made him the best whore operator on the watch, but then they began talking about other things because Gus never joked back and it was not as much fun as picking on Bonelli who had a caustic tongue and was quick at repartee.

'Hey, Marty,' said Farrell to Hunter who was trying to pencil out a follow-up to a vice complaint. He held his forehead in a smooth brown hand while the pencil moved jerkily and stopped often while Hunter laughed at something Bonelli said. It was obvious that Hunter would rather work with Bonelli than any of the others, but Sergeant Anderson figured the deployment carefully so that certain men were working on certain nights because he had fixed opinions on supervision and deployment. He informed them that he was very close to his degree in government and he had twelve units in psychology and only *he* was in a position to know who should work with whom, and Bonelli had whispered gruffly, 'How did this cunt get on the vice squad?'

'Hey, Marty,' Farrell repeated, until Hunter looked up. 'How come you people are always complaining that there aren't enough blacks in this job or that group or something and then when we *do* use enough you still bitch. Listen to this article in the *Times*, "The NAACP sought a class action on behalf of all the men on death's row because it contends a disproportionate number of them are Negroes."'

'People are never satisfied,' said Hunter.

'By the way, Marty, you getting your share of that white liberal pussy that's floating around the *ghetto* these days?' asked Bernbaum.

'Marty's going to pass the sergeant's exam this time, ain't you, Marty?' said Bonelli. 'He'll get forty points on his own and they'll give him forty more for being black.'

'And when we get to be on top, first thing I'm going to do is go after your woman, Sal,' said Hunter, glancing up from his report.

'Oh, Christ, Marty, do me a favor, go after Elsie right now, will you? That bitch does nothing but talk about marriage anymore and me with three divorces behind me. I need another wife like...'

'Do any of you have any rubbers?' asked Sergeant Anderson, suddenly walking into the working area of the vice office separated from his desk by a row of lockers.

'No, if we think a broad is bad enough for rubbers, we generally get a head job,' said Farrell, his close-set blue eyes examining Anderson with humor.

'I was referring to the use of rubbers for evidence containers,' said Anderson coldly. 'We still use them to pour drinks into, don't we?'

'We got a box in the locker, Mike,' said Bonelli, and they became quiet when they saw he disliked Farrell's joke. 'Working a bar tonight?'

'We've had a complaint about The Cellar for two weeks now. I thought we'd try to take it.'

'They serving after hours?' asked Farrell.

'If you could take time out from your joke writing and look at the vice complaints you'd see that the bartender at The Cellar lives in an apartment upstairs and that after two o'clock he sometimes invites customers up to the pad where he continues to operate a bar. After hours.'

'We'll try it for you tonight, Mike,' said Bonelli with his conciliatory tone, but Gus thought that the heavily browed brown eyes were not conciliatory. They fixed Anderson with a bland expression.

'I want to work it myself,' said Anderson. 'I'll meet you and Plebesly at Third and Western at eleven and we'll decide then whether we go together or separate.'

'I can't go at all,' said Bonelli. 'I made too many pinches around there. The bartender knows me.'

'Might be a good idea for you to go in with one of us,' said Bernbaum, scratching his wiry brush of red hair with a pencil. 'We could have a drink and leave. They wouldn't suspect the joint was full of cops. They'd probably be satisfied that everything was cool after us two left.'

'I think there's a couple of whores working in there,' said Hunter. 'Me and Bonelli were in there one night and there was an ugly little brunette and another old bat that sure looked like hookers.'

'Alright, we'll all meet at Andre's Restaurant at eleven and talk it over,' said Anderson going back to his desk. 'And another thing, the streetwalkers are getting pretty thick out there on Sunday and Monday nights, I hear. They must know those are the vice squad's nights off so some of you are going to start working Sundays.'

'You guys see those magazines the day watch picked up at a trick pad?' asked Bernbaum, and the conversation again picked up now that Anderson was finished.

'I seen enough of that garbage to last me a lifetime,' said Bonelli.

'No, these weren't regular nudie mags,' said Bernbaum. 'These were pinup mags, but somebody had taken about a hundred Polaroid pictures of guys' dicks and cut them out and stuck them on the girls in the magazines.'

'Psychos. The world is full of psychos,' said Farrell.

'By the way, are we working fruits tonight, Marty?' asked Petrie.

'Lord, no. We busted enough last week to last all month.'

'Think I'll go on days for a while,' said Bernbaum. 'I'd like to work books. Get me away from all these slimes you have to bust at night.'

'Well I'll guarantee you, bookmakers are assholes,' said Bonelli. 'They're mostly Jews, ain't they?'

'Oh yeah, the Mafia's all Jews too,' said Bernbaum. 'I think there's a few Italian bookmakers up on Eighth Street last I heard.'

Gus felt Bonelli look at him when Bernbaum said it and he knew Bonelli was thinking about Lou Scalise, the bookmaking agent and collector for the loan sharks whom Bonelli hated with a hatred that now made Gus's palms sweat as he thought of it.

'Incidentally, Petrie,' said Marty Hunter, slamming the logbook, 'the next time we take a fighter, how about using the sap on *him*, not on *me*. Last night we take Biff's Cocktail Lounge for serving a drunk and when we try to bust the drunk he starts a fight and *I* get sapped by my partner.'

'Bullshit, Marty. I just grazed your elbow with the sap.'

'Anytime more than one policeman jumps a suspect the policeman ends up getting hurt,' said Farrell. 'I remember the night we had that fairy lumberjack.' They laughed and Farrell looked appealingly to Bonelli. 'Yeah, the guy was a lumberman from Oregon. And he's a suck*or* not a suck*ee*. Comes to LA and wears eye shadow. Anyway, he's swishing around Lafayette Park and gropes Bonelli, remember, Sal?'

'I'll never forget that asshole.'

'Anyway, there were five of us in the park that night and for fifteen minutes we all battle that puke. He threw me in the pond and threw Steve in there twice. We thumped the shit out of each other with saps and it finally ended when Sal held his head underwater for a few minutes. He never did get sapped or even hurt and every one of us policemen had to get patched up.'

'Funny thing,' said Bernbaum, 'when Sal had him about half drowned and he was panicky and all, know what he does? He yells, "Help, police!" Imagine that, with five policemen all over him, he yells that.'

'He know you were policemen?' asked Gus.

'Sure he knew,' said Farrell. 'He said to Bonelli, "Ain't no cop in the world can take me." He didn't figure on five, though.'

'I had a guy yell that one time when I was in full uniform,' said Bernbaum. 'Funny what people say when you're wrestling them off to jail.'

'Garbage,' said Bonelli. 'Garbage.'

'You handle these assholes, you got to wash your hands *before* you take a leak,' said Hunter.

'Remember the time the swish kissed you, Ben?' said Farrell to Bernbaum, and the ruddy-faced young policeman winced in disgust.

'Walked into a bar where we got a complaint some fruits were dancing,' said Hunter, 'and this little blond swish flits right up to Ben as we were sitting at the bar and plants a smack right on his kisser and then he dances away into the dark. Ben goes to the head and washes his mouth with hand soap and we leave without even working the joint.'

'I heard enough. I'm going to take a crap and then we're going to work,' said Bonelli standing up, scratching his stomach and lumbering toward the toilet across the hall.

'You say you're going in there to give birth to a sergeant?' said Farrell, winking at Petrie who shook his head and whispered, 'Anderson doesn't appreciate your humor.'

When Bonelli returned, he and Gus gathered their binoculars and small flashlights and batons which they would put under the seat of the vice car in case of emergency. After reassuring Anderson they wouldn't forget to meet him they went to their car without deciding what they were going to do.

'Want to work complaints, or whores?' asked Bonelli.

'We got some crappy three eighteens,' said Gus. 'One about the floating card game in the hotel sounds like fun, but it only goes on Saturdays.'

'Yeah, let's work whores,' said Bonelli.

'Tail or operate?'

'Feel like operating?'

'I don't mind. I'll get my car,' said Gus.

'Got enough gas? That cheap prick Anderson won't break loose with any more operating money till next week. You'd think it was his bread and not the city's.'

'I've got gas,' said Gus. 'I'll take a sweep around Washington and La Brea and meet you in the back of the drive-in in fifteen minutes. Sooner, if I get a whore.'

'Get a whore. We need the pinches. This's been a slim month.'

Gus drove down West Boulevard to Washington and over Washington toward La Brea, but he hadn't gotten two blocks on Washington until he spotted two prostitutes. He was preparing to swing in toward the curb when he saw one was Margaret Pearl whom he had arrested almost three months ago when he first came to the vice squad and she would surely recognize him so he drove past. Already the pulse beat was advancing.

Gus remembered how it had been when he had first come to vice, or rather, he did not remember clearly. Those first nights and those first few arrests were difficult to envision coherently. There was a red cloud of fear enveloping his memory of those nights and that was something else he could not understand. Why did he see or rather feel a red mist about his memories when he was very much afraid? Why were all such memories red-tinged? Was it blood or fire or what? He had been so thoroughly frightened that the prostitutes had come to his car with their offers without questioning his identity. They hadn't dreamed he was a cop, and he had been a vastly successful vice operator. Now that he had some confidence and was no longer afraid except of things he should be afraid of, he was having to work much harder to get an offer. He was being turned down occasionally by girls who suspected he might be a policeman. Still, he could get twice the girls that any of the others could, only because he looked less like a policeman than any of them. Bonelli had told him it was not just his size. He was actually as tall and heavy as Marty Hunter. It was his diffidence, and Bonelli said that was a shame because the meek would inherit this miserable earth and Gus was too nice a guy to get stuck with it.

Gus hoped he would spot a white whore tonight. He had only arrested a few white whores and these were in bars on Vermont. He had never gotten a white streetwalker, although there were some of them here in this Negro half of Wilshire Division, but there weren't many. He thought Wilshire Division was a good division to work because of the variety. He could leave this Negro section and drive to the northwest boundaries of the division and be on the Miracle Mile and Restaurant Row. There was great variety in a few square miles. He was glad they had transferred him here, and almost immediately he had been marked as a future vice officer by his watch commander Lieutenant Goskin who had finally recommended him when the opening came. Gus wondered how many of his academy classmates were working plainclothes assignments yet. It was good, and it would be very good when the nauseating fear at last disappeared, the fear of being on the streets alone without the security of the blue uniform and badge. There was not too much else to really fear because if you were careful you would never have to fight anyone alone. If you were careful, you would always have Bonelli with you and Bonelli was as powerful and reassuring as Kilvinsky, but of course he did not have Kilvinsky's intellect.

Gus reminded himself that he had not answered Kilvinsky's last letter and he would do that tomorrow. It had worried him. Kilvinksy did not talk of the fishing and the lake and the peaceful mountains anymore. He talked of his children and his ex-wife and Kilvinsky had never talked of them when he had been here. He told of how his youngest son had written him and how his answer to the boy had been returned unopened and how he and his ex-wife had promised themselves years ago that it would be better if the boy forgot him, but he didn't say why. Gus knew that he had never gone East to visit them at his wife's home, and Gus never knew why, and he thought he would give a great deal to learn Kilvinsky's secrets. The latest letters indicated that Kilvinsky wanted to tell someone, wanted to tell Gus, and Gus decided to ask the big man to come to Los Angeles for a visit before the summer ended. Lord, it would be good to see his friend, Gus thought.

Then Gus realized he also had to send a check to his mother and John because it was less painful than going to see them and hearing how they could no longer make it on seventy-five a month from him even with the welfare check, because things were so dear today and poor John can't work, what with his slipped disc which Gus knew was an excuse for workman's compensation and a free ride from Gus. He was ashamed of his disgust as he thought of those weaklings and then he thought of Vickie. He wondered why his mother and his brother and his wife were all weaklings and depended so completely on him, and anger made him feel better as always, purged him. He saw a chubby Negro prostitute wiggling down Washington Boulevard toward Cloverdale. He pulled to the curb beside her and feigned the nervous smile which used to come so naturally.

'Hi baby,' said the prostitute looking in the window of his car as Gus went through his act of looking around as though fearful of seeing police.

'Hello,' said Gus. 'Want a ride?'

'I ain't out here to ride, baby,' said the prostitute watching him closely. 'At least I ain't out here to ride no cars.'

'Well I'm ready for anything,' said Gus, careful not to use any of the forbidden words of entrapment, even though Sal often argued with him that it is obviously impossible to entrap a whore, and he should only worry about entrapment later while writing the report because following the rules of the game was crazy. But Gus had answered that the rules made it all *civilized*.

'Look, Officer,' said the girl suddenly, 'why don't you go on up to the academy and play yourself a nice game of handball?'

'What?' said Gus blandly, as she examined his eyes.

'Jist a joke, baby,' she said finally. 'We got to be careful of vice officers.'

'Vice officers? Where?' said Gus gunning his motor. 'Maybe we better forget all about this.'

'Don't git nervous, honey,' she said, getting in the car and moving over to him. I'll give you such a nice French that you goin' to be glad you came down here tonight and don't worry none about the vice, I got them all paid off. They never bother me.'

'Where should I drive?' asked Gus.

'Down La Brea there. The Notel Motel. They got electric beds that vibrate and mirrors on the walls and ceilings and I got my own room reserved and it ain't goin' to cost you nothin' extra. It's all yours for fifteen dollars.'

'That sounds about right,' said Gus turning around and bouncing into the drive-in parking lot where Bonelli waited and Sal smiled through the heavy whiskers when he saw the prostitute.

'Hi baby, how's tricks?' said Bonelli opening the door for her.

Tricks was fine, Mr. Bonelli, till I hit on this one,' said the girl looking at Gus in disbelief. 'I would a swore he was a trick. He really a cop?'

Gus showed the prostitute his badge and got back in the car.

'He looks too motherfuckin' peaceable to be a cop,' said the prostitute in disgust as Gus drove out of the lot for another try before they made the long drive to Lincoln Heights jail.

Gus swept the block twice and then made a wider arc and finally decided to drive north on La Brea toward Venice where he had seen prostitutes the last few nights, and then he saw three Cadillacs parked side by side in the motel parking lot. He recognized a prostitute standing outside the purple Cadillac talking to Eddie Parsons and Big Dog Hanley and another Negro pimp he didn't recognize. Gus remembered the time they had arrested Big Dog when Gus had just arrived in Wilshire Division last year and was still working uniform patrol. They had stopped Big Dog for an unsafe lane change and while Gus was writing the ticket, his partner Drew Watson, an aggressive and inquisitive policeman, had spotted the pearl handle of a .22 revolver protruding from under the seat. He had retrieved it and arrested Big Dog, taking him to the detectives who, since Big Dog was a pimp, and had a five-page rap sheet, decided to book him for robbery, impound his car, and book his roll of flashmoney as evidence. When they counted out the bills which came to eight hundred dollars and told Big Dog they were booking the money, he broke down and wept, begging the detective not to book his money because it had been done to him before and it took months to get it back and it was *his* money so please don't book it. This surprised Gus in that Big Dog was at once the most insolent and arrogant of all the pimps and here he was begging for his roll and crying. Then Gus realized that without the roll and the Cadillac he was nothing, and Big Dog knew it and realized that the other pimps and prostitutes knew it, and he would lose everything. It would be taken away by pimps with a bankroll who commanded respect.

Then Gus saw the white prostitute at Venice and La Brea. He accelerated but she had already reached a red Cadillac hardtop and she was alone and getting in the driver's side when Gus slowed and double-parked next to her. He smiled his carefully rehearsed smile which had seldom failed so far.

'Looking for me, sweetie?' asked the girl, and up close she did not look nearly as good although the tight silver pants and black jersey fit well. Gus could see even in this light that the swirling blond hair was a wig and the makeup was garish.

'I think you're the one I've been looking for,' Gus smiled.

'Pull up in front of me and park,' said the girl. 'Then walk on back here and let's talk.'

Gus pulled in at the curb and turned his lights out, slipped the holstered two-inch Smith & Wesson under the seat, got out, and walked back to the Cadillac and up to the driver's side.

'Looking for action, sweetie?' asked the girl with a smile that Gus thought was rehearsed as carefully as his. 'Sure am,' he shot back with his own version of a smile.

'How much you willing to spend?' she said coyly and reached out the window with a long clawed finger and ran it seductively over his torso while she felt for a gun and he smiled to himself because he had left the gun in the car.

She seemed satisfied not feeling a gun or other evidence that he was a policeman and she apparently saw little use in wasting more time. 'How about a nice ten-dollar fuck?' she said.

'You don't mince words,' said Gus, pulling out the badge he had in his back pocket. 'You're under arrest.'

'Oh crap,' moaned the girl. 'Man, I just got out of jail. Oh no,' she wailed.

'Let's go,' said Gus, opening the door of the Cadillac. 'Awright, lemme get my purse,' she spat, but turned the key and cramped the wheel hard to the left as the Cadillac lurched forward and Gus, not knowing why, leaped on the side of the car and in only seconds he was clinging to the back of the seat and standing on nothing as the powerful car sped east on Venice. He reached desperately across for the keys, but she drove her little fist into his face and he slid back and tasted the blood from his nose. His eye caught the speedometer registering sixty and quickly seventy and his lower body was swept backward in a rush of wind and he clung to the seat as the cursing prostitute swerved the Cadillac across three lanes attempting to hurl him to his death and now for the first time he was conscious of exactly what he was doing and he prayed to God the body would not fail him now and it would just cling – that was all – just cling.

There were other cars on Venice. Gus knew this from the blasting horns and squeal of tires but he kept his eyes closed and clung as she beat at his hands with a purse and then with a high-heeled shoe as the Cadillac swerved and skidded on Venice Boulevard. Gus tried to remember a simple prayer from his boyhood because he knew there would be a jarring flaming crash but he couldn't remember the prayer and suddenly there was a giddy sliding turn and he knew this was the end and now he would be hurtled through space like a bullet, but then the car righted itself and was speeding back westbound on Venice the way it had come and Gus thought if he could reach his gun, if he dared release the grip of one hand, he would take her with him to the grave and then he remembered the gun was in his car and he thought if he could crank the wheel now at eighty miles an hour he could flip the Cadillac, and that would be as good as the gun. He wanted to, but the body would not obey and would only cling stubbornly to the back cushion of the seat. Then the prostitute began pushing the door open as she cut the wheel back and forth and the force hurtled his feet straight back and Gus found his voice, but it was a whisper and she was shrieking curses and the car tape deck had somehow been turned as loudly as it would go and the music from the car stereo and roar of the wind and screams of the prostitute were deafening and he shouted in her ear, 'Please, please, let me go! I won't arrest you if you'll let me go. Slow down and let me jump!'

She answered by cutting the wheel recklessly to the right and saying, 'Die, you dirty little motherfucker.'

Gus saw La Brea coming up and the traffic was moderate when she slashed through the red light at ninety miles an hour and Gus heard the unmistakable screech and crash but still they flew and he knew another car had crashed in the intersection and then all lanes were blocked east and west just west of La Brea as a stream of fire trucks lumbered north at the next intersection. The prostitute slammed on her brakes and turned left on a dark residential street, but made the turn much too sharply and the Cadillac slid and righted and careened to the right and up over a lawn taking out twenty feet of picket fence which hurtled in clattering fragments over the hood of the car and cracked the windshield of the Cadillac which sliced across lawns and through hedges with the prostitute riding the burning brakes and the lawns hurtling by were coming slower and slower and Gus guessed the car was going only thirty miles an hour when he let go but he hit the grass with a shock and his body coiled and rolled without command but he was still rolling when he crashed into a parked car and sat there for a long moment as the earth moved up and down. Then he was on his feet as the lights were being turned on all over the block and the neighborhood dogs had gone mad and the Cadillac was now almost out of sight.

Gus then started to run as the people poured from the houses. He was almost at La Brea when he began to feel the pain in his hip and his arm and several other places and he wondered why he was running, but right now it was the only thing that made sense. So he ran faster and faster and then he was at his car and driving, but his legs, although they would run, would not be still enough to maneuver the car, and twice he had to stop and rub them before reaching the station. He drove his car to the rear of the station and went in the back door and down to the bathroom where he examined his gray face which was badly scratched and bruised from the blows. When he washed away the blood it didn't look bad but his left knee was mushy and the sweat dried cold on his chest and back. Then he noticed the terrible smell and his stomach turned as he realized what it was and he hurried to the locker thankful that he kept a sport coat and slacks in case he tore his clothing prowling or in case an assignment demanded a dressier appearance. He crept back down to the restroom and cleansed his legs and buttocks, sobbing breathlessly in shame and fear and relief.

After he was washed, he put on the clean slacks and rolled the trousers and soiled underwear into a ball and threw the stinking bundle outside in the trash can at the rear of the station. He got back in the car and drove to the drive-in where he knew Bonelli would be frantic because he had been gone almost an hour and he was still uncertain if he could carry off the lie when he drove to the rear of the restaurant. He found Bonelli with two radio cars who had begun a search for Gus. He told the lie which he had formulated while the tears choked him as he drove to the restaurant. He had to lie because if they knew they had a policeman who was so stupid he would jump on the side of a car, why they would kick him off the squad, and rightly so, for such an officer certainly would need more seasoning – if not a psychiatrist. So he told them an elaborate lie about a prostitute who had hit him in the face with a shoe and had leaped from his car and how he had chased her through alleys on foot for a half hour and finally lost her. Bonelli had told him it was dangerous to go off alone away from your car but he was so damned glad to see Gus was alright that he dropped it at that not even noticing the clothes change, and they drove to the Main Jail. Several times Gus thought he would break down and weep and in fact he twice stifled a sob. But he did not break down and after an hour or so his legs and hands stopped shaking completely. But he could not eat and when they stopped later for a hamburger he had almost gotten sick at the sight of food.

'You look awful,' said Bonelli, after he had eaten and they were cruising down Wilshire Boulevard. Gus was looking out the window at the street and the cars and people, feeling not elated at being still alive but darkly depressed. He wished for a moment that the car had overturned during that bowel-searing moment when she had skidded and he knew they were doing ninety.

'I guess that hassle with the whore was a little too much for me,' Gus said.

'How far you say you chased that whore?' asked Bonelli with a look of disbelief.

'Several blocks I guess. Why?'

'I happen to know you run like a cougar. How come you couldn't catch her?'

'Well, the truth is, she kicked me in the balls, Sal. I was ashamed to tell you. I was lying in the alley for twenty minutes.'

'Well, why in the hell didn't you say you caught a nut shot for chrissake? No wonder you been looking sick all night. I'm taking you home.'

'No. No, I don't want to go home,' said Gus and thought he would analyze later why he preferred being at work even now when he was despairing of everything.

'Suit yourself, but I want you to really go through that whore mug book tomorrow night and keep looking till you find that bitch. We're going to get a warrant for battery on a police officer.'

'I told you, Sal, she was a new one. I never saw her before.'

'We'll find the cunt,' said Bonelli and seemed content with Gus's explanation. Gus felt better now and his stomach hardly hurt at all. He sat back and wondered where he would get the money for his mother this payday because the furniture payment was due, but he decided not to worry about it because thinking about his mother and John always made his stomach tighten up and he had had enough of that tonight.

At eleven o'clock, Sal said, 'Guess we better go see the boy leader, huh?'

'Okay,' Gus mumbled, unaware that he had been dozing.

'You sure you don't want to go home?'

'I feel fine.'

They met Anderson at the restaurant looking sour and impatient as he sipped a cup of creamy coffee and tapped on a table with a teaspoon.

'You're late,' he muttered as they sat down.

'Yeah,' said Bonelli.

'I took a booth so we wouldn't be overheard,' said Anderson, worrying the tip of the sparse moustache with the handle of the teaspoon.

'Yeah, can't be too careful when you're in this business,' said Bonelli, and Anderson glanced sharply at the stony brown eyes looking for irony.

'The others aren't coming. Hunter and his partner got a couple whores and the others took a game.'

'Dice?'

'Cards,' said Anderson and Gus became irritated as he always did when Anderson referred to Hunter and *his partner* or *the others* when there were only eight of them altogether and he should know their names well enough by now.

'The three of us working the bar?' asked Bonelli.

'Not you. They know you so you stay outside. I've got a good place picked out for surveillance across the street in an apartment house parking lot. You be there when we bring out an arrestee, or if we get invited to the apartment for after-hour drinking like I hope, we may just have a drink and leave and call for reinforcements.'

'Don't forget to pour the drink in the rubber,' said Sal.

'Of course,' said Anderson.

'Don't pour too much. Those rubbers break if you pour too much booze in.'

'I can manage,' said Anderson.

'Especially *that* rubber. Don't pour too much in.'

'Why?'

'I used that one on my girl friend Bertha last night. It ain't brand-new anymore.'

Anderson looked at Bonelli for a second and then chortled self-consciously.

'He thinks I'm joking,' said Bonelli to Gus.

'Great kidders,' said Anderson. 'Let's get going. I'm anxious to do police work.'

Bonelli shrugged to Gus as they followed Anderson to his car and drove behind him to within a block of The Cellar where they decided Anderson and Gus would go in separately at five-minute intervals. They might find an excuse to get together once inside, but they were going to act like strangers.

Once inside, Gus wasn't interested in arrests or police work or anything but the drink in front of him when he sat at the leather-padded bar. He drank two whiskeys with soda and ordered a third, but the peace-giving warmth started before he had finished the second and he wondered if his was the type of personality that was conducive to alcoholism. He guessed it was, and that was one reason he seldom drank, but it was mainly that he hated the taste except for whiskey and soda which he could tolerate. Tonight they were good, and his hand began to beat time to the blaring jukebox and for the first time he looked around the bar. It was a good noisy crowd for a week night. The bar was crowded as were the booths and the tables were almost all occupied. After his third drink he noticed Sergeant Anderson sitting alone at a tiny round table, sipping a cocktail and staring hard at Gus before getting up and going to the jukebox.

Gus followed and fumbled in his pocket for a quarter as he approached the glowing machine which flickered green and blue light across the intense face of Anderson.

'Good crowd,' said Gus, pretending to pick out a recording. Gus noticed that his mouth was getting numb and he was light-headed and the music made his heart beat fast. He finished the drink in his hand.

'Better take it easy on the drinking,' whispered Anderson. 'You'll have to be sober if we're going to operate this place.' Anderson punched a selection and pretended to search for another.

'You operate better if you look like one of the boozers,' said Gus, and surprised himself because he never contradicted sergeants, least of all Anderson whom he feared.

'Make your drink last,' said Anderson. 'But don't overdo it that way either or they'll suspect you're vice.'

'Okay,' said Gus. 'Shall we sit together?'

'Not yet,' said Anderson. 'There're two women at the table directly in front of me. I think they're hustlers, but I'm not sure. It wouldn't hurt to try for a prostitution offer. If we get it, we could always try to use them to duke us into the upstairs drinking. Then we could bust them when we bust the after-hours place.'

'Good plan,' said Gus, belching wetly.

'Don't talk so loud for crying out loud.'

'Sorry,' said Gus, belching again.

'You go back to the bar and watch me. If I'm not doing well with the women you stroll over to their table and hit on them. If you score, I'll invite myself over again.'

'Okay,' said Gus and Anderson punched the last record on the jukebox and the buzz of voices in the bar threatened to drown out the jukebox until Gus's ears popped and he knew most of the buzz was in his head and he thought of the speeding Cadillac, became frightened, and forced it from his mind.

'Go back to your table now,' whispered Anderson. 'We've been standing here too long.'

'Shouldn't I play a record? That's what I came here for,' said Gus, pointing to the glowing machine.

'Oh yes,' said Anderson. 'Play something first.'

'Okay,' said Gus, belching again.

'You better take it easy with the booze,' said Anderson, as he strode back to his table.

Gus found the blurred record labels too hard to read and just punched the first three buttons on the machine. He liked the hard rock that was now being played and he found his fingers snapping and his shoulders swaying as he returned to the bar and had another whiskey and soda which he drank furtively hoping Anderson would not see. Then he ordered another and picked his way through the crowd to the two women at the table who did indeed look like prostitutes, he thought.

The younger of the two, a slightly bulging silver-tipped brunette in a gold sheath, smiled at Gus immediately as he stood, tapping a foot to the music, in front of their table. He sipped his drink and gave them both a leer which he knew they would respond to, and he glanced at Anderson who glared morosely over his drink and he almost laughed because he hadn't felt so happy in months and he knew he was getting drunk. But his sensibility had become actually more acute, he thought, and he saw things in perspective and God, life was good. He leered from the younger one to the bleached fat one who was fifty-five if she was a day, and the fat one blinked at Gus through alcoholic blue eyes and Gus guessed she was not a true professional hooker, but just a companion for the younger. She would probably join in if the opportunity arose, but who in hell would pay money for the hag?

'All alone?' slurred the older one, as Gus stood before them, growing hilarious now, as he bounced and swayed to the music which was building to a crescendo of drums and electric guitar.

'Nobody's alone as long as there's music and drink and love,' said Gus, toasting each of them with the whiskey and soda and then pouring it down as he thought how damned eloquent that was, and if he could only remember it later.

'Well, sit down and tell me more, you cute little thing,' said the old blonde pointing to the empty chair.

'May I buy you girls a drink?' asked Gus, leaning both elbows on the table and thinking how the younger one really wasn't too bad except for her bad nose which was bent to the right and her fuzzy eyebrows which began and ended nowhere, but she had enormous breasts and he stared at them frankly and then hurled a lewd smile in her face as he snapped his fingers for the waitress who was giving Anderson another drink.

Both women ordered manhattans and he had whiskey and soda and noticed Anderson looked angrier than usual. Anderson finished two drinks while the fat blonde told a long obscene joke about a little Jew and a blue-eyed camel and Gus roared even though he failed to get the punch line, and when he calmed himself the old blonde said, 'We didn't even get introduced. I'm Fluffy Largo. This is Poppy La Farge.'

'My name is Lance Jeffrey Savage,' said Gus, standing shakily and bowing to both giggling women.

'Ain't he the cutest little shit?' said Fluffy to Poppy.

'Where do you work, Lance?' asked Poppy letting her hand rest against her forearm as she dipped her torso forward revealing a half inch more cleavage.

'I work at a cantaloupe factory,' said Gus staring at Poppy's breasts. 'I mean a dress factory,' he added looking up to see if they caught it.

'Cantaloupes,' said Fluffy and burst into a high whooping laugh that ended in a snort.

Damn good, thought Gus. That was damn good. And he wondered how he could so easily think of such spectacularly funny things tonight, and then he looked over at Anderson who was paying for another drink and Gus said to the women, 'Hey, see that guy over there?'

'Yeah, the bastard tried to pick us up a minute ago,' said Fluffy, scratching her vast belly and pulling up a slipping bra strap which had dropped below the shoulder onto the flabby pink bicep.

'I know him,' said Gus. 'Let's invite him over.'

'You know him?' asked Poppy. 'He looks like a cop to me.'

'Hah, hah, hah,' said Gus. 'A cop. I knew that sucker for five years. He used to own a string of gas stations. His old lady divorced him though and now he's down to three. Always has plenty of bread on him, though.'

'Don't you have any bread, Lance?' asked Fluffy suddenly.

'Just seventy-five bucks,' said Gus. 'That enough?'

'Well,' Fluffy smiled. 'We expect to show you a good time after this joint closes and naturally, all good things are expensive.'

'What kind of dresses you like, Fluffy?' asked Gus expansively. 'I carry samples in my car and I want to see you dolls in some fine goods.'

'Really?' said Poppy with a huge grin. 'Do you have any size four-teens?'

'I got 'em, baby,' said Gus.

'You got a twenty-two and a half?' asked Fluffy. 'This old green rag is falling apart.'

'I got 'em, Fluffy,' said Gus and now he was annoyed because he had absolutely no feeling in his lower jaw, mouth and tongue.

'Listen, Lance,' said Poppy, pulling her chair next to his. 'We usually don't sleep with nobody for less than a hundred a night each. But maybe for those dresses, I could let you have it for oh, fifty bucks, and maybe we could talk Fluffy into a twenty-five dollar ride. What do you say, Fluff? He's a damned nice guy.'

'He's a cute little shit,' said Fluffy. 'I'll do it.'

'Okay, dolls,' said Gus, holding up three fingers to the waitress, even though he sensed Anderson was glaring at him through the smoky darkness.

'Why don't we get started now?' asked Poppy. 'It's almost one o'clock.'

'Not yet,' said Gus. 'I hear they swing after hours in this joint. What say we try to get in upstairs after two? After a few drinks and a little fun, we can head for the motel.'

'George charges a lot for drinks upstairs,' said Poppy. 'You only got seventy-five bucks and we need it worse than George.'

'Listen,' Gus muttered, pitying for a moment a drowning fly who thrashed in a ringed puddle on the cluttered table. 'I got a plan. Let's invite that guy I know over here and we'll take him with us upstairs to George's place after the bar closes. And we'll all drink off his money. He's loaded. And then after we drink for a while the three of us'll ditch him and head for the pad. I hate to go to bed yet, I'm having too much fun.'

'You don't know what fun is, you cute little shit,' said Fluffy, squeezing Gus's thigh with a pudgy pink hand and lurching forward heavily into Gus as she tried to kiss him on the cheek with a mouth that looked like a deflated tire tube.

'Cut that out, Fluff,' said Poppy. 'Crissake, you get thrown in jail for drunk and what're we going to do?'

'She isn't drunk,' said Gus drunkenly, as his elbow slipped off the table from the weight of Fluffy's heavy body.

'We better get out of here and head for the motel right now,' said Poppy. 'You two are going to fuck up the whole deal if you get busted like a couple common winos.'

'Just a minute,' said Gus, waving a hand toward where he thought Anderson would be.

'We don't want that guy,' said Poppy.

'Shut up, Poppy,' said Gus.

'Shut up, Poppy,' said Fluffy. 'The more, the fuckin' merrier.'

'This is the last time I take you with me, Fluffy,' said Poppy, taking a big swallow of the cocktail.

'You wanted me?' asked Anderson, and Gus looked up at the red-eyed sergeant standing over him.

'Sure, sure,' mumbled Gus. 'Sit down ... Chauncey. Girls, this is Chauncey Dunghill, my old friend. Chauncey, meet Fluffy and Poppy, my new friends.' Gus held his whiskey up in a toast to the three of them and swallowed a gulp he could hardly taste.

'Pleased to meet you,' said Anderson stiffly and Gus squinted at the sergeant and remembered that Bonelli had told him that Anderson could not operate bars because he got high on two drinks, being a teetotaler except when duty called. Gus smiled and leaned over the table seeing the peculiar angle of Anderson's eyes.

'Ol' Chaunce has to catch up with us,' said Gus, 'if he wants to come with us to George's private bar for a few belts after two.'

'Shit,' said Poppy.

'Private bar?' said Anderson with a crafty look at Gus, toying with his sparse moustache.

'Sure, these girls are taking us upstairs. They know this guy George and he's got a swinging after-hours joint and you can come as long as you buy all the drinks, right, girls?'

'Tha's right,' said Fluffy and kissed Gus on the cheek with a jarring collision and Gus winced in spite of the drink in him and wondered about the diseases prostitutes' mouths must carry. He furtively spilled a little whiskey on his hand and dabbed it on the spot to kill the germs.

'You buying drinks, Chauncey?' asked Fluffy with a challenge in her voice as she looked at Anderson like a boxer eyeing an opponent.

'Four drinks,' said Anderson to the waitress.

'Two for you,' said Gus.

'What?'

'You got to catch up.'

'Well?' said the bored waitress, hesitating.

'You catch up or we don't take you upstairs,' said Gus.

'Bring me two daiquiris,' said Anderson and glared at Gus who giggled all through the joke about the Jew and the blue-eyed camel which Fluffy repeated for Anderson.

'Chug-a-lug the drink,' Gus commanded to Anderson when the daiquiris arrived.

'I'll drink as I please,' said Anderson.

'Chug-a-lug, mudder-fug,' commanded Fluffy, and the purple pouches under her eyes bulged ominously. Gus cheered as Anderson put the first drink away and smiled weakly at Poppy who was now smoking and nursing her drink.

Gus leered in earnest at her bulging breasts and told Fluffy a joke about a one-titted stripper who couldn't twirl a tassle, but he forgot how it ended and he stopped in the middle. Fluffy whooped and snorted and said it was the funniest joke she ever heard.

When Anderson finished his second drink, he signaled for five more and now grinned gaily at Poppy, asking her if she had ever been a dancer because she had wonderful legs.

'Chug-a-lug,' said Anderson when the drinks arrived.

'Mudder-fug,' said Fluffy, and exploded in cackles, bumping heads painfully with Gus.

'This is all right,' said Anderson, after his glass was drained, and he picked up his next. 'I'm catching up, Poppy.'

'Something's goin' to happen,' Poppy whined. 'You can't get drunk in this business, Fluffy.'

'I'm not drunk. Lance's drunk,' said Fluffy. 'Chauncey's drunk too.'

'You're a beautiful girl and I really mean it, Poppy,' said Anderson, and Gus roared, 'Oooooh, stop it, Chauncey, you're killing me,' and then Gus giggled in a prolonged burst of hilarity which threatened to suffocate him. When he recovered he saw that everyone on that side of the bar was laughing at him and that made him laugh harder and he only stopped when Fluffy grabbed him in a bulging embrace, called him a cute little shit, and kissed him on the open mouth. She probably went around the world tonight, he thought, cringing in horror. He took a hurried drink, swishing it around in his mouth and held up his hand for another.

'You had enough to drink,' said Anderson with a surly slurred voice.

'Speak for yourself, Chauncey,' said Gus trying not to think of how prostitutes used their mouths, as he became nauseous.

'We all had enough to drink,' said Poppy. 'I know something's going to go wrong.'

'You're really a lovely girl, Poppy,' said Anderson as he spilled half his drink on her gold purse.

'Bunch of fuckin' drunks,' said Poppy.

'I'm sorry, Poppy,' said Anderson. 'Really I am.'

Anderson finished his drink and ordered another round even though Poppy had not touched her last one, and finally Anderson drank his and Poppy's two manhattans when Fluffy dared him to. Gus had a headache and still felt nauseous as he remembered hearing a whore in the wagon saying she once gave twenty-two head jobs in one night, and he looked at Fluffy's mouth which had actually touched the inside of his. He sloshed more of the drink around in his mouth and pushed Fluffy away each time she leaned over and squeezed his thigh and now he found he was becoming angry at everything while only moments ago he was happy. He glared at Anderson's sparse moustache and thought what a miserable son of a bitch he was.

'I'm not feeling too good, Poppy,' said Anderson who had been patting her hand and telling her that business was bad and he only made fifty thousand last year as she looked as though she didn't believe him.

'Let's all get out of here,' said Poppy. 'Can you still walk, Fluffy?'

'I can dance,' growled Fluffy, whose head seemed to be sinking lower into the mass of her body.

'I'm getting sick,' said Anderson.

'Kiss the son of a bitch,' whispered Gus suddenly into Fluffy's ear.

'What?' asked Fluffy, swiping at an indomitable drop of moisture which clung to the ball of her nose.

'Grab that bastard like you did me around the arms and give him a big sloppy kiss and make sure you stick your old tongue right in there.'

'But I don't even like the shithead,' Fluffy whispered.

'I'll give you an extra five bucks later,' whispered Gus.

'Okay,' said Fluffy, leaning over the table and knocking an empty glass on the floor as she pinned the arms of the surprised Anderson and ground her mouth against his until he could manage the leverage to plop her back in the chair.

'Why did you do that?' Anderson gasped.

''Cause I love you, you shithead,' said Fluffy and when the waitress passed with a tray of beers for the adjoining table, Fluffy grabbed a beer from the tray and stuck her chin in the foam and said, 'Look at me, I'm a billy goat.' Anderson paid for the beer and tipped the angry waitress two dollars.

'Come on, Fluffy,' said Poppy after the waitress left, 'let's go to the restroom and wash your goddamn face and then we're getting Lance and going to the motel right now. Understand, Lance?'

'Sure, sure, Poppy, whatever you say,' said Gus, grinning at the outraged Anderson and feeling happy again.

When they were gone Anderson lurched forward, almost fell to the floor and looked painfully at Gus. 'Plebesly, we're too goddamn drunk to do our job. Do you realize that?'

'We're not drunk, Sergeant. You're drunk,' said Gus.

'I'm getting sick, Plebesly,' pleaded Anderson.

'Know what Fluffy told me, Sergeant?' said Gus. 'She told me she worked in a whorehouse all day and blew twenty-two guys.'

'She did?' said Anderson, holding his hand to his mouth.

'She said she gives around the world or straight French 'cause it's too much trouble to screw and she'll go right up the old poop chute if a guy wants it.'

'Don't tell me that, Plebesly,' said Anderson. 'I'm sick, Plebesly.'

'I'm sorry she kissed you, Sergeant,' said Gus, 'I'm sorry 'cause those spermatozoas are probably swarming down your friggin' throat right this minute and swishing their tails against your friggin' tonsils.'

Anderson cursed and stumbled sideways, heading for the exit. His handcuffs fell out and clashed to the floor. Gus stooped carefully, retrieved the handcuffs and weaved his way through the tables after Anderson. Even on the sidewalk outside Gus could hear Poppy's curse when she found the table empty. Then Gus crossed the street, carefully following the wavy white line to the opposite curb. It seemed like a mile to the darkened parking lot where he found Anderson vomiting beside his car and Bonelli looking at Gus with affection.

'What happened in there?' asked Bonelli.

'We drank with two whores.'

'Didn't they hit on you? Didn't you get an offer?'

'Yes, but there's too much between us now. I couldn't bear to arrest them.'

'You drank Anderson under the table, kid,' Bonelli grinned.

'Under the friggin' table. I really did, Sal,' Gus squeaked.

'How do you feel?'

'I'm getting sick.'

'Come on,' said Bonelli, throwing a big hairy arm around Gus's shoulder and patting him on the cheek. "Let's go get you some coffee, son."

FIFTEEN
Conception

The transfer to Seventy-seventh Street station had been a demoralizing blow. Now, after his fourth week in the division Roy could still not believe they would do this to him. He knew that most of his academy class had been transferred to three divisions but he hoped he might escape the third one. After all, he was well liked in Central Division and he had already worked Newton Street and didn't dream they would make him work another black division. But then again, he should have expected it. Everything the Department did was senseless and illogical and none of the command officers cared in the least about intangibles like morale as long as they were efficient, icily efficient, and as long as the public knew and appreciated their efficiency. But Christ, Roy thought, Seventy-seventh Division! Fifty-ninth Place and Avalon, Slauson and Broadway, Ninety-second and Beach, One Hundred and Third, all of Watts for that matter! It was Newton Street magnified ten times, it was violence and crime, and every night he was wading through blood.

The stores, the offices, even the churches looked like fortresses with bars and grates and chains protecting doors and windows and he had even seen private uniformed guards in churches during services. It was impossible.

'Let's go to work,' said Lieutenant Feeney to the night watch officers. Feeney was a laconic twenty-year man with a melancholy face who seemed to Roy a decent watch commander, but he had to be because in this hellish division a rigid disciplinarian would drive the men to mutiny.

Roy put on his cap, jammed the flashlight in the sap pocket and picked up his books. He hadn't heard a single thing that was said at roll call. He was getting worse about that lately. Someday he'd miss something important. They must occasionally say something important, he thought.

Roy did not walk down the stairs with Rolfe, his partner. The laughter and voices of the others angered him for no apparent reason. The uniform clung wetly on this hot evening and chafed and hung like an oppressive blue pall. Roy dragged himself to the radio car and was glad it was Rolfe's turn to drive tonight. He hadn't the energy. It would be a sultry night as well as hot.

Roy wrote his name mechanically in the log and wrote Rolfe's name on the line below. He made a few other notations, then slammed the notebook as Rolfe drove out of the station parking lot and Roy turned the windwing so that what breeze there was cooled him a little.

'Anything special you want to do tonight?' asked Rolfe, a young, usually smiling ex-sailor who had been a policeman just one year and who still had a bubbling exuberance for police work that Roy found annoying.

'Nothing special,' said Roy, closing the windwing when he lit a cigarette which tasted bad.

'Let's drive by Fifty-ninth and Avalon,' said Rolfe. 'We haven't been giving the pill pushers too much attention lately.'

'Okay,' Roy sighed, thinking that only one more night and then he was off for three. And then he began thinking of Alice, the buxom nurse who for six months he watched leaving the apartment house across the street from his, but whom he never tried before last week because he was keeping well satisfied by fair and fragile Jenny, the steno who only lived across the hall. Jenny was so available and so convenient and so eager for love at any hour, sometimes too eager. She insisted on lovemaking when he was exhausted from an overtime shift and any sane person should have been long asleep. He would stumble into his apartment and close the door quietly and before he could even get into his pajamas she would be in his bedroom, having heard him enter and having used the key he never should have given her. He would turn around suddenly when he felt her presence in the silent room and she would burst into a fit of giggling because she had scared hell out of him. She would be in her nightgown, not a well-shaped girl, far too thin, but very pretty and insatiable in her lust. He knew there were other men too despite what Jenny said, but he didn't give a damn because she was too much for him anyway, and besides, now that he had met Alice, milky, scrubbed and starched Alice, and had luxuriated in her yielding softness one fortunate night last week, now he was going to have to discourage Jenny.

'Looks like a good crowd this evening,' said Rolfe. Roy wished he would be quiet when he was thinking about Alice and her splendid gourd-shaped breasts which in themselves provided him with hours of excitement and wonder. If Jenny was two feverish eyes, Alice was two peace-giving breasts. He wondered if there lived a woman whom he could think of as a whole person. He didn't think of Dorothy at all anymore. But then he realized he never thought of anyone as a whole person anymore. Carl was a mouth, an open mouth that criticized incessantly. His father was a pair of eyes, not devouring him like Jenny's, but entreating him, mournful eyes that wanted him to submit to the suffocation of his and Carl's tyranny.

'If only I could add an S to the Fehler and Son sign,' his father had pleaded. 'Oh Roy, I'd pay a fortune for that privilege.' And then he had come to think of his mother as only a pair of hands, clasped hands, moist hands, talking hands which cajoled, 'Roy, Roy, we never see you anymore and when are you leaving that city and coming home where you belong, Roy?'

Then he thought of Becky, and he felt his heart race. He could think of her as a whole person. She was scampering about now and she seemed so happy to see him when he came. He would never let a week pass without seeing her and to hell with Dorothy and her fat-assed henpecked fiancé, because he would never let a weekend pass without seeing Becky. Never. He would bring her presents, spend whatever he wished, and they could go to hell.

The evening dragged even though many radio calls were being given to Seventy-seventh cars. He was afraid to ask for code seven for fear they'd get a call. His stomach was rumbling. He should have eaten lunch today.

'Ask for seven,' said Rolfe.

'Twelve-A-Five requesting code seven at the station,' said Roy, wishing that he had packed something better than a cheese sandwich in his lunch. It was too close to payday to be buying dinner. He wished there were more eating spots on Seventy-seventh Street. He had long since decided that free food was not unprofessional. Everyone accepted meals and the restaurant proprietors did not seem to mind. They wanted policemen in the place or they wouldn't do it. But he and Rolfe had no eating spot in their district that would even feed them at a discount.

'Twelve-A-Five, continue patrol,' said the operator, 'and handle this call: See the woman, unknown trouble, eleven-o-four, east Ninety-second Street, code two.'

Roy rogered the call and turned to Rolfe. 'Shit! I'm starving.'

'I hate unknown trouble calls,' said Rolfe. 'They always make me nervous. I like to know what to expect.'

'This goddamned jungle,' said Roy, flipping his cigarette out the window. 'You don't get off on time, you miss your meals, fifteen radio calls a night. I've got to get a transfer.'

'Do you really feel that way?' asked Rolfe, turning to Roy with a surprised look. 'I like it here. The time passes fast. We're so busy that it's time to go home when I feel like I just came to work. All this action is pretty exciting to me.'

'You'll get over that crap,' said Roy. 'Turn left here. This is Ninety-second.'

There was a woman in a clean white turban standing in the front yard of the house next to eleven-o-four. Rolfe parked and she waved nervously as they got out of the car.

'Evening,' said Rolfe as they approached the woman, putting on their caps.

'I'm the one that called, Mr. PO-lice,' she whispered. 'They's a lady in that house that is terrible drunk all the time. She got a new baby, one of them preemeys, jist a tiny bug of a chil', and she always drunk, 'specially when her man at work, and he at work tonight.'

'She bothering you?' asked Roy.

'It the baby, Mr. PO-lice,' said the woman, her arms folded over the ample stomach, as she glanced several times at the house. 'She dropped that chil' on the ground last week. I seed her, but my husband say it ain't none our business, but tonight she was staggerin' around that front porch wif the chil' again and she almost fell right off the porch and I tol' my husband I was calling the PO-lice and tha's what I done.'

'Okay, we'll go have a talk with her,' said Roy, walking toward the one-story frame house with a rotting picket fence.

Roy walked carefully up the dangerous porch steps and stood by habit to one side of the doorway as Rolfe stood to the other side and knocked. They heard the shuffling of feet and a crash and then they knocked again. After more than a minute a woman with oily ringlets opened the door and stared at the policemen with watery little eyes.

'What you want?' she asked, weaving from side to side as she held tightly to the doorknob for support.

'We were told you might be having some trouble,' said Rolfe with his young easy smile. 'Mind if we come in? We're here to help you.'

'I know how the PO-lices helps,' said the woman, bumping the doorway with her wide shoulder during a sudden lurch sideways.

'Look, lady,' said Roy, 'we were told your baby might be in some danger. How about showing us that the baby's okay and we'll be on our way.'

'Get off my porch,' said the woman as she prepared to close the door, and Roy shrugged at Rolfe because they couldn't force their way in with no more cause than her being drunk. Roy decided to stop and buy a hamburger to go with the cheese sandwich that he had begun to crave. Then the baby shrieked. It was not a petulant baby scream of anger or discomfort, but it was a full-blown scream of pain or terror and Rolfe was through the door before the shriek died. Pushing past the drunken woman he bounded across the small living room into the kitchen. Roy was just entering the house when Rolfe emerged from the kitchen carrying the incredibly tiny nightgown-clad baby in his arms.

'She laid the baby on the kitchen table next to her ashtray,' said Rolfe, awkwardly rocking the moaning brown-skinned infant. 'It got hold of the burning cigarette. Hand's burned, and the stomach too. Look at the hole in the nightgown. Poor thing.' Rolfe glared at the angry woman over his shoulder as he cradled the baby in one big arm away from the mother who looked on the verge of a drunken decision.

'Give me my chil',' she said stepping toward Rolfe.

'Just a minute, lady,' said Roy, grabbing her by a surprisingly hard bicep. 'Partner, I think we've got enough to book her for child endangering. Lady, you're under ar ...' She drove an elbow into the side of Roy's neck and his head struck the edge of the door with a painful shock and he heard Rolfe shout as she lunged for him and Roy stared transfixed as he saw the fragile, screaming baby being pulled by the woman who had the left arm and Rolfe who had the right leg in one hand while his other hand clawed the air in horror and helplessness.

'Let it go, Rolfe,' Roy shouted, as the woman jerked backward viciously and Rolfe followed her, unwilling to surrender the wailing infant completely.

Finally Rolfe released the child, and Roy shuddered as the woman fell heavily back into a chair holding the baby by one leg across her lap.

'Let her keep it, Rolfe!' Roy shouted, still unable to decide what to do because they would surely kill it, but Rolfe had pounced on the woman who was digging and punching at his face, still holding the baby in a death grip, first by the leg, then by the arm when Rolfe pulled a hand free. Roy leaped forward when she grabbed the now silent baby by the throat.

'My God, my God,' Roy whispered, as he tore the fingers free one at a time while Rolfe pinned the woman's other arm and she cursed and spat and he had the last finger twisted free and was lifting the trembling little body in one hand when the woman's head snapped forward and her teeth closed first on Roy's hand and he shouted in sudden pain. She released him and bit at the child as Rolfe grabbed the woman's neck, and tried to force the head back, but the large white teeth flashed and snapped again and again at the baby, and then the baby shrieked once more, long and loud. Roy pulled the infant and the nightgown ripped away in the woman's mouth and Roy did not look at the baby, but ran to the bedroom with it and put it on the bed and came back to help Rolfe handcuff her.

It was after midnight when they got the woman booked and the baby admitted to the hospital. It was too late to eat now and Roy could not eat anyway and he told himself for the tenth time to stop thinking about what the baby's body looked like there on the shockingly white table in the emergency ward. Rolfe had also been unusually silent for the past hour or so.

'Someone else tried to bite me once,' Roy said suddenly as he puffed on a cigarette and leaned back in the car as Rolfe was driving them to the station to complete the reports. 'It wasn't like this at all. It was a man and he was white, and there was no excuse at all. I was trying to get away from him. It was in a restroom.'

Rolfe looked at him curiously and Roy said, 'I was working vice. He was trying to devour me. People are cannibals I guess. They just eat each other. Sometimes they don't even have the decency to kill you before they eat you.'

'Hey, there's a waitress I know pretty good down at a restaurant at a Hundred-fifteenth and Western. I go there after work for coffee all the time. How about us stopping there for a few minutes before we go to the station? We could at least drink some coffee and unwind. And who knows, maybe we'll get hungry. I think she'd bounce for a free meal if the boss isn't there.'

'Why not?' said Roy, thinking the coffee sounded good and it would be a pleasure to drive through the west side of the division for a change, which was only part Negro and relatively peaceful. Roy hoped he could work Ninety-one next month and get as far west and south as the division went. He had to get away from black faces. He was starting to change toward them and he knew it was wrong. But still it was happening.

They were only two blocks from the restaurant and Roy was already feeling reassured at seeing the predominantly white faces driving and walking by when Rolfe said, 'Fehler, did you look in that liquor store we just passed?'

'No, why?' asked Roy.

'There was nobody behind the counter,' said Rolfe.

'So he went in the back room,' said Roy. 'Look, do you want to play cops and robbers or do we get some coffee?'

'I'm just going to have a look,' said Rolfe, making a U-turn and driving north again while Roy shook his head and vowed to ask for an older, more settled partner next month.

Rolfe parked across the street from the store and they watched the interior for a second. They saw a sandy-haired man in a yellow sport shirt run from the back room to the cash register where he punched several keys, and then they saw him clearly shove the gun inside his belt.

'Officers need help, One one three and Western!' Rolfe whispered into the radio, and then he was out of the car, hatless, flashlight in hand, running low to the north side of the building. He evidently remembered Roy who was just getting around the front of the car because he stooped, turned, and pointed to the rear door indicating that he would take the rear and then he disappeared in the shadows streaking for the darkness of the rear alley.

Roy debated a moment where he should place himself, thought of lying across the hood of a car that was parked directly in front of the store and was probably the suspect's car, but changed his mind and decided to get behind the corner of the building at the southwest corner where he could have a clear line of fire if the man came out the front. He began trembling, wondered for a moment if he could shoot a man, and decided not to think about that.

Then he saw that one of the cars in the bar parking lot next door was occupied by a man and woman who sat in the front seat apparently oblivious to the policeman's presence. Roy saw that they would be directly in the line of fire of the gunman if he would shoot at Roy hiding behind the corner of the building. His conscience nagged and his hand trembled more, and he thought if I leave here to run across the vacant lot and tell them to get the hell out, he might come out the door and I'll be caught out of position. But Jesus Christ, he might kill them and I'd never be able to forget ... Then he decided, and made a dash to the yellow Plymouth thinking: Stupid bastard, probably sitting there playing with her tits and doesn't even know they might get killed. Roy was beside the car and he saw the girl look at him wide-eyed as he held his revolver at his side. The man opened the door quickly.

'Get that car the hell out of here,' said Roy and he never forgot the foolish grin and the look of patent unconcern on the face of the little freckled man who leveled the sawed-off shotgun. Then the yellow and red flame crashed into him and he flew back across the sidewalk. He slid off the curb into the gutter where he lay on his side weeping because he could not get up and he had to get up because he could see the slimy intestines wet in the moonlight flopping out of his lower stomach in a pile. They began touching the street and Roy strained to turn over. He heard footsteps and a man said, 'Goddammit Harry, get in!' and another male voice said, 'I didn't even know they was out here!' Then the car started and roared across the sidewalk and off the curb and it sounded like more footsteps farther away. He heard Rolfe shouting 'Stop! Stop!' and heard four or five shots and tires squeal. Then he remembered that the intestines were lying on the street and he was filled with horror because they were lying there in the filthy street getting dirty and he began to cry. He squirmed a little to get on his back and get them bunched up because if he could just shovel them back inside and brush the dirt off them he knew he'd be alright because they were oh so dirty now. But he couldn't lift them. His left arm wouldn't move and it hurt so much to try to reach across the bubbling hole with his right arm so he began to cry again, and thought: Oh, if only it would rain. Oh, why can't it rain in August, and suddenly as he cried, he was deafened by thunder and the lightning flashed and clattered and the rain poured down on him. He thanked God and cried tears of joy because the rain was washing all the dirt off the heap of guts that was hanging out. He watched them shine wet red in the rain, clean and red, as all the filth was flushed away and he was still crying happily when Rolfe leaned over him. There were other policemen there and none of them were wet from the rain. He couldn't understand that.

Roy could not have said how long he had been in the police ward of Central Receiving Hospital. Could not at this moment say if it was days or weeks. It was always the same: blinds drawn, the hum of the air conditioning, the patter of soft-soled footsteps, whispers, needles and tubes which were endlessly inserted and withdrawn, but now he guessed perhaps three weeks had passed. He wouldn't ask Tony who sat there reading a magazine by the inadequate night light with a grin on his effeminate face.

'Tony,' said Roy, and the little male nurse put the magazine on the table and walked to the bed.

'Hello Roy,' Tony smiled. 'Woke up, huh?'

'How long I been sleeping?'

'Not too long, two, three hours, maybe,' said Tony. 'You were restless tonight. I thought I'd sit in here, I figured you'd wake up.'

'It hurts tonight,' said Roy, sliding the cover back to look at the hole covered with light gauze. It no longer bubbled and sickened him but it could not be sutured because of its size and had to heal on its own. It had already begun to shrink a little.

'It looks good tonight, Roy,' Tony smiled. 'Pretty soon no more I.V.'s, you'll be eating real food.'

'It hurts like hell.'

'Dr. Zelko says you're doing wonderfully, Roy. I'll bet you're out of here in two more months. And back to work in six. Light duty of course. Maybe you can work the desk for a while.'

'I need something for the pain tonight.'

'I can't. I've had specific orders about that. Dr. Zelko says we were giving you too many injections.'

'Screw Dr. Zelko! I need something. Do you know what adhesions are? Your goddamn guts tighten up and come together like they were glued. Do you know what that's like?'

'Now, now,' said Tony, wiping Roy's forehead with a towel.

'Look how my leg's swollen. There's a nerve that's damaged. Ask Dr. Zelko. I need something. That nerve keeps me in terrible pain.'

'I'm sorry, Roy,' said Tony, his smooth little face contorted with concern. 'I wish I could do more for you. You're our number one patient ...'

'Shove it!' said Roy and Tony walked back to his chair, sat down, and continued reading.

Roy stared at the holes in the acoustical ceiling and counted rows but he soon tired of that. When the pain was really bad and they wouldn't give him his medication he sometimes thought of Becky and that helped a little. He thought that Dorothy had been here once with Becky but he couldn't be sure. He was about to ask Tony, but Tony was his night nurse and he wouldn't know if they had visited him. His father and mother had been here several times and Carl had come at least once in the beginning. He remembered that. He had opened his eyes one afternoon and seen Carl and his parents, and the wound started hurting again and his cries of anguish had sent them out and brought the delicious indescribable injection that was all he lived for now. Some policemen had come, but he couldn't say just who. He thought he remembered Rolfe, and Captain James, and he thought he saw Whitey Duncan once through a sheet of fire. Now he was getting frightened because his stomach was clenching like a painful fist as though it didn't belong to him and acted on its own in defiance of the waves of anguish that were punishing it.

'What do I look like?' asked Roy suddenly.

'Pardon, Roy?' said Tony, jumping to his feet.

'Get me a mirror. Hurry up.'

'What for, Roy?' Tony smiled, opening the drawer of the table in the corner of the private room.

'Have you ever had a really bad stomachache?' asked Roy. 'One that made you sick clear through?'

'Yes,' said Tony, bringing the small mirror over to Roy's bed.

'Well it was nothing. Nothing, do you understand?'

'I can't give you anything,' said Tony, holding the mirror up for Roy.

'Who's that?' said Roy, and the fear swelled and pounded and swelled in him as he looked at the thin gray face with the dark-rimmed eyes and the thousands of greasy globules of sweat that roughened the texture of the face that stared at him in horror.

'You don't look bad at all, now. We thought we were going to lose you for the longest time. Now we know you're going to be alright.'

'I've got to have some medication, Tony. I'll give you twenty dollars. Fifty. I'll give you fifty dollars.'

'Please, Roy,' said Tony returning to his chair.

'If I only had my gun,' Roy sobbed.

'Don't talk like that, Roy.'

'I'd blow my brains out. But first I'd kill you, you little cocksucker.'

'You're a cruel man. And I don't have to stand for your insults. I've done everything I could for you. We all have. We've done everything to save you.'

'I'm sorry I called you that. You can't help it if you're a fruit. I'm sorry. Please get some medication. I'll give you a hundred dollars.'

'I'm going out. You ring if you really need me.'

'Don't go. I'm afraid to be alone with it. Stay here. I'm sorry. Please.'

'Alright. Forget it,' Tony grumbled, sitting down.

'Dr. Zelko has terrible eyes,' said Roy.

'What do you mean?' Tony sighed, putting down the magazine.

'There's hardly any iris. Just two round black little balls like two slugs of double ought buckshot. I can't bear his eyes.'

'Is that the kind of buckshot that hit you, Roy?'

'No. I'd be stinking up a coffin now if it had been double ought buck. It was number seven and a half birdshot. You ever hunt?'

'No.'

'He hit me from less than two feet away. Some hit my Sam Browne but I got most of it. He was such a silly-looking man. That's why I didn't bring the gun up. He was so silly-looking I just couldn't believe it. And he was a white man. And that sawed-off shotgun was so silly-looking and monstrous I couldn't believe that either. Maybe if he'd been a regular-looking man and had a regular handgun I could've brought my gun up, but I just held it there at my side and he looked so damned silly when he fired.'

'I don't want to hear it. Stop talking about it, Roy.'

'You asked me. You asked about the buckshot, didn't you?'

'I'm sorry I did. I'd just better go out for a while and maybe you can sleep.'

'Go ahead!' Roy sobbed. 'All of you can leave me. Look at what you've done to me though. Look at my body. You made me a freak, all you bastards. I got a huge open hole in my belly and you put another one in me and now I can wake up and find a pile of shit on my chest.'

'You had to have a colostomy, Roy.'

'Yeah? How would you like to have an asshole in your stomach? How would you like to wake up and look at a bag of shit on your chest?'

'I always clean it up as soon as I see it. Now you try to ...'

'Yeah,' he cried, weeping openly now, 'you made me a freak. I got a bloody pussy that won't close and an asshole in front that I can't control and they're both here on my stomach where I've got to look at them. I'm a goddamn freak.' Then Roy wept and the pain worsened but he wept more and the pain made him weep harder and harder until he gasped and tried to stop so that he could control the inexorable pain that he prayed would kill him instantly in one huge crashing red and yellow ball of fire.

Tony wiped his face and was about to speak when Roy's sobbing subsided and he gasped, 'I ... I've got to ... to turn over. It's killing me like this. Please, help me. Help me get on my stomach for a little while.'

'Sure, Roy,' said Tony, gently lifting him and then letting the bed down flat and taking the pillow away as Roy rested on the throbbing burning wound and sobbed spasmodically and blew his nose in the tissue Tony gave him.

Roy lay like this for perhaps five minutes and then he could bear it no more and turned, but Tony had stepped out into the corridor. He thought the hell with it he'd turn himself over and maybe the effort would kill him and that would be fine. He raised up on an elbow, feeling the sweat streaming over his rib cage and then moved as quickly as he could and fell on his back again. He felt the sweat flowing freely over his entire body. He felt something else and pulled the Scotch tape loose and glanced at the wound and screamed.

'What is it?' said Tony, running into the room.

'Look at it!' said Roy, staring at the fibrous bloody clump which protruded from the wound.

'What the hell?' said Tony, looking toward the hall and then back at Roy with confusion in his eyes.

Roy gaped at the wound and then at Tony and seeing the worried little face on the nurse began to giggle.

'I'll get a doctor, Roy,' said Tony.

'Wait a minute,' said Roy, laughing harder now. 'I don't need a doctor. Oh Christ, this is too funny.' Roy gasped and stopped laughing when another spasm struck him but even the pain could not completely destroy the humor of it. 'Do you know what that mess is, Tony? That's the god-damn wadding!'

'The what?'

'The wadding of the shotgun shell! It finally worked itself out. Look close. There's even some shot mixed in there. Two little pieces of shot. Oh Christ, that's funny. Oh, Christ. Go make the announcement to the staff that there was a happy event in the police ward. Tell them that Dr. Zelko's monster strained his new pussy and gave birth to a three-ounce pile of bloody wadding. And it had eyes like Dr. Zelko! Oh Christ, that's funny.'

'I'll get a doctor, Roy. We'll clean that up.'

'Don't try taking my baby away, you goddamn faggot! I once saw a nigger try to eat her baby when I did that to her. Oh Christ, this is too funny,' Roy gasped, wiping the tears away.

August 1964

SIXTEEN
The Saint

Serge stretched and yawned, then put his feet on the desk in the deserted juvenile office at Hollenbeck station. He smoked and wondered when his partner Stan Blackburn would return. Stan had asked Serge to wait in the office while he did some 'personal business' which Serge knew to be a woman whose divorce was not final, who had three children that were old enough to get him into trouble when the romance finally ended. An officer would get at least a suspension for conduct unbecoming, when an adulterous affair was brought to the Department's attention. Serge wondered if he would tomcat around – if – he married.

Serge had accepted the assignment as a juvenile officer only because he was assured he would not be transferred to Georgia Street Station but could remain here in Hollenbeck and work the night watch J-Car. He decided that the juvenile background would look good in his record when he went up for promotion. But first he would have to pass the written exam and it would be extremely doubtful that he would manage that since he couldn't imagine himself knuckling down to a rigid study program. He hadn't been able to make himself study even in his college classes and he smiled as he recalled the brave ambition of a few years ago to work diligently for the degree and advance quickly in his profession. After several false starts, he was now a government major at Cal State and had only accumulated thirty-three units.

But he enjoyed his work here at Hollenbeck and he made more than enough money to support himself. He had a surprisingly sound savings program and he couldn't see any farther than perhaps detective sergeant here at Hollenbeck. That would be enough, he thought. At the end of his twenty years he would be forty-three years old and able to draw forty percent of his salary the rest of his life which would certainly not be lived here in Los Angeles, or anywhere near Los Angeles. He thought of San Diego. It was pleasant down there, but not in the city, some suburb perhaps. There should be a woman and children somewhere in his plans, he knew. It could not be avoided indefinitely. And it was true that he was more and more becoming restless and sentimental. The home and hearth television stories were starting to interest him slightly.

He had been seeing a great deal of Paula. No other girl had ever stirred this much interest in him. She was not a beauty, but she was attractive and her clear gray eyes held your attention unless she was wearing tight-fitting clothes and then she became extremely interesting. He knew she would marry him. She had hinted often enough that she wanted a family. He told her you'd better get started because you're now twenty-two, and she asked him if he'd like to sire her a couple of kids. When he said, 'My pleasure,' she said they'd have to be legitimate.

Paula had other assets. Her father, Dr. Thomas Adams, was a successful dentist in Alhambra, and would probably bestow a small piece of property on a lucky son-in-law since Paula was his only child and overly indulged. Paula had taken apartment number twelve in his building, formerly occupied by a steno named Maureen Ball, and Serge had hardly noticed the change in women and had begun dating Paula without a break in stride. He knew that some evening, after a good dinner and more than a few martinis, he would probably go through the formality of asking her, and tell her to go ahead and inform the family to prepare the marriage feast because, what the hell, he couldn't go on aimlessly forever.

At eight-thirty the sun had fallen and it was cool enough to take a ride around Hollenbeck. Serge was wishing Stan Blackburn would come back and he was trying to decide whether to resume reading the treatise on the California constitution for the summer school class he wished he hadn't taken, or whether to read a novel which he had brought to work tonight because he knew he would be waiting in the office for several hours.

Blackburn came whistling through the door just as Serge made the decision of the novel over the California constitution. Blackburn had a simpering smile on his face and the evidence of his personal business was easy to see.

'Better wipe the lipstick off your shirt front,' said Serge.

'Wonder how it got way down there,' said Blackburn with a knowing wink at his mark of conquest.

Serge had seen her once when Blackburn had parked in the alley next to her duplex, and gone inside for a moment. Serge wouldn't have bothered with her even without the dangers of an estranged husband, and children who might report to Daddy.

Blackburn ran a comb through his thinning gray hair, straightened his tie, and dabbed at the lipstick on his white shirt.

'Ready to go to work?' asked Serge, swinging his feet off the desk.

'I don't know. I'm kind of tired,' Blackburn chuckled.

'Let's go, Casanova,' said Serge, shaking his head. 'I guess I better drive so you can rest and restore yourself.'

Serge decided to drive south on Soto and east toward the new Pomona freeway right-of-way. Sometimes in the late afternoon if it wasn't too hot, he liked to watch the workmen scurrying about to complete another vast

Los Angeles complex of steel and concrete, obsolete before it is finished, guaranteed to be strangled by cars one hour after its opening. One thing the freeway had done, it had broken up *Los Gavilanes*. The doctrine of eminent domain had succeeded in gang busting where the police, probation department, and juvenile court had failed – *Los Gavilanes* had dissolved when the state bought the property and the parents of *Los Gavilanes* scattered through East Los Angeles.

Serge decided to drive through the concrete paths at Hollenbeck Park to check for juvenile gang activity. They hadn't made an arrest for a week, mostly because of Blackburn's time-consuming romantic meetings, and Serge hoped they might spot something tonight. He liked to do just enough work to keep the sergeant off his back, although nothing had yet been said about their lack of accomplishment this week.

As Serge drove toward the boathouse, a figure disappeared in the bushes and they heard a hollow clunk as a bottle hastily dropped, struck a rock.

'See who that was?' asked Serge as Blackburn lazily ran the spotlight over the bushes.

'Looked like one of the Pee Wees. Bimbo Zaragoza, I think.'

'Drinking a little wine, I guess.'

'Yeah, that's not like him. He's a glue head.'

'Any port in a storm.'

'Port. Hah, that's pretty good.'

'Think we can drive down below and catch him?'

'No, he's clear across the lake by now.' Blackburn leaned back and closed his eyes.

'We better make a pinch tonight,' said Serge.

'Nothing to worry about,' said Blackburn, eyes still closed as he took the wrappers off two sticks of gum and shoved them in his mouth.

As Serge came out of the park onto Boyle Street he saw two more Pee Wees but Bimbo was not with them. The smaller one he recognized as Mario Vega, the other he couldn't recall.

'Who's the big one?' he asked.

Blackburn opened one eye and shined the light on the two boys who grinned and began walking toward Whittier Boulevard.

'Ape man, they called him. I forget his real name.'

As they passed the boys, Serge snorted at the exaggerated cholo walk of ape man: toes turned out, heels digging in, arms swinging freely, this was the trademark of the gang member. This and the curious deliberate ritual chewing on imaginary chewing gum. One wore Levis, the other khakis slit at the bottoms at the seams to 'hang tough' over the black polished shoes. Both wore Pendleton shirts buttoned at the cuff to hide the puncture marks which, if they had them, would bring the status of the addict. And both wore navy watch caps as they wear in youth camp, and this showed they were ex-cons whether or not they actually were.

Serge caught a few words of the conversation when they drove slowly past the boys, mostly muffled Spanish obscenities. Then he thought of the books which talked of the formalism of Spanish insults in which acts are only implied. Not so in familiar informal Mexican, he thought. A Mexican insult or vulgarism could surpass in color even the English equivalent. The Chicanos had given life to the Spanish obscenity.

Serge had decided that Blackburn was asleep when at ten past ten the Communications operator said, 'All Hollenbeck units, and Four-A-Forty-three, a four-eighty-four suspect just left twenty-three eleven Brooklyn Avenue running eastbound on Brooklyn and south on Soto. Suspect is male, Mexican, thirty-five to forty, five feet eight to ten, a hundred and sixty to a hundred and seventy, black hair, wearing a dirty short-sleeved red turtleneck shirt, khaki pants, carrying a plaster statue.'

Serge and Blackburn were on Brooklyn approaching St. Louis when the call came out. They passed the scene of the theft and Serge saw the radio car parked in front, the dome light on and an officer sitting inside. The other officer was in the store talking with the proprietor.

Serge double-parked for a moment beside the radio car, and read 'Luz del Día Religious Store' on the window.

'What did he get?' he called to the officer who was a new rookie that Serge didn't know.

'A religious statue, sir,' said the young officer, probably thinking they were worthy of the 'sir' since they were plainclothesmen. Serge was glad to see that his drowsing partner at least opened his eyes when he talked to the rookie. He hated to disillusion the young ones too quickly.

Serge turned south on Soto and began glancing around for the thief. He turned east on First and north on Matthews and spotted the red turtleneck lurching down the street. The witness had given an excellent description he thought, but she didn't say he was drunk.

'Here he comes,' said Serge.

'Who?'

'The four-eighty-four suspect from the religious store. This has to be him. Look.'

'Yeah, that must be him,' said Blackburn, lighting up the weaving drunk with the spotlight. The drunk threw his hands in front of his face.

Serge stopped a few feet in front of the man and they both got out.

'Where's the statue?' asked Blackburn.

'I ain't got nothing, sir,' said the man, watery-eyed and bloated. His turtleneck was purple with the stains of a hundred pints of wine.

'I know this guy,' said Blackburn. 'Let's see, Eddie ... Eddie something.'

'Eduardo Onofre Esquer,' said the man, swaying precariously. 'I 'member you, sir. You bosted me lots of times for drunk.'

'Yeah. Eddie was one of the Brooklyn Avenue winos for years. Where you been, Eddie?'

'I got a jeer last time, sir. I been in the county for a jeer.'

'A year? For drunk?'

'Not for drunk. Petty theft, sir. I was choplifting a couple pairs of woman's stocking to sell for a drink.'

'And now you're doing the same damn thing,' said Blackburn. 'You know petty theft with a prior is a felony. You're going to go for a felony this time.'

'Please sir,' sobbed Eddie. 'Don' bost me this time.'

'Get in, Eddie,' said Serge. 'Show us where you threw it.'

'Please don' bost me,' said Eddie, as Serge started the car and drove east on Michigan.

'Which way, Eddie?' asked Serge.

'I didn' throw it, sir. I set it down at the church when I saw what it was.'

Blackburn's spotlight lighted up the white robe and black cowl and black face of Martin de Porres on the steps in front of the drab gray building on Breed Street.

'When I saw what it was, I put it there on the steps of the church.'

'That ain't no church,' said Blackburn. 'That's a synagogue.'

'Anyway, I put it there for the priest to find,' said Eddie. 'Please don' bost me, sir. I'll go straight home to my room if you give me a break. I won' steal no more. I swear on my mother.'

'What do you say, partner?' asked Serge, grinning.

'What the hell. We're juvenile officers, ain't we?' said Blackburn. 'Eddie's no juvenile.'

'Go home, Eddie,' said Serge, reaching over the seat and unlocking the rear door of the car.

'Thank you, sir,' said Eddie. 'Thank you. I'm going home.' Eddie stumbled over the curb, righted himself and staggered down the sidewalk toward home as Serge retrieved the statue from the steps of the synagogue.

'Thank you, sir,' Eddie shouted over his shoulder. 'I didn' know what I was taking. I swear to God I wouldn' steal a saint.'

'You about ready to eat?' asked Blackburn, after they left black Martin at the religious store, telling the proprietor they found him undamaged on the sidewalk two blocks away, and that perhaps the thief had a conscience and could not steal Martin de Porres. The proprietor said, '*Quizás, quizás. Quién sabe?* We like to think of a thief with a soul.'

Blackburn offered the old man a cigarette and said, 'We've got to believe there are good ones, eh señor? Young men like my *compañero* here, they don't need anything, but when they get a little older like you and me they need some faith, eh?'

And the old man nodded, puffed on the cigarette and said, 'It is very true, señor.'

'Ready to eat?' Serge asked Blackburn.

Blackburn was silent for a minute, then said, 'Take me to the station, will you, Serge?'

'What for?'

'I want to make a call. You go eat, and pick me up later.'

Now what the hell's going on? Serge thought. This guy had more personal problems than any partner he ever had.

'I'm going to call my wife,' said Blackburn.

'You're separated, aren't you?' asked Serge, and was then sorry he said it because innocent remarks like that could leave an opening for a lurid confession of marital problems.

'Yeah, but I'm going to call her and ask her if I can come home. What am I doing living in a bachelor pad? I'm forty-two years old. I'm going to tell her we can make it if we have faith.'

That's just swell, Serge thought. Black Martin worked his magic on the horny old bastard.

Serge dropped Blackburn at the station and drove back to Brooklyn deciding he'd have some Mexican food. Some *carnitas* sounded good and there were a couple of places on Brooklyn that gave policemen half price and made *carnitas* Michoacán style.

Then he thought of Mr. Rosales' place. He hadn't been there in a few months and there was always Mariana who looked better and better each time he stopped. One of these days he might ask her out to a movie. Then he realized he hadn't dated a Mexican girl since high school.

He didn't see Mariana when he first entered the restaurant. He had been coming in once or twice a month, but had missed the last few months – because of a thirty-day vacation and a waitress that Blackburn was trying to seduce at a downtown drive-in who was unaccountably interested in the old boy and was supplying them with hot dogs, hamburgers, and occasional pastramis courtesy of the boss who did not know she was doing it.

'Ah, Señor Duran,' said Mr. Rosales, waving Serge to a booth. 'We have not seen you. How are you? Have you been sick?'

'Vacation, Mr. Rosales,' said Serge. 'Am I too late to eat?'

'No, of course not. Some *carnitas*? I have a new cook from Guanajuato. She can make delicious *barbacoa* and *birria*.'

'Maybe just a couple tacos, Mr. Rosales. And coffee.'

'Tacos. *Con todo*?'

'Yes, lots of chile.'

'Right away, Señor Duran,' said Mr. Rosales, going to the kitchen, and Serge waited but it was not Mariana who returned with the coffee, it was another girl, older, thinner, inexperienced as a waitress, who spilled a little coffee while pouring.

Serge drank the coffee and smoked until she brought him the tacos. He was not as hungry as he thought, even though the new cook made them just as good as the last one. Every bit of fat was trimmed off the tiny chunks of pork and the onions were grated with care, with cilantro sprinkled over the meat. The chile sauce, Serge thought, was the best he ever tasted, but still he was not as hungry as he thought.

Midway through the first taco, he caught Mr. Rosales' eye and the little man hurried to his table. 'More *café?*' he asked.

'No, this is fine. I was just wondering, where's Mariana? New job?'

'No,' he laughed. 'Business is so good I have two waitresses now. I have sent her to the market. We ran out of milk tonight. She will be back soon.'

'How's her English? Improving?'

'You will be surprised. She is a very smart one. She talks much better than I do.'

'Your English is beautiful, Mr. Rosales.'

'Thank you. And your Spanish, señor? I have never heard you speaking Spanish. I thought you were Anglo until I learned your name. You are half Anglo, perhaps? Or a real Spaniard?'

'Here she comes,' said Serge, relieved to have Mariana interrupt the conversation. She was carrying two large bags and closed the door with her foot, not seeing Serge who took a grocery bag from her hand.

'Señor Duran!' she said, her black eyes glowing. 'How good it is to see joo.'

'How good it is to hear you speak such beautiful English,' Serge smiled, and nodded to Mr. Rosales, as he helped her take the milk to the kitchen.

Serge returned to the table and ate heartily while Mariana put on an apron and came to his table with a fresh pot of coffee.

'Two more tacos, Mariana,' he said, noting with approval that she had gained a few pounds and was now rounding into womanhood.

'Joo are hungry tonight, Señor Duran? We have missed you.'

'I'm hungry tonight, Mariana,' he said. 'I've missed you too.'

She smiled and returned to the kitchen and he was surprised that he could have forgotten that clean white smile. Now that he saw it again, he thought it astonishing that he could have forgotten. It was still too thin and delicate a face. The forehead was ample, the upper lip still a bit long, the black eyes heavy-lashed and full of life. It was still the madonna face. He knew the tiny fire of longing still lived in spite of what the world had told him, and that flame was glowing red hot at this moment. He thought he'd let it smolder for a while because it was not unpleasant.

When Mariana brought the second plate of tacos, he brushed against her fingers. 'Let me hear you speak English,' he said.

'What do joo wish me to say?' she laughed, self-consciously.

'First of all, stop calling me señor. You know my name, don't you?'

'I know it.'

'What is it?'

'Sergio.'

'Serge.'

'I cannot say that word. The end is too harsh and difficult. But Sergio is soft and easy to say. Try it jurself.'

'Ser-hee-oh.'

'Ay, that sounds berry comic. Can you no' say Sergio?' she laughed. 'Sergio. Two sounds. No more. No' three sounds.'

'Of course,' he smiled. 'My mother called me Sergio.'

'Joo see,' she laughed. 'I knew that joo could say it. But why don' joo ever talk Spanish?'

'I've forgotten,' he smiled, and thought, you couldn't help smiling at her. She was a delightful little child. 'You're a dove,' he said.

'What is a dove?'

'*Una paloma.*'

'But that is my name. Mariana Paloma.'

'It fits. You're a little dove.'

'I am no' so little. It is that joo are a big man.'

'Did you ever see a man so big in your country?'

'No' many,' she said.

'How old are you, Mariana, nineteen?'

'Jas.'

'Say yes.'

'Jes.'

'Y-y-yes.'

'J-j-jes.'

They both laughed and Serge said, 'Would you like me to teach you to say yes? Yes is easy to say.'

'I wish to learn all English words,' she answered, and Serge felt ashamed because her eyes were innocent, and she didn't understand. Then he thought, for God's sake, there are plenty of girls even if Paula wasn't enough which she most certainly was. What would it prove to take a simple child like this? Had he lived so long alone that self-gratification had become the only purpose for living?

Still he said, 'You don't work Sundays, do you?'

'No.'

'Would you like to go somewhere with me? To dinner? Or to a theater? Have you ever seen a real play? With music?'

'Joo want me to go with joo? *De veras?*'

'If Mr. Rosales will let you.'

'He will let me go anywhere with joo. He thinks joo are a good man. Joo mean it?'

'I mean it. Where shall we go?'

'To a lake. Can we go to a lake? In the afternoon? I will bring food. I have never seen a lake in this country.'

'Okay, a picnic,' he laughed. 'We call it a picnic when people bring food and go to a lake.'

'That is another hard word,' she said.

Serge thought several times on Saturday of calling Mr. Rosales' restaurant and calling off the outing. He never was aware of having any particular respect for himself. He realized that he was always one who wanted only to get along, to do things the easiest, least painful way, and if he could have a woman, a book, or a movie, and get drunk at least once a month, he thought that he had mastered life. But now there was the lust for the girl and it was not that he was Don Quixote, he thought, but it was a totally unnecessary bit of cruelty to take a child like her who had seen or done nothing in a short difficult life, and to whom he must seem something special with a one-year-old Corvette and expensive gaudy sports coats which Paula bought for him. He was degenerating, he thought. In three years he'd be thirty. What would he be then?

In order to sleep Saturday night, he made a solemn promise to himself that under no circumstance would he engage in a cheap seduction of a girl who was the ward of a kindly old man who had done him no harm. And besides, he grinned wryly, if Mr. Rosales found out, there would be no more free meals for the Hollenbeck policemen. Free meals were harder to come by than women – even if she were truly the Virgin of Guadalajara.

He picked her up at the restaurant because that Sunday she had to work two hours from ten until noon when the afternoon girl came on. Mr. Rosales seemed very glad to see him and she had a shopping bag full of food which she called her 'chopping sack'. Mr. Rosales waved to them as they drove away from the restaurant and Serge checked his tank because he intended to drive all the way to Lake Arrowhead. If she wanted a lake, he'd give her the best, he thought, complete with lakeside homes that should open those gleaming black eyes as wide as silver pesos.

'I didn't know if joo would come,' she smiled.

'Why do you say that?'

'Joo are always joking with Señor Rosales and with the other girl and me. I thought maybe it was a joke.'

'You were ready, weren't you?'

'I still thought it was maybe a joke. But I went to a berry early Mass and prepared the food.'

'What kind of food? Mexican?'

'*Claro*. I am *Mexicana*? No?'

'You are,' he laughed. 'You are *muy Mexicana*.'

'And joo are completely an American. I cannot believe that joo could have a name like Sergio Duran.'

'Sometimes I can't believe it either, little dove.'

'I like that name,' she smiled, and Serge thought she's not a wilting flower, this one. She carries her face uplifted and looks right in your eye, even when she's blushing because you've made her terribly self-conscious.

'And I like your red dress. And I like your hair down, long like that.'

'A waitress cannot wear her hair like this. Sometimes I think I chould cut the hair like American girls.'

'Never do that!' he said. 'You're not an American girl. Do you want to be one?'

'Only sometimes,' she said, looking at him seriously, and then they were silent for a while but it was not an uncomfortable silence. Occasionally she would ask him about a town they passed or an unusual building. She amazed him by noticing and knowing the names of several species of flowers that were used to decorate portions of the San Bernardino Freeway. And she knew them in English.

She surprised him again when she said, 'I love the flowers and plants so much, Señor Rosales was telling me I chould perhaps study botany instead of language.'

'Study?' he said in amazement. 'Where?'

'I am starting college in Se'tember,' she smiled. 'My teacher at my English class says that my reading of English is good and that I will speak also berry good after I begin to study in college.'

'College!' he said. 'But little girls from Mexico don't come here and go to college. It's wonderful! I'm very glad.'

'Thank joo,' she smiled. 'I am happy that joo are pleased with me. My teacher says that I may do well even though I have no' too much ed-joocation because I read and write so good in Spanish. My mother was also a berry good reader and had a good ed-joocation before she married my poor father who had none.'

'Is your mother alive?'

'No, not for three years.'

'Your father is?'

'Oh jes, he is a big strong man. Always berry alive. But not so much as before Mamá died. I have ten junger sisters. I will earn money and I will send for them one by one unless they marry before I earn money.'

'You're an ambitious girl.'

'What means this?'

'You have great strength and desire to succeed.'

'It is nothing.'

'So you'll study botany, eh?'

'I will study English and Spanish,' she said. 'I can be a teacher in perhaps four jeers or a translator in less time working for the courthouse if I work hard. Botany is just a foolish thought. Could joo see me as an ed-joocated woman?'

'I can't see you as a woman at all,' he said, even as he studied her ripe young body. 'You're just a little dove to me.'

'Ah, Sergio,' she laughed, 'joo get such things from the books. I used to watch joo, before we became friends, when I would serve the food to joo and jour *compañero*, the other policeman. Joo would carry books in the coat pocket and read while eating. There is not a place in the real life for little doves. Joo must be strong and work berry hard. Still, I like to hear joo say that I am a dove.'

'You're only nineteen years old,' he said.

'A Mexican girl is a woman long before. I am a woman, Sergio.'

They drove again in silence and Serge deeply enjoyed her enjoyment of the passing miles, and vineyards, and towns, which he scarcely noticed.

Mariana was as impressed with the lake as he knew she would be. He rented a motorboat, and for an hour showed her the lakeside Arrowhead homes. He knew she was speechless at such wealth.

'But there are so many!' she exclaimed. 'There must be so many rich ones.'

'They're many,' he said. 'And I'll never be one of them.'

'But that is not important,' she said, leaning an inch closer to him as he steered the boat out into open water. The bright sunlight reflecting off the water hurt his eyes and he put his sunglasses on. She looked a deeper bronze, and the wind caught her deep brown hair and swept it back at least twelve inches from the nape of her exposed neck. It was four o'clock and the sun was still hot when they finished the lunch on a rocky hill on the far side of the lake which Serge had discovered another time with another girl who liked picnics and making love in open places.

'I thought you were bringing Mexican food,' said Serge, finishing his fifth piece of tender chicken and washing it down with strawberry soda which was kept chilled by a plastic bucket of ice in the bottom of the shopping bag.

'I heard that Americans take *pollo frito* on a pic-nic,' she laughed. 'I was told that all Americans expected it.'

'It's delicious,' he sighed, thinking he hadn't had strawberry soda lately. He wondered again why strawberry is by far the favorite flavor of Mexicans, and any Good Humor man in East Los Angeles carries an extra box of strawberry sundaes and Popsicles.

'Señora Rosales wanted me to bring *chicharrones* and beer for joo, but I didn't, because I thought joo would like the other better.'

'I loved your lunch, Mariana,' he smiled, wondering how long it had been since he tasted the rich crispy pork rinds. Then he realized he had never tasted *chicharrones* with beer because when his mother made them he was too young to drink beer. He found himself suddenly yearning for some *chicharrones* and a cold glass of beer. You always want what you don't have at the moment, he thought.

He watched Mariana as she cleaned up the picnic things, putting the paper plates in an extra shopping bag she brought. In a few minutes he would not have known anyone had eaten there. She was a totally efficient girl, he thought, and she looked dazzling in the red dress and black sandals. She had lovely toes and feet, brown and smooth like the rest of her. He got a sharp pain in the lower part of his chest as he thought about the rest of her and remembered the vow of abstinence he had made to the person he was growing to respect the least in all the world.

When she finished she sat next to him and drew her knees up and put her hands on her knees and her chin on her hands.

'Joo want to know something?' she asked gazing at the water.

'What?'

'I never have seen a lake. Not here. Not in Mexico. Only in movies. This is my first real lake to see.'

'Do you like it?' he asked, feeling his palms become a little moist. The pain returned to his chest as his mouth turned dry.

'Joo have given me a fine day, Sergio,' she said looking at him with heaviness in her voice.

'So you've enjoyed it?'

'Jas.'

'Not jas,' he laughed. 'Yes.'

'Jes,' she smiled.

'Like this. Y-y-yes. Here, put your chin forward just a little bit.' He held her chin in his fingers and tugged lightly. But her whole face came forward to him.

'Yes,' he said, and his fingers trembled. 'I told you I'd teach you to say yes.'

'Yes,' she said.

'You said it.'

'Yes, Sergio, oh, yes, yes,' she breathed.

'Fly away, little dove,' he said not knowing the strange hollow voice. 'Please fly away,' he said, and yet he held her shoulders fearing she would.

'Yes, Sergio, yes.'

'You're making a mistake, little dove,' he whispered, but her lip touched his cheek.

'I say yes, Sergio. For you, yes. *Para tí*, yes, yes.'

SEVENTEEN
Kiddy Cops

L ucy was merely attractive, but her eyes were alert and missed nothing and devoured you when you were talking to her. Yet you were never uncomfortable because of it. Instead, you succumbed to being devoured and you liked it. Yes, you liked it. Gus took his gaze from the road and examined her long legs, crossed at the ankle, hose sheer, pale and subtle. She sat relaxed much like a male partner and smoked and watched the street as Gus cruised, much like a male partner would, but it was nothing like working with a male partner. With some of the other policewomen there was no difference, except you had to be more careful and not get involved in things where there was the slightest element of danger. Not if you could help it, because a policewoman was still a woman, nothing more, and you were responsible for her safety, being the male half of the team. With some policewoman partners it was almost like being with a man, but not with Lucy. Gus wondered why he liked being devoured by those brown eyes which crinkled at the corners. He was normally shriveled by eyes which looked too hard.

'Think you're going to stay with police work, Lucy?' asked Gus, turning on Main Street thinking she would probably enjoy touring the skid row streets. Most new policewomen did.

'I love it, Gus,' she said. 'It's a fascinating job. Especially here in Juvenile Division. I don't think working the women's jail would've been nearly as good.'

'I don't think so either. I can't picture you in there pushing those bull daggers around.'

'I can't either,' she grimaced, 'but I guess sooner or later I'll get assigned there.'

'Maybe not,' said Gus. 'You're a good juvenile officer, you know. For just being a few weeks out of the academy I'd say you're exceptional. They may keep you in Juvenile.'

'Oh sure, I'm indispensable,' she laughed.

'You're smart and quick and you're the first policewoman I ever enjoyed working with. Most policemen don't like working with women.' He pretended to watch the road very closely as he said it because he felt the brown eyes. He hadn't meant to say this. It was only 7:00 P.M., not dark yet, and he didn't want to blush and let her see it. But then, she would probably even see it in the dark with those eyes.

'That's a fine compliment, Gus,' said Lucy. 'You've been a patient teacher.'

'Oh, I don't know it all myself yet,' said Gus, working hard at not blushing by thinking of other things as he talked, like where they would eat, and that they should walk through the Main Street bus depot and look for runaway juveniles because Sunday night was a slow night, or maybe they should cruise through Elysian Park and look for the kids who would surely be there on a Sunday drinking beer on the grass. Lieutenant Dilford loved them to make arrests for minors' possession of alcohol and Dilford treated it like patrol watch commanders treated good felony arrests.

'You've been working Juvenile about six months, haven't you?' asked Lucy.

'About five months now. I've still got lots to learn.'

'Where did you work before that, Central Vice?'

'Wilshire Vice.'

'I can't picture you as a vice officer,' she laughed. 'When I worked Lincoln Heights Jail on weekend assignments, the vice officers would be in and out all night. I can't picture you as a vice officer.'

'I know. I don't look man enough to be a vice officer, do I?'

'Oh, I didn't mean that, Gus,' she said, uncrossing her ankles and drilling him with her brown eyes. When they were working they darkened her face which was smooth and milky. 'I didn't mean that at all. In fact, I didn't like them because they were loud and talked to policewomen like they talked to their whores. I didn't think all that bravado made them more manly. I think that being quiet and gentle and having some humility is very manly, but I didn't see many vice officers like that.'

'Well, they have to construct some kind of defense against all the sordid things they see,' said Gus, elated because she as much as admitted that she was fond of him and saw things in him. Then he became disgusted and thought viciously, you simpering little bastard. He thought of Vickie who was recovering from an appendectomy and he hoped she would sleep tonight, and he swore that he would stop this childish flirtation before it went any further because Lucy would soon see it even though she was not a self-conscious person and did not notice such things. But when she did, finally, she would probably say, that's not what I meant, that's not what I meant at all. Simpering little bastard, he thought again, and peeked in the rearview mirror at his sandy receding hair which was hardly noticeable. In a few years he would be completely bald and he wondered if he would still be dreaming of a bright, pale, brown-eyed girl who would smile in pity or perhaps revulsion if she knew the thoughts he had about her.

'What time should we check out the unfit home?' asked Lucy, and Gus was glad she had changed the subject. He couldn't help smiling at the man walking up Hill Street who turned his head to look at Lucy as they passed. He remembered how men used to turn like that to look at Vickie when they were first married, before she got so heavy. He thought of how he and Lucy must look, two young people, he in a suit and tie and white shirt and her in a modest green dress which fit so well. They might be going to dinner, or to the Bowl for a concert, or to the Sports Arena. Of course, all the street people recognized the plain four-door Plymouth as a police car, and knew the man and woman were juvenile officers, but to anyone else they might just be lovers.

'What time, Gus?'

'It's twenty after seven.'

'No,' she laughed. 'What time do we check out the unfit home the lieutenant mentioned?'

'Oh, let's do it now. Sorry, I was dreaming.'

'How's your wife recovering from her appendectomy?' asked Lucy. Gus hated to talk about Vickie to her, but she always asked things about his family as partners did, often in the early morning hours when things were quiet and partners talked.

'She's getting along all right.'

'How's your little one? He's talking, isn't he?'

'Chattering,' Gus smiled, and he never hesitated to talk about his children to her because she wanted to hear, he was sure of it.

'They look so beautiful in the pictures. I'd love to see them some time.'

'I'd like you to,' said Gus.

'I hope it's quiet tonight.'

'Why? The night passes slow when it's quiet.'

'Yes, but I can get you talking then,' she laughed. 'I learn more about being a cop in the late hours when I get you talking.'

'You mean when I tell you all the things Kilvinsky taught me?' he smiled.

'Yes, but I bet you're a better teacher than your friend Kilvinsky was.'

'Oh, no. Kilvinsky was the best,' said Gus, his face burning again. 'That reminds me, I've got to write him. He hasn't been answering my letters lately and I'm worried. Ever since he took the trip East to see his ex-wife and children.'

'Are you sure he came back?'

'Yes. I got one letter right after he came back, but it didn't say anything.'

'Isn't it strange that he never visited his own children before that?'

'He must've had a reason,' said Gus.

'I don't think you could abandon your children like that.'

'He didn't abandon them,' said Gus quickly. 'Kilvinsky wouldn't do that. He's just a mysterious man, that's all. He must've had good reasons.'

'If your wife ever left you, you wouldn't abandon your children, Gus, not you. Not for any reason.'

'Well, I can't judge him,' said Gus, glad darkness was settling on downtown as he stopped for a light.

'He's not the father you are, I bet,' said Lucy and she was watching him again.

'Oh, you're wrong,' said Gus. 'Kilvinsky would be a good father. He'd be as good a father as anyone could want. He could tell you things, and when he talked you knew he was right. Things seemed all in place when he explained them.'

'It's getting dark.'

'Let's go handle the unfit home,' said Gus, growing uneasy at the deprecating talk about Kilvinsky.

'Okay, it was on West Temple, wasn't it?'

'It might be a phony call.'

'Anonymous?'

'Yeah, a woman called the watch commander and said a neighbor in apartment twenty-three had a cruddy pad and left a little kid alone all the time.'

'I haven't been in a real unfit home yet,' said Lucy. 'They've all turned out to be false alarms.'

'Remember how to tell a real unfit?' smiled Gus.

'Sure. If you stomp your foot and the roaches are so tame they don't run, then you know it's a real unfit.'

'Right,' Gus grinned. 'And if we could bottle the smell we'd win every case in court.'

Gus drove through the Second Street tunnel and over the Harbor Freeway and turned north, then west on Temple, the setting sun glowing dirty pink on the horizon. It had been a smoggy day.

'I bet it's the white apartment building,' said Lucy pointing toward the three-story stucco with an imitation stone façade.

'Eighteen thirteen. That's it,' said Gus parking in front and wondering if he had enough money to buy a decent dinner tonight. With anyone else he ate hamburgers or brown bagged it, but Lucy ate well and liked a hot dinner. He went along with her, pretending this was what he wanted too, even though he had less than five dollars to last until payday, and less than a half tank of gas in his car. Monday night he had an argument with Vickie over the check to his mother which had shrunk to forty-five dollars a month because John was in the army, thank God.

The argument was so violent it made him sick. Lucy had noticed his depression the next evening. And now he thought of how he had blurted it out to Lucy that night, and how kind she had been and how ashamed he had been and still was that he had told her. Yet it had lifted his spirits. And come to think of it, she hadn't asked to eat in a real restaurant since that night, and she had insisted on buying the coffee or Cokes more often than she should.

It was built to wear only for a time, like so many southern California apartment houses. Gus parked in front and they climbed the twenty-four steps to the second floor. Gus noticed that the metal railing, which only vaguely resembled wrought iron, was loose. He drew his hand back and guessed that someday a drunk would stagger from his apartment door and hit the railing and plunge twenty feet to the concrete below, but being drunk, he would probably receive only abrasions. Apartment twenty-three was in the back. The drapes were drawn and the door was closed, and this alone made Gus suspect there was no one home, because in all the other occupied apartments the doors were open. All had outside screen doors and the people were trying to catch the evening breeze because it had been a hot smoggy day.

Gus knocked and rang the tinny chime and knocked again. Finally, Lucy shrugged and they turned to go and Gus was glad because he didn't feel like working; he felt like driving through Elysian Park pretending to look for juvenile drinkers and just look at Lucy and talk to her perhaps on the upper road on the east side near the reservoir which looked like black ice in the moonlight.

'You the cops?' whispered a woman who suddenly appeared inside the dusty screen door of apartment number twenty-one.

'Yes. Did you call?' asked Gus.

'I'm the one,' said the woman. 'I called but I said I didn't want nobody to know I called. They aren't home now, but the kid's in there.'

'What seems to be the problem?' asked Gus.

'Well, come on in. It looks like I'm going to get involved anyway,' she muttered holding the screen and licking the absurdly made-up lips which were drawn on halfway to her nose. In fact, all her makeup had a theatrical exaggeration designed for an audience that must be far away.

'I talked to some Lieutenant Whatzizname and told him that place isn't fit for pigs most of the time and the kid gets left alone and I never see him outside hardly. Last night he was screaming and screaming and I think the old man was beating him 'cause the old lady was screaming too.'

'Do you know the people in that apartment?' asked Gus.

'Lord, no. They're trash,' said the woman, uncoiling a wiry wisp of blond hair with gray roots. 'They only been living here a month and they go out almost every night and sometimes they have a babysitter, a cousin or something, staying with their kid. And sometimes they got nobody staying with him. I learned long time ago to mind my own business but today it was so damn hot they had the door open and I happened to walk by and the place looks like a slit trench and I know what a slit trench is because I like war novels. There was dog crap from this dirty little terrier they got, and food and other crud all over the floor and then when they left the kid today I just said what the hell, I'll call and remain anonymous but now it looks like I can't be anonymous, huh?'

'How old is the child?' asked Gus.

'Three. A little boy. He hardly never comes outside. The old man's a souse. The mother seems okay. Just a dirty little mouse, you know what I mean. A souse and a mouse. I think the old man pushes her around when he's drunk, but it don't matter much to her probably, because she's usually drunk when he is. Fine neighbors. This place had class a few years ago. I'm moving.'

'How old are they? The parents?'

'Young people. Not thirty I don't think. Dirty people though.'

'You sure the little boy's in there alone? Right now?'

'I saw them leave, Officer. I'm sure. He's in there. He's a quiet little guy. Never hear a peep out of him. He's in there.'

'What apartment is the landlady in? We'll need a passkey.'

'Martha went to the movies tonight. She told me she was going. I never thought about the key.' The woman shook her head and tugged at the frayed waistband of the olive stretch pants that were never meant to be stretched so much.

'We can't just break the door down on this information.'

'Why not? The kid's only three and he's in there alone.'

'No,' said Gus, shaking his head. 'He could be in there and maybe they took him when you weren't looking. Maybe a lot of things. We'll just have to come back later when they're home and try to get invited inside to take a look around.'

'Goddamn,' said the woman. 'The one time in my life I call a cop and try to do a decent thing and look what happens.'

'Let me go try the door,' said Gus. 'Maybe it's open.'

'The one time I call the cops,' said the woman to Lucy as Gus stepped outside and walked down the walkway to number twenty-three. He opened the screen and turned the knob and the door slid open.

'Lucy,' he called, and stepped inside the stifling apartment, looking carefully for the 'dirty little terrier' that might suddenly grab him by the ankle. He stepped around a moist stinking brown heap in the center of the floor and decided the dog must be large for a terrier. Then he heard the pat pat on the vinyl tile floor and the gaunt gray dog appeared from the bathroom, looked at Gus, wagged his stumpy tail, yawned, and returned to the bathroom. Gus glanced in the empty bedroom and pointed to the pile on the floor when Lucy entered and she walked around it and followed him into the living room.

'Dirty people,' said the woman, who had followed Lucy inside.

'This certainly isn't bad by unfit home standards,' explained Gus. 'It has to be really dangerous. Broken windows, leaky stove. Clothes hanging over an open flame. Knee-deep in defecation, not just a pile on the floor.

And garbage laying around. Clogged toilet. I've seen places where the wall seems to move and then you realize that it's a solid sheet of roaches. This isn't bad. And there's no child in that bedroom.'

'He's here I tell you!'

'Look for yourself,' said Gus, and stood aside as the woman bounced into the bedroom. Her cheeks shook with every step, she walked so heavily.

It was now quite dark and Lucy switched on the hall light and walked toward the small bathroom.

'He's got to be here,' said the woman. 'I watched them leave.'

'Gus!' said Lucy, and he came to the bathroom door as she switched on the light and he saw the little boy on the floor by the bathtub curled up with the dog on a pile of bath towels. The boy was asleep and even before Lucy turned on the light Gus saw the absurd purple rings around his eyes and the swollen mouth cracked and raw from a recent beating. The boy slobbered and wheezed and Gus guessed the nose was broken. The coagulation had the nostrils blocked and Gus saw the way the hand was bent.

'Dirty people,' whispered the woman, and then began crying at once, and Lucy took her out without Gus saying anything. Lucy was back in a moment and neither of them spoke as Lucy lifted him in her arms and took him to the bedroom where he didn't awaken until she had him dressed. Gus marveled at her strength and how she gently managed the broken wrist and never woke him until they were starting out of the apartment.

The boy saw Gus first when he awoke and the swollen eyes stared for a second and then through pain or terror the fearful moaning started which never ceased for the hour they were with the boy.

'We'll be back,' said Gus to the woman who stood sobbing in the doorway of her apartment. Gus tried to take the boy when they started down the stairway, but when he touched the boy he recoiled and uttered a shriek. Lucy said, 'It's okay, Gus, he's afraid of you. There, there, darling.' And she patted him as Gus shined his light on the stairway for her. In a few moments they were driving to Central Receiving Hospital and each time Gus got too near the little boy, the moan became a terrible cry so he let Lucy handle him.

'He doesn't even look three years old,' said Gus when they parked in the hospital parking lot. 'He's so little.'

Gus waited in the hallway while they worked on the boy and when a second doctor was called in to look at the arm, Gus peered through the door and saw the first doctor, a floppy-haired young man, nod to the second doctor and point to the little boy whose battered face, green and blue and purple in the naked light, looked as though it had been painted by a surrealist gone mad. 'Dig the crazy downface,' said the first doctor with a bitter smile.

Lucy came out in fifteen minutes and said, 'Gus, his rectum was stitched up!'

'His rectum?'

'It had been stitched up! Oh Christ, Gus, I know it's usually the father in these sex things, but Christ, I can't believe it.'

'Was it a professional stitching job?'

'Yes. A doctor did it. Why wouldn't the doctor notify the police? Why?'

'There are doctors,' said Gus.

'He's afraid of men, Gus. He was just as much afraid of the doctor as he was of you. The nurse and I had to pet him and talk to him so the doctor could get near him.' Lucy looked for a moment like she would cry but instead she lit a cigarette and walked with Gus to the phone and waited until he phoned the watch commander.

'He's a bright child,' said Lucy, as Gus waited for the lieutenant to come to the phone. 'When the nurse asked him who did that to his rectum, he said, "Daddy did it 'cause I'm a bad boy". Oh Christ, Gus ...'

It was eleven o'clock before they completed their reports on the boy who was admitted to General Hospital. The parents hadn't returned home yet and Lieutenant Dilford had another team staked out on the apartment. Gus and Lucy resumed patrol.

'There's no sense thinking about it,' said Gus when Lucy was silent for a half hour.

'I know,' she said, forcing a smile and Gus thought of her comforting the child and thought how beautiful she had looked then.

'My gosh, it's almost eleven,' said Gus. 'You hungry?'

'No.'

'But can you eat?'

'You eat. I'll have coffee.'

'Let's both have coffee,' said Gus, driving to a restaurant on Sunset Boulevard where there were booths for two and anyone who noticed them would think they were lovers or perhaps a young married couple. Gus thought of how he was wrinkling at the corners of his mouth much like his mother. He smiled, because on second thought no one would believe he was a *young* lover.

When they were seated in the booth in the bright spacious restaurant Gus noticed the rusty smear on the shoulder of her dress and he thought again of how she had been with the child, of how strong she was in every way and how capable. He wondered what it would be like to live your life with someone whom you did not have to take care of and he wondered what it would be like to have someone take care of you occasionally, or at least pretend to. The anger started to build when he thought of Vickie and his mother and at least the army could take care of his brother for a few years. Gus vowed that if his mother let John freeload off her when he returned from the service that she would do it on her county check because he would refuse to give her another cent. As soon as he thought this he knew it was a lie because he too was basically a weakling, his only strength being that he could earn a living. When it came down to it he would go on giving them money because he was too much of a weakling to do otherwise. How much easier would life be, he wondered, being married to a strong girl like Lucy.

'You've got blood on your dress,' said Gus, nodding to the smear on her shoulder and he was immediately sorry he said it because he should be trying to cheer her up.

'I don't care,' she said, not bothering to look at it, and something had been building up in him. At that moment he almost blurted something. If those steady eyes had been on him instead of on the table he probably would have blurted it but he didn't, and was glad he didn't, because she probably would have looked at him sadly and said, 'But that's not what I meant at all.'

Gus noticed the three teen-age girls in the large booth across from them gossiping in shrill voices and smoking compulsively as they tried in vain to handle the two little boys who kept slipping unnoticed to the floor and scampering down the aisle between the booths.

One of the girls with a proud bulging belly smiled often at the children of her adolescent girl friends, who had no doubt long since found the mystery of motherhood to be quite different from what had been anticipated. All three girls had ugly hairdos, high, teased, and bleached, and Gus thought that Vickie had been a mother that young. Then the guilt, which he knew was foolish, began to come again, but he forgot it when one of the young mothers grabbed the red-haired tot and cracked him across the face as she whispered, 'Sit down and behave, you little son of a bitch.'

Their coffee was half drunk when Lucy said, 'Have you been thinking about the little boy, Gus?'

'Not at all,' said Gus.

'Isn't it hard not to?'

'No it's not. Not after you get the hang of it. And you should learn that as soon as you can, Lucy.'

'What should I think about?'

'Your own problems. That's what I've been doing. Worrying about my own petty problems.'

'Tell me about *your* problems, Gus,' said Lucy. 'Give me something else to worry about.'

'Well, we haven't made a juvenile arrest for three days. The boss is going to be getting at us. That's something to worry about.'

'Do you *really* like juvenile work, Gus? I mean all things considered do you like being a kiddy cop?'

'I do, Lucy. It's not easy to explain, but it's like, well, especially with the little ones, I like the job because *we* protect them. Take the boy tonight. His father will be arrested and maybe the D.A. will be able to show that he did those things to the boy and maybe he won't. The boy will be a very bad witness or I miss my guess. Maybe the mother will tell the truth, but that's doubtful. And by the time the lawyers, headshrinkers, and criminologists have their say, nothing much will happen to him. But at least we got the boy out of there. I'm sure juvenile court won't give him back to them. Maybe we've saved his life. I like to think that we protect the children. To tell you the truth, if the door'd been locked I would've broken it down. I'd just about made up my mind. We're the only ones who can save the little kids from their parents.'

'Wouldn't you like to take a man like that and make him confess?' said Lucy, smashing her cigarette butt in the ashtray.

'I used to think I could torture the truth out of people,' Gus smiled, 'but after I was a policeman for a while and saw and arrested some of the really bad ones, I found that I didn't even want to touch them or be with them. I'd never make the grade in a medieval dungeon.'

'I had a very proper and square upbringing,' said Lucy, sipping her coffee as Gus stared at a place on her white collarbone where the brown hair touched it and caressed it when she moved her head even slightly. He was disgusted because his heart was racing and his hands were clammy. So he stopped staring at that tender patch of flesh. 'My dad teaches high school, like I told you, and Mother would have trouble believing that a parent would even let his child go around without freshly washed drawers. They're good people, you know? How can good people conceive of the existence of really bad people? I was going to be a social worker until I found what LAPD was paying policewomen. How could I ever be a social worker now that I've caught the scent of evil? People aren't basically good after all, are they?'

'But maybe they're not bad, either.'

'But they're not good, damn it. All my professors told me they were good! And people lie. God, how they lie. I can't get over how people lie.'

'That was the single most difficult thing for me to learn,' Gus said. 'I believed people for my first year or so on the job. No matter what anybody said. I wouldn't even listen to Kilvinsky. All my life I believed what people told me was the truth, and I was a lousy policeman until I got over that mistake. Now I know they'll lie when the truth would help. They'll lie when their lives depend on the truth.'

'What a rotten way to make a living,' said Lucy.

'Not for a man. For a woman, maybe. But you'll find someone and get married. You won't be doing this all your life.' Gus avoided her eyes when he said it.

'I'll be sure not to marry a policeman. That would mean I couldn't escape it.'

'Cops are terrible husbands anyway,' Gus smiled. 'Divorce rate is sky high.'

'You're a cop and you're not a terrible husband.'

'How do you know?' he said, and then was caught and trapped by the brown eyes.

'I know you. Better than I've ever known anyone.'

'Well,' said Gus, 'I don't know ... well ...' and then he gave up and succumbed to the unblinking eyes, a happy gray rabbit surrendering to the benevolent lethal embrace of the fox, and he decided that wherever the conversation went from here he would go with it willingly. Now his heart hammered joyfully.

'You're a good policeman,' she said. 'You know how things are and yet you're gentle and compassionate, especially with kids. That's a rare thing you know. How can you know what people are and still treat them like they were good?'

'People are weak. I guess I'm resigned to handling weak people. I guess I know them because I'm so weak myself.'

'You're the strongest man I've ever known, and the gentlest.'

'Lucy, I want to buy you a drink after work tonight. We'll just have time for one before the bars close. Will you stop at Marty's Lounge with me?'

'I don't think so.'

'Oh, I don't mean anything by it,' said Gus, cursing himself for saying such a silly thing, because he meant everything by it and of course she knew he meant everything by it.

'This will be our last night together,' said Lucy.

'What do you mean?'

'The lieutenant asked me tonight if I'd like to be loaned to Harbor Juvenile starting tomorrow and if it worked out maybe it could be permanent. I told him I'd like to think about it. I've decided.'

'But that's too far to drive! You live in Glendale.'

'I'm a single girl who lives in an apartment. I can move.'

'But you like police work! The Harbor will be too dull. You'll miss the action you get around here.'

'Was it terrible growing up without a father, Gus?' she asked suddenly.

'Yes, but ...'

'Could you ever do that to your children?'

'What?'

'Could you ever make them grow up without a father, or with a weekend father, twice a month?'

He wanted to say 'yes' to the eyes that he knew wanted him to say 'yes', but he faltered. He often thought later that if he hadn't faltered he might have said 'yes', and where would things have gone if he had merely said 'yes'. But he did not say 'yes', he said nothing for several seconds, and her mouth smiled and she said, 'Of course you couldn't. And that's the kind of man I want to marry me and give me babies. I should've found you about three kids ago. Now how about taking me to the station? I'm going to ask the lieutenant if I can go home. I have a rotten headache.'

There must be something he could say but the more he thought, the less sense all this made. His brain was whirling when he parked in the station lot and while Lucy was putting her things away he decided that now, this moment, he would meet her in the parking lot at her car and he would tell her something. They would work out something because if he didn't do it now, right now, he never would. And his very life, no, his soul was on the line.

'Oh, Plebesly,' said Lieutenant Dilford, stepping out of his office and beckoning to Gus.

'Yes, sir?' said Gus, entering the watch commander's office.

'Sit down for a second, Gus. I've got some bad news for you. Your wife called.'

'What happened?' asked Gus, leaping to his feet. 'The kids? Did something happen?'

'No, no. Your wife and kids are okay. Sit down, Gus.'

'My mother?' asked Gus, ashamed at his relief that it was his mother, not his children.

'It's your friend Andy Kilvinsky, Gus. I knew him well when I worked University years ago. Your wife said that she was called tonight by a lawyer up in Oregon. Kilvinsky left you a few thousand dollars. He's dead, Gus. He shot himself.'

Gus heard the lieutenant's voice droning monotonously for several seconds before he got up and walked to the front door, and the lieutenant was nodding and saying something as though he approved. But Gus did not know what he was saying as he walked weak-legged down the stairway to his car in the parking lot. He was out of the parking lot and on his way home before he started to cry and he thought of Kilvinsky and cried for him. His head bent in anguish and he thought incoherently of the little boy tonight and of all fatherless children. He could no longer see the road. Then he thought of himself and his grief and shame and anger. The tears came like lava. He pulled to the curb and the tears scalded him and his body was convulsed by shuddering sobs for all the silent misery of life. He no longer knew for whom he wept and he was past caring. He wept alone.

EIGHTEEN
The Huckster

'I'm sure glad they sent me to Seventy-seventh Street,' said Dugan, the ruddy-faced little rookie who had been Roy's partner for a week. 'I've learned a hell of a lot from working a Negro division. And I've had good partners breaking me in.'

'Seventy-seventh Street is as good a place to work as any,' said Roy, thinking how glad he'd be when the sun dropped below the elevated Harbor freeway. The streets would begin to cool and the uniform would become bearable.

'You been here quite a while now, haven't you, Roy?'

'About fifteen months. You're busy in this division. There's always something happening so you're busy. There's no time to sit and think, and time passes. That's why I like it.'

'You ever work in a white division?'

'Central,' Roy nodded.

'Is it the same as a black division?'

'It's slower. Not as much crime so it's slower. Time passes slower. But it's the same. People are all murderous bastards, they're just a little darker down here.'

'How long have you been back to work, Roy? If you don't mind talking about it. As soon as I transferred in, I heard right away about how you were shot. Not many guys have ever survived a shotgun blast in the stomach, I guess.'

'Not many.'

'I guess you hate to talk about it.'

'I don't hate to but I'm tired talking about it. I talked about it for the past five months when I was working light duty on the desk. I told the story a thousand times to every curious policeman who wanted to see how I screwed up and got myself shot like that. I'm just tired telling it. You don't mind?'

'Oh, hell no, Roy. I understand completely. You *are* feeling okay, now, aren't you? I mean I'll be glad to drive *and* keep books any night you want to take it easy.'

'I'm okay, Dugan,' Roy laughed. 'I played three hard games of handball last week. I'm doing fine, physically.'

'I figure I'm lucky to have an experienced partner who's been around and done everything. But I ask too many questions sometimes. I have a big Irish mouth that I can't control sometimes.'

'Okay, partner,' Roy smiled.

'Anytime you want me to shut up just say the word.'

'Okay, partner.'

'Twelve-A-Nine, Twelve-A-Nine, see the woman, four five nine report, eighty-three twenty-nine south Vermont, apartment B as in boy.'

'Twelve-A-Nine, roger,' said Dugan, and Roy turned into the orange and purple smog-streaked sunset and drove leisurely to the call.

'I used to think most burglaries happened at night,' said Dugan. 'When I was a civilian, I mean. I guess the biggest portion happen during the day when people aren't home.'

'That's right,' said Roy.

'Most burglars wouldn't go in an occupied pad at night, would they?'

'Too dangerous,' said Roy, lighting a cigarette, which tasted better than the last, now that it was cooling off.

'I'd sure like to nail a good burglar one of these nights. Maybe we'll get one tonight.'

'Maybe,' Roy answered, turning south on Vermont Avenue from Florence.

'I'm going to continue my education,' said Dugan. 'I picked up a few units since getting out of the navy but now I'm going to get serious and go after a degree in police science. You going to school, Roy?'

'No.'

'You ever go?'

'I used to.'

'Got quite a ways to go for your degree?'

'Twenty units maybe.'

'Is that all? That's terrific. You going to sign up this semester?'

'Too late.'

'You *are* going to finish?'

'Of course I am,' said Roy and his stomach began to burn from a sudden wave of indigestion and a shudder of nausea followed. Indigestion brought nausea now. His stomach would never be reliable again he supposed, and this bright-eyed rookie was upsetting his stomach with his prying, and his exasperating innocence.

That would change, Roy thought. Not abruptly, but gradually. Life would steal his innocence a bit at a time like an owl steals chicks until the nest is empty and awesome in its loneliness.

'That looks like the pad, partner,' said Dugan, putting on his cap and opening the door before Roy stopped the car.

'Wait'll I stop, Dugan,' said Roy. 'I don't want you breaking a leg. This is only a report call.'

'Oh, sorry,' Dugan smiled, reddening.

It was an upstairs apartment at the rear. Dugan tapped on the door lightly with the butt of his flashlight as Roy usually did, and as he probably had seen Roy do. Roy also noticed that Dugan had switched to Roy's brand of cigarettes and had bought a new three-cell, big-headed flashlight like Roy's even though his five-cell was only a few weeks old. I always wanted a son, Roy thought, sardonically, as he watched Dugan knock and step carefully to the side of the door as Roy had taught him to do on any call no matter how routine, at any time. And he always had his right hand free, carrying the report notebook and the flashlight in the left. He kept his hat on when they entered a house until they were absolutely sure what they had and only then did they sit down and remove the hats and relax. But Roy never relaxed anymore even when he wanted to relax, even as he concentrated on relaxation, because he must if his stomach would ever heal. He could not afford an ulcer now, could never afford one. He wanted so to relax. But now Dorothy was hounding him to let her new fat middle-aged husband adopt Becky. He had told her he'd see them both dead first and Dorothy had been trying to reach him through his mother whom Dorothy had always found an intercessor. And he was thinking of Becky and how she said 'Daddy' and how incredibly beautiful and golden she was. The apartment door was opened by a girl who was not beautiful and golden but Roy thought immediately that she was attractive. She was dark-brown-skinned, too dark he thought, even though her eyes were light brown and flecked with black specks that reminded him of the flecks in his daughter's eyes. Roy guessed she was his age or older and he thought the natural African hairdo was attractive on black women even though he despised it on the men. At least she didn't go in for dangling bone or iron earrings and other pretentious Africana. Just the hairdo. That was alright, he thought. It was natural.

She waved them in and pointed carelessly to the ransacked apartment. Roy saw that the molding had been pried from the door with a quarter-inch screwdriver which was then used to easily shim the door.

'These wafer locks aren't worth anything,' said Roy, touching the lock with his flashlight.

'Now you tell me,' she smiled and shook her head sadly. 'They cleaned me out. They really did.'

She was surprisingly tall, he noticed, as she stood next to him, not having to tilt her face very much to look in his eyes. He guessed she was five feet nine. And she was shapely.

'Did you touch anything?' asked Dugan.

'No.'

'Let's see if we can find some nice smooth items that prints can be lifted from,' said Dugan, putting his notebook down and prowling around the apartment.

'This happen while you were at work?' asked Roy, sitting on a high stool at the kitchen bar.

'Yes.'

'Where do you work?'

'I'm a dental technician. I work downtown.'

'Live alone?'

'Yes.'

'What all is missing?'

'Color TV set. A wristwatch, Polaroid camera. Clothes. Just about everything I own that's worth a damn.'

'That's a shame,' said Roy, thinking that she was *very* shapely and thinking that he had never tried a black woman and had not tried any woman since recovering from the wound, except for Velma, the overweight beautician whom he had met through his mother's neighbor Mrs. Smedley. Velma hadn't been interesting enough to attract him more than once every two or three weeks and he wondered if the buckshot hadn't done something to diminish his sex drive, and if it did, what the hell, it would be natural for him to lose the full appreciation of one of the few pleasures life seemed to hold for every poor son of a bitch it finally murdered.

'Is there much of a chance of getting the TV back?' she asked.

'Do you know the serial number?'

'Afraid not,' she said.

'Not too much chance then.'

'Do most burglaries go unsolved?'

'In a way they do. I mean they're not officially cleared. The stolen property is never recovered because burglars sell it real fast to fences or in pawnshops or just to no-questions-asked-people they meet on the street. The burglars usually get caught sooner or later and sometimes the detectives know they're good for lots and lots of jobs, maybe dozens or hundreds, but they usually don't get the property back.'

'So the guilty get caught sooner or later, but it doesn't help their victims, is that it?'

'That's about it.'

'Bastards,' she whispered.

Why doesn't she move, Roy thought. Why doesn't she move farther west to the periphery of the black district. Even if she can't get completely away from it she could move to the salt and pepper periphery where there's less crime. But what the hell, he thought. Some white burglar with a kink would probably strangle her in her bed some night. You can't get away from evil. It leaps all barriers, racial or otherwise.

'It'll take a long time to replace all your losses,' said Roy.

'You bet,' she said, turning away because there were tears glistening, dampening the heavy fringe of real eyelash. 'Want some coffee?'

'Sure,' said Roy, glad that Dugan was still rummaging in the bedroom.

As he watched her going from the stove to a cupboard he thought: maybe I could go for a little of that. Maybe all of the simple animal pleasures aren't gone for me.

'I'm going to fortify my coffee,' she said, handing him a gold-rimmed cup and saucer, cream pitcher, and sugar bowl. She returned to the cupboard, brought out a fifth of unopened Canadian bourbon, cracked the seal and poured a liberal shot into the coffee.

'I never drink alone,' she said, 'but tonight I think I'll get loaded. I feel rotten!'

Roy's eyes roved from the girl to the bottle and back and then to the bottle and he told himself that he was not in any danger yet. He only drank because he enjoyed it, because he needed to relax and if the drinking was not good for his stomach, the therapeutic value of a whiskey tranquilizer more than made up for its ill effects. At least he was not interested in drugs. It could have happened in the hospital. It happened to lots of people with long-term painful injuries who were kept on medication. He could get through his shift without a drink, he knew. But he wasn't harming anyone. A few ounces of whiskey always sharpened his wits and not a partner had ever suspected, least of all not little Dugan.

'If I weren't on duty, I'd join you,' said Roy.

'Too bad,' she said, not looking at him as she took a sip, grimaced, and took a larger one.

'If I were off duty I wouldn't let you drink alone,' he said, and watched the glance she gave him and then she turned away and sipped the coffee again and did not answer.

'Might as well get the report started,' said Dugan, coming back into the living room. 'There's a jewelry box and a few other things in there that might have latent fingerprints on them. I've stacked them in the corner. The print man will be out tonight or tomorrow to dust the dresser and those items.'

'I won't be here tomorrow. I work during the day.'

'Maybe he can come tonight if he's not too busy,' said Dugan.

'He'll come tonight. I'll make sure. I'll tell him you're a special friend of mine,' said Roy, and she looked at him again and he saw no sign.

'Well, might as well get started on this report, ma'am,' said Dugan. 'Can I have your name?'

'Laura Hunt,' she said, and this time Roy thought he saw in her eyes a sign.

As they were driving back to the station, Roy began to get jittery. It was not happening as often lately, he told himself. It was not nearly as bad now that he was back in the radio car. Those months of working the desk had been bad, though. He had periodic pain and his nerves were bothering him. He kept a bottle in the trunk of his car and made frequent trips to the parking lot. He worried that Lieutenant Crow, the watch commander, suspected something, but he had never been questioned. He never overdid it. He only drank enough to relax or to assuage the pain or to fight the depression. Only two times did he overdo it, unable to complete his tour of duty. He feigned sickness on those occasions, an attack of nausea he had said, and had gone to the lonely apartment, being careful to keep the speedometer needle pegged at thirty-five miles an hour and concentrating on the elusive white line in the highway. It was much better now that he was in the radio car again. Everything was better. And being back in the old apartment was good for him.

The months of living with his parents had been as damaging to his emotions as anything else. And Carl – with his fat little children and his impeccable wife Marjorie and his new car and his goddamn belly hanging over his belt even though he wasn't thirty years old – Carl was unbearable: 'We can still find a spot for you, Roy. Of course, you couldn't expect to start as an *equal* partner, but eventually ... after all, it *is* the family business and you *are* my brother ... I always thought you could be a businessman if you just made up your mind to grow up and now I hope your brush with death has made you come to your senses and realize where you belong and abandon your whims. You remember Roy when I was a child I wanted to be a policeman too and a fireman but I outgrew them and you've admitted that you don't really like your job and if you don't you can never expect to be a really successful policeman if there is such a thing and Roy you must realize by now that you're never going to get your degree in criminology. Roy, you haven't the desire to hit the books again and I don't blame you because why in the hell would you want to be a criminologist anyway and oh you don't want to be one anymore well Roy that's the best news I've heard from you in some time well we can make a place for you in the business and someday soon it can be changed to Fehler and Sons and someday Roy it will be Fehler Brothers and God knows Dad and Mom would be so pleased and I'll do everything I can to bring you along and make you the kind of businessman worthy of the family name and you know it will be different than working for a boss who is an impersonal taskmaster because I know your faults and weaknesses Roy. God knows we all have them and I'll make allowances because after all you *are* my brother.'

When Roy had at last decided to come back to duty and move to the apartment again it had been Carl who was the most bewildered by it all. Christ, I need to relax, Roy thought, looking at Dugan who was driving slowly checking license numbers against the hot sheet. Dugan checked thousands of license numbers against the hot sheet.

'Drive to Eighty-second and Hoover,' said Roy.

'Okay, Roy. What for?'

'I want to use the call box.'

'To call the station? I thought we were going in with the burglary report anyway.'

'I want to call R & I. And I don't want to go in just yet. Let's patrol for a while.'

'Okay. There's a call box just down the street.'

'Doesn't work.'

'Sure it does. I just used it the other night.'

'Look, Dugan. Take me to Eighty-second and Hoover. You know that's the call box I always use. It works all the time and I like to use it.'

'Okay, Roy,' Dugan laughed. 'I guess I'll start developing habits too when I get a little more experience.'

Roy's heart thumped as he stood behind the opened metal door of the call box and drank hopefully. He might only have to make one call to R & I tonight, he thought grimly. He'd have to be extremely careful with a rookie like Dugan. His throat and stomach were still burning but he drank again and again. He was very nervous tonight. Sometimes it happened like this. His hands would become clammy and he would feel light-headed and he had to relax. He screwed the lid back on the bourbon and replaced the bottle in the call box. Then he stood for a moment sucking and chewing on three breath mints and an enormous wad of chewing gum. He returned to the car where Dugan was impatiently tapping on the steering wheel.

'Let's go to the station now, Dugan my lad,' said Roy, already more relaxed, knowing the depression would dissolve.

'Now? Okay, Roy. But I thought you said later.'

'Got to go to the can,' Roy grinned, lighting a cigarette and whistling a themeless tune as Dugan accelerated.

While Dugan was in the report room getting a DR number for his burglary report, Roy started, wavered, and started again for the parking lot. He debated with himself as he stood by the door of his yellow Chevrolet, but then he realized that another drink could not possibly do more than relax him a bit more and completely defeat the towering specter of depression that was the hardest thing to combat unassisted. He looked around, and seeing no one in the dark parking lot, unlocked the Chevrolet, removed the pint from the glove compartment and took a large fiery mouthful. He capped the bottle, hesitated, uncapped it and took another, then one more, and put the bottle away.

Dugan was ready when he walked back in the station.

'Ready to go, Roy?' Dugan smiled.

'Let's go, my boy,' Roy chuckled, but before they had patrolled for half an hour, Roy had to call R & I from the call box at Eighty-second and Hoover.

At 11:00 P.M. Roy was feeling marvelous and he began thinking about the girl. He thought of her bottle too and wondered if she were feeling as fine as he was. He also thought of her smooth lithe body.

'That was a pretty nice-looking girl, that Laura Hunt,' said Roy.

'Who?' asked Dugan.

'That broad. The burglary report. You know.'

'Oh, yeah, pretty nice,' said Dugan. 'Wish I could write a ticket. I haven't got a mover yet this month. Trouble is, I haven't learned to spot them yet. Unless a guy blasts right through a red light three seconds late or something obvious like that.'

'She was put together,' said Roy. 'I liked that, didn't you?'

'Yeah. Do you know a good spot to sit? Some good spot where we could get a sure ticket?'

'An apple orchard, huh? Yeah, drive down Broadway, I'll show you an apple orchard, a stop sign that people hate to stop for. We'll get you six tickets if you want them.'

'Just one will do. I think I should try to write one mover a day. What do you think?'

'One every other day is enough to keep the boss happy. We got more to do than write tickets in this goddamn division. Hadn't you noticed?'

'Yes,' laughed Dugan, 'I guess we're busy with more serious things down here.'

'How old are you, Dugan?'

'Twenty-one, why?'

'Just wondering.'

'I look young, don't I?'

'About eighteen. I knew you had to be twenty-one to get on the job, but you look about eighteen.'

'I know. How old are you, Roy?'

'Twenty-six.'

'Is that all? I thought you were older. I guess because I'm a rookie, everyone seems much older.'

'Before we get that ticket, drive down Vermont.'

'Any place in particular?'

'To the apartment. Where we took the burglary report.'

'Any special reason?' asked Dugan, looking at Roy warily, exposing large portions of the whites of his large, slightly protruding eyes, and the eyes shining in the darkness made Roy laugh.

'I'm going to do a little pubic relations, Dugan my boy. I mean public relations.'

Dugan drove silently and when they reached the apartment building he turned off on the first side street and shut his lights off.

'I'm still on probation, Roy. I don't want to get in trouble.'

'Don't worry,' Roy chuckled, dropping his flashlight on the street as he got out of the car.

'What should I do?'

'Wait right here, what else? I'm just going to try to set something up for later. I'll be back in two minutes for heaven's sake.'

'Oh, that's good. It's just that I'm on probation,' said Dugan as Roy strode unsteadily to the front of the building and almost laughed aloud as he stumbled on the first step.

'Hello,' he grinned, before she had a chance to speak, while the door chime still echoed through the breezeway. 'I'm almost off duty and I wondered if you were really going to get drunk. I plan to, and one sad drunk always seeks out another, doesn't he?'

'I'm not really surprised to see you,' she said, holding a white robe at the bosom, not looking particularly friendly or unfriendly.

'I really *am* sad,' he said, still standing in the doorway. 'The only sadder face I've seen lately is yours. The way you were tonight. I thought we could have a few drinks and sympathize with each other.'

'I have a head start on you,' she said, unsmiling, pointing to the fifth on the breakfast bar that was no longer full.

'I can catch up,' said Roy.

'I have to get up early and go to work tomorrow.'

'I won't stay long. Just a drink or two and a friendly pair of eyes is all I need.'

'Can't you find the drink and eyes at home?'

'Only the drink. My place is as lonely as this one.'

'What time do you get off?'

'Before one. I'll be here before one.'

'That's late as hell.'

'Please.'

'Alright,' she said, and smiled a little for the first time and closed the door softly, as he crept down the stairway, holding the handrail in a tight grip.

'We got a call,' said Dugan. 'I was about to come and get you.'

'What is it?'

'Go to the station, code two. Wonder what's up?'

'Who knows?' said Roy, lighting a cigarette, and opening a fresh stick of gum in case he would be talking to a sergeant at the station.

Sergeant Schumann was waiting in the parking lot when they arrived, along with two other radio car teams. Roy walked carefully when they parked their car and joined the others.

'Okay, everyone's here, I guess,' said Schumann, a young sergeant with an imperious manner who annoyed Roy.

'What's up?' asked Roy, knowing that Schumann would make an adventure out of an assignment to write parking tickets.

'We're going to tour Watts,' said Schumann. 'We've gotten several letters in the last week from Councilman Gibbs' office and a couple from citizens' groups complaining about the drunken loafers on the streets in Watts. We're going to clean them up tonight.'

'You better rent a couple semi's then,' said Betterton, a cigar-smoking veteran, 'one little B wagon ain't going to hold the drunks that hang out on one corner.'

Schumann cleared his throat and smiled self-consciously as the policemen laughed, all except Benson, a Negro who did not laugh, Roy noticed.

'Well, we're going to make some arrests, anyway,' said Schumann. 'You men know all the spots around a Hundred and Third and down around Imperial and maybe Ninety-second and Beach. Fehler, you and your partner take the wagon. You other men, take your cars. That'll make six policemen so you shouldn't have any trouble. Stick together. Fill the wagon first, then scoop up a few in your radio cars and bring them in. Not here, take them to Central Jail. I'll make sure it's okay at Central. That's all. Good hunting.'

'Oh, sweet Jesus,' Betterton groaned, as they walked to their cars. 'Good hunting. Did you hear that? Oh, sweet Jesus. I'm glad I retire in a couple years. This is the new breed? Good hunting, men. Oh, Jesus.'

'Want me to drive the wagon, Roy?' asked Dugan eagerly.

'Of course. You're driving the car tonight, aren't you? You drive the wagon.'

'You don't need a chauffeur's license, do you?'

'It's just a beat-up panel truck, Dugan,' said Roy as they walked to the rear parking lot. Then Roy stopped, saying, 'I just thought of something. I want to get a fresh pack of cigarettes from my car. Get the wagon and meet me in front of the station.'

Roy could hear Dugan racing the engine of the wagon as he fumbled in the darkness for his car keys and at last was forced to use the flashlight, but this side of the parking lot was still and quiet and he knew he was worrying unnecessarily. He wouldn't do it if he weren't feeling a little depressed again. Finally he unlocked the car, held the button on the door post in so the overhead light stayed out as he opened the bottle one-handed, expertly, and sat with his legs out of the car ready to jump out in case he heard footsteps. He finished the pint in four or five swallows and felt in the glove compartment for the other but couldn't find it, and he realized there was no other. He had finished it this morning. Funny, he chuckled silently, that's pretty funny. Then he locked the car and walked woodenly to the wagon which Dugan was revving in front of the station. He chewed the mints as he walked and lit a cigarette he didn't really want.

'Might be kind of fun working a drunk wagon,' said Dugan, 'I've never done it before.'

'Oh yeah,' said Roy. 'Soon as a drunk pukes on you or rubs his shit-covered pants against your uniform, let me know how you like it.'

'Never thought of that,' said Dugan. 'Do you think I should get my gloves? I bought some.'

'Leave them. We'll just hold the door open and let the other guys throw the drunks in.'

The rattling bumping panel truck was making Roy slightly sick as he leaned his head out the window. The summer breeze felt good. He began to doze and awakened with a start when Dugan drove over the curb into the parking lot at Ninety-second and Beach and the arrests began.

'Maybe we'll find somebody with a little marijuana or something,' said Dugan, jumping out of the wagon as Roy looked sleepily at the throng of Negroes, who had been drinking in the parked cars, shooting dice against the back wall of the liquor store, standing, sitting, reclining in discarded chairs, or on milk crates, or on hoods and bumpers of ancient cars which always seemed to be available in any vacant lot or field in Watts. There were even several women among them in the darkness and Roy wondered what the hell was the attraction in these loitering places amid the rubble and broken glass. But then he remembered what some of the houses were like inside and he guessed the smell outdoors was certainly an improvement, although it wasn't any too good because in the loitering places were always packs of prowling hungry dogs and lots of animal and human excrement and lots of winos with all the smells they brought with them. Roy walked carefully to the rear of the wagon and slid the steel bolt back and opened the double doors. He staggered as he stepped back and this annoyed him. Got to watch that, he thought, and then the thought of a drunken police-man loading drunks in the drunk wagon struck him as particularly funny. He began giggling and had to sit in the wagon for a few minutes until he could control his mirth.

They arrested four drunks, one of whom was a ragpicker, lying almost unnoticed against the wall behind three overflowing trash cans. He held a half-eaten brown apple in one bony yellow hand and they had to carry him and flip him into the wagon onto the floor. The other drunks sitting on the benches on each side of the wagon didn't seem to notice the foul bundle at their feet.

They patrolled One Hundred and Third and then drove down Wilmington. In less than a half hour the wagon was filled with sixteen men and each radio car held three more. Betterton waved to Roy and sped ahead toward the Harbor Freeway and downtown as the slower wagon rumbled and clunked along.

'Mustn't be too comfortable back there,' said Dugan, 'maybe I should drive slower.'

'They can't feel anything,' said Roy, and this struck him as very amusing. 'Don't take the freeway,' said Roy. 'Let's go on the surface streets. But first go up Hoover.'

'What for?'

'I want to call the station.'

'We can go by the station, Roy,' said Dugan.

'I want to call in. No sense going in. It's out of the way.'

'Well, your favorite call box is out of the way, Roy. I think you can use another call box.'

'Do as I ask you, please,' said Roy deliberately. 'I always use the same call box.'

'I think I know why. I'm not completely stupid. I'm not driving to that call box.'

'Do as I say, goddamnit!'

'Alright, but I don't want to work with you anymore. I'm afraid to work with you, Roy.'

'Fine. Go tell Schumann tomorrow that you and me have a personality conflict. Or I'll tell him. Or tell him whatever you want.'

'I won't tell him the truth. Don't worry about that. I'm no fink.'

'Truth? What the hell is the truth? If you've got that figured out, let *me* know, not Schumann.'

Roy sat silently as Dugan drove obediently to the call box and parked in the usual place. Roy went to the box and tried to put his car key in the lock, then he tried his house key, and finally used the call box key. This was very funny too and restored his good humor. He opened it and drank until he finished. He threw it behind the hedge as he always did after his last call of the evening, and he laughed aloud as he walked back to the wagon when he wondered what the resident there thought when he found an empty half-pint in his flower garden each morning.

'Drive up Central Avenue,' said Roy. 'I want to drive through Newton and see if I see any of the guys I used to know.' He was talking slightly slurred now. But as long as he knew it he'd be alright. He was always very careful. He put three fresh sticks of gum in his mouth and smoked as Dugan drove silently.

'This was a good division to work,' said Roy, looking at the hundreds of Negroes still on the streets at this hour. 'People never go home in Newton Street. You can find thousands of people on the corners at five in the morning. I learned a lot here. I used to have a partner named Whitey Duncan. He taught me a lot. He came to see me when I was hurt. When not many other guys came, he came to see me. Four or five times Whitey came and brought me magazines and cigarettes. He died a few months ago. He was a goddamn drunk and died of cirrhosis of the liver just like a goddamn drunk. Poor old drunk. He liked people too. Really liked them. That's the worst kind of drunk to be. That'll kill you fast. Poor old fat bastard.'

Roy began dozing again and checked his watch. After they got rid of the drunks and got back to the station it would be end of watch and he could change clothes and go see her. He didn't really still want her so much physically, but she had eyes he could talk to, and he wanted to talk. Then Roy saw the huge crowd at Twenty-second and Central.

'There's a place you can always get a load of drunks,' said Roy, noticing that his face was becoming numb.

Dugan stopped for the pedestrians and Roy had a hilarious thought.

'Hey, Dugan, you know what this wagon reminds me of? An Italian huckster that used to peddle vegetables on our street when I was a kid. His panel truck was just like this one, smaller maybe, but it was blue and closed in like this one and he'd bang on the side and yell, "Ap–ple, ra–dish, coo–cumbers for sale!"' Roy began laughing uproariously and Dugan's worried look made him laugh even harder. 'Turn left quick and drive through the parking lot where all those assholes are standing around shuckin' and jivin'. Drive through there!'

'What for, Roy? Damn it, you're drunk!'

Roy reached across the cab and turned the wheel sharply to the left, still chuckling.

'Okay, let go,' said Dugan, 'I'll drive through, but I promise you I'm not working with you tomorrow night or ever!'

Roy waited until Dugan was halfway through the parking lot, parting the worried throngs of loiterers before him, moving slowly toward the other driveway and the street. Some of the more drunken ones scurried away from the wagon. Roy leaned out the window and slapped the side of the blue panel truck three times and shouted, 'Nig–gers, nig–gers, niggers for sale!'

August 1965

NINETEEN
The Queue

It was bad on Wednesday. The Hollenbeck policemen listened in disbelief to their police radios which broadcast a steady flow of help and assistance calls put out by the officers from Seventy-seventh Street Station.

'The riot is starting,' said Blackburn as he and Serge patrolled nervously in the juvenile car but could not concentrate on anything but what was happening in the southeast part of the city.

'I don't think it'll be a real riot,' said Serge.

'I tell you it's starting,' said Blackburn, and Serge wondered if he could be right as he listened to the frantic operators sending cars from several divisions into Seventy-seventh Street where crowds apparently were forming at One Hundred Sixteenth Street and Avalon Boulevard. By ten o'clock a command post had been set up at Imperial and Avalon and a perimeter patrol was activated. It was obvious to Serge as he listened that there were insufficient police units to cope with a deteriorating situation.

'I tell you it's starting,' said Blackburn. 'It's LA's turn. Burn, burn, burn. Let's get the hell to a restaurant and eat because we ain't going home tonight I tell you.'

'I'm ready to eat,' said Serge. 'But I'm not going to worry too much yet.'

'I tell you they're ready to rip loose,' said Blackburn, and Serge could not determine if his partner was glad of it or not. Perhaps he's glad, thought Serge. After all, his life had been rather uneventful since his wife sued him for divorce and he was afraid to be caught in any more adulterous situations until the case was decided.

'Where do we want to eat?' asked Serge.

'Let's go to Rosales' place. We ain't ate there in a couple weeks. At least I haven't. Is it still on with you and the little waitress?'

'I see her once in a while,' said Serge.

'Sure don't blame you,' said Blackburn. 'She's turned out real nice. Wish I could see somebody. Anybody. Doesn't she have a cousin?'

'Nope?'

'I can't see my own women. My goddamn wife got my notebook with every goddamn number in it. I'm afraid she's got the places staked out. I wish I had one she didn't know about.'

'Can't you wait until your divorce goes to trial?'

'Wait? Goddamn. You know I'm a man that needs my pussy. I ain't had a goddamn thing for almost three months. By the way, your little girl friend ain't working as much as she used to, is she?'

'She's going to college,' said Serge. 'She still works some. I think she'll be working tonight.'

'What's with your other girl friend? That blonde that picked you up that night at the station. It still on with her?'

'Paula? It's more or less on, I guess.'

'Bet she wants to marry you, right? That's what all those cunts want. Don't do it, I'm telling you. You got the life now, boy. Don't change it.'

Serge could never control his heartbeat when he was near her and that was the thing that most annoyed him. When they left their car parked at the curb and entered the restaurant only minutes before Mr. Rosales put up the closed sign, his heart galloped, and Mr. Rosales nodded his gray head and waved them to a booth. He had thought for months that Mr. Rosales had guessed how it was with him and Mariana, but there had been no indication, and at last, he decided it was only the tattered remnants of his conscience fluttering in the hot wind of his passion. He made it a point not to meet her more than once a week, sometimes less, and he always brought her home early and feigned perfect innocence even though they had just spent several hours in a tiny motel room which the management kept for Hollenbeck policemen who only had to show a badge in lieu of payment. He thought at first that it would be only a short time before the inevitable melodrama would begin and she would wail and weep that she couldn't go on like this in a cheap motel and that her tears would destroy the pleasure – but it hadn't happened yet. When he was making love to Mariana it was the same no matter where, and it seemed to be so with her also. She had never complained and there were never any serious promises made by either of them. He was glad it was so, and yet he waited anxiously for the melodrama. Surely it would come.

And making love with Mariana was something to analyze, he thought, but he had as yet been unable to understand how she alone had made it so different. It wasn't only because he had been her first, because he had felt like this with that dark-eyed little daughter of the bracero when he was fifteen, and he was certainly not the first with that one, and sometimes he was not the first on any given evening with that one. It was not only that he had been first, it was that he was purged each time when it was over. Her heat burned him from the inside out and he was at peace. She opened his pores and drained the impurities. That was why he kept coming back for more although it was difficult enough to single-handedly match the sexual prowess of Paula who was suspecting there was another girl and was demanding more and more of him until the ultimatum and melodrama was certainly overdue with Paula also. Paula had almost exploded in tears two nights before when they were watching an inane television movie and he had commented on the aging spinster in the story who was unhappily pursuing a fat little stockbroker who was not able to break the stranglehold of a domineering wife.

'Show a little pity!' she almost shouted when he snorted at the miserable woman. 'Where's your compassion? She's scared to death of being alone. She needs love, damn it. Can't you see that she has no love?'

He decided to be careful after that, very careful about what he said because the end was very near. He would have to decide whether to marry Paula or not. And if he didn't, he decided he would probably never marry because the prospects would never again be this good.

He thought this as they waited for Mariana to come from the kitchen and take their order, but she didn't come. Mr. Rosales himself came to the table with coffee and a writing pad and Serge said, 'Where is she?' and watched closely but detected nothing in the eyes or manner of the proprietor who said, 'I thought she should study tonight. I told her to stay home and study. She does so well with her studies. I do not want her to become too tired or upset because of overwork or anything else.' He glanced at Serge when he said 'anything else', and it was not a malicious glance, but now Serge was positive the old man knew how it was, but Christ, anyone with any intelligence would know that he wasn't taking her out several times a month this past year just to hold her hand. Christ, he was almost twenty-nine years old and she was twenty. What the hell did anybody expect?

Serge toyed with his food, and Blackburn as usual devoured everything in sight and without much urging finished most of what Serge didn't eat.

'Worried about the riot?' asked Blackburn. 'Don't blame you. Makes me a little queasy to think that they might do here what they did in the East.'

'It'll never be like that here,' said Serge. 'We're not going to tolerate the bullshit as long as they did back East.'

'Yeah, we're the best Department in the country,' said Blackburn. 'That's what our press notices say. But I want to know how a few hundred bluesuits are going to turn back a black ocean of people.'

'It won't be like that, I'm sure it won't.'

They were all held over in Hollenbeck that night. But at 3:00 A.M. they were permitted to secure, and Blackburn only shrugged when Serge told him that it was evidently quelled and that tomorrow things would be normal.

But on Thursday things were not normal and at 7:05 P.M. a crowd of two thousand again gathered at One Hundred Sixteenth and Avalon and units from Central, University, Newton and Hollenbeck were rushed to the trouble spot. At 10:00 P.M. Serge and Blackburn had given up all pretense of patrolling and sat in the station parking lot listening to the police radio in disbelief as did four of the uniformed officers who were preparing to leave for the Watts area.

Shots were fired at a police vehicle at Imperial Highway and Parmelee, and an hour later Serge heard a sergeant being denied a request for tear gas.

'I guess they don't think the sergeant knows what the fuck is going on out there,' said Blackburn. 'I guess they think he should reason with them instead of using gas on them.'

The word came again a few hours past midnight that they would be sent to Watts and Serge and Blackburn were given permission to secure. Serge had called Mariana at the restaurant at ten-thirty and she had agreed to meet him in front of the Rosales house whenever he could get there. She often studied until late in the morning and Serge would come by when the Rosales family was asleep. He would park across the street in the shade of an elm and she would come out to the car and it would always be better than he remembered. He could not seem to hold the moment in his mind. Not the moment with Mariana. He could not remember the catharsis of her lovemaking. He could only remember that it was like bathing in a warm pool in the darkness and he felt refreshed and never at any time did he think it was not good for *him*. For *her*, he wondered.

He almost didn't stop because it was fifteen past two, but the light was burning and so he stopped, knowing that if she were awake she would hear. In a moment he saw her tiptoe out the front door wearing the soft blue robe and filmy pink nightgown he had come to know so well even though he had never seen it in the light. But he knew the feel of it well and his mouth became dry as he held a hand over the dome light and opened the door for her.

'I thought you would not come,' she said when he stopped kissing her for a moment.

'I had to come. You know I can't stay away very long.'

'It is the same with me, Sergio, but wait. Wait!' she said, pushing his hands away.

'What is it, little dove?'

'We should talk, Sergio. It is exactly one year since we went to the mountain and I saw my first lake. Do you remember?'

This is it, he thought almost triumphantly. I knew it would come. And though he dreaded the weeping, he was glad it would be finally ended. The waiting.

'I remember the mountain and the lake.'

'I regret nothing, Sergio. You should know that.'

'But?' he said, lighting a cigarette, preparing for an embarrassing scene. Paula will be next, he thought. After Mariana.

'But it is so much better if it should stop now while we both feel what we feel for each other.'

'You're not pregnant, are you?' Serge said suddenly as the thought struck him that this was what she was preparing to tell him.

'Poor Sergio,' she smiled sadly. 'No, *querido*, I am not. I have learned all the ways of prevention well even though they shame me. Poor Sergio. And what if I was? Do you think I would go away with your baby in my stomach? To Guadalajara perhaps? And live my poor life out raising your child and yearning only for your arms? I have told you before, Sergio, you read too many books. I have my own life to live. It is as important to me as yours is to you.'

'What the hell is this? What are you driving at?' He couldn't see her eyes in the darkness and he didn't like any of this. She had never talked like this before and it was unnerving him. He wanted to turn on the light to be sure it was her.

'I cannot pretend I can get over you easy, Sergio. I cannot pretend I do not love you enough to live like this. But it would not be forever. Sooner or later, you would marry your other one and please do not tell me there is not another one.'

'I won't, but ...'

'Please, Sergio, let me finish. If you can be a whole man by marrying your other one, then do it. Do something, Sergio. Find out what you must do. And I say this: if you find it is my kind of life you want to share, then come to this house. Come on a Sunday in the afternoon like you did the first time when we went to the lake in the mountain. Tell Señor Rosales what you wish to say to me, because he is my father here. Then if he approves, come to me and say it. And then it will be announced in the church and we will not touch each other as we have done, until the night of the marriage. And I will marry you in a white dress, Sergio. But I will not wait for you forever.'

Serge groped for the light switch, but she grabbed his hand and when he reached for her desperately she pulled away.

'Why do you talk like this with such a strange voice? My God, Mariana, what've I done?'

'Nothing, Sergio. You have done absolutely nothing. But it has been a year. I was a Catholic before. But since we had our love, I have not been to confession or Communion.'

'So that's it,' he nodded. 'The goddamn religion's got you all confused. Do you feel sinful when we make love? Is that it?'

'It is not only that, Sergio, but it is partly that. I went to confession last Saturday. I am again a child of God. But it is not only that. I want you, Sergio, but only if you are a complete man. I want Sergio Duran, a *complete* man. Do you understand?'

'Mariana,' he said in bleak frustration, but when he reached for her she opened the door and was gliding barefoot across the shadowy street. 'Mariana!'

'You must never return, Sergio,' she whispered, her voice breaking for an instant, 'unless you come as I have said.' He squinted through the darkness

497

and saw her standing for a moment straight and still, the long blue robe fluttering against her calves. Her chin was uplifted as always, and he felt the pain in his chest grow sharper and thought for one horrible moment that he was being ripped in two and only part of him sat there mute before this ghostly apparition whom he had thought he knew and understood.

'And if you come, I will wear white. Do you hear me? I will wear white, Sergio!'

On Friday, the thirteenth of August, Serge was awakened at noon by Sergeant Latham who shouted something in the phone as Serge sat up in bed and tried to make his brain function.

'Are you awake, Serge?' asked Latham.

'Yeah, yeah,' he said, finally. 'Now I am. What the hell did you say?'

'I said that you've got to come in right away. All the juvenile officers are being sent to Seventy-seventh Street Station. Do you have a uniform?'

'Yeah, Christ, I think so. I got it here somewhere.'

'Are you sure you're awake?'

'Yeah, I'm awake.'

'Okay, dig your blue suit out of mothballs and put it on. Take your baton, flashlight and helmet. Don't wear a necktie and don't bother taking your soft hat. You're going into combat, man.'

'What's happening now?' asked Serge, his heart already beginning to advance its rhythm.

'Bad. It's bad. Just get the hell down to Seventy-seventh. I'll be there myself as soon as I get all our people there.'

Serge cursed as he cut his face twice while shaving. His light-brown eyes were watery, the irises trapped in a web of scarlet. The toothpaste and mouthwash did not cleanse his mouth of the vile taste which the pint of scotch had left there. He had drunk and read until an hour past daybreak after Mariana had left him there babbling to himself in the darkness and he hadn't yet thought it all out. How could he have been so wrong about his little dove who was in fact a hunting hawk, strong and independent. Was he the predator or the prey? She didn't need him the way he had gleefully imagined. When the hell would he be right about someone or something? And now, with a brain-cracking headache and a stomach twisted with anxiety and seething alcohol, and perhaps two hours' sleep, he was going into he knew not what, where he might need every bit of physical strength and mental alertness to save his very life.

When this insanity in the streets was over and things returned to normal he would marry Paula, he thought. He would accept as much of her father's dowry as was offered and play house and live as comfortably as he possibly could. He would stay away from Mariana because it was only her youth and virginity that had attracted him in the first place as it would have attracted any reasonably degenerate hedonist. Now he could see that stewing over that had been stupidly romantic because it appeared that she had taken more than he had. He doubted whether she were feeling as miserable as he was at this very moment and he suddenly thought, let them shoot me, let some black son of a bitch shoot me. I'm not capable of finding peace. Maybe there's no such thing. Maybe it exists only in books.

Serge found that he could not buckle the Sam Browne and had to let it out a notch. He had been drinking more lately and was not playing handball as much since he was trying to handle two women. The waistband of the blue woolen trousers was hard to button and he had to suck in his stomach to fasten both buttons. He still looked slim enough in the tight-fitting heavy woolen uniform, he thought, and decided to concentrate on such trivialities as his growing stomach because he could not afford at this moment to be caught in a swamp of depression. He was going into something that no policeman in this city had ever before been asked to face and his death wish might be happily granted by some fanatic. He knew himself well enough to know that he was definitely afraid to die and therefore probably did not really want to.

Serge saw the smoke before he was five miles from Watts and realized then what policemen had been saying for two days, that this conflagration would not remain on One Hundred and Sixteenth Street or even on One Hundred and Third, but that it would spread through the entire southern metropolitan area. The uniform was unbearable in the heat and even the sunglasses didn't stop the sun from cutting his eyes and boiling his brain. He looked at the helmet beside him on the seat and dreaded putting it on. He stayed on the Harbor Freeway to Florence Avenue then south on Broadway to Seventy-seventh Station which was as chaotic as he expected, with scores of police cars going and coming and newsmen roaming aimlessly about looking for escorts into the perimeter, and the scream of sirens from ambulances, fire trucks and radio cars. He parked on the street as close as he could get to the station and was waved wildly to the watch commander's office by the desk officer who was talking into two telephones, looking like he was feeling about as miserable as Serge. The watch commander's office was jammed with policemen and reporters who were being asked to remain outside by a perspiring sergeant with a face like a dried apple. The only one who seemed to have some idea of what was happening was a balding lieutenant with four service stripes on his sleeve. He sat calmly at a desk and puffed on a brown hooked pipe.

'I'm Duran from Hollenbeck Juvenile,' said Serge.

'Okay, boy, what're your initials?' asked the lieutenant.

'S,' said Serge.

'Serial number?'

'One o five eight three.'

'Hollenbeck Juvenile, you say?'

'Yes.'

'Okay, you'll be known as Twelve-Adam-Forty-five. You'll team up with Jenkins from Harbor and Peters from Central. They should be out in the parking lot.'

'Three-man cars?'

'You'll wish it was six,' said the lieutenant, making an entry in a logbook. 'Pick up two boxes of thirty-eight ammo from the sergeant out by the jail. Make sure there's one shotgun in your car and an extra box of shotgun rounds. What division are you from, boy?' said the lieutenant to the small policeman in an oversized helmet who came in behind him. Serge then recognized him as Gus Plebesly from his academy class. He hadn't seen Plebesly in perhaps a year, but he didn't stop. Plebesly's eyes were round and blue as ever. Serge wondered if he looked as frightened as Plebesly.

'You drive,' said Serge. 'I don't know the division.'

'Neither do I,' said Jenkins. He had a bobbing Adam's apple and blinked his eyes often. Serge could see that he was not the only one who wished he were somewhere else.

'Do you know Peters?' asked Serge.

'Just met him,' said Jenkins. 'He ran inside to take a crap.'

'Let's let him drive,' said Serge.

'Suits me. You want the shotgun?'

'You can have it.'

'I'd rather have my blanket and teddy bear right now,' said Jenkins.

'This him?' asked Serge, pointing at the tall, loose-jointed man striding toward them. He seemed too long for his uniform pants which stopped three inches above the shoes, and the shirt cuffs were too short. He was pretty well built and Serge was glad. Jenkins didn't seem too impressive and they'd probably need lots of muscle before this tour of duty ended.

Serge and Peters shook hands and Serge said, 'We've elected you driver, okay?'

'Okay,' said Peters, who had two service stripes on his sleeve, making him senior officer in the car. 'Either of you guys know the division?'

'Neither of us,' said Jenkins.

'That makes it unanimous,' said Peters. 'Let's go before I talk myself into another bowel movement. I got eleven years on this job but I never saw what I saw here last night. Either of you here last night?'

'Not me,' said Serge.

'I was on station defense at Harbor Station,' said Jenkins, shaking his head.

'Well pucker up your asshole and get a good grip on the seat because I'm telling you you aren't going to believe this is America. I saw this in Korea, sure, but this is America.'

'Cut it out, or you'll be loosening up *my* bowels,' said Jenkins, laughing nervously.

'You'll be able to shit through a screen door without hitting the wire, before too long,' said Peters.

Before driving three blocks south on Broadway, which was lined on both sides by roving crowds, a two–pound chunk of concrete crashed through the rear window of the car and thudded against the back of the front seat cushion. A cheer went up from forty or more people who were spilling from the corner of Eighty-first and Broadway as the Communications operator screamed: 'Officer needs help, Manchester and Broadway! Officer needs assistance, One O Three and Grape! Officer needs assistance, Avalon and Imperial!' And then it became difficult to become greatly concerned by the urgent calls that burst over the radio every few seconds, because when you sped toward one call another came out in the opposite direction. It seemed to Serge they were chasing in a mad S-shape configuration through Watts and back toward Manchester never accomplishing anything but making their car a target for rioters who pelted it three times with rocks and once with a bottle. It was incredible, and when Serge looked at the unbeliev-ing stare of Jenkins he realized what he must look like. Nothing was said during the first forty-five minutes of chaotic driving through the littered streets which were filled with surging chanting crowds and careening fire engines. Thousands of felonies were being committed with impunity and the three of them stared and only once or twice did Peters slow the car down as a group of looters were busy at work smashing windows. Jenkins aimed the shotgun out the window, and as soon as the groups of Negroes broke from the path of the riot gun, Peters would accelerate and drive to another location.

'What the hell are we doing?' asked Serge finally, at the end of the first hour in which few words were spoken. Each man seemed to be mastering his fear and incredulity at the bedlam in the streets and at the few, very few police cars they actually saw in the area.

'We're staying out of trouble until the National Guard gets here, that's what,' said Peters. 'This is nothing yet. Wait till tonight. You ain't seen nothing yet.'

'Maybe we should do something,' said Jenkins. 'We're just driving around.'

'Well, let's stop at a Hundred and Third,' said Peters angrily. 'I'll let you two out and you can try and stop five hundred niggers from carrying away the stores. You want to go down there? How about up on Central Avenue? Want to get out of the car up there? You saw it. How about on Broadway? We can clear the intersection at Manchester. There's not much looting there. They're only chunking rocks at every black and white that drives by. I'll let you boys clear the intersection there with your shotgun. But just watch out they don't stick that gun up your ass and fire all five rounds.'

'Want to take a rest and let me drive?' asked Serge quietly.

'Sure, you can drive if you want to. Just wait till it gets dark. You'll get action soon enough.'

When Serge took the wheel he checked his watch and saw it was ten minutes until 6:00 P.M. The sun was still high enough to intensify the heat that hung over the city from the fires which seemed to be surrounding them on the south and east but which Peters had avoided. Roving bands of Negroes, men, women, and children, screamed and jeered and looted as they drove past. It was utterly useless, Serge thought, to attempt to answer calls on the radio which were being repeated by babbling female Communications operators, some of whom were choked with sobs and impossible to understand.

It was apparent that most of the activity was in Watts proper, and Serge headed for One Hundred and Third Street feeling an overwhelming desire to create some order. He had never felt he was a leader but if he could only gather a few pliable men like Jenkins who seemed willing to obey, and Peters who would submit to more apparent courage, Serge felt he *could* do something. Someone had to do something. They passed another careening police car every five minutes or so, manned by three helmeted officers who all seemed as disorganized and bewildered as themselves. If they were not pulled together soon, it could not be stopped at all, Serge thought. He sped south on Central Avenue and east to Watts substation where he found what he craved more than he had ever craved for a woman – a semblance of order.

'Let's join that group,' said Serge, pointing to a squad of ten men who were milling around the entrance of the hotel two doors from the station. Serge saw there was a sergeant talking to them and his stomach uncoiled a little. Now he could abandon the wild scheme he was formulating which called for a grouping of men which he was somehow going to accomplish through sheer bravado because goddammit, someone had to do something. But they had a sergeant, and he could follow. He was glad.

'Need some help?' asked Jenkins as they joined the group.

The sergeant turned and Serge saw a two-inch gash on his left cheek-bone caked with dust and coagulation but there was no fear in his eyes. His sleeves were rolled up to the elbow, showing massive forearms, and on closer examination Serge saw fury in the green eyes of the sergeant. He looked like he could do something.

'See what's left of those stores on the south side?' said the sergeant, whose voice was raspy, Serge thought, from screaming orders in the face of this black hurricane which must be repelled.

'See those fucking stores that aren't burning?' the sergeant repeated. 'Well they're full of looters. I just drove past and lost every window in my fucking car before I reached Compton Avenue. I think there's about sixty looters or more in those three fucking stores on the south and I think there's at least a hundred in the back because they drove a truck right through the fucking rear walls and they're carrying the places away.'

'What the hell can we do about it?' asked Peters, as Serge watched the building on the north side three blocks east burning to the ground while the firemen waited near the station apparently unable to go in because of sniper fire.

'I'm not ordering nobody to do nothing,' said the sergeant, and Serge saw he was much older than he first appeared, but he was not afraid and he was a sergeant. 'If you want to come with me, let's go in those stores and clean them out. Nobody's challenged these motherfuckers here today. I tell you nobody's stood up to them. They been having it their own way.'

'It might be ten to one in there,' said Peters, and Serge felt his stomach writhing again, and deliberately starting to coil.

'Well I'm going in,' said the sergeant. 'You guys can suit yourselves.'

They all followed dumbly, even Peters, and the sergeant started out at a walk, but soon they found themselves trotting and they would have run blindly if the sergeant had, but he was smart enough to keep the pace at a reasonably ordered trot to conserve energy. They advanced on the stores and a dozen looters struggled with the removal of heavy appliances through the battered front windows and didn't even notice them coming.

The sergeant shattered his baton on the first swing at a looter, and the others watched for an instant as he dove through the store window, kicking a sweat-soaked shirtless teen-ager who was straining at the foot of a king-sized bed which he and another boy were attempting to carry away headboard and all. Then the ten policemen were among them swinging batons and shouting. As Serge was pushed to the glass-littered floor of the store by a huge mulatto in a bloody undershirt he saw perhaps ten men run in the rear door of the store hurling bottles as they ran, and Serge, as he lay in the litter of broken glass which was lacerating his hands, wondered about the volume of alcoholic beverage bottles which seemed to supply the mighty arsenal of missiles that seemed to be at the fingertips of every Negro in Watts. In that insane moment he thought that Mexicans do not drink so much and there wouldn't be this many bottles lying around Hollenbeck. Then a shot rang out and the mulatto who was by now on his feet began running and Jenkins shouldered the riot gun and fired four rounds toward the rear of the store. When Serge looked up, deafened from the explosions twelve inches from his ear, he saw the black reinforcements, all ten lying on the floor, but then one stood up and then another and another, and within a few seconds nine of them were streaking across the devastated parking lot. The looters in the street were shouting and dropping their booty and running.

'I must have shot high,' said Jenkins and Serge saw the pellet pattern seven feet up on the rear wall. They heard screaming and saw a white-haired toothless Negro clutching his ankle which was bleeding freely. He tried to rise, fell, and crawled to a mutilated queen-sized gilded bed. He crawled under it and curled his feet under him.

'They're gone,' said the sergeant in wonder. 'One minute they were crawling over us like ants and now they're gone!'

'I didn't mean to shoot,' said Jenkins. 'One of them fired first. I saw the flash and I heard it. I just started shooting back.'

'Don't worry about it,' said the sergeant. 'Goddamn! They're gone. Why the hell didn't we start shooting two nights ago? Goddamn! It really works!'

In ten minutes they were on their way to General Hospital and the moans of the old Negro were getting on Serge's nerves. He looked at Peters who was sitting against the door of the car, his helmet on the seat beside him, his thinning hair plastered down with sweat as he stared at the radio which had increased in intensity as they sped northbound on the Harbor Freeway. The sky was black now on three sides as the fires were leaping over farther north.

'We'll be there in a minute,' said Serge. 'Can't you stop groaning for a while?'

'Lord, it hurts,' said the old man who rocked and squeezed the knee six inches above the wet wound which Jenkins seemed unwilling to look at.

'We'll be there in a minute,' said Serge, and he was glad it was Jenkins who had shot him, because Jenkins was his partner and now they would book him at the prison ward of General Hospital and that meant they could leave the streets for an hour or two. He felt the need to escape and order his thinking which had begun to worry him because blind fury could certainly get him killed out there.

'Must have hit him with one pellet,' said Peters dully. 'Five rounds. Sixty pellets of double ought buck and one looter gets hit in the ankle by one little pellet. But I'll bet before this night's over some cop will get it from a single shot from a handgun fired at two hundred yards by some asshole that never shot a gun before. Some cop'll get it tonight. Maybe more than just one.'

How did I get stuck with someone like him? Serge thought. I needed two strong partners today and look what I got.

Jenkins held the elbow of the scrawny old man as he limped into the hospital and up the elevator to the prison ward. After booking the prisoner they stopped at the emergency entrance where Serge had his cut hands treated and after they were washed he saw that the cuts were very superficial and a few Band-Aids did the trick. At nine o'clock they were driving slowly south on the Harbor Freeway and the Communications operators were reciting the calls perfunctorily – calls which, before this madness, would have sent a dozen police cars speeding from all directions but now had become as routine as a family dispute call. 'Officer needs help! Four Nine and Central!' said the operator. 'Officer needs help, Vernon and Central!

Officer needs assistance, Vernon and Avalon! Officer needs assistance, One one five and Avalon! Looting, Vernon and Broadway! Looting, Five eight and Hoover! Looters, Four three and Main!' Then another operator would cut in and recite her list of emergencies which they had given up trying to assign to specific cars because it was obvious now to everyone that there weren't enough cars to even protect each other, let alone quell the looting and burning and sniping.

Serge blundered into a sniper's line of fire on Central Avenue, which was badly burned. They had to park across from a flaming two-story brick building and hide behind their car because two fire trucks had come in behind them and blocked the street and had then been abandoned when the sniping started. The sniping, for all but the combat veterans of Korea and World War II, was a terrible new experience. As Serge hid for forty minutes behind his car and fired a few wild shots at the windows of a sinister yellow apartment building where someone said the snipers were hiding, he thought this the most frightening part of all. He wondered if a police force could cope with snipers and remain a police force. He began thinking that something was going on here in this riot, something monumental for all the nation, perhaps an end of something. But he had better keep his wits about him and concentrate on that yellow building. Then the word was passed by a grimy young policeman in a torn uniform who crawled to their position on his stomach that the National Guard had arrived.

At five past midnight they responded to a help call at a furniture store on south Broadway where three officers had an unknown number of looters trapped inside. One officer swore that when a lookout had ducked inside after the police car drove up, he had seen a rifle in the looter's hands, and another policeman who worked this area said that the office of this particular furniture store contained a small arsenal because the owner was a nervous white man who had been robbed a dozen times.

Serge, without thinking, ordered Peters and one of the policemen from the other teams to the rear of the store where a blue-clad white-helmeted figure was already crouched in the shadows, his shotgun leveled at the back door. They went without question, and then Serge realized he was giving commands and thought wryly, at last you are a leader of men and will probably get a slug in your big ass for your trouble. He looked around and several blocks south on Broadway he saw an overturned car still smoldering and the incessant crackling of pistol fire echoed through the night, but for five hundred yards in each direction it was surprisingly quiet. He felt that if he could do something in this gutted skeleton of a furniture store, then a vestige of sanity would be preserved and then he thought that that in itself was insane thinking.

'Well, what's next, Captain?' said the wrinkled grinning policeman who knelt next to him behind the cover of Serge's radio car. Jenkins had the riot gun resting across the deck lid of the car pointed at the store front with its gaping jagged opening where plate glass used to be.

'I guess I *am* giving orders,' Serge smiled. 'You can do what you want, of course, but somebody ought to take charge. And I make the biggest target.'

'That's a good enough reason,' said the policeman. 'What do you want to do?'

'How many you think are in there?'

'A dozen, maybe.'

'Maybe we should wait for more help.'

'We've had them trapped for twenty minutes, and we put in maybe five requests for help. You guys are the only ones we've seen. I'd say offhand there isn't any help around right now.'

'I think we ought to arrest everyone in that store,' said Serge. 'We've been racing around all night getting shot at and clubbing people and mostly chasing them from one store to another and one street to another. I think we ought to arrest everyone in that store right now.'

'Good idea,' said the wrinkled policeman. 'I haven't actually made a pinch all night. I just been acting like a goddamn infantryman, crawling and running and sniping. This is Los Angeles not Iwo Jima.'

'Let's book these assholes,' Jenkins said angrily.

Serge stood up and ran in a crouch to a telephone pole a few feet to the side of the storefront.

'You people in there,' Serge shouted, 'come out with your hands on top of your head!' He waited for thirty seconds and looked toward Jenkins. He shook his head and pointed to the barrel of the riot gun.

'You people come out or we're going to kill every goddamn one of you,' Serge shouted. 'Come out! Now!'

Serge waited another silent half minute and felt the fury returning. He had only momentary seizures of anger tonight. Mostly it was fear, but occasionally the anger would prevail.

'Jenkins, give them a volley,' Serge commanded. 'This time aim low enough to hit somebody.' Then Serge leveled his revolver at the store front and fired three rounds into the blackness and the flaming explosions of the riot gun split the immediate silence. He heard nothing for several seconds until the ringing echo ceased and then he heard a wail, shrill and ghostly. It sounded like an infant. Then a man cursed and shouted, 'We comin' out. Don't shoot us. We comin' out.'

The first looter to appear was about eight years old. He wept freely, his hands held high in the air, his dirty red short pants hanging to the knees, and the loose sole of his left shoe flip-flopped on the pavement as he crossed the sidewalk and stood wailing now in the beam of Jenkins' spotlight.

A woman, apparently the child's mother, came next holding one hand high while the other dragged along a hysterical girl of ten who babbled and held a hand over her eyes to ward off the white beam of light. The next two out were men, and one of them, an old one, was still repeating, 'We comin', don't shoot,' and the other had his hands clasped on top of his head staring sullenly into the beam of light. He muttered obscenities every few seconds.

'How many more in there?' Serge demanded.

'Oney one,' said the old man. 'God, they's oney one, Mabel Simms is in there, but I think you done killed her.'

'Where's the one with the rifle?' asked Serge.

'They ain't no rifle,' said the old man. 'We was jist tryin' to git a few things before it was too late. Ain't none of us stole a thing these three days and ever' body else had all these new things and we jist decided to git us somethin'. We jist live across the street, Officer.'

'There was a man with a rifle ducked in that fucking doorway when we drove up,' said the wrinkled policeman. 'Where is he?'

'That was me, Mister PO-liceman,' said the old man. 'It wan't no rifle. It was a shovel. I was jist bustin' all the glass out the window so my grandkids wouldn't git cut goin' in. I never stole in all my life befo', I swear.'

'I'll take a look,' said the wrinkled policeman, entering the blackened store carefully, and Jenkins followed, the twin beams of their flashlights crisscrossing in the darkness for more than three minutes. They came out of the store one on each side of an immense black woman whose ringlets hung in her eyes. She murmured, 'Jesus, Jesus, Jesus.' They half-carried her out to where the others were as she let out an awesome shriek of despair.

'Where's she hit?' asked Serge.

'I don't think she's hit,' said the wrinkled policeman as he released her and let her bulk slide to the pavement where she pounded her hands on the concrete and moaned.

'Kin I look at her?' asked the old man. 'I been knowin' her for ten years. She live next do' to me.'

'Go ahead,' said Serge, and watched while the old man labored to get the big woman sitting upright. He supported her with great effort and patted her shoulder while he talked too low for Serge to hear.

'She ain't hurt,' said the old man. 'She jist scared to death like the rest of us.'

Like all of us, Serge thought, and then he thought that this was a very fitting end to the military campaign of Serge Duran, leader of men. It was about as he should have expected. Reality was always the opposite of what he at first anticipated. He knew this for certain now, therefore it was about as he should have expected.

'You going to book them?' asked the wrinkled policeman.

'You can have them,' said Serge.

'Don't fight over us, you honky motherfuckers,' said the surly muscled man whose hands were unclasped now and hung loosely at his sides.

'You get those hands on top of your head, or I'll open your belly,' said the wrinkled policeman, as he stepped forward and jammed the muzzle of the shotgun in the man's stomach. Serge saw the finger tighten on the trigger when the Negro instinctively touched the barrel, but then the Negro looked in the wrinkled policeman's eyes and removed his hand as though the barrel was on fire. He clasped the hands on top of his head.

'Why didn't you try to pull it away?' the wrinkled policeman whispered. 'I was going to make you let go.'

'You can have them,' said Serge. 'We're leaving.'

'We'll take this one,' said the wrinkled policeman. 'The rest of you people get your asses home and stay there.'

Jenkins and Peters agreed that they should go to Seventy-seventh Station because they might get relieved since they had been on duty now twelve hours. It did seem that things had quieted down a bit even though Watts substation was under some type of sniper siege, but there were apparently enough units there, so Serge drove to the station and thought he had not died like the heroes of his novels, even though he was at least as neurotic and confused as any of them. He suddenly remembered that last month during a two-day stretch of staying in the apartment and reading, he had read a book on T. E. Lawrence and maybe the romantic heroism of books had triggered his irresistible urge to surround and capture the furniture store which had ended in low comedy. Mariana said he read too many books. But it wasn't just that. It was that things were breaking apart. He was accustomed to the feeling lately that *he* was breaking apart, but now everything was fragmented – not in two reasonably neat sections but in jagged chaotic slivers and chunks, and he was one of society's orderers, as trite as it sounded. Even though he had never felt particularly idealistic before, now, surrounded by darkness and fire and noise and chaos, he, suddenly given the opportunity, had to create a tiny bit of order in that gutted store on south Broadway. But what good had it done? It had ended as all his attempts to do a worthy thing invariably ended. That was why marriage to Paula, and getting drunk occasionally and spending Paula's father's money seemed a most appropriate life for Serge Duran.

To the surprise of all three of them, they were relieved when they reached the station. They muttered a brief good-bye to each other and hurried to their cars before someone changed his mind and made them stay for the rest of the night. Serge drove home by the Harbor Freeway and the skies were still glowing red but it was apparent that the National Guard was making a difference. There were far fewer fires and after reaching Jefferson he turned around and saw no more fires. Instead of going straight to the apartment he stopped at an all-night hamburger stand in Boyle Heights and for the first time in thirteen hours, now that he was back in Hollenbeck Division, he felt safe.

The night man knew Serge as a juvenile officer in plainclothes and he shook his head when Serge walked inside and sat down in the deserted diner.

'What's it like down there?' asked the night man.

'It's still pretty bad,' said Serge running his fingers through his hair, sticky and matted from the helmet and soot and sweat. His hands were filthy, but there was no restroom for the customers and he decided to just have a cup of coffee and go home.

'I almost didn't know you in the uniform,' said the night man. 'You're always wearing a suit.'

'We're all in uniform today,' said Serge.

'I can understand,' said the night man, and Serge thought his sparse moustache made him look like Cantinflas although he was a tall man.

'Good coffee,' said Serge, and so was the cigarette, and his stomach unwound for the last time that night as the hot coffee splashed into it.

'I don't know why the boss wants me here,' said the night man. 'There have been few customers. Everyone's staying at home because of the *mallate*. But I shouldn't use that word. Nigger is a terrible word and *mallate* means the same thing but is even worse.'

'Yes.'

'I don't think the blacks would try to burn the east side. They don't get along with us Mexicans, but they respect us. They know we'd kill them if they tried to burn our homes. They don't fear the Anglo. No one fears the Anglo. Your people are growing weak.'

'I wouldn't be surprised,' said Serge.

'I've noticed that here in this country, the Mexican is forced to live close to black people because he's poor. When I first came here the Mexicans wanted to get away from the black who is exactly unlike a Mexican, and to live near the Anglo who is more nearly the same. But the things that've been happening, the softness of the Anglo, and the way you tell the world you're sorry for feeding them, and the way you take away the Negro's self-respect by giving everything to him, I'm starting to think that the Mexican should avoid the Anglo. I can tell you these things? I won't offend you? I talk so much tonight. I'm sick to my heart because of the riot.'

'I'm not an easily offended Anglo,' said Serge. 'You can talk to me like I was a Mexican.'

'Some police officers who work in the *barrios* seem *muy Mexicano* to me,' smiled the night man. 'You, señor, even look a little *Mexicano*, mostly around the eyes, I think.'

'You think so?'

'I meant that as a compliment.'

'I know.'

'When I came to this country twelve years ago, I thought it was bad that the Mexicans lived mostly in the east side here where the old ways were kept. I even thought we should not teach our children *la lengua* because they should completely learn to be Americans. I've looked closely and I believe that the Anglos in this place accept us almost like other Anglos. I used to feel very proud to be accepted like an Anglo because I know of the bad treatment of Mexicans not too long ago. But as I watched you grow weak and fearful that you wouldn't have the love of the world, then I thought: look, Armando – *Mira, hombre, los gabachos* are nothing to envy. You wouldn't be one of them if you could. If a man tried to burn your house or hold a knife at your belly you kill him and no matter his color. If he broke your laws you would prove to him that it's painful to do such a thing. Even a child learns that the burning coal hurts if you get close. Don't the gringos teach this to their children?'

'Not all of us.'

'I agree. You seem to say, touch it six or five times and maybe it burns and maybe not. Then he grows to be a man and runs through your streets and it's not all his fault because he never learned the hot coal burns. I think I'm glad to live in your country, but only as a Mexican. Forgive me, señor, but I wouldn't be a gringo. And if your people continue to grow weak and corrupt I'll leave your comforts and return to Mexico because I don't wish to see your great nation fall.'

'Maybe I'll go with you,' said Serge. 'Got any room down there?'

'In Mexico there's room for all,' smiled the night man, carrying a fresh coffeepot to the counter. 'Would you like me to tell you of Mexico? It always makes me glad to talk of Yucatán.'

'I'd like that,' said Serge. 'Are you from Yucatán?'

'Yes. It's far, far. You know of the place?'

'Tell me about it. But first, can I use your bathroom? I've got to wash. And can you fix me something to eat?'

'Certainly, señor. Go through that door. What would you like to eat. Ham? Eggs? Bacon?'

'We're going to talk about Mexico. I should eat Mexican food. How about *menudo*? You'd be surprised how long it's been since I ate *menudo*.'

'I have *menudo*,' laughed the night man. 'It's not excellent, but it passes.'

'Do you have corn tortillas?'

'Of course.'

'How about lemon? And oregano?'

'I have them, señor. You know about *menudo*. Now I'm ashamed to give you my poor *menudo*.'

Serge saw that it was after four but he wasn't the least bit sleepy and he felt suddenly exhilarated yet relaxed. But mostly he was hungry. He laughed in the mirror at the grimy sweat-stained face and thought, God, how I'm hungry for *menudo*.

Suddenly Serge popped his head out the door, his hands still covered with suds. 'Tell me, señor, have you traveled a lot in Mexico?'

'I know the country. *De veras.* I know my Mexico.'

'Have you been to Guadalajara?'

'It's a beautiful city. I know it well. The people are wonderful, but all the people of Mexico are wonderful and will treat you very good.'

'Will you tell me about Guadalajara too? I want to know about that city.'

'A pleasure, señor,' chuckled the night man. 'To have someone to talk to at this lonely hour is a pleasure, especially someone who wants to hear about my country. I'd give you free *menudo* even if you were not a policeman.'

It was seven o'clock when Serge was driving home, so full of *menudo* and tortillas he hoped he wouldn't get a stomachache. He wished he had some *yerba buena* like his mother used to fix. It never failed to help a stomachache and he couldn't afford to be ill because in exactly six hours he would have to get up and be ready for another night. The news on the car radio indicated that looting and burning was expected to resume heavily today.

Serge took Mission Road instead of the freeway and there on North Mission Road he saw something that made him brake sharply and slow to fifteen miles per hour and stare. Eight or ten men, one woman, and two small boys, were lined up at the door of a restaurant which was not yet open. They carried pots and pans of all shapes, but each pot was ample in size and Serge realized they were waiting for the resturant to open so they could buy a pot of *menudo* and take it home because they were sick or someone in the house was sick from drinking too much on Friday night. There was not a Mexican who did not believe with all his soul that *menudo* cured hangovers and because they believed, it did in fact cure the hangover, and even though his stomach felt like a goatskin bag pumped full of the stuff, he would have stopped and bought some more to keep for later if he had a pot. Then he looked at his helmet, but the liner was too grimy from oil and soot to carry *menudo* in, and he accelerated the Corvette and headed for his bed.

He felt he would sleep better than he had in weeks even though he had seen the beginning of the end of things, because now that they had a taste of anarchy, and saw how easy it is to defeat the civil authority, there would be more and it would be the white revolutionary who would do it. This was the beginning, and the Anglos were neither strong enough nor realistic enough to stop it. They doubted everything, especially themselves. Perhaps they had lost the capacity to believe. They could never believe in the miracle in a pot of *menudo*.

As he looked in the rearview mirror, the queue of forlorn Mexicans with their *menudo* pots had disappeared, but in a few moments their spirits would be soaring he thought, because the *menudo* would make them well.

'They are not good Catholics,' Father McCarthy had said, 'but they are so respectful and they believe so well.' *Andale pues*, Serge thought. To bed.

TWENTY
The Chase

'Good thing they're too fucking dumb to make fire bombs out of wine bottles,' said Silverson and Gus cringed as a rock skidded over the already dented deck lid and slammed against the already cracked rear window. A glass fragment struck the Negro policeman whose name Gus had already forgotten, or perhaps it was buried there among the ruins of his rational mind which had been annihilated by terror.

'Shoot that motherfucker that ...' screamed Silverson to Gus, but then sped away from the mob before finishing the sentence.

'Yeah, those Coke bottles aren't breaking,' said the Negro policeman. 'If that last one would've broke, we'd have a lap full of flaming gasoline right now.'

They had been out only thirty minutes, Gus thought. He knew it was only thirty because it was now five till eight and still it wasn't dark and it had been seven-twenty-five when they drove from the parking lot at Seventy-seventh Station because it was written here on his log. He could see it. It had only been thirty minutes ago. So how could they survive twelve hours of this? They had been told they would be relieved in twelve hours, but of course they would all be dead.

'Friday the thirteenth,' muttered Silverson, slowing down now that they had run the gauntlet on Eighty-sixth Street where a mob of fifty young Negroes appeared from nowhere and a cocktail had bounced off the door but failed to burst. This happened after someone had cracked the side window with a rock. Now Gus stared at another rock which was lying on the floor at his feet and he thought, we've only been out thirty minutes. Isn't that incredible?

'Some organization we got,' said Silverson, turning back east toward Watts where most of the radio calls seemed to be emanating at the moment. 'I never worked this crummy division in my life. I don't know my ass from pork sausage.'

'I never worked down here either,' said the Negro policeman. 'How about you, Plebesly? It is Plebesly, isn't it?'

'No, I don't know the streets,' said Gus, holding the shotgun tightly against his belly and wondering if the paralysis would fade because he was sure he could not get out of the car, but then he supposed that if they succeeded in breaking a fire bomb inside, his instinct would get him out. Then he thought of himself on fire.

'They just tell you here's a box of thirty-eights and a shotgun and point out two other guys and say take a car and go out there. It's ridiculous,' said Silverson. 'None of us ever worked down here before. Hell, man, I worked Highland Park for twelve years. I don't know my ass from sliced salami down here.'

'Some guys got called down here last night,' said the soft-spoken Negro policeman. 'I work Wilshire, but I didn't get called down here last night.'

'The whole goddamn Department's here tonight,' said Silverson. 'Where in the hell's Central Avenue? There was an assistance call on Central Avenue.'

'Don't worry about it,' said the Negro policeman. 'There'll be another one any minute.'

'Look at that!' said Silverson, and aimed the radio car down the wrong side of San Pedro Street as he accelerated toward a market where a band of eight or ten men were systematically carrying out boxes of groceries.

'Those brazen assholes,' said the Negro policeman and he was out and running toward the storefront after the already fleeing looters as soon as Silverson parked. To his surprise, Gus's body functioned and his arm opened the door and his legs carried him, unsteadily, but still carried him, at a straight-legged lope toward the storefront. The Negro policeman had a tall very black man by the shirt front and palmed him across the face with his gloved hands which were probably sap gloves because the man spun backward and fell through the yawning hole in the plate glass, screaming as his arm was raked and bloodied by the jagged edge.

The others scattered through back and side doors and in a few seconds only the three policemen and the bleeding looter stood in the gutted store.

'Lemme go,' pleaded the looter to the Negro policeman. 'We're both black. You're just like me.'

'I'm not nothin' like you, bastard,' said the Negro policeman, showing great strength by lifting the looter one-handed. 'I am nothing whatever like you.'

A peaceful hour passed while they took their looter to the station and engaged in what had to pass for booking, but which required only a skeleton of an arrest report and no booking slip at all. This hour passed much too quickly for Gus who found that hot coffee knotted his stomach even more. Before he could believe it they were back on the streets, only now night had come. The small arms fire was crackling through the darkness. He had fooled them for five years, thought Gus. He had almost fooled himself, but tonight they would know, and he would know. He wondered if it would be as he always feared, himself trembling like a rabbit before the deadly eye at the last moment. This is how he always thought it would be at the instant when the great fear came, whatever that fear was, which irrevocably paralyzed his disciplined body and brought the final mutiny of body against mind.

'Listen to that gunfire,' said Silverson as they were back on Broadway and the sky glowed from a dozen fires. He had to take several detours on their patrol to nowhere in particular, because of the fire engines blocking streets.

'This is crazy,' said the Negro policeman, who Gus knew by now was named Clancy.

It is the natural tendency of things toward chaos, Gus thought. It's a very basic natural law Kilvinsky always said, and only the order makers could temporarily halt its march, but eventually there will certainly be darkness and chaos, Kilvinsky had said.

'Look at that asshole,' said Clancy, and shined his spotlight on a lone looter who was reaching through a window of a liquor store feeling for a quart of clear liquid that rested there, miraculously whole among the broken glass. 'We ought to give that bastard some sidewalk surgery. Wonder how he'd like a lobotomy by Dr. Smith and Dr. Wesson?'

Clancy was carrying the shotgun now and as Silverson stopped the car Clancy fired a blast into the air behind the man who did not turn but continued his probing, and when he reached the bottle he turned a scowling brown face to the naked light, and walked slowly away from the store with his prize.

'Son of a bitch, we're whipped,' said Silverson and drove away from the lonely snarling figure who continued his inexorable pace in the darkness.

For another hour it was the same: speeding to calls only to arrive in time to chase fleeting shapes in the darkness as the Communications operators continued a barrage of help and assistance and looting calls until all calls were routine and they wisely decided that the main order of business would be protecting each other and surviving the night uninjured.

But at 11:00 P.M. as they were scattering a group intent on burning a large food market on Santa Barbara Avenue, Silverson said, 'Let's catch a couple of these assholes. Can you run, Plebesly?'

'I can run,' said Gus grimly, and he knew, somehow knew he could run. In fact, he had to run, and this time when Silverson squealed into the curb and fleeting shadows faded into darker shadow there was another shadow pursuing fleeter than the rest. The last looter hadn't gotten a hundred feet from the store when Gus overtook him and slammed the heel of his hand in the back of the looter's head. He heard him fall and grind along the sidewalk, and from the shouts he knew that Clancy and Silverson had grabbed him. Gus pursued the next shadow and within a minute he was streaking down Forty-seventh Street through the residential darkness after the second shadow and another shadow a half block ahead. Despite the Sam Browne and the strangeness of a helmet, and the baton clacking against the metal of his belt, he felt unencumbered, and swift, and free. He ran like he ran in the academy, like he still ran at least twice a week during his workouts, and he was doing the thing he did best in all the world. Suddenly he knew that none of them could stand up to him. And though he was afraid, he knew he would endure and his spirit ignited as the sweat boiled him and the warm wind fed the fire as he ran and ran.

He caught the second shadow near Avalon and saw that the man was huge with a triangular neck that sloped from ear to shoulder but he was easy to sidestep when he made two or three halfhearted lunges toward Gus and then collapsed in a gasping heap without being struck by the baton that Gus held ready. He handcuffed the looter to the bumper bracket of a recently wrecked car that was squatting at the curb where the man fell.

Gus looked up and the third shadow hadn't made another three hundred feet but jogged painfully toward Avalon Boulevard, looking often over his shoulder and Gus was running again, easy striding, loose, letting his body run as the mind rested, which is the only way to run successfully. The shadow was getting larger and larger and was in the blue glow of the street lamp when Gus was on him. The looter's eyes blinked back in disbelief at the oncoming policeman. Gus was panting but bounded forward still strong when the exhausted man turned and stumbled toward a pile of litter beside a smoldering building and came up with a piece of two by four. He held it in both hands like a ball bat.

He was perhaps twenty, six feet two, and fierce. Gus was afraid, and though his mind told him to use his gun because that was the only sensible thing to do, he reached instead for his baton and circled the man who sucked and rattled at the air and Gus was sure he would cave in. But still the man held the two by four as Gus circled him. Drops of sweat plinked on the concrete sidewalk at his feet and his white shirt was completely transparent now and clung to him.

'Drop that,' said Gus. 'I don't want to hit you.'

The looter continued to back away and the heavy wood wavered as more eye white showed than a moment before.

'Drop that or I'll smash you,' said Gus. 'I'm stronger than you.'

The board slid from the looter's hands and clunked to the pavement and he caved and lay there gasping while Gus wondered what to do with him. He wished he had taken Silverson's handcuffs, but it had happened so fast. His body had just started the chase and left his mind behind, but now his mind had caught up with the body and was all together.

Then he saw a black and white roaring down Avalon. He stepped into the street and waved it down and in a few minutes he was back on Santa Barbara and reunited with Silverson and Clancy who were astonished by his feat. They took all three looters to the station where Silverson told the jailer how his 'little partner' had caught the three looters, but Gus still found that his stomach rebelled at coffee and would accept only water, and forty-five minutes later when they went back on the streets he was still trembling and perspiring badly and told himself, what did you expect? That it would now all vanish like in a war movie? That you who feared everything for a lifetime now would dramatically know no fear? He completed the night as he had begun it, quivering, at moments near panic, but there was a difference: he knew the body would not fail him even if the mind would bolt and run with graceful antelope leaps until it vanished. The body would remain and function. It was his destiny to endure, and knowing it he would never truly panic. And this, he thought, would be a splendid discovery in any coward's life.

TWENTY-ONE
The Golden Knight

W hat the hell's going on? Roy thought, standing in the middle of the intersection of Manchester and Broadway gaping at the crowd of two hundred on the northeast corner and wondering if they would break in the bank. The sun was still bright and hot. Then he heard a crash and saw that the group of one hundred on the northwest corner had broken in the windows of the storefronts and were beginning to loot. What the hell's happening, thought Roy, and gained little solace from the faces of the policemen near him who seemed as bewildered as he. Then they smashed the windows at the southwest corner and Roy thought, my God, a hundred more gathered and I didn't even see them! Suddenly only the southeastern side of the intersection was clear and most of the policemen were retreating to this side of the street except one stocky policeman who charged a pocket of six or eight Negroes with their arms full of men's clothing who were strolling to a double-parked Buick. The policeman struck the first man in the back with the point of the baton and brought the second one to his knees with a skillful slashing blow across the leg, and then the policeman was hit full in the face with a milk crate thrown from the crowd and he was being kicked by eighteen or twenty men and women. Roy joined a squad of six rescuers who ran across Manchester. They dragged him away and were pelted by a hail of stones and bottles, one of which struck Roy on the elbow and caused him to cry out.

'Where do the rocks come from?' asked a gray-haired, beefy policeman with a torn uniform shirt. 'How in the hell do they find so many rocks lying around in a city street?'

After they got the injured man to a radio car, the dozen officers returned to the intersection through which all vehicle traffic had been diverted. Officers and mob watched each other amid the screams and taunts and laughter and blaring radios. Roy never knew who fired the first shot, but the gunfire erupted. He fell to his stomach and began to tremble and crawled into the doorway of a pawnshop holding both arms over his stomach. Then he thought of removing the white helmet and holding it over his stomach, but he realized how futile it would be. He saw three or four more radio cars roaring into the chaotic intersection as the crowds panicked and broke into and away from the confused policemen who were shouting conflict-ing orders to each other. No one knew where the gunfire was coming from.

Roy stayed in the doorway and protected his stomach as the rumors came of snipers on every roof and that they were firing from the crowd and then several policemen began firing at a house on the residential street just south of Manchester. Soon the house was riddled with shotgun and revolver fire, but Roy never saw the outcome because a frantic policeman waved them north again and when he ran a hundred yards he saw a dead Negro blocking the sidewalk, shot through the neck, and another dead in the middle of the street. This can't be true, Roy thought. It's broad daylight. This is America. Los Angeles. And then he fell to his stomach again because he saw the brick hurtling end over end toward him and it shattered the plate glass window behind him. A cheer went up from thirty Negroes who had appeared in the alley to the left and a young policeman ran up to Roy as he was getting up. The young policeman said, 'The one in the red shirt threw the brick,' and he aimed coolly at the running Negroes and fired the riot gun. The blast took two of the men down. The man in red held his leg screaming and another in a brown shirt limped to his feet and was pulled into a mob of cursing looters where he disappeared as the looters scurried away from the young policeman with the riot gun. Then Roy heard two small pops and saw a tiny flash in the midst of the retreating crowd and the car window next to Roy shattered.

'Show yourself, you bastard,' the young policeman shouted to the invis-ible sniper and then turned his back on them and walked slowly away. 'This isn't real,' he muttered to Roy. 'Is it?'

Then Roy saw something extraordinary: a young black with a full beard and a black beret and silk undershirt, a fiercely militant-looking young man, stepped in front of a mob of fifty and told them to go home and that the police were not their enemies, and other things equally provocative. He had to be removed from the area in a car under guard when the mob turned on him and kicked him unconscious in less than a minute, before the policemen could drive them off.

The sirens shrieked and two ambulances and a police car containing six policemen drove up. Roy saw there was a sergeant with them. He was young and almost everyone ignored him as he tried in vain to create order at least among the squad of policemen, but it took almost an hour to get the dead and wounded to the hospital and the temporary morgue. The Watts riot had begun in earnest this Friday afternoon.

Roy was ordered by the sergeant to arrest a wounded man in a red shirt, and he was teamed with two other policemen. They took the man to the prison ward of the County Hospital in a radio car with a windshield and rear window completely destroyed by rocks. The paint on the white door was scorched from a fire bomb and Roy was glad to be taking the long drive to the hospital. He hoped his new partners would not be too anxious to return to the streets.

It was after dark when they were driving again toward Seventy-seventh Street Station and by now Roy and his partners knew each other. Each had started the afternoon with different partners until the chaos at Manchester and Broadway, but what the hell did it matter, they decided, who was working with whom. They made a pact to stay one with the other and to provide mutual protection, not to stray far from each other, because they had only one shotgun, Roy's, and it was not reassuring at all, not on this night, but at least it was something.

'It's not nine o'clock yet,' said Barkley, a ten-year policeman from Harbor Division with a face like a bruised tomato who had, for their first two hours together, mumbled over and over that 'it was unbelievable, all so, unbelievable', until he was asked to please shut up by Winslow, a fifteen-year policeman from West Los Angeles Division who was the driver and a slow careful driver he was, Roy thought. Roy was thankful he had a veteran driving.

Roy sat alone in the back seat cradling the shotgun, a box of shotgun shells on the seat next to him. He had not fired the gun yet, but he had made the decision to fire at anyone who threw a rock or fire bomb at them, and at anyone who shot or aimed a gun at them or looked like he was aiming a gun at them. They were shooting looters. Everyone knew it. He decided he would not shoot looters, but he was glad some of the others were doing it. They had seen a semblance of order begin in the bursts of initial gunfire. Only deadly force could destroy this thing and he was glad they were shooting looters, but he decided he would not shoot looters. And he would try not to shoot anyone. And he would shoot no one in the stomach.

In one of my rare displays of humanity I will blow their heads off, he thought. Under no circumstance will I shoot a man in the stomach.

'Where you want to go, Fehler?' asked Winslow, rolling a cigar from side to side in his wide mouth. 'You know the area best.'

'Sounds like Central Avenue and Broadway and a Hundred and Third are getting hit the hardest,' said Barkley.

'Let's try Central Avenue,' said Roy, and at 9:10 P.M. when they were only two blocks from Central Avenue the fire department requested assistance because they were being fired on in a six-block stretch of Central Avenue.

Roy felt the heat when they were still half a block from Central and Winslow parked as close to the inferno as he could get. Roy was perspiring freely and by the time they jogged the five hundred feet to the first besieged fire truck they were all sweating and the night air was scorching Roy's lungs and the pop pop pop of gunfire was coming from several directions. Roy began to develop a fierce stomachache, one which could not be relieved by a bowel movement, and a ricochet pinged off the concrete sidewalk. The three policemen dived for the fire truck and huddled next to a filthy, yellow-helmeted, wide-eyed fireman.

It was not Central Avenue, Roy thought. It was not even possible that the signpost which pointed Forty-sixth Street east and west and Central Avenue north and south could be right. He had worked Newton Street. He had patrolled these streets with dozens of other partners, with partners now dead even, like Whitey Duncan. This street was a vivid part of his learning. He had been educated in southeast Los Angeles and Central Avenue had been a valuable schoolroom, but this hissing inferno was not Central Avenue. Then Roy for the first time noticed the two cars overturned and burning. He suddenly could not remember what kind of buildings had been there on Forty-seventh and Forty-sixth that were now sheets of flame two hundred feet high. If this happened a year ago I would certainly not believe it, he thought. I would simply believe that it was a fantastic seizure of d.t.'s and I would take another drink. Then he thought of Laura, and he was astonished that now, even now, as he lay by the big wheel of the fire engine and the sounds of gunfire and sirens and growling flames were all around him, even now, he could get the empty ache within him that would be filled warmly when he thought of holding her, and how she stroked his hair as no one, not Dorothy, not his mother, no woman, had done. He had guessed he loved her when the yearning for drink began to wane, and he knew it when, three months after their affair began, he realized that she aroused the same feeling within him that Becky did, who was now talking clearly and was assuredly a brilliant child – not simply beautiful, but stunning. Roy ached again as he thought of Becky, ethereal, bright, and golden – and Laura, dusky and real, altogether real, who had begun to put him together, Laura, who was five months younger than he, but who seemed years older, who used pity and compassion and love and anger until he stopped drinking after he was suspended sixty days for being found drunk on duty, and who lived with him and kept him for those sixty days in her apartment, and who said nothing, but only watched him with those tawny tragic eyes when he began to resemble a man again and decided to return to his own apartment. She said nothing about that since, and he still came to her three or four nights a week because he still needed her badly. She watched him, always watched him with those liquid eyes. With Laura the sex made it perfect but was far, far from all of it, and that was another reason he knew he loved her. He had been on the verge of a decision about her for weeks and even months and he began to tremble as he thought that if it weren't for the ache and the warmth which always came when he thought of Becky or Laura, if it weren't for this feeling he could evoke in himself, then now, now in the blood and hate and fire and chaos, he would turn the riot gun around and look in the great black eye of the twelve gauge and jerk the trigger. Then he guessed he was far from healthy yet, despite Laura's reassurance, or he wouldn't think such thoughts. Suicide was madness, he had always been taught to believe, but what was this around him, if not madness? He began to get light-headed and decided to stop thinking so hard. His palms were dripping wet and leaving tiny drops of moisture on the receiver of the shotgun. Then he worried about the moisture rusting the piece. He wiped the receiver with his sleeve until he realized what he was doing and laughed aloud.

'You guys come with me!' shouted a sergeant, crouching as he ran past the fire engine. 'We got to clean these snipers out and get the firemen working before the whole goddamn city burns down.'

But though they walked along Central Avenue in groups of three for over an hour they never saw a sniper but only heard, and they chased and occasionally shot at shadowy figures who scurried in and out of gutted storefronts that were not in flames. Roy did not shoot because the conditions had not been met. Still, he was glad the others were shooting. When Central Avenue reached the point that it was burning more or less quietly and there was little left to steal, Winslow suggested they go elsewhere, but first they should stop at a restaurant and eat. When they asked which restaurant he had in mind, he waved an arm and they followed him to the car and found that the two remaining unbroken windows had been smashed out in their absence and the upholstery had been cut, but not the tires strangely enough, so Winslow drove to a restaurant on Florence Avenue that he said he had noticed earlier. They walked through a gigantic hole in the wall of the cafe where a car must have smashed through. Roy guessed the car had probably been driven by some terrified white man passing through the riot area who had been attacked by the mobs that were stopping traffic and beating whites earlier in the day when they owned the streets before the shooting started. Then again it could have been a looter's car which the police had chased until he crashed through the restaurant in spectacular fashion. What difference did it make? Roy thought.

'Shine your flashlight over here,' said Winslow, removing six hamburger patties from the refrigerator which was not running. 'They're still cold. It's okay,' said Winslow. 'See if you can find the buns in that drawer, Fehler. I think the mustard and stuff is behind you there on the little table.'

'The gas still works,' said Barkley, propping his flashlight on the counter with the beam directed on the griddle. 'I'm a pretty good cook. Want me to get them started?'

'Go head on, brother,' said Winslow in an affected Negro accent, as he squeezed a head of lettuce he found on the floor, peeling away the outer leaves and dropping them in a cardboard box. They ate and drank several bottles of soda pop which were not cold enough, but it wasn't at all bad there in the darkness and it was after midnight when they finished and sat smoking, looking at each other as the ceaseless crackling small arms fire and ubiquitous smell of smoke reminded them that they had to go back.

Finally it was Barkley who said, 'Might as well get back out there. But I wish they hadn't broke our windows out. You know, the one thing that scares me most is that a cocktail will come flying in the car and bust, and fry us. If we only had windows we could roll them up.'

Roy was more impressed with Winslow as the night wore on. He drove through Watts and west and north through the rest of the gutted city as though he were on routine patrol. He seemed to be listening carefully to the garbled endless, breathless calls that were blaring out at them over the radio. Finally one of the operators with a girlish voice began sobbing hysterically as she was jabbering a string of twelve emergency calls to 'any unit in the vicinity', and she and all of them must realize by now that there were no units in certain vicinities, and if there were they were hard pressed to save their own asses and to hell with anything else. But at 3:00 A.M. Winslow stopped the car on Normandie Avenue which was exceptionally dark except for a building burning in the distance and they watched a gang of perhaps thirty looters ransacking a clothing store and Winslow said, 'There's too many of them for us to handle, wouldn't you say?'

'They might have guns,' said Barkley.

'See the car out front, the green Lincoln?' said Winslow. 'I'm going after them when they leave. We'll get some of them at least. It's about time we threw some looters in jail.'

Three men got in the car and even from a half block away in the darkness, Roy could see that the back seat of the Lincoln was filled with suits and dresses. The Lincoln pulled away from the curb and Winslow said, 'Dirty motherfuckers,' and the radio car roared forward. Winslow turned on his headlights and red lights and they passed the clothing store and crossed Fifty-first Street at eighty miles per hour and the chase was on.

The driver of the Lincoln was a good driver but his brakes were not good and the police car had tremendous brakes and could corner better. Winslow ate up the ground which separated them and didn't listen to Barkley who was shouting directions at him. Roy sat silently in the rear seat and wished they had seat belts in the back seat too. He could see that Winslow was oblivious of both of them and would catch that Lincoln if it killed all of them and then they were going northbound on Vermont. Roy did not look at the speedometer but knew they were traveling in excess of one hundred and this was of course absolutely insane because there were thousands of looters, thousands! But Winslow wanted *these* looters and Barkley shouted, 'Soldiers!' and Roy saw a National Guard roadblock two blocks north and the Lincoln's driver, a hundred feet ahead, saw it too and burned out the rest of his brakes trying to turn left before reaching the roadblock. A National Guardsman began firing a machine gun and Winslow jammed on his brakes when they saw the muzzle flashes and heard the clug-a-clug-a-clug-a-clug and saw the tracers explode on the asphalt closer to them than to the Lincoln. Roy was horrified to see that the Lincoln did not crash as he was sure it would. The driver made the turn and was speeding west on a narrow dark residential street and Winslow doggedly made the turn and Roy wondered if he could lean out the window and fire the riot gun, or perhaps his revolver because that Lincoln had to be stopped before Winslow killed them all. He was surprised to discover how badly he wanted to live now, and he saw Laura's face for an instant and was thrown against the door handle when Winslow made an impossible right turn and picked up two hundred feet on the Lincoln.

Winslow, trying to conserve power, wasn't using his siren and Roy had lost count of the other cars they had almost hit, but he was thankful that at this hour in this part of the city, there were few civilian autos on the street and Barkley uttered a joyful whoop when the Lincoln bounced over the curb turning left again, and slammed against a parked car. The Lincoln was still skidding in a tight circle when the three looters were leaping out, and Winslow, jaw set, was driving across the sidewalk at the fleeing driver, a slim Negro who was running down the middle of the sidewalk with an occasional terrified glance over his shoulder at the approaching headlights. Roy realized that Winslow was going to run him down as he drove the radio car down the residential sidewalk taking corners off fences and running over shrubbery with the radio car that was too wide for the sidewalk. They were less than thirty feet from the looter when he turned the last time and his mouth opened in a soundless shriek as he dived over a chain link fence. Winslow skidded past him, cursed, and leaped out of the car. Roy and Barkley were out in a second but Winslow, amazingly agile for his size and age, was already over the fence and crashing through the rear yard. Roy heard four shots and then two more as he threw the riot gun over the fence and scrambled after it, ripping his trousers, but in a moment Winslow came walking back reloading his revolver.

'He got away,' said Winslow. 'The motherfucking nigger got away. I'd give a thousand dollars for one more shot at him.'

When they got back in the car Winslow circled the block and returned to the looter's green Lincoln which sat awkwardly in the middle of the street, steam hissing from the broken radiator.

Winslow stepped slowly from the radio car and asked Roy for the riot gun. Roy gave him the gun and shrugged at Barkley as Winslow stepped to the car and fired two flaming blasts at the rear tires. Then he stepped to the front of the car and smashed out the headlights with the butt of the gun and then broke the windshield. Then he circled the car, his shotgun ready like it was a dangerous wounded thing that might yet attack, and he slammed the gun butt into both side windows. Roy looked toward the houses on both sides of the street, but all were dark. The residents of southeast Los Angeles, who had always known how to mind their own business, were not curious at any sounds they heard *this* night.

'That's enough, Winslow,' Barkley shouted. 'Let's get the hell out of here.'

But Winslow opened the car door and Roy could not see what he was doing. In a second he emerged with a large piece of fabric and Roy watched him in the beam of the headlights as he put his pocket knife away. He removed the gas cap and shoved the piece of material into the tank and dripped gasoline on the street beneath the tank.

'Winslow, are you nuts?' shouted Barkley. 'Let's get the hell out of here!'

But Winslow ignored him and made his trickle of gasoline extend a safe distance from the Lincoln and then he shoved the soaked piece of cloth back into the tank except for two feet of it which hung to the ground. He ran to the mouth of the gasoline stream and lit it and there was a small smothered explosion almost instantly and the car was burning well as Winslow got back in the radio car and drove away in the relaxed careful manner of before.

'How can you fight them without getting just like them?' said Winslow finally to his silent partners. 'I'm just a nigger now, and you know what? I feel pretty good.'

Things became a little quieter after three, and at 4:00 A.M. they drove to Seventy-seventh Station, and after working a fifteen-hour watch, Roy was relieved. He was too tired to change into his civilian clothes, and was certainly too tired to drive to his apartment. And even if he weren't, he would not go home tonight. There was only one place in the world, he would go tonight. It was exactly four-thirty when he parked in front of Laura's apartment. He could not hear the pop of gunfire now. This part of Vermont had been untouched by fire and almost untouched by looting. It was very dark and still. He only knocked twice when she opened the door.

'Roy! What time is it?' she asked, in a yellow nightgown and robe, and already he felt the pleasurable ache.

'I'm sorry to come so late. I had to, Laura.'

'Well, come in. You look like you're about to fall on your face.'

Roy entered and she switched on a lamp and held his arms as she watched him in her unique way. 'You're a mess. You're really a filthy mess. Take your uniform off and I'll fill the bath. Are you hungry?'

Roy shook his head as he walked into the familiar comfortable bedroom and unhooked the Sam Browne, letting it fall to the floor. Then, remembering how tidy Laura was, he pushed it with his foot into the corner by the closet and sat heavily in a padded, pink and white bedroom chair. He took his shoes off and sat for a minute wanting a cigarette but too tired to light one.

'Want a drink, Roy?' asked Laura, leaving the bathroom as the tub filled with a sound of rushing restorative water.

'I don't need a drink, Laura. Not even tonight.'

'One drink won't hurt you. Not anymore.'

'I don't want one.'

'Okay, baby,' she said, picking up his shoes and putting them in the bottom of the closet.

'What the hell would I do without you?'

'I haven't seen you for four days. I guess you've been busy.'

'I was going to come Wednesday night. That's when this thing started, but we had to work overtime. And yesterday too. And then tonight, Laura, tonight was the worst, but I had to come tonight. I couldn't stay away any longer.'

'I'm very sorry about all this, Roy,' she said, pulling off his damp black socks, as he thanked her silently for helping him.

'Sorry about what?'

'About the riot.'

'Why? Did you start it?'

'I'm black.'

'You're not black and I'm not white. We're lovers.'

'I'm a Negro, Roy. Isn't that why you moved back home in your apartment? You knew I wanted you to stay with me.'

'I think I'm too tired to talk about that, Laura,' said Roy, standing up and kissing her and then he took off the dusty shirt which was sticking to him. She hung up the shirt and the trousers and he left his shorts and T-shirt on the bathroom floor. He glanced at the concave scar on his abdomen and stepped into the steaming suds-filled tub. Never had a bath felt better. He leaned back with his eyes closed and set his mind free and dozed for a moment, then felt her presence. She was sitting on the floor beside the tub watching him.

'Thank you, Laura,' he said, loving the flecks in the light brown eyes, and the smooth brown skin and the graceful fingers she laid against his shoulder.

'What do you suppose I see in you?' she smiled, caressing his neck. 'It must be the attraction of opposites, don't you think? Your golden hair and golden body. You're the most beautiful man I know. Think that's it?'

'That's just gold plate,' said Roy. 'There's nothing but pot metal underneath.'

'There's plenty underneath.'

'If there's anything, you put it there. There was nothing when you found me last year.'

'*I* was nothing,' she corrected him.

'You're everything. You're beauty and love and kindness, but mostly you're order. I need order right now, Laura. I'm very scared, you know. There's chaos out there.'

'I know.'

'I haven't been this afraid since you dried me out and taught me not to be afraid. God, you should see what chaos looks like, Laura.'

'I know. I know,' she said, still stroking his neck.

'I can't stay away from you anymore,' he said, staring at the faucet which dripped sporadically into the suds. 'I didn't have the guts to stay with you, Laura. I need peace and tranquility and I knew we'd face hatred together and I didn't have the guts. But now that I've been back in that lonely apartment I don't have the guts to be away from you and now that I've been in that darkness and madness tonight, I could never make it without you and ...'

'Don't talk anymore, Roy,' she said, getting up. 'Wait until tomorrow. See how you feel tomorrow.'

'No,' he said, grabbing her arm with a wet, soapy hand. 'You can't depend on tomorrow. I tell you the way it is out there, you mustn't depend on tomorrow. I live for you now. You can never get rid of me now. Never.' Roy pulled her down and kissed her on the mouth and then kissed the palm of her hand, and she stroked his neck with the other hand, saying, 'Baby, baby,' as she always did and which never failed to soothe him.

They were still awake, lying naked on their backs with only a sheet over them when the sun rose in Los Angeles.

'You should go to sleep,' she whispered. 'You've got to go back to the street tonight.'

'It won't be bad now,' he said.

'Yes. Maybe the National Guard will have things under control.'

'It doesn't matter if they don't. It still won't be bad now. My vacation begins September first. It'll surely be over by then. Do you mind getting married in Las Vegas? We can do it without waiting.'

'We don't have to get married. It doesn't matter if we're not married.'

'I still have a conventional bone or two in my body, I guess. Do it for me.'

'Alright. For you.'

'Weren't you brought up to respect the institution of marriage?'

'My daddy was a Baptist preacher,' she laughed.

'Well then it's settled. I was brought up a Lutheran, but we never went to church very much except when appearances demanded it, so I think we'll raise our children as Baptists.'

'I'm nothing now. Not a Baptist. Nothing.'

'You're everything.'

'Do we have a right to have children?'

'You're goddamn right we do.'

'The golden knight and his dark lady,' she said. 'But we'll suffer, you and me. I promise you. You don't know what a holy war is.'

'We'll win.'

'I've never seen you so happy.'

'I've never been so happy.'

'Do you want to know why I loved you from the first?'

'Why?'

'You weren't like other white men that flirted with me and that asked me out on dates to their apartments or maybe to some out of the way pretty nice place where lots of mixed couples go. I never really could trust a white man because I could see that they saw something in me that they wanted, but it wasn't me.'

'What was it?'

'I don't know. Just lust maybe, for a little brown animal. Primitive vitality of a Negro, that sort of thing.'

'My, you're intellectual tonight.'

'It's morning.'

'This morning then.'

'Then there were white liberals who would've taken me to a governor's ball, but I think with people like that almost any Negro would do. I don't trust those people either.'

'Then there was me.'

'Then there was you.'

'Old Roy the wino.'

'Not anymore.'

'Because I borrowed some of your guts.'

'You're such a humble man that I get annoyed with you.'

'I used to be arrogant and conceited.'

'I can't believe that.'

'Neither can I anymore. But it's true.'

'You were different than any white man I ever met. You needed something from me, but it was something one human being could give another and it had nothing to do with my being Negro. You always looked at me as a woman and a person, do you know that?'

'Guess I'm just not the lusty type.'

'You're very lusty,' she laughed. 'You're a marvelous lusty lover and right now you're too silly to talk to.'

'Where'll we go for a honeymoon?'

'Do we have to have one of those too?'

'Of course,' said Roy. 'I'm conventional, remember?'

'San Francisco is a fine city. Have you ever been there?'

'No, let's go to San Francisco.'

'It's also a very tolerant city. You've got to consider things like that now.'

'It's so quiet,' said Roy. 'For a while last night when I was most afraid I thought the sound of the fire would never stop. I thought I'd always hear the fire roaring in my ears.'

TWENTY-TWO

Reunion

'I hear we're going back to almost normal deployment starting tomor-row,' said Roy. It pleased him to say it because he and Laura had decided that as soon as the riot was completely finished and he could do it, he would ask for some special days off and they would go to San Francisco for a week after being married in Las Vegas where they might stay for a few days, but then again they might go from Vegas to Tahoe for a night ... 'Sure will be nice to get off the twelve-hour shifts,' said Roy in a burst of exuberance at the thought of doing it, and now that he and Laura were going to do it all his doubts dissolved.

'I've had enough of it,' said Serge Duran as he made a lazy U-turn on Crenshaw where they were on perimeter patrol and Roy liked the solid way Duran drove, in fact he liked Duran whom he had only seen a dozen times during these five years and whom he never bothered to get to know. But they had been together only two hours tonight and he liked him and was glad that when the perimeter patrols were set that Duran had told the sergeant, 'Let me work with my two classmates Fehler and Plebesly.' And Gus Plebesly seemed like a very decent sort and Roy hoped he might become good friends with both these men. He became acutely aware that he had no real friends among policemen, had never made any, but he was going to change that, he was changing lots of things.

'Now that the riot's just about done, it's hard to believe it happened,' said Gus, and Roy thought that Plebesly had aged more than five years. He remembered Plebesly as a timid man, perhaps the smallest in their class, but he seemed taller now and solider. Of course he remembered Plebesly's inhuman stamina and smiled as he thought of how his endurance had been a threat to their P.T. instructor, Officer Randolph.

'It's not hard to believe it happened when you drive down Central Avenue or a Hundred and Third Street,' said Serge. 'Were you down there on Friday night, Roy?'

'I was there,' said Roy.

'I think we were there too,' said Gus, 'but I was too scared to know for sure.'

'Likewise, brother,' said Roy.

'But I was so scared I can hardly remember most of the things that happened,' said Gus, and Roy saw that the shy grin was the same, and so was the deprecatory manner that used to annoy Roy because he was too stupid in those days to see that it was thoroughly genuine.

'I was thinking the same thing just today,' said Serge. 'Friday night is already becoming a kind of mist in my mind. I can't remember big chunks of it. Except the fear, of course.'

'You feel that way too, Serge?' said Gus. 'How about you, Roy?'

'Sure, Gus,' said Roy. 'I was scared to death.'

'Be damned,' said Gus and was silent and Roy guessed that Gus felt reassured. It was comforting to talk with a policeman who, like himself, was obviously filled with doubts, and he pitied Gus now and felt the tug of friendship.

'Did you ever finish college, Roy?' asked Serge. 'I remember talking to you in the academy about your degree in criminology. You were pretty close to it then.'

'I never got any closer, Serge,' laughed Roy and was surprised to discover no irony in the laugh and he guessed he was finally making peace with Roy Fehler.

'I never built up too many units myself,' said Serge, nodding his understanding. 'Sorry now that I didn't, with our first sergeant exam coming up. How about you, Gus? You go to school?'

'Off and on,' said Gus. 'I hope to have my bachelor's in business administration in about a year.'

'Good for you, Gus,' said Roy. 'We'll be working for you one of these days.'

'Oh, no,' said Gus, apologetically. 'I haven't really studied for the sergeant's exam, and besides, I freeze in test situations. I know I'll fail miserably.'

'You'll be a great sergeant, Gus,' said Serge, and he seemed to mean it. Roy felt drawn to both of them and he wanted them to know about his coming marriage – wanted them to know about Laura, about a white policeman with a black wife and whether they thought he was mad, because he was sure they were compassionate men. But even if they thought him a fool and proved it by polite embarrassment it wouldn't change a thing.

'It's getting dark, thank goodness,' said Gus. 'It was so smoggy and hot today. I'd sure like to go for a swim. I've got a neighbor with a pool. Maybe I'll ask him tomorrow.'

'How about tonight?' said Serge. 'After we get off. I've got a pool in my apartment building. We might as well take advantage of it because I'm moving in a few weeks.'

'Where you moving?' asked Gus.

'My girl and I have a pad picked out to buy. It'll be lawn mowing and weed pulling instead of moonlight swims, I guess.'

'You're getting married?' asked Roy. 'I'm getting married as soon as I can get a week off.'

'You're tumbling too?' smiled Serge. 'That's reassuring.'

'I thought you were already married, Roy,' said Gus.

'I was when we were in the academy. I was divorced not long after that.'

'Have kids, Roy?' asked Gus.

'A little girl,' said Roy, and then he thought of her last Sunday when he had brought her to Laura's apartment. He thought of how Laura had played with her and made Becky love her.

'You didn't go sour on marriage?' asked Serge.

'Nothing wrong with marriage,' said Roy. 'It gives you children and Gus can tell you what children give you.'

'Couldn't make it without them,' said Gus.

'How long you been married, Gus?' asked Serge.

'Nine years. All my life.'

'How old are you?'

'Twenty-seven.'

'What's your girl's name, Serge?' asked Roy as he had an idea.

'Mariana.'

'How about having that swim tomorrow?' said Roy. 'Maybe Gus and his wife and Laura and I could come over to your place and meet your fiancée and we could have a swim and a few beers before we go to work tomorrow afternoon.' It was done, he thought. It would be the first test.

'Okay,' said Serge, with enthusiasm. 'Can you make it, Gus?'

'Well, my wife hasn't been feeling well lately, but maybe she'd like to come over even if she won't swim. I'd sure like to come.'

'That's fine. I'll be expecting you,' said Serge. 'How about ten o'clock in the morning?'

'Fine,' said Gus, and Roy thought this would be the best way for him to see. To just bring her and see. The hell with apologies and warnings. Let them see her, lots of her, long-legged and shapely and incomparable in a bathing suit. Then he'd know how it would be, what he could expect.

'Would it be too much ...' Gus hesitated. 'I mean, I hate to ask you ... If your landlady wouldn't like it, or if maybe you don't want a bunch of noisy kids around ... I could understand ...'

'You want to bring your kids?' Serge smiled.

'I would.'

'Bring them,' said Serge. 'Mariana loves kids. She wants six or eight.'

'Thanks,' said Gus. 'My kids will be thrilled. That's a beautiful name your fiancée has – Mariana.'

'Mariana Paloma,' said Serge.

'That's Spanish, isn't it?' asked Gus.

'She's Mexican,' said Serge. 'From Guadalajara.'

'Come to think of it, isn't Duran a Spanish name?'

'I'm Mexican too,' said Serge.

'I'll be damned. That never occurred to me,' said Roy, looking at Serge for some Mexican features and finding none, except perhaps something about the shape of his eyes.

'Are you of Mexican descent on both sides?' asked Gus. 'You don't look it.'

'One hundred percent,' Serge laughed. 'I guess I'm probably more Mexican than anyone I know.'

'You speak Spanish then?' asked Gus.

'Hardly at all,' Serge answered. 'When I was a boy I did, but I've forgotten. I guess I'll learn again though. I went to Mariana's home Sunday afternoon, and after I got the blessing of Mr. Rosales, her *padrino*, I went to her and tried to ask her in Spanish. I think it ended up more in English than Spanish. I must've been a hell of a sight, a big stammering clown with an armload of white roses.'

'I'll bet you were just smashing,' Roy grinned, wondering if he looked as contented as Serge.

'Mariana's informed me we'll talk only Spanish in our house until my Spanish is at least as good as her English.'

'That's very nice,' said Gus, and Roy wondered if she had required courting in the old Mexican manner. He wondered if Serge had known her a long time before he kissed her. I'm getting corny, Roy smiled to himself.

'Usually Mexican men dominate their women,' said Serge, 'until they get old and then Mama is the boss and the old boys pay for their tyranny. But I'm afraid Mariana and I are starting out the other way around.'

'Nothing wrong with a strong woman,' said Roy. 'A policeman needs one.'

'Yes,' said Gus, gazing at the blazing sunset. 'Not many guys can do this job alone.'

'Well, we're *veteranos*, now,' said Serge. 'Five years. We can sew a hash mark on our sleeves, I thought we were going to have a class reunion after five years.'

'That would've been nice,' said Gus. 'We can have a small reunion party tomorrow afternoon. If they bring us all back to the command post maybe we can work together again tomorrow night.'

'I really think we'll be going back to our divisions tomorrow,' said Serge. 'This riot is over.'

'I wonder how long the experts will screw around with their cause theories?' said Roy.

'This is just the beginning,' said Serge. 'They'll appoint commissions, and intellectuals who know two or three Negroes will demonstrate their expertise in race relations and this will be only the beginning. Negroes are no better and no worse than whites. I think they'll do whatever they can get away with and whatever is expected of them, and from now on there'll be lots of Negroes living up to their angry black man press notices.'

'Do you think blacks are the same as whites?' asked Roy to Gus, who was still watching the sunset.

'Yes,' said Gus absently. 'I learned it five years ago from my first partner who was the best policeman I ever knew. Kilvinsky used to say that most people are like plankton that can't fight the currents but only drift with the waves and tides, and some are like benthos which can do it but have to crawl along the slimy ocean floor to do it. And then others are like nekton which can actually fight the currents but don't have to crawl on the bottom to do it but it's so hard on the nekton that they must be very strong. I guess he figured the best of us were like the nekton. Anyway, he always said that in the big dark sea, the shape or shade of the poor suffering little things didn't matter at all.'

'Sounds like he was a philosopher,' Roy smiled.

'Sometimes I think I made a mistake becoming a cop,' said Serge. 'I look back over these five years and the frustrations have been bad but I guess there's nothing I'd rather do.'

'I saw an editorial today that said it was just deplorable that so many people had been shot and killed in the riot,' said Gus. 'The guy said, "We must assume that police can shoot to *wound*. Therefore it follows that the police must be intentionally killing all these people."'

'That's a screwed-up syllogism,' said Serge. 'But you can't blame the ignorant bastards. They've seen a thousand movies that prove you can wing a guy or shoot a gun out of his hands. What the hell, you can't blame them.'

'Just a pile of plankton dumped in a sea of concrete, eh, Gus?' said Roy.

'I guess I don't really regret the job,' said Gus. 'I guess I think I know something that most people don't.'

'All we can do is try to protect ourselves,' said Roy. 'We sure as hell can't change them.'

'And we can't save them,' said Gus. 'Nor ourselves. Poor bastards.'

'Hey, this conversation is getting too damned depressing,' said Roy suddenly. 'The riot's over. Better days are coming. We're having a swimming party tomorrow. Let's cheer up.'

'Okay, let's try to catch a crook,' said Serge. 'A good felony pinch always lifts my spirits. You used to work this area, didn't you, Gus?'

'Sure,' said Gus, straightening up and smiling. 'Drive west toward Crenshaw. I know where there's some drop-off spots for hot rollers. Maybe we can pick up a car thief.'

Roy was the first to see the woman waving to them from the car parked near the phone booth on Rodeo Road.

'I think we got a citizen's call,' said Roy.

'That's okay, I was getting tired driving around anyway,' said Serge. 'Maybe she has an insurmountable problem we can surmount.'

'It got dark fast tonight,' Gus observed. 'A couple of minutes ago I was enjoying the sunset and now, bang, it's dark.'

Serge parked beside the woman who squirmed out of the Volkswagen awkwardly and shuffled over to their car in her bedroom slippers and bathrobe which fought to conceal her expansive largeness.

'I was just going to the phone booth to call the cops,' she puffed, and before he was out of the car Roy smelled the alcoholic breath and examined the red face and weedy dyed red hair.

'What's the problem, ma'am?' said Gus.

'My old man is nuts. He's been drinking and not going to work lately and not supporting me and my kids and beating hell out of me whenever he feels like it and tonight he's completely nuts and he kicked me right in the side. The bastard. I think he broke a rib.' The woman writhed inside the bathrobe and touched her ribs.

'You live far from here?' asked Serge.

'Just down the street on Coliseum,' said the woman. 'How about coming home and throwing him out for me?'

'He your legal husband?' asked Serge.

'Yeah, but he's nuts.'

'Okay, we'll follow you home and have a talk with him.'

'You can't talk to him,' the woman insisted, getting back inside the Volkswagen. 'The bastard's crazy tonight.'

'Okay, we'll follow you home,' said Roy.

'Breaks the monotony, anyway,' said Gus, as they drove behind the little car and Roy put the shotgun down on the floor in the back and wondered if they should lock it in the front when they went in the woman's residence or would it be alright here on the floor if the car doors were locked. He decided to leave it on the floor.

'Is this neighborhood mostly white?' asked Serge to Gus.

'It's mixed,' said Gus. 'It's mixed clear out to La Cienega and up into Hollywood.'

'If this town has a ghetto it's the biggest goddamn ghetto in the world,' said Serge. 'Some ghetto. Look up there in Baldwin Hills.'

'Fancy pads,' said Gus. 'That's a mixed neighborhood too.'

'I think the broad in the VW is the best pinch we'll see tonight,' said Roy. 'She almost creamed that Ford when she turned.'

'She's loaded,' said Serge. 'Tell you what, if she smashes into somebody we'll just take off like we don't know her. I figured she was too drunk to drive when she waddled out of that car and lit my cigarette with her breath.'

'Must be that apartment house,' said Gus, flashing the spotlight on the number over the door as Serge pulled in behind the Volkswagen which she parked four feet from the curb.

'Three-Z-Ninety-one, citizen's call, forty-one twenty-three, Coliseum Drive,' said Gus into the mike.

'Don't forget to lock your door,' said Roy. 'I left the shotgun on the floor.'

'I'm not going in,' said the woman. 'I'm afraid of him. He said he'd kill me if I called the cops on him.'

'Your kids in there?' asked Serge.

'No,' she breathed. 'They ran next door when we started fighting. I guess I should tell you there's a gun in there and he's nuts as hell tonight.'

'Where's the gun?' asked Gus.

'Bedroom closet,' said the woman. 'When you take him, you can take that too.'

'We don't know if we're taking anybody yet,' said Roy. 'We're going to talk to him first.'

Serge started up the steps first as she said, 'Number twelve. We live in number twelve.'

They passed through a landscaped archway and into a court surrounded by apartments. There was a calm lighted swimming pool to their left and a sun deck with ping-pong tables to the right. Roy was surprised at the size of the apartment building after passing through the deceiving archway.

'Very nice,' said Gus, obviously admiring the swimming pool.

'Twelve must be this way,' said Roy, walking toward the tile staircase surrounded by face-high ferns. Roy thought he could still smell the woman's alcoholic breath when a frail chalky man in a damp undershirt stepped from behind a dwarfed twisted tree and lunged toward Roy who turned on the stairway. The man pointed the cheap .22 revolver at Roy's stomach and fired once and as Roy sat down on the stairway in amazement the sounds of shouts and gunfire and a deathless scream echoed through the vast patio. Then Roy realized he was lying at the foot of the staircase alone and it was quiet for a moment. Then he was aware that it was his stomach.

'Oh, not there,' said Roy and he clamped his teeth on his tongue and fought the burst of hysteria. The shock. It can kill. The shock!

Then he pulled the shirt open and unbuckled the Sam Browne and looked at the tiny bubbling cavity in the pit of his stomach. He knew he could not survive another one. Not there. Not in the guts. He had no guts left!

Roy unclamped his teeth and had to swallow many times because of the blood from his ripped tongue. It didn't hurt so much this time, he thought, and he was astonished at his lucidity. He saw that Serge and Gus were kneeling beside him, ashen-faced. Serge crossed himself and kissed his thumbnail.

It was *much* easier this time. By God, it was! The pain was diminishing and an insidious warmth crept over him. But no, it was all wrong. It shouldn't happen now. Then he panicked as he realized that it shouldn't happen now because he was starting to know. Oh, please, not now, he thought. I'm starting to know.

'Know, know,' said Roy. 'Know, know, know, know.' His voice sounded to him hollow and rhythmic like the tolling of a bell. And then he could no longer speak.

'*Santa Maria*,' said Serge taking his hand. '*Santa Maria* ... where's the goddamn ambulance? *Ay, Dios mío* ... Gus, he's cold. *Sóbale las manos* ...'

Then Roy heard Gus sob, 'He's gone, Serge. Poor Roy, poor poor man. He's gone.'

Then Roy heard Serge say, 'We should cover him. Did you hear him? He was saying no to death. *No, no, no*, he said. *Santa Maria!*'

I am not dead, Roy thought. It is monstrous to say I am dead. And then he saw Becky walking primly through a grassy field and she looked so grown up he said Rebecca when he called her name and she came smiling to her father, the sun glistening off her hair, more golden than his had ever been.

'*Dios te salve Maria, llena de gracia, el Señor es contigo* ...' said Serge.

'I'll cover him. I'll get a blanket from somebody,' said Gus. 'Please, somebody, give me a blanket.'

Now Roy released himself to the billowy white sheets of darkness and the last thing he ever heard was Sergio Durán saying, '*Santa Maria*,' again and again.

THE BLUE KNIGHT

To my parents and to Upton Birnie Brady

WEDNESDAY
the First Day

ONE

The wheel hummed and Rollo mumbled Yiddish curses as he put rouge on the glistening bronze surface.

'There ain't a single blemish on this badge,' he said.

'Sure there is, Rollo,' I said. 'Look closer. Between the *s* in *Los* and the big *A* in *Angeles*. I scratched it on the door of my locker.'

'There ain't a single blemish on this badge,' said Rollo, but he buffed, and in spite of his bitching I watched bronze change to gold, and chrome become silver. The blue enamelled letters which said 'Policeman', and '4207', jumped out at me.

'Okay, so now are you happy?' he sighed, leaning across the display case, handing me the badge.

'It's not too bad,' I said, enjoying the heft of the heavy oval shield, polished to a lustre that would reflect sunlight like a mirror.

'Business ain't bad enough, I got to humour a crazy old cop like you.' Rollo scratched his scalp, and the hair, white and stiff, stood like ruffled chicken feathers.

'What's the matter, you old gonif, afraid some of your burglar friends will see a bluesuit in here and take their hot jewellery to some other crook?'

'Ho, ho! Bob Hope should watch out. When you get through sponging off the taxpayers you'll go after his job.'

'Well, I've gotta go crush some crime. What do I owe you for the lousy badge polishing?'

'Don't make me laugh, I got a kidney infection. You been free-loading for twenty years, now all of a sudden you want to pay?'

'See you later, Rollo. I'm going over to Seymour's for breakfast. He appreciates me.'

'Seymour too? I know Jews got to suffer in this world, but not all of us in one day.'

'Good-bye, old shoe.'

'Be careful, Bumper.'

I strolled outside into the burning smog that hung over Main Street. I started to sweat as I stopped to admire Rollo's work. Most of the ridges had been rounded off long ago, and twenty years of rubbing gave it unbelievable brilliance. Turning the face of the shield to the white sun, I watched the gold and silver take the light. I pinned the badge to my shirt and looked at my reflection in the blue plastic that Rollo has over his front windows. The plastic was rippled and bubbled and my distorted reflection made me a freak. I looked at myself straight on, but still my stomach hung low and made me look like a blue kangaroo, and my ass was two nightsticks wide. My jowls hung to my chest in that awful reflection and my big rosy face and pink nose were a deep veiny blue like the colour of my uniform which somehow didn't change colours in the reflection. It was ugly, but what made me keep looking was the shield. The four-inch oval on my chest glittered and twinkled so that after a second or two I couldn't even see the blue man behind it. I just stood there staring at that shield for maybe a full minute.

Seymour's delicatessen is only a half block from Rollo's jewellery store, but I decided to drive. My black-and-white was parked out front in Rollo's no parking zone because this downtown traffic is so miserable. If it weren't for those red kerbs there'd be no place to park even a police car. I opened the white door and sat down carefully, the sunlight blasting through the windshield making the seat cushion hurt. I'd been driving the same black-and-white for six months and had worked a nice comfortable dip in the seat, so I rode cosy, like in a worn friendly saddle. It's really not too hard to loosen up seat springs with two hundred and seventy-five pounds.

I drove to Seymour's and when I pulled up in front I saw two guys across Fourth Street in the parking lot at the rear of the Pink Dragon. I watched for thirty seconds or so and it looked like they were setting something up, probably a narcotics buy. Even after twenty years I still get that thrill a cop gets at seeing things that are invisible to the square citizen. But what was the use? I could drive down Main Street anytime and see hugger-muggers, paddy hustlers, till-tappers, junkies, and then waste six or eight man-hours staking out on these small-timers and maybe end up with nothing. You only had time to grab the sure ones and just make mental notes of the rest.

The two in the parking lot interested me so I decided to watch them for a minute. They were dumb strung-out hypes. They should've made me by now. When I was younger I used to play the truth game. I hardly ever played it anymore. The object of the game is simple: I have to explain to an imaginary black-robed square (His Honour) how Officer William A. Morgan *knows* that those men are committing a criminal act. If the judge finds that I didn't have sufficient probable cause to stop, detain, and search my man, then I lose the game. Illegal search and seizure – case dismissed.

I usually beat the game whether it's imaginary or for real. My courtroom demeanour is very good, pretty articulate for an old-time copper, they say. And such a simple honest kisser. Big innocent blue eyes. Juries loved me. It's very hard to explain the 'know'. Some guys never master it. Let's see,

I begin, I *know* they are setting up a buy because of ... the clothing. That's a good start, the clothing. It's a suffocating day, Your Honour, and the tall one is wearing a long-sleeved shirt buttoned at the cuff. To hide his hype marks, of course. One of them is still wearing his 'county shoes'. That tells me he just got out of county jail, and the other one, yes, the other one – you only acquire that frantic pasty look in the joint: San Quentin, Folsom, maybe. He's been away a long time. And I would find out they'd just been in the Pink Dragon and no one but a whore, hype, pill-head, or other hustler would hang out in that dive. And I'd explain all this to my judge too, but I'd be a little more subtle, and then I'd be stopped. I could explain to my imaginary jurist but never to a real one about the instinct – the stage in this business when, like an animal, you can *feel* you've got one, and it can't be explained. You *feel* the truth, and you know. Try telling *that* to the judge, I thought. Try explaining *that*, sometime.

Just then a wino lurched across Main Street against the red light and a Lincoln jammed on the binders almost creaming him.

'Goddamnit, come over here,' I yelled when he reached the sidewalk.

'Hi, Bumper,' he croaked, holding the five-sizes-too-big pants around his bony hips, trying his best to look sober as he staggered sideways.

'You almost got killed, Noodles,' I said.

'What's the difference?' he said, wiping the saliva from his chin with his grimy free hand. The other one gripped the pants so hard the big knuckles showed white through the dirt.

'I don't care about you but I don't want any wrecked Lincolns on my beat.'

'Okay, Bumper.'

'I'm gonna have to book you.'

'I'm not that drunk, am I?'

'No, but you're dying.'

'No crime in that.' He coughed then and the spit that dribbled out the corner of his mouth was red and foamy.

'I'm booking you, Noodles,' I said, mechanically filling in the boxes on the pad of drunk arrest reports that I carried in my hip pocket like I was still walking my beat instead of driving a black-and-white.

'Let's see, your real name is Ralph M. Milton, right?'

'Millard.'

'Millard,' I muttered, filling in the name. I must've busted Noodles a dozen times. I never used to forget names or faces.

'Let's see, eyes bloodshot, gait staggering, attitude stuporous, address transient....'

'Got a cigarette?'

'I don't use them, Noodles,' I said, tearing out the copies of the arrest report. 'Wait a minute, the nightwatch left a half pack in the glove compartment. Go get them while I'm calling the wagon.'

545

The wino shuffled to the radio car while I walked fifty feet down the street to a call box, unlocked it with my big brass key, and asked for the B-wagon to come to Fourth and Main. It would've been easier to use my car radio to call the wagon, but I walked a beat too many years to learn new habits.

That was something my body did to me, made me lose my foot beat and put me in a black-and-white. An ankle I broke years ago when I was a slick-sleeved rookie chasing a purse-snatcher, finally decided it can't carry my big ass around anymore and swells up every time I'm on my feet a couple of hours. So I lose my foot beat and got a radio car. A one-man foot beat's the best job in this or any police department. It always amuses policemen to see the movies where the big hood or crooked politician yells, 'I'll have you walking a beat, you dumb flatfoot,' when really it's a sought-after job. You got to have whiskers to get a foot beat, and you have to be big and good. If only my legs would've held out. But even though I couldn't travel it too much on foot, it was still *my* beat, all of it. Everyone knew it all belonged to me more than anyone.

'Okay, Noodles, give this arrest report to the cops in the wagon and don't lose the copies.'

'You're not coming with me?' He couldn't shake a cigarette from the pack with one trembling hand.

'No, you just lope on over to the corner and flag 'em down when they drive by. Tell 'em you want to climb aboard.'

'First time I ever arrested myself,' he coughed, as I lit a cigarette for him, and put the rest of the pack and the arrest report in his shirt pocket. 'See you later.'

'I'll get six months. The judge warned me last time.'

'I hope so, Noodles.'

'I'll just start boozing again when they let me out. I'll just get scared and start again. You don't know what it's like to be scared at night when you're alone.'

'How do you know, Noodles?'

'I'll just come back here and die in an alley. The cats and rats will eat me anyway, Bumper.'

'Get your ass moving or you'll miss the wagon.' I watched him stagger down Main for a minute and I yelled, 'Don't you believe in miracles?'

He shook his head and I turned back to the guys in the parking lot again just as they disappeared inside the Pink Dragon. Someday, I thought, I'll kill that dragon and drink its blood.

I was too hungry to do police work, so I went into Seymour's. I usually like to eat breakfast right after rollcall and here it was ten o'clock and I was still screwing around.

Ruthie was bent over one of the tables scooping up a tip. She was very attractive from the rear and she must've caught me admiring her out of the corner of her eye. I suppose a blue man, dark blue in black leather, sets off signals in some people.

'Bumper,' she said, wheeling around. 'Where you been all week?'

'Hi, Ruthie,' I said, always embarrassed by how glad she was to see me.

Seymour, a freckled redhead about my age, was putting together a pastrami sandwich behind the meat case. He heard Ruthie call my name and grinned.

'Well, look who's here. The finest cop money can buy.'

'Just bring me a cold drink, you old shlimazel.'

'Sure, champ.' Seymour gave the pastrami to a take-out customer, made change, and put a cold beer and a frosted glass in front of me. He winked at the well-dressed man who sat at the counter to my left. The beer wasn't opened.

'Whadda you want me to do, bite the cap off?' I said, going along with his joke. No one on my beat had ever seen me drink on duty.

Seymour bent over, chuckling. He took the beer away and filled my glass with buttermilk.

'Where you been all week, Bumper?'

'Out there. Making the streets safe for women and babies.'

'Bumper's here!' he shouted to Henry in the back. That meant five scrambled eggs and twice the lox the paying customers get with an order. It also meant three onion bagels, toasted and oozing with butter and heaped with cream cheese. I don't eat breakfast at Seymour's more than once or twice a week, although I knew he'd feed me three free meals every day.

'Young Slagel told me he saw you directing traffic on Hill Street the other day,' said Seymour.

'Yeah, the regular guy got stomach cramps just as I was driving by. I took over for him until his sergeant got somebody else.'

'Directing traffic down there is a job for the young bucks,' said Seymour, winking again at the businessman who was smiling at me and biting off large chunks of a Seymour's Special Corned Beef on Pumpernickel Sandwich.

'Meet any nice stuff down there, Bumper? An airline hostess, maybe? Or some of those office cuties?'

'I'm too old to interest them, Seymour. But let me tell you, watching all that young poon, I had to direct traffic like this.' With that I stood up and did an imitation of waving at cars, bent forward with my legs and feet crossed.

Seymour fell backward and out came his high-pitched hoot of a laugh. This brought Ruthie over to see what happened.

'Show her, Bumper, please,' Seymour gasped, wiping the tears away.

Ruthie waited with that promising smile of hers. She's every bit of forty-five, but firm, and golden blonde, and very fair – as sexy a wench as I've ever seen. And the way she acted always made me know it was there for me, but I'd never taken it. She's one of the regular people on my beat and it's because of the way *they* feel about me, all of them, the people on my beat. Some of the smartest bluecoats I know have lots of broads but won't even cop a feel on their beats. Long ago I decided to admire her big buns from afar.

'I'm waiting, Bumper,' she said, hands on those curvy hips.

'Another funny thing happened while I was directing traffic,' I said, to change the subject. 'There I was, blowing my whistle and waving at cars with one hand, and I had my other hand out palm up, and some little eighty-year-old lady comes up and drops a big fat letter on my palm. "Could you please tell me the postage for this, Officer?" she says. Here I am with traffic backed up clear to Olive, both arms out and this letter on my palm. So, what the hell, I just put my feet together, arms out, and rock back and forth like a scale balancing, and say, "That'll be twenty-one cents, ma'am, if you want it to go airmail." "Oh *thank* you, Officer," she says.'

Seymour hooted again and Ruthie laughed, but things quieted down when my food came, and I loosened my Sam Browne for the joy of eating. It annoyed me though when my belly pressed against the edge of the yellow Formica counter.

Seymour had a flurry of orders to go which he took care of and nobody bothered me for ten minutes or so except for Ruthie who wanted to make sure I had enough to eat, and that my eggs were fluffy enough, and also to rub a hip or something up against me so that I had trouble thinking about the third bagel.

The other counter customer finished his second cup of coffee and Seymour shuffled over.

'More coffee, Mister Parker?'

'No, I've had plenty.'

I'd never seen this man before but I admired his clothes. He was stouter than me, soft fat, but his suit, not bought off the rack, hid most of it.

'You ever met Officer Bumper Morgan, Mister Parker?' asked Seymour.

We smiled, both too bloated and lazy to stand up and shake hands across two stools.

'I've heard of you, Officer,' said Parker. 'I recently opened a suite in the Roxman Building. Fine watches. Stop around anytime for a special discount.' He put his card on the counter and pushed it halfway towards me. Seymour shoved it the rest of the way.

'Everyone around here's heard of Bumper,' Seymour said proudly.

'I thought you'd be a bigger man, Officer,' said Parker. 'About six foot seven and three hundred pounds, from some of the stories I've heard.'

'You just about got the weight right,' said Seymour.

I was used to people saying I'm not as tall as they expected, or as I first appeared to be. A beat cop has to be big or he'll be fighting all the time. Sometimes a tough, feisty little cop resents it because he can't walk a foot beat, but the fact is that most people don't fear a little guy and a little guy'd just have to prove himself all the time, and sooner or later somebody'd take that nightstick off him and shove it up his ass. Of course I was in a radio car now, but as I said before, I was still a beat cop, more or less.

The problem with my size was that my frame was made for a guy six feet five or six instead of a guy barely six feet. My bones are big and heavy, especially my hands and feet. If I'd just have grown as tall as I was meant to, I wouldn't have the goddamn weight problem. My appetite was meant for a giant, and I finally convinced those police doctors who used to send 'fat man letters' to my captain ordering me to cut down to two hundred and twenty pounds.

'Bumper's a one-man gang,' said Seymour. 'I tell you he's fought wars out there.' Seymour waved at the street to indicate the 'out there'.

'Come on, Seymour,' I said, but it was no use. This kind of talk shrivelled my balls, but it did please me that a newcomer like Parker had heard of me. I wondered how special the 'special discount' would be. My old watch was about finished.

'How long ago did you get this beat, Bumper?' asked Seymour, but didn't allow me to answer. 'Well, it was almost twenty years. I know that, because when Bumper was a rookie, I was a young fella myself, working for my father right here. It was real bad then. We had B-girls and zoot-suiters and lots of crooks. In those days there was plenty of guys that would try the cop on the beat.'

I looked over at Ruthie, who was smiling.

'Years ago, when Ruthie worked here the first time, Bumper saved her life when some guy jumped her at the bus stop on Second Street. He saved you, didn't he, Ruthie?'

'He sure did. He's my hero,' she said, pouring me a cup of coffee.

'Bumper's always worked right here,' Seymour continued. 'On foot beats and now in a patrol car since he can't walk too good no more. His twenty-year anniversary is coming up, but we won't let him retire. What would it be like around here without the champ?'

Ruthie actually looked scared for a minute when Seymour said it, and this shook me.

'When is your twentieth year up, Bumper?' she asked.

'End of this month.'

'You're not even considering pulling the pin, are you, Bumper?' asked Seymour, who knew all the police lingo from feeding the beat cops for years.

'What do *you* think?' I asked, and Seymour seemed satisfied and started telling Parker a few more incidents from the Bumper Morgan legend. Ruthie kept watching me. Women are like cops, they sense things. When Seymour finally ran down, I promised to come back Friday for the Deluxe Businessman's Plate, said my good-byes, and left six bits for Ruthie which she didn't put in her tip dish under the counter. She looked me in the eye and dropped it right down her bra.

I'd forgotten about the heat and when it hit me I decided to drive straight for Elysian Park, sit on the grass, and smoke a cigar with my radio turned up loud enough so I wouldn't miss a call. I wanted to read about last night's Dodger game, so before getting in the car I walked down to the smoke shop. I picked up half a dozen fifty-cent cigars, and since the store recently changed hands and I didn't know the owner too well, I took a five out of my pocket.

'From you? Don't be silly, Officer Morgan,' said the pencil-necked old man, and refused the money. I made a little small talk in way of payment, listened to a gripe or two about business, and left, forgetting to pick up a paper. I almost went back in, but I never make anyone bounce for two things in one day. I decided to get a late paper across the street from Frankie the dwarf. He had his Dodger's baseball cap tilted forward and pretended not to see me until I was almost behind him, then he turned fast and punched me in the thigh with a deformed little fist.

'Take that, you big slob. You might scare everybody else on the street, but I'll get a fat lock on you and break your kneecap.'

'What's happening, Frankie?' I said, while he slipped a folded paper under my arm without me asking.

'No happenings, Killer. How you standing up under this heat?'

'Okay, I guess.' I turned to the sports page while Frankie smoked a king-sized cigarette in a fancy silver holder half as long as his arm. His tiny face was pinched and ancient but he was only thirty years old.

A woman and a little boy about four years old were standing next to me, waiting for the red light to change.

'See that man,' she said. 'That's a policeman. He'll come and get you and put you in jail if you're bad.' She gave me a sweet smile, very smug because she thought I was impressed with her good citizenship.

Frankie, who was only a half head taller than the kid, took a step towards them and said, 'That's real clever, lady. Make him scared of the law. Then he'll grow up hating cops because *you* scared him to death.'

'Easy, Frankie,' I said, a little surprised.

The woman lifted the child and the second the light changed she ran from the angry dwarf.

'Sorry, Bumper,' Frankie smiled. 'Lord knows I'm not a cop lover.'

'Thanks for the paper, old shoe,' I said, keeping in the shade, nodding to several of the local characters and creeps who gave me a 'Hi, Bumper'.

I sauntered along towards Broadway to see what the crowds looked like today and to scare off any pickpockets that might be working the shoppers. I fired up one of those fifty-centers which are okay when I'm out of good hand-rolled custom-mades. As I rounded the corner on Broadway I saw six of the Krishna cult performing in their favourite place on the west sidewalk. They were all kids, the oldest being maybe twenty-five, boys and girls, shaved heads, a long single pigtail, bare feet with little bells on their ankles, pale orange saris, tambourines, flutes and guitars. They chanted and danced and put on a hell of a show there almost every day, and there was no way old Herman the Devil-drummer could compete with them. You could see his jaw flopping and knew he was screaming but you couldn't hear a word he said after they started *their* act.

Up until recently, this had been Herman's corner, and even before I came on the job Herman put in a ten-hour day right here passing out tracts and yelling about demons and damnation, collecting maybe twelve bucks a day from people who felt sorry for him. He used to be a lively guy, but now he looked old, bloodless, and dusty. His shiny black suit was threadbare and his frayed white collar was grey and dirty and he didn't seem to care anymore. I thought about trying to persuade him one more time to move down Broadway a few blocks where he wouldn't have to compete with these kids and all their colour and music. But I knew it wouldn't do any good. Herman had been on his beat too long. I walked to my car thinking about him, poor old Devil-drummer.

As I was getting back in my saddle seat I got a burning pain in the gut and had to drop a couple of acid eaters. I carried pockets full of white tablets. Acid eaters in the right pocket and bubble breakers in the left pocket. The acid eaters are just antacid pills and the bubble breakers are for gas and I'm cursed with both problems, more or less all the time. I sucked an acid eater and the fire died. Then I thought about Cassie because that sometimes settled my stomach. The decision to retire at twenty years had been made several weeks ago, and Cassie had lots of plans, but what she *didn't* know was that I'd decided last night to make Friday my last day on duty. Today, tomorrow, and Friday would be it. I could string my vacation days together and run them until the end of the month when my time was officially up.

Friday was also to be her last day at LA City College. She'd already prepared her final exams and had permission to leave school now, while a substitute instructor took over her classes. She had a good offer, a 'wonderful opportunity' she called it, to join the faculty of an expensive girls' school in northern California, near San Francisco. They wanted her up there now, before they closed for the summer, so she could get an idea how things were done. She planned on leaving Monday, and at the end of the month when I retired, coming back to Los Angeles where we'd get married, then we'd go back to the apartment she'd have all fixed up and ready. But I'd decided to leave Friday and go with her. No sense fooling around any longer, I thought. It would be better to get it over with and I knew Cruz would be happy about it.

Cruz Segovia was my sergeant, and for twenty years he'd been the person closest to me. He was always afraid something would happen and he made me promise him I wouldn't blow this, the best deal of my life. And Cassie *was* the best deal, no doubt about it. A teacher, a divorced woman with no kids, a woman with real education, not just a couple college degrees. She was young-looking, forty-four years old, and had it all.

So I started making inquiries about what there was for a retired cop around the Bay area and damned if I didn't luck out and get steered into a good job with a large industrial security outfit that was owned by an ex-LAPD inspector I knew from the old days. I got the job of security chief at an electronics firm that has a solid government contract, and I'd have my own office and car, a secretary, *and* be making a hundred more a month than I was as a cop. The reason he picked me instead of one of the other applicants who were retired captains or inspectors is that he said he had enough administrators working for him and he wanted one real iron-nutted street cop. So this was maybe the first time I ever got rewarded for doing police work and I was pretty excited about starting something new and seeing if real police techniques and ideas couldn't do something for industrial security which was usually pretty pitiful at best.

The thirtieth of May, the day I'd officially retire, was also my fiftieth birthday. It was hard to believe I'd been around half a century, but it was harder to believe I'd lived in this world thirty years before I got my beat. I was sworn in as a cop on my thirtieth birthday, the second oldest guy in my academy class, the oldest being Cruz Segovia, who had tried three times to join the Department but couldn't pass the oral exam. It was probably because he was so shy and had such a heavy Spanish accent, being an El Paso Mexican. But his grammar was beautiful if you just bothered to listen past the accent, and finally he got an oral board that was smart enough to listen.

I was driving through Elysian Park as I was thinking these things and I spotted two motor cops in front of me, heading towards the police academy. The motor cop in front was a kid named Lefler, one of the hundred or so I've broken in. He'd recently transferred to Motors from Central and was riding tall in his new shiny boots, white helmet, and striped riding britches. His partner breaking him in on the motor beat was a leather-faced old fart named Crandall. He's the type that'll get hot at a traffic violator and screw up your public relations programme by pulling up beside him and yelling, 'Grab a piece of the kerb, asshole.'

Lefler's helmet was dazzling white and tilted forward, the short bill pulled down to his nose. I drove up beside him and yelled, 'That's a gorgeous skid lid you got there, boy, but pull it up a little and lemme see those baby blues.'

Lefler smiled and goosed his bike a little. He was even wearing expensive black leather gloves in this heat.

'Hi, Bumper,' said Crandall, taking his hand from the bar for a minute. We rode slow side by side and I grinned at Lefler, who looked self-conscious.

'How's he doing, Crandall?' I asked. 'I broke him in on the job. He's Bumper-ized.'

'Not bad for a baby,' Crandall shrugged.

'I see you took his training wheels off,' I said, and Lefler giggled and goosed the Harley again.

I could see the edge of the horseshoe cleats on his heels and I knew his soles were probably studded with iron.

'Don't go walking around my beat with those boots on, kid,' I yelled. 'You'll be kicking up sparks and starting fires.' I chuckled then as I remembered seeing a motor cop with two cups of coffee in his gloved hands go right on his ass one time because of those cleats.

I waved at Lefler and pulled away. Young hotdogs, I thought. I was glad I was older when I came on the job. But then, I knew I would never have been a motor officer. Writing traffic tickets was the one part of police work I didn't like. The only good thing about it was it gave you an excuse to stop some suspicious cars on the pretext of writing a ticket. More good arrests came from phony traffic stops than anything else. More policemen got blown up that way, too.

I decided, what the hell, I was too jumpy to lay around the park reading the paper. I'd been like a cat ever since I'd decided about Friday. I hardly slept last night. I headed back towards the beat.

I should be patrolling for the burglar, I thought. I really wanted him now that I only had a couple of days left. He was a daytime hotel creeper and hitting maybe four to six hotel rooms in the best downtown hotels every time he went to work. The dicks talked to us at rollcall and said the M.O. run showed he preferred weekdays, especially Thursday and Friday, but a lot of jobs were showing up on Wednesdays. This guy would shim doors which isn't too hard to do in any hotel since they usually have the world's worst security, and he'd burgle the place whether the occupants were in or not. Of course he waited until they were in the shower or napping. I loved catching burglars. Most policemen call it fighting ghosts and give up trying to catch them, but I'd rather catch a hot prowl guy than a stickup man any day. And any burglar with balls enough to take a pad when the people are home is every bit as dangerous as a stickup man.

I decided I'd patrol the hotels by the Harbour Freeway. I had a theory this guy was using some sort of repairman disguise since he'd eluded all stakeouts so far, and I figured him for a repair or delivery truck. I envisioned him as an out-of-towner who used the convenient Harbour Freeway to come to his job. This burglar was doing ding-a-ling stuff on some of the jobs, cutting up clothing, usually women's or kids', tearing the crotch out of underwear, and on a recent job he stabbed the hell out of a big teddy bear that a little girl left on the bed covered up with a blanket. I was glad the people weren't in when he hit *that* time. He was kinky, but a clever burglar, a lucky burglar. I thought about patrolling around the hotels, but first I'd go see Glenda. She'd be rehearsing now, and I might never see her again. She was one of the people I owed a good-bye to.

I entered the side-door of the run-down little theatre. They mostly showed skin flicks now. They used to have a halfway decent burlesque house here, with some fair comics and good-looking girls. Glenda was something in those days. The 'Gilded Girl' they called her. She'd come out in a gold sheath and peel to a golden G-string and gold pasties. She was tall and graceful, and a better-than-average dancer. She played some big-time clubs off and on, but she was thirty-eight years old now and after two or three husbands she was back down on Main Street competing with beaver movies between reels, and taxi dancing part-time down the street at the ballroom. She was maybe twenty pounds heavier, but she still looked good to me because I saw her like she used to be.

I stood there in the shadows backstage and got accustomed to the dark and the quiet. They didn't even have anyone on the door anymore. I guess even the weinie waggers and bustle rubbers gave up sneaking in the side door of this hole. The wallpaper was wet and rusty and curling off the walls like old scrolls. There were dirty costumes laying around on chairs. The popcorn machine, which they activated on weekend nights, was leaning against the wall, one leg broken.

'The cockroaches serve the popcorn in this joint. You don't want any, Bumper,' said Glenda, who had stepped out of her dressing room and was watching me from the darkness.

'Hi, kid.' I smiled and followed her voice through the dark to the dimly lit little dressing room.

She kissed me on the cheek like she always did, and I took off my hat and flopped down on the ragged overstuffed chair beside her make-up table.

'Hey, Saint Francis, where've all the birdies gone?' she said, tickling the bald spot on my crown. She always laid about a hundred old jokes on me every time we met.

Glenda was wearing net stockings with a hole in one leg and a sequined G-string. She was nude on top and didn't bother putting on a robe. I didn't blame her, it was so damn hot today, but she didn't usually go around like this in front of me and it made me a little nervous.

'Hot weather's here, baby,' she said, sitting down and fixing her make-up. 'When you going back on nights?'

Glenda knew my M.O. I work days in the winter, night-watch in the summer when the Los Angeles sun starts turning the heavy bluesuit into sackcloth.

'I'll never go back on nights, Glenda,' I said casually. 'I'm retiring.'

She turned around in her chair and those heavy white melons bounced once or twice. Her hair was long and blonde. She always claimed she was a real blonde but I'd never know.

'You won't quit,' she said. 'You'll be here till they kick you out. Or till you die. Like me.'

'We'll both leave here,' I said, smiling because she was starting to look upset. 'Some nice guy'll come along and ...'

'Some nice guy took me out of here three times, Bumper. Trouble is I'm just not a nice girl. Too fucked up for any man. You're just kidding about retiring, aren't you?'

'How's Sissy?' I said, to change the subject.

Glenda answered by taking a package of snapshots out of her purse and handing them to me. I'm farsighted now and in the dimness I couldn't really see anything but the outline of a little girl holding a dog. I couldn't even say if the dog was real or stuffed.

'She's beautiful,' I said, knowing she was. I'd last seen her several months ago when I drove Glenda home from work one night.

'Every dollar you ever gave me went into a bank account for her just like we agreed at first,' said Glenda.

'I know that.'

'I added to it on my own too.'

'She'll have something someday.'

'Bet your ass she will,' said Glenda, lighting a cigarette.

I wondered how much I'd given Glenda over the past ten years. And I wondered how many really good arrests I'd made on information she gave me. She was one of my big secrets. The detectives had informants who they paid but the bluesuits weren't supposed to be involved in that kind of police work. Well, I had my paid informants too. But I didn't pay them from any Department money. I paid them from my pocket, and when I made the bust on the scam they gave me, I made it look like I lucked on to the arrest. Or I made up some other fanciful story for the arrest report. That way Glenda was protected and nobody could say Bumper Morgan was completely nuts for paying informants out of his own pocket. The first time, Glenda turned me a federal fugitive who was dating her and who carried a gun and pulled stickups. I tried to give her twenty bucks and she refused it, saying he was a no-good asshole and belonged in the joint and she was no snitch. I made her take it for Sissy who was a baby then, and who had no dad. Since then over the years I've probably laid a thousand on Glenda for Sissy. And I've probably made the best pinches of any cop in Central Division.

'She gonna be a blondie like momma?' I asked.

'Yeah,' she smiled. 'More blonde than me though. And about ten times as smart. I think she's smarter already. I'm reading books like mad to keep up with her.'

'Those private schools are tough,' I nodded. 'They teach them something.'

'You notice this one, Bumper?' She smiled, coming over to me and sitting on the arm of the chair. She was smiling big and thinking about Sissy now. 'The dog's pulling her hair. Look at the expression.'

'Oh yeah,' I said, seeing only a blur and feeling one of those heavy chi-chis resting on my shoulder. Hers were big and natural, not pumped full of plastic like so many these days.

'She's peeved in this one,' said Glenda, leaning closer, and it was pressed against my cheek, and finally one tender doorbell went right into my ear.

'Damn it, Glenda!' I said, looking up.

'What?' she answered, moving back. She got it, and laughed her hard hoarse laugh. Then her laugh softened and she smiled and her big eyes went soft and I noticed the lashes were dark beneath the eyes and not from mascara. I thought Glenda was more attractive now than she ever was.

'I have a big feeling for you, Bumper,' she said, and kissed me right on the mouth. 'You and Sissy are the only ones. You're what's happening, baby.'

Glenda was like Ruthie. She was one of the people who belonged to the beat. There were laws that I made for myself, but she was almost naked and to me she was still so beautiful.

'Now,' she said, knowing I was about to explode. 'Why not? You never have and I always wanted you to.'

'Gotta get back to my car,' I said, jumping up and crossing the room in three big steps. Then I mumbled something else about missing my radio calls, and Glenda told me to wait.

'You forgot your hat,' she said, handing it to me.

'Thanks,' I said, putting the lid on with one shaky hand. She held the other one and kissed my palm with a warm wet mouth.

'Don't think of leaving us, Bumper,' she said and stared me in the eye.

'Here's a few bucks for Sissy,' I said, fumbling in my pocket for a ten.

'I don't have any information this time,' she said, shaking her head, but I tucked it inside her G-string and she grinned.

'It's for the kid.'

There were some things I'd intended asking her about some gunsel I'd heard was hanging out in the skin houses and taxi-dance joints, but I couldn't trust myself alone with her for another minute. 'See you later, kid,' I said weakly.

'Bye, Bumper,' she said as I picked my way through the darkness to the stage door. Aside from the fact that Cassie gave me all I could handle, there was another reason I tore myself away from her like that. Any cop knows you can't afford to get too tight with your informant. You try screwing a snitch and you'll be the one that ends up getting screwed.

TWO

After leaving Glenda it actually seemed cool on the street. Glenda never did anything like that before. Everyone was acting a little ding-a-ling when I mentioned my retirement. I didn't feel like climbing back inside that machine and listening to the noisy chatter on the radio.

It was still morning now and I was pretty happy, twirling my stick as I strolled along. I guess I *swaggered* along. Most beat officers swagger. People expect you to. It shows the hangtoughs you're not afraid, and people expect it. Although they expect an older cop to cock his hat a little so I always do that too.

I still wore the traditional eight-pointed hat and used a leather thong on my stick. The Department went to more modern round hats, like Air Force hats, and we all have to change over. I'd wear the eight-pointed police hat to the end, I thought. Then I thought about Friday as being the end and I started a fancy stick spin to keep my mind off it. I let the baton go bouncing off the sidewalk back up into my hand. Three shoe shine kids were watching me, two Mexican, one Negro. The baton trick impressed the hell out of them. I strung it out like a Yo-Yo, did some back twirls and dropped it back into the ring in one smooth motion.

'Want a choo chine, Bumper?' said one of the Mexican kids.

'Thanks, pal, but I don't need one.'

'It's free to you,' he said, tagging along beside me for a minute.

'I'm buying juice today, pal,' I said, flipping two quarters up in the air which one of them jumped up and caught. He ran to the orange juice parlour three doors away with the other two chasing him. The shoe shine boxes hung around their necks with ropes and thudded against their legs as they ran.

These little kids probably never saw a beat officer twirl a stick before. The Department ordered us to remove the leather thongs a couple of years ago, but I never did and all the sergeants pretend not to notice as long as I borrow a regulation baton for inspections.

The stick is held in the ring now by a big rubber washer like the one that goes over the pipe in the back of your toilet. We've learned new ways to use the stick from some young Japanese cops who are karate and akido experts.

557

We use the blunt end of the stick more and I have to admit it beats hell out of the old caveman swing. I must've shattered six sticks over guys' heads, arms and legs in my time. Now I've learned from these Nisei kids how to swing that baton in a big arc and put my whole ass behind it. I could damn near drive it through a guy if I wanted to, and never hurt the stick. It's very graceful stuff too. I feel I can do twice as well in a brawl now. The only bad thing is, they convinced the Department brass that the leather thong was worthless. You see, these kids were never real beat men. Neither were the brass. They don't understand what the cop twirling his stick really means to people who see him stroll down a quiet street throwing that big shadow in an eight-pointed hat. Anyway, I'd never take off the leather thong. It made me sick to think of a toilet washer on a police weapon.

I stopped by the arcade and saw a big muscle-bound fruit hustler standing there. I just looked hard at him for a second, and he fell apart and slithered away. Then I saw two con guys leaning up against a wall flipping a quarter, hoping to get a square in a coin stack. I stared at them and they got nervous and skulked around to the parking lot and disappeared.

The arcade was almost deserted. I remember when the slimeballs used to be packed in there solid, asshole to belly button, waiting to look at the skin show in the viewer. That was a big thing then. The most daring thing around. The vice squad used to bust guys all the time for masturbating. There were pecker prints all over the walls in front of the viewer. Now you can walk in any bar or movie house down there and see live skin shows, or animal flicks, and I don't mean Walt Disney stuff. It's women and dogs, dykes and donkeys, dildos and whips, fags, chickens, and ducks. Sometimes it's hard to tell who or what is doing what to who or what.

Then I started thinking about the camera club that used to be next door to the arcade when nudity was still a big thing. It cost fifteen bucks to join and five bucks for every camera session. You got to take all the pictures of a naked girl you wanted, as long as you didn't get closer than two feet and as long as you didn't touch. Of course, most of the 'photographers' didn't even have film in their cameras, but the management knew it and never bothered putting in real camera lights and nobody complained. It was really so innocent.

I was about to head back to my car when I noticed another junkie watching me. He was trying to decide whether to rabbit or freeze. He froze finally, his eyes roaming around too casually, hitting on everything but me, hoping he could melt into the jungle. I hardly ever bust hypes for marks anymore, and he looked too sick to be holding, but I thought I recognized him.

'Come here, man,' I called and he came slinking my way like it was all over.

'Hello, Bumper.'

'Well, hello, Wimpy,' I said to the chalk-faced hype. 'It took me a minute to recognize you. You're older.'

'Went away for three years last time.'

'How come so long?'

'Armed robbery. Went to Q behind armed robbery. Violence don't suit me. I shoulda stuck to boosting. San Quentin made me old, Bumper.'

'Too bad, Wimpy. Yeah, now I remember. You did a few gas stations, right?'

He *was* old. His sandy hair was streaked with grey and it was patchy. And his teeth were rotting and loose in his mouth. It was starting to come back to me like it always does: Herman (Wimpy) Brown, a lifelong hype and a pretty good snitch when he wanted to be. Couldn't be more than forty but he looked a lot older than me.

'I wish I'd never met that hangtough, Barty Mendez. Remember him, Bumper? A dope fiend shouldn't never do violent crime. You just ain't cut out for it. I coulda kept boosting cigarettes out of markets and made me a fair living for quite a while.'

'How much you boosting now, Wimpy?' I said, giving him a light. He was clammy and covered with gooseflesh. If he knew anything he'd tell me. He wanted a taste so bad right now, he'd snitch on his mother.

'I don't boost anywhere near your beat, Bumper. I go out to the west side and lift maybe a couple dozen cartons of smokes a day outta those big markets. I don't do nothing down here except look for guys holding.'

'You hang up your parole yet?'

'No, I ain't running from my parole officer. You can call in and check.' He dragged hard on the cigarette but it wasn't doing much good.

'Let's see your arms, Wimpy,' I said, taking one bony arm and pushing up the sleeve.

'You ain't gonna bust me on a chickenshit marks case, are you, Bumper?'

'I'm just curious,' I said, noticing the inner elbows were fairly clean. I'd have to put on my glasses to see the marks and I never took my glasses to work. They stayed in my apartment

'Few marks, Bumper, not too bad,' he said, trying a black-toothed smile. 'I shrink them with haemorrhoid ointment.'

I bent the elbow and looked at the back of the forearm. 'Damn, the whole Union Pacific could run on those tracks!' I didn't need glasses to see those swollen abscessed wounds.

'Don't bust me, Bumper,' he whined. 'I can work for you like I used to. I gave you some good things, remember? I turned the guy that juked that taxi dancer in the alley. The one that almost cut her tit off, remember?'

'Yeah, that's right,' I said, as it came back to me. Wimpy *did* turn that one for me.

'Don't these P.O.'s ever look at your arms?' I asked, sliding the sleeves back down.

'Some're like cops, others're social workers. I always been lucky about drawing a square P.O. or one who really digs numbers, like how many guys he's rehabilitating. They don't want to *fail* you, you know? Nowadays they give you dope and call it something else and say you're cured. They show you statistics, but I think the ones they figure are clean are just dead, probably from an overdose.'

'Make sure *you* don't O.D., Wimpy,' I said, leading him away from the arcade so we could talk in private while I was walking him to the corner call box to run a make.

'I liked it inside when I was on the programme, Bumper. Honest to God. C.R.C. is a good place. I knew guys with no priors who shot phony needle holes in their arms so they could go there instead of to Q. And I heard Tehachapi is even better. Good food, and you don't hardly work at all, and group therapy where you can shuck, and there's these trade schools there where you can jive around. I could do a nickel in those places and I wouldn't mind. In fact, last time I was sorta sorry they kicked me out after thirteen months. But three years in Q broke me, Bumper. You know you're really in the joint when you're in that place.'

'Still think about geezing when you're inside?'

'Always think about that,' he said, trying to smile again as we stopped next to the call box. There were people walking by but nobody close. 'I need to geez bad now, Bumper. Real bad.' He looked like he was going to cry.

'Well, don't flip. I might not bust you if you can do me some good. Start thinking real hard, while I run a make to see if you hung it up.'

'My parole's good as gold,' he said, already perking up now that he figured I wasn't going to book him for marks. 'You and me could work good, Bumper. I always trusted you. You got a rep for protecting your informants. Nobody never got a rat jacket behind your busts. I know you got an army of snitches, but nobody never got a snitch jacket. You take care of your people.'

'You won't get a jacket either, Wimpy. Work with me and nobody knows. Nobody.'

Wimpy was sniffling and cotton-mouthed so I unlocked the call box and hurried up with the wants check. I gave the girl his name and birthdate, and lit his cigarette while we waited. He started looking around. He wasn't afraid to be caught informing, he was just looking for a connection: a peddler, a junkie, anybody that might be holding a cap. I'd blow my brains out first, I thought.

'You living at a halfway house?' I asked.

'Not now,' he said. 'You know, after being clean for three years I thought I could do it this time. Then I went and fixed the second day out, and I was feeling so bad about it I went to a kick pad over on the east side and asked them to sign me in. They did and I was clean three more days, left the kick pad, scored some junk, and had a spike in my arm ever since.'

'Ever fire when you were in the joint?' I asked, trying to keep the conversation going until the information came back.

'I never did. Never had the chance. I heard of a few guys. I once saw two guys make an outfit. They were expecting half a piece from somewheres. I don't know what they had planned, but they sure was making a fit.'

'How?'

'They bust open this light bulb and one of them held the filament with a piece of cardboard and a rag and the other just kept heating it up with matches, and those suckers stretched that thing out until it was a pretty good eyedropper. They stuck a hole in it with a pin and attached a plastic spray bottle to it and it wasn't a bad fit. I'd a took a chance and stuck it in my arm if there was some dope in it.'

'Probably break off in your vein.'

'Worth the chance. I seen guys without a spike so strung out and hurting they cut their arm open with a razor and blow a mouthful of dope right in there.'

He was puffing big on the smoke. His hands and arms were covered with the jailhouse tattoos made from pencil lead shavings which they mix with spit and jab into their arms with a million pinpricks. He probably did it when he was a youngster just coming up. Now he was an old head and had professional tattoos all over the places where he shoots junk, but nothing could hide those tracks.

'I used to be a boss booster at one time, Bumper. Not just a cigarette thief. I did department stores for good clothes and expensive perfume, even jewellery counters which are pretty tough to do. I wore two-hundred-dollar suits in the days when only rich guys wore suits that good.'

'Work alone?'

'All alone, I swear. I didn't need nobody. I looked different then. I was good looking, honest I was. I even talked better. I used to read a lot of magazines and books. I could walk through these department stores and spot these young kids and temporary sales help and have them give me their money. *Give* me their money, I tell you.'

'How'd you work that scam?'

'I'd tell them Mister Freeman, the retail manager, sent me to pick up their receipts. He didn't want too much in the registers, I'd say, and I'd stick out my money bag and they'd fill it up for Mister Freeman.' Wimpy started to laugh and ended up wheezing and choking. He settled down after a minute.

'I sure owe plenty to Mister Freeman. I gotta repay that sucker if I ever meet him. I used that name in maybe fifty department stores. That was my real father's name. That's really *my* real name, but when I was a kid I took the name of this bastard my old lady married. I always played like my real old man would've did something for us if he'd been around, so this way he did. Old Mister Freeman must've gave me ten grand. Tax free. More than most old men ever give their kids, hey, Bumper?'

'More than mine, Wimpy,' I smiled.

'I did real good on that till-tap. I looked so nice, carnation and all. I had another scam where I'd boost good stuff, expensive baby clothes, luggage, anything. Then I'd bring it back to the salesman in the store bag and tell him I didn't have my receipt but would they please give me back my money on account of little Bobby wouldn't be needing these things because he smothered in his crib last Tuesday. Or old Uncle Pete passed on just before he went on his trip that he saved and dreamed about for forty-eight years and I couldn't bear to look at this luggage anymore. Honest, Bumper, they couldn't give me the bread fast enough. I even made *men* cry. I had one woman beg me to take ten bucks from her own purse to help with the baby's funeral. I took that ten bucks and bought a little ten-dollar bag of junk and all the time I was cutting open that balloon and cooking that stuff I thought, "Oh you baby. You really are my baby." I took that spike and dug a little grave in my flesh and when I shoved that thing in my arm and felt it going in, I said, "Thank you, lady, thank you, thank you, this is the best funeral my baby could have."' Wimpy closed his eyes and lifted his face, smiling a little as he thought of his baby.

'Doesn't your P.O. ever give you a urinalysis or anything?' I still couldn't get over an old head like him not having his arms or urine checked when he was on parole, even if he *was* paroled on a non-narcotics beef.

'Hasn't yet, Bumper. I ain't worried if he does. I always been lucky with P.O.'s. When they put me on the urine programme I came up with the squeeze-bottle trick. I just got this square friend of mine, old Homer Allen, to keep me supplied with a fresh bottle of piss, and I kept that little plastic squeeze bottle full and hanging from a string inside my belt. My dumb little P.O. used to think he was sneaky and he'd catch me at my job or at home at night sometimes and ask for a urine sample and I'd just go to the john with him right behind me watching, and I'd reach in my fly and fill his little glass bottle full of Homer's piss. He thought he was real slick, but he never could catch me. He was such a square. I really liked him. I felt like a father to that kid.'

The girl came to the phone and read me Wimpy's record, telling me there were no wants.

'Well, you're not running,' I said, hanging up the phone, closing the metal call box door, and hanging the brass key back on my belt.

'Told you, Bumper. I just saw my P.O. last week. I been reporting regular.'

'Okay, Wimpy, let's talk business,' I said.

'I been thinking, Bumper, there's this dog motherfucker that did me bad one time. I wouldn't mind you popping him.'

'Okay,' I said, giving him a chance to rationalize his snitching, which all informants have to do when they start out, or like Wimpy, when they haven't snitched for a long time.

'He deserves to march,' said Wimpy. 'Everybody knows he's no good. He burned me on a buy one time. I bring him a guy to score some pot. It's not on consignment or nothing, and he sells the guy catnip and I told him I knew the guy good. The guy kicked my ass when he found out it was catnip.'

'Okay, let's do him,' I said. 'But I ain't interested in some two- or three-lid punk.'

'I know, Bumper. He's a pretty big dealer. We'll set him up good. I'll tell him I got a guy with real bread and he should bring three kilos and meet me in a certain place and then maybe you just happen by or something when we're getting it out of the car and we both start to run but you go after him, naturally, and you get a three-key bust.'

'No good. I can't run any more. We'll work out something else.'

'Any way you want, Bumper. I'll turn anybody for you. I'll roll over on anybody if you give me a break.'

'Except your best connection.'

'That's God you're talking about. But I think right this minute I'd even turn my connection for a fix.'

'Where's this pot dealer live? Near my beat?'

'Yeah, not far. East Sixth. We can take him at his hotel. That might be the best way. You can kick down the pad and let me get out the window. At heart he's just a punk. They call him Little Rudy. He makes roach holders out of chicken bones and folded-up matchbooks and all that punk-ass bullshit. Only thing is, don't let me get a jacket. See, he knows this boss dyke, a real mean bull dagger. Her pad's a shooting gallery for some of us. If she knows you finked, she'll sneak battery acid in your spoon and laugh while you mainline it home. She's a *dog* motherfucker.'

'Okay, Wimpy, when can you set it up?'

'Saturday, Bumper, we can do it Saturday.'

'No good,' I said quickly, a gas pain slicing across my stomach. 'Friday's the latest for anything.'

'Christ, Bumper. He's out of town. I know for sure. I think he's gone to the border to score.'

'I can't wait past Friday. Think of somebody else then.'

'Shit, lemme think,' he said, rapping his skinny fingers against his temple. 'Oh yeah, I got something. A guy in the Rainbow Hotel. A tall dude, maybe forty, forty-five, blondish hair. He's in the first apartment to the left on the second floor. I just heard last night he's a half-ass fence. Buys most anything you steal. Cheap, I hear. Pays less than a dime on the dollar. A righteous dog. He deserves to fall. I hear these dope fiends bring radios and stuff like that, usually in the early morning.'

'Okay, maybe I'll try him tomorrow,' I said, not really very interested.

'Sure, he might have lots of loot in the pad. You could clear up all kinds of burglaries.'

'Okay, Wimpy, you can make it now. But I want to see you regular. At least three times a week.'

'Bumper, could you please loan me a little in advance?'

'You gotta be kidding, Wimpy! Pay a junkie in advance?'

'I'm in awful bad shape today, Bumper,' he said with a cracked whispery voice, like a prayer. He looked as bad as any I'd ever seen. Then I remembered I'd never see him again. After Friday I'd never see any of them again. He couldn't do me any good and it was unbelievably stupid, but I gave him a ten, which was just like folding up a sawbuck and sticking it in his arm. He'd be in the same shape twelve hours from now. He stared at the bill like he didn't believe it at first. I left him there and walked back to the car.

'We'll get that pothead for you,' he said. 'He's sloppy. You'll find seeds between the carpet and the moulding outside the door in the hall. I'll get you lots of probable cause to kick over the pad.'

'I know how to take down a dope pad, Wimpy,' I said over my shoulder.

'Later, Bumper, see you later,' he yelled, breaking into a coughing spasm.

THREE

I always try to learn something from the people on my beat, and as I drove away I tried to think if I learned anything from all Wimpy's chatter. I'd heard this kind of bullshit from a thousand hypes. Then I thought of the haemorrhoid ointment for shrinking hype marks. That was something new. I'd never heard that one before. I always try to teach the rookies to keep their mouths shut and learn to listen. They usually give more information than they get when they're interrogating somebody. Even a guy like Wimpy could teach you something if you just give him a chance.

I got back in my car and looked at my watch because I was starting to get hungry. Of course I'm always hungry, or rather, I always want to eat. But I don't eat between meals and I eat my meals at regular times unless the job prevents it. I believe in routine. If you have rules for little things, rules you make up yourself, and if you obey these rules, your life will be in order. I only alter routines when I have to.

One of the cats on the daywatch, a youngster named Wilson, drove by in his black-and-white but didn't notice me because he was eyeballing some hype that was hot-footing it across Broadway to reach the crowded Grand Central Market, probably to score. The doper was moving fast like a hype with some gold in his jeans. Wilson was a good young copper, but sometimes when I looked at him like this, in profile when he was looking somewhere else, that cowlick of his and that kid nose, and something else I couldn't put my finger on, made me think of someone. For a while it bothered me and then one night last week when I was thinking so hard about getting married, and about Cassie, it came to me – he reminded me of Billy a little bit, but I pushed it out of my mind because I don't think of dead children or any dead people, that's another rule of mine. But I *did* start thinking of Billy's mother and how bad my first marriage had been and whether it could have been good if Billy had lived, and I had to admit that it *could* have been good, and it would have lasted if Billy had lived.

Then I wondered how many bad marriages that started during the war years had turned out all right. But it wasn't just that, there was the other thing, the dying. I almost told Cruz Segovia about it one time when we used to be partners and we were working a lonely morning watch at three a.m., about how my parents died, and how my brother raised me and how he died, and how my son died, and how I admired Cruz because he had his wife and all those kids and gave himself away to them fearlessly. But I never told him, and when Esteban, his oldest son, died in Vietnam, I watched Cruz with the others, and after the crushing grief he still gave himself away to them, completely. But I couldn't admire him for it anymore. I could marvel at it, but I couldn't admire it. I don't know what I felt about it after that.

Thinking all these foolish things made a gas bubble start, and I could imagine the bubble getting bigger and bigger. Then I took a bubble buster, chewed it up and swallowed it, made up my mind to start thinking about women or food or something good, raised up, farted, said 'Good morning, Your Honour,' and felt a whole lot better.

FOUR

It always made me feel good just to drive around *without* thinking, so I turned off my radio and did just that. Pretty soon, without looking at my watch, I knew it was time to eat. I couldn't decide whether to hit Chinatown or Little Tokyo today. I didn't want Mexican food, because I promised Cruz Segovia I'd come to his pad for dinner tonight and I'd get enough Mexican food to last me a week. His wife Socorro knew how I loved *chile relleno* and she'd fix a dozen just for me.

A few burgers sounded good and there's a place in Hollywood that has the greatest burgers in town. Every time I go to Hollywood I think about Myrna, a broad I used to fool around with a couple years ago. She was an unreal Hollywood type, but she had a good executive job in a network television studio and whenever we went anywhere she'd end up spending more bread than I would. She loved to waste money, but the thing she really had going as far as I was concerned is that she looked just like Madeleine Carroll whose pictures we had all over our barracks during the war. It wasn't just that Myrna had style and elegant, springy tits, it's that she really looked like a woman and acted like one, except that she was a stone pothead and liked to improvise *too* much sexually. I'm game for anything reasonable, but sometimes Myrna was a little too freaky about things, and she also insisted on turning me on, and finally I tried smoking pot one time with her, but I didn't feel good high like on fine Scotch. On her coffee table she had at least half a key and that's a pound of pot and that's trouble. I could just picture me and her getting hauled off to jail in a nark ark. So it was a bummer, and I don't know if it's the overall depressant effect of pot or what, but I crashed afterwards, down, down, down, until I felt mean enough to kick the hell out of her. But then, come to think of it, I guess Myrna liked that best of all anyway. So, Madeleine Carroll or not, I finally shined her on and she gave up calling me after a couple weeks, probably having found herself a trained gorilla or something.

There was one thing about Myrna that I'd never forget – she was a great dancer, not a good dancer, a *great* dancer, because Myrna could completely stop thinking when she danced. I think that's the secret. She could dig hard rock and she was a real snake. When she moved on a dance floor, often as not, everyone would stop and watch. Of course they laughed at me – at first. Then they'd see there were *two* dancers out there. It's funny about dancing, it's like food or sex, it's something you do and you can just forget you *have* a brain. It's all body and deep in your guts, especially the hard rock. And hard rock's the best thing to happen to music. When Myrna and me were really moving, maybe at some kid place on the Sunset Strip, our bodies joined. It wasn't just a sex thing, but there *was* that too, it was like our bodies really made it together and you didn't even have to *think* anymore.

I used to always experiment by doing the funky chicken when we first started out. I know it's getting old now, but I'd do it and they'd all laugh, because of the way my belly jumped and swayed around. Then I'd always do it again right near the end of the song, and nobody laughed. They smiled, but nobody laughed, because they could see by then how graceful I really am, despite the way I'm built. Nobody's chicken was as funky as mine, so I always stood there flapping my elbows and bowing my knees just to test them. And despite the raw animal moves of Myrna, people also looked at *me*. They watched both of us dance. That's one thing I miss about Myrna.

I didn't feel like roaming so far from my beat today so I decided on beef teriyaki and headed for J-town. The Japanese have the commercial area around First and Second Streets between Los Angeles Street and Central Avenue. There are lots of colourful shops and restaurants and professional buildings. They also have their share of banks and lots of money to go in them. When I walked in the Geisha Doll on First Street, the lunch hour rush was just about over and the mama-san shuffled over with her little graceful steps like she was still twenty instead of sixty-five. She always wore a silk slit-skirted dress and she really didn't look too bad for an old girl. I always kidded her about a Japanese wearing a Chinese dress and she would laugh and say, 'Make moah China ting in Tokyo than all China. And bettah, goddam betcha.' The place was plush and dark, lots of bamboo, beaded curtains, hanging lanterns.

'Boom-pah san, wheah you been hide?' she said as I stepped through the beads.

'Hello, Mother,' I said, lifting her straight under the arms and kissing her on the cheek. She only weighed about ninety pounds and seemed almost brittle, but once I didn't do this little trick and she got mad. She expected it and all the customers got a kick out of watching me perform. The cooks and all the pretty waitresses and Sumi, the hostess, dressed in a flaming orange kimono, expected it too. I saw Sumi tap a Japanese customer on the shoulder when I walked in.

I usually held the mama-san up like this for a good minute or so and snuggled her a little bit and joked around until everyone in the place was giggling, especially the mama-san, and then I put her down and let her tell anyone in shouting distance how 'stlong is owah Boom-pah'. My arms are good even though my legs are gone, but she was like a paper doll, no weight at all. She always said '*owah* Boom-pah', and I always took it to mean I belonged to J-town too and I liked the idea. Los Angeles policemen are very partial to Buddha heads because sometimes they seem like the only ones left in the world who really appreciate discipline, cleanliness, and hard work. I've even seen motor cops who'd hang a ticket on a one-legged leper, let a Nip go on a good traffic violation because they contribute practically nothing to the crime rate even though they're notoriously bad drivers. I've been noticing in recent years though that Orientals have been showing up as suspects on crime reports. If they degenerate like everyone else there'll be no *group* to look up to, just individuals.

'We have a nice table for you, Bumper,' said Sumi with a smile that could almost make you forget food – almost. I started smelling things: tempura, rice wine, teriyaki steak. I have a sensitive nose and can pick out individual smells. It's really only *individual* things that count in this world. When you lump everything together you get goulash or chop suey or a greasy stew pot. I hated food like that.

'I think I'll sit at the *sushi* bar,' I said to Sumi, who once confessed to me her real name was Gloria. People expected a geisha doll to have a Japanese name, so Gloria, a third generation American, obliged them. I agreed with her logic. There's no sense disappointing people.

There were two other men at the *sushi* bar, both Japanese, and Mako who worked the *sushi* bar smiled at me but looked a little grim at the challenge. He once told Mama that serving Boom-pah alone was like serving a *sushi* bar full of *sumos*. I couldn't help it, I loved those delicate little rice balls, moulded by hand and wrapped in strips of pink salmon and octopus, abalone, tuna and shrimp. I loved the little hidden pockets of horseradish that surprised you and made your eyes water. And I loved a bowl of soup, especially soybean and seaweeed, and to drink it from the bowl Japanese style. I put it away faster than Mako could lay it out and I guess I looked like a buffalo at the *sushi* bar. Much as I tried to control myself and use a little Japanese self-discipline, I kept throwing the chow down and emptying the little dishes while Mako grinned and sweated and put them up. I knew it was no way to behave at the *sushi* bar in a nice restaurant, this was for gourmets, the refined eaters of Japanese cuisine, and I attacked like a blue locust, but God, eating *sushi* is being in heaven. In fact, I'd settle for that, and become a Buddhist if heaven was a *sushi* bar.

There was only one thing that saved me from looking too bad to a Japanese – I could handle chopsticks like one of them. I first learned in Japan right after the war, and I've been coming to the Geisha Doll and every other restaurant here in J-town for twenty years so it was no wonder. Even without the bluesuit, they could look at me click those sticks and know I was no tourist passing through. Sometimes though, when I didn't think about it, I ate with both hands. I just couldn't devour it fast enough.

In cooler weather I always drank rice wine or hot sake with my meal, today, ice water. After I'd finished what two or three good-sized Japanese would consume, I quit and started drinking tea while Mama and Sumi made several trips over to make sure I had enough and to see that my tea was hot enough and to try to feed me some tempura, and the tender fried shrimp looked so good I ate half a dozen. If Sumi wasn't twenty years too young I'd have been awful tempted to try her too. But she was so delicate and beautiful and so *young*, I lost confidence even thinking about it. And then too, she was one of the people on my beat, and there's that thing, the way they think about me. Still, it always helped my appetite to eat in a place where there were pretty women. But until I was at least half full, I have to say I didn't notice women or anything else. The world disappears for me when I'm eating something I love.

The thing that always got to me about Mama was how much she thanked me for eating up half her kitchen. Naturally she would never let me pay for my food, but she always thanked me about ten times before I got out the door. Even for an Oriental she really overdid it. It made me feel guilty, and when I came here I sometimes wished I could violate the custom and pay her. But she'd fed cops before I came along and she'd feed them after, and that was the way things were. I didn't tell Mama that Friday was going to be my last day, and I didn't start thinking about it because with a barrel of *sushi* in my stomach I couldn't afford indigestion.

Sumi came over to me before I left and held the little teacup to my lips while I sipped it and she said, 'Okay Bumper, tell me an exciting cops-and-robbers story.' She did this often, and I'm sure she was aware how she affected me up close there feeling her sweet breath, looking at those chocolate-brown eyes and soft skin.

'All right, my little lotus blossom,' I said, like W. C. Fields, and she giggled. 'One spine tingler, coming up.'

Then I reverted to my normal voice and told her about the guy I stopped for blowing a red light at Second and San Pedro one day and how he'd been here a year from Japan and had a California licence and all, but didn't speak English, or pretended not to so he could try to get out of the ticket. I decided to go ahead and hang one on him because he almost wiped out a guy in the crosswalk, and when I got it written he refused to sign it, telling me in pidgin, 'Not gear-tee, not gear-tee,' and I tried for five minutes to explain that the signature was just a promise to appear and he could have a jury trial if he wanted one and if he didn't sign I'd have to book him. He just kept shaking his head like he didn't savvy and finally I turned that ticket book over and drew a picture on the back. Then I drew the same picture for Sumi. It was a little jail window with a stick figure hanging on the bars. He had a sad turned-down mouth and slant eyes. I'd showed him the picture and said, 'You sign now, maybe?' and he wrote his name so fast and hard he broke my pencil lead.

Sumi laughed and repeated it in Japanese for Mama. When I left after tipping Mako they all thanked me again until I really *did* feel guilty. That was the only thing I didn't like about J-town. I wished to hell I could pay for my meal there, though I confess I never had that wish anywhere else.

Frankly, there was practically nothing to spend my money on. I ate three meals on my beat. I could buy booze, clothes, jewellery, and everything else you could think of at wholesale or less. In fact, somebody was always giving me something like that as a gift. I had my bread stop and a dairy that supplied me with gallons of free ice cream, milk, cottage cheese, all I wanted. My apartment was very nice and rent-free, even including utilities, because I helped the manager run the thirty-two units. At least he thought I helped him. He'd call me when he had a loud party or something, and I'd go up, join the party, and persuade them to quiet down a little while I drank their booze and ate their canapés. Once in a while I'd catch a peeping tom or something, and since the manager was such a mouse, he thought I was indispensable. Except for girlfriends and my informants it was always hard to find anything to spend my money on. Sometimes I actually went a week hardly spending a dime except for tips. I'm a big tipper, not like most policemen.

When it came to accepting things from people on my beat I did have one rule – no money. I felt that if I took money, which a lot of people tried to give me at Christmas time, I'd be getting bought. I never felt bought though if a guy gave me free meals or a case of booze, or a discounted sports coat, or if a dentist fixed my teeth at a special rate, or an optometrist bounced for a pair of sunglasses half price. These things weren't money, and I wasn't a hog about it. I never took more than I could personally use, or which I could give to people like Cruz Segovia or Cassie, who recently complained that her apartment was beginning to look like a distillery. Also I never took anything from someone I might end up having to arrest. For instance, before we started really hating each other, Marvin Heywood, the owner of the Pink Dragon, tried to lay a couple of cases of Scotch on me, and I mean the best, but I turned him down. I'd known from the first day he opened that place it would be a hangout for slime-balls. Every day was like a San Quentin convention in that cesspool. And the more I thought of it, the more I got burned up thinking that after I retired nobody would roust the Dragon as hard as I always did. I caused Marvin a sixty-day liquor licence suspension twice, and I probably cost him two thousand a month in lost business since some of the hoods were afraid to come there because of me.

I jumped in my car and decided to cruise by the Dragon for one last shot at it. When I parked out back, a hype in the doorway saw me and ran down the steps to tell everybody inside the heat was coming. I took my baton, wrapped the thong around my hand which they teach you not to do now, but which I've been doing for twenty years, and I walked down the concrete stairway to this cellar bar, and through the draped doorway. The front is framed by a pink dragon head. The front doorway is the mouth of the beast, the back door is under the tail. It always made me mad just to see the big dumb-looking dragon-mouth door. I went in the back door, up the dragon's ass, tapping my stick on the empty chairs and keeping my head on a swivel as I let my eyes get accustomed to the gloom. The pukepots were all sitting near the back. There were only about ten customers now in the early afternoon, and Marvin, all six feet six inches of him, was at the end of the bar grinning at a bad-looking bull dyke who was putting down a pretty well-built black stud in an arm wrestle.

Marvin was grinning, but he didn't mean it, he knew I was there. It curdled his blood to see me tapping on the furniture with my stick. That's why I did it. I always was as badge heavy and obnoxious as I could be when I was in there. I'd been in two brawls here and both times I knew Marvin was just wetting his shorts wishing he had the guts to jump in on me, but he thought better of it.

He weighed at least three hundred pounds and was damned tough. You had to be to own this joint, which catered to bookmakers, huggermugger whores, paddy hustlers, speed freaks, fruits and fruit hustlers, and ex-cons of both sexes and all ages. I'd never quite succeeded in provoking Marvin into attacking me, although it was common knowledge on the street that a shot fired at me one night from a passing car was some punk hired by Marvin. It was after that, even though nothing was ever proved, that I really began standing on the Dragon's tail. For a couple of months his business dropped to nothing with me living on his doorstep, and he sent two lawyers to my captain and the police commission to get me off his back. I relented as much as I had to, but I still gave him fits.

If I wasn't retiring there'd be hell to pay around here because once you get that twenty years service in, you don't have to pussyfoot around so much. I mean no matter what kind of trouble you get into, nobody can ever take your pension away for any reason, even if they fire you. So if I were staying, I'd go right on. Screw the lawyers, screw the police commission. I'd land on that Dragon with both boondockers. And as I thought that, I looked down at my size thirteen triple E's. They were beat officer shoes, high top, laces with eyelets, ankle supporting, clumsy, round toes, beat officer shoes. A few years ago they were actually popular with young black guys, and almost came into style again. They called them 'old man comforts' and they were soft and comfortable, but ugly as hell, I guess, to most people. I'd probably always wear them. I'd sunk my old man comforts in too many deserving asses to part with them now.

Finally Marvin got tired watching the arm wrestlers and pretending he didn't see me.

'Whadda you want, Morgan?' he said. Even in the darkness I could see him getting red in the face, his big chin jutting.

'Just wondering how many scumbags were here today, Marvin,' I said in a loud voice which caused four or five of them to look up. These days we're apt to get disciplinary action for making brutal remarks like that, even though these assholes would burst their guts laughing if I was courteous or even civil.

The bull dyke was the only righteous female in the place. In this dive you almost have to check everybody's plumbing to know whether it's interior or exterior. The two in dresses were drags, the others were fruit hustlers and flimflam guys. I recognized a sleazy bookmaker named Harold Wagner. One of the fruit hustlers was a youngster, maybe twenty-two or so. He was still young enough to be offended by my remark, especially since it was in front of the queen in the red mini who probably belonged to him. He mumbled something under his breath and Marvin told him to cool it since he didn't want to give me an excuse to make another bust in the place. The guy looked high on pot like most everyone these days.

'He your new playmate, Roxie?' I said to the red dress queen, whose real name I knew was John Jeffrey Alton.

'Yes,' said the queen in a falsetto voice, and motioned to the kid to shut his mouth. He was a couple inches taller than me and big chested, probably shacking with Roxie now and they split what they get hustling. Roxie hustles the guys who want a queen, and the kid goes after the ones who want a jocker. This jocker would probably become a queen himself. I always felt sorry for queens because they're so frantic, searching, looking. Sometimes I twist them for information, but otherwise I leave them alone.

I was in a rotten mood thinking nobody would roust the Dragon after I was gone. They were all glaring at me now, especially Marvin with his mean grey eyes and knife mouth.

One young guy, too young to know better, leaned back in his chair and made a couple of oinks and said, 'I smell pig.'

I'd never seen him before. He looked like a college boy slumming. Maybe in some rah-rah campus crowd beer joint I'd just hee-haw and let him slide, but here in the Pink Dragon the beat cops rule by force and fear. If they stopped being afraid of me I was through, and the street would be a jungle which it is anyway, but at least now you can walk through it watching for occasional cobras and rabid dogs. I figured if it weren't for guys like me, there'd be no trails through the frigging forest.

'Oink, oink,' he said again, with more confidence this time, since I hadn't responded. 'I sure do smell pig.'

'And what do pigs like best?' I smiled, slipping the stick back in my baton ring. 'Pigs like to clean up garbage, and I see a pile.' Still smiling I kicked the chair legs and he went down hard throwing a glass of beer on

Roxie who forgot the falsetto and yelled, 'Shithouse mouse!' in a pretty good baritone when the beer slid down his bra.

I had the guy in a wristlock before he knew what fell on him, and was on my way out the door, with him walking backwards, but not too fast in case someone else was ready.

'You bastard!' Marvin sputtered. 'You assaulted my customer. You bastard! I'm calling my lawyer.'

'Go right on, Marvin,' I said, while the tall kid screamed and tippy-toed to the door because the upward thrust of the wristlock was making him go as high as he could. The smell of pot was hanging on his clothes but the euphoria wasn't dulling the pain of the wristlock. When you've got one that's really loaded you can't crank it on too hard because they don't react to pain, and you might break a wrist trying to make them flinch. This guy felt it though, and he was docile, ow, ow, owing all the way out. Marvin came around the bar and followed us to the door.

'There's witnesses!' he boomed. 'This time there's witnesses to your dirty, filthy false arrest of my customer! What's the charge? What're you going to charge him with?'

'He's drunk, Marvin,' I smiled, holding the wristlock with one hand, just in case Marvin was mad enough. I was up, high up, all alive, ready to fly.

'It's a lie. He's sober. He's sober as you.'

'Why, Marvin,' I said, 'he's drunk in public view and unable to care for himself. I'm obliged to arrest him for his own protection. He *has* to be drunk to say what he did to me, don't you agree? And if you're not careful I might think you're trying to interfere with my arrest. You wouldn't like to try interfering with my arrest would you, Marvin?'

'We'll get you, Morgan,' Marvin whispered helplessly. 'We'll get your job one of these days.'

'If you slimeballs could have my job I wouldn't want it,' I said, let down because it was over.

The kid wasn't as loaded as I thought when I got him out of there into the sunshine and more or less fresh Los Angeles air.

'I'm not drunk,' he repeated all the way to the Glass House, shaking his mop of blond hair out of his face since I had his hands cuffed behind his back. The Glass House is what the street people call our main police building because of all the windows.

'You *talked* your way into jail, boy,' I said, lighting a cigar.

'You can't just put a sober man in jail for drunk because he calls you a pig,' said the kid, and by the way he talked and looked, I figured him for an upper-middle-class student hanging out downtown with the scumbags for a perverse kick, and also because he was at heart a scumbag himself.

'More guys talk themselves into jail than get there any other way,' I said.

'I demand an attorney,' he said.

'Call one soon as you're booked.'

'I'll bring those people to court. They'll testify I was sober. I'll sue you for false arrest.'

'You wouldn't be getting a cherry, kid. Guys tried to sue me a dozen times. And you wouldn't get those assholes in the Dragon to give you the time of day if they had a crate full of alarm clocks.'

'How can you book me for *drunk*? Are you prepared to swear before God that I was drunk?'

'There's no God down here on the beat, and anyway He'd never show his face in the Pink Dragon. The United States Supreme Court decisions don't work too well down here either. So you see, kid, I been forced to write my own laws, and you violated one in there. I just have to find you guilty of contempt of cop.'

FIVE

After I got the guy booked I didn't know what the hell to do. I had this empty feeling now that was making me depressed. I thought about the hotel burglar again, but I felt lazy. It was this empty feeling. I was in a black mood as I swung over towards Figueroa. I saw a mailbox handbook named Zoot Lafferty standing there near a public phone. He used to hang around Main and then Broadway and now Figueroa. If we could ever get him another block closer to the Harbour Freeway maybe we could push the bastard off the overpass sometime, I thought, in the mood for murder.

Lafferty always worked the businessmen in the area, taking the action and recording the bets inside a self-addressed stamped envelope. And he always hung around a mailbox and a public phone booth. If he saw someone that he figured was a vice cop, he'd run to the mailbox and deposit the letter. That way there'd be no evidence like betting markers or owe sheets the police could recover. He'd have the customers' bets the next day when the mail came, and in time for collection and payment. Like all handbooks though, he was scared of plain-clothes vice-cops but completely ignored uniformed policemen.

So one day when I was riding by, I slammed on the binders, jumped out of the black-and-white, and fell on Zoot's skinny ass before he could get to the mailbox. I caught him with the markers and they filed a felony bookmaking charge. I convicted him in Superior Court after I convinced the judge that I had a confidential reliable informant tell me all about Zoot's operation, which was true, and that I hid behind a bush just behind the phone booth and overheard the bets being taken over the phone, which was a lie. But I convinced the judge and that's all that matters. He had to pay a two-hundred-and-fifty-dollar fine and was given a year's probation, and that same day, he moved over here to Figueroa away from my beat where there are no bushes anywhere near his phone booth.

As I drove by Zoot, he waved at me and grinned and stood by the mailbox. I wondered if we could've got some help with the Post Office special agents to stop this flimflam, but it would've been awful hard and not worth the effort. You can't tamper with someone's mail very easy. Now, as I looked at his miserable face for the last time, my black mood got blacker and I thought, I'll bet no other uniformed cop ever takes the trouble to shag him after I'm gone.

Then I started thinking about bookmaking in general, and got even madder, because it was the kind of crime I couldn't do anything about. I saw the profits reaped from it all around me, and I saw the people involved in it, and knew some of them, and yet I couldn't do anything because they were so well organized and their weapons were so good and mine were so flimsy. The money was so unbelievably good that they could expand into semi-legitimate businesses and drive out competition because they had the racket money to fall back on, and the legitimate businesses couldn't compete. And also they were tougher and ruthless and knew other ways to discourage competition. I always wanted to get one of them good, someone like Red Scalotta, a big book, whose fortune they say can't be guessed at. I thought all these things and how mad I get every time I see a goddamn lovable Damon-Runyon-type bookmaker in a movie. I started thinking then about Angie Caputo, and got a dark kind of pleasure just picturing him and remembering how another old beat man, Sam Giraldi, had humbled him. Angie had never realized his potential as a hood after what Sam did to him.

Sam Giraldi is dead now. He died last year just fourteen months after he retired at twenty years' service. He was only forty-four when he had a fatal heart attack, which is particularly a policeman's disease. In a job like this, sitting on your ass for long periods of time and then moving in bursts of heart-cracking action, you can expect heart attacks. Especially since lots of us get so damned fat when we get older.

When he ruined Angie Caputo, Sam was thirty-seven years old but looked forty-seven in the face. He wasn't very tall, but had tremendous shoulders, a meaty face, and hands bigger than mine, all covered with heavy veins. He was a good handball player and his body was hard as a spring-loaded sap. He'd been a vice officer for years and then went back to uniform. Sam walked Alvarado when I walked downtown, and sometimes he'd drive over to my beat or I'd come over to him. We'd eat dinner together and talk shop or talk about baseball, which I like and which he was fanatic about. Sometimes, if we ate at his favourite delicatessen on Alvarado, I'd walk with him for a while and once or twice we even made a pretty good pinch together like that. It was on a wonderful summer night when a breeze was blowing off the water in MacArthur Park that I met Angie Caputo.

It seemed to be a sudden thing with Sam. It struck like a bullet, the look on his face, and he said, 'See that guy? That's Angie Caputo, the pimp and bookmaker's agent.' And I said, 'So what?' wondering what the hell was going on, because Sam looked like he was about to shoot the guy who was just coming out of a bar and getting ready to catch the eight o'clock show at the burlesque house out there on his beat.

'He hangs out further west, near Eighth Street,' said Sam. 'That's where

took back offices where I seized records that could prove, *prove* the guy was a millionaire book. And I convicted them and saw them get pitiful fines time after time and I *never* saw a bookmaker go to state prison even though it's a felony. Let somebody else work bookmaking I finally decided, and I came back to uniform. But Angie's different. I know him. All my life I knew him, and I live right up Serrano there, in the apartments. That's *my* neighbourhood. I use that cleaners where the old man works. Sure he was my snitch but I liked him. I never paid him. He just told me things. He got a kid's a schoolteacher, the old man does. The books'll be scared now for a little while after what I done. They'll respect us for a little while.'

I had to agree with everything Sam said, but I'd never seen a guy worked over that bad before, not by a cop anyway. It bothered me. I worried about us, Sam and me, about what would happen if Caputo complained to the Department, but Sam was right. Caputo kept his mouth shut and I admit I was never sorry for what Sam did. When it was over I felt something and couldn't put my finger on it at first, and then one night laying in bed I figured it out. It was a feeling of something being *right*. For one of the few times on this job I saw an untouchable touched. I felt my thirst being slaked a little bit, and I was never sorry for what Sam did.

But Sam was dead now and I was retiring, and I was sure there weren't many other bluesuits in the division who could nail a bookmaker. I turned my car around and headed back towards Zoot Lafferty, still standing there in his pea green slack suit. I parked the black-and-white at the kerb, got out, and very slow, with my sweaty uniform shirt sticking to my back, I walked over to Zoot who opened the package door on the red and blue mailbox and stuck his arm inside. I stopped fifteen feet away and stared at him.

'Hello, Morgan,' he said, with a crooked phony grin that told me he wished he'd have slunk off long before now. He was a pale, nervous guy, about forty-five years old, with a bald freckled skull.

'Hello, Zoot,' I said, putting my baton back inside the ring, and measuring the distance between us.

'You got the rocks off once by busting me, Morgan. Why don't you go back over to your beat, and get outta my face? I moved clear over here to Figueroa to get away from you and your fucking beat, what more do you want?'

'How much action you got written down, Zoot?' I said, walking closer. 'It'll inconvenience the shit out of you to let it go in the box, won't it?'

'Goddamnit, Morgan,' said Zoot, blinking his eyes nervously, and scratching his scalp which looked loose and rubbery. 'Why don't you quit rousting people. You're an old man, you know that? Why don't you just fuck off outta here and start acting like one.'

When the slimeball said that, the blackness I felt turned blood red, and I sprinted those ten feet as he let the letter slide down inside the box. But he didn't get his hand out. I slammed the door hard and put my weight against it and the metal door bit into his wrist and he screamed.

'Zoot, it's time for you and me to have a talk.' I had my hand on the mailbox package door, all my weight leaning hard, as he jerked for a second and then froze in pain, bug-eyed.

'Please, Morgan,' he whispered, and I looked around, seeing there was a lot of car traffic but not many pedestrians.

'Zoot, before I retire I'd like to take a real good book, just one time. Not a sleazy little handbook like you but a real bookmaker, how about helping me?'

Tears began running down Zoot's cheeks and he showed his little yellow teeth and turned his face to the sun as he pulled another time on the arm. I pushed harder and he yelped loud, but there were noisy cars driving by.

'For God's sake, Morgan,' he begged. 'I don't know anything. Please let my arm out.'

'I'll tell you what, Zoot. I'll settle for your phone spot. Who do you phone your action in to?'

'They phone *me*,' he gasped, as I took a little weight off the door.

'You're a liar,' I said, leaning again.

'Okay, okay, I'll give you the number,' he said, and now he was blubbering outright and I got disgusted and then mad at him and at me and especially at the bookmaker I'd never have a chance to get, because he was too well protected and my weapons were puny.

'I'll break your goddamn arm if you lie,' I said, with my face right up to his. A young, pretty woman walked by just then, looked at Zoot's sweaty face and then at mine, and damned near ran across the street to get away from us.

'It's six-six-eight-two-seven-three-three,' he sobbed.

'Repeat it.'

'Six-six-eight-two-seven-three-three.'

'One more time, and it better come out the same.'

'Six-six-eight-two-seven-three-three. Oh, Christ!'

'How do you say it when you phone in the action?'

'Dandelion. I just say the word Dandelion and then I give the bets. I swear, Morgan.'

'Wonder what Red Scalotta would say if he knew you gave me that information?' I smiled, and then I let him go when I saw by his eyes that I'd guessed right and he was involved with that particular bookmaker.

He pulled his arm out and sat down on the kerb, holding it like it was broken and cursing under his breath as he wiped the tears away.

'How about talking with a vice cop about this?' I said, lighting a fresh cigar while he began rubbing his arm which was probably going numb.

'You're a psycho, Morgan!' he said, looking up. 'You're a real psycho if you think I'd fink on anybody.'

'Look, Zoot, you talk to a vice cop like I say, and we'll protect you. You won't get a jacket. But if you don't, I'll personally see that Scalotta gets the word that you gave me the phone number and the code so we could stiff in a bet on the phone clerk. I'll let it be known that you're a paid snitch and when he finds out what you told me you know what? I bet he'll believe it. You ever see what some gunsel like Bernie Zolitch can do to a fink?'

'You're the most rottenest bastard I ever seen,' said Zoot, standing up, very shaky, and white as paste.

'Look at it this way, Zoot, you co-operate just this once, we'll take one little pukepot sitting in some phone spot and that'll be all there is to it. We'll make sure we come up with a phony story about how we got the information like we always do to protect an informant, and nobody'll be the wiser. You can go back to your slimy little business and I give you my word I'll never roust you again. Not personally, that is. And you probably know I always keep my word. Course I can't guarantee you some *other* cop won't shag you sometime.'

He hesitated for a second and then said, 'I'll settle for *you* not rousting me no more, Morgan. Those vice cops I can live with.'

'Let's take a ride. How's your arm feeling?'

'Fuck you, Morgan,' he said, and I chuckled to myself and felt a little better about everything. We drove to Central Vice and I found the guy I wanted sitting in the office.

'Why aren't you out taking down some handbook, Charlie?' I said to the young vice cop who was leaning dangerously back in a swivel chair with his crepe-soled sneak shoes up on a desk doping the horses on a scratch sheet.

'Hi, Bumper,' he grinned, and then recognized Zoot who he himself probably busted a time or two.

'Mr. Lafferty decide to give himself up?' said Charlie Bronski, a husky, square-faced guy with about five years on the department. I broke him in when he was just out of the academy. I remembered him as a smart aggressive kid, but with humility. Just the kind I liked. You could teach that kind a little something. I wasn't ashamed to say he was Bumper-ized.

Charlie got up and put on a green striped, short-sleeved ivy-league shirt over the shoulder holster which he wore over a white T-shirt.

'Old Zoot here just decided to repent his evil ways, Charlie,' I said, glancing at Zoot who looked as sad as anyone I'd ever seen.

'Let's get it over with, Morgan, for chrissake,' said Zoot. 'And you got to swear you'll keep it confidential.'

'Swear, Charlie,' I said.

'I swear,' said Charlie. 'What's this all about?'

'Zoot wants to trade a phone spot to us.'

'For what?' asked Charlie.

'For nothing,' said Zoot, very impatient. 'Just because I'm a good fuck-ing citizen. Now you want the information or not?'

'Okay,' Charlie said, and I could tell he was trying to guess how I squeezed Zoot. Having worked with me for a few months, Charlie was familiar with my M.O. I'd always tried to teach him and other young cops that you can't be a varsity letterman when you deal with these barfbags. Or rather, you *could* be, and you'd probably be the one who became a captain, or Chief of Police or something, but you can bet there'd always have to be the guys like me out on the street to make you look good up there in that ivory tower by keeping the assholes from taking over the city.

'You wanna give us the relay, is that it?' said Charlie, and Zoot nodded, looking a little bit sick.

'*Is* it a relay spot? Are you sure?' asked Charlie.

'I'm not sure of a goddam thing,' Zoot blubbered, rubbing his arm again. 'I only came 'cause I can't take this kind of heat. I can't take being rousted and hurt.'

Charlie looked at me, and I thought that if this lifelong handbook, this ex-con and slimeball started crying, I'd flip. I was filled with loathing for a pukepot like Zoot, not because he snitched, hell, everybody snitches when the twist is good enough. It was this crybaby snivelling stuff that I couldn't take.

'Damn, Zoot!' I finally exploded. 'You been a friggin' scammer all your life, fracturing every friggin' law you had nuts enough to crack, and you sit here now acting like a pious nun. If you wanna play your own tune you better damn well learn to dance to it, and right now you're gonna do the friggin' boogaloo, you goddamn haemorrhoid!'

I took a step towards Zoot's chair and he snapped up straight in his seat saying, 'Okay, Morgan, okay. Whadda you want? For God's sake I'll tell you what you wanna know! You don't have to get tough!'

'Is the number you phone a relay?' repeated Charlie calmly.

'I think so,' Zoot nodded. 'Sounds like some goofy broad don't know nothing about the business. I been calling this same broad for six months now. She's probably just some stupid fucking housewife, sitting on a hot seat and taking them bets for somebody she don't even know.'

'Usually record them on Formica,' Charlie explained to me, 'then some-body phones her several times a day and takes the action she wrote down. She can wipe the Formica in case the vice cops come busting down her door. She probably won't even know who pays her or where the phone calls come from.'

'Fuck no, she ain't gonna know,' said Zoot, looking at me. 'This shit's too big, Morgan. It's too goddamn big. You ain't gonna bother nobody by rousting me. You don't understand, Morgan. People *want* us in business. What's a guy get for bookmaking? Even a big guy? A fucking fine. Who does time? You ever see a book get joint time?' said Zoot to Charlie, who shook his head. 'Fuck no, you ain't and you ain't going to. Everybody bets with bookies for chrissake and those that don't, they like some other kind of vice. Give up, Morgan. You been a cop all these years and you don't know enough to give up fighting it. You can't save this rotten world.'

'I ain't trying to, Zoot,' I said. 'I just love the friggin' battle!'

I went down the hall to the coffee room, figuring that Charlie should be alone with Zoot. Now that I had played the bad guy, he could play the good guy. An interrogation never works if it's not private, and Charlie was a good bullshitter. I had hopes he could get more out of Zoot because I had him loosened up. Anytime you get someone making speeches at you, you have a chance. If he's shaky about one thing, he might be about something else. I didn't think you could buy Zoot with money, he was too scared of everything. But being scared of us as well as the mob, he could be gotten to. Charlie could handle him.

Cruz Segovia was in the coffee room working on his log. I came in behind him. There was no one else in the room and Cruz was bent over the table writing in his log. He was so slim that even in his uniform he looked like a little boy bent over doing his homework. His face was still almost the same as when we were in the academy and except for his grey hair he hadn't changed much. He was barely five feet eight and sitting there he looked really small.

'*Qué pasó, compadre*,' I said, because he always said he wished I was Catholic and could have been the godfather for his last seven kids. His kids considered me their godfather anyway, and he called me *compadre*.

'*Órale, panzón*,' he said, like a pachuco, which he put on for me. He spoke beautiful Spanish and could also read and write Spanish, which is rare for a Mexican. He was good with English too, but the barrios of El Paso Texas died hard, and Cruz had an accent when he spoke English.

'Where you been hiding out all day?' I said, putting a dime in the machine and getting Cruz a fresh cup, no cream and double sugar.

'You bastard,' he said. 'Where've *I* been hiding. Communication's been trying to get *you* all day! Don't you know that funny little box in your car is called a radio and you're supposed to listen for your calls and you're even supposed to handle them once in a while?'

'*Chale, chale*. Quit being a sergeant,' I said. 'Gimme some slack. I been bouncing in and out of that black-and-white machine so much I haven't heard anything.'

'You'll be a beat cop all your life,' he said, shaking his head. 'You have no use at all for your radio, and if you didn't have your best friend for a sergeant, your big ass'd be fired.'

'Yeah, but I got him,' I grinned, poking him in the shoulder and making him swear.

'Seriously, Bumper,' he said, and he didn't have to say 'seriously' because his large black eyes always turned down when he was serious. 'Seriously, the skipper asked me to ask you to pay a little more attention to the radio. He heard some of the younger officers complaining about always handling the calls in your district because you're off the radio walking around so much.'

'Goddamn slick-sleeved rookies,' I said, hot as hell, 'they wouldn't know a snake in the grass if one jumped up and bit them on the dick. You seen these goddamn rookies nowadays, riding down the friggin' streets, ogling all the cunt, afraid to put on their hats because it might ruin their hair styles. Shit, I actually saw one of these pretty young fuzz sitting in his black-and-white spraying his hair! I swear, Cruz, most of these young cats wouldn't know their ass from a burnt biscuit.'

'I know, Bumper,' Cruz nodded with sympathy. 'And the skipper knows a whole squad of these youngsters couldn't do half the police work you old-timers do. That's why nobody says anything to you. But *hombre*, you have to handle some calls once in a while instead of walking that beat.'

'I know,' I said, looking at my coffee.

'Just stay on the air a little more.'

'Okay, okay, you're the *macho*. You got the *huevos de oro*.'

Cruz smiled now that he was through stepping on my meat. He was the only one that ever nagged me or told me what to do. When someone else had ideas along those lines, they'd hit Cruz with them, and if he thought I needed talking to, he'd do it. They figured I'd listen to Cruz.

'Don't forget, *loco*, you're coming to dinner tonight.'

'Can you see me forgetting dinner at your pad?'

'You sure Cassie can't come with you?'

'She sure wishes she could. You know Friday's the last day for her at school and they're throwing a little party for her. She *has* to be there.'

'I understand,' said Cruz. 'What day is she actually going up north? She decided yet?'

'Next week she'll be packed and gone.'

'I don't know why you don't just take your vacation now and cut out with her. What's the sense of waiting till the end of the month? That vacation pay isn't worth being away from her for a few weeks, is it? She might come to her senses and ask herself why the hell she's marrying a mean old bastard like Bumper Morgan.'

I wondered why I didn't tell Cruz that I'd decided to do just that. What the hell was the secret? Friday was going to be my last day. I never cared anything about the vacation pay. Was I really afraid to say it?

'Gonna be strange leaving everything,' I muttered to my coffee cup.

'I'm glad for you, Bumper,' said Cruz, running his slim fingers through his heavy grey hair. 'If I didn't have all the kids I'd get the hell out too, I swear. I'm glad you're going.'

Cruz and me had talked about it lots of times the last few years, ever since Cassie came along and it became inevitable that I'd marry her and probably pull the pin at twenty years instead of staying thirty like Cruz had to do. Now that it was here though, it seemed like we'd never discussed it at all. It was so damn strange.

'Cruz, I'm leaving Friday,' I blurted. 'I'm going to see Cassie and tell her I'll leave Friday. Why wait till the end of the month?'

'That's fine, *'mano!'* Cruz beamed, looking like he'd like to cut loose with a yelp, like he always did when he was drunk.

'I'll tell her today.' Now I felt relieved, and drained the last of the coffee as I got up to leave. 'And I don't give a damn if I loaf for a month. I'll just take it easy till I feel like starting my new job.'

'That's right!' said Cruz, his eyes happy now. 'Sit on that big fat *nalgas* for a year if you want to. They want you as security chief. They'll wait for you. And you have forty per cent coming every month, and Cassie's got a good job, and you still have a good bank account, don't you?'

'Hell, yes,' I answered, walking towards the door. 'I never had to spend much money, with my beat and all.'

'Shhh,' Cruz grinned. 'Haven't you heard? We're the new breed of professionals. We don't accept gratuities.'

'Who said anything about gratuities? I only take tribute.'

Cruz shook his head and said, '*Ahí te huacho,*' which is anglicized slang meaning I'll be seeing, or rather, watching for you.

'*Ahí te huacho,*' I answered.

After I left Cruz I went back to the vice squad office and found Zoot hanging his head, and Charlie downright happy, so I figured Charlie had done all right.

'I'd like to talk to you alone for a minute, Bumper,' said Charlie, leading me into the next room and closing the door while Zoot sat there looking miserable.

'He told me lots more than he thinks he did,' said Charlie. He was charged up like any good cop should be when he has something worthwhile.

'He thinks you're taking me off his back?' I asked.

'Yeah,' Charlie smiled. 'Play along. He thinks I'm going to save him from you. Just lay off him for a while, okay, Bumper? He told me he's planning on moving his territory out of the division to Alvorado in a couple of weeks but he has to stay around Figueroa for the time being. I told him I'd talk to you.'

'Tell Zoot he doesn't have to worry about old Bumper anymore,' I said, getting another gas pain. I vowed to myself I'd lay off the soy sauce next time I ate in J-town.

'Yeah, he'll be a problem for the Rampart vice squad then,' said Charlie, not getting my meaning.

'Want me to take him back to Fig?'

'I'll take him,' said Charlie. 'I want to talk a little more.'

'Do me a favour?'

'Sure, Bumper.'

'You think there's any chance of something going down because of what Zoot told you?'

'There's a damn good chance. Zoot half-ass copped that he thinks the broad at the relay spot that takes his action is Reba McClain, and if it is we might be able to swing real good with her.'

'How's that?'

'She's Red Scalotta's girlfriend. We took her down in another relay about six months ago and she got probation with a six months' jail sentence hanging. She's a meth head and an ex-con and stir crazy as hell. Kind of a sex thing. She's got a phobia about jails and bull dykes and all that. Real ding-a-ling, but a gorgeous little toadie. We were just talking last week about her and if we could shag her and catch her dirty we might get to Scalotta through her. She's a real shaky bitch. I think she'd turn her mama to stay on the street. You bringing in Zoot with that phone number was a godsend.'

'Okay, then I'm really going to ask the favour.'

'Sure.'

'Take her today or tomorrow at the latest. If she gives you something good, like a back office, take it down on Friday.'

'A back office! Jesus, I don't think she'll have that kind of information, Bumper. And hell, Friday is just two days away. Sometimes you stake out for weeks or months to take a back office. Jesus, that's where the book's records are kept. We'd have to get a search warrant and that takes lots of information beforehand. Why Friday?'

'I'm going on vacation. I want to be in on this one, Charlie. I never took a back office. I want it real bad, and it has to be before I go on vacation.'

'I'd do it for you, Bumper, if I could, you know that, but Friday's only two days away!'

'Just do police work like I taught you, with balls and brains and some imagination. That's all I ask. Just try, okay?'

'Okay,' Charlie said. 'I'll give it a try.'

Before I left I put on an act for Zoot so he'd think Charlie was his protector. I pretended I was mad at Charlie and Charlie pretended he was going to stop me from any future attempts to stuff Zoot down the goddamn mail chute.

SIX

After I got in my car I remembered the friendly ass bite Cruz gave me and I picked up the hand mike and said, 'One-X-L-Forty-five, clear.'

'One-X-L-Forty-five, handle this call,' said the operator, and I grumbled and wrote the address down. 'Meet One-L-Thirty, Ninth and Broadway.'

'One-X-L-Forty-five, roger,' I said disgustedly, and thought, that's what I get for clearing. Probably some huge crisis like taking a chickenshit theft report from some fatass stockbroker who got his wallet lifted while he was reading dirty magazines at the dirty bookstore on Broadway.

One-X-L-Thirty was a rookie sergeant named Grant who I didn't know very well. He wore one five-year hashmark showing he had between five and ten years on. I'd bet it was a whole lot closer to five. He had a ruddy, smooth face and a big vocabulary. I never heard him swear at any rollcall he conducted. I couldn't trust a policeman who didn't swear once in a while. You could hardly describe certain things you see and feelings you have in this job without some colourful language.

Grant was south of Ninth near Olympic, out of his car, pacing up and down as I drove up. I knew it was snobbish but I couldn't call a kid like him 'Sergeant'. And I didn't want to be out and out rude so I didn't call these young sergeants by their last names. I didn't call them anything. It got awkward sometimes, and I had to say, 'Hey pal', or 'Listen bud' when I wanted to talk to one of them. Grant looked pretty nervous about something.

'What's up?' I asked, getting out of my car.

'We have a demonstration at the Army Induction Centre.'

'So?' I said, looking down the street at a group of about fifteen marchers picketing the building.

'A lot of draftees go in and out and there could be trouble. There're some pretty militant-looking types in that picket line.'

'So what're we gonna do?'

'I just called you because I need someone to stand by and keep them under surveillance. I'm going in to talk to the lieutenant about the advisability of calling a tactical alert. I'd like you to switch to frequency nine and keep me advised of any status change.'

'Look, pal, this ain't no big thing. I mean, a tactical alert for fifteen ragtag flower sniffers?'

'You never know what it can turn into.'

'Okay,' and I sighed, even though I tried not to, 'I'll sit right here.'

'Might be a good idea to drive closer. Park across the street. Close enough to let them see you but far enough to keep them from trying to bait you.'

'Okay, pal,' I muttered, as Grant got in his car and sped towards the station to talk to Lieutenant Hilliard, who was a cool old head and wouldn't get in a flap over fifteen peace marchers.

I pulled out in the traffic and a guy in a blue Chevvy jumped on his brakes even though he was eighty feet back and going slow. People get black-and-white fever when they see a police car and they do idiotic things trying to be super careful. I've seem them concentrate so hard on one facet of safe driving, like giving an arm signal, that they bust right through a red light. That's black-and-white fever for you.

The marchers across Broadway caught my eye when two of them, a guy and a girl, were waving for me to come over. They seemed to be just jiving around but I thought I better go over for several reasons. First of all, there might really be something wrong. Second, if I didn't, it looked like hell for a big bad copper to be afraid to approach a group of demonstrators. And third, I had a theory that if enough force could be used fast enough in these confrontations there'd *be* no riot. I'd never seen real force used quick enough yet, and I thought, what the hell, now was my chance to test my theory since I was alone with no sergeants around.

These guys, at least a few of them, two black guys, and one white, bearded scuz in a dirty buckskin vest and yellow headband, looked radical enough to get violent with an overweight middle-aged cop like myself, but I firmly believed that if one of them made the mistake of putting his hands on me and I drove my stick three inches in his oesophagus, the others would yell police brutality and slink away. Of course I wasn't sure, and I noticed that the recent arrivals swelled their numbers to twenty-three. Only five of them were girls. That many people could stomp me to applesauce without a doubt, but I wasn't really worried, mainly because even though they were fist shaking, most of them looked like middle-class white people just playing at revolution. If you have a few hungry-looking professionals like I figured the white guy in the headband to be, you could have trouble. Some of these could lend their guts to the others and set them off, but he was the only one I saw.

I drove around the block so I didn't have to make an illegal U-turn in front of them, made my illegal U-turn on Olympic, came back and parked in front of the marchers, who ignored me and kept marching and chanting, 'Hell no, we won't go.' And 'Fuck Uncle Sam, and Auntie Spiro,' and several other lewd remarks mostly directed at the President, the governor, and the mayor. A few years ago, if a guy yelled 'fuck' in a public place in the presence of women or children, we'd have to drag his ass to jail.

'Hi, Officer, I love you,' said one little female peace marcher, a cute blonde about seventeen, wearing two inches of false eyelashes that looked upside-down, and ironed-out shoulder-length hair.

'Hi, honey, I love you too,' I smiled back, and leaned against the door of my car. I folded my arms and puffed a cigar until the two who had been waving at me decided to walk my way.

They were whispering now with another woman and finally the shorter girl, who was not exactly a girl, but a woman of about thirty-five, came right up. She was dressed like a teenager with a short yellow mini, violet panty hose, granny glasses, and white lipstick. Her legs were too damned fat and bumpy and she was wearing a theatrical smile with a cold arrogant look beneath it. Up close, she looked like one of the professionals, and seemed to be a picket captain. Sometimes a woman, if she's the real thing, can be the detonator much quicker than a man can. This one seemed like the real thing, and I looked her in the eye and smiled while she toyed with a heavy peace medal hanging around her neck. Her eyes said, 'You're just a fat harmless cop, not worth my talents, but so far you're all we have here, and I don't know if an old bastard like you is even intelligent enough to know when he's being put down.'

That's what I saw in her eyes, and her phony smile, but she said nothing for a few more minutes. Then a car from one of the network stations rolled up and two men got out with a camera and mike.

The interest of the marchers picked up now that they were soon to be on tape, and the chanting grew louder, the gestures more fierce, and the old teenybopper in the yellow dress finally said, 'We called you over because you looked very forlorn. Where're the riot troops, or are you all we get today?'

'If you get *me*, baby, you ain't gonna want any more,' I smiled through a puff of cigar smoke, pinning her eyeballs, admiring the fact that she didn't bat an eye even though I knew damn well she was expecting the business-like professional clichés we're trained to give in these situations. I'd bet she was even surprised to see me slouching against my car like this, showing such little respect for this menacing group.

'You're not supposed to smoke in public, are you, Officer?' She smiled, a little less arrogant now. She didn't know what the hell she had here, and was going to take her time about setting the bait.

'Maybe a real policeman ain't supposed to, but this uniform's just a shuck. I rented this ill-fitting clown suit to make an underground movie about this fat cop that steals apples and beats up flower children and old mini-skirted squatty-bodies with socks to match their varicose veins in front of the US Army Induction Centre.'

Then she lost her smile completely and stormed back to the guy in the headband who was also much older than he first appeared. They whispered and she looked at me as I puffed on the cigar and waved at some of the marchers who were putting me on, most of them just college-age kids having a good time. A couple of them sincerely seemed to like me even though they tossed a few insults to go along with the crowd.

Finally, the guy in the headband came my way shouting encouragement to the line of marchers who were going around and around in a long oval in front of the door, which was being guarded by two men in suits who were not policemen, but probably military personnel. The cameraman was shooting pictures now, and I hid my cigar and sucked in a few inches of gut when he photographed me. The babe in the yellow dress joined the group after passing out some Black Panther pins and she marched without once looking at me again.

'I hear you don't make like the other cops we've run into in these demonstrations,' said the guy with the headband, suddenly standing in front of me and grinning. 'The LAPD abandoning the oh so firm but courteous approach? Are you a new police riot technique? A caricature of a fat pig, a jolly jiveass old cop that we just can't get mad at? Is that it? They figure we couldn't use you for an Establishment symbol? Like you're too fucking comical looking, is that it?'

'Believe it or not, Tonto,' I said, 'I'm just the neighbourhood cop. Not a secret weapon, nothing for lumpy legs to get tight-jawed about. I'm just your local policeman.'

He twitched a little when I mentioned the broad so I guessed she might be his old lady. I figured they probably taught sociology IA and IB in one of the local junior colleges.

'Are you the only swine they're sending?' he asked, smiling not quite so much now which made me very happy. It's hard even for professionals like him to stay with a smirk when he's being rapped at where it hurts. He probably just *loves* everything about her, even the veiny old wheels. I decided, screw it, I was going to take the offensive with these assholes and see where it ended.

'Listen, Cochise,' I said, the cigar between my teeth, 'I'm the only old pig you're gonna see today. All the young piglets are staying in the pen. So why don't you and old purple pins just take your Che handbooks and cut out. Let these kids have their march with no problems. And take those two dudes with the naturals along with you.' I pointed to the two black guys who were standing ten feet away watching us. 'There ain't gonna be any more cops here, and there ain't gonna be any trouble.'

'You *are* a bit refreshing,' he said, trying to grin, but it was a crooked grin. 'I was getting awfully sick of those unnatural pseudo professionals with their businesslike platitudes, pretending to look right through us when really they wanted to get us in the back room of some police station and beat our fucking heads in. I must say you're refreshing. You're truly a vicious fascist and don't pretend to be anything else.'

Just then the mini-skirted broad walked up again. 'Is he threatening you, John?' she said in a loud voice, looking over her shoulder, but the guys with the camera and mike were at the other end of the shouting line of marchers.

'Save it till they get to this end,' I said, as I now estimated her age to be closer to forty. She was a few years older than he was and the mod camouflage looked downright comical. 'Want some bubble gum, little girl?' I said.

'Shut your filthy mouth,' he said, taking a step towards me. I was tight now, I wound myself up and was ready. 'Stay frosty, Sitting Bull,' I smiled. 'Here, have a cigar.' I offered one of my smokes, but he wheeled and walked away with old lumpy clicking along behind him.

The two black guys hadn't moved. They too were professionals, I was positive now, but they were a different kind. If anything went down, I planned to attack those two right away. They were the ones to worry about. They both wore black plastic jackets and one wore a black cossack hat. He never took his eyes off me. He'd be the very first one I'd go after, I thought. I kept that flaky look, grinning and waving at any kid who gave me the peace sign, but I was getting less and less sure I could handle the situation. There were a couple of other guys in the group that might get froggy if someone leaped, and I've seen what only two guys can do if they get you down and put the boots to you, let alone nine or ten.

I hated to admit it but I was beginning to wish Grant would show up with a squad of bluecoats. Still, it was a quiet demonstration, as quiet as these things go, and there was probably nothing to worry about, I thought.

The march continued as it had for a few more minutes, with the young ones yelling slogans, and then headband and mini-skirt came back with six or eight people in tow. These kids were definitely collegiate, wearing flares or bleach-streaked Levis. Some of the boys had muttonchops and moustaches, most had collar-length hair, and two of them were pretty, suntanned girls. They looked friendly enough and I gave them a nod of the head when they stopped in front of me.

One particularly scurvy-looking slimeball walked up, smiled real friendly, and whispered, 'You're a filthy, shit-eating pig.'

I smiled back and whispered, 'Your mother eats bacon.'

'How can we start a riot with no riot squad?' another said.

'Careful, Scott, he's not just a pig, he's a wild boar, you dig?' said the mini-skirt who was standing behind the kids.

'Maybe *you* could use a little bore, sweetheart, maybe that's your trouble,' I said, looking at the guy in the headband, and two of the kids chuckled.

'You seem to be the only Establishment representative we have at the moment, maybe you'd like to rap with us,' said Scott, a tall kid with a scrubbed-looking face and a mop of blond hair. He had a cute little baby hanging on his arm and she seemed amused.

'Sure, just fire away,' I said, still leaning back, acting relaxed as I puffed. I was actually beginning to *want* to rap with them. One time when I asked some young sergeant if I could take a shot at the 'Policeman Bill' programme and go talk to a class of high-schooled kids, he shined me on with a bunch of crap, and I realized then that they wanted these flat-stomached, clear-eyed, handsome young recruiting-poster cops for these jobs. I had my chance now and I liked the idea.

'What's your first name, Officer Morgan?' asked Scott, looking at my nameplate, 'and what do you think of street demonstrations?'

Scott was smiling and I could hardly hear him over the yelling as the ring of marchers moved twenty feet closer to us to block the entrance more effectively after the fat bitch in yellow directed them to do it. Several kids mugged at the cameraman and waved 'V' signs at him and me. One asshole, older than the others, flipped me the bone and then scowled into the camera.

'That's it, smile and say pig, you pukepot,' I mumbled, noticing the two black cossacks were at the other end of the line of marchers talking to purple legs. Then I turned to Scott. 'To answer your question, my name's Bumper Morgan and I don't mind demonstrations except that they take us cops away from our beats, and believe me we can't spare the time. Everybody loses when we're not on patrol.'

'What do you patrol, the fucking barnyard?' said one little shitbird wearing shades and carrying a poster that showed a white army officer telephoning a black mother about her son being killed in Vietnam. She was shown in a corner of the poster and there was a big white cop clubbing her with an oversized baton.

'That poster doesn't make sense,' I said. 'It's awful damn lame. You might as well label it, "Killed by the running dogs of imperialism!" I could do a lot better than that.'

'Man, that's *exactly* what I told him,' Scott laughed, and offered me a cigarette.

'No thanks,' I said, as he and his baby doll lit one. 'Now that one's sort of clever,' I said, pointing to a sign which said 'Today's pigs are tomorrow's porkchops.'

None of the other kids had anything to say yet, except the shithead with the poster, who yelled, 'Like, what're we doing talking to this fucking fascist lackey?'

'Look,' I said, 'I ain't gonna lay down and play dead just because you say "fuck" pretty good. I mean nobody's shocked by that cheap shit any more, so why don't we just talk quiet to each other. I wanna hear what you guys got to say.'

'Good idea,' said another kid, a black, with a wild natural, wire-rim glasses, and a tiger tooth necklace, who almost had to shout because of the noise. 'Tell us why a man would want to be a cop. I mean really. I'm not putting you on, I want to know.'

He was woofing me, because he winked at the blond kid, but I thought I'd *tell* them what I liked about it. What the hell, I liked having all these kids crowded around listening to me. Somebody then moved the marchers' line a little north again and I could almost talk in a normal voice.

'Well, I like to take lawbreakers off the street,' I began.

'Just a minute,' said the black kid, pushing his wire-rims up on his nose. 'Please, Officer, no euphemisms. I'm from Watts.' Then he purposely lapsed into a Negro drawl and said, 'I been knowin' the PO-lice all mah life.' The others laughed and he continued in his own voice. 'Talk like a *real* cop and tell us like it is, without any bullshit. You know, use that favourite expression of LAPD – "asshole", I believe it is.' He smiled again after he said all this and so did I.

'What part of Watts you live in?' I asked.

'One-O-Three and Grape, baby,' he answered.

'Okay, I'll talk plainer. I'm a cop because I love to throw assholes in jail, and if possible I like to send them to the joint.'

'That's more like it,' said the black kid. 'Now you're lookin' so good and soundin' so fine.'

The others applauded and grinned at each other.

'Isn't that kind of a depressing line of work?' asked Scott. 'I mean, don't you like to do something *for* someone once in a while instead of *to* them?'

'I figure I do something *for* someone every time I make a good bust. I mean, you figure every real asshole you catch in a dead bang burglary or robbery's tore off probably a hundred people or so before you bring him down. I figure each time I make a pinch I save a hundred more, maybe even more lives. And I'll tell you, most victims are people who can't afford to be victims. People who can afford it have protection and insurance and aren't so vulnerable to all these scummy haemorrhoids. Know what I mean?'

Scott's little girlfriend was busting to throw in her two cents, but three guys popped off at once, and finally Scott's voice drowned out the others. 'I'm a law student,' he said, 'and I intend to be your adversary someday in a courtroom. Tell me, do you really get satisfaction when you send a man away for ten years?'

'Listen, Scott,' I said, 'in the first place even Eichmann would stand a fifty–fifty chance of not doing ten years nowadays. You got to be a boss crook to pull that kind of time. In fact, you got to work at it to even *get* to state prison. Man, some of the cats I put away, I wouldn't give them ten years, I'd give them a god-damned lobotomy if I could.'

I dropped my cigar because these kids had me charged up now. I figured they were starting to respect me a little and I even tried for a minute to hold in my gut but that was uncomfortable, and I gave it up.

'I saw a big article in some magazine a few years ago honouring these cops,' I continued. '"These are not pigs" the article said, and it showed one cop who'd delivered some babies, and one cop who'd rescued some people in a flood, and one cop who was a goddamn boy scout troop leader or something like that. You know, I delivered two babies myself. But we ain't being paid to be midwives or lifeguards or social workers. They got other people to do those jobs. Let's see somebody honour some copper because the guy made thirty good felony pinches a month for ten years and sent a couple of hundred guys to San Quentin. Nobody ever gives an award to him. Even his sergeant ain't gonna appreciate that, but he'll get on his ass for not writing a traffic ticket every day because the goddamn city needs the revenue and there's no room in prisons anyway.'

I should've been noticing things at about this time. I should've noticed that the guy in the headband and his old lady were staying away from me and so were the two black guys in the plastic jackets. In fact, all the ones I spotted were staying at the other end of the line of marchers who were quieting down and starting to get tired. I should've noticed that the boy, Scott, the other blond kid, and the tall black kid, were closer to me than the others, and so was the cute little twist hanging on Scott's arm and carrying a huge heavy-looking buckskin handbag.

I noticed nothing, because for one of the few times in my life I wasn't being a cop. I was a big, funny-looking, blue-suited donkey and I thought I was home-run king belting them out over the fences. The reason was that I was somewhere I'd never been in my life. I was on a soapbox. Not a stage but a soapbox. A stage I could've handled. I can put on the act people want and expect, and I can still keep my eyes open and not get carried away with it, but this goddamned soapbox was something else. I was making speeches, one after another, about things that meant something to me, and all I could see was the loving gaze of my audience, and the sound of my own voice drowned out all the things that I should've been hearing and seeing.

'Maybe police departments should only recruit college graduates,' Scott shrugged, coming a step closer.

'Yeah, they want us to solve crimes by these "scientific methods", whatever that means. And what do us cops do? We kiss ass and nod our heads and take federal funds to build computers and send cops to college and it all boils down to a cop with sharp eyes and an ability to talk to people who'll get the goddamn job done.'

'Don't you think that in the age that's coming, policemen will be obsolete?' Scott's little girfriend asked the question and she looked so wide-eyed I had to smile.

'I'm afraid not, honey,' I said. 'As long as there's people, there's gonna be lots of bad ones and greedy ones and weak ones.'

'How can you feel that way about people and still care at all about helping them as you say you do when you arrest somebody?' she asked, shaking her head. She smiled sadly, like she felt sorry for me.

'Hell, baby, they ain't much but they're all we got. It's the only game in town!' I figured that was obvious to anybody and I started to wonder if they weren't still a little young. 'By the way, are most of you social science and English majors?'

'Why do you say that?' asked the black kid, who was built like a ball-player.

'The surveys say you are. I'm just asking. Just curious.'

'I'm an engineering major,' said the blond kid, who was now behind Scott, and then for the first time I was aware how close in on me these certain few were. I was becoming aware how polite they'd been to me. They were all activists and college people and no doubt had statistics and slogans and arguments to throw at me, yet I had it all my way. They just stood there nodding, smiling once in a while, and let me shoot my face off. I knew that something wasn't logical or right, but I was still intrigued with the sound of my own voice and so the fat blue maharishi said, 'Anything else about police work you'd like to talk about?'

'Were you at Century City?' asked the little blonde.

'Yeah, I was there, and it wasn't anything like you read in the underground newspapers or on those edited TV tapes.'

'It wasn't? I was there,' said Scott.

'Well, I'm not gonna deny some people got hurt,' I said, looking from one face to another for hostility. 'There was the President of the United States to protect and there were thousands of war protestors out there and I guarantee you that was no bullshit about them having sharpened sticks and bags of shit and broken bottles and big rocks. I bet *I* could kill a guy with a rock.'

'You didn't see any needless brutality?'

'What the hell's brutality?' I said. 'Most of those bluecoats out there are just kids *your* age. When someone spits in his face, all the goddamn discipline in the world ain't gonna stop him or any normal kid from getting that other cat's teeth prints on his baton. There's times when you just *gotta* play a little catch-up. You know what five thousand screaming people look like? Sure, we got some stick time in. Some scumbags, all they respect is force. You just gotta kick ass and collect names. Anybody with any balls woulda whaled on some of those pricks out there.' Then I remembered the girl. 'Sorry for the four-letter word, miss,' I said as a reflex action.

'Prick is a five-letter word,' she said, reminding me of the year I was living in.

Then suddenly, the blond kid behind Scott got hostile. 'Why do we talk to a pig like this? He talks about helping people. What's he do besides beat their heads in, which he admits? What do you do in the ghettos of Watts for the black people?'

Then a middle-aged guy in a clergyman's collar and a black suit popped through the ring of young people. 'I work in the eastside Chicano barrios,' he announced. 'What do you do for the Mexicans except exploit them?'

'What do *you* do?' I asked, getting uncomfortable at the sudden change of mood here, as several of the marchers joined the others and I was backed up against the car by fifteen or twenty people.

'I fight for the Chicanos. For brown power,' said the clergyman.

'You ain't brown,' I observed, growing more nervous.

'Inside I'm brown!'

'Take an enema,' I mumbled, standing up straight, as I realized that things were wrong, all wrong.

Then I caught a glimpse of the black cossack hat to the left behind two girls who were crowding in to see what the yelling was all about, and I saw a hand flip a peace button at me, good and hard. It hit me in the face, the pin scratching me right under the left eye. The black guy looked at me very cool as I spun around, mad enough to charge right through the crowd.

'You try that again and I'll ding your bells, man,' I said, loud enough for him to hear.

'Who?' he said, with a big grin through the moustache and goatee.

'Who, my ass,' I said. 'You ain't got feet that fit on a limb. I'm talking to *you*.'

'You fat pig,' he sneered and turned to the crowd. 'He wants to arrest me! You pick out a black, that the way you do it, Mister PO-lice?'

'If anything goes down, I'm getting *you* first,' I whispered, putting my left hand on the handle of my stick.

'He wants to arrest me,' he repeated, louder now. 'What's the charge? Being black? Don't I have any rights?'

'You're gonna get your rites,' I muttered. 'Your *last* rites.'

'I should kill you,' he said. 'There's fifty braves here and we should kill you for all the brothers and sisters you pigs murdered.'

'Get it on, sucker, anytime you're ready,' I said with a show of bravado because I was really scared now.

I figured that many people let loose could turn me into a doormat in about three minutes. My breath was coming hard. I tried to keep my jaw from trembling and my brain working. They weren't going to get me down on the ground. Not without a gun in my hand. I decided it wouldn't be that easy to kick *my* brains in. I made up my mind to start shooting to save myself, and I decided I'd blow up the two Black Russians, Geronimo, and Purple Legs, not necessarily in that order.

Then a hand reached out and grabbed my necktie, but it was a breakaway tie, and I didn't go with it when the hand pulled it into the crowd. At about the same time the engineering major grabbed my badge, and I instinctively brought up my right hand, holding his hand on my chest, backing up until his elbow was straight. Then I brought my left fist up hard just above his elbow and he yelped and drew back. Several other people also drew back at the unmistakable scream of pain.

'Off the pig! Off the pig!' somebody yelled. 'Rip him off!'

I pulled my baton out and felt the black-and-white behind me now and they were all screaming and threatening, even the full-of-shit padre.

I would've jumped in the car on the passenger side and locked the door but I couldn't. I felt the handle and it was locked, and the window was rolled up, and I was afraid that if I fooled around unlocking it, somebody might get his ass up and charge me.

Apparently the people inside the induction centre didn't know a cop was about to get his ticket cancelled, because nobody came out. I could see the cameraman fighting to get through the crowd which was spilling out on the street and I had a crazy wish that he'd make it. That's the final vanity, I guess, but I kind of wanted him to film Bumper's Last Stand.

For a few seconds it could've gone either way and then the door to my car opened and hit me in the back, scaring the shit out of me.

'Get your butt in here, Bumper,' said a familiar voice, which I obeyed. The second I closed the door something hit the window almost hard enough to break the glass and several people started kicking at the door and fender of my black-and-white.

'Give me the keys,' said Stan Ludlow, who worked Intelligence Division. He was sitting behind the wheel, looking as dapper as always in a dark green suit and mint-coloured necktie.

I gave him the keys from my belt and he drove away from the kerb as I heard something else chunk off the fender of the car. Four radio cars each containing three Metro officers pulled up at the induction centre as we were leaving, and started dispersing the group.

'You're the ugliest rape victim I ever saw,' said Stan, turning on Ninth Street and parking behind a plain-clothes police car where his partner was waiting.

'What the hell you talking about?'

'Had, man. You just been had.'

'I had a feeling something wasn't right,' I said, getting sick because I was afraid to hear what I figured he was going to say. 'Did they set me up?'

'Did they set you up? No, they didn't have to. You set yourself up! Christ, Bumper, you should know better than to make speeches to groups like that. What the hell made you do it?'

Stan had about fifteen years on the job and was a sergeant, but he was only about forty and except for his grey sideburns he looked lots younger. Still, I felt like a dumb little kid sitting there now. I felt like he was lots older and a damn sight wiser and took the assbite without looking at him.

'How'd you know I was speechmaking, Stan?'

'One of them is one of us,' said Stan. 'We had one of those guys wired with a mike. We listened to the whole thing, Bumper. We called for the Metro teams because we knew what was going to happen. Damn near didn't get to you quick enough though.'

'Who were the leaders?' I was trying to save a grain or two of my pride.

'The bitch in the yellow dress and the guru in the headband?'

'Hell no,' said Stan, disgustedly. 'Their names are John and Marie French. They're a couple of lames trying to groove with the kids. They're nothing. She's a self-proclaimed revolutionary from San Pedro and he's her husband. As a matter of fact he picked up our undercover man and drove him to the demonstration today when they were sent by the boss. French is mostly used as errand boy. He drives a VW bus and picks up everybody that needs a ride to all these peace marches. He's nothing. Why, did you have them figured for the leaders?'

'Sort of,' I mumbled.

'You badmouthed them, didn't you?'

'Sort of. What about the two in the Russian hats?'

'Nobody,' said Stan. 'They hang around all the time with their Panther buttons and get lots of pussy, but they're nobody. Just opportunists. Professional blacks.'

'I guess the guy running the show was a tall nice-looking kid named Scott?' I said, as the lights slowly turned on.

'Yeah, Scott Hairston. He's from UCLA. His sister Melba was the little blonde with the peachy ass who was hanging on his arm. She was the force behind subversive club chapters starting on her high school campus when she was still a bubblegummer. Their old man, Simon Hairston's an attorney and a slippery bastard, and his brother Josh is an old-time activist.'

'So the bright-eyed little baby was a goddamn viper, huh? I guess they've passed me by, Stan.'

Stan smiled sympathetically and lit my cigar for me. 'Look, Bumper, these kids've been weaned on this bullshit. You're just a beginner. Don't feel too bad. But for God's sake, next time don't start chipping with them. No speeches, please!'

'I must've sounded like a boob,' I said, and I could feel myself flushing clear to my toes.

'It's not that so much, Bumper, but that little bitch Melba put you on tape. She always solicits casual comments from cops. Sometimes she has a concealed hand mike with a wire running up her sleeve down to a box in her handbag. She carrying a big handbag today?'

I didn't have to answer. Stan saw it on the sick look on my face.

'They'll edit your remarks, Bumper. I heard some of them from the mike *our* guy was wearing. Christ, you talked about stick time and putting teeth marks on your baton and kicking ass and collecting names.'

'But all that's not how I meant it, Stan.'

'That's the way your comments'll be presented – out of context. It'll be printed that way in an underground newspaper or maybe even in a daily if Simon Hairston gets behind it.'

'Oooooh,' I said, tilting my hat over my eyes and slumping down in my seat.

'Don't have a coronary on me, Bumper,' said Stan. 'Everything's going to be all right.'

'All right? I'll be the laughingstock of the Department!'

'Don't worry, Melba's tapes're going to disappear.'

'The undercover man?'

Stan nodded.

'Bless him,' I breathed. 'Which one was he? Not the kid whose arm I almost broke?'

'No,' Stan laughed, 'the tall black kid. I'm only telling you because we're going to have to use him as a material witness in a few days anyway, and we'll have to disclose his identity. We got secret indictments on four guys who make pretty good explosives in the basement of a North Hollywood apartment building. He's been working for me since he joined the Department thirteen months ago. We have him enrolled in college. Nice kid. Hell of a basketball player. He can't wait to wear a bluesuit and work a radio car. He's sick of mingling with all these revolutionaries.'

'How do you know he can get the tape?'

'He's been practically living in Melba's skivvies for at least six months now. He'll sleep with her tonight and that'll be it.'

'Some job,' I said.

'He doesn't mind that part of it,' Stan chuckled. 'He's anxious to see how all his friends react when they find out he's the heat. Says he's been using them as whipping boys and playing the outraged black man role for so long, they probably won't believe it till they actually see him in the blue uniform with that big hateful shield on his chest. And wait'll Melba finds out she's been balling a cop. You can bet she'll keep that a secret.'

'Nobody's gonna hear about me then, huh, Stan?'

'I'll erase the tape, Bumper,' said Stan, getting out of the car. 'You know, in a way it worked out okay. Scott Hairston was expecting a hundred marchers in the next few hours. He didn't want trouble yet. You wrecked his game today.'

'See you later, Stan,' I said, trying to sound casual, like I wasn't totally humiliated. 'Have a cigar, old shoe.'

I was wrung out after that caper and even though it was getting late in the afternoon, I jumped on the Harbour Freeway and started driving south, as fast as traffic would permit, with some kind of half-baked idea about looking at the ocean. I was trying to do something which I usually do quite well, controlling my thoughts. It wouldn't do any good at all to stew over what happened, so I was trying to think about something else, maybe food, or Cassie, or how Glenda's jugs looked today – something good. But I was in a dark mood, and nothing good would come, so I decided to think of absolutely nothing which I can also do quite well.

I wheeled back to my seat and called the lieutenant, telling him about the ruckus at the induction centre, leaving out all the details of course, and he told me the marchers dispersed very fast and there were only a few cars still at the scene. I knew there'd hardly be any mention of this one, a few TV shots on the six o'clock news and that'd be it. I hung up and got back in my car, hoping the cameraman hadn't caught me smoking the cigar. That's another silly rule, no smoking in public, as if a cop is a Buckingham Palace guard.

SEVEN

I drove around some more, cooling off, looking at my watch every few seconds, wanting this day to end. The noisy chatter on the radio was driving me nuts so I turned it off. Screw the radio, I thought, I never made a good pinch from a radio call. The good busts come from doing what I do best, walking and looking and talking to people.

I had a hell of an attack of indigestion going. I took four antacid tablets from the glove compartment and popped them all but I was still restless, squirming around on the seat. Cassie's three o'clock class would be finished now so I drove up Vermont to Los Angeles City College and parked out front in the red zone even though when I do that I always get a few digs from the kids or from teachers like, 'You can do it but we get tickets for it.' Today there was nobody in front and I didn't get any bullshit which I don't particularly mind anyway, since nobody including myself really likes authority symbols. I'm always one of the first to get my ass up when the brass tries to restrict my freedom with some idiotic rules.

I climbed the stairs leisurely, admiring the tits on some suntanned, athletic-looking, ponytailed gym teacher. She was in a hurry and took the stairs two at a time, still in her white shorts and sneakers and white jersey that showed all she had, and it was plenty. Some of the kids passing me in the halls made all the usual remarks, calling me Dick Tracy and Sheriff John, and there were a few giggles about Marlene somebody holding some pot and then Marlene squealed and giggled. We didn't used to get snickers about pot, and that reminded me of the only argument concerning pot that made any sense to me. Grass, like booze, breaks the chain and frees the beast, but does it so much easier and quicker. I've seen it thousands of times.

Cassie was in her office with the door opened talking to a stringy-haired bubblegummer in a micro-mini that showed her red-flowered pantygirdle when she sat down.

'Hi,' said Cassie, when she saw me in the doorway. The girl looked at me and then back at Cassie, wondering what the fuzz was here for.

'We'll just be a minute,' said Cassie, still smiling her clean white smile, and I nodded and walked down the hall to the water fountain thinking how damn good she looked in that orange dress. It was one of the twenty or so that I'd bought her since we met, and she finally agreed with me that she looked better in hot colours, even though she thought it was part of any man's M.O. to like his women in flaming oranges and reds.

Her hair was drawn back today and either way, back or down, her hair was beautiful. It was thick brown, streaked with silver, not grey, but real untouched silver, and her figure was damn good for a girl her age. She was tanned and looked more like a gym teacher than a French teacher. She always wore a size twelve and sometimes could wear a ten in certain full styles. I wondered if she still looked so good because she played tennis and golf or because she didn't have any kids when she was married, but then, Cruz's wife Socorro had a whole squad of kids and though she was a little overweight she still looked almost as good as Cassie. Some people just keep it all, I guess, which almost made me self-conscious being with this classy-looking woman when we went places together. I always felt like everyone was thinking, 'He must have bread or she'd never be with him.' But it was useless to question your luck, you just had to grab on when you had the chance, and I did. And then again, maybe I was one of those guys that's ugly in an attractive sort of way.

'Well?' said Cassie, and I turned my head and saw her standing in the doorway of her office, still smiling at me as I went over her with my eyes. The kid had left.

'That's the prettiest dress you have,' I said, and I really meant it. At that moment she'd never looked better, even though some heavy wisps of hair were hanging on her cheeks and her lipstick was almost all gone.

'Why don't you admire my mind instead of my body once in a while like I do yours?' she grinned.

I followed her into the office and stepped close, intending to give her a kiss on the cheek. She surprised me by throwing her arms around my neck and kissing me long and hot, causing me to drop my hat on the floor and get pretty aroused even though we were standing in an open doorway and any minute a hundred people would walk past. When she finally stopped, she had the lazy dazzling look of a passionate woman.

'Shall we sweep everything off that damned desk?' she said in a husky voice, and for a minute or two I thought she would've. Then a bell rang and doors started opening and she laughed and sat down on her desk showing me some very shapely legs and you would never guess those wheels had been spinning for forty odd years. I plopped down in a leather chair, my mouth woolly dry from having that hot body up against me.

'Are you sure you won't come to the party tonight?' she said finally, lighting a cigarette.

'You know how I feel about it, Cassie,' I said. 'This is *your* night. Your friends and the students want to have you to themselves. I'll have you forever after that.'

'Think you can handle me?' she asked, with a grin, and I knew from her grin she meant sexually. We had joked before about how I awoke this in her, which she said had been dormant since her husband left her seven years ago and maybe even before that, from what I knew of the poor crazy guy. He was a teacher like Cassie, but his field was chemistry.

We supposed that some of her nineteen-year-old students, as sex-obsessed as they are these days, might be making love more often than we did, but she didn't see how they could. She said it had never been like this with her, and she never knew it could be so good. Me, I've always appreciated how good it was. As long as I can remember, I've been horny.

'Come by the apartment at eleven,' she said. 'I'll make sure I'm home by then.'

'That's pretty early to leave your friends.'

'You don't think I'd sit around drinking with a bunch of educators when I could be learning at home with Officer Morgan, do you?'

'You mean I can teach a teacher?'

'You're one of the tops in your field.'

'You have a class tomorrow morning,' I reminded her.

'Be there at eleven.'

'A lot of these teachers and students that don't have an early class tomorrow are gonna want to jive and woof a lot later than that. I think you ought to stay with them tonight, Cassie. They'd expect you to. You can't disappoint the people on your beat.'

'Well, all right,' she sighed. 'But I won't even see you tomorrow night because I'll be dining with those two trustees. They want to give me one final look, and casually listen to my French to make sure I'm not going to corrupt the already corrupted debs at their institution. I suppose I can't run off and leave *them* either.'

'It won't be long till I have you all to myself. Then *I'll* listen to your French and let you corrupt the hell out of me, okay?'

'Did you tell them you're retiring yet?' She asked the question easily, but looked me straight in the eye, waiting, and I got nervous.

'I've told Cruz,' I said, 'and I got a surprise for you.'

'What?'

'I've decided that Friday's gonna be my last day. I'll start my vacation Saturday and finish my time while I'm on vacation. I'll be going with you.'

Cassie didn't yell or jump up or look excited or anything, like I thought she would. She just went limp like her muscles relaxed suddenly, and she slipped off the desk and sat down on my lap where there isn't any too much room, and with her arms doubled around the top of my neck she started kissing me on the face and mouth and I saw her eyes were wet and soft like her lips, and next thing I know, I heard a lot of giggling. Eight or ten kids were standing in the hall watching us through the open door, but Cassie didn't seem to hear, or didn't care. I did though because I was sitting there in my bluesuit, being loved up and getting turned on in public.

'Cassie,' I gasped, nodding towards the door, and she got up, and calmly shut the door on the kids like she was ready to start again.

I stood and picked up my hat from the floor. 'Cassie, this is a school. I'm in uniform.'

Cassie started laughing very hard and had to sit down in the chair I'd been in, leaning back, and holding her hands over her face as she laughed. I thought how sexy even her throat was, the throat usually being the first thing to show its age, but Cassie's was sleek.

'I wasn't going to rape you,' she said at last, still chuckling between breaths.

'Well, it's just that you teachers are so permissive these days, I thought you might try to do me on the desk like you said.'

'Oh, Bumper,' she said finally, holding her arms out, and I came over and leaned down and she kissed me eight or ten warm times all over my face.

'I can't even begin to tell you how I feel now that you're really going to do it,' she said. 'When you said you actually *are* finishing up this Friday, and that you told Cruz Segovia, I just went to pieces. That was relief and joy you saw on my face when I closed the door, Bumper, not passion. Well, maybe a *little* of it was.'

'We've been planning all along, Cassie, you act like it was really a shock to you.'

'I've had nightmares about it. I've had fantasies awake and asleep of how after I'd gone, and got our apartment in San Francisco, you'd phone me one bitter night and tell me you weren't coming, that you just could never leave your beat.'

'Cassie!'

'I haven't told you this before, Bumper, but it's been gnawing at me. Now that you've told Cruz, and it's only two more days, I know it's coming true.'

'I'm not married to my goddamn job, Cassie,' I said, thinking how little you know about a woman, even one as close as Cassie. 'You should've seen what happened to me today. I was flim-flammed by a soft-nutted little kid. He made a complete ass out of me. He made me look like a *square*.'

Cassie looked interested and amused, the way she always does when I tell her about my job.

'What happened?' she asked, as I pulled out my last cigar and fired it up so I could keep calm when the humiliation swept over me.

'A demonstration at the Army Induction Centre. A kid, a punkass kid, conned me and I started blabbing off about the job. Rapping real honest with him I was, and I find out later he's a professional revolutionary, probably a Red or something, and oh, I thought I was so goddamn hip to it.

I been living too much on my beat, Cassie. Too much being the Man, I guess. Believing I could outsmart any bastard that skated by. Thinking the only ones I never could really get to were the organized ones, like the bookmakers and the big dope dealers. But *sometimes* I could do things that even hurt *them*. Now there's new ones that've come along. And they have organization. And I was like a baby, they handled me so easy.'

'What the hell did you *do*, Bumper?'

'Talked. I talked to them straight about things. About thumping assholes that needed thumping. That kind of thing. I made *speeches*.'

'Know what?' she said, putting her long-fingered hand on my knee. 'Whatever happened out there, whatever you said, I'll bet wouldn't do you or the Department a damn bit of harm.'

'Oh yeah, Cassie? You should've heard me talking about when the President was here and how we busted up the riot by busting up a skull or three. I was marvellous.'

'Do you know a *gentle* way to break up riots?'

'No, but we're supposed to be professional enough not to talk to civilians the way we talk in police locker rooms.'

'I'll take Officer Morgan over one of those terribly wholesome, terribly tiresome TV cops, and I don't think there's a gentle way to break up riots, so I think you should stop worrying about the whole thing. Just think, pretty soon you won't have any of these problems. You'll have a real position, an important one, and people working under you.'

'I got to admit, it gets me pretty excited to think about it. I bet I can come up with ways to improve plant security that those guys never dreamed of.'

'Of course you can.'

'No matter what I do, you pump me up,' I smiled. 'That's why I wanted you for my girl in spite of all your shortcomings.'

'Well, you're my Blue Knight. Do you know you're a knight? You joust and live off the land.'

'Yeah, I guess you might say I live off my beat, all right. 'Course I don't do much jousting.'

'Just *rousting*?'

'Yeah, I've rousted a couple thousand slimeballs in my time.'

'So you're my Blue Knight.'

'Wait a minute, kid,' I said. 'You're only getting a *former* knight if you get me.'

'What do you mean "if"?'

'It's okay to shuck about me being some kind of hero or something, but when I retire I'm just a has-been.'

'Bumper,' she said, and laughed a little, and kissed my hand like Glenda did. That was the second woman to kiss my hand today, I thought. 'I'm not dazzled by authority symbols. It's really *you* that keeps me kissing your hands.' She did it again and I've always thought that having a woman kiss your hands is just almost more than a man can take. 'You're going to an important job. You'll be an executive. You have an awful lot to offer, especially to me. In fact, you have so much maybe I should share it.'

'I can only handle one woman at a time, baby.'

'Remember Nancy Volger, from the English department?'

'Yeah, you want to share me with her?'

'Silly,' she laughed. 'Nancy and her husband were married twelve years and they didn't have any children. A couple of years ago they decided to take a boy into their home. He's eleven now.'

'They adopted him?'

'No, not exactly. They're foster parents.' Cassie's voice became serious. 'She said being a foster parent is the most rewarding thing they've ever done. Nancy said they'd almost missed out on knowing what living is and didn't realize it until they got the boy.

Cassie seemed to be searching my face just then. Was she thinking about *my* boy? I'd only mentioned him once to her. Was there something she wanted to know?

'Bumper, after we get married and settled in our home, what would you say to *us* becoming foster parents? Not really adopting a child if you didn't want to, but being foster parents, sharing. You'd be someone for a boy to look up to and learn from.'

'A kid! But I never thought about a family!'

'I've been thinking about this for a long time, and after seeing Nancy and hearing about their life, I think about how wonderful it would be for us. We're not old yet, but in ten or fifteen more years when we *are* getting old, there'd be someone else for both of us.' She looked in my eyes and then down. 'You may think I'm crazy, and I probably am, but I'd like you to give it some thought.'

That hit me so hard I didn't know what to say, so I grinned a silly grin, kissed her on the cheek, said 'I'm end of watch in fifteen minutes. Bye, old shoe,' and left.

She looked somehow younger and a little sad as she smiled and waved at me when I'd reached the stairway. When I got in my black-and-white I felt awful. I dropped two pills and headed east on Temple and cursed under my breath at every asshole that got in my way in this rush-hour traffic. I couldn't believe it. Leaving the Department after all these years and getting married was change enough, but a kid! Cassie had asked me about my ex-wife one time, just once, right after we started going together. I told her I was divorced and my son was dead and I didn't go into it any further. She never mentioned it again, never talked about kids in that way.

Damn, I thought, I guess every broad in the world should drop a foal at least once in her life or she'll never be happy. I pushed Cassie's idea out of my mind when I drove into the police building parking lot, down to the lower level where it was dark and fairly cool despite the early spring heat wave. I finished my log, gathered up my ticket books, and headed for the office to leave the log before I took off the uniform. I never wrote traffic tickets but they always issued me the ticket books. Since I made so many good felony pinches they pretty well kept their mouths shut about me not writing tickets, still, they always issued me the books and I always turned them back in just as full. That's the trouble with conformists, they'd never stop giving me those ticket books.

After putting the log in the daywatch basket I jived around with several of the young nightwatch coppers who wanted to know when I was changing to nights for the summer. They knew my M.O. too. Everybody knew it. I hated anyone getting my M.O. down too good like that. The most success-ful robbers and burglars are the ones who change their M.O.'s. They don't give you a chance to start sticking little coloured pins in a map to plot their movements. That reminded me of a salty old cop named Nails Grogan who used to walk Hill Street.

About fifteen years ago, just for the hell of it, he started his own crime wave. He was teed off at some chickenshit lieutenant we had then, named Wall, who used to jump on our meat every night at rollcall because we weren't catching enough burglars. The way Wall figured this was that there were always so many little red pins on the pin maps for night-time business burglaries, especially around Grogan's beat. Grogan always told me he didn't think Wall ever really read a burglary report and didn't know shit from gravy about what was going on. So a little at a time Nails started changing the pins every night before rollcall, taking the pins out of the area around his beat and sticking them in the east side. After a couple of weeks of this, Wall told the rollcall what a hell of a job Grogan was doing with the burglary problem in his area, and restricted the ass chewing to guys that worked the eastside cars. I was the only one that knew what Grogan did and we got a big laugh out of it until Grogan went too far and pinned a full-blown crime wave on the east side, and Lieutenant Wall had the captain call out the Metro teams to catch the burglars. Finally the whole hoax was exposed when no one could find crime reports to go with all the pins.

Wall was transferred to the morning watch, which is our graveyard shift, at the old Lincoln Heights jail. He retired from there a few years later. Nails Grogan never got made on that job, but Wall knew who screwed him, I'm sure. Nails was another guy that only lived a few years after he retired. He shot himself. I got a chill thinking about that, shook it off, and headed for the locker room where I took off the bluesuit and changed into my herring-bone sports coat, grey slacks, and lemon yellow shirt, no tie. In this town you can usually get by without a tie anywhere you go.

Before I left, I plugged in my shaver and smoothed up a little bit. A couple of the guys were still in the locker room. One of them was an ambitious young bookworm named Wilson, who as usual was reading while sitting on the bench and slipping into his civvies. He was going to college three or four nights a week and always had a textbook tucked away in his police notebook. You'd see him in the coffee room or upstairs in the cafeteria going through it all the time. I'm something of a reader myself but I could never stand the thought of doing it because you had to.

'What're you reading?' I asked Wilson.

'Oh, just some criminal law,' said Wilson, a thin youngster with a wide forehead and large blue eyes. He was a probationary policeman, less than a year on the job.

'Studying for sergeant already?' said Hawk, a cocky, square-shouldered kid about Wilson's age, who had two years on, and was going through his badge-heavy period.

'Just taking a few classes.'

'You majoring in police science?' I asked.

'No, I'm majoring in government right now. I'm thinking about trying for law school.' He didn't look right at me and I didn't think he would. This is something I've gotten used to from the younger cops, especially ones with some education, like Wilson. They don't know how to act when they're with old-timers like me. Some act salty like Hawk, trying to strut with an old beat cop, and it just looks silly. Others act more humble than they usually would, thinking an old lion like me would claw their ass for making an honest mistake out of greenness. Still others, like Wilson, pretty much act like themselves, but like most young people, they think an old fart that's never even made sergeant in twenty years must be nearly illiterate, so they generally restrict all conversation to the basics of police work to spare you, and they generally look embarrassed like Wilson did now, to admit to you that they read books. The generation gap is as bad in this job as it is in any other except for one thing: the hazards of the job shrink it pretty fast. After a few brushes with danger, a kid pretty much loses his innocence, which is what the generation gap is really all about – innocence.

'Answer me a law question,' said Hawk, putting on some flared pants. We're too GI to permit mutttonchops or big moustaches or he'd surely have them. 'If you commit suicide can you be prosecuted for murder?'

'Nobody ever has,' Wilson smiled, as Hawk giggled and slipped on a watermelon-coloured velvet shirt.

'That's only because of our permissive society,' I said, and Wilson glanced at me and grinned.

'What's that book in your locker, Wilson,' I asked, nodding towards a big paperback on the top shelf.

'*Guns of August*.'

'Oh yeah, I read that,' I said, 'I've read a hundred books about the First World War. Do you like it?'

'I do,' he said, looking at me like he discovered the missing link. 'I'm reading it for a history course.'

'I read T. E. Lawrence's *Seven Pillars of Wisdom* when I was on my First World War kick. Every goddamn word. I had maps and books spread all over my pad. That little runt only weighed in at about a hundred thirty, but thirty pounds of that was brains and forty was balls. He was a boss warrior.'

'A loner,' Wilson nodded, really looking at me now.

'Right. That's what I dig about him. I would've liked him even better if he hadn't written it all so intimate for everyone to read. But then if he hadn't done that, I'd never have appreciated him. Maybe a guy like that finally gets tired of just enjoying it and *has* to tell it all to figure it all out and see if it means anything in the end.'

'Maybe you should write your memoirs when you're through, Bumper,' Wilson smiled. 'You're as well known around here as Lawrence ever was in Arabia.'

'Why don't you major in history?' I said. 'If I went to college that'd be my meat. I think after a few courses in criminal law the rest of law school'd be a real drag, torts and contracts and all that bullshit. I could never plough through the dust and cobwebs.'

'It's exciting if you like it,' said Wilson, and Hawk looked a little ruffled that he was cut out of the conversation so he split.

'Maybe so,' I said. 'You must've had a few years of college when you came on the Department.'

'Two years,' Wilson nodded. 'Now I'm halfway through my junior year. It takes forever when you're a full-time cop and a part-time student.'

'You can tough it out,' I said, lighting a cigar and sitting down on the bench, while part of my brain listened to the youngster and the other part was worrying about something else. I had the annoying feeling you get, that can sometimes be scary, that I'd been here with him before and we talked like this, or maybe it was somebody else, and then I thought, yes, that was it, maybe the cowlick in his hair reminded me of Billy, and I got an empty tremor in my stomach.

'How old're you, Wilson?'

'Twenty-six,' he said, and a pain stabbed me and made me curse and rub my pot. Billy would've been twenty-six too!

'Hope your stomach holds out when you get my age. Were you in the service?'

'Army,' he nodded.

'Vietnam?'

'Yeah,' he nodded.

'Did you hate it?' I asked, expecting that all young people hated it.

'I didn't like the *war*. It scared hell out of me, but I didn't mind the *army* as much as I thought I would.'

'That's sort of how I felt,' I smiled. '*I* was in the Marine Corps for eight years.'

'Korea?'

'No, I'm even older than that,' I smiled. 'I joined in forty-two and got out in fifty, then came on the police department.'

'You stayed in a long time,' he said.

'Too long. The war scared me too, but sometimes peace is just as bad for a military man.'

I didn't tell him the truth because it might tune him out, and the truth was that it *did* scare me, the war, but I didn't hate it. I didn't exactly like it, but I didn't hate it. It's fashionable to hate war, I know, and I wanted to hate it, but I never did.

'I swore when I left Vietnam I'd never fire another gun and here I am a cop. Figure that out,' said Wilson.

I thought that was something, having him tell *me* that. Suddenly the age difference wasn't there. He was telling me things he probably told his young partners during lonely hours after two a.m. when you're fighting to keep awake or when you're 'in the hole' trying to hide your radio car, in some alley where you can doze uncomfortably for an hour, but you never really rest. There's the fear of a sergeant catching you, or there's the radio. What if you *really* fall asleep and a hot call comes out and you miss it?

'Maybe you'll make twenty years without ever firing your gun on duty,' I said.

'Have you had to shoot?'

'A few times,' I nodded, and he let it drop like he should. It was only civilians who ask you, 'What's it feel like to shoot someone?' and all that bullshit which is completely ridiculous, because if you do it in war or you do it as a cop, it doesn't feel like anything. If you do what has to be done, why *should* you feel anything? I never have. After the fear for your own life is past, and the adrenalin slows, nothing. But people generally can't stand truth. It makes a lousy story so I usually give them their clichés.

'You gonna stay on the job after you finish law school?'

'If I ever finish I might leave,' he laughed. 'But I can't really picture myself ever finishing.'

'Maybe you won't want to leave by then. This is a pretty strange kind of job. It's ... intense. Some guys wouldn't leave if they had a million bucks.'

'How about you?'

'Oh, I'm pulling the pin,' I said. 'I'm almost gone. But the job gets to you. The way you see everyone so exposed and vulnerable.... And there's nothing like rolling up a good felon if you really got the instinct.'

He looked at me for a moment and then said, 'Rogers and I got a good two-eleven suspect last month. They cleared five holdups on this guy. He had a seven-point-six-five-millimetre pistol shoved down the back of his waistband when we stopped him for a traffic ticket. We got hinky because he was sweating and dry-mouthed when he talked to us. It's really something to get a guy like that, especially when you never know how close you came. I mean, he was just sitting there looking from Rogers to me, measuring, thinking about blowing us up. We realized it later, and it made the pinch that much more of a kick.'

'That's part of it. You feel more alive. Hey, you talk like you're Bumperized and I didn't even break you in.'

'We worked together one night, remember?' said Wilson. 'My first night out of the academy. I was more scared of you than I was of the assholes on the street.'

'That's right, we *did* work together. I remember now,' I lied.

'Well, I better get moving,' said Wilson, and I was disappointed. 'Got to get to school. I've got two papers due next week and haven't started them.'

'Hang in there, Wilson. Hang tough,' I said, as I locked my locker.

I walked to the parking lot and decided to tip a few at my neighbourhood pub near Silverlake before going to Cruz's house. The proprietor was an old pal of mine who used to own a decent bar on my beat downtown before he bought this one. He was no longer on my beat of course, but he still bounced for drinks, I guess out of habit. Most bar owners don't pop for too many policemen, because they'll take advantage of it, policemen will, and they'll be so many at your watering hole you'll have to close the goddamn doors. Harry only popped for me and a few detectives he knew real well.

It was five o'clock when I parked my nineteen-fifty-one Ford in front of Harry's. I'd bought the car new and was still driving it. Almost twenty years and I only had a hundred and thirty thousand miles on her, and the same engine. I never went anywhere except at vacation time or sometimes when I'd take a trip to the river to fish. Since I met Cassie I've used the car more than I ever had before, but even with Cassie I seldom went far. We usually went to the movies in Hollywood, or to the Music Centre to see light opera, or to the Bowl for a concert which was Cassie's favourite place to go, or to Dodger Stadium which was mine. Often we went out to the Strip to go dancing. Cassie was good. She had all the moves, but she couldn't get the hang of letting her body do it all. With Cassie the mind was always there. One thing I decided I wouldn't get rid of when I left LA was my Ford. I wanted to see just how long a car could live if you treated it right.

Harry was alone when I walked in the little knotty-pine tavern which had a pool table, a few sad booths, and a dozen bar stools. The neighbourhood business was never very good. It was quiet and cool and dark in there and I was glad.

'Hi, Bumper,' he said, drawing a draught beer in a frosted glass for me.

'Evening, Harry,' I said, grabbing a handful of pretzels from one of the dishes he had on the bar. Harry's was one of the few joints left where you could actually get something free, like pretzels.

'How's business, Bumper?'

'Mine's always good, Harry,' I said, which is what policemen always answer to that question.

'Anything exciting happen on your beat lately?' Harry was about seventy, an ugly little goblin with bony shoulder blades who hopped around behind the bar like a sparrow.

'Let's see,' I said, trying to think of some gossip. Since Harry used to own a bar downtown, he knew a lot of the people I knew. 'Yeah, remember Frog LaRue?'

'The little hype with the stooped-over walk?'

'That one.'

'Yeah,' said Harry. 'I must've kicked that junkie out of my joint a million times after you said he was dealing dope. Never could figure out why he liked to set up deals in my bar.'

'He got his ass shot,' I said.

'What'd he do, try to sell somebody powdered sugar in place of stuff?'

'No, a narco cop nailed him.'

'Yeah? Why would anyone shoot Frog? He couldn't hurt nobody but himself.'

'Anybody can hurt somebody, Harry,' I said. 'But in this case it was a mistake. Old Frog always kept a blade on the window sill in any hotel he stayed at. And the window'd be open even in the dead of winter. That was his M.O. If someone came to his door who he thought was cops, Frog'd slit the screen and throw his dope and his outfit right out the window. One night the narcs busted in the pad when they heard from a snitch that Frog was holding, and old Froggy dumped a spoon of junk out the window. He had to slit the screen to do it and when this narc came crashing through the door, his momentum carried him clear across this little room, practically on to Frog's bed. Frog was crouched there with the blade still in his hand. The partner coming through second had his gun drawn and that was it, he put two almost in the ten ring of the goddamn bull's eye.' I put my fist on my chest just to the right of the heart to show where they hit him.

'Hope the poor bastard didn't suffer.'

'Lived two days. He told about the knife bit to the detectives and swore how he never would've tried to stab a cop.'

'Poor bastard,' said Harry.

'At least he died the way he lived. Armload of dope. I heard from one of the dicks that at the last they gave him a good stiff jolt of morphine. Said old Frog laying there with two big holes in his chest actually looked happy at the end.'

'Why in the hell don't the state just give dope to these poor bastards like Frog?' said Harry, disgustedly.

'It's the high they crave, not just feeling healthy. They build up such a tolerance you'd have to keep increasing the dose and increasing it until you'd have to give them a fix that'd make a pussycat out of King Kong. And heroin substitutes don't work with a stone hype. He wants the *real* thing. Pretty soon you'd be giving him doses that'd kill him anyway.'

'What the hell, he'd be better off. Some of them probably wouldn't complain.'

'Got to agree with you there,' I nodded. 'Damn straight.'

'Wish that bitch'd get here,' Harry mumbled, checking the bar clock.

'Who's that?'

'Irma, the goofy barmaid I hired last week. You seen her yet?'

'Don't think so,' I said, sipping the beer, so cold it hurt my teeth.

'Sexy little twist,' said Harry, 'but a kook, you know? She'll steal your eyes out if you let her. But a good body. I'd like to break her open like a shotgun and horsefuck her.'

'Thought you told me you were getting too old for that,' I said, licking the foam off my upper lip, and finishing the glass, which Harry hurried to refill.

'I am, God knows, but once in a while I get this terrible urge, know what I mean? Sometimes when I'm closing up and I'm alone with her.... I ain't stirred the old lady for a couple years, but I swear when I'm with Irma I get the urge like a young stallion. I'm not *that* old, you know. Not by a long shot. But you know how my health's always been. Lately there's been this prostate problem. Still, when I'm around this Irma I'm awful randy. I feel like I could screw anything from a burro to a cowboy boot.'

'I'll have to see this wench,' I smiled.

'You won't take her away from me, will you, Bumper?'

I thought at first he was kidding and then I saw the desperate look on his face. 'No, of course not, Harry.'

'I really think I could make it with her, Bumper. I been depressed lately especially with this prostate, but I could be a man again with Irma.'

'Sure, Harry.' I'd noticed the change coming over him gradually for the past year. He sometimes forgot to pick up bar money, which was very unusual for him. He mixed up customers' names and sometimes told you things he'd told you the last time he saw you. Mostly that, repeating things. A few of the other regular customers mentioned it when we played pool out of earshot. Harry was getting senile and it was not only sad, it was scary. It made my skin crawl. I wondered how much longer he'd be able to run the joint. I laid a quarter on the bar, and sure enough, he absently picked it up. The first time I ever bought my own drink in Harry's place.

'My old lady can't last much longer, Bumper. I ever tell you that the doctor's only give her a year?'

'Yeah, you told me.'

'Guy my age can't be alone. This prostate thing, you know I got to stand there and coax for twenty minutes before I can take a leak. And you don't know how lovely it is to be able to sit down and take a nice easy crap. You know, Bumper, a nice easy crap is a thing of beauty.'

'Yeah, I guess so.'

'I could do all right with a dame like Irma. Make me young again, Irma could.'

'Sure.'

'You try to go it alone when you get old and you'll be rotting out a coffin liner before you know it. You got to have somebody to keep you alive. If you don't, you might die without even knowing it. Get what I mean?'

'Yeah.'

It was so depressing being here with Harry that I decided to split, but one of the local cronies came in.

'Hello, Freddie,' I said, as he squinted through six ounces of eyeglasses into the cool darkness.

'Hi, Bumper,' said Freddie, recognizing my voice before he got close enough to make me through his half-inch horn-rims. Nobody could ever mistake his twangy voice which could get on your nerves after a bit. Freddie limped over and laid both arthritic hands on the bar knowing I'd bounce for a couple drinks.

'A cold one for Freddie,' I said, suddenly afraid that Harry wouldn't even know him. But that was ridiculous, I thought, putting a dollar on the bar, Harry's deterioration was only beginning. I usually bought for the bar when there were enough people in there to make Harry a little coin, trouble is, there were seldom more than three or four customers in Harry's at any one time anymore. I guess everyone runs from a man when he starts to die.

'How's business, Bumper?' asked Freddie, holding the mug in both his hands, fingers like crooked twigs.

'My business's always good, Freddie.'

Freddie snuffled and laughed. I stared at Freddie for a few seconds while he drank. My stomach was burning and Harry had me spooked. Freddie suddenly looked ancient too. Christ, he probably was at least sixty-five. I'd never thought about Freddie as an older guy, but suddenly he was. Little old men they were. I had nothing in common with them now.

'Girls keeping you busy lately, Bumper?' Harry winked. He didn't know about Cassie or that I stopped chasing around after I met her.

'Been slowing down a little in that department, Harry,' I said.

'Keep at it, Bumper,' said Harry, cocking his head to one side and nodding like a bird. 'The art of fornication is something you lose if you don't practise it. The eye muscles relax, you get bifocals like Freddie. The love muscles relax, whatta you got?'

'Maybe he *is* getting old, Harry,' said Freddie, dropping his empty glass on its side as he tried to hand it to Harry with those twisted hands.

'Old? You kidding?' I said.

'How about you, Freddie?' said Harry. 'You ain't got arthritis of the cock, have you? When was the last time you had a piece of ass?'

'About the last time you did,' said Freddie sharply.

'Shit, before my Flossie got sick, I used to tear off a chunk every night. Right up till when she got sick, and I was sixty-eight years old then.'

'Haw!' said Freddie, spilling some beer over the gnarled fingers. 'You ain't been able to do anything but lick it for the past twenty years.'

'Yeah?' said Harry, nodding fast now, like a starving little bird at a feed tray. 'You know what I did to Irma here one night? Know what?'

'What?'

'I laid her right over the table there. What do you think of that, wise guy?'

'Haw. Haw. Haw,' said Freddie who had been a little bit fried when he came in and was really feeling it now.

'All you can do is read about it in those dirty books,' said Harry. 'Me, I don't read about it, I do it! I threw old Irma right over that bar there and poured her the salami for a half hour!'

'Haw. Haw. Haw,' said Freddie. 'It'd take you that long to find that shrivelled up old cricket dick. Haw. Haw. Haw.'

'What's the sense of starting a beef?' I muttered to both of them. I was getting a headache. 'Gimme a couple aspirin will you, Harry?' I said, and he shot the grinning Freddie a pissed-off look, and muttering under his breath, brought me a bottle of aspirin and a glass of water.

I shook out three pills and pushed the water away, swallowing the pills with a mouthful of beer. 'One more beer,' I said, 'and then I gotta make it.'

'Where you going, Bump? Out to hump?' Harry leered, and winked at Freddie, forgetting he was supposed to be mad as hell.

'Going to a friend's house for dinner.'

'Nice slice of tail waiting, huh?' said Harry, nodding again.

'Not tonight. Just having a quiet dinner.'

'Quiet dinner,' said Freddie. 'Haw. Haw. Haw.'

'Screw you, Freddie,' I said, getting mad for a second as he giggled in his beer. Then I thought, Jesus, I'm getting loony too.

The phone rang and Harry went to the back of the bar to answer it. In a few seconds he was bitching at somebody, and Freddie looked at me, shaking his head.

'Harry's going downhill real fast, Bumper.'

'I know he is, so why get him pissed off?'

'I don't mean to,' said Freddie. 'I just lose my temper with him sometimes, he acts so damned nasty. I heard the doctors're just waiting for Flossie to die. Any day now.'

I thought of how she was ten years ago, a fat, tough old broad, full of hell and jokes. She fixed such good cold-cut sandwiches I used to make dinner out of them at least once a week.

'Harry can't make it without her,' said Freddie. 'Ever since she went away to the hospital last year, he's been getting more and more childish, you noticed?'

I finished my beer and thought, I've *got* to get the hell out of here.

'It happens only to people like Harry and me. When you love somebody and need them so much especially when you're old, and then lose them, that's when it happens to you, when your mind rots like Harry's. Better your body goes like Flossie's. Flossie's the lucky one, you know. You're lucky too. You don't love nobody and you ain't married to nothing but that badge. Nothing can ever touch you, Bumper.'

'Yeah, but how about when you get too old to do the job, Freddie? How about then?'

'Well, I never thought about that, Bumper.' Freddie tipped the mug and dribbled on his chin. He licked some foam off one knotted knuckle. 'Never thought about that, but I'd say you don't have to worry about it. You get a little older and charge round the way you do and somebody's bound to bump you off. It might sound cold, but what the hell, Bumper, look at *that* crazy old bastard.' He waved a twisted claw towards Harry still yelling in the phone. 'Screwing everything with his imagination and a piece of dead skin. Look at me. What the hell, dying on your beat wouldn't be the worst way to go, would it?'

'Know why I come to this place, Freddie? It's just the most cheerful goddamn drinking establishment in Los Angeles. Yeah, the conversation is stimulating and the atmosphere is very jolly and all.'

Harry came back before I could get away from the bar. 'Know who that was, Bumper?' he said, his eyes glassy and his cheeks pale. He had acne as a young man and now his putty-coloured cheeks looked corroded.

'Who was it,' I sighed, 'Irma?'

'No, that was the hospital. I spent every cent I had, even with the hospital benefits, and now she's been put in a big ward with a million other old, dying people. And still I got to pay money for one thing or another. You know, when Flossie finally dies there ain't going to be nothing left to bury her. I had to cash in the insurance. How'll I bury old Flossie, Bumper?'

I started to say something to soothe Harry, but I heard sobbing and realized Freddie had started blubbering. Then in a second or two Harry started, so I threw five bucks on the bar for Freddie and Harry to get bombed on, and I got the hell away from those two without even saying good-bye. I've never understood how people can work in mental hospitals and old people's homes and places like that without going nuts. I felt about ready for the squirrel tank right now just being around those two guys for an hour.

EIGHT

Ten minutes later I was driving my Ford north on the Golden State Freeway and I started getting hungry for Socorro's enchiladas. I got to Eagle
Rock at dusk and parked in front of the big old two-storey house with the
neat lawn and flower gardens on the sides. I was wondering if Socorro
planted vegetables in the back this year, when I saw Cruz in the living
room standing by the front window. He opened the door and stepped out
on the porch, wearing a brown sports shirt and old brown slacks and his
house slippers. Cruz didn't have to dress up for me, and I was glad to come
here and see everyone comfortable, as though I belonged here, and in a way
I did. Most bachelor cops have someplace like Cruz's house to go to once in
a while. Naturally, you can get a little ding-a-ling if you live on the beat and
don't ever spend some time with decent people. So you find a friend or a
relative with a family and go there to get your supply of faith replenished.

I called Cruz my old roomie because when we first got out of the police
academy twenty years ago, I moved into this big house with him and
Socorro. Dolores was a baby, and Esteban a toddler. I took a room upstairs
for over a year and helped them with their house payments until we were
through paying for our uniforms and guns, and were both financially on
our feet. That hadn't been a bad year and I'd never forget Socorro's cooking. She always said she'd rather cook for a man like me who appreciated
her talent than a thin little guy like Cruz who never ate much and didn't
really appreciate good food. Socorro was a slender girl then, twelve years
younger than Cruz, nineteen years old, with two kids already, and the
heavy Spanish accent of El Paso which is like that of Mexico itself. They'd
had a pretty good life I guess, until Esteban insisted on joining the army
and was killed two years ago. They weren't the same after that. They'd
never be the same after that.

'How do you feel, *oso*?' said Cruz, as I climbed the concrete stairs to his
porch. I grinned because Socorro had first started calling me '*oso*' way back
in those days, and even now some of the policemen call me 'bear' from
Socorro's nickname.

'You hurting, Bumper?' Cruz asked. 'I heard those kids gave you some
trouble at the demonstration today.'

618

'I'm okay,' I answered. 'What'd you hear?'

'Just that they pushed you around a little bit. *Hijo la*—. Why does a man your age get involved in that kind of stuff? Why don't you listen to me and just handle your radio calls and let those young coppers handle the militants and do the hotdog police work?'

'I answered a radio call. That's how it started. That's what I get for having that goddamn radio turned on.'

'Come on in, you stubborn old bastard,' Cruz grinned, holding the wood frame screen door open for me. Where could you see a wood frame screen door these days? It was an old house, but preserved. I loved it here. Cruz and me once sanded down all the woodwork in the living room, even the hardwood floor, and refinished it just as it had been when it was new.

'What're we having?' Cruz asked, brushing back his thick grey-black hair and nodding towards the kitchen.

'Well, let's see,' I sniffed. I sniffed again a few times, and then took a great huge whiff. Actually I couldn't tell, because the chile and onion made it hard to differentiate, but I took a guess and pretended I knew.

'*Chile renello, carnitas* and *cilantro* and onion. And ... let's see ... some *enchiladas*, some *guacamole*.'

'I give up,' Cruz shook his head. 'The only thing you left out was rice and beans.'

'Well hell, Cruz, *arroz y frijoles*, that goes without saying.'

'An animal's nose.'

'Sukie in the kitchen?'

'Yeah, the kids're in the backyard, some of them.'

I went through the big formal dining room to the kitchen and saw Socorro, her back to me, ladling out a huge wooden spoonful of rice into two of the bowls that sat on the drainboard. She was naturally a little the worse for wear after twenty years and nine kids, but her hair was as long and black and shiny rich as ever, and though she was twenty pounds heavier, she still was a strong, lively-looking girl with the whitest teeth I'd ever seen. I snuck up behind her and tickled her ribs.

'Ay!' she said, dropping the spoon. 'Bumper!'

I gave her a hug from the back while Cruz chuckled and said, 'You didn't surprise him, he smelled from the door and knew just what you fixed for him.'

'He's not a man, this one,' she smiled, 'no man ever had a nose like that.'

'Just what I told him,' said Cruz.

'Sit down, Bumper,' said Socorro, waving to the kitchen table, which, big and old as it was, looked lost in the huge kitchen. I'd seen this kitchen when there wasn't a pathway to walk through, the day after Christmas when all the kids were young and I'd brought them toys. Kids and toys literally covered every foot of linoleum and you couldn't even see the floor then.

'Beer, Bumper?' asked Cruz, and opened two cold ones without me answering. We still liked drinking them out of the bottle, both of us, and I almost finished mine without taking it away from my mouth. And Cruz, knowing my M.O. so well, uncapped another one.

'Cruz told me the news, Bumper. I was thrilled to hear it,' said Socorro, slicing an onion, her eyes glistening from the fumes.

'About you retiring right away and going with Cassie when she leaves,' said Cruz.

'That's good, Bumper,' said Socorro. 'There's no sense hanging around after Cassie leaves. I was worried about that.'

'Sukie was afraid your *puta* would seduce you away from Cassie if she was up in San Francisco and you were down here.'

'*Puta?*'

'The beat,' said Cruz, taking a gulp of the beer. 'Socorro always calls it Bumper's *puta*.'

'*Cuidao!*' said Sorocco to Cruz. 'The children are right outside the window.' I could hear them laughing, and Nacho yelled something then, and the girls squealed.

'Since you're leaving, we can talk about her, can't we, Bumper?' Cruz laughed. 'That beat is a *puta* who seduced you all these years.'

Then for the first time I noticed from his grin and his voice that Cruz had had a few before I got there. I looked at Socorro who nodded and said, 'Yes, the old *borracho*'s been drinking since he got home from work. Wants to celebrate Bumper's last dinner as a bachelor, he says.'

'Don't be too rough on him,' I grinned. 'He doesn't get drunk very often.'

'Who's drunk?' said Cruz, indignantly.

'You're on your way, *penjedo*,' said Socorro, and Cruz mumbled in Spanish, and I laughed and finished my beer.

'If it hadn't been for that *puta*, Bumper would've been a captain by now.'

'Oh, sure,' I said, going to the refrigerator and drawing two more beers for Cruz and me. 'Want one, Sukie?'

'No, thanks,' said Socorro, and Cruz burped a couple times.

'Think I'll go outside and see the kids,' I said, and then I remembered the presents in the trunk of my car that I bought Monday after Cruz invited me to dinner.

'Hey, you roughnecks,' I said when I stepped out, and Nacho yelled, 'Buuuum-per,' and swung towards me from a rope looped over the limb of a big oak that covered most of the yard.

'You're getting about big enough to eat hay and pull a wagon, Nacho,' I said. Then four of them ran towards me chattering about something, their eyes all sparkling because they knew damn well I'd never come for dinner without bringing them something.

'Where's Dolores?' I asked. She was my favourite now, the oldest after Esteban, and was a picture of what her mother had been. She was a college junior majoring in physics and engaged to a classmate of hers.

'Dolores is out with Gordon, where else?' said Ralph, a chubby ten-year-old, the baby of the family who was a terror, always raising some kind of hell and keeping everyone in an uproar.

'Where's Alice?'

'Over next door playing,' said Ralph again, and the four of them, Nacho, Ralph, María, and Marta, were all about to bust, and I was enjoying it even though it was a shame to make them go through this.

'Nacho,' I said nonchalantly, 'would you please take my car keys and get some things out of the trunk?'

'I'll help,' shrieked Marta.

'I will,' said María, jumping up and down, a little eleven-year-old dream in a pink dress and pink socks and black patent leather shoes. She was the prettiest and would be heartbreakingly beautiful someday.

'I'll go alone,' said Nacho. 'I don't need no help.'

'The hell you will,' said Ralph.

'You watch your language, Rafael,' said María, and I had to turn around to keep from busting up at the way Ralph stuck his chubby little fanny out at her.

'Mama,' said María. 'Ralph did something dirty!'

'Snitch,' said Ralph, running to the car with Nacho.

I strolled back into the kitchen still laughing, and Cruz and Socorro both were smiling at me because they knew how much I got a bang out of their kids.

'Take Bumper in the living room, Cruz,' said Socorro. 'Dinner won't be ready for twenty minutes.'

'Come on, Bumper,' said Cruz, taking four cold ones out of the refrigerator, and a beer opener. 'I don't know why Mexican women get to be tyrants in their old age. They're so nice and obedient when they're young.'

'Old age. Huh! Listen to the *viejo*, Bumper,' she said, waving a wooden spoon in his direction, as we went into the living room and I flopped in Cruz's favourite chair because he insisted. He pushed the ottoman over and made me put my feet up.

'Damn, Cruz.'

'Got to give you extra special treatment tonight, Bumper,' he said, opening another beer for me. 'You look dog tired, and this may be the last we have you for a long time.'

'I'll only be living one hour away by air. You think Cassie and me aren't gonna come to LA once in a while? And you think you and Socorro and the kids aren't gonna come see us up there?'

'The whole platoon of us,' he laughed.

'We're gonna see each other plenty, that's for sure,' I said, and fought against the down feeling that I was getting because I realized we probably would *not* be seeing each other very often at all.

'Yeah, Bumper,' said Cruz, sitting across from me in the other old chair, almost as worn and comfortable as this one. 'I was afraid that jealous bitch would never let you go.'

'You mean my beat?'

'Right.' He took several big gulps on the beer and I thought about how I was going to miss him.

'How come all the philosophizing tonight? Calling my beat a whore and all that?'

'I'm waxing poetic tonight.'

'You also been tipping more than a little *cerveza*.'

Cruz winked and peeked towards the kitchen where we could hear Socorro banging around. He went to an old mahogany hutch that was just inside the dining room and took a half-empty bottle of mescal out of the bottom cabinet.

'That one have a worm in it?'

'If it did I drank it,' he whispered. 'Don't want Sukie to see me drinking it. I still have a little trouble with my liver and I'm not supposed to.'

'Is that the stuff you bought in San Luis? That time on your vacation?'

'That's it, the end of it.'

'You won't need any liver if you drink that stuff.'

'It's good, Bumper. Here, try a throatful or two.'

'Better with salt and lemon.'

'Pour it down. You're the big *macho*, damn it. Drink like one.'

I took three fiery gulps and a few seconds after they hit bottom I regretted it and had to drain my bottle of beer while Cruz chuckled and sipped slowly for his turn.

'Damn,' I wheezed and then the fire fanned out and my guts uncoiled and I felt good. Then in a few minutes I felt better. That was the medicine my body needed.

'They don't always have salt and lemon lying around down in Mexico,' said Cruz, handing me back the mescal. 'Real Mexicans just mix it with saliva.'

'No wonder they're such tough little bastards,' I wheezed, taking another gulp, but only one this time, and handing it back.

'How do you feel now, *'mono*?' Cruz giggled, and it made me start laughing, his silly little giggle that always started when he was half-swacked.

'I feel about half as good as you,' I said, and splashed some more beer into the burning pit that was my stomach. But it was a different fire entirely than the one made by the stomach acid, this was a friendly fire, and after it smouldered it felt great.

'Are you hungry?' asked Cruz.

'Ain't I always?'

'You are,' he said, 'you're hungry for almost everything. Always. I've often wished I was more like you.'

'Like me?'

'Always feasting, on *everything*. Too bad it can't go on forever. But it can't. I'm damn glad you're getting out now.'

'You're drunk.'

'I am. But I know what I'm talking about, *'mano*. Cassie was sent to you. I prayed for that.' Then Cruz reached in his pocket for the little leather pouch. In it was the string of black carved wooden beads he carried for luck. He squeezed the soft leather and put it away.

'Did those beads really come from Jerusalem?'

'They did, that's no baloney. I got them from a missionary priest for placing first in my school in El Paso. "First prize in spelling to Cruz Guadalupe Segovia," the priest said, as he stood in front of the whole school, and I died of happiness that day. I was thirteen, just barely. He got the beads in the Holy Land and they were blessed by Pius XI.'

'How many kids did you beat out for the prize?'

'About six entered the contest. There were only seventy-five in the school altogether. I don't think the other five contestants spoke any English. They thought the contest would be in Spanish but it wasn't, so I won.'

We both laughed at that. 'I never won a thing, Cruz. You're way ahead of me.' It was amazing to think of a real man like Cruz carrying those wooden beads. In this day and age!

Then the front door banged open and the living room was filled with seven yelling kids, only Dolores being absent that night, and Cruz shook his head and sat back quietly drinking his beer and Socorro came into the living room and tried to give me hell for buying all the presents, but you couldn't hear yourself over the noisy kids.

'Are these real big-league cleats?' asked Nacho as I adjusted the batting helmet for him and fixed the chin strap which I knew he'd throw away as soon as the other kids told him big leaguers don't wear chin straps.

'Look! Hot pants!' María squealed, holding them up against her adolescent body. They were sporty, blue denim with a bib, and patch pockets.

'Hot pants?' Cruz said. 'Oh, no!'

'They even wear them to school, Papa. They do. Ask Bumper!'

'Ask Bumper,' Cruz grumbled and drank some more beer.

The big kids were there then too, Linda, George, and Alice, all high school teenagers, and naturally I bought clothes for them. I got George a box of mod-coloured long-sleeved shirts and from the look in his eyes I guess I couldn't have picked anything better.

After all the kids thanked me a dozen times, Socorro ordered them to put everything away and called us to dinner. We sat close together on different kinds of chairs at the huge rectangular oak table that weighed a ton. I know because I helped Cruz carry it in here twelve years ago when there was no telling how many kids were going to be sitting around it.

The youngest always said the prayers aloud. They crossed themselves and Ralph said grace, and they crossed themselves again and I was drooling because the *chiles rellenos* were on a huge platter right in front of me. The big *chiles* were stuffed with cheese and fried in a light fluffy batter, and before I could help myself, Alice was serving me and my plate was filled before any one of those kids took a thing for themselves. Their mother and father never said anything to them, they just did things like that.

'You *do* have *cilantro*,' I said, salivating with a vengeance now. I knew I smelled that wonderful spice.

Marta, using her fingers, sprinkled a little extra *cilantro* over my *carnitas* when I said that, and I bit into a soft, handmade flour tortilla crammed with *carnitas* and Socorro's own *chile* sauce.

'Well, Bumper?' said Cruz after I'd finished half a plateful which took about thirty-five seconds.

I moaned and rolled my eyeballs and everybody laughed because they knew that look so well.

'You see, Marta,' said Socorro. 'You wouldn't hate to cook so much if you could cook for somebody like Bumper who appreciates your work.'

I grinned with a hog happy look, washing down some *chile relleno* and enchilada with three big swigs of cold beer. 'Your mother is an artist!'

I finished three helpings of *carnitas*, the tender little chunks of pork which I covered with Socorro's *chile* and *cilantro* and onion. Then, after everyone was finished and there were nine pairs of brown eyes looking at me in wonder, I heaped the last three *chiles rellenos* on my plate and rolled one up with the last flour tortilla and the last few bites of *carnitas* left in the bowl, and nine pairs of brown eyes got wider and rounder.

'*Por Dios*, I thought I made enough for twenty,' said Socorro.

'You did, you did, Sukie,' I said, enjoying being the whole show now, and finishing it in three big bites. 'I'm just extra hungry tonight, and you made it extra good, and there's no sense leaving leftovers around to spoil.' With that I ate half a *chile relleno* and swallowed some beer and looked around at all the eyes, and Nacho burped and groaned. We all busted up, Ralph especially, who fell off his chair on to the floor holding his stomach and laughing so hard I was afraid he'd get sick. It was a hell of a thing when you think of it, entertaining people by being a damn glutton, just to get attention.

After dinner we cleared the table and I got roped into a game of Scrabble with Alice and Marta and Nacho with the others kibitzing, and all the time I was swilling cold beer with an occasional shot of mescal that Cruz brought out in the open now. By nine o'clock when the kids had to go to bed I was pretty well lubricated.

They all kissed me good night except George and Nacho, who shook hands, and there were no arguments about going to bed, and fifteen minutes later it was still and quiet upstairs. I'd never seen Cruz or Socorro spank any of them. Of course the older ones spanked hell out of the younger ones, I'd seen that often enough. After all, everyone in this world needs a thumping once in a while.

We took the leaf out of the table and replaced the lace tablecloth and the three of us went into the living room. Cruz was pretty well bombed out, and after Socorro complained, he decided not to have another beer. I had a cold one in my right hand, and the last of the mescal in my left.

Cruz sat next to Socorro on the couch and he rubbed his face which was probably as numb as hell. He gave her a kiss on the neck.

'Get out of here,' she grumbled. 'You smell like a stinking wino.'

'How can I smell like a wino. I haven't had any wine,' said Cruz.

'Remember how we used to sit like this after dinner back in the old days,' I said, realizing how much the mescal had affected me, because they were both starting to look a little fuzzy.

'Remember how little and skinny Sukie was,' said Cruz, poking her arm.

'I'm going to let you have it in a minute,' said Socorro, raising her hand which was a raw, worn-out-looking hand for a girl her age. She wasn't quite forty years old.

'Sukie was the prettiest girl I'd ever seen,' I said.

'I guess she was,' said Cruz with a silly grin.

'And still is,' I added. 'And Cruz was the handsomest guy I ever saw outside of Tyrone Power or maybe Clark Gable.'

'You really think Tyrone Power was better looking?' said Cruz, grinning again as Socorro shook her head, and to me he honestly didn't look a bit different now than he ever had, except for the grey hair. Damn him for staying young, I thought.

'Speaking of pretty girls,' said Socorro, 'let's hear about your new plans with Cassie.'

'Well, like I told you, she was gonna go up north to an apartment and get squared away at school. Then after the end of May when Cruz and me have our twenty years, she'd fly back here and we'd get married. Now I've decided to cut it short. I'll work tomorrow and the next day and run my vacation days and days off together to the end of the month when I officially retire. That way I can leave with Cassie, probably Sunday morning or Monday, and we'll swing through Las Vegas and get married on the way.'

'Oh, Bumper, we wanted to be with you when you got married,' said Socorro, looking disappointed.

'What the hell, at our age getting married ain't no big thing,' I said.

'We love her, Bumper,' said Socorro. 'You're lucky, very lucky. She'll be perfect for you.'

'What a looker.' Cruz winked and tried to whistle, but he was too drunk.

Socorro shook her head and said '*sinvergüenza,*' and we both laughed at him.

'What're you going to do Friday?' asked Socorro. 'Just go into rollcall and stand up and say you're retiring and this is your last day?'

'Nope, I'm just gonna fade away. I'm not telling a soul and I hope you haven't said anything to anyone, Cruz.'

'Nothing,' said Cruz, and he burped.

'I'm just cutting out like for my regular two days off, then I'm sending a registered letter to Personnel Division and one to the captain. I'll just sign all my retirement papers and mail them in. I can give my badge and I.D. card to Cruz before I leave and have him turn them in for me so I won't have to go back at all.'

'You'll have to come back to LA for your retirement party,' said Cruz. 'We're sure as hell going to want to throw a retirement party for you.'

'Thanks, Cruz, but I never liked retirement parties anyway. In fact I think they're miserable. I appreciate the thought but no party for me.'

'Just think,' said Socorro. 'To be starting a new life! I wish Cruz would leave the job too.'

'You said it,' said Cruz, his eyes glassy though he sat up straight. 'But with all our kids, I'm a thirty-year man. Thirty years, that's a lifetime. I'll be an old man when I pull the pin.'

'Yeah, I guess I'm lucky,' I said. 'Remember when we were going through the academy, Cruz? We thought we were old men then, running with all those kids twenty-one and twenty-two years old. Here you were thirty-one, the oldest guy in the class, and I was close behind you. Remember Mendez always called us *elefante y ratoncito*?'

'The elephant and the mouse,' Cruz giggled.

'The two old men of the class. Thirty years old and I thought I knew something then. Hell, you're still a baby at that age. We were both babies.'

'We were babies, *'mano,*' said Cruz. 'But only because we hadn't been out there yet.' Cruz waved his hand towards the streets. 'You grow up fast out there and learn too much. It's no damn good for a man to learn as much as you learn out there. It ruins the way you think about things, and the way you feel. There're certain things you should believe and if you stay out there for twenty years you can't still believe them any more. That's not good.'

'You still believe them, don't you, Cruz?' I asked, and Socorro looked at us like we were two raving drunks, which we probably were, but we understood, Cruz and me.

'I still believe them, Bumper, because I want to. And I have Sukie and the kids. I can come home, and then the other isn't real. You've had no one to go to. Thank God for Cassie.'

'I've got to go fix school lunches. Excuse me, Bumper,' said Socorro, and she gave us that shake of the head which meant, it's time to leave the drunken cops to their talk. But Cruz hardly ever got drunk, and she didn't really begrudge him, even though he had trouble with his liver.

'I never could tell you how glad we were when you first brought Cassie here for dinner, Bumper. Socorro and me, we stayed awake in bed that night and talked about it and how God must've sent her, even though you don't believe in God.'

'I believe in the *gods*, you know that,' I grinned, gulping the beer after I took the last sip of the mescal.

'There's only one God, goddamnit,' said Cruz.

'Even your God has three faces, goddamnit,' I said, and gave him a glance over the top of my beer bottle, making him laugh.

'Bumper, I'm trying to talk to you seriously.' And his eyes turned down at the corners like always. I couldn't woof him any more when his eyes did that.

'Okay.'

'Cassie's the answer to a prayer.'

'Why did you waste all your prayers on me?'

'Why do you think, *penjedo*? You're my brother, *mi hermano*.'

That made me put the beer down, and I straightened up and looked at his big eyes. Cruz was struggling with the fog of the mescal and beer because he wanted to tell me something. I wondered how in hell he had ever made the Department physical. He was barely five-eight in his bare feet, and he was so damn skinny. He'd never gained a pound, but outside of Esteban, he had the finest-looking face you would ever see.

'I didn't know you thought that much about Cassie and me.'

'Of course I did. After all, I prayed her here for you. Don't you see what you were heading for? You're fifty years old, Bumper. You and some of the other old beat cops've been the *machos* of the streets all these years, but Lord, I could just see you duking it out with some young stud or chasing somebody out there and all of a sudden just lying down on that street to die. You realize how many of our classmates had heart attacks already?'

'Part of being a policeman,' I shrugged.

'Not to mention some asshole blowing you up,' said Cruz. 'You remember Driscoll? He had a heart attack just last month, and he's not nearly as fat as you, and a few years younger, and I'll bet he never does anything harder than lift a pencil. Like you today, all alone, facing a mob, like a rookie! What the hell, Bumper, you think I want to be a pallbearer for a guy two hundred and eighty pounds?'

'Two seventy-five.'

'When Cassie came, I said, "Thank God, now Bumper's got a chance". I worried though. I knew you were smart enough to see how much woman you had, but I was afraid that *puta* had too strong a grip on you.'

'Was it *you* that kept getting me assigned to the north end districts all the time? Lieutenant Hilliard kept telling me it was a mistake every time I bitched about it.'

'Yeah, I did it. I tried to get you away from your beat, but I gave up. You just kept coming back down anyway and that meant nobody was patrolling the north end, so I didn't accomplish anything. I can guess what it was to you, being *el campeón* out there, having people look at you the way they do on your beat.'

'Yeah, well it isn't so much,' I said, nervously fidgeting with the empty bottle.

'You know what happens to old cops who stay around the streets too long.'

'What?' I said, and the enchilada caught me and bit into the inside of my gut.

'They get too old to do police work and they become *characters*. That's what I'd hate to see. You just becoming an old character, and maybe getting yourself hurt bad out there before you realize you're too old. Just too old.'

'I'm not that old yet. Damn it, Cruz!'

'No, not for civilian life. You have lots of good years ahead of you. But for a warrior, it's time to quit, *'mano*. I was worried about her going up there and you coming along in a few weeks. I was afraid the *puta* would get you alone when Cassie wasn't there. I'm so damn glad you're leaving with Cassie.'

'So am I, Cruz,' I said, lowering my voice like I was afraid to let myself hear it. 'You're right. I've half thought of these things. You're right. I think I'd blow my brains out if I ever got as lonely as some I've seen, like some of those people on my beat, homeless wandering people, that don't belong anywhere....'

'That's it, Bumper. There's no place for a man alone, not really. You can get along without love when you're young and strong. Some guys can, guys like you. Me, I never could. And nobody can get along without it when he gets old. You shouldn't be afraid to love, *'mano*.'

'Am I, Cruz?' I asked, chewing two tablets because a mailed fist was beating on my guts from the inside. 'Is that why I feel so unsure of myself now that I'm leaving? Is that it?'

I could hear Socorro humming as she made lunches for the entire tribe. She would write each one's name on his lunch sack and put it in the refrigerator.

'Remember when we were together in the old days? You and me and Socorro and the two kids? And how you hardly ever spoke about your previous life even when you were drunk? You only said a little about your brother Clem who was dead, and your wife who'd left you. But you really told us more, much more about your brother. Sometimes you called him in your sleep. But mostly you called someone else.'

I was rocking back now, holding my guts which were throbbing, and all the tablets in my pocket wouldn't help.

'You never told us about your boy. I always felt bad that you never told *me* about him, because of how close we are. You only told me about him in your sleep.'

'What did I say?'

'You'd call "Billy", and you'd say things to him. Sometimes you'd cry, and I'd have to go in and pick up your covers and pillow from the floor and cover you up because you'd thrown them clear off the bed.'

'I never dreamed about him, never!'

'How else would I know, *'mano*?' he said softly. 'We used to talk a lot about it, Socorro and me, and we used to worry about a man who'd loved a brother and a son like you had. We wondered if you'd be afraid to love again. It happens. But when you get old, you've got to. You've *got* to.'

'But you're safe if you *don't*, Cruz!' I said, flinching from the pain. Cruz was looking at the floor, not used to talking to me like this, and he didn't notice my agony.

'You're safe, Bumper, in one way. But in the way that counts, you're in danger. Your soul is in danger if you don't love.'

'Did you believe that when Esteban was killed? Did you?'

Cruz looked up at me, and his eyes got even softer than normal and turned way down at the corners because he was being most serious. His heavy lashes blinked twice and he sighed. 'Yes. Even after Esteban, and even though he was the oldest and you always feel a little something extra for the firstborn. Even after Esteban was killed I felt this to be the truth. After the grief, I knew it was God's truth. I believed it, even then.'

'I think I'll get a cup of coffee. I have a stomach ache. Maybe something warm....'

Cruz smiled and leaned back in his chair. Socorro was finishing the last of the lunches and I chatted with her while we warmed up the coffee. The stomach ache started to fade a little.

I drank the coffee and thought about what Cruz said which made sense, and yet, every time you get tied up to people something happens and that cord is cut, and I mean really cut with a bloody sword.

'Shall we go in and see how the old boy's doing?'

'Oh sure, Sukie,' I said, putting my arm around her shoulder. Cruz was stretched out on the couch snoring.

'That's his drinking sleep. We'll never wake him up,' she said. 'Maybe I just better get his pillow and a blanket.'

'He shouldn't be sleeping on the couch,' I said. 'It's draughty in this big living room.' I went over to him and knelt down.

'What're you going to do?'

'Put him to bed,' I said, picking him up in my arms.

'Bumper, you'll rupture yourself.'

'He's light as a baby,' I said, and he *was* surprisingly light. 'Why the hell don't you make him eat more?' I said, following Socorro up the stairs.

'You know he doesn't like to eat. Let me help you, Bumper.'

'Just lead the way, Mama. I can handle him just fine.'

When we got in their bedroom I wasn't even breathing hard and I laid him on the bed, on the sheets. She had already pulled back the covers. Cruz was rattling and wheezing now and we both laughed.

'He snores awful,' she said as I looked at the little squirt.

'He's the only *real* friend I ever made in twenty years. I know millions of people and I see them and eat with them and I'll miss things about all of them, but it won't be like something inside is gone, like with Cruz.'

'Now you'll have Cassie. You'll be ten times closer with her.' She held my hand then. Both her hands were tough and hard.

'You sound like your old man.'

'We talk about you a lot.'

'Good night,' I said, kissing her on the cheek. 'Cassie and me are coming by before we leave to say good-bye to all of you.'

'Good night, Bumper.'

'Good night, old shoe,' I said to Cruz in a loud voice and he snorted and blew and I chuckled and descended the stairs. I let myself out after turning out the hall light and locking the door.

When I went to bed that night I started getting scared and didn't know why. I wished Cassie was with me. After I went to sleep I slept very well and didn't dream.

THURSDAY
the Second Day

NINE

The next morning I worked on my badge for five minutes, and my boondockers were glistening. I was kind of disappointed when Lieutenant Hilliard didn't have an inspection, I was looking so good. Cruz looked awful. He sat at the front table with Lieutenant Hilliard and did a bad job of reading off the crimes. Once or twice he looked at me and rolled his eyes which were really sad this morning because he was so hung over. After rollcall I got a chance to speak to him for a minute.

'You look a little *crudo*,' I said, trying not to smile.

'What a bastard you are,' he moaned.

'It wasn't the mescal. I think you swallowed the worm.'

'A complete bastard.'

'Can you meet me at noon? I wanna buy you lunch.'

'Don't even talk about it,' he groaned, and I had to laugh.

'Okay, but save me your lunch hour tomorrow. And pick out the best, most expensive place in town. Someplace that doesn't bounce for bluecoats. That's where we're going for my last meal as a cop.'

'You're actually going to *pay* for a meal on duty?'

'It'll be a first,' I grinned, and he smiled but he acted like it hurt to grin.

'*Ahí te haucho,*' I said, heading for the car.

'Don't forget you have court this afternoon, *'mano*,' he said, always nagging me.

Before getting in my black-and-white I looked it over. It's always good to pull out the back seat before you leave, in case some innocent rookie on the nightwatch let one of his sneaky prisoners stash his gun down there, or a condom full of heroin, or a goddamn hand grenade. It takes so long to make a policeman out of some of these kids, nothing would surprise me. But then I reminded myself what it was like to be twenty-two. They're right in the middle of growing up, these babies, and it's awful tough growing up in that bluecoat as twenty-two-year-old Establishment symbols. Still, it chills my nuts the way they stumble around like civilians for five years or so, and let people flimflam them. Someday, I thought, I'll probably find a dead midget jammed down there behind the friggin' seat.

As soon as I hit the bricks and started cruising I began thinking about the case I had this afternoon. It was a preliminary hearing on a guy named Landry and the dicks had filed on him for being an ex-con with a gun, and also filed one count for possession of marijuana. I didn't figure to have any problems with the case. I'd busted him in January after I'd gotten information on this gunsel from a snitch named Knobby Booker, who worked for me from time to time, and I went to a hotel room on East Sixth Street on some phony pretext I couldn't completely remember until I reread the arrest report. I busted Landry in his room while he was taking a nap in the middle of the afternoon. He had about two lids of pot in a sandwich bag in a drawer by his bed to give him guts when he pulled a robbery, and a fully loaded US Army forty-five automatic under his mattress. He damned near went for it when I came through the door, and I almost blew him up when he started for it. In fact, it was a Mexican standoff for a few seconds, him with his hand an inch or so under the mattress, and me crouching and coming to the bed, my six-inch Smith aimed at his upper lip, and warning about what I was going to do if he didn't pull his hand out very slow, and he did.

Landry had gotten out on five thousand dollars' bail which some old broad put up for him. He'd been a half-assed bit actor on TV and movies a few years back, and was somewhat of a gigolo with old women. He jumped bail and was rearrested in Denver and extradited, and the arrest was now four months old. I didn't remember all the details, but of course I would read the arrest report and be up on it before I testified. The main thing of course was to hold him to answer at the prelim without revealing my informant Knobby Booker, or without even letting anyone know I *had* an informant. It wasn't too hard if you knew how.

It was getting hot and smoggy and I was already starting to sweat in the armpits. I glanced over at an old billboard on Olive Street which said, 'Don't start a boy on a life of crime by leaving your keys in the car,' and I snorted and farted a couple of times in disgust. It's the goddamn do-gooder P.R. men, who dream up slogans like that to make everybody but the criminals feel guilty, who'll drive all *real* cops out of this business one of these days.

As I pulled to the kerb opposite the Grand Central Market, a wino staggering down Broadway sucking on a short dog saw me, spun around, fell on his ass, dropped his bottle, and got up as though nothing happened. He started walking away from the short dog, which was rolling around on the sidewalk spilling sweet lucy all over the pavement.

'Pick up the dog, you jerk,' I called to him. 'I ain't gonna bust you.'

'Thanks, Bumper,' he said sheepishly and picked up the bottle. He waved, and hustled back down Broadway, a greasy black coat flapping around his skinny hips.

I tried to remember where I knew him from. Of course I knew him from the beat, but he wasn't just a wino face. There was something else. Then I saw through the gauntness and grime and recognized him and smiled because these days it always felt good to remember and prove to yourself that your memory is as sharp as ever.

They called him Beans. The real name I couldn't recall even though I'd had it printed up on a fancy certificate. He almost caused me to slug another policeman about ten years ago and I'd never come close to doing that before or since.

The policeman was Herb Slovin and he finally got his ass canned. Herb was fired for capping for a bail bondsman and had a nice thing going until they caught him. He was working vice and was telling everybody he busted to patronize Laswell Brothers Bail Bonds, and Slim Laswell was kicking back a few bucks to Herb for each one he sent. That's considered to be as bad as stealing, and the Department bounced his ass in a hurry after he was caught. He would've gone behind something else though if it hadn't been that. He was a hulking, cruel bastard and so horny he'd mount a cage if he thought there was a canary in there. I figured sooner or later he'd fall for broads or brutality.

It was Beans that almost caused me and Herb to tangle. Herb hated the drunk wagon. 'Niggers and white garbage,' he'd repeat over and over when something made him mad which was most of the time. And he called the wagon job 'the N.H.I. detail'. When you asked him what that stood for he'd say 'No Humans Involved', and then he let out with that donkey bray of his. We were working the wagon one night and got a call on Beans because he was spread-eagled prone across San Pedro Street blocking two lanes of traffic, out cold. He'd puked and wet all over himself and didn't even wake up when we dragged him to the wagon and flipped him in on the floor. There was no problem. We both wore gloves like most wagon cops, and there were only two other winos inside. About ten minutes later when we were on East Sixth Street, we heard a ruckus in the back and had to stop the wagon and go back there and keep the other two winos from kicking hell out of Beans who woke up and was fighting mad for maybe the first time in his life. I'd busted him ten or twenty times for drunk and never had any trouble with him. You seldom have to hassle a stone wino like Beans.

They quieted down as soon as Herb opened the back door and threatened to tear their heads off, and I was just getting back in the wagon when Beans, sitting by the door, said, 'Fuck you, you skin-headed jackass!' I cracked up laughing because Herb was bald, and with his long face and big yellow teeth and the way he brayed when he laughed, he *did* look like a skin-headed jackass.

Herb, though, growled something, and snatched Beans right off the bench, out of the wagon into the street, and started belting him back and forth across the face with his big gloved hand. I realized from the thuds that they were sap gloves and Beans's face was already busted open and bleeding before I could pull Herb away and push him back, causing him to fall on his ass.

'You son of a bitch,' he said, looking at me with a combination of surprise and blood red anger. He almost said it like a question he was so surprised.

'He's a wino, man,' I answered, and that should've been enough for any cop, especially a veteran like Herb who had twelve years on the job at that time and knew that you don't beat up defenceless winos no matter what kind of trouble they give you. That was one of the first things we learned in the old days from the beat cops who broke us in. When a man takes a swing at you or actually hits you, you have the right to kick ass, that goes without saying. It doesn't have to be tit for tat, and if some asshole gives you tit, you tat his goddamn teeth down his throat. That way, you'll save some other cop from being slugged by the same pukepot if he learns his lesson from you.

But every real cop also knows you don't beat up winos. Even if they swing at you or actually hit you. Chances are it'll be a puny little swing and you can just handcuff him and throw him in jail. Cops know very well how many fellow policemen develop drinking problems themselves, and there's always the thought in the back of your mind that there on the sidewalk, but for the gods, sleeps old Bumper Morgan.

Anyway, Herb had violated a cop's code by beating up the wino and he knew it, which probably saved us a hell of a good go right there on East Sixth Street. And I'm not at all sure it might not've ended by me getting my chubby face changed around by those sap gloves because Herb was an ex-wrestler and a very tough bastard.

'Don't you ever try that again,' he said to me, as we put Beans back inside and locked the door.

'I won't, if you never beat up a drunk when you're working with me,' I answered casually, but I was tense and coiled, ready to go, even thinking about unsnapping my holster because Herb looked damned dangerous at that moment, and you never know when an armed man might do something crazy. He was one of those creeps that carried an untraceable hideout gun and bragged how if he ever killed somebody he shouldn't have, he'd plant the gun on the corpse and claim self-defence. The mood was interrupted by a radio call just then, and I rogered it and we finished the night in silence. The next night Herb asked to go back to a radio car because him and me had a 'personality conflict'.

Shortly after that Herb went to vice and got fired, and I forgot all about that incident until about a year later on Main Street, when I ran into Beans again. That night I got into a battle with two guys I'd watched pull a pigeon drop on some old man. I'd stood inside a pawnshop and watched them through binoculars while they flimflammed him out of five hundred bucks.

They were bad young dudes, and the bigger of the two, a block-faced slob with an eighteen-inch neck, was giving me a pretty good go, even though I'd already cracked two of his ribs with my stick. I couldn't finish him because the other one kept jumping on my back, kicking and biting, until I ran backward and slammed into a car and brick wall, with him between me and the object. I did this twice and he kept hanging on and then somebody from the crowd of about twenty assholes who were gathered around enjoying the fight barrelled in and tackled the little one and held him on the sidewalk until I could finish the big one by slapping him across the Adam's apple with the stick.

The other one gave up right then and I cuffed the two of them together and saw that my helper was old Beans the wino, sitting there throwing up, and bleeding from a cut eye where the little dude clawed him. I gave Beans a double sawbuck for that and took him to a doctor, and I had the Captain's adjutant print up a beautiful certificate commending Beans for his good citizenship. Of course, I lied and said Beans was some respectable businessman who saw the fight and came to my aid. I couldn't tell them he was a down-and-out wino or they might not have done it. It was nicely framed and had Beans's real name on it, which I couldn't for the life of me remember now. I presented it to him the next time I found him bombed on East Sixth Street and he really seemed to like it.

As I remembered all this, I felt like calling him back and asking him if he still had it, but I figured he probably sold the frame for enough to buy a short dog, and used the certificate to plug the holes in his shoe. It's always best not to ask too many questions of people or to get to know them too well. You save yourself disappointment that way. Anyway, Beans was half a block away now, staggering down the street cradling the wine bottle under his greasy coat.

I took down my sunglasses which I keep stashed behind the visor in my car and settled down to cruise and watch the streets and relax even though I was too restless to really relax. I decided not to wait, but to cruise over to the school and see Cassie, who would be coming in early like she always did on Thursdays. She'd feel like I did, like everything she did these last days at school would be for the last time. But at least she knew she'd be doing similar things in another school.

I parked out front and got a few raspberries from students for parking my black-and-white in the no parking zone, but I'd be damned if I'd walk clear from the faculty lot. Cassie wasn't in her office when I got there, but it was unlocked so I sat at her desk and waited.

The desk was exactly like the woman who manned it: smart and tidy, interesting and feminine. She had an odd-shaped ceramic ashtray on one side of the desk which she'd picked up in some junk store in west LA There was a small, delicately painted oriental vase that held a bunch of dying violets which Cassie would replace first thing after she arrived. Under the plastic cover on the desk blotter Cassie had a screwy selection of pictures of people she admired, mostly French poets. Cassie was long on poetry and tried to get me going on haiku for a while, but I finally convinced her I don't have the right kind of imagination for poetry. My reading is limited to history and to new ways of doing police work. I liked one poem Cassie showed me about woolly lambs and shepherds and wild killer dogs. I understood that one all right.

The door opened and Cassie and another teacher, a curvy little chicken in a hot pink mini, came giggling through the door.

'Oh!' said the young broad. 'Who are you?' The blue uniform shocked her. I was sitting back in Cassie's comfortable leather-padded desk chair.

'I am the Pretty Good Shepherd,' I said, puffing on my cigar and smiling at Cassie.

'Whatever that means,' said Cassie, shaking her head, putting down a load of books, and kissing me on the cheek much to the surprise of her friend.

'You must be Cassie's fiancé,' the friend laughed as it suddenly hit her. 'I'm Maggie Carson.'

'Pleased to meet you, Maggie. I'm Bumper Morgan,' I said, always happy to meet a woman, especially a young one, who shakes hands, and with a firm friendly grip.

'I've heard about Cassie's policeman friend, but it surprised me, seeing that uniform so suddenly.'

'We've all got our skeletons rattling, Maggie,' I said. 'Tell me, what've you done that makes you jump at the sight of the fuzz?'

'All right, Bumper,' Cassie smiled. I was standing now, and she had me by the arm.

'I'll leave you two alone,' said Maggie, with a sly wink, just as she'd seen and heard it in a thousand corny love movies.

'Nice kid,' I said, after Maggie closed the door and I kissed Cassie four or five times.

'I missed you last night,' said Cassie, standing there pressed up against me, smelling good and looking good in her yellow sleeveless dress. Her arms were red tan, her hair down, touching her shoulders.

'Your dinner date tonight still on?'

'Afraid so,' she murmured.

'After tomorrow we'll have all the time we want together.'

'Think we'll ever have all the time we want?'

'You'll get sick of seeing me hanging around the pad.'

'Never happen. Besides, you'll be busy launching that new career.'

'I'm more worried about the other career.'

'Which one?'

'Being the kind of husband you think I'll be. I wonder if I'll be really good for you.'

'Bumper!' she said, stepping back and looking to see if I meant it, and I tried a lopsided grin.

I kissed her then, as tenderly as I could, and held her. 'I didn't mean it the way it came out.'

'I know. I'm just a very insecure old dame.'

I could've kicked my ass for blurting out something that I knew would hurt her. It was like I wanted to hurt her a little for being the best thing that ever happened, for saving me from becoming a pitiful old man trying to do a young man's work, and doing brass balls police work was definitely a young man's work. I never could've been an inside man. Never a jailer, or a desk officer, or a supply man handing out weapons to guys doing the real police work. Cassie was saving me from that nightmare. I was getting out while I was still a man alive, with lots of good years ahead. And with somebody to care about. I got a vicious gas pain just then, and I wished I wasn't standing there with Cassie so I could pop a bubble breaker.

'I guess *I'm* the silly one,' said Cassie.

'If you only knew how bad I want out, Cassie, you'd stop worrying.' I patted her back like I was burping her when really I was wishing I could burp myself. I could feel the bubble getting bigger and floating up in my stomach.

'All right, Bumper Morgan,' she said. 'Now what day are we actually leaving Los Angeles? I mean actually? As man and wife. We've got a million things to do.'

'Wait till tomorrow night, me proud beauty,' I answered. 'Tomorrow night when we have some time to talk and to celebrate. Tomorrow night we make all the plans while having a wonderful dinner somewhere.'

'In my apartment.'

'Okay.'

'With some wonderful champagne.'

'I'll supply it.'

'Police discount?'

'Naturally. My last one.'

'And we celebrate tomorrow being the last day you'll ever have to put on that uniform and risk your neck for a lot of people who don't appreciate it.'

'Last day I risk my neck,' I nodded. 'But I never did risk it for anyone but myself. I had some fun these twenty years, Cassie.'

'I know it.'

'Even though sometimes it's a rotten job I wouldn't wish on anyone, still, I had good times. And any risks were for Bumper Morgan.'

'Yes, love.'

'So get your heart-shaped fanny in gear and get your day's work done. I still got almost two days of police work left to do.' I stepped away from her and picked up my hat and cigar.

'Coming by this afternoon?'

'Tomorrow.'

'Tonight,' she said. 'I'll get away before midnight. Come to my apartment at midnight.'

'Let's get some sleep tonight, baby. Tomorrow's the last day for us both on our jobs. Let's make it a good one.'

'I don't like my job as well since you charged into my life, do you know that?'

'Whadda you mean?'

'The academic life. I was one of the students who never left school. I loved waddling around with a gaggle of egg-heads, and then *you* had to come along, so, so ... I don't know. And now nothing seems the same.'

'Come on down, kid, I like your earthy side better.'

'I want you to come tonight,' she said, looking me dead in the eye.

'I'd rather be with you tonight than with anyone in the world, you know that, but I really ought to go by Abd's Harem and say good-bye to my friends there. And there're a few other places.'

'You mustn't disappoint people,' she smiled.

'You should try not to,' I said, heating up from the way she looked me in the eye just then.

'It's getting tough to make love to you lately.'

'A couple more days.'

'See you tomorrow,' she sighed. 'I think I'll jump you here in my office when I get my hands on you.'

'On duty?' I frowned, and put my hat on, tipping it at a jaunty angle because, let's face it, you feel pretty good when a woman like Cassie's quivering to get you in bed.

'Good-bye, Bumper,' she smiled sadly.

'Later, kid. See you later.'

As soon as I cleared after leaving Cassie I got a radio call.

'One-X-L-Forty-five, One-X-L-Forty-five,' said the female communications operator, 'see the man at the hotel, four-twenty-five South Main, about a possible d.b.'

'One-X-L-Forty-five, roger,' I said, thinking this will be my last dead body call.

An old one-legged guy with all the earmarks or a reformed alky was standing in the doorway of the fleabag hotel.

'You called?' I said, after parking the black-and-white in front and taking the stick from the holder on the door and slipping it through the ring on my belt.

'Yeah. I'm Poochie the elevator boy,' said the old man. 'I think a guy might be dead upstairs.'

'What the hell made you think so?' I said sarcastically, as we started up the stairs and I smelled the d.b. from here. The floorboards were torn up and I could see the ground underneath.

The old guy hopped up the stairs pretty quick on his one crutch without ever stopping to rest. There were about twenty steps up to the second floor where the smell could drop you and would, except that most of the tenants were bums and winos whose senses, all of them, had been killed or numbed. I almost expected the second storey to have a dirt floor, the place was so crummy.

'I ain't seen this guy in number two-twelve for oh, maybe a week,' said Poochie, who had a face like an axe, with a toothless puckered mouth.

'Can't you smell him?'

'No,' he said, looking at me with surprise. 'Can you?'

'Never mind,' I said, turning right in the hallway. 'Don't bother telling me where two-twelve is, I could find it with my eyes closed. Get me some coffee.'

'Cream and sugar?'

'No, I mean dry coffee, right out of the can. And a frying pan.'

'Okay,' he said, without asking dumb questions, conditioned by fifty years of being bossed around by cops. I held a handkerchief over my nose, and opened a window in the hallway which led out on the fire escape in the alley. I stuck my head out but it didn't help, I could still smell him.

After a long two minutes Poochie came hopping back on his crutch with a frying pan and the coffee.

'Hope there's a hot plate in here,' I said, suddenly thinking there might not be, though lots of the transient hotels had them, especially in the rooms used by the semi-permanent boarders.

'He's got one,' nodded Poochie, handing me the passkey. The key turned but the door wouldn't budge.

'I coulda told you it wouldn't open. That's why I called you. Scared old man, Herky is. He keeps a bolt on the door whenever he's inside. I already tried to get in.'

'Move back.'

'Going to break it?'

'Got any other suggestions?' I said, the handkerchief over my face, breathing through my mouth.

'No, I think I can smell him now.'

I booted the door right beside the lock and it crashed open, ripping the jamb loose. One rusty hinge tore free and the door dangled there by the bottom hinge.

'Yeah, he's dead,' said Poochie, looking at Herky who had been dead for maybe five days, swollen and steamy in this unventilated room which not only had a hot plate, but a small gas heater that was raging on an eighty-five degree day.

'Can I look at him?' said Poochie, standing next to the bed, examining

Herky's bloated stomach and rotting face. His eyelids were gone and the eyes stared silver and dull at the elevator boy who grinned toothlessly and clucked at the maggots on Herky's face and swollen sex organs.

I ran across the room and banged on the frame until I got the window open. Flies were crawling all over the glass, leaving wet tracks in the condensation. Then I ran to the hot plate, lit it, and threw the frying pan on the burner. I dumped the whole can of coffee on the frying pan, but the elevator boy was enjoying himself so much he didn't seem to mind my extravagance with his coffee. In a few minutes the coffee was burning, and a pungent smoky odour was filling the room, almost neutralizing the odour of Herky.

'You don't mind if I look at him?' asked Poochie again.

'Knock yourself out, pal,' I answered, going for the door.

'Been dead a while hasn't he?'

'Little while longer and he'd have gone clear through the mattress.'

I walked to the pay phone at the end of hall on the second floor. 'Come with me, pal,' I called, figuring he'd roll old Herky as soon as my back was turned. It's bad enough getting rolled when you're alive.

I put a dime in the pay phone and dialled operator. 'Police department,' I said, then waited for my dime to return as she rang the station. The dime didn't come. I looked hard at Poochie who turned away, very innocently.

'Someone stuffed the goddamn chute,' I said. 'Some asshole's gonna get my dime when he pulls the stuffing out later.'

'Bunch of thieves around here, Officer,' said Poochie, all puckered and a little chalkier than before.

I called the dicks and asked for one to come down and take the death report, then I hung up and lit a cigar, not that I really wanted one, but any smell would do at the moment.

'Is it true they explode like a bomb after a while?'

'What?'

'Stiffs. Like old Herky.

'Damn,' said the elevator boy, grinning big and showing lots of gums, upper and lower. 'Some of these guys like Herky got lots of dough hidden around,' he said, winking at me.

'Yeah, well let's let him keep it. He's had it this long.'

'Oh, I didn't mean we should take it.'

'Course not.'

'It's just that these coroner guys, they get to steal anything they find laying around.'

'How long's old Herky been living here?' I asked, not bothering to find out his whole name. I'd let the detective worry about the report.

'Off and on, over five years I know of. All alone. Never even had no friends. Nobody. Just laid up there in that room sucking up the sneaky pete. Used to drink a gallon a day. I think he lived off his social security.

Pay his rent, eat a little, drink a little. I never could do it myself. That's why I'm elevator boy. Can't make it on that social security.'

'You ever talk to him?'

'Yeah, he never had nothing to say though. No family. Never been married. No relatives to speak of. Really alone, you know? I got me eight kids spread all over this damn country. I can go sponge off one of them ever' once in a while. Never gonna see old Poochie like that.' He winked and tapped his chest with a bony thumb. 'Guys like old Herky, they don't care about nobody and nobody cares about them. They check out of this world grabbing their throat and staring around a lonely hotel room. Those're the guys that swell up and pop all over your walls. Guys like old Herky.' The elevator boy thought about old Herky popping, and he broke out in a snuffling croupy laugh because that was just funny as hell.

I hung around the lobby waiting for the detective to arrive and relieve me of caring for the body. While I was waiting I started examining both sides of the staircase walls. It was the old kind with a scalloped moulding about seven feet up, and at the first landing there were dirty finger streaks below the moulding while the rest of the wall on both sides was uniformly dirty, but unsmudged. I walked to the landing and reached up on the ledge, feeling a toilet-paper-wrapped bundle. I opened it and found a complete outfit: eyedropper, hypodermic needle, a piece of heavy thread, burned spoon, and razor blade.

I broke the eyedropper, bent the needle, and threw the hype kit in the trash can behind the rickety desk in the lobby.

'What's that?' asked the elevator boy.

'A fit.'

'A hype outfit?'

'Yeah.'

'How'd you know it was there?'

'Elementary, my dear Poochie.'

'That's pretty goddamn good.'

The detective came in carrying a clipboard full of death reports. He was one of the newer ones, a young collegiate-looking type. I didn't know him. I talked to him for a few minutes and the elevator boy took him back to the body.

'Never catch old Poochie going it alone,' he called to me with his gums showing. 'Never gonna catch old Poochie busting like a balloon and plastered to your wallpaper.'

'Good for you, Poochie,' I nodded, taking a big breath out on the sidewalk, thinking I could still smell the dead body. I imagined that his odour was clinging to my clothes and I goosed the black-and-white, ripping off some rubber in my hurry to get away from that room.

I drove around for a while and started wondering what I should work on. I thought about the hotel burglar again and wondered if I could find Link

Owens, a good little hotel creeper, who might be able to tell me something about this guy that'd been hitting us so hard. All hotel burglars know each other. Sometimes you see so many of them hanging around the lobbies of the better hotels, it looks like a thieves' convention. Then I got the code-two call to go to the station.

TEN

Code two means hurry up, and whenever policemen get that call to go to the station they start worrying about things. I've had a hundred partners tell me that: 'What did I do wrong? Am I in trouble? Did something happen to the old lady? The kids?' I never had such thoughts, of course. A code-two call to go to the station just meant to me that they had some special shit detail they needed a man for, and mine happened to be the car they picked.

When I got to the watch commander's office, Lieutenant Hilliard was sitting at his desk reading the morning editorials, his millions of wrinkles deeper than usual, looking as mean as he always did when he read the cop-baiting letters to the editor and editorial cartoons which snipe at cops. He never stopped reading them though, and scowling all the way.

'Hi, Bumper,' he said, glancing up. 'One of the vice officers wants you in his office. Something about a bookmaker you turned for them?'

'Oh yeah, one of my snitches gave him some information yesterday. Guess Charlie Bronski needs to talk to me some more.'

'Going to take down a bookie, Bumper?' Hilliard grinned. He was a hell of a copper in his day. He wore seven service stripes on his left forearm, each one signifying five years' service. His thin hands were knobby and covered with bulging blue veins. He had trouble with bone deterioration now, and walked with a cane.

'I'm a patrol officer. Can't be doing vice work. No time.'

'If you've got something going with Bronski, go ahead and work on it. Vice caper or not, it's all police work. Besides, I've never seen many uniformed policemen tear off a bookmaker. That's about the only kind of pinch you've never made for me, Bumper.'

'We'll see what we can do, Lieutenant,' I smiled, and left him there, scowling at the editorials again, an old man that should've pulled the pin years ago. Now he'd been here too long. He couldn't leave or he'd die. And he couldn't do the work anymore, so he just sat and talked police work to other guys like him who believed police work meant throwing lots of bad guys in jail and that all your other duties were just incidental. The young officers were afraid to get close to the watch commander's office when he was in there. I've seen rookies call a sergeant out into the hall to have him approve a report so they wouldn't have to take it to Lieutenant Hilliard. He demanded excellence, especially on reports. Nobody's ever asked that of the young cops who were TV babies, not in all their lives. So he was generally avoided by the men he commanded.

Charlie Bronski was in his office with two other vice officers when I entered.

'What's up, Charlie?' I asked.

'We had some unbelievable luck, Bumper. We ran the phone number and it comes back to an apartment on Hobart near Eighth Street, and Red Scalotta hangs around Eighth Street quite a bit when he's not at his restaurant on Wiltshire. I'm betting that phone number you squeezed out of Zoot goes right into Reba McClain's pad just like I hoped. She always stays by Red, but never *too* close. Red's been married happily for thirty years and has a daughter in Stanford and a son in medical school. Salt of the earth, that asshole is.'

'Gave nine thousand last year to two separate churches in Beverly Hills,' said one of the other vice officers, who looked like a wild young head with his collar-length hair, and beard, and floppy hat with peace and pot buttons all over it. He wore a cruddy denim shirt cut off at the shoulders and looked like a typical Main Street fruit hustler.

'And God returns it a hundredfold,' said the other vice officer, Nick Papalous, a melancholy-looking guy, with small white teeth. Nick had a big Zapata moustache, sideburns, and wore orange-flowered flares. I'd worked with Nick several times before he went to vice. He was a good cop for being so young.

'You seemed pretty hot on taking a book, Bumper, so I thought I'd see if you wanted to go with us. This isn't going to be a back office, but it might lead to one, thanks to your friend Zoot. What do you say, want to come?'

'Do I have to change to civvies?'

'Not if you don't want to. Nick and Fuzzy here are going to take the door down. You and me could stiff in the call from the pay phone at the corner. Your uniform wouldn't get in the way.'

'Okay, let's go,' I said, anxious for a little action, glad I didn't have to take the uniform off. 'Never went on a vice raid before. Do we have to circumcise our watches and all that?'

'I'll do the door,' Nick grinned. 'Fuzzy'll watch out the window and keep an eyeball on you and Bumper down at the pay phone on the corner. When you get the bet stiffed, Fuzz'll see your signal and give me the okay and down goes the door.'

'Kind of tough kicking, ain't it, Nick, in those crêpe soled, sneak-and-peek shoes you guys wear?'

'Damn straight, Bumper,' Nick smiled. 'I could sure use those size-twelve boondockers of yours.'

'Thirteens,' I said.

'Wish I could take down the door,' said Fuzzy. 'Nothing I like better than John Wayne-ing a goddamn door.'

'Tell Bumper why you can't, Fuzzy,' Nick grinned.

'Got a sprained ankle and a pulled hamstring,' said Fuzzy, taking a few limping steps to show me. 'I was off duty for two weeks.'

'Tell Bumper how it happened,' said Nick, still grinning.

'Freakin' fruit,' said Fuzzy, pulling off the wide-brimmed hat and throwing back his long blond hair. 'We got a vice complaint about this fruit down at the main library, hangs around out back and really comes on strong with every young guy he sees.'

'Fat mother,' said Charlie. 'Almost as heavy as you, Bumper. And strong.'

'Damn!' said Fuzzy, shaking his head, looking serious even though Nick was still grinning. 'You shoulda seeen the arms on that animal! Anyway, I get picked to operate him, naturally.'

"Cause you're so pretty, Fuzzy,' said Charlie.

'Yeah, anyway, I go out there, about two in the afternoon, and hang around a little bit, and sure enough, there he is standing by that scrub oak tree and I don't know which one's the freakin' tree for a couple minutes, he's so wide. And I swear I never saw a hornier fruit in my life 'cause I just walked up and said, "Hi". That's all, I swear.'

'Come on, Fuzzy, you winked at him,' said Charlie, winking at me.

'You asshole,' said Fuzzy. 'I swear I just said, "Hi, Brucie," or something like that, and this mother grabbed me. Grabbed me! In a bear hug! He pinned my arms! I was shocked, I tell you! Then he starts bouncing me up and down against his fat belly, saying, "You're so cute. You're so cute. You're so cute."'

Then Fuzzy stood up and started bouncing up and down with his arms against his sides and his head bobbing. 'Like this I was,' said Fuzzy. 'Like a goddamn rag doll bouncing, and I said, "Y-y-y-you're u-u-u-under a-a-a-arrest," and he stopped loving me and said, "What?" and I said, "YOU'RE UNDER ARREST, YOU FAT ZOMBIE!" And he threw me. Threw me! And I rolled down the hill and crashed into the concrete steps. And you know what happens then? My partner here lets him get away. He claims he couldn't catch the asshole and the guy couldn't run no faster than a pregnant alligator. My brave partner!'

'Fuzzy really wants that guy bad,' Charlie grinned. 'I tried to catch him, honest, Fuzzy.' Then to me, 'I think Fuzzy fell in love. He wanted that fat boy's phone number.'

'Yuk!' said Fuzzy, getting a chill as he thought about it. 'We got a warrant for that prick for battery on a police officer. Wait'll I get him. I'll get that prick in a choke hold and lobotomize him!'

'By the way, what's the signal you use for crashing in the pad?' I asked.

'We always give it this,' said Charlie, pumping his closed fist up and down.

'Double time,' I smiled. 'Hey, that takes me back to my old infantry days.' I felt good now, getting to do something a little different. Maybe I should've tried working vice, I thought, but no, I've had lots more action and lots more variety on my beat. That's where it's at. That's where it's really at.

'Reba must have some fine, fine pussy,' said Fuzzy, puffing on a slim cigar and cocking his head at Charlie. I could tell by the smell it was a ten- or fifteen-center. I'd quit smoking first, I thought.

'She's been with Red a few years now,' said Nick to Fuzzy. 'Wait'll you meet her. Those mug shots don't do her justice. Good-looking snake.'

'You cold-blooded vice cops don't care how good-looking a broad is,' I said, needling Charlie. 'All a broad is to you is a booking number. I'll bet when some fine-looking whore thinking you're a trick lays down and spreads her legs, you just drop that cold badge right on top of her.'

'Right on her bare tummy,' said Nick. 'But I'll bet Reba has more than a nice tight pussy. A guy like Scalotta could have a million broads. She must give extra good head or something.'

'That's what I need, a little skull,' said Fuzzy, leaning back in a swivel chair, his soft-soled shoes propped up on a desk. He was a pink-faced kid above the beard, not a day over twenty-four, I'd guess.

'A *little* skull'd be the first you ever had, Fuzzy,' said Nick.

'Ha!' said Fuzzy, the cigar clenched in his teeth. 'I used to have this Chinese girlfriend that was a go-go dancer....'

'Come on, Fuzzy,' said Charlie, 'let's not start those lies about all the puss you got when you worked Hollywood. Fuzzy's laid every toadie on Sunset Boulevard three times.'

'I can tell you yellow is mellow,' Fuzzy leered. 'This chick wouldn't ball nobody but me. She used to wet her pants playing with the hair on my chest.' Fuzzy stood up then, and flexed his biceps.

Nick, always a man of few words, said, 'Siddown, fruit-bait.'

'Anyway, Reba ain't just a good head job,' said Charlie. 'That's not why Scalotta keeps her. He's a leather freak and likes to savage a broad. Dresses her up in animal skins and whales the shit out of her.'

'I never really believed those rumours,' said Nick.

'No shit?' said Fuzzy, really interested now.

'We had a snitch tell us about it one time,' said Charlie. 'The snitch said Red Scalotta digs dykes and whips and Reba's his favourite. The snitch told us it's the only way Red can get it up any more.'

'He *is* an old guy,' said Fuzzy seriously. 'At least fifty, I think.'

'Reba's a stone psycho, I tell you,' said Charlie. 'Remember when we busted her, Nick? How she kept talking all the way to jail about the bull daggers and how they'd chase her around the goddamn jail cell before she could get bailed out.'

'That broad got dealt a bum hand,' said Nick.

'Ain't got a full deck even now,' Charlie agreed.

'She's scared of butches and yet she puts on dyke shows for Red Scalotta?' said Fuzzy, his bearded baby face split by a grin as he pictured it.

'Let's get it over with,' said Charlie. 'Then we can spend the rest of the day shooting pool in a nice cool beer bar, listening to Fuzzy's stories about all those Hollywood groupies.'

Nick and Fuzzy took one vice car and I rode with Charlie in another one. It's always possible there could be more than one in the pad, and they wanted room for prisoners.

'Groovy machine, Charlie,' I said, looking over the vice car which was new and air-conditioned. It was gold with mags, a stick, and slicks on the back. The police radio was concealed inside the glove compartment.

'It's not bad,' said Charlie, 'especially the air conditioning. Ever see air conditioning in a police car, Bumper?'

'Not the ones I drive, Charlie,' I said, firing up a cigar and Charlie tore through the gears to show me the car had some life to it.

'Vice is lots of fun, Bumper, but you know, some of the best times were when I walked with you on your beat.'

'How long'd you work with me, Charlie, coupla months?'

'About three months. Remember, we got that burglar that night? The guy that read the obituaries?'

'Oh, yeah,' I said, not remembering that it was Charlie who'd been with me. When they have you breaking in rookies, they all kind of merge in your memory, and you don't remember them very well as individuals.

'Remember? We were shaking this guy just outside the Indian beer bar near Third, and you noticed the obituary column folded up in his shirt pocket? Then you told me about how some burglars read the obituaries and then burgle the pads of the dead people after the funeral when chances are there's nobody going to be there for a while.'

'I remember,' I said, blowing a cloud of smoke at the windshield, thinking how the widow or widower usually stays with a relative for a while. Rotten M.O., I can't stand grave robbing. Seems like your victim ought to have some kind of chance.

'We got a commendation for that pinch, Bumper.'

'We did? I can't remember.'

'Of course I got one only because I was with you. That guy burgled ten or fifteen pads like that. Remember? I was so green I couldn't understand why he carried a pair of socks in his back pocket and I asked you if many of these transient types carried a change of socks with them. Then you showed me the stretch marks in the socks from his fingers and explained how they wear them for gloves so's not to leave prints. You never put me down even when I asked something that dumb.'

'I always liked guys to ask questions,' I said, beginning to wish Charlie'd shut up.

'Hey, Charlie,' I said, to change the subject, 'if we take a good phone spot today, what're the chances it could lead to something big?'

'You mean like a back office?'

'Yeah.'

'Almost no chance at all. How come you're so damned anxious to take a back?'

'I don't know. I'm leaving the job soon and I never really took a big crook like Red Scalotta. I'd just like to nail one.'

'Christ, I never took anyone as big as Scalotta either. And what do you mean, you're leaving? Pulling the pin?'

'One of these days.'

'I just can't picture you retiring.'

'*You're* leaving after twenty years, aren't you?'

'Yeah, but not *you*.'

'Let's forget about it,' I said, and Charlie looked at me for a minute then opened the glove compartment and turned to frequency six for two-way communication with the others.

'One-Victor-One to One-Victor-Two,' said Charlie.

'One-Victor-Two, go,' said Nick.

'One-Victor-One, I think it's best to park behind on the next street east, that's Harvard,' said Charlie. 'If anybody happens to be looking they wouldn't see you go in through the parking area in the rear.'

'Okay, Charlie,' said Nick, and in a few minutes we were there. Eighth Street is all commercial buildings with several bars and restaurants, and the residential north-south streets are lined with apartment buildings. We gave them a chance to get to the walkway on the second floor of the apartment house, and Charlie drove about two hundred feet south of Eighth on Harvard. We walked one block to the public telephone on the southwest corner at Hobart. After a couple of minutes, Fuzzy leaned over a wrought iron railing on the second floor and waved.

'Let's get it on, Bumper,' said Charlie, dropping in a dime. Charlie hung up after a second. 'Busy.'

'Zoot give you the code and all that?'

'Twenty-eight for Dandelion is the code,' Charlie nodded. 'This is a relay phone spot. If it was a relay call-back we might have some problems.'

'What's the difference?' I asked, standing behind the phone booth so someone looking out of the apartment wouldn't see the bluesuit.

'A call-back is where the bettor or the handbook like Zoot calls the relay, that's like I'm going to do now. Then every fifteen minutes or so the back office calls the relay and gets the bettor's number and calls the bettor himself. I think we'd have a poor chance with that kind of setup because back office clerks are sharper than some dummy sitting on the hot seat at a phone spot. Last time we took Reba McClain it was a regular relay spot where the bettor calls her and she writes the bets on a Formica board and then the back office calls every so often and she reads off the bets and wipes the Formica clean. It's better for us that way because we always try to get some physical evidence if we can move quick enough.'

'The Formica?'

'Yeah,' Charlie nodded. 'Some guys kick in the door and throw something at the guy on the hot seat to distract him so he can't wipe the bets off. I've seen cops throw a tennis ball in the guy's face.'

'Why not a baseball?'

'That's not a bad idea. You'd make a good vice cop, Bumper.'

'Either way the person at the phone spot doesn't know the phone number or address of the back office?' I asked.

'Hell no. That's why I was telling you the chances are nil.'

Charlie dropped the dime in again and again hung it up.

'Must be doing a good business,' I said.

'Red Scalotta's relay spots always do real good,' said Charlie. 'I know personally of two Superior Court judges that bet with him.'

'Probably some cops too,' I said.

'Righteous,' he nodded. 'Everybody's got vices.'

'Whadda you call that gimmick where the phone goes to another pad?'

'A tap out,' said Charlie. 'Sometimes you bust in an empty room and see nothing but a phone jack and a wire running out a window, and by the time you trace the wire down to the right apartment, the guy in the relay spot's long gone. Usually with a tap out, there's some kind of alarm hooked up so he knows when you crash in the decoy pad. Then there's a toggle relay, where a call can be laid off to another phone line. Like for instance the back office clerk dials the relay spot where the toggle switch is and he doesn't hang up. Then the bettor calls the relay and the back can take the action himself. All these gimmicks have disadvantages though. One of the main ones is that bettors don't like call-back setups. Most bettors are working stiffs and maybe on their coffee breaks they have only a few minutes to get in to their bookie, and they don't have ten or fifteen minutes to kill waiting for call-backs and all that crap. The regular relay spot with some guy or maybe some housewife earning a little extra bread by sitting on the hot seat is still the most convenient way for the book to operate.'

'You get many broads at these phone spots?'

'We sure do. We get them in fronts and backs. That is, we get them in the relay phone spots as well as back offices. We hear Red Scalotta's organization pays a front clerk a hundred fifty a week and a back clerk three hundred a week. That's a good wage for a woman, considering it's tax free. A front clerk might have to go to jail once in a while but it ain't no big thing to her. The organization bails them out and pays all legal fees. Then they go right back to work. Hardly any judge is going to send someone to county jail for bookmaking, especially if she's female. And they'll never send anyone to state prison. I know a guy in the south end of town with over eighty bookmaking arrests. He's still in business.'

'Sounds like a good business.'

'It's a joke, Bumper. I don't know why I stay at it, I mean trying to nail them. We hear Red Scalotta's back offices gross from one to two million a year. And he probably has at least three backs going. That's a lot of bread even though he only nets eleven to sixteen per cent of that. And when we take down these agents and convict them, they get a two-hundred-and-fifty-dollar fine. It's a sick joke.'

'You ever get Red Scalotta himself?'

'Never. Red'll stay away from the back offices. He's got someone who takes care of everything. Once in a while we can take a front and on rare occasions a back and that's about all we have hope for. Well, let's try to duke our bet in again.'

Charlie dropped in his dime and dialled the number. Then he looked excited and I knew someone answered.

'Hello,' said Charlie, 'this is twenty-eight for Dandelion. Give me number four in the second, five across. Give me a two-dollar, four-horse round robin in the second. The number two horse to the number four in the third to the number six in the fourth to number seven in the fifth.'

Then Charlie stiffed in a few more bets for races at the local track, Hollywood Park, which is understood, unless you specify an Eastern track. Midway through the conversation, Charlie leaned out the phone booth and pumped his fist at Fuzzy, who disappeared inside the apartment building. Charlie motioned to me and I took off my hat and squeezed into the hot phone booth with him. He grinned and held the phone away from his ear, near mine.

I heard the crash over the phone, and the terrified woman scream and a second later Nick's voice came over the line and said, 'Hello, sweetheart, would you care for a round robin or a three-horse parley today?'

Charlie chuckled and hung up the phone and we hopped back in the vice car and drove to the apartment house, parking in front.

When we got to the second floor, Fuzzy was smooth talking an irate landlady who was complaining about the fractured door which Nick was propping shut for privacy. A good-looking dark-haired girl was sitting on the couch inside the apartment crying her eyes out.

'Hi, Reba,' Charlie grinned as we walked in and looked around.

'Hello, Mister Bronski,' she wailed, drenching the second of two handkerchiefs she held in her hands.

'The judge warned you last time, Reba,' said Charlie. 'This'll make your third consecutive bookmaking case. He told you you'd get those six months he suspended. You might even get a consecutive sentence on top of it.'

'Please, Mister Bronski,' she wailed, throwing herself face down on the couch and sobbing so hard the whole couch shook.

She was wearing a very smart jersey blouse and skirt, and a matching blue scarf was tied around her black hair. Her fair legs had a very light spattering of freckles on them. She was a fine-looking girl, very Irish.

Charlie took me in the frilly sweet-smelling bedroom where the phone was. Reba had smeared half the bets off a twelve-by-eighteen chalkboard, but the other bets were untouched. A wet cloth was on the floor where the board was dropped along with the phone.

'I'll bet she wet her pants again this time,' said Charlie, still grinning as he examined the numbers and x's on the chalkboard which told the track, race, handicap position and how much to win, place or show. The bettor's identification was written beside the bets. I noticed that K.L. placed one hell of a lot of bets, probably just before Charlie called.

'We're going to squeeze the shit out of her,' Charlie whispered. 'You think Zoot was shaky, wait'll you hear this broad. A real ding-a-ling.'

'Go ahead,' Nick was saying to someone on the phone when we came back into the living room. Fuzzy was nodding politely to the landlady and locking her out by closing the broken door and putting a chair in front of it.

'Right. Got it,' said Nick, hanging up. A minute later the phone rang again.

'Hello,' said Nick. 'Right. Go ahead.' Every few seconds he mumbled, 'Yeah,' as he wrote down bets. 'Got it.' He hung up.

'Nick's taking some bets mainly just to fuck up Scalotta,' Charlie explained to me. 'Some of these guys might hit, or they might hear Reba got knocked over, and then they'll claim they placed their bet and there'll be no way to prove they didn't, so the book'll have to pay off or lose the customers. That's where we get most of our tips, from disgruntled bettors. It isn't too often a handbook like Zoot Lafferty comes dancing in, anxious to turn his bread and butter.'

'Mister Bronski, can I talk to you?' Reba sobbed, as Nick and then Fuzzy answered the phone and took the bets.

'Let's go in the other room,' said Charlie, and we followed Reba back into the bedroom where she sat down on the soft, king-sized bed and wiped away the wet mascara.

'I got no time for bullshit, Reba,' said Charlie. 'You're in no position to make deals. We got you by the curlies.'

'I know, Mister Bronski,' she said, taking deep breaths. 'I ain't gonna bullshit you. I wanna work with you. I swear I'll do anything. But please don't let me get this third case. That Judge Bowers is a bastard. He told me if I violated my probation, he'd put me in. Please, Mister Bronski, you don't know what it's like there. I couldn't do six months. I couldn't even do six days. I'd kill myself.'

'You want to work for me? What could you do?'

'Anything. I know a phone number. Two numbers. You could take two other places just like this one. I'll give you the numbers.'

'How do you know them?'

'I ain't dumb, Mister Bronski. I listen and I learn things. When they're drunk or high they talk to me, just like all men.'

'You mean Red Scalotta and his friends?'

'Please, Mister Bronski, I'll give you the numbers, but you can't take me to jail.'

'That's not good enough, Reba,' said Charlie, sitting down in a violet-coloured satin chair next to a messy dressing table. He lit a cigarette as Reba glanced from Charlie to me, her forehead wrinkled, chewing her lip. 'That's not near good enough,' said Charlie.

'Whadda you want, Mister Bronski? I'll do anything you say.'

'I want the back,' said Charlie easily.

'What?'

'I want one of Red's back offices. That's all. Keep your phone spots. If we take too much right away it'll burn you and I want you to keep working for Red. But I want his back office. I think you can help me.'

'Oh God, Mister Bronski. Oh Mother of God, I don't know about things like that, I swear. How would I know? I'm just answering phones here. How would I know?'

'You're Red's girlfriend.'

'Red has other girlfriends!'

'You're his *special* girlfriend. And you're smart. You listen.'

'I don't know things like that, Mister Bronski. I swear to God and His Mother. I'd tell you if I knew.'

'Have a cigarette,' said Charlie, and pushed one into Reba's trembling hand. I lit it for her and she glanced up like a trapped little rabbit, choked on the smoke, then took a deep breath, and inhaled down the right pipe. Charlie let her smoke for a few seconds. He had her ready to break, which is what you want, and you shouldn't wait, but she was obviously a ding-a-ling and you had to improvise when your subject is batty. He was letting her unwind, letting her get back a little confidence. Just for a minute.

'You wouldn't protect Red Scalotta if it meant your ass going to jail, would you, Reba?'

'Hell no, Mister Bronski, I wouldn't protect my mother if it meant that.'

'Remember when I busted you before? Remember how we talked about those big hairy bull dykes you meet in jail? Remember how scared you were? Did any of them bother you?'

'Yes.'

'Did you sleep in jail?'

'No, they bailed me out.'

'What about after you get your six months, Reba? Then you have to sleep in jail. Did you see any dildoes in jail?'

'What's that?'

'Phony dicks.'

'I hate those things,' she shuddered.

'How would you like to wake up in the middle of the night with two big bull dykes working on you? And what's more, how would you feel if you really started *liking* it? It happens all the time to girls in jail. Pretty soon you're a stone butch, and then you might as well cut off that pretty hair, and strap down those big tits, because you're not a woman anymore. Then you can lay up in those butch pads with a bunch of bull daggers and a pack of smelly house cats and drop pills and shoot junk because you can't stand yourself.'

'Why're you doing this to me, Mister Bronski?' said Reba, starting to sob again. She dropped the cigarette on the carpet and I picked it up and snuffed it. 'Why do men like to hurt? You all hurt!'

'Does Red hurt you?' asked Charlie calmly, sweating a little as he lit another cigarette with the butt of the last one.

'Yes! He hurts!' she yelled, and Fuzzy stuck his head in the door to see what the shouting was about, but Charlie motioned him away while Reba sobbed.

'Does he make you do terrible things?' asked Charlie, and she was too hysterical to see he was talking to her like she was ten years old.

'Yes, the bastard! The freaky bastard. He hurts me! He likes to hurt, that fucking old freak!'

'I'll bet he makes you do things with bull daggers,' said Charlie, glancing at me, and I realized I broke him in right. He wasn't a guy to only stick it in halfway.

'He *makes* me do it, Mister Bronski,' said Reba. 'I don't enjoy it, I swear I don't. I hate to do it with a woman. I wasn't raised like that. It's a terrible sin to do those things.'

'I bet you don't like taking action for him either. You hate sitting on this hot seat answering the phones, don't you?'

'I *do* hate it, Mister Bronski. I *do* hate it. He's so goddamn cheap. He just won't give me money for anything. He makes me always work for it. I have to do those things with them two or three nights a week. And I have to sit here in this goddamn room and answer those goddamn phones and every minute I know some cop might be ready to break down the door and take me to jail. Oh, please help me, Mister Bronski.'

'Stop protecting him then,' said Charlie.

'He'll kill me, Mister Bronski,' said Reba, and her pretty violet eyes were wide and round and her nostrils were flared, and you could smell the fear on her.

'He won't kill you, Reba,' said Charlie soothingly. 'You won't get a jacket. He'll never know you told me. We'll make it look like someone else told.'

'No one else *knows*,' she whispered, and her face was dead white.

'We'll work it out, Reba. Stop worrying, we know how to protect people that help us. We'll make it look like someone else set it up. I promise you, he'll never know you told.'

'Tell me you swear to God you'll protect me.'

'I swear to God I'll protect you.'

'Tell me you swear to God I won't go to jail.'

'We've got to book you, Reba. But you know Red'll bail you out in an hour. When your case comes up I'll personally go to Judge Bowers and you won't go to jail behind that probation violation.'

'Are you a hundred per cent sure?'

'I'm almost a hundred per cent sure, Reba. Look, I'll talk for you myself. Judges are always ready to give people another break, you know that.'

'But that Judge Bowers is a bastard!'

'I'm a hundred per cent sure, Reba. We can fix it.'

'You got another cigarette?'

'Let's talk first. I can't waste any more time.'

'If he finds out, I'm dead. My blood'll be on you.'

'Where's the back?'

'I only know because I heard Red one night. It was after he'd had his dirty fun with me and a girl named Josie that he brought with him. She was as sick and filthy as Red. And he brought another guy with him, a Jew named Aaron something.'

'Bald-headed guy, small, glasses and a grey moustache?'

'Yeah, that's him,' said Reba.

'I know of him,' said Charlie, and now he was squirming around on the velvet chair, because he had the scent, and I was starting to get it too, even though I didn't know who in the hell Aaron was.

'Anyway, this guy Aaron just watched Josie and me for a while and when Red got in bed with us, he told Aaron to go out in the living room and have a drink. Red was high as a kite that night, but at least he wasn't mean. He didn't hurt me. Can I please have that cigarette, Mister Bronski?'

'Here,' said Charlie, and his hand wasn't quite as steady, which is okay, because that showed that good information could still excite him.

'Tastes good,' said Reba, dragging hard on the cigarette. 'Afterwards, Red called a cab for Josie and sent her home, and him and Aaron started talking and I stayed in the bedroom. I was supposed to be asleep, but like I say, I'm not dumb, Mister Bronski, and I always listen and try to learn things.

'Aaron kept talking about the "laundry", and at first I didn't get it even though I knew that Red was getting ready to move one of his back offices. And even though I never saw it, or any other back office, I knew about them from talking to bookie agents and people in the business. Aaron was worrying about the door to the laundry and I figured there was something about the office door being too close to the laundry door, and Aaron tried to argue Red into putting another door in the back near an alley, but Red thought it would be too suspicious.

'That was all I heard, and then one day, when Red was taking me to his club for dinner, he said he had to stop by to pick up some cleaning, and he parks by this place near Sixth and Kenmore, and he goes in a side door and comes out after a few minutes and says his suits weren't ready. Then I noticed the sign on the window. It was a Chinese laundry.' Reba took two huge drags, blowing one through her nose as she drew on the second one.

'You're a smart girl, Reba,' said Charlie.

'I ain't guaranteeing this is the right laundry, Mister Bronski. In fact, I ain't even sure the laundry they were talking about had anything to do with the back office. I just *think* it did.'

'I think you're right,' said Charlie.

'You gotta protect me, Mister Bronski. I got to live with him, and if he knows, I'll die. I'll die in a bad way, a *real* bad way, Mister Bronski. He told me once what he did to a girl that finked on him. It was thirty years ago, and he talked about it like it was yesterday, how she screamed and screamed. It was so awful it made me cry. You got to protect me!'

'I will, Reba. I promise. Do you know the address of the laundry?'

'I know,' she nodded. 'There were some offices or something on the second floor, maybe like some business offices, and there was a third floor but nothing on the windows in the third floor.'

'Good girl, Reba,' Charlie said, taking out his pad and pencil for the first time, now that he didn't have to worry about his writing breaking the flow of the interrogation.

'Charlie, give me your keys,' I said. 'I better get back on patrol.'

'Okay, Bumper, glad you could come.' Charlie flipped me the keys. 'Leave them under the visor. You know where to park?'

'Yeah, I'll see you later.'

'I'll let you know what happens, Bumper.'

'See you, Charlie. So long, kid,' I said to Reba.

'Bye,' she said, wiggling her fingers at me like a little girl.

ELEVEN

It was okay driving back to the Glass House in the vice car because of the air conditioning. Some of the new black-and-whites had it, but I hadn't seen any yet. I turned on the radio and switched to a quiet music station and lit a cigar. I saw the temperature on the sign at a bank and it said eighty-two degrees. It felt hotter than that. It seemed awfully muggy.

After I crossed the Harbour Freeway I passed a large real estate office and smiled as I remembered how I cleaned them out of business machines one time. I had a snitch tell me that someone in the office bought several office machines from some burglar, but the snitch didn't know who bought them or even who the burglar was. I strolled in the office one day during their lunch hour when almost everyone was out and told them I was making security checks for a burglary prevention programme the police department was sponsoring. A cute little office girl with a snappy fanny took me all around the place and I checked their doors and windows and she helped me write down the serial number of every machine in the place so that the police department would have a record if they were ever stolen. Then as soon as I got back to the station, I phoned Sacramento and gave them the numbers and found that thirteen of the nineteen machines had been stolen in various burglaries around the greater Los Angeles area. I went back with the burglary dicks and impounded them along with the office manager. IBM electric typewriters are just about the hottest thing going right now. Most of the machines are sold by the thieves to 'legitimate' business men who, like everyone else, can't pass up a good buy.

It was getting close to lunch time and I parked the vice car at the police building and picked up my black-and-white, trying to decide where to have lunch. Olvera Street was out, because I'd had Mexican food with Cruz and Socorro last night. I thought about Chinatown, but I'd been there Tuesday, and I was just about ready to go to a good hamburger joint I know of when I thought about Odell Bacon. I hadn't had any bar-b-que for a while, so I headed south on Central Avenue to the Newton Street area and the more I thought about some bar-b-que the better it sounded and I started salivating.

I saw a Negro woman get off a bus and walk down a residential block from Central Avenue and I turned on that street for no reason, to get over to Avalon. Then I saw a black guy on the porch of a whitewashed frame house. He was watching the woman and almost got up from where he was sitting until he saw the black-and-white. Then he pretended to be looking at the sky and sat back, a little too cool, and I passed by and made a casual turn at the next block and then stomped down and gave her hell until I got to the first street north. Then I turned east again, south on Central, and finally made the whole block, deciding to come up the same street again. It was an old scam around here for purse snatchers to find a house where no one was home and sit on the stoop of the house near a bus stop, like they lived at the pad, and when a broad walked by, to run out, grab the purse, and then cut through the yard to the next street where a car would be stashed. Most black women around here don't carry purses. They carry their money in their bras out of necessity, so you don't see that scam used too much anymore, but I would've bet this guy was using it now. And this woman had a big brown leather purse. You just don't get suspicious of a guy when he approaches you from the porch of a house in your own neighbourhood.

I saw the woman in mid-block and I saw the guy walking behind her pretty fast, I got overanxious and pushed a little too hard on the accelerator, instead of gliding along the kerb, and the guy turned around, saw me, and cut to his right through some houses. I knew there'd be no sense going after him. He hadn't done anything yet, and besides, he'd lay up in some backyard like these guys always do and I'd never find him. I just went on to Odell Bacon's Bar-b-que, and when I passed the woman I glanced over and smiled, and she smiled back at me, a pleasant-looking old ewe. There were white sheep and black sheep and there were wild dogs and a few Pretty Good Shepherds. There'd be one sheep herder less after tomorrow, I thought.

I could smell the smoky meat a hundred yards away.

They cooked it in three huge old-fashioned brick ovens. Odell and his brother Nate were both behind the counter when I walked in. They wore sparkling white cook's uniforms and hats and aprons even though they served the counter and watched the register and didn't have to do the cooking anymore. The place hadn't started to fill up for lunch yet. Only a few white people ate there, because they're afraid to come down here into what is considered the ghetto, and right now there were only a couple customers in the place and I was the only paddy. Everyone in South LA knew about Bacon's Bar-b-que though. It was the best soul food and bar-b-que restaurant in town.

'Hey Bumper,' said Nate, spotting me first. 'What's happenin', man?' He was the younger, about forty, coffee brown. He had well-muscled arms from working construction for years before he came in as Odell's partner.

'Nothing to it, Nate,' I grinned. 'Hi, Odell.'

'Aw right, Bumper,' said Odell, and smiled big. He was a round-faced fat man. 'I'm aw right. Where you been? Ain't seen you lately.'

'Slowing down,' I said. 'Don't get around much these days.'

'That'll be the day,' Nate laughed. 'When ol' Bumper can't get it on, it ain't worth gittin'.'

'Some gumbo today, Bumper?' asked Odell.

'No, I think I'll have me some ribs,' I said, thinking the gumbo did sound good, but the generous way these guys made it, stuffed full of chicken and crab, it might spoil me for the bar-b-que and my system was braced for the tangy down-home sauce that was their speciality, the like of which I'd never had anywhere else.

'Guess who I saw yestiday, Bumper?' said Odell, as he boxed up some chicken and a hot plate of beef, french fries and okra for a take-out customer.

'Who's that?'

'That ponk you tossed in jail that time, 'member? That guy that went upside ol' Nate's head over a argument about paying his bill, and you was just comin' through the door and you rattled his bones but good. 'Member?'

'Oh yeah, I remember. Sneed was his name. Smelled like dog-shit.'

'That's the one,' Nate nodded. 'Didn't want him as a customer no how. Dirty clothes, dirty body, dirty mouf.'

'Lucky you didn't get gangrene when that prick hit you, Nate,' I said.

'Ponk-ass bastard,' said Nate, remembering the punch that put him out for almost five minutes. 'He come in the other day. I recognized him right off, and I tol' him to git his ass out or I'd call Bumper. He musta' 'membered the name, 'cause he got his ass out wif oney a few cuss words.'

'He remembered me, huh?' I grinned as Odell set down a cold glass of water, and poured me a cup of coffee without asking. They knew of course that I didn't work Newton Street Station and they only bounced for the Newton Street patrol car in the area, but after that Sneed fight, they always fed *me* free too, and in fact, always tried to get me to come more often. But I didn't like to take advantage. Before that, I used to come and pay half price like any uniformed cop would do.

'Here come the noonday rush,' said Nate, and I heard car doors slam and a dozen black people talking and laughing came in and took the large booths in the front. I figured them for teachers. There was a high school and two grade schools close by and the place was pretty full by the time Nate put my plate in front of me. Only it wasn't a plate, it was a platter. It was always the same. I'd ask for ribs, and I'd get ribs, a double portion, and a heap of beef, oozing with bar-b-que sauce, and some delicious fresh bread that was made next door, and an ice-cream scoop of whipped butter. I'd sop the bread in the bar-b-que and either Nate or Odell would ladle fresh hot bar-b-que on the platter all during the meal. With it I had a huge cold mound of delicious slaw, and only a few fries because there wasn't much room for anything else. There just was no fat on Odell's beef. He was too proud to permit it, because he was almost sixty years old and hadn't learned the new ways of cutting corners and chiselling.

After I got over the first joy of remembering exactly how delicious the beef was, one of the waitresses started helping at the counter because Odell and Nate were swamped. She was a buxom girl, maybe thirty-five, a little bronzer than Nate, with a modest natural hairdo, which I like, not a way-out phony Afro. Her waist was very small for her size and the boobs soared out over a flat stomach. She knew I was admiring her and didn't seem to mind, and as always, a good-looking woman close by made the meal perfect.

'Her name's Trudy,' said Odell, winking at me, when the waitress went to the far end of the counter. His wink and grin meant she was fair game and not married or anything. I used to date another of his waitresses once in a while, a plump, dusky girl called Wilma who was a thirty-two-year-old grandmother. She finally left Odell's and got married for the fourth time. I really enjoyed being with her. I taught her the swim and the jerk and the boogaloo when they first came out. I learned them from my Madeleine Carroll girlfriend.

'Thanks, Odell,' I said. 'Maybe next time I come in I'll take a table in her section.'

'Anything funny happen lately, Bumper?' asked Nate after he passed some orders through to the kitchen.

'Not lately.... Let's see, did I ever tell you about the big dude I stopped for busting a stop sign out front of your place?'

'Naw, tell us,' said Odell, stopping with a plate in his hand.

'Well, like I say, this guy blew the stop sign and I chased him and brought him down at Forty-first. He's a giant, six-feet-seven maybe, heavier than me. All muscle. I ran a make on him over the radio while I'm writing a ticket. Turns out there's a traffic warrant for his arrest.'

'Damn,' said Nate, all ears now. 'You had to fight him?'

'When I tell him there's this warrant he says, "Too bad, man. I just ain't going to jail." Just that cool he said it. Then he steps back like he's ready.'

'Guddamn,' said Odell.

'So then it just comes to me, this idea. I walk over to the police car and pick up the radio and say in a loud voice, "One-X-L-Forty-five requesting an ambulance at Forty-first and Avalon." The big dude, he looks around and says, "What's the ambulance for?" I say, "That's for you, asshole, if you don't get in that car."

'So he gets in the car and halfway to jail he starts chuckling, then pretty soon he really busts up. "Man," he says, "you really flimflammed my ass. This is the first time I ever laughed my way to jail."'

'Gud-damn, Bumper,' said Odell. 'You're somethin' else. Gud-damn.' Then they both went off laughing to wait on customers.

I finished the rest of the meat, picked the bones, and sopped up the last of the bread, but I wasn't happy now. In fact, it was depressing there with a crowd of people and the waitresses rushing around and dishes clattering, so I said good-bye to Nate and Odell. Naturally, I couldn't tip them even though they personally served me, so I gave two bucks to Nate and said, 'Give it to Trudy. Tell her it's an advance tip for the good service she's gonna give me next time when I take a table in her section.'

'I'll tell her, Bumper,' Nate grinned as I waved and burped and walked out the door.

As I was trying to read the temperature again over a savings and loan office, the time flashed on the marquee. It was one-thirty, which is the time afternoon court always convenes. It dawned on me that I'd forgotten I had to be at a preliminary hearing this afternoon!

I cursed and stomped on it, heading for the new municipal court annexe on Sunset, near the Old Mission Plaza, and then I slowed down and thought, what the hell, this is the last time I'll ever go to court on duty. I may get called back to testify after I'm retired, but this'll be the last time *on duty* as a working cop, and I'd never been late to court in twenty years. So what the hell, I slowed down and cruised leisurely to the court building.

I passed one of the Indian bars on Main Street, and saw two drunken braves about to duke it out as they headed for the alley in back, pushing and yelling at each other. I knew lots of Payutes and Apaches and others from a dozen Southwest tribes, because so many of them ended up downtown here on my beat. But it was depressing being with them. They were so defeated, those that ended up on Main Street, and I was glad to see them in a fist-fight once in a while. At least that proved they could strike back a little bit, at something, even if it was at another drunken tribal brother. Once they hit my beat they were usually finished, or maybe long before they arrived here. They'd become winos, and many of the women, fat, five-dollar whores. You wanted to pick them up, shake them out, send them somewhere, in some direction, but there didn't seem to be anywhere an Indian wanted to go. They were hopeless, forlorn people. One old beat cop told me they could break your heart if you let them.

I saw a Gypsy family walking to a rusty old Pontiac in a parking lot near Third and Main. The mother was a stooped-over hag, filthy, with dangling earrings, a peasant blouse, and a full red skirt hanging lopsided below her knees. The man walked in front of her. He was four inches shorter and skinny, about my age. A very dark unshaven face turned my way, and I recognized him. He used to hang around downtown and work with a Gypsy dame on pigeon drops and once in a while a Jamaican switch. The broad was probably his old lady, but I couldn't remember the face just now. There were three kids following: a dirty, beautiful teenage girl dressed like her mother, a ragtag little boy of ten or so, and a curly-haired little doll of four who was dressed like mama also.

I wondered what kind of scam they were working on now, and I tried to think of his name and couldn't, and I wondered if he'd remember me. As late as I was for court, I pulled to the kerb.

'Hey, just a minute,' I called.

'What, what, what?' said the man. 'Officer, what's the problem? What's the problem? Gypsy boy. I'm just a Gypsy boy. You know me, don't you, Officer? I talked with you before, ain't I? We was just shopping, Officer. Me and my babies and my babies' mother.'

'Where's your packages?' I asked, and he squinted from the bright sunshine and peered into the car from the passenger side. His family all stood like a row of quail, and watched me.

'We didn't see nothing we liked, Officer. We ain't got much money. Got to shop careful.' He talked with his hands, hips, all his muscles, especially those dozen or so that moved the mobile face, in expressions of hope and despair and honesty. Oh, what honesty.

'What's your name?'

'Marcos. Ben Marcos.'

'Related to George Adams?'

'Sure. He was my cousin, God rest him.'

I laughed out loud then, because every Gypsy I'd ever talked to in twenty years claimed he was cousin to the late Gypsy king.

'I know you, don't I, Officer?' he asked, smiling then, because I had laughed, and I didn't want to leave because I enjoyed hearing the peculiar lilt to the Gypsy speech, and I enjoyed looking at his unwashed children who were exceptionally beautiful, and I wondered for the hundredth time whether a Gypsy could ever be honest after centuries of living under a code which praised deceit and trickery and theft from all but other Gypsies. Then I was sad because I'd always wanted to really know the Gypsies. That would be the hardest friendship I would ever make, but I had it on my list of things to accomplish before I die. I knew a clan leader named Frank Serna, and once I went to his home in Lincoln Heights and ate dinner with a houseful of his relatives, but of course they didn't talk about things they usually talked about, and I could tell by all the nervous jokes that having an outsider and especially a cop in the house was a very strange thing for the clan. Still, Frank asked me back, and when I had time I was going to work on breaking into the inner circle and making them trust me a little because there were Gypsy secrets I wanted to know. But I could never hope to do it without being a cop, because they'd only let me know them if they first thought I could do them some good, because all Gypsies lived in constant running warfare with cops. It was too late now, because I would *not* be a cop, and I would *never* get to learn the Gypsy secrets.

'We can go now, Officer?' said the Gypsy, holding his hands clasped together, in a prayerful gesture. 'It's very hot for my babies' mama here in the sun.'

I looked at the Gypsy woman then, looked at her face and she was *not* a hag, and not as old as I first thought. She stood much taller now and glared at me because her man was licking my boots and I saw that she had once been as pretty as her daughter, and I thought of how I had so often been accused of seeing good things in all women, even ones who were ugly to my partners, and I guessed it was true, that I exaggerated the beauty of all women I knew or ever saw. I wondered about that, and I was wallowing in depression now.

'Please, sir. Can we go now?' he said, the sweat running down the creases in his face, and on his unwashed neck.

'Go your way, Gypsy,' I said, and dug out from the kerb, and in a few minutes I was parked and walking in the court building.

TWELVE

'Been waiting for you, Bumper,' said the robbery detective, a wrinkled old-timer named Miles. He had been a robbery detective even before I came on the job and was one of the last to still wear a wide-brimmed felt hat. They used to be called the 'hat squad', and the wide felt hat was their trademark, but of course in recent years no one in Los Angeles wore hats like that. Miles was a stubborn old bastard though, he still wore his, and a wide-shouldered, too-big suit coat with two six-inch guns, one on each hip, because he was an old robbery detective and the hat squad legend demanded it and other policemen expected it.

'Sorry I'm late, Miles,' I said.

'That's okay, the case just got sent out to Division Forty-two. Can you handle this by yourself? I got another prelim in Forty-three and a couple of rookie arresting officers for witnesses. If I ain't in there to tell this young D.A. how to put on his case, we might lose it.'

'Sure, I'll handle it. Am I the only witness?'

'You and the hotel manager.'

'Got the evidence?'

'Yeah, here it is.' Miles pulled a large manila envelope out of his cheap plastic briefcase and I recognized the evidence tag I had stuck on there months ago when I made the arrest.

'The gun's in there and the two clips.'

'Too bad you couldn't file a robbery.'

'Yeah, well like I explained to you right after that caper, we were lucky to get what we did.'

'You filed an eleven-five-thirty too, didn't you?'

'Oh yeah. Here's the pot, I almost forgot.' Miles reached back in the briefcase and pulled out an analysed-evidence envelope with my seal on it that contained the marijuana with the chemist's written analysis on the package.

'How many jobs you figure this guy for?'

'I think I told you four, didn't I?'

'Yeah.'

'Now we think he done six. Two in Rampart and four here in Central.'

'It's a shame you couldn't make him on at least one robbery.'

'You're telling me. I had him in a regular show-up and I had a few private mug-shot show-ups, and I talked and coaxed and damned near threatened my victims and witnesses and the closest I could ever come was one old broad who said he *looked* like the bandit.'

'Scumbag really did a good job with make-up, huh?'

'Did a hell of a job,' Miles nodded. 'Remember, he was an actor for a while and he did a hell of a good job with paint and putty. But shit, the M.O. was identical, the way he took mom and dad markets. Always asked for a case of some kind of beer they were short of and when they went back for the beer, boom, he pulled the forty-five automatic and took the place down.'

'He ever get violent?'

'Not in the jobs in Central. I found out later he pistol-whipped a guy in one of the Rampart jobs. Some seventy-year-old grocery clerk decided he was Wyatt Earp and tried to go for some fucked-up old thirty-two he had stashed under the counter. Landry really laid him open. Three times across the eyes with the forty-five. He blinded him. Old guy's still in the hospital.'

'His P.O. going to violate him?'

'This asshole has a rabbit's foot. He finished his parole two weeks before you busted him. Ain't that something else? Two weeks!'

'Well, I better get in there,' I said. 'Some of these deputy D.A.'s get panicky when you're not holding their hands. You got a special D.A. for this one?'

'No. It's a dead bang case. You got him cold. Shouldn't be any search and seizure problems at all. And even though we know this guy's a good robber, we ain't got nothing on him today but some low-grade felonies, ex-con with a gun and possession of pot.'

'Can't we send him back to the joint with his record?'

'We're going to try. I'll stop in the courtroom soon as I can. If you finish before me, let me know if you held him to answer.'

'You got doubts I'll hold him?' I grinned, and headed for the courtroom, feeling very strange as I had all day. The last time I wore a bluesuit into a courtroom, I thought.

The courtroom was almost empty. There were only three people in the audience, two older women, probably the kind that come downtown and watch criminal trials for fun, and a youngish guy in a business suit who was obviously a witness and looked disgusted as hell about being here. Since these courtrooms are for preliminary hearings only, there was no jury box, just the judge's bench and witness box, the counsel tables, the clerk's desk, and a small desk near the railing for the bailiff.

At least I'll be through hassling with this legal machinery, I thought, which cops tend to think is designed by a bunch of neurotics because it seems to go a hundred miles past the point where any sane man would've stopped. After a felony complaint is filed, the defendant is arraigned and then has a preliminary hearing which amounts to a trial. This takes the place of a grand jury indictment and it's held to see if there's good enough cause to bind him over to superior court for trial, and then he's arraigned again in superior court, and later has a trial. Except that in between there're a couple of hearings to set aside what you've done already. In capital cases there's a separate trial for guilt and another for penalty, so that's why celebrated California cases drag on for years until they cost so much that everybody gives up or lets the guy cop to a lesser included offence.

We have a very diligent bunch of young public defenders around here who, being on a monthly salary and not having to run from one good paying client to another, will drive you up a wall defending a chickenshit burglary like it was the Sacco-Vanzetti trial. The D.A.'s office has millions of very fine crimes to choose from and won't issue a felony complaint unless they're pretty damned sure they can get a conviction. But then, there aren't that many real felony convictions, because courts and prisons are so overcrowded. A misdemeanour plea is accepted lots of times even from guys with heavyweight priors.

All this would make Los Angeles a frustrating place to be a cop if it weren't for the fact that the West in general is not controlled by the political clubhouse, owing to the fact that our towns are so sprawling and young. This means that in my twenty years I could bust *any* deserving son of a bitch, and I never got bumrapped except once when I booked an obnoxious French diplomat for drunk driving after he badmouthed me. I later denied to my bosses that he told me of his diplomatic immunity.

But in spite of all the bitching by policemen there's one thing you can't deny: it's still the best system going, and even if it's rough on a cop, who the hell would want to walk a beat in Moscow or Madrid, or anywhere in between? We gripe for sympathy but most of us know that a cop's never going to be loved by people in general, and I say if you got to have lots of love, join the fire department.

I started listening a little bit to the preliminary hearing that was going on. The defendant was a tall, nice-looking guy named John Trafford, about twenty-seven years old, and his pretty woman, probably his wife, was in the courtroom. He kept turning and making courageous gestures in her direction which wasn't particularly impressing Judge Martha Redford, a tough, severe-looking old girl who I had always found to be a fair judge, both to the people and to the defence. There was a fag testifying that this clean-cut-looking young chap had picked him up in a gay bar and gone to the fag's pad, where after an undescribed sex act the young defendant, who the fag called Tommy, had damn near cut his head off with a kitchen knife. And then he ransacked the fruit's pad and stole three hundred blood-soaked dollars which were found in his pocket by two uniformed coppers who shagged him downtown at Fifth and Main where he later illegally parked his car.

The defence counsel was badgering the fruit, an effeminate little man about forty years old, who owned a photography studio, and the fruit wasn't without sympathy for the defendant as he glanced nervously at his friend 'Tommy', and I thought this was darkly humorous and typical. Weak people need people so much they'd forgive anything. I didn't think the defence counsel was succeeding too well in trying to minimize the thing as just another fruitroll, since the hospital record showed massive transfusions and a hundred or so sutures needed to close up the neck wounds of the fruit.

The young defendant turned around again and shot a long sad glance at pretty little mama who looked brave, and after Judge Redford held him to answer on the charges of attempted murder and robbery, his lawyer tried to con her into a bail reduction because the guy had never been busted before except once for wife beating.

Judge Redford looked at the defendant then, staring at his handsome face and calm eyes, and I could tell she wasn't listening to the deputy D.A. who was opposing the bail reduction and recounting the savagery of the cutting. She was just looking at the young dude and he was looking at her. His blond hair was neatly trimmed and he wore a subdued pin-striped suit.

Then she denied the motion for bail reduction, leaving the huge bail on this guy and I was sure she saw what I saw in his face. He was one to be reckoned with. You could see the confidence and intelligence in his icy expression. And power. There's real power you can feel when it's in a guy like this and it even gave me a chill. You can call him a psychopath or say that he's evil, but whatever he is, he's the deadly Enemy, and I wondered how many other times his acts ended in blood. Maybe it was him that ripped the black whore they dug out of a garbage pile on Seventh Street last month, I thought.

You've got to respect the power to harm in a guy like him, and you've got to be scared by it. It sure as hell scared Her Honour, and after she refused to lower the bail he smiled a charming boyish smile at her and she turned away. Then he looked at his teary wife again and smiled at her, and then he felt me watching and I caught his eye and felt *myself* smiling, and my look was saying: I know you. I know you very well. He looked at me calmly for a few seconds, then his eyes sort of glazed over and the deputy led him out of court. Now that I knew he hung around downtown, I thought, I'd be watching for that boy on my beat.

The judge left the bench and the deputy D.A., a youngster whose muttonchops and moustache didn't fit, started reading the complaint to get ready for my case.

Timothy Landry, my defendant, was led in by a deputy sheriff. A deputy public defender was handling the case since Landry was not employed, even though Miles figured he'd stolen ten thousand or so.

He was a craggy-looking guy, forty-four years old, with long, dyed black hair that was probably really grey, and a sallow face that on some guys never seems to get rosy again after they do some time in the joint. He had the look of an ex-con all over him. His bit movie parts were mostly westerns, a few years back, right after he got out of Folsom.

'Okay, Officer,' said the young D.A., 'where's the investigator?'

'He's busy in another court. I'm Morgan, the arresting officer. I'm handling the whole thing. Dead bang case. You shouldn't have any problems.'

He probably had only a few months' experience. They stick to these deputy D.A.'s in the preliminary hearings to give them instant courtroom experience handling several cases a day, and I figured this one hadn't been here more than a couple of months. I'd never seen him before and I spent lots of time in court because I made so many felony pinches.

'Where's the other witness?' asked the D.A., and for the first time I looked around the courtroom and spotted Homer Downey, who I'd almost forgotten was subpoenaed in this case. I didn't bother talking with him to make sure he knew what he'd be called on to testify to, because his part in it was so insignificant you almost didn't need him at all, except as probable cause for me going in the hotel room on an arrest warrant.

'Let's see,' muttered the D.A. after he'd talked to Downey for a few minutes. He sat down at the counsel table reading the complaint and running his long fingers through his mop of brown hair. The public defender looked like a well-trimmed ivy-leaguer, and the D.A., who's theoretically the law and order guy, was mod. He even wore round granny glasses.

'Downey's the hotel manager?'

'Right,' I said as the D.A. read my arrest report.

'On January thirty-first, you went to the Orchid Hotel at eight-two-seven East Sixth Street as part of your routine duties?'

'Right. I was making a check of the lobby to roust any winos that might've been hanging around. There were two sleeping it off in the lobby and I woke them up intending to book them when all of a sudden one of them runs up the stairs, and I suddenly felt I had more than a plain drunk so I ordered the other one to stay put and I chased the first one. He turned down the hall to the right on the third floor and I heard a door close and was almost positive he ran into room three-nineteen.'

'Could you say if the man you chased was the defendant?'

'Couldn't say. He was tall and wore dark clothes. That fleabag joint is dark even in the daytime, and he was always one landing ahead of me.'

'So what did you do?'

'I came back down the stairs, and found the first guy gone. I went to the manager, Homer Downey, and asked him who was living in room three-nineteen, and I used the pay telephone in the lobby and ran a warrant check through R and I and came up with a fifty-two dollar traffic warrant for Timothy Landry, eight-twenty-seven East Sixth Street. Then I asked the manager for his key in case Landry wouldn't open up and I went up to three-nineteen to serve the warrant on him.'

'At this time you thought the guy that ran in the room was Landry?'

'Sure,' I said, serious as hell.

I congratulated myself as the D.A. continued going over the complaint because that wasn't a bad story now that I went back over it again. I mean I felt I could've done better, but it wasn't bad. The truth was that a half hour before I went in Landry's room I'd promised Knobby Booker twenty bucks if he turned something good for me, and he told me he tricked with a whore the night before in the Orchid Hotel and that he knew her pretty good and she told him she just laid a guy across the hall and had seen a gun under his pillow while he was pouring her the pork.

With that information I'd gone in the hotel through the empty lobby to the manager's room and looked at his register, after which I'd gotten the passkey and gone straight to Landry's room where I went in and caught him with the gun and the pot. But there was no way I could tell the truth and accomplish two things : protecting Knobby, and convicting a no-good dangerous scumbag that should be back in the joint. I thought my story was very good.

'Okay, so then you knew there was a guy living in the room and he had a traffic warrant out for his arrest, and you had reason to believe he ran from you and was in fact hiding in his room?'

'Correct. So I took the passkey and went to the room and knocked twice and said, "Police officer".'

'You got a response?'

'Just like it says in my arrest report, counsel. A male voice said, "What is it?" and I said, "Police officer, are you Timothy Landry?" He said, "Yeah, what do you want?" and I said, "Open the door, I have a warrant for your arrest."'

'Did you tell him what the warrant was for?'

'Right, I said a traffic warrant.'

'What did he do?'

'Nothing. I heard the window open and knew there was a fire escape on that side of the building, and figuring he was going to escape, I used the passkey and opened the door.'

'Where was he?'

'Sitting on the bed by the window, his hand under the mattress. I could see what appeared to be a blue steel gun barrel protruding a half inch from the mattress near his hand, and I drew my gun and made him stand up where I could see from the doorway that it *was* a gun. I handcuffed the defendant and at this time informed him he was under arrest. Then in plain view on the dresser I saw the waxed-paper sandwich bag with the pot in it. A few minutes later, Homer Downey came up the stairs, and joined me in the defendant's room and that was it.'

'Beautiful probable cause,' the D.A. smiled. 'And real lucky police work.'

'Real luck,' I nodded seriously. 'Fifty per cent of good police work is just that, good luck.'

'We shouldn't have a damn bit of trouble with Chimel or any other search and seizure cases. The contraband narcotics was in plain view, the gun was in plain view, and you got in the room legally attempting to serve a warrant. You announced your presence and demanded admittance. No problem with eighty-forty-four of the penal code.'

'Right.'

'You only entered when you felt the man whom you held a warrant for was escaping?'

'I didn't hold the warrant,' I reminded him. 'I only knew about the existence of the warrant.'

'Same thing. Afterwards, this guy jumped bail and was rearrested recently?'

'Right.'

'Dead bang case.'

'Right.'

After the public defender was finished talking with Landry he surprised me by going to the rear of the courtroom and reading my arrest report and talking with Homer Downey, a twitchy little chipmunk who'd been manager of the Orchid for quite a few years. I'd spoken to Homer on maybe a half-dozen occasions, usually like in this case, to look at the register or to get the passkey.

After what seemed like an unreasonably long time, I leaned over to the D.A. sitting next to me at the counsel table. 'Hey, I thought Homer was the people's witness. He's grinning at the P.D. like he's a witness for the defence.'

'Don't worry about it,' said the D.A. 'Let him have his fun. That public defender's been doing this job for exactly two months. He's an eager beaver.'

'How long you been doing it?'

'Four months,' said the D.A., stroking his moustache, and we both laughed.

The P.D. came back to the counsel table and sat with Landry, who was dressed in an open-throat, big-collared brown silk shirt, and tight chocolate pants. Then I saw an old skunk come in the courtroom. She had hair dyed like his, and baggy pantyhose and a short skirt that looked ridiculous on a woman her age, and I would've bet she was one of his girlfriends, maybe even the one he jumped bail on, who was ready to forgive. I was sure she was his baby when he turned around and her painted old kisser wrinkled in a smile. Landry looked straight ahead, and the bailiff in the court was not as relaxed as he usually was with an in-custody felony prisoner sitting at the counsel table. He too figured Landry for a bad son of a bitch, you could tell.

Landry smoothed his hair back twice and then seldom moved for the rest of the hearing.

Judge Redford took the bench again and we all quieted down and came to order.

'Is your true name Timothy G. Landry?' she asked the defendant, who was standing with the public defender.

'Yes, Your Honour.'

Then she went into the monotonous reading of the rights even though they'd been read to Landry a hundred times by a hundred cops and a dozen other judges, and she explained the legal proceeding to him which *he* could have explained to *her*, and I looked at the clock, and finally, she tucked a wisp of straight grey hair behind her black horn-rimmed glasses and said, 'Proceed.'

She was a judge I always liked. I remembered once in a case where I'd busted three professional auto thieves in a hot Buick, she'd commended me in court. I'd stopped these guys cruising on North Broadway through Chinatown and I knew, *knew* something was wrong with them and something wrong with the car when I noticed the *rear* licence plate was bug-spattered, but the licence, the registration, the guy's driver's licence, everything checked out. But I felt it and I knew. And then I looked at the identification tag, the metal tag on the door post with the spot-welded rivets, and I stuck my fingernail under it and one guy tried to split, and only stopped when I drew the six-inch and aimed at his back and yelled, 'Freeze, asshole, or name your beneficiary.'

Then I found that the tag was not spot-welded on, but was glued, and I pulled it off and later the detectives made the car as a Long Beach stolen. Judge Redford said it was good police work on my part.

The D.A. was ready to call his first witness, who was Homer Downey, and who the D.A. needed to verify the fact that he rented the room to Landry, in case Landry later at trial decided to say he was just spending the day in a friend's pad and didn't know how the gun and pot got in there. But the P.D. said, 'Your Honour, I would move at this time to exclude all witnesses who are not presently being called upon to testify.'

I expected that. P.D.'s always exclude all witnesses. I think it's the policy of their office. Sometimes it works pretty well for them, when witnesses are getting together on a story, but usually it's just a waste of time.

'Your Honour, I have only two witnesses,' said the D.A., standing up. 'Mr. Homer Downey and Officer Morgan the arresting officer, who is acting as my investigating officer. I would request that he be permitted to remain in the courtroom.'

'The investigating officer will be permitted to remain, Mr. Jeffries,' she said to the public defender. 'That doesn't leave anyone we can exclude, does it?'

Jeffries, the public defender, blushed because he hadn't enough savvy to look over the reports to see how many witnesses there were, and the D.A. and I smiled, and the D.A. was getting ready to call old Homer when the P.D. said, 'Your Honour, I ask that if the arresting officer is acting as the district attorney's investigating officer in this case, that he be instructed to testify first, even if it's out of order, and that the other witness be excluded.'

The D.A. with his two months' extra courtroom experience chuckled out loud at that one. 'I have no objection, Your Honour,' he said.

'Let's get on with it, then,' said the judge, who was getting impatient, and I thought maybe the air-conditioner wasn't working right because it was getting close in there.

She said, 'Will the district attorney please have his other witness rise?'

After Downey was excluded and told to wait in the hall the D.A. finally said, 'People call Officer Morgan,' and I walked to the witness stand and the court clerk, a very pleasant woman about the judge's age, said, 'Do you solemnly swear in the case now pending before this court to tell the truth, the whole truth, and nothing but the truth, so help you God?'

And I looked at her with my professional witness face and said, 'Yes, I do.'

That was something I'd never completely understood. In cases where I wasn't forced to embellish, I always said, 'I do,' and in cases where I was fabricating most of the probable cause, I always made it more emphatic and said, '*Yes*, I do.' I couldn't really explain that. It wasn't that I felt guilty when I fabricated, because I didn't feel guilty, because if I hadn't fabricated, many many times, there were people who would have been victimized and suffered because I wouldn't have sent half the guys to the joint that I sent over the years. Like they say, most of the testimony by all witnesses in a criminal case is just lyin' and denyin'. In fact, everyone expects the *defence* witnesses to 'testilie' and would be surprised if they didn't.

'Take the stand and state your name, please,' said the clerk.

'William A. Morgan, M-O-R-G-A-N.'

'What is your occupation and assignment?' asked the D.A.

'I'm a police officer for the City of Los Angeles assigned to Central Division.'

'Were you so employed on January thirty-first of this year?'

'Yes, sir.'

'On that day did you have occasion to go to the address of eight-twenty-seven East Sixth Street?'

'Yes, sir.'

'At about what time of the day or night was that?'

'About one-fifteen p.m.'

'Will you explain your purpose for being at that location?'

'I was checking for drunks who often loiter and sleep in the lobby of the Orchid Hotel, and do damage to the furniture in the lobby.'

'I see. Is this lobby open to the public?'

'Yes, it is.'

'Had you made drunk arrests there in the past?'

'Yes, I had. Although, usually, I just sent the drunks on their way, my purpose being mainly to protect the premises from damage.'

'I see,' said the D.A., and my baby blues were getting wider and rounder and I was polishing my halo. I worked hard on courtroom demeanour, and when I was a young cop, I used to practise in front of a mirror. I had been told lots of times that jurors had told deputy D.A.'s that the reason they convicted a defendant was that Officer Morgan was so sincere and honest-looking.

Then I explained how I chased the guy up the stairs and saw him run in room three-nineteen, and how naturally I was suspicious then, and I told how Homer showed me the register and I read Timothy Landry's name. I phoned R and I and gave them Landry's name and discovered there was a traffic warrant out for his arrest, and I believed he was the man who had run in three-nineteen. I wasn't worried about what Homer would say, because I *did* go to his door to get the passkey of course, and I *did* ask to see the register, and as far as Homer knew about the rest of it, it was the gospel.

When I got to the part about me knocking on the door and Landry answering and telling me he was Timothy Landry, I was afraid Landry was going to fly right out of his chair. That was his first indication I was embellishing the story a bit, and the part about the window opening could have been true, but the bastard snorted so loud when I said the gun was sticking out from under the mattress, that the P.D. had to poke him in the ribs and the judge shot him a sharp look.

I was sweating a little at that point because I was pissed off that a recent case made illegal the search of the premises pursuant to an arrest. Before this, I could've almost told the whole truth, because I would've been entitled to search the whole goddamn room which only made good sense. Who in the hell would waste four hours getting a search warrant when you didn't have anything definite to begin with, and couldn't get one issued in the first place?

So I told them how the green leafy substance resembling marijuana was in plain view on the dresser, and Landry rolled his eyes up and smacked his lips in disgust because I got the pot out of a shoe box stashed in the closet. The P.D. didn't bother taking me on *voir dire* for my opinion that the green leafy substance was pot, because I guessed he figured I'd made a thousand narcotics arrests, which I had.

In fact, the P.D. was so nice to me I should've been warned. The D.A. introduced the gun and the pot and the P.D. stipulated to the chemical analysis of the marijuana, and the D.A. introduced the gun as people's exhibit number one and the pot as people's number two. The P.D. never objected to anything on direct examination and my halo grew and grew until I must've looked like a bluesuited monk, with my bald spot and all. The P.D. never opened his mouth until the judge said, 'Cross,' and nodded towards him.

'Just a few questions, Officer Morgan,' he smiled. He looked about twenty-five years old. He had a very friendly smile.

'Do you recall the name on the hotel register?'

'Objection, Your Honour,' said the D.A. 'What name, what are we ...'

The judge waved the D.A. down, not bothering to sustain the objection as the P.D. said, 'I'll rephrase the question, Your Honour. Officer, when you chased this man up the stairs and then returned to the manager's apartment did you look at the name on the register or did you ask Mr. Downey who lived there?'

'I asked for the register.'

'Did you read the name?'

'Yes, sir.'

'What was the name?'

'As I've testified, sir, it was the defendant's name, Timothy G. Landry.'

'Did you then ask Mr. Downey the name of the man in three-nineteen?'

'I don't remember if I did or not. Probably not, since I read the name for myself.'

'What was the warrant for, Officer? What violation?'

'It was a vehicle code violation, counsel. Twenty-one four-fifty-three-A, and failure to appear on that traffic violation.'

'And it had his address on it?'

'Yes, sir.'

'Did you make mention of the warrant number and the issuing court and the total bail and so forth on your police report?'

'Yes, sir, it's there in the report,' I said, leaning forward just a little, just a hint. Leaning was a sincere gesture, I always felt.

Actually it was two hours after I arrested Landry that I discovered the traffic warrant. In fact, it was when I was getting ready to compose a plausible arrest report, and the discovery of a traffic warrant made me come up with this story.

'So you called into the office and found out that Timothy G. Landry of that address had a traffic warrant out for his arrest?'

'Yes, sir.'

'Did you use Mr. Downey's phone?'

'No, sir, I used the pay phone in the hall.'

'Why didn't you use Mr. Downey's phone? You could've saved a dime.' The P.D. smiled again.

'If you dial operator and ask for the police you get your dime back anyway, counsel. I didn't want to bother Mr. Downey further, so I went out in the hall and used the pay phone.'

'I see. Then you went back upstairs with the key Mr. Downey gave you?'

'Yes, sir.'

'You knocked and announced yourself and made sure the voice inside was Timothy Landry, for whom you had knowledge that a warrant existed?'

'Yes, sir. The male voice said he was Timothy Landry. Or rather he said yes when I asked if he was Timothy Landry.' I turned just a little towards the judge, nodding my head ever so slightly when I said this. Landry again rolled his eyeballs and slumped down in his seat at that one.

'Then when you heard the window opening and feared your traffic warrant suspect might escape down the fire escape, you forced entry?'

'I used the passkey.'

'Yes, and you saw Mr. Landry on the edge of the bed as though getting ready to go out the window?'

'Yes, that's right.'

'And you saw a metal object protruding from under the mattress?'

'I saw a blue metal object that I was sure was a gun barrel, counsel,' I corrected him, gently.

'And you glanced to your right and there in plain view was the object marked people's two, the sandwich bag containing several grams of marijuana?'

'Yes, sir.'

'I have no further questions of this witness,' said the P.D., and now I was starting to worry a little, because he just went over everything as though he were the D.A. on direct examination. He just made our case stronger by giving me a chance to tell it again.

What the hell? I thought, as the judge said, 'You may step down.'

I sat back at the counsel table and the D.A. shrugged at my questioning look.

'Call your next witness,' said the judge, taking a sip of water, as the bailiff got Homer Downey from the hall. Homer slouched up to the stand, so skinny the crotch of his pants was around his knees. He wore a dirty white shirt for the occasion and a frayed necktie and the dandruff all over his thin brown hair was even visible from the counsel table. His complexion was as yellow and bumpy as cheese pizza.

He gave his name, the address of the Orchid Hotel, and said he had been managing the place for three years. Then the D.A. asked him if I contacted him on the day of the arrest and looked at his register and borrowed his passkey, and if some ten minutes later did he come to the defendant's room and see me with the defendant under arrest, and how long had the defendant lived there, and did he rent the room to the defendant and only the defendant, and did all the events testified to occur in the city and county of Los Angeles, and Homer was a fairly good talker and a good witness, also very sincere, and was finished in a few minutes.

When direct examination was finished the public defender stood up and started pacing like in the Perry Mason shows and the judge said, 'Sit down, counsel,' and he apologized and sat down like in a real courtroom, where witnesses are only approached by lawyers when permission is given by the judge and where theatrical stuff is out of the question.

'Mister Downey, when Officer Morgan came to your door on the day in question, you've testified that he asked to see your register, is that right?'

'Yes.'

'Did he ask you who lived in three-nineteen?'

'Nope, just asked to see the register.'

'Do you remember whose name appeared on the register?'

'Sure. His.' Downey pointed at Landry, who stared back at him.

'By him, do you mean the defendant in this case? The man on my right?'

'Yes.'

'And what's his name?'

'Timothy C. Landowne.'

'Would you repeat that name, please, and spell it?'

My heart started beating hard then, and the sweat broke out and I said to myself, 'Oh no, oh no!'

'Timothy C. Landowne. T-I-M ...'

'Spell the last name please,' the P.D. smiled and I got sick.

'Landowne. L-A-N-D-O-W-N-E.'

'And the middle initial was C as in Charlie?'

'Yes, sir.'

'Are you sure?'

'Sure I'm sure. He's been staying at the hotel for four, five months now. And he even stayed a couple months last year.'

'Did you ever see the name Timothy G. Landry on any hotel records? That's L-A-N-D-R-Y?'

'No.'

'Did you ever see the name anywhere?'

'No.'

I could feel the D.A. next to me stiffen as he finally started to catch on.

'Did you at any time tell Officer Morgan that the man in three-nineteen was named Timothy G. Landry?'

'No, because that's not his name as far as I know, and I never heard that name before today.'

'Thank you, Mister Downey,' said the public defender, and I could feel Landry, grinning with his big shark teeth, and I was trying hard to come up with a story to get out of this. I knew at that moment, and admitted to myself finally and forever, that I should've been wearing my glasses years before this, and could no longer do police work or anything else without them, and if I hadn't been so stupid and had my glasses on, I would've seen that the name on that register was a half-assed attempt at an alias on the part of Landry, and even though the traffic warrant was as good as gold and really belonged to him, I couldn't possibly have got the right information from R and I by giving the computer the wrong name. And the judge would be sure of that in a minute because the judge would have the defendant's make sheet. And even as I was thinking it she looked at me and whispered to the court clerk who handed her a copy of the make sheet and nowhere in his record did it show he used an alias of Landowne. So I was trapped, and then Homer nailed the coffin tight.

'What did the officer do after you gave him the key?'

'He went out the door and up the stairs.'

'How do you know he went up the stairs?'

'The door was open just a crack. I put my slippers on in a hurry because I wanted to go up there too so's not to miss the action. I thought something might happen, you know, an arrest and all.'

'You remember my talking to you just before this hearing and asking you a few questions, Mister Downey?'

'Yes, sir.'

'Do you remember my asking you about the officer using the pay phone in the lobby to call the police station?'

'Yes, sir,' he said, and I had a foul taste in my mouth and I was full of gas and had branding iron indigestion pains and no pills for them.

'Do you remember what you said about the phone?'

'Yes, sir, that it didn't work. It'd been out of order for a week and I'd called the phone company, and in fact I was mad because I thought maybe they came the night before when I was out because they promised to come, and I tried it that morning just before the officer came and it was still broke. Buzzed real crazy when you dropped a dime in.'

'Did you drop a dime in that morning?'

'Yes, sir. I tried to use it to call the phone company and it didn't matter if I dialled or not, it made noises so I used my own phone.'

'You could *not* call on that phone?'

'Oh no, sir.'

'I suppose the phone company would have a record of your request and when they finally fixed the phone?'

'Objection, Your Honour,' said the D.A. weakly. 'Calls for a conclusion.'

'Sustained,' said the judge, looking only at me now, and I looked at Homer just for something to do with my eyes.

'Did you go upstairs behind the officer?' asked the P.D. again, and now the D.A. had slumped in his chair and was tapping with a pencil, and I'd passed the point of nervous breathing and sweat. Now I was cold and thinking, thinking about how to get out of this and what I would say if they recalled me to the stand, if either of them recalled me, and I thought the defence might call me because I was *their* witness now, they owned me.

'I went upstairs a little bit after the officer.'

'What did you see when you got up there?'

'The officer was standing outside Mister Lansdowne's room and like listening at the door. He had his hat in his hand and his ear was pressed up to the door.'

'Did he appear to see you, or rather, to look in your direction?'

'No, he had his back to my end of the hall and I decided to peek from around the corner, because I didn't know what he was up to and maybe there'd be a big shoot-out or something, and I could run back down the stairs if something dangerous happened.'

'Did you hear him knock on the door?'

'No, he didn't knock.'

'Objection,' said the D.A. 'The witness was asked ...'

'All right,' said the judge, holding her hand up again as the D.A. sat back down.

'Did you ever *hear* the officer knock?' the judge asked the witness.

'No, sir,' said Homer to the judge, and I heard a few snickers from the rear of the court, and I thanked the gods that there were only a few spectators and none of them were cops.

'Did the officer say anything while you were there observing?' asked the P.D.

'Nothing.'

'How long did you watch him?'

'Two, three minutes, maybe longer. He knelt down and tried to peek in the keyhole, but I had them all plugged two years ago because of hotel creepers and peeping toms.'

'Did you ... strike that, did the officer say anything that you could hear while you were climbing the stairway?'

'I never heard him say nothing,' said Homer, looking bewildered as hell, and noticing from my face that something was sure as hell wrong and I was very unhappy.

'Then what did he do?'

'Used the key. Opened the door.'

'In what way? Quickly?'

'I would say careful. He like turned the key slow and careful, and then he pulled out his pistol and then he seemed to get the bolt turned, and he kicked open the door and jumped in the room with the gun out front.'

'Could you hear any conversation then?'

'Oh yeah,' he giggled, through gapped, brown-stained teeth. 'The officer yelled something to Mister Landowne.'

'What did he say? His *exact* words if you remember.'

'He said, "Freeze asshole, you move and you're wallpaper".'

I heard all three spectators laugh at that one, but the judge didn't think it was funny and neither did the D.A., who looked almost as sick as I figured I looked.

'Did you go in the room?'

'Yes, sir, for a second.'

'Did you see anything unusual about the room?'

'No. The officer told me to get out and go back to my room so I did.'

'Did you notice if anything was on the dresser?'

'I didn't notice.'

'Did you hear any other conversation between the officer and the defendant?'

'No.'

'Nothing at all?'

'The officer warned him about something.'

'What did he say?'

'It was about Mister Landowne not trying anything funny, something like that. I was walking out.'

'What did he say?'

'Well, it's something else not exactly decent.'

'We're grown up. What did he say?'

'He said, "You get out of that chair and I'll shove this gun so far up your ass there'll be shit on the grips". That's what he said. I'm sorry.' Homer turned red and giggled nervously and shrugged at me.

'The defendant was sitting in a chair?'

'Yes.'

'Was it his own gun the officer was talking about?'

'Objection,' said the D.A.

'I'll rephrase that,' said the P.D. 'Was the officer holding his own gun in his hand at that time?'

'Yes, sir.'

'Did you see the other gun at that time?'

'No, I never saw no other gun.'

The P.D. hesitated for a long, deadly silent minute and chewed on the tip of his pencil, and I almost sighed out loud when he said, 'I have no further questions,' even though it was much too late to feel relieved.

'I have a question,' said Judge Redford, and she pushed her glasses up over a hump on her thin nose and said, 'Mister Downey, did you happen to go into the lobby any time that morning *before* the officer arrived?'

'No.'

'You never went out or looked out into the lobby area?'

'Well, only when the officer drove up in front. I saw the police car parked in front, and I was curious and I started out the door and then I saw the officer climbing the front steps of the hotel and I went back inside to put a shirt and shoes on so's to look presentable in case he needed some help from me.'

'Did you look into the lobby?'

'Well, yes, it's right in front of my door, ma'am.'

'Who was in the lobby?'

'Why, nobody.'

'Could you see the entire lobby? All the chairs? Everywhere in the lobby area?'

'Why sure. My front door opens right on the lobby and it's not very big.'

'Think carefully. Did you see two men sleeping anywhere near the lobby area?'

'There was nobody there, Judge.'

'And where was the officer when you were looking into the empty lobby?'

'Coming in the front door, ma'am. A couple seconds later he came to my door and asked about the room and looked at the register like I said.'

My brain was burning up now like the rest of me, and I had an idiotic story ready when they recalled me about how I'd come into the lobby once and then got out and come in again when Homer saw me and thought it was the first entry. And I was prepared to swear the phone worked, because what the hell, anything was possible with telephone problems. And even if that bony-assed, dirty little sneak followed me up the stairs, maybe I could convince them I called to Landry *before* Downey got up there, and what the hell, Downey didn't know if the marijuana was on the dresser or in the closet, and I was trying to tell myself everything would be all right so I could keep the big-eyed honest look on my kisser because I needed it now if ever in my life.

I was waiting to be recalled and I was ready even though my right knee trembled and made me mad as hell, and then the judge said to the public defender and the D.A., 'Will counsel please approach the bench?'

Then I knew it was all over and Landry was making noises and I could feel the shark grin as his head was turned towards me. I just stared straight ahead like a zombie and wondered if I'd walk out of this courtroom in handcuffs for perjury, because anyone in the world could see that dumb shit Homer Downey was telling the stone truth and didn't even know what the P.D. was doing to me.

When they came back to the table after talking with the judge, the D.A. smiled woodenly at me and whispered, 'It was the name on the register. When the public defender realized that Homer didn't know Landry's real name, he asked him about the register. It was the register that opened it all up for him. She's going to dismiss the case. I don't know what to advise you, Officer. I've never had anything like this happen before. Maybe I should call my office and ask what to do if ...'

'Would you care to offer a motion to dismiss, Mister Jeffries?' asked the judge to the public defender, who jumped to his feet and did just that, and then she dismissed the case and I hardly heard Landry chuckling all over the place and I knew he was shaking hands with that baby-faced little python that defended him. Then Landry leaned over the public defender and said, 'Thanks, stupid,' to me, but the P.D. told him to cool it. Then the bailiff had his hand on my shoulder and said, 'Judge Redford would like to see you in her chambers,' and I saw the judge had left the bench and I walked like a toy soldier towards the open door. In a few seconds I was standing in the middle of this room, and facing a desk where the judge sat looking towards the wall which was lined with bookcases full of law books. She was taking deep breaths and thinking of what to say.

'Sit down,' she said, finally, and I did. I dropped my hat on the floor and was afraid to stoop down to pick it up I was so dizzy.

'In all my years on the bench I've never had that happen. Not like that. I'd like to know why you did it.'

'I want to tell you the truth,' I said, and my mouth was leathery. I had trouble forming the words. My lips popped from the dryness every time I opened my mouth. I had seen nervous suspects like that thousands of times when I had them good and dirty, and they knew I had them.

'Maybe I should advise you of your constitutional rights before you tell me anything,' said the judge, and she took off her glasses and the bump on her nose was more prominent. She was a homely woman and looked smaller here in her office, but she looked stronger too, and aged.

'The hell with my rights!' I said suddenly. 'I don't give a damn about my rights, I want to tell you the truth.'

'But I intend to have the district attorney's office issue a perjury complaint against you. I'm going to have that hotel register brought in, and the phone company's repairman will be subpoenaed and so will Mister Downey of course, and I think you'll be convicted.'

'Don't you even care about what I've got to say?' I was getting mad now as well as scared, and I could feel the tears coming to my eyes, and I hadn't felt anything like this since I couldn't remember when.

'What can you say? What can anyone say? I'm awfully disappointed. I'm sickened in fact.' She rubbed her eyes at the corners for a second and I was bursting and couldn't hold on.

'*You're* disappointed? *You're* sickened? What the hell do you think I'm feeling at this minute? I feel like you got a blowtorch on the inside of my guts and you won't turn it off and it'll never be turned off, that's what I feel, Your Honour. Now can I tell the God's truth? Will you at least let me tell it?'

'Go ahead,' she said, and lit a cigarette and leaned back in the padded chair and watched me.

'Well, I have this snitch, Your Honour. And I've got to protect my informants, you know that. For his own personal safety, and so he can continue to give me information. And the way things are going in court nowadays with everyone so nervous about the defendant's rights, I'm afraid to even mention confidential informants like I used to, and I'm afraid to try to get a search warrant because the judges are so damn hinky they call damn near every informant a material witness, even when he's not. So in recent years I've started ... exploring ways around.'

'You've started lying.'

'Yes, I've started lying! What the hell, I'd hardly ever convict any of these crooks if I didn't lie at least a little bit. You know what the search and seizure and arrest rules are like nowadays.'

'Go on.'

Then I told her how the arrest went down, exactly how it went down, and how I later got the idea about the traffic warrant when I found out he had one. And when I was finished, she smoked for a good two minutes and didn't say a word. Her cheeks were eroded and looked like they were hacked out of a rocky cliff. She was a strong old woman from another century as she sat there and showed me her profile and finally she said, 'I've seen witnesses lie thousands of times. I guess every defendant lies to a greater or lesser degree and most defence witnesses stretch hell out of the truth, and of course I've seen police officers lie about probable cause. There's the old hackneyed story about feeling what appeared to be an offensive weapon like a knife in the defendant's pocket and reaching inside to retrieve the knife and finding it to be a stick of marijuana. That one's been told so many times by so many cops it makes judges want to vomit. And of course there's the furtive movement like the defendant is shoving something under the seat of the car. That's always good probable cause for a search, and likewise that's overdone. Sure, I've heard officers lie before, but nothing is black and white in this world and there are degrees of truth and untruth, and like many other judges who feel police officers cannot possibly protect the public these days, I've given officers the benefit of the doubt in probable cause situations. I never really believed a Los Angeles policeman would *completely* falsify his entire testimony as you've done today. That's why I feel sickened by it.'

'I didn't falsify it all. He had the gun. It *was* under the mattress. He *had* the marijuana. I just lied about where I found it. Your Honour, he's an active bandit. The robbery dicks figure him for six robberies. He's beaten an old man and blinded him. He's ...'

She held up her hand and said, 'I didn't figure he was using that gun to stir his soup with, Officer Morgan. He has the look of a dangerous man about him.'

'You could see it too!' I said. 'Well ...'

'Nothing,' she interrupted. 'That means nothing. The higher courts have given us difficult law, but by God, it's the law!'

'Your Honour,' I said slowly. And then the tears filled my eyes and there was nothing I could do. 'I'm not afraid of losing my pension. I've done nineteen years and over eleven months and I'm leaving the Department after tomorrow, and officially retiring in a few weeks, but I'm not afraid of losing the money. That's not why I'm asking, why I'm *begging* you to give me a chance. And it's not that I'm afraid to face a perjury charge and go to jail, because you can't be a crybaby in this world. But Judge, there are people, policemen, and other people, people on my beat who think I'm something special. I'm one of the ones they really look up to, you know? I'm not just a character, I'm a hell of a cop!'

'I know you are,' she said. 'I've noticed you in my courtroom many times.'

'You have?' Of course I'd been in her courtroom as a witness before, but I figured all bluecoats looked the same to blackrobes. 'Don't get down on us, Judge Redford. Some coppers don't lie at all, and others only lie a little like you said. Only a few like me would do what I did.'

'Why?'

'Because I care, Your Honour, goddamnit. Other cops put in their nine hours and go home to their families twenty miles from town and that's it, but guys like me, why I got nobody and I want nobody. I do my living on my beat. And I've got things inside me that make me do these things against my better judgment. That proves I'm dumber than the dumbest moron on my beat.'

'You're not dumb. You're a clever witness. A very clever witness.'

'I never lied that much before, Judge. I just thought I could get away with it. I just couldn't read that name right on that hotel register. If I could've read that name right on the register I never would've been able to pull off that traffic warrant story and I wouldn't've tried it. And I probably wouldn't be in this fix, and the reason I couldn't really see that name and only assumed it must've been Landry is because I'm fifty years old and far-sighted, and too stubborn to wear my glasses, and kidding myself that I'm thirty and doing a young man's job when I can't cut it any more. I'm going out though, Judge. This clinches it if I ever had any doubts. Tomorrow's my last day. A knight. Yesterday somebody called me a Blue Knight. Why do people say such things? They make you think you're really something and so you got to win a battle every time out. Why should I care if Landry walks out of here? What's it to *me*? Why do they *call* you a knight?'

She looked at me then and put the cigarette out and I'd never in my life begged anyone for anything, and never licked anyone's boots. I was glad she was a woman because it wasn't quite so bad to be licking a woman's boots, not *quite* so bad, and my stomach wasn't only burning now, it was hurting in spasms, like a big fist was pounding inside in a jerky rhythm. I thought I'd double over from the pain in a few minutes.

'Officer Morgan, you fully agree, don't you, that we can call off the whole damn game and crawl back in primeval muck if the orderers, the enforcers of the law, begin to operate outside it? You understand that there could be no civilization, don't you? You know, don't you, that I as well as many other judges am terribly aware of the overwhelming numbers of criminals on those streets whom you policemen must protect us from? You cannot always do it and there are times when you are handcuffed by court decisions that presume the goodness of people past all logical presumption. But don't you think there are judges, and yes, even defence attorneys, who sympathize with you? Can't you see that you, you policemen of all people, must be more than you are? You must be patient and above all, honest. Can't you see if you go outside the law regardless of how absurd it seems, in the name of enforcing it, that we're all doomed? Can't you see these things?'

'Yes. Yes, I know, but old Knobby Booker doesn't know. And if I had to name him as my snitch he might get a rat jacket and somebody might rip him off. ...' And now my voice was breaking and I could hardly see her because it was all over and I knew I'd be taken out of this courtroom and over to the county jail. 'When you're alone out there on that beat, Your Honour, and everyone knows you're the Man.... The way they look at you ... and how it feels when they say, "You're a champ, Bumper. You're a warlord. You're a Knight, a Blue Knight. ..." And then I could say no more and said no more that day to that woman.

The silence was buzzing in my ears and finally she said, 'Officer Morgan, I'm requesting that the deputy district attorney say nothing of your per-jured testimony in his report to his office. I'm also going to request the public defender, the bailiff, the court reporter and the clerk, not to reveal what happened in there today. I want you to leave now so I can wonder if I've done the right thing. We'll never forget this, but we'll take no further action.'

I couldn't believe it. I sat for a second, paralysed, and then I stood up and wiped my eyes and walked towards the door and stopped and didn't even think to thank her, and looked around, but she was turned in her chair and watching the book stacks again. When I walked through the courtroom, the public defender and the district attorney were talking quietly and both of them glanced at me. I could feel them look at me, but I went straight for the door, holding my stomach, and waiting for the cramps to subside so I could think.

I stepped into the hall and remembered vaguely that the gun and narcot-ics evidence were still in the courtroom, and then thought the hell with it, I had to get out in the car and drive with the breeze in my face before the blood surging through my skull blew the top of my head off.

I went straight for Elysian Park around the back side, got out of the car, filled my pockets with acid eaters from the glove compartment, and climbed the hill behind the reservoir. I could smell eucalyptus, and the dirt was dry and loose under my shoes. The hill was steeper than I thought and I was sweating pretty good after just a few minutes of walking. Then I saw two park peepers. One had binoculars to see the show better. They were watching the road down below where couples sit in their cars at any hour of the day or night under the trees and make love.

'Get outta my park, you barfbags,' I said, and they turned around and saw me standing above them. They both were middle-aged guys. One of them, with fishbelly pale skin, wore orange checkered pants and a yellow turtle-neck and had the binoculars up to his face. When I spoke he dropped them and bolted through the brush. The other guy looked indignant and started walking stiff-legged away like a cocky little terrier, but when I took a few steps towards him, cursing and growling, he started running too, and I picked up the binoculars and threw them at him, but missed and they bounced off a tree and fell in the brush. Then I climbed the hill clear to the top and even though it was smoggy, the view was pretty good. By the time I flopped on the grass and took off my Sam Browne and my hat, the stomach cramps were all but gone. I fell asleep almost right away and slept an hour there on the cool grass.

THIRTEEN

When I woke up, the world tasted horrible and I popped an acid eater just to freshen my mouth. I laid there on my back for a while and looked up at a bluejay scampering around on a branch.

'Did you shit in my mouth?' I said, and then wondered what I'd been dreaming about because I was sweaty even though it was fairly cool here. A breeze blowing over me felt wonderful. I saw by my watch it was after four and I hated to get up but of course I had to. I sat up, tucked in my shirt, strapped on the Sam Browne and combed back my hair which was tough to do, it was so wild and wiry. And I thought, I'll be glad when it all falls out and then I won't have to screw around with it any more. It was hell sometimes when even your hair wouldn't obey you. When you had no control over anything, even your goddamn hair. Maybe I should use hair spray, I thought, like these pretty young cops nowadays. Maybe while I still had some hair I should get those fifteen-dollar haircuts and ride around in a radio car all day, spraying my hair instead of booking these scumbags, and then I could stay out of trouble, then no judge could throw me in jail for perjury, and disgrace me, and ruin everything I've done for twenty years, and ruin everything they all think about me, all of them, the people on the beat.

One more day and it's over, thank Christ, I thought, and half stumbled down the hill to my car because I still wasn't completely awake.

'One-X-L-Forty-five, One-X-L-Forty-five, come in,' said the communications operator, a few seconds after I started the car. She sounded exasperated as hell, so I guess she'd been trying to get me. Probably a major crisis, like a stolen bicycle, I thought.

'One-X-L-Forty-five, go,' I said disgustedly into the mike.

'One-X-L-Forty-five, meet the plain-clothes officer at the southeast corner of Beverly and Vermont in Rampart Division. This call has been approved by your watch commander.'

I rogered the call and wondered what was going on and then despite how rotten I felt, how disgusted with everything and everybody, and mostly this miserable crummy job, despite all that, my heart started beating a little bit harder, and I got a sort of happy feeling bubbling around inside me because I knew it had to be Charlie Bronski. Charlie must have something, and next thing I knew I was driving huckety-buck over Temple, slicing through the heavy traffic and then bombing it down Vermont, and I spotted Charlie in a parking lot near a market. He was standing beside his car looking hot and tired and mad, but I knew he had something or he'd never call me out of my division like this.

'About time, Bumper,' said Charlie. 'I been trying to reach you on the radio for a half-hour. They told me you left court a long time ago.'

'Been out for investigation, Charlie. Too big to talk about.'

'I wonder what *that* means,' Charlie smiled, with his broken-toothed, Slavic, hard-looking grin. 'I got something so good you won't believe it.'

'You busted Red Scalotta!'

'No, no, you're dreaming,' he laughed. 'But I got the search warrant for the back that Reba told us about.'

'How'd you do it so fast?'

'I don't actually have it yet. I'll have it in fifteen minutes when Nick and Fuzzy and the Administrative Vice team get here. Nick just talked to me on the radio. Him and Fuzzy just left the Hall of Justice. They got the warrant and the Ad Vice team is on the way to assist.'

'How the hell did you do it, Charlie?' I asked, and now I'd forgotten the judge, and the humiliation, and the misery, and Charlie and me were grinning at each other because we were both on the scent. And when a real cop gets on it, there's nothing else he can think about. Nothing.

'After we left Reba I couldn't wait to get started on this thing. We went to that laundry over near Sixth and Kenmore. Actually, it's a modern dry cleaning and laundry establishment. They do the work on the premises and it's pretty damned big. The building's on the corner and takes in the whole ground floor, and I even saw employees going up to the second floor where they have storage or something. I watched from across the street with binoculars and Fuzzy prowled around the back alley and found the door Reba said Aaron was talking about.'

'Who in the hell *is* Aaron, Charlie?'

'He's Scalotta's think man. Aaron Fishman. He's an accountant and a shrewd organizer and he's got everything it takes but guts, so he's a number two man to Scalotta. I never saw the guy, I only heard about him from Ad Vice and Intelligence. Soon as Reba described that little Jew I knew who she was talking about. He's Scalotta's link with the back offices. He protects Red's interests and hires the back clerks and keeps things moving. Dick Reemey at Intelligence says he doesn't think Red could operate without Aaron Fishman. Red's drifting away from the business more and more, getting in with the Hollywood crowd. Anyway, Fuzzy, who's a nosy bastard, went in the door to the laundry and found a stairway that was locked, and a door down. He went down and found a basement and an old vented furnace and a trash box, and he started sifting through and found a few adding machine tapes all ending in five's and zero's, and he even found a few charred pieces of owe sheets and a half-burned scratch sheet. I'll bet Aaron would set fire to his clerk if he knew he was that careless.'

Charlie chuckled for a minute and I lit a cigar and looked at my watch.

'Don't worry about the time, Bumper, the back office clerks don't leave until an hour or so past the last post. He's got to stay and figure his tops.'

'Tops?'

'Top sheets. This shows each agent's code and lists his bettors and how much was won and lost.'

'Wonder how Zoot Lafferty did today?' I laughed.

'Handbooks like Zoot get ten per cent hot or cold, win or lose,' said Charlie. 'Anyway, Fuzzy found a little evidence to corroborate Reba, and then came the most unbelievable tremendous piece of luck I ever had in this job. He's crawling around down there in the basement like a rat, picking up burned residue, and next thing he sees is a big ugly guy standing stone still in the dark corner of the basement. Fuzzy almost shit his pants and he didn't have a gun or anything because you don't really need weapons when you're working books. Next thing, this guy comes towards him like the creature from the black lagoon and Fuzzy said the door was behind the guy and just as he's thinking about rushing him with his head down and trying to bowl him over on his ass, the giant starts talking in a little-boy voice and says "Hello, my name is Bobby. Do you know how to fix electric trains?"

'And next thing Fuzzy knows this guy leads him to a little room in the back where there's a bed and a table and Fuzzy has to find a track break in a little electric train set that Bobby's got on his table, and all the time the guy's standing there, his head damn near touching the top of the doorway he's so big, and making sure Fuzzy fixes it.'

'Well, what ...'

'Lemme finish,' Charlie laughed. 'Anyway, Fuzzy gets the train fixed and the big ox starts banging Fuzzy on the back and shoulders out of sheer joy, almost knocking Fuzzy's bridgework loose, and Fuzzy finds out this moron is the cleanup man, evidently some retarded relative of the owner of the building, and he lives there in the basement and does the windows and floors and everything in the place.

'There're some offices on the second floor with a completely different stairway, Fuzzy discovers, and this locked door is the only way up to this part of the third floor except for the fire escape in back and the ladder's up and chained in place. This giant, Bobby, says that the third floor is all storage space for one of the offices on the second floor except for "Miss Terry's place", and then he starts telling Fuzzy how he likes Miss Terry and how she brings him pies and good things to eat every day, so Fuzzy starts pumping him and Bobby tells him how he hardly ever goes in Miss Terry's place, but he washes the windows once in a while and sometimes helps her with something. And with Fuzzy prodding, he tells about the wooden racks where all the little yellow cards are with the numbers. Those're the ABC professional-type markers of course, and he tells about the adding machine, two adding machines, in fact, and when Fuzzy shows him the burned National Daily Reporter, Bobby says, yeah, those are always there. In short, he completely describes an élite bookmaking office right up to the way the papers are bundled and filed.'

'You used this Bobby for your informant on the search warrant affidavit?'

'Yeah. I didn't have to mention anything about Reba. According to the affidavit, we got the warrant solely on the basis of this informant Bobby and our own corroborative findings.'

'You'll have to use the poor guy in court?'

'He'll certainly have to be named,' said Charlie.

'How old a guy is he?'

'I don't know, fifty, fifty-five.'

'Think they'll hurt him?'

'Why should they? He doesn't even know what he's doing. They can see that. They just fucked up, that's all. Why should they hurt a dummy?'

'Because they're slimeballs.'

'Well, you never know,' Charlie shrugged. 'They might. Anyway, we got the warrant, Bumper. By God, I kept my promise to you.'

'Thanks, Charlie. Nobody could've done better. You got anybody staked on the place?'

'Milburn. He works in our office. We'll just end up busting the broad, Terry. According to the dummy she's the only one ever comes in there except once in a while a man comes in, he said. He couldn't remember what the man looked like. This is Thursday. Should be a lot of paper in that back office. If we get enough of the records we can hurt them, Bumper.'

'A two-hundred-and-fifty-dollar fine?' I sniffed.

'If we get the right records we can put Internal Revenue on them. They can tax ten per cent of gross for the year. And they can go back as far as five years. That hurts, Bumper. That hurts even a guy as big as Red Scalotta, but it's tough to pull it off.'

'How're you going in?'

'We first decided to use Bobby. We can use subterfuge to get in if we can convince the court that we have information that this organization will attempt to destroy records. Hell, they all do that. Fuzzy thought about using Bobby to bang on the lower door to the inside stairway and call Terry and have Terry open the door which she can buzz open. We could tell Bobby it's a game or something, but Nick and Milburn voted us down. They thought when we charged through the door and up the steps through the office door and got Terry by the ass, old Bobby might decide to end the game. If he stopped playing I imagine he'd be no more dangerous than a brahma bull. Anyway, Nick and Milburn were afraid we'd have to hurt the dummy so they voted us down.'

'So how'll you do it?'

'We borrowed a black policewoman from Southwest Detectives. We got her in a blue dungaree apron suit like the black babes that work pressing downstairs. She's going to knock on the downstairs door and start yelling something unintelligible in a way-out suede dialect, and hope Terry buzzes her in. Then she's going to walk up the steps and blab something about a fire in the basement and get as close to Terry as she can, and we hope she can get right inside and get her down on the floor and sit on her because me and Nick'll be charging up that door right behind her. The Administrative Vice team'll follow in a few minutes and help us out since they're the experts on a back-office operation. You know, I only took one back office before so this'll be something for me too.'

'Where'll I be?'

'Well, we got to hide you with your bluesuit, naturally, so you can hang around out back, near the alley behind the solid wood fence on the west side. After we take the place I'll open the back window and call you and you can come on in and see the fruits of your labour with Zoot Lafferty.'

'What'll you do about getting by your star witness?'

'The dummy? Oh, Fuzzy got stuck with that job since he's Bobby's best pal,' Charlie chuckled. 'Before any of us even get in position Fuzzy's going in to get Bobby and walk him down the street to the drugstore for an ice cream sundae.'

'One-Victor-One to Two, come in,' said a voice over frequency six.

'That's Milburn at the back office,' said Charlie, hurrying to the radio.

'Go, Lem,' said Charlie over the mike.

'Listen, Charlie,' said Milburn. 'A guy just went in that doorway outside. It's possible he could've turned left into the laundry, I couldn't tell, but I think he made a right to the office stairway.'

'What's he look like, Lem?' asked Charlie.

'Caucasian, fifty-five to sixty, five-six, hundred fifty, bald, moustache, glasses. Dressed good. I think he parked one block north and walked down because I saw a white Cad circle the block twice and there was a bald guy driving and looking around like maybe for heat.'

'Okay, Lem, we'll be there pretty quick,' said Charlie, hanging up the mike, red-faced and nodding at me without saying anything.

'Fishman,' I said.

'Son of a bitch,' said Charlie. 'Son of a bitch. He's there!'

Then Charlie got on the mike and called Nick and the others, having trouble keeping his voice low and modulated in his excitement, and it was affecting me and my heart started beating. Charlie told them to hurry it up and asked their estimated time of arrival.

'Our E.T.A. is five minutes,' said Nick over the radio.

'Jesus, Bumper, we got a chance to take the office and Aaron Fishman at the same time! That weaselly little cocksucker hasn't been busted since the depression days!'

I was still happy as hell for Charlie, but looking at it realistically, what the hell was there to scream about? They had an idiot for an informant, and I didn't want to throw cold water, but I knew damn well the search warrant stood a good chance of being traversed, especially if Bobby was brought into court as a material witness and they saw his I.Q. was less than par golf. And if it wasn't traversed, and they convicted the clerk and Fishman, what the hell would happen to them, a two-hundred-fifty-dollar fine? Fishman probably had four times that much in his pants pocket right now. And I wasn't any too thrilled about I.R.S. pulling off a big case and hitting them in the bankbook, but even if they did, what would it mean? That Scalotta couldn't buy a new whip every time he had parties with sick little girls like Reba? Or maybe Aaron Fishman would have to drive his Cad for two years without getting a new one? I couldn't see anything to get ecstatic about when I considered it all. In fact, I was feeling lower by the minute, and madder. I prayed Red Scalotta would show up there too and maybe try to resist arrest, even though my common sense told me nothing like that would ever happen, but if it did . . .

'There should be something there to destroy the important records,' said Charlie, puffing on a cigarette and dancing around impatiently waiting for Nick and the others to drive up.

'You mean like flash paper? I've heard of that,' I said.

'They sometimes use that, but mostly in fronts,' said Charlie. 'You touch a flame or a cigarette to it and it goes up in one big flash and leaves no residue. They also got this dissolving paper. You drop it in water and it dissolves with no residue you can put under a microscope. But sometimes in backs they have some type of small furnace they keep charged where they can throw the real important stuff. Where the hell is that Nick?'

'Right here, Charlie,' I said, as the vice car sped across the parking lot. Nick and Fuzzy and the Negro policewoman were inside and another car was following with the two guys from Administrative Vice.

Everybody was wetting their pants when they found out Aaron Fishman was in there, and I marvelled at vice officers, how they can get excited about something that is so disappointing, and depressing, and meaningless, when you thought about it. And then Charlie hurriedly explained to the Ad Vice guys what a uniformed cop was doing there, saying it started out as my caper. I knew one of the Ad Vice officers from when he used to work Central Patrol and we jawed and made plans for another five minutes, and finally piled into the cars.

We turned north on Catalina from Sixth Street before getting to Kenmore and then turned west and came down Kenmore from the north. The north side of Sixth Street is all apartment buildings and to the south

is the Miracle Mile, Wilshire Boulevard. Sixth Street itself is mostly commercial buildings. Everybody parked to the north because the windows
were painted on the top floor of the building on this side. It was the blind
side, and after a few minutes everybody got ready when Fuzzy was seen
through binoculars skipping down the sidewalk with Bobby, who even from
this distance looked like Gargantua. With the giant gone the stronghold
wasn't quite so impregnable.

In a few minutes they were all hustling down the sidewalk and I circled
around the block on foot and came in behind the wooden fence and I was
alone and sweating in the sunshine, wondering why the hell I wanted this
so bad, and how the organization would get back on its feet, and another of
Red's back offices would just take as much of the action as it could until a
new back could be set up, and Aaron would get his new Cad in two years.
And he and Red would be free to enjoy it all and maybe someone like me
would be laying up in a county jail for perjury in the special tank where
they keep policemen accused of crimes, because a policeman put in with
the regular pukepots would live probably about one hour at best.

This job didn't make sense. How could I have told myself for twenty
years that it made any sense at all? How could I charge around that beat,
a big blue stupid clown, and pretend that anything made any sense at all?
Judge Redford *should've* put me in jail, I thought. My brain was boiling in
the sunshine, the sweat running in my eyes and burning. That would've
been a consistent kind of lunacy at least. What the hell are we doing here
like this?

Then suddenly I couldn't stand it there alone, my big ass only partly
hidden by the fence, and I walked out in the alley and over to the fire
escape of the old building. The iron ladder was chained up like an ancient
fearsome drawbridge. A breach of fire regulation to chain it up, I thought,
and I looked around for something to stand on, and spotted a trash can by
the fence which I emptied and turned upside down under the ladder. And
then in a minute I was dangling there like a fat sweaty baboon, tearing my
pants on the concrete wall, scuffing my shoes, panting, and finally sobbing,
because I couldn't get my ass up there on a window ledge where I could
then climb over the railing on the second floor.

I fell back once, clear to the alley below. I fell hard on my shoulder,
and thought if I'd been able to read that hotel register I'd never have been
humiliated like that, and I thought of how I was of no value whatever to
this operation which was in itself of no value because if I couldn't catch
Red Scalotta and Aaron Fishman by the rules, then they would put *me* in
jail. And I sat on my ass there in the alley, panting, my hands red and sore
and my shoulder hurting, and I thought then, if I go to the dungeon and
Fishman goes free, then *I'm* the scumbag and *he's* the Blue Knight, and I
wondered how he would look in my uniform.

Then I looked up at that ladder and vowed that I'd die here in this alley if I didn't climb that fire escape. I got back on the trash can and jumped up, grabbing the metal ladder and feeling it drop a little until the chain caught it. Then I shinnied up the wall again, gasping and sobbing out loud, the sweat like vinegar in my eyes, and got one foot up and had to stop and try to breathe in the heat. I almost let go and thought how that would make sense too if I fell head first now on to the garbage can and broke my fat neck. Then I took a huge breath and knew if I didn't make it now I never would make it, and I heaved my carcass up, up, and then I was sitting on the window ledge and surprisingly enough I still had my hat on and I hadn't lost my gun. I was perched there on the ledge in a pile of birdshit, and a fat grey pigeon sat on the fire escape railing over me. He cooed and looked at me gasping and grimacing and wondered if I was dangerous.

'Get outta here, you little prick,' I whispered, when he crapped on my shoulder. I swung my hat at him and he squawked and flew away.

Then I dragged myself up carefully, keeping most of my weight on the window ledge, and I was on the railing and then I climbed over and was on the first landing of the fire escape where I had to rest for a minute because I was dizzy. I looked at my watch and saw that the policewoman should be about ready to try her flimflam now, so, dizzy or not, I climbed the second iron ladder.

It was steep and long to the third floor, one of those almost vertical iron ladders like on a ship, with round iron hand railings. I climbed as quietly as I could, taking long deep breaths. Then I was at the top and was glad I wouldn't have to make the steep descent back down. I should be walking out through the back office if everything went right. When Charlie opened the back door to call to me, I'd be standing right here watching the door instead of crouched in some alley. And if I heard any doors breaking, or any action at all, I'd kick in the back door here, and maybe *I'd* be the first one inside the place, and maybe I'd do something else that could land me in jail, but the way I felt this moment, maybe it would be worth it because twenty years didn't mean a goddam thing when Scalotta and Fishman could wear *my* uniform and I could wear jail denims with striped patch pockets and lay up there in the cop's tank at the county jail.

Then I heard a crash and I knew the scam hadn't worked because this was a door breaking far away, way down below, which meant they'd had to break in that first door, run up those steps clear to the third floor and break in the other door, and then I found myself kicking on the back door which I didn't know was steel reinforced with a heavy bar across it. It wouldn't go, and at that moment I didn't know how sturdy they had made it and I thought it was a regular door and I was almost crying as I kicked it because I couldn't even take down a door anymore and I couldn't do *anything* anymore. But I kicked, and kicked, and finally I went to the window on the left and kicked right through it, cutting my leg. I broke out the glass with my hands and I lost my hat and cut my forehead on the glass and was raging and yelling something I couldn't remember when I stormed through that room and saw the terrified young woman and the trembling bald little man by the doorway, their arms full of boxes. They looked at me for a second and then the woman started screaming and the man went out the door, turned right and headed for the fire escape with me after him. He threw the bar off the steel door and was back out on the fire escape, a big cardboard box in his arms crammed with cards and papers, and he stopped on the landing and saw how steep that ladder was. He was holding tight to the heavy box and he turned his back to the ladder and gripped the box and was going to try to back down the iron stairs when I grabbed him with my bloody hands and he yelled at me as two pigeons flew in our faces with a whirr and rattle of wings.

'Let me go!' he said, the little greenish sacs under his eyes bulging. 'You ape, let me go!'

And then I don't know if I just let him go or if I put pressure against him. I honestly don't know, but it doesn't really make any difference, because pulling away from me like he was, and holding that box like Midas's gold, I knew exactly what would happen if I just suddenly did what he was asking.

So I don't know for sure if I shoved him or if I just released him, but as I said, the result would've been the same, and at this moment in my life it was the only thing that made the slightest bit of sense, the only thing I could do for any of it to make any sense at all. He would never wear my bluesuit, never, if I only did what he was asking. My heart was thumping like the pigeon's wing, and I just let go and dropped my bleeding hands to my sides.

He pitched backward then, and the weight of the box against his chest made him fall head first, clattering down the iron ladder like an anchor being dropped. He was screaming and the box had broken open and markers and papers were flying and sailing and tumbling through the air. It *did* sound like an anchor chain feeding out, the way he clattered down. On the landing below where he stopped, I saw his dentures on the first rung of the ladder not broken, and his glasses on the landing, broken, and the cardboard box on top of him so you could hardly see the little man doubled over beneath it. He was quiet for a second and then started whimpering, and finally sounded like a pigeon cooing.

'What happened, Bumper?' asked Charlie, running out on the fire escape, out of breath.

'Did you get all the right records, Charlie?'

'Oh my God, what happened?'

'He fell.'

'Is he dead?'

'I don't think so, Charlie. He's making a lot of noises.'

'I better call for an ambulance,' said Charlie. 'You better stay here.'

'I intend to,' I said, and stood there resting against the railing for five minutes watching Fishman. During that time, Nick and Charlie went down and unfolded him and mopped at his face and bald head, which was broken with huge lacerations.

Charlie and me left the others there and drove slowly in the wake of the screaming ambulance which was taking Fishman to Central Receiving Hospital.

'How bad is your leg cut?' asked Charlie, seeing the blood, a purple wine colour when it soaks through a policeman's blue uniform.

'Not bad, Charlie,' I said, dabbing at the cuts on my hands.

'Your face doesn't look bad. Little cut over your eye.'

'I feel fine.'

'There was a room across from the back office,' said Charlie. 'We found a gas-fed burn oven in there. It was fired up and vented through the roof. They would've got to it if you hadn't crashed through the window. I'm thankful you did it, Bumper. You saved everything for us.'

'Glad I could help.'

'Did Fishman try to fight you or anything?'

'He struggled a little. He just fell.'

'I hope the little asshole dies. I'm thinking what he means to the organization and what he is, and I hope the little asshole dies, so help me God. You know, I thought you pushed him for a minute. I thought you did it and I was glad.'

'He just fell, Charlie.'

'Here we are, let's get you cleaned up,' said Charlie, parking on the Sixth Street side of Central Receiving where a doctor was going into the ambulance that carried Fishman. The doctor came out in a few seconds and waved them on to General Hospital where there are better surgical facilities.

'How's he look, doctor?' asked Charlie, as we walked through the emergency entrance.

'Not good,' said the doctor.

'Think he'll die?' asked Charlie.

'I don't know. If he doesn't, he may wish he had.'

The cut on my leg took a few stitches but the ones on my hands and face weren't bad and just took cleaning and a little germ killer. It was almost seven o'clock when I finished my reports telling how Fishman jerked out of my grasp and how I got cut.

When I left, Charlie was dictating his arrest report to a typist.

'Well, I'll be going now, Charlie,' I said, and he stopped his dictation and stood up and walked behind me a little way down the hall and looked for a second like he was going to shake hands with me.

'Thanks, Bumper, for everything. This is the best vice pinch I've ever been in on. We got more of their records than I could've dreamed of.'

'Thanks for cutting me in on it, Charlie.'

'It was *your* caper.'

'Wonder how Fishman's doing?' I said, getting a sharp pain and feeling a bubble forming. I popped two tablets.

'Fuzzy called out there about a half hour ago. Couldn't find out much. I'll tell you one thing, I'll bet Red Scalotta has to get a new accountant and business adviser. I'll bet Fishman'll have trouble adding two-digit numbers after this.'

'Well, maybe it worked out right.'

'Right? It was more than that. For the first time in years I feel like maybe there *is* some justice in the world, and even though they fuck over you and rub it in your face and fuck over the law itself, well, now for the first time I feel like maybe there's other hands in it, and these hands'll give you some justice. I feel like the hand of God pushed the man down those stairs.'

'The hand of God, huh? Yeah, well I'll be seeing you, Charlie. Hang in there, old shoe.'

'See you, Bumper,' said Charlie Bronski, his square face lit up, eyes crinkled, the broken tooth showing.

The locker room was empty when I got there, and after I sat down on the bench and started unlacing my boon-dockers, I suddenly realized how sore I was. Not the cuts from the glass, that was nothing. But my shoulder where I fell in that alley, and my arms and back from dangling there on that fire escape, when I couldn't do what any young cop could do – pull my ass up six feet in the air. And my hands were blistered and raw from hanging there and from clawing at the concrete wall trying to get that boost. Even my ass was sore, deep inside, the muscles of both cheeks, from kicking against that steel reinforced door and bouncing off it like a tennis ball, or maybe in my case like a lumpy medicine ball. I was very very sore all over.

In fifteen minutes I'd gotten into my sports coat and slacks, and combed my hair as best I could, which just means rearranging what resembles a bad wiring job, and slipped on my loafers, and was driving out of the parking lot in my Ford. The gas pains were gone, and no indigestion. Then I thought of Aaron Fishman again, folded over, his gouged head twisted under the puny little body with the big cardboard box on top. But I stopped that nonsense right there, and said, no, no, you won't haunt my sleep because it doesn't matter a bit that I made you fall. I was just the instrument of some force in this world that, when the time is right, screws over almost every man, good or bad, rich or poor, and usually does it just when the man can bear it least.

FOURTEEN

It was dark now, and the spring night, and the cool breeze, even the smog, all tasted good to me. I rolled the windows down to suck up the air, and jumped on the Hollywood Freeway, thinking how good it would be at Abd's Harem with a bunch of happy Arabs.

Hollywood was going pretty good for a Thursday night, Sunset and Hollywood Boulevards both being jammed with cars, mostly young people, teeny boppers who've literally taken over Hollywood at night. The place has lost the real glamour of the forties and early fifties. It's a kid's town now, and except for a million hippies, fruits and servicemen, that's about all you see around the Strip and the main thoroughfares. It's a very depressing place for that reason. The clubs are mostly bottomless skin houses and psychedelic joints, but there're still some places you can go, some excellent places to eat.

I'd come to know Yasser Hafiz and the others some ten or twelve years ago when I was walking my beat on Main Street. One night at about two a.m., I spotted a paddy hustler taking a guy up the back stairs of the Marlowe Hotel, a sleazy Main Street puke hole used by whores and fruits and paddy hustlers. I was alone because my partner, a piss-poor excuse for a cop named Syd Bacon, was laying up in a hotel room knocking a chunk off some bubble-assed taxi dancer he was going with. He was supposed to meet me back on the beat at one-thirty but never showed up.

I hurried around the front of the hotel that night and went up the other stairway and hid behind the deserted clerk's desk, and when the paddy hustler and his victim came that way down the hall, I jumped inside the small closet at the desk. I was just in time because the paddy hustler's two partners came out of a room two doors down and across the hall.

They were whispering, and one of them faded down the front stairway to watch the street. The second walked behind the desk, turned the lamp on and pretended to be reading a newspaper he carried with him. They were black of course. Paddy hustling was always a Negro flimflam and that's where the name came from, but lately I've seen white hustlers using this scam on other paddies.

'Say, brother,' said the hustler who was with the paddy. I left the door open a crack and saw the paddy was a well-dressed young guy, bombed out of his skull, weaving around where he stood, trying hard to brush his thick black hair out of his eyes. He'd lost his necktie somewhere, and his white dress shirt was stained from booze and unbuttoned.

'Wha's happenin', blood?' said the desk clerk, putting down his paper.

'Alice in tonight?' said the first one, acting as the procurer. He was the bigger of the two, a very dark-skinned guy, tall and fairly young.

'Yeah, she's breathin' fire tonight,' said the other one. He was young too. 'Ain't had no man yet and that bitch is a nymphomaniac!'

'Really,' said the procurer. 'Really.'

'Let's go, I'm ready,' said the paddy, and I noticed his Middle East accent.

'Jist a minute, man,' said his companion. 'That whore is fine pussy, but she is a stone thief, man. You better leave the wallet with the desk clerk.'

'Yeah, I kin put it in the night safe,' said the bored-looking guy behind the desk. 'Never tell when that whore might talk you into a all-night ride and then rob your ass when you falls asleep.'

'Right, brother,' said the procurer.

The paddy shrugged and took out his wallet, putting it on the desk.

'Better leave the wristwatch and ring too,' warned the desk clerk.

'Thank you,' the paddy nodded, obeying the desk clerk, who removed an envelope from under the counter, which he had put there for the valuables.

'Kin I have my five dollars now?' asked the first man. 'And the clerk'll take the five for Alice and three for the room.'

'All right,' said the paddy, unsteadily counting out thirteen dollars for the two men.

'Now you go on in number two-thirty-seven there,' said the desk clerk, pointing to the room where the first one had come out. 'I'll buzz Alice's room and she be in there in 'bout five minutes. And baby, you better hold on 'cause she move like a steam drill.'

The paddy smiled nervously and staggered down the hall, opening the door and disappearing inside.

'Ready, blood?' grinned the desk clerk.

'Le's go,' said the big one, chuckling as the clerk turned off the lamp.

I'd come out of the closet without them seeing, and stood at the desk now, with my Smith pointed at the right eyeball of the desk clerk. 'Want a room for the night, gentlemen?' I said. 'Our accommodations ain't fancy, but it's clean and we can offer two very square meals a day.'

The procurer was the first to recover, and he was trying to decide whether to run or try something more dangerous. Paddy hustlers didn't usually carry guns, but they often carried blades or crude saps of some kind. I aimed at *his* eyeball to quiet down his busy mind. 'Freeze, or name your beneficiary,' I said.

'Hey, Officer, wha's happenin'?' said the desk clerk with a big grin showing lots of gold. 'Where you come from?'

'Down the chimney. Now get your asses over there and spread-eagle on the wall!'

'Sheee-it, this is a humbug, we ain't done nothin',' said the procurer.

'Shit fuck,' grumbled the desk clerk.

This was in the days when we still believed in wall searches, before so damn many policemen got shot or thumped by guys who practised coming out of that spread-eagled position. I abandoned it a few years before the Department did, and I put hot suspects on their knees or bellies. But at this time I was still using the wall search.

'Move your legs back, desk clerk!' I said to the smaller one, who was being cute, barely leaning forward. He only shuffled his feet a few inches so I kicked him hard behind the right knee and he screamed and did what I told him. The scream brought the paddy out.

'Is something wrong?' asked the paddy who was half-undressed, trying to look sober as possible.

'I'm saving you from being flimflammed, asshole,' I said. 'Get your clothes on and come out here.' He just stood there gaping. Then I yelled, 'Get dressed, stupid,' my gun in my left hand still pointing at the spread-eagled paddy hustlers, and my handcuffs in my right hand getting ready to cuff the two hustlers together, and my eyes drilling the dipshit victim who stood there getting ready to ask more dumb questions. I didn't see or hear the third paddy hustler, a big bull of a kid, who'd crept up the front stairway when he heard the ruckus. If he'd been an experienced hustler instead of a youngster he'd have left the other two and gone his way. But being inexperienced, he was loyal to his partners, and just as I was getting ready to kick the paddy in the ass to get him moving, two hundred pounds falls on my back and I'm on the floor fighting for my gun and my life with all three hustlers.

'Git the gun, Tyrone!' yelled the desk clerk to the kid. 'Jist git the *gun!*'

The procurer was cursing and hitting me in the face, head, and neck, anywhere he could, and the desk clerk was working on my ribs while I tried to protect myself with my left arm. All my thoughts were on the right arm, and hand, and the gun in the hand, which the kid was prying on with both his strong hands, For a few seconds everything was quiet, except for the moans and breathing and muffled swearing of the four of us, and then the kid was winning and almost had the gun worked loose when I heard a godawful Arab war cry and the paddy cracked the desk clerk over the head with a heavy metal ashtray.

Then the paddy was swinging it with both hands and I ducked my head, catching a glancing blow on the shoulder that made me yelp and which left a bruise as big as your first. The fourth or fifth swing caught the procurer in the eyes and he was done, laying there holding his bleeding face and yelling, 'YOW, YOW, YOW,' like somebody cut his nuts off.

The kid lost his stomach at this point and said, 'Aw right, aw right, aw right,' raising his hands to surrender and scooting back on his ass with his hands in the air until he backed against the wall.

I was so sick and trembling I could've vomited and I was ready to kill all three of them, except that the desk clerk and the procurer looked half-dead already. The kid was untouched.

'Stand up,' I said to the kid, and when he did, I put my gun in the holster, reached for my beavertail, and sapped him across the left collarbone. That started him yelling and bitching, and he didn't stop until we got him to the hospital, which made me completely disgusted. Up until then I had some respect for him because he was loyal to his friends and had enough guts to jump a cop who had a gun in his hand. But when he couldn't suffer in silence, he lost my respect. I figured this kind of cry-baby'd probably make a complaint against me for police brutality or something, but he never did.

'What can I do, sir?' asked the paddy after I had the three hustlers half-way on their feet. I was trying to stay on mine as I leaned against the desk and covered them with the gun. This time I kept my eyes open.

'Go downstairs and put a dime in the pay phone and dial operator,' I panted, still not sure how sober he was, even though he damn near decapitated all of us. 'Ask for the police and tell them an officer needs assistance at the Marlowe Hotel, Fifth and Main.'

'Marlowe Hotel,' said the paddy. 'Yes, sir.'

I never found out what he said over the phone, but he must've laid it on pretty good because in three minutes I had patrol units, vice cops, felony cars, and even some dicks who rolled from the station. There were more cops than tenants at the Marlowe and the street out front was lined with radio cars, their red lights glowing clear to Sixth Street.

The paddy turned out to be Yasser's oldest son, Abd, the one the Harem was named for, and that was how I got to know them. Abd stayed with me for several hours that night while I made my reports, and he seemed like a pretty good guy after he had a dozen cups of coffee and sobered up. He had a very bad recollection of the whole thing when we went to court against the paddy hustlers, and he ended up testifying to what I told him happened before we went in the courtroom. That part about saving my ass, he never did remember, and when I drove him home to Hollywood after work that night, in gratitude for what he did for me, he took me in the house, woke up his father, mother, uncle, and three of his brothers to introduce me and tell them that I saved him from being robbed and killed by three bandits. Of course he never told them the whole truth about how the thing went down in a whorehouse, but that was okay with me, and since he really thought *I* saved *him* instead of the other way around, and since he really enjoyed having been saved even though it didn't happen, and making me the family hero, what the hell, I let him tell it the way he believed it happened so as not to disappoint them.

It was about that time that Yasser and his clan had moved here from New York where they had a small restaurant. They had pooled every cent they could lay hands on to buy the joint in Hollywood, liquor licence and all, and had it remodelled and ready to open. We sat in Yasser's kitchen that night, all of us, drinking *arak* and wine, and then beer, and I picked out the name for the new restaurant.

It's a corny name, I know, but I was drunk when I picked it and I could've done better. But by then I was such a hero to them they wouldn't have changed it for anything. They insisted on me being a kind of permanent guest of Abd's Harem. I couldn't pay for a thing in there and that's why I didn't come as often as I wanted to.

I drove in the parking lot in back of Abd's Harem instead of having the parking lot attendant handle the Ford, and I came in through the kitchen.

'*Al-sâm 'alaykum, Baba,*' I said to Yasser Hafiz Hammad, a squat, completely bald old man with a heavy grey moustache, who had his back to me as he mixed up a huge metal bowlful of *kibbi* with clean powerful hands which he dipped often in ice water so the *kibbi* wouldn't stick to them.

'Bumper! *Wa-'alaykum al-salãm,*' he grinned through the great moustache. He hugged me with his arms, keeping his hands free, and kissed me on the mouth. That was something I couldn't get over about Arabs. They didn't usually kiss women in greeting, only men.

'Where the hell you keep yourself, Bumper?' he said, dipping a spoon in the raw *kibbi* for me to sample it. 'We don't see you much no more.'

'Delicious, *Baba,*' I said.

'Yes, but is it ber-fect?'

'It's ber-fect, *Bubba.*'

'You hungry, eh, Bumper?' he said, returning to the *kibbi* and making me some little round balls which he knew I'd eat raw. I liked raw *kibbi* every bit as good as baked, and *kibbi* with yogurt even better.

'You making *labaneeyee* tonight, *Baba?*'

'Sure, Bumper. Damn right. What else you want? *Sfeeha? Bamee?* Anything you want. We got lots of dish tonight. Bunch of Lebanese and Syrian guys in the banquet room. Ten entrées they order special. Son of a bitch, I cook all goddamn day. When I get rest, I coming out and have a goddamn glass of *arak* with you, okay?'

'Okay, *Baba,*' I said, finishing the *kibbi* and watching Yasser work. He kneaded the ground lamb and cracked wheat and onion and cinnamon and spices, after dipping his hands in the ice water to keep the mixture pliable. This *kibbi* was well stuffed with pine nuts and the meat was cooked in butter and braised. When Yasser got it all ready he spread the *kibbi* over the bottom of a metal pan and the *kibbi* stuffing over the top of that, and another layer of *kibbi* on top of that. He cut the whole pan into little diamond shapes and then baked it. Now I couldn't decide whether to have the *kibbi* with yogurt or the baked *kibbi*. What the hell, I'll have them both, I thought. I was pretty hungry now.

'Look, Bumper,' said Yasser Hafiz, pointing to the little footballs of *kibbi* he'd been working on all day. He'd pressed hollows into the centre and stuffed them with lamb stuffing and was cooking them in a yogurt sauce.

Yeah, I'll have both, I thought. I decided to go in and start on some appetizers. I was more than hungry all of a sudden and not quite so tired, and all I could think of was the wonderful food of Abd's Harem.

Inside, I spotted Ahmed right away, and he grinned and waved me to a table near the small dance area where one of his dancers could shove her belly in my face. Ahmed was tall for an Arab, about thirty years old, the youngest of Yasser's sons, and had lived in the States since he was a kid. He'd lost a lot of the Arab ways and didn't kiss me like his father and his uncles did, when the uncles were here helping wait tables or cooking on a busy weekend night.

'Glad you could come tonight, Bumper,' said Ahmed with a hint of a New York accent, since his family had lived there several years before coming to Los Angeles. When he talked to the regular customers though, he put on a Middle East accent for show.

'Think I'll have some appetizers, Ahmed. I'm hungry tonight.'

'Good, Bumper, good,' said Ahmed, his dark eyes crinkling at the corners when he grinned. 'We like to see you eat.' He clapped his hands for a good-looking, red-haired waitress in a harem girl's outfit, and she came over to the table..

Abd's Harem was like all Middle East restaurants, but bigger than most. There were Saracen shields on the walls, and scimitars, and imitation Persian tapestries, and the booths and tables were dark and heavy, leather-padded, and studded with hammered bronzework. Soothing Arab music drifted through the place from several hidden speakers.

'Bring Bumper some lamb tongue, Barbara. What else would you like, Bumper?'

'A little *humos tahini*, Ahmed.'

'Right. *Humos* too, Barbara.'

Barbara smiled at me and said, 'A drink, Bumper?'

'All right, I'll have *arak*.'

'If you'll excuse me, Bumper,' said Ahmed, 'I've got to take care of the banquet room for the next hour. Then I'll join you and we'll have a drink together.'

'Go head on, kid,' I nodded. 'Looks like you're gonna have a nice crowd.'

'Business is great, Bumper. Wait'll you see our new belly dancer.'

I nodded and winked as Ahmed hurried towards the banquet room to take care of the roomful of Arabs. I could hear them from where I sat, proposing toasts and laughing. They seemed pretty well lubricated for so early in the evening.

The appetizers were already prepared and the waitress was back to my table in a few minutes with the little slices of lamb's tongue, boiled and peeled and seasoned with garlic and salt, and a good-sized dish of *humos*, which makes the greatest dip in the world. She gave me more *humos* than any of the paying customers get, and a large heap of the round flat pieces of warm Syrian bread covered with a napkin. I dipped into the *humos* right away with a large chunk of the Syrian bread and almost moaned out loud it was so delicious. I could taste the sesame seeds even though they were ground into the creamy blend of garbanzo beans, and I poured olive oil all over it, and dipped lots of oil up in my bread. I could also taste the clove and crushed garlic and almost forgot the lamb tongue I was enjoying the *humos* so much.

'Here's your *arak*, Bumper,' said Barbara, bringing me the drink and another dish of *humos* a little smaller than the first. 'Yasser says not to let you ruin your dinner with the tongue and *humos*.'

'No chance, kid,' I said, after swallowing a huge mouthful of tongue and bread. I gulped some *arak* so I could talk. 'Tell *Baba* I'm as hungry as a tribe of Bedouins and I'll eat out his whole kitchen if he's not careful.'

'And as horny as a herd of goats?'

'Yeah, tell him that too,' I chuckled. That was a standing joke between Yasser and Ahmed and me that all the girls had heard.

Now that the starvation phase was over I started to feel pain in my leg and shoulder. I poured some water into the clear *arak*, turning it milky. I glanced around to make sure no one could see and I loosened up my belt and smiled to myself as I smelled the food all through the place. I nibbled now, and tried not to be such a crude bastard, and I sipped my *arak*, getting three refills from Barbara who was a fast and good waitress. Then the pain started to go away.

I saw Ahmed running between kitchen, bar, and banquet room, and I thought that Yasser was lucky to have such good kids. All his sons had done well, and now the last one was staying in the business with him. The Arab music drifted softly through the place and mingled with the food smell, and I was feeling damn warm now. In about an hour the band would be here, a three-piece Armenian group who played exotic music for the belly dancer that I was anxious to see. Ahmed really knew his dancers.

'Everything okay, Bumper?' Ahmed called in an Arab accent since other customers were around.

'Okay,' I grinned, and he hurried past on one of his trips to the kitchen.

I was starting to sway with the sensual drums and I was feeling much better, admiring the rugs hanging on the walls, and other Arabian Nights decorations like water pipes that kids used now for smoking dope, and the swords up high enough on the walls so some drunk couldn't grab them and start his own dance. Abd's Harem was a very good place, I thought. Really an oasis in the middle of a tacky, noisy part of Hollywood which was generally so phony I couldn't stand it.

I noticed that Khalid, one of Yasser's brothers, was helping in the bar tonight. I figured as soon as he saw me I'd get another big hairy kiss.

'Ready, Bumper?' said Barbara, smiling pretty, and padding quietly up to my table with a huge tray on a food cart.

'Yeah, yeah,' I said, looking at the dishes of baked *kibbi*, *kibbi* with yogurt, stuffed grape leaves and a small skewer of shish kebab.

'Yasser said to leave room for dessert, Bumper,' said Barbara as she left me there. I could think of nothing at times like these, except the table in front of me, and I waged a tough fight against myself to eat slowly and savour it, especially the grape leaves which were a surprise for me, because Yasser doesn't make them all the time. I could taste the mint, fragrant and tangy in the yogurt that I ladled over the grape leaves, pregnant with lamb and rice, succulent parsley, and spices. Yasser added just the right amount of lemon juice for my taste.

After a while, Barbara returned and smiled at me as I sat sipping my wine, at peace with the world.

'Some pastry, Bumper? *Baklawa?*'

'Oh no, Barbara,' I said, holding my hand up weakly. 'Too rich. No *baklawa*, no.'

'All right,' she laughed. 'Yasser has something special for you. Did you save a little room?'

'Oh no,' I said painfully, as she took away the cartload of empty plates.

Arabs are so friendly and hospitable, and they like so much to see me eat, I would've hated to do something horrible like up-chucking all his hard work. My belly was bulging so much I had to move the chair back two inches, and my shirt was straining to pop open. I thought of Fatstuff in the old 'Smilin' Jack' cartoon strip and remembered how I used to laugh at the poor bastard always popping his buttons, when I was young and slim.

A few minutes later Barbara came back with an oversized sherbet glass.

'*Moosh moosh!*' I said. 'I haven't had *moosh moosh* for a year.'

Barbara smiled and said, 'Yasser says that Allah sent you tonight because Yasser made your favourite dessert today and thought about you.'

'*Moosh moosh!*' I said as Barbara left me, and I scooped up a mouthful and let it lay there on my tongue, tasting the sweet apricot and lemon rind, and remembering how Yasser's wife, Yasmine, blended the apricot and lemon rind and sugar, and folded the apricot purée into the whipped cream before it was chilled. They all knew it was my very favourite. So I ended up having two more cups of *moosh moosh* and then I was really through. Barbara cleared the table for the last time and Ahmed and Yasser both joined me for ten minutes.

There's an Arab prayer which translates something like, 'Give me a good digestion, Lord, and something to digest'. It was the only prayer I ever heard that I thought made a lot of sense, and I thought that if I believed in God I wouldn't lay around begging from him and mumbling a lot of phony promises. This particular Arab prayer said all I'd say to Him, and all I'd expect of Him, so even though I didn't believe, I said it before and after I ate dinner in Abd's Harem. Sometimes I even said it at other times. Sometimes even at home I said it.

When the Armenians arrived, I was happy to see the *oud* player was old Mr. Kamian. He didn't often play at Abd's Harem any more. His grandsons Berge and George were with him, and anyone could see they were his grandsons, all three being tall, thin, with hawk noses and dark-rimmed blazing eyes. Berge would play the violin and George, the youngest, a boy not yet twenty, would play the *darouka* drums. It was just a job to the two young ones. They were good musicians, but it was old Kamian I would hear as he plucked and stroked those *oud* strings with the quill of an eagle feather. It's a lute-like instrument and has no frets like a guitar. Yet the old man's fingers knew exactly where to dance on that *oud* neck, so fast it was hard to believe. It gave me goose bumps and made it hard to swallow when I saw that old man's slender, brittle-looking fingers dart over those twelve strings.

Once I was there in the afternoon when they were rehearsing new dancers, and old Kamian was telling Armenian tales to Berge's children. I sat there hidden behind a beaded curtain and heard Kamian tell about the fiery horses of Armenia, and pomegranates full of pearls and rubies, and about Hazaran-Bulbul, the magic nightingale of a thousand songs. He made me feel like a kid that day listening to him, and ever since, when I hear him play the *oud*, I could almost climb aboard one of those fiery horses.

Another time when I was here late at night listening to Mr. Kamian play, his oldest son Leon sat with me drinking Scotch and told me the story of his father, how he was the only survivor of a large family which totalled, cousins and all, half of a village that was massacred by Turkish soldiers. Mr. Kamian was fifteen years old then, and his body was left in a big ditch with those of his parents, brothers, sisters, everyone in his entire world.

'The thing that saved him that day was the *smell* of death,' said Leon, who spoke five languages, English with only a slight accent, and like all Armenians, loved to tell stories. 'As he lay there, my father wanted to be dead with the others. It wasn't the sight or idea of death that made him drag himself up and out of that ditch, it was the smell of rotting bodies which at last was the only unbearable thing, and which drove him to the road and away from his village forever.

'For almost a year he wandered, his only possession an *oud* which he rescued from a plundered farmhouse. One night when he was huddling alone in the wilderness like Cain, feeling like the only human being left on earth, he became very angry that God would let this happen, and like the child he was, he *demanded* a sign from Him, and he waited and listened in the darkness, but he heard only the wind howling across the Russian steppes. Then he wondered how he could ever have believed in a God who would let this happen to Armenia, His tiny Christian island in a sea of Islam. There was no sign, so he strummed the *oud* and sang brave songs into the wind all that night.

'The very next night the boy was wandering through a village very much like his had been, and of course he passed hundreds of starving refugees on the road. He took off from the road to find a place to sleep in the trees where someone wouldn't kill him just to steal the *oud*. There in the woods he saw a black sinister shape rising from the ground, and the first thing the boy thought was that it was a *dev*, one of those fearsome Armenian ogres his *nany* used to tell him about. He raised the flimsy *oud* like it was an axe and prepared to defend himself. Then the dark form took shape and spoke to him in Armenian from beneath a ragged cloak, 'Please, do you have something to eat?'

'The boy saw a child in the moonlight, covered with sores, stomach bloated, barely able to walk. Her teeth were loose, eyes and gums crusted, and a recently broken nose made it hard for her to breathe. He examined her face and saw that at no time could that face have been more than homely, but now it was truly awful. He spoke to her a few moments and found she was thirteen years old, a wandering refugee, and he remembered the proud and vain demand he had made of God the night before. He began to laugh then and suddenly felt stronger. He couldn't stop laughing and the laughter filled him with strength. It alarmed the girl, and he saw it, and finally he said, "The God of Armenians has a sense of humour. How can you doubt someone with a sense of humour like His? You're to come with me, my little *dev*."

'"What do you want of me, sir?" she asked, very frightened now.

'"What do you want of me, sir?" she asked, very at you. "What do you have to offer? Everything has been taken from you and everything has been done to you. What could anyone in the world possibly want of you now? Can you think of what it is, the thing I want?"

'"No, sir."

'"There is only one thing left. To *love* you, of course. We're good for no more than this. Now come with me. We're going to find *our* Armenia."

'She went with the half-starved, wild-eyed boy. They survived together and wandered to the Black Sea, somehow got passage, and crossed on foot through Europe, through the war and fighting, ever westward to the Atlantic, working, having children. Finally, in 1927, they and five children, having roamed half the world, arrived in New York, and from force of habit more than anything, kept wandering west, picking up jobs along the way until they reached the Pacific Ocean. Then my mother said, "This is as far as we go. This ocean is too big." And they stopped, had four more children, sixty-one grandchildren, and so far, ten great grandchildren, more than forty with the Kamian name that would not die in the ditch in Armenia. Most of his sons and grandsons have done well, and he still likes to come here sometimes once a week and play his *oud* for a few people who understand.'

So that was the story of old Kamian, and I didn't doubt any of it, because I've known a lot of tough bastards in my time that could've pulled off something like that, but the thing that amazed me, that I couldn't really understand, is how he could've taken the little girl with him that night. I mean he could've helped her, sure. But he purposely *gave* himself to her that night. After what he'd already been through, he up and *gave* himself to somebody! That was the most incredible thing about Mr. Kamian, that, and how the hell his fingers knew exactly where to go on that *oud* when there were no frets to guide them.

'You eat plenty, Bumper?' asked Yasser, who came to the table with Ahmed, and I responded by giving him a fatcat grin and patting him on the hand, and whispering '*shukran*' in a way that you would know meant thanks without knowing Arabic

'Maybe you'll convert me, feeding me like that. Maybe I'll become a Moslem,' I added.

'What you do during Ramadan when you must fast?' laughed Yasser.

'You see how *big* Abd's kids?' said Yasser, lifting his apron to reach for his wallet, and laying some snapshots on me that I pretended I could see.

'Yeah, handsome kids,' I said, hoping the old man wouldn't start showing me all his grandkids. He had about thirty of them, and like all Arabs, was crazy about children.

Ahmed spoke in Arabic that had to do with the banquet room, and Yasser seemed to remember something.

'Scoose me, Bumper,' said the old boy, 'I come back later, but I got things in the kitchen.'

'Sure, *Baba*,' I said, and Ahmed smiled as he watched his father strut back to the kitchen, the proud patriarch of a large family, and the head of a very good business, which Abd's Harem certainly was.

'How old is your father now?'

'Seventy-five,' said Ahmed. 'Looks good, doesn't he?'

'Damn good. Tell me, can he still eat like he used to, say ten, fifteen years ago?'

'He eats pretty well,' Ahmed laughed. 'But no, not like he used to. He used to eat like you, Bumper. It was a joy to watch him eat. He says food doesn't taste quite the same any more.'

I started getting gas pains, but didn't pop a tablet because it would be rude for Ahmed to see me do that after I'd just finished such a first-rate dinner.

'It'd be a terrible thing for your appetite to go,' I said. That'd be almost as bad as being castrated.'

'Then I never want to get *that* old, Bumper,' Ahmed laughed, with the strength and confidence of only thirty years on this earth. 'Of course there's a third thing, remember, your digestion? Got to have that, too.'

'Oh, yeah,' I said. 'Got to have digestion or appetite ain't worth a damn.'

Just then the lights dimmed, and a bluish spot danced around the small bandstand as the drums started first. Then I was amazed to see Laila Hammad run out to the floor, in a gold-and-white belly dancer's costume, and the music picked up as she stood there, chestnut hair hanging down over her boobs, fingers writhing, and working the *zils*, those little golden finger cymbals, hips swaying as George's hands beat a blood-beating rhythm on the *darbuka*. Ahmed grinned at me as I admired her strong golden thighs.

'How do you like our new dancer?'

'Laila's your dancer?'

'Wait'll you see her,' said Ahmed, and it was true, she really was something. There was art to the dancing, not just lusty gyrations, and though I'm no judge of belly dancing, even I could see it.

'How old is she now?' I said to Ahmed, watching her mobile stomach, and the luxuriant chestnut hair, which was all her own, and now hung down her back and then streamed over her wonderful-looking boobs.

'She's nineteen,' said Ahmed, and I was very happy to see how good-looking she'd turned out.

Laila had worked as a waitress here for a few years, even when she was much too young to be doing it, but she always looked older, and her father, Khalil Hammad, was a cousin of Yasser's, who lingered for years with cancer, running up tremendous hospital bills before he finally died. Laila was a smart, hard-working girl, and helped support her three younger sisters. Ahmed once told me Laila never really knew her mother, an American broad who left them when they were little kids. I'd heard Laila was working in a bank the last couple years and doing okay.

You could really see the Arab blood in Laila now, in the sensual face, the nose a little too prominent but just suiting her, and in the wide full mouth, and glittering brown eyes. No wonder they were passionate people, I thought, with faces like that. Yes, Laila was a jewel, like a fine half-Arab mare with enough American blood to give good height and those terrific thighs. I wondered if Ahmed had anything going with her. Then Laila started 'sprinkling salt' as the Arabs say. She revolved slowly on the ball of one bare foot, jerking a hip to each beat of the *darbuka*. And if there'd been a small bag of salt tied to the throbbing hip, she would've made a perfect ring of salt on the floor around her. It's a hot, graceful move, not hard at all. I do it myself to hardrock music.

When Laila was finished with her dance and ran off the floor and the applause died down I said, 'She's beautiful, Ahmed. Why don't you con her into marrying you?'

'Not interested,' said Ahmed, shaking his head. He leaned over the table and took a sip of wine before speaking. 'There're rumours, Bumper. Laila's supposed to be whoring.'

'I can't believe that,' I said, remembering her again as a teenage waitress who couldn't even put her lipstick on straight.

'She left her bank job over a year ago. Started belly dancing professionally. You never knew her when she was a real little tot. I remember her when she was three years old and her aunts and uncles taught her to dance. She was the cutest thing you ever saw. She was a smart little girl.'

'Where did you hear she was tricking?'

'In this business you hear all about the dancers,' said Ahmed. 'You know, she's one of the few belly dancers in town that's really an Arab, or rather, half-Arab. She's no cheapie, but she goes to bed with guys if they can pay the tariff. I hear she gets two hundred a night.'

'Laila's had a pretty tough life, Ahmed,' I said. 'She had to raise little sisters. She never had time to be a kid herself.'

'Look, I'm not blaming her, Bumper. What the hell, I'm an American. I'm not like the old folks who wait around on the morning after the wedding to make sure there's blood on the bridal sheets. But I have to admit that whoring bothers me. I'm just not that Americanized, I guess. I used to think maybe when Laila got old enough ... well, it's too late now. I shouldn't have been so damn busy these last few years. I let her get away and now ... it's just too late.'

Ahmed ordered me another drink, then excused himself, saying he'd be back in a little while. I was starting to feel depressed all of a sudden. I wasn't sure if the talk about Laila set it off or what, but I thought about her selling her ass to these wealthy Hollywood creeps. Then I thought about Freddie and Harry, and Poochie and Herky, and Timothy G. for goddamn Landry, but that was *too* depressing to think about. Suddenly for no reason I thought about Esteban Segovia and how I used to worry that he really would become a priest like he wanted to be when he returned from Vietnam, instead of a dentist like I always wanted him to be. That dead boy was about Laila's age when he left. Babies. Nobody should die a baby.

All right, Bumper, I said to myself, let's settle down to some serious drinking. I called Barbara over and ordered a double Scotch on the rocks even though I'd mixed my drinks too much and had already more than enough.

After my third Scotch I heard a honey-dipped voice say, 'Hi, Bumper.'

'Laila!' I made a feeble attempt at getting up, as she sat down at my table, looking smooth and cool in a modest white dress, her hair tied back and hanging down one side, her face and arms the colour of a golden olive.

'Ahmed told me you were here, Bumper,' she smiled, and I lit her cigarette, liberated women be damned, and called Barbara over to get her a drink.

'Can I buy you a drink, kid?' I asked. 'It's good to see you all grown up, a big girl and all, looking so damn gorgeous.'

She ordered a bourbon and water and laughed at me, and I knew for sure I was pretty close to being wiped out. I decided to turn it off after I finished the Scotch I held in my hand.

'I was grown up last time you saw me, Bumper,' she said, grinning at my clownish attempts to act sober. 'All men appreciate your womanhood better when they see your bare belly moving for them.'

I thought about what Ahmed had told me, and though it didn't bother me like it did Ahmed, I was sorry she had to do it, or that she *thought* she had to do it.

'You mean that slick little belly was moving for ol' Bumper?' I said, trying to kid her like I used to, but my brain wasn't working right.

'Sure, for you. Aren't you the hero of this whole damned family?'

'Well, how do you like dancing for a living?'

'It's as crummy as you'd expect.'

'Why do you do it?'

'You ever try supporting two sisters on a bank teller's wage?'

'Bullshit,' I said too loud, one elbow slipping out from under me. 'Don't give me that crybaby stuff. A dish like you, why you could marry any rich guy you wanted.'

'Wrong, Bumper. I could screw any rich guy I wanted. And get paid damn well for it.'

'I wish you wouldn't talk like that, Laila.'

'You old bear,' she laughed, as I rubbed my face which had no feeling whatever. 'I know Ahmed told you I'm a whore. It just shames the hell out of these Arabs. You know how subtle they are. Yasser hinted around the other day that maybe I should change my name now that I'm show biz. Hammad's too ordinary, he said. Maybe something more American. They're as subtle as a boot in the ass. How about Feinberg or Goldstein, Bumper? I'll bet they wouldn't mind if I called myself Laila Feinberg. That'd explain my being a whore to the other Arabs, wouldn't it? They could start a rumour that my mother was a Jew.'

'What the hell're you telling *me* all this for?' I said, suddenly getting mad. 'Go to a priest or a headshrinker, or go to the goddamn mosque and talk to the Prophet, why don't you? I had enough problems laid on me today. Now you?'

'Will you drive me home, Bumper? I do want to talk to you.'

'How many more performances you got to go?' I asked, not sure I could stay upright in my chair if I had another drink.

'I'm through. Marsha's taking my next one for me. I've told Ahmed I'm getting cramps.'

711

I found Ahmed and said good-bye while Laila waited for me in the parking lot. I tipped Barbara fifteen bucks, then I staggered into the kitchen, thanked Yasser, and kissed him on the big moustache while he hugged me and made me promise to come to his house in the next few weeks.

Laila was in the parking lot doing her best to ignore two well-dressed drunks in a black Lincoln. When they saw me staggering across the parking lot in their direction the driver stomped on it, laid a patch of rubber, and got the hell out.

'Lord, I don't blame them,' Laila laughed. 'You look wild and danger-ous, Bumper. How'd you get those scratches on your face?'

'My Ford's right over there,' I said, walking like Frankenstein's monster so I could stay on a straight course.

'The same old car? Oh, Bumper.' She laughed like a kid and she put my arm around her and steered me to my Ford, but around to the passenger-side. Then she patted my pockets, found my keys, got them, pushed me in, and closed the door after me.

'Light-fingered broad,' I mumbled. You ever been a hugger-mugger?'

'What was that, Bumper?' she said, getting behind the wheel and crank-ing her up.

'Nothing, nothing,' I mumbled, rubbing my face again.

I dozed while Laila drove. She turned the radio on and hummed, and she had a pretty good voice too. In fact, it put me to sleep, and she had to shake me awake when we got to her pad.

'I'm going to pour you some muddy Turkish coffee and we're going to talk,' she said, helping me out of the Ford, and for a second the sidewalk came up in my eyes, but I closed them and stood there and everything righted itself.

'Ready to try the steps, Bumper?'

'As I'll ever be, kid.'

'Let's get it on,' she said, my arm around her wide shoulders, and she guided me up. She was a big strong girl. Ahmed was nuts, I thought. She'd make a hell of a wife for him or *any* young guy.

It took some doing but we reached the third floor of her apartment building, a very posh place, which was actually three L-shaped buildings scattered around two Olympic-sized pools. Mostly catered to swinging singles which reminded me of the younger sisters.

'The girls home?' I asked.

'I live alone during the school year, Bumper. Nadia lives in the dorm at USC. She's a freshman. Dalal boards at Ramona Convent. She'll be going to college next year.'

'Ramona Convent? I thought you were a Moslem.'

'I'm nothing.'

We got in the apartment and Laila guided me past the soft couch, which looked pretty good to sleep on, and dumped me in a straight-backed kitchen chair after taking off my sports coat and hanging it in a closet.

'You even wear a gun off duty?' she asked as she ladled out some coffee and ran some water from the tap.

'Yeah,' I said, not knowing what she was talking about for a minute, I was so used to the gun. 'This job makes you a coward. I don't even go out without it in this town any more, except to Harry's bar or somewhere in the neighbourhood.'

'If I saw all the things you have, maybe I'd be afraid to go out without one too,' she shrugged.

I didn't know I was dozing again until I smelled Laila there shaking me awake, a tiny cup of Turkish coffee thick and dark on a saucer in front of me. I smelled her sweetness and then I felt her cool hand again and then I saw her wide mouth smiling.

'Maybe I should spoon it down your throat till you get sober.'

'I'm okay,' I said, rubbing my face and head.

I drank the coffee as fast as I could even though it scalded my mouth and throat. Then she poured me another, and I excused myself, went to the head, took a leak, washed my face in cold water, and combed my hair. I was still bombed when I came back, but at least I wasn't a zombie.

Laila must've figured I was in good enough shape. 'Let me turn on some music, Bumper, then we can talk.'

'Okay.' I finished the second cup almost as fast as the first and poured myself a third.

The soft stirring song of an Arab girl singer filled the room for a second and then Laila turned down the volume. It's a wailing kind of plaintive sound, almost like a chant at times, but it gets to you, at least it did to me, and I always conjured up mental pictures of the Temple of Karnak, and Giza, and the streets of Damascus, and a picture I once saw of a Bedouin on a pink granite cliff in the blinding sun looking out over the Valley of the Kings. I saw in his face that he knew more about history, even though he was probably illiterate, than I ever would, and I promised myself I'd go there to die when I got old. If I ever *did* get old, that is.

'I still like the old music,' Laila smiled, nodding towards the stereo set. 'Most people don't like it. I can put on something else if you want.

'Don't touch it,' I said, and Laila looked in my eyes and seemed glad.

'I need your help, Bumper.'

'Okay, what is it?'

'I want you to talk to my probation officer for me.'

'You're on probation? What for?'

'Prostitution. The Hollywood vice cops got three of us in January. I pleaded guilty and was put on probation.'

'Whadda you want me to do?'

'I wasn't given *summary* probation like my lousy thousand-dollar lawyer promised. I got a tough judge and I have to report to a P.O. for two years. I want to go somewhere and I need permission.'

'Where you going?'

'Somewhere to have a baby. I want to go somewhere, have my baby, adopt it out, and come back.'

She saw the 'Why me? Why in the hell me?' look in my eyes.

'Bumper, I need you for this. I don't want my sisters to know anything. Nothing, you hear? They'd only want to raise the baby and for God's sake, it's hard enough making it in this filthy world when you know who the hell your two parents are and have them to raise you. I've got a plan and you're the only one my whole damned tribe would listen to without question. They trust you completely. I want you to tell Yasser and Ahmed and all of them that you don't think I should be dancing for a living, and that you have a friend in New Orleans who has a good-paying office job for me. And then tell the same thing to my P.O. and convince her it's the truth. Then I'll disappear for seven or eight months and come back and tell everyone I didn't like the job or something. They'll all get mad as blazes but that'll be it.'

'Where the hell you going?'

'What's it matter?' she shrugged. 'Anywhere to have the kid and farm it out. To New Orleans. Wherever.'

'You're not joining the coat hanger corps, are you?'

'An abortion?' she laughed. 'No, I figure when you make a mistake you should have the guts at least to see it through. I won't shove it down a garbage disposal. I was raised an Arab and I can't change.'

'You got any money?'

'I've got thirteen thousand in a bank account. I'd like you to handle it for me and see that the girls have enough to get them through the summer while they're living here in my apartment. If everything goes right I'll be back for a New Year's Eve party with just you and me and the best bottle of Scotch money can buy.'

'Will you have enough to live on?' I asked, knowing where she got the thirteen thousand.

'I've got enough,' she nodded.

'Listen, goddamn it, don't lie to me. I'm not gonna get involved if you're off somewhere selling your ass in a strange town with a foal kicking around in your belly.'

'I wouldn't take any chances,' she said, looking deep in my eyes again. 'I swear it. I've got enough in another account to live damn well for the whole time I'll be gone. I'll show you my bankbooks. And I can afford to have the kid in a good hospital. A private room if I want it.'

'Wow!' I said, getting up, light-headed and dizzy. I stood for a second and shuffled into the living room, dropping on the couch and laying back. I noticed that the red hose on Laila's crystal and gold narghile was uncoiled.

Those pipes are fine decorator items but they never work right unless you stuff all the fittings with rags like Laila's was. I often smoked mint-flavoured. Turkish tobacco with Yasser. Laila smoked hashish. There was a black-and-white mosaic inlaid box sitting next to the narghile. The lid was open and it was half full of hash, very high-grade, expensive, shoe-leather hash, pressed into dark flat sheets like the sole of your shoe.

Laila let me alone and cleared the kitchen table. What a hell of a time. First the decision to retire. And after I told Cassie, everything seemed right. And then Cassie wants a kid! And a goddamn pack of baby Bolsheviks make an ass out of me. Humiliate me! Then perjury, for chrissake. I felt like someone was putting out cigars on the inside of my belly, which was so hard and swollen I couldn't see my knees unless I sat up straight. But at least I got a back office, even if I did almost die in the pigeon shit.

'What a day,' I said when Laila came in and sat down on the end of the couch.

'I'm sorry I asked you, Bumper.'

'No, no, don't say that. I'll do it. I'll help you.'

She didn't say anything, but she got up and came over and sat on the floor next to me, her eyes wet, and I'll be a son of a bitch if she didn't kiss my hand!

Laila got up then, and without saying anything, took my shoes off, and I let her lift my legs up and put them on the couch. I felt like a beached walrus laying there like that, but I was still swacked. In fact, I felt drunker now laying down, and I was afraid the room would start spinning, so I wanted to start talking. 'I had a miserable goddamn day.'

'Tell me about it, Bumper,' said Laila, sitting there on the floor next to me and putting her cool hand on my hot forehead as I loosened my belt. I knew I was gone for the night. I was in no shape to get up, let alone drive home. I squirmed around until my sore shoulder was settled against a cushion.

'Your face and hands are cut and your body's hurting.'

'Guess I can sleep here, huh?'

'Of course. How'd you get hurt?'

'Slipped and fell off a fire escape. Whadda you think about me retiring, Laila?'

'Retiring? Don't be ridiculous. You're too full of hell.'

'I'm in my forties, goddamnit. No, I might as well level with you. I'll be fifty this month. Imagine that. When I was born Warren G. Harding was a new President!'

'You're too alive. Forget about it. It's too silly to think about.'

'I was sworn in on my thirtieth birthday, Laila. Know that?'

'Tell me about it,' she said, stroking my cheek now, and I felt so damn comfortable I could've died.

'You weren't even born then. That's how long I been a cop.'

'Why'd you become a cop?'

'Oh, I don't know.'

'Well, what did you do *before* you became a cop?'

'I was in the Marine Corps over eight years.'

'Tell me about it.'

'I wanted to get away from the hometown, I guess. There was nobody left except a few cousins and one aunt. My brother Clem and me were raised by our grandmother, and after she died, Clem took care of me. He was a ripper, that bastard. Bigger than me, but didn't look anything like me. A handsome dog. Loved his food and drink and women. He owned his own gas station and just before Pearl Harbor, in November it was, he got killed when a truck tyre blew up and he fell back into the grease pit. My brother Clem died in a filthy grease pit, killed by a goddamn tyre! It was ridiculous. There was nobody else I gave a damn about so I joined the Corps. Guys actually *joined* in those days, believe it or not. I got wounded twice, once at Saipan and then in the knees at Iwo, and it almost kept me off the Department. I had to flimflam the shit out of that police surgeon. You know what? I didn't hate war. I mean, why not admit it? I didn't hate it.'

'Weren't you ever afraid?'

'Sure, but there's something about danger I like, and fighting was something I could do. I found that out right away and after the war I shipped over for another hitch and never did go back to Indiana. What the hell, I never had much there anyway. Billy was here with me and I had a job I liked.'

'Who's Billy?'

'He was my son,' I said, and I heard the air-conditioner going and I knew it was cool, because Laila looked so crisp and fresh, and yet my back was soaked and the sweat was pouring down my face and slipping beneath my collar.

'I never knew you were married, Bumper.'

'It was a hundred years ago.'

'Where's your wife?'

'I don't know. Missouri, I think. Or dead maybe. It's been so long. She was a girl I met in San Diego, a farm girl. Lots of them around out here on the coast during the war. They drifted out to find defence work, and some of them boozed it too much. Verna was a pale, skinny little thing. I was back in San Diego from my first trip over. I had a chest full of ribbons and had a cane because my first hit was in the thigh. That's one reason my legs aren't worth a shit today, I guess. I picked her up in a bar and slept with her that night and then I started coming by whenever I got liberty and next thing you know, before I ship out, she says she's knocked up. I had the feeling so many guys get, that they're gonna get bumped off, that their number's up, so we got drunk one night and I took her to a justice of the peace in Arizona and married her. She got an allotment and wrote me all the time and I didn't think too much about her till I got hit the second time and went home for good. And there she was, with my frail, sickly Billy. William's my real name, did you know that?'

'No, I didn't.'

'So anyway, I screwed up, but just like you said, Laila, there was no sense anybody else suffering for it so I took Verna and Billy and we got a decent place to stay in Oceanside, and I thought, what the hell, this is a pretty fair life. So I re-enlisted for another hitch and before long I was up for master sergeant. I could take Verna okay. I mean I gotta give her credit, after Billy came she quit boozing and kept a decent house. She was just a poor dumb farm girl but she treated me and Billy like champs, I have to admit. I was lucky and got to stay with Headquarters Company, Base, for five years, and Billy was to me, like ... I don't know, standing on a granite cliff and watching all the world from the Beginning until Now, and for the first time there was a reason for it all. You understand?'

'Yes, I think so.'

'You won't believe this, but when he was barely four years old he printed a valentine card for me. He could print and read at four years old, I swear it. He asked his mother how to make the words and then he composed it himself. It said, "Dad. I love you. Love, Billy Morgan." Just barely four years old. Can you believe that?'

'Yes, I believe you, Bumper.'

'But like I said, he was a sickly boy like his mother, and even now when I tell you about him, I can't picture him. I put him away mentally, and it's not possible to picture how he looked, even if I try. You know, I read where only schizophrenics can control subconscious thought, and maybe I'm schizoid, I don't doubt it. But I can do it. Sometimes when I'm asleep and I see a shadow in a dream and the shadow is a little boy wearing glasses, or he has a cowlick sticking up in the back, I wake up. I sit straight up in my bed, wide awake. I cannot picture him either awake or asleep. You're smart to adopt out your kid, Laila.'

'When did he die?'

'When he was just five. Right after his birthday, in fact. And it shouldn't have surprised me really. He was anaemic and he had pneumonia twice as a baby, but still, it *was* a surprise, you know? Even though he was sick so long, it *was* a surprise, and after that, Verna seemed dead too. She told me a few weeks after we buried him that she was going home to Missouri and I thought it was a good idea so I gave her all the money I had and I never saw her again.

'After she left, I started drinking pretty good, and once, on weekend liberty, I came to LA and got so drunk I somehow ended up at El Toro Marine Base with a bunch of other drunken jarheads instead of at Camp Pendleton where I was stationed. The M.P.'s at the gate let the other drunks through, but of course my pass was wrong, so they stopped me. I was mean drunk then, and confused as hell, and I ended up swinging on the two M.P.'s

'I can hardly remember later that night in the El Toro brig. All I really recall was two brig guards, one black guy and one white guy, wearing khaki pants and skivvy shirts, dragging me off the floor of the cell and taking me in the head where they worked me over with billies and then to the showers to wash off the blood. I remember holding on to the faucets with my head in the sink for protection, and the billies landing on my arms and ribs and kidneys and the back of my head. That was the first time my nose was ever broken.'

Laila was still stroking my face and listening. Her hands felt cool and good.

'After that, they gave me a special courtmartial, and after all the M.P.'s testified, my defence counsel brought out a platoon or so of character witnesses, and even some civilians, wives of the marines who lived near Verna and Billy and me. They all talked about me, and Billy, and how extra smart and polite he was. Then the doctor who treated me in the brig testified as a defence witness that I was unbalanced at the time of the fight and not responsible for my actions, even though he had no psychiatric training. My defence counsel got away with it and when it was over I didn't get any brig time. I just got busted to buck sergeant

'Is it hot in here, Laila?'

'No, Bumper,' she said, stroking my cheek with the back of her fingers.

'Well, anyway, I took my discharge in the spring of nineteen-fifty and fooled around a year and finally joined the Los Angeles Police Department.'

'Why did you do it, Bumper? The police force?'

'I don't know. I was good at fighting, I guess that's why. I thought about going back in the Corps when Korea broke out, and then I read something that said, "Policemen are soldiers who act alone", and I figured that was the only thing I hated about the military, that you couldn't act alone very much. And as a cop I could do it all myself, so I became a cop.'

'You never heard from Verna?' asked Laila quietly, and suddenly I was cold and damp and getting chills laying there.

'About six years after I came on the job I got a letter from a lawyer in Joplin. I don't know how he found me. He said she'd filed for divorce and after that I got the final papers. I paid his fee and sent her about five hundred I'd saved, to get her started. I always hoped maybe she found some nice working stiff and went back to the farm life. She was one who couldn't make it by herself. She'd have to love somebody and then of course she'd have to suffer when something took them away from her, or maybe when they left on their own. She'd never learn you gotta suffer *alone* in this world. I never knew for sure what happened to her. I didn't try to find out because I'd probably just discover she was a wino and a street-walking whore and I'd rather think otherwise.'

'Bumper?'

'What?'

'Please take my bed tonight. Go in and shower and take my bed. You're dripping wet and you'll get sick if you stay here on the couch.'

'I'll be okay. You should see some of the places I've slept. Just give me a blanket.'

'Please.'

She began trying to lift me and that almost made me laugh out loud. She was a strong girl, but no woman was about to raise Bumper Morgan, two hundred and seventy-five pounds anytime, and almost three hundred this night with all of me cold dead weight from the booze.

'Okay, okay,' I grumbled, and found I wasn't too drunk when I stood up. I made my way to her bedroom, stripped, and jumped in the shower, turning it on cold at the end. When I was through I dried in her bath towel which smelled like woman, took the wet gauze bandage off my leg, and felt better than I had all day. I rinsed my mouth with toothpaste, examined my meat-red face and red-webbed eyes, and climbed in her bed naked, which is the only way to sleep, winter or summer.

The bed smelled like her too, or rather it smelled like woman, since all women are pretty much the same to me. They all smell and feel the same. It's the essence of womanhood, that's the thing I need.

I was dozing when Laila came in and tiptoed to the shower and it seemed like seconds later when she was sitting on the bed in a sheer white nightgown whispering to me. I smelled lilac, and then woman, and I came to with her velvet mouth all over my face.

'What the hell?' I mumbled, sitting up.

'I touched you tonight,' said Lalia. 'You told me things. Maybe for the first time in years, Bumper, I've really touched another person!' She put her hand on my bare shoulder.

'Yeah, well that's enough touching for one night,' I said, disgusted with myself for telling her all those personal things, and I took her hand off my shoulder. Now I'd have to fly back to LA in a couple of weeks to set this thing up with Laila and her family. Everyone was complicating my life lately.

'Bumper,' she said, drawing her feet up under her and laughing pretty damn jolly for this time of night. 'Bumper, you're wonderful. You're a wonderful old panda. A big blue-nosed panda. Do you know your nose is blue?'

'Yeah, it gets that way when I drink too much,' I said, figuring she'd been smoking hash, able to see right through the nightie at her skin which was now exactly the colour of apricots. 'I had too many blood vessels busted too many times there on my nose.'

'I want to get under the covers with you, Bumper.'

'Look, kid,' I said. 'You don't owe me a goddamn thing. I'll be glad to help you flimflam your family.'

'You've let me touch you, Bumper,' she said, and the warm wide velvet mouth was on me again, my neck and cheek, and all that chestnut hair was covering me until I almost couldn't think about how ridiculous this was.

'Goddamnit,' I said, holding her off. 'This is a sickening thing you're doing. I knew you since you were a little girl. Damn it, kid, I'm an old bag of guts and you're still just a little child to me. This is unnatural!'

'Don't call me kid. And don't stop me from having you.'

'*Having* me? You're just impressed by cops. I'm a father symbol. Lots of girls feel like that about cops.'

'I hate cops,' she answered, her boobs wobbling against my arms, which were getting tired. 'It's you I want because you're more man than I've ever had my hands on.'

'Yeah, I'm about six cubic yards,' I said, very shaky.

'That's not what I meant,' she said, her hands going over me, and she was kissing me again and I was doing everything I could to avoid the pleasures of a thousand and one nights.

'Listen, I couldn't if I wanted to,' I groaned. 'You're just too young, I just couldn't do it with a kid like you.'

'Want to bet?'

'Don't Laila.'

'How can a man be so aware and be so square,' she smiled, standing up and slipping off the nightie.

'It's just the bluesuit,' I said with a voice gone hoarse and squeaky. 'I probably look pretty sharp to you in my uniform.'

Laila busted up then, falling on the bed and rolling on her stomach, laughing for a good minute. I smiled weakly, staring at her apricot ass and those thunder thighs, thinking it was over. But after she stopped laughing she smiled at me softer than ever, whispered in Arabic, and crept under the sheet.

FRIDAY
the Last Day

FIFTEEN

I woke up Friday morning with a terrible hangover. Laila was sprawled half on top of me, a big smooth naked doe, which was the reason I woke up. After living so many years alone I don't like sleeping with anyone. Cassie, who I made love to maybe a hundred times, had never slept with me, not all night. We'd have to get twin beds, Cassie and me. I just can't stand to be too close to anybody for too long.

Laila didn't wake up and I took my clothes into the living room and dressed, leaving a note that said I'd get in touch in a week or so, to work out the details of handling her bank account and dumping a load of snow on Yasser and the family.

Before I left I crept back into the bedroom to look at her this last time. She was sprawled on her stomach, sleek and beautiful.

'*Sal m*, Laila,' I whispered. A thousand *sal ms*, little girl.'

I very carefully made my way down the stairs of Laila's apartment house to my car parked in front, and I felt a little better when I got out on the road with the window down driving on to the Hollywood Freeway on a windy, not too smoggy day.

Then I thought for a few minutes about how it had been with Laila and I was ashamed because I always prided myself on being something more than the thousands of ugly old slimeballs you see in Hollywood with beautiful young babies like her. She did it because she was grateful and neurotic and confused and I took advantage. I'd always picked on someone my own size all my life, and now I was no better than any other horny old fart.

I went home and had a cold shower and a shave and I felt more or less human after some aspirin and three cups of coffee that started the heartburn going for the day. I wondered if after a few months of retirement my stomach might begin to rebuild itself, and who knows, maybe I'd have digestive peace.

I got to the Glass House a half hour early and by the time I shined my black high-top shoes, buffed the Sam Browne, hit the badge with some rouge and a cloth, I was sweating a little and feeling much improved. I put on a fresh uniform since the one from yesterday was covered with blood and birdshit. When I pinned on the gleaming shield and slid the scarred baton through the chrome ring on my Sam Browne I felt even better.

At rollcall Cruz was sitting as usual with the watch commander, Lieutenant Hilliard, at the table in front of the room, and Cruz glanced at me several times like he expected me to get up and make a grand announcement that this was my last day. Of course I didn't, and he looked a little disappointed. I hated to disappoint anyone, especially Cruz, but I wasn't going out with a trumpet blare. I really wanted Lieutenant Hilliard to hold an inspection this morning, my last one, and he did. He limped down the line and said my boondockers and my shield looked like a million bucks and he wished some of the young cops looked half as sharp. After inspection I drank a quart or so from the water fountain and I felt better yet.

I meant to speak to Cruz about our lunch date, but Lieutenant Hilliard was talking to him so I went out to the car, and decided to call him later. I fired up the black-and-white, put my baton in the holder on the door, tore off the paper on my writing pad, replaced the old hot sheet, checked the back seat for dead midgets, and drove out of the station. It was really unbelievable. The *last time*.

After hitting the bricks, I cleared over the air, even though I worried that I'd get a burglary report or some other chickenshit call before I could get something in my stomach. I couldn't stand the idea of anything heavy just now so I turned south on San Pedro and headed for the dairy, which was a very good place to go for hangover cures, at least it always was for me. It was more than a dairy, it was the plant and home office for a dairy that sold all over Southern California, and they made very good speciality products like cottage cheese and buttermilk and yogurt, all of which are wonderful for hangovers, if you're not too far gone. I waved at the gate guard, got passed into the plant, and parked in front of the employees' store, which wasn't opened yet.

I saw one of the guys I knew behind the counter setting up the cash register and I knocked on the window.

'Hi, Bumper,' he smiled, a young guy, with deep-set green eyes and a mop of black hair. 'What do you need?'

'Plasma, pal,' I said, 'but I'll settle for yogurt.'

'Sure. Come on in, Bumper,' he laughed, and I passed through, heading for the tall glass door to the cold room where the yogurt was kept. I took two yogurts from the shelf, and he gave me a plastic spoon when I put them on the counter.

'That all you're having, Bumper?' he asked, as I shook my head and lifted the lid and spooned out a half pint of blueberry which I finished in three or four gulps and followed with a lime. And finally, what the hell, I thought, I grabbed another, French apple, and ate it while the guy counted his money and said something to me once or twice which I nodded at, and I smiled through a mouthful of cool creamy yogurt that was coating my stomach, soothing me, and making me well.

'Never saw anyone put away yogurt like that, Bumper,' he said after I finished.

I couldn't remember this young guy's name, and wished like hell they wore their names on the grey work uniform because I always like to make a little small talk and call someone by name when he's feeding me. It's the least you can do.

'Could I have some buttermilk?' I asked, after he threw the empty yogurt containers in a gleaming trash can behind the counter. The whole place sparkled, being a dairy, and it smelled clean, and was nice and cool.

'Why sure, Bumper,' he said, leaving the counter and coming back with a pint of cold buttermilk. Most of the older guys around the dairy wouldn't bring me a pint container, and here I was dying of thirst from the booze. Rather than say anything I just tipped it up and poured it down, only swallowing three times to make him realize his mistake.

'Guess I should've brought you a quart, huh?' he said after I put the milk carton down and licked my lips.

I smiled and shrugged and he went in the back, returning with a quart.

'Thanks, pal,' I said. 'I'm pretty thirsty today.' I tipped the quart up and let it flow thick and delicious into my mouth, and then I started swallowing, but not like before, more slowly. When I finished it I was really fit again. I was well. I could do anything now.

'Take a quart with you?' he said. 'Would you like more yogurt or some cottage cheese?'

'No thanks,' I said. I don't believe in being a hog like some cops I've worked with. 'Gotta get back to the streets. Friday mornings get pretty busy sometimes.'

I really should've talked a while. I knew I should, but I just didn't feel like it. It was the first time this guy ever served me so I said the thing that all policemen say when they're ninety per cent sure what the answer will be.

'How much do I owe you?'

'Don't mention it,' he said, shaking his head. 'Come see us any time, Bumper.'

While driving out the main gate of the dairy, I fired up a fresh cigar which I knew couldn't possibly give me indigestion because my stomach was so well coated I could eat tin cans and not notice.

Then I realized that was the last time I'd ever make my dairy stop. Damn, I thought, everything I do today will be for the last time. Then I suddenly started hoping I'd get some routine calls like a burglary report or maybe a family dispute which I usually hated refereeing. I wouldn't even mind writing a traffic ticket today.

It would've been something, I thought, really something to have stayed on the job after my twenty years. You have your pension in the bag then, and you own your own mortgage, having bought and paid for them with twenty years' service. Regardless of what you ever do or don't do you have a forty per cent pension the rest of your life, from the moment you leave the Department. Whether you're fired for pushing a slimeball down the fire escape, or whether you're booked for lying in court to put a scumbag where he ought to be, or whether you bust your stick over the hairy little skull of some college brat who's tearing at your badge and carrying a tape recorder at a demonstration, no matter what you do, they got to pay you that pension. If they have to, they'll mail those cheques to you at San Quentin. Nobody can take your pension away. Knowing that might make police work even a little *more* fun, I thought. It might give you just a little more push, make you a little more aggressive. I would've liked to have done police work knowing that I owned my own mortgage.

As I was cruising I picked a voice out of the radio chatter. It was the girl with the cutest and sexiest voice I ever heard. She was on frequency thirteen today, and she had her own style of communicating. She didn't just come on the horn and answer with clipped phrases and impersonal 'rogers'. Her voice would rise and fall like a song, and getting even a traffic accident call from her, which patrol policemen hate worst because they're so tedious, was somehow not quite so bad. She must've been hot for some cop in unit Four-L-Nine because her voice came in soft and husky and sent a shiver through me when she said, 'Foah-L? Ninah, rrrrrrraj-ahh!'

'Now that's the way to roger a call, I thought. I was driving nowhere at all, just touring the beat, looking at people I knew and ones I didn't know, trying not to think of all the things I'd never do out here. I was trading them for things I'd *rather* do, things any sane man would rather do, like be with Cassie and start my new career and live a civilized normal life. Funny I should think of it as *civilized*, that kind of life. That was one of the reasons I'd always wanted to go to North Africa to die.

I always figured kind of vaguely that if somebody didn't knock me off and I lasted say thirty years, I'd pull the pin then because I could never do my kind of police work past sixty. I really thought I could last that long though. I thought that if I cut down on the groceries and the drinking and the cigars, maybe I could last out here on the streets until I was sixty. Then I'd have learned almost all there was to learn here. I'd know all the secrets I always wanted to know and I'd hop a jet and go to the Valley of the Kings and look out there from a pink granite cliff and see where all civilization started, and maybe if I stayed there long enough and didn't get drunk and fall off a pyramid, or get stomped to death by a runaway camel, or ventilated by a Yankee-hating Arab, maybe if I lasted there long enough, I'd find out the last thing I wanted to know: whether *civilization* was worth the candle after all.

Then I thought of what Cruz would say if I ever got drunk enough to tell him about this. He'd say, "*Mano*, let yourself love, and give yourself away. You'll get your answer. You don't need a sphinx or a pink granite cliff.'

'Hi, Bumper,' a voice yelled, and I turned from the glare of the morning sun and saw Percy opening his pawnshop.

'Hi, Percy,' I yelled back, and slowed down to wave. He was a rare animal, an honest pawnbroker. He ran hypes and other thieves out of his shop if he ever suspected they had something hot. And he always demanded good identification from a customer pawning something. He was an honest pawnbroker, a rare animal.

I remembered the time Percy gave me his traffic ticket to take care of because this was the first one he'd ever gotten. It was for jaywalking. He didn't own a car. He hated them and took a bus to the shop every day. I just couldn't disillusion old Percy by letting him know that I couldn't fix a ticket, so I took it and paid it for him. It's practically impossible to fix a ticket any more in this town. You have to know the judge or the City Attorney. Lawyers take care of each other of course, but a cop can't fix a ticket. Anyway, I paid it, and Percy thought I fixed it and wasn't disappointed. He thought I was a hell of a big man.

Another black-and-white cruised past me going south. The cop driving, a curly-haired kid named Nelson, waved, and I nodded back. He almost rear-ended a car stopped at the red light because he was looking at some chick in hot pants going into an office building. He was a typical young cop, a thought. Thinking of pussy instead of police work. And just like all these cats, Nelson loved talking about it. I think they all love talking about it these days more than they love doing it. That gave me a royal pain in the ass. I guess I've had more than my share in my time. I've had some good stuff for an ugly guy, but by Maggie's muff, I never talked about screwing a dame, not with anybody. In my day, a guy was unmanly if he did that. But your day is over after this day, I reminded myself, and swung south on Grand.

Then I heard a Central car get a report call at one of the big downtown hotels and I knew the hotel burglar had hit again. I'd give just about anything, I thought, to catch that guy today. That'd be like quitting after your last home run, like Ted Williams. A home run your last time up. That'd be something. I cruised around for twenty minutes and then drove to the hotel and parked behind the black-and-white that got the call. I sat there in my car smoking a cigar and waited another fifteen minutes until Clarence Evans came out. He was a fifteen-year cop, a tall stringbean who I used to play handball with before my ankles got so bad.

We had some good games. It's especially fun to play when you're working nightwatch and you get up to the academy about one a.m. after you finish work, and play three hard fast games and take a steam bath. Except Evans didn't like the steam bath, being so skinny. We always took a half case of beer with us and drank it up after we showered. He was one of the first Negroes I worked with as a partner when LAPD became completely integrated several years ago. He was a good copper and he liked working with me even though he knew I always preferred working alone. On night-watch it's comforting sometimes to have someone riding shotgun or walking beside you. So I worked with him and lots of other guys even though I would've rather had a one-man beat or an 'L' car that you work alone, 'L' for lonesome. But I worked with him because I never could disappoint anyone that wanted to work with me that bad, and it made the handball playing more convenient.

Then I saw Clarence coming out of the hotel carrying his report notebook. He grinned at me, came walking light-footed over to my car, opened the door and sat down.

'What's happening, Bumper?'

'Just curious if the hotel creeper hit again, Clarence.'

'Took three rooms on the fifth floor and three on the fourth floor,' he nodded.

'The people asleep?'

'In four of them. In the other ones, they were down in the bar.'

'That means he hit before two a.m.'

'Right.'

'I can't figure this guy,' I said, popping an antacid tablet. 'Usually he works in the daytime but sometimes in the early evening. Now he's hitting during the night when they're in and when they're not in. I never heard of a hotel burglar as squirrelly as this guy.'

'Maybe that's it,' said Evans. 'A squirrel. Didn't he try to hurt a kid on one job?'

'A teddy bear. He stabbed hell out of a big teddy bear. It was all covered up with a blanket and looked like a kid sleeping.'

'That cat's a squirrel,' said Evans.

'That would explain why the other hotel burglars don't know anything,' I said, puffing on the cigar and thinking. 'I never did think he was a pro, just a lucky amateur.'

'A lucky looney,' said Evans. 'You talked to all your snitches?' He knew my M.O. from working with me. He knew I had informants, but like everyone else he didn't know how many, or that I paid the good ones.

'I talked to just about everyone I know. I talked to a hotel burglar who told me he'd already been approached by three detectives and that he'd tell us if he knew anything, because this guy is bringing so much heat on all the hotels he'd like to see us get him.'

'Well, Bumper, if anybody lucks on to the guy I'm betting you will,' said Evans, putting on his hat and getting out of the car.

'Police are baffled but an arrest is imminent,' I winked, and started the car. It was going to be a very hot day.

I was given a report call at Pershing Square, an injury report. Probably some pensioner fell off his soapbox and was trying to figure how he could say there was a crack in the sidewalk and sue the city. I ignored the call for a few minutes and let her assign it to another unit. I didn't like to do that. I always believed you should handle the calls given to you, but damn it, I only had the rest of the day and that was it, and I thought about Oliver Horn and wondered why I hadn't thought about him before. I couldn't waste time on the report call so I let the other unit handle it and headed for the barbershop on Fourth Street.

Oliver was sitting on a chair on the sidewalk in front of the shop. His ever-present broom was across his lap, and he was dozing in the sunshine.

He was the last guy in the world you would ever want to die and come back looking like. Oliver was built like a walrus with one arm cut off above the elbow. It was done maybe forty years ago by probably the worst surgeon in the world. The skin just flapped over and hung there. He had orange hair and a big white belly covered with orange hair. He long ago gave up trying to keep his pants up, and usually they barely gripped him below the gut so that his belly button was always popping out at you. His shoelaces were untied and destroyed from stepping on them because it was too hard to tie them one-handed, and he had a huge lump on his chin. It looked like if you squeezed it, it'd break a window. But Oliver was surprisingly clever. He swept out the barbershop and two or three businesses on this part of Fourth Street, including a bar called Raymond's where quite a few ex-cons hung out. It was close to the big hotels and a good place to scam on the rich tourists. Oliver didn't miss anything and had given me some very good information over the years.

'You awake, Oliver?' I asked.

He opened one blue-veined eyelid. 'Bumper, how's it wi'choo?'

'Okay, Oliver. Gonna be a hot one again today.'

'Yeah, I'm gettin' sticky. Let's go in the shop.'

'Don't have time. Listen, I was just wondering, you heard about this burglar that's been ripping us downtown here in all the big hotels for the past couple months?'

'No, ain't heard nothin'.'

'Well, this guy ain't no ordinary hotel thief. I mean he probably ain't none of the guys you ordinarily see around Raymond's, but he might be a guy that you would *sometimes* see there. What the hell, even a ding-a-ling has a drink once in a while, and Raymond's is convenient when you're getting ready to rape about ten rooms across the street.'

'He a ding-a-ling?'

'Yeah.'

'What's he look like?'

'I don't know.'

'How can I find him then, Bumper?'

'I don't know, Oliver. I'm just having hunches now. I think the guy's done burglaries before. I mean he knows how to shim doors and all that. And like I say, he's a little dingy. I think he's gonna stab somebody before too long. He carries a blade. A *long* blade, because he went clear through a mattress with it.'

'Why'd he stab a mattress?'

'He was trying to kill a teddy bear.'

'You been drinkin', Bumper?'

I smiled, and then I wondered what the hell I was doing here because I didn't know enough about the burglar to give a snitch something to work with. I was grabbing at any straw in the wind so I could hit a home run before walking off the field for the last time. Absolutely pathetic and sickening, I thought, ashamed of myself.

'Here's five bucks,' I said to Oliver. 'Get yourself a steak.'

'Jeez, Bumper,' he said, 'I ain't done nothin' for it.'

'The guy carries a long-bladed knife and he's a psycho and lately he takes these hotels at any goddamn hour of the day or night. He just might go to Raymond's for a drink sometime. He just might use the rest room while you're cleaning up and maybe he'll be tempted to look at some of the stuff in his pockets to see what he stole. Or maybe he'll be sitting at the bar and he'll pull a pretty out of his pocket that he just snatched at the hotel, or maybe one of these sharp hotel burglars that hangs out at Raymond's will know something, or say something, and you're always around there. Maybe anything.'

'Sure, Bumper, I'll call you right away I hear anything at all. Right away, Bumper. And you get any more clues you let me know, hey, Bumper?'

'Sure, Oliver, I'll get you a good one from my clues closet.'

'Hey, that's aw right,' Oliver hooted. He had no teeth in front, upper or lower. For a long time he had one upper tooth in front.

'Be seeing you, Oliver.'

'Hey, Bumper, wait a minute. You ain't told me no funny cop stories in a long time. How 'bout a story?'

'I think you heard them all.'

'Come on, Bumper.'

'Well, let's see, I told you about the seventy-five-year-old nympho I busted over on Main that night?'

'Yeah, yeah,' he hooted, 'tell me that one again. That's a good one.'

'I gotta go, Oliver, honest. But say, did I ever tell you about the time I caught the couple in the back seat up there in Elysian Park in one of those maker's acres?'

'No, tell me, Bumper.'

'Well, I shined my light in there and here's these two down on the seat, the old boy throwing the knockwurst to his girlfriend, and this young partner I'm with says, "What're you doing there?" And the guy gives the answer ninety per cent of the guys do when you catch them in that position: "Nothing, Officer."'

'Yeah, yeah,' said Oliver, his shaggy head bobbing.

'So I say to the guy, "Well, if *you* ain't doing anything, move over there and hold my flashlight and lemme see what *I* can do."'

'Whoooo, that's funny,' said Oliver. 'Whoooo, Bumper.'

He was laughing so hard he hardly saw me go, and I left him there holding his big hard belly and laughing in the sunshine.

I thought about telling Oliver to call Central Detectives instead of me, because I wouldn't be here after today, but what the hell, then I'd have to tell him *why* I wouldn't be here, and I couldn't take another person telling me why I should or should not retire. If Oliver ever called, somebody'd tell him I was gone, and the information would eventually get to the dicks. So what the hell, I thought, pulling back into the traffic and breathing exhaust fumes. It would've been really something though, to get that burglar on this last day. Really something.

I looked at my watch and thought Cassie should be at school now, so I drove to City College and parked out front. I wondered why I didn't feel guilty about Laila. I guess I figured it wasn't really my fault.

Cassie was alone in the office when I got there. I closed the door, flipped my hat on a chair, walked over, and felt that same old amazement I've felt a thousand times over how well a woman fits in your arms, and how soft they feel.

'Thought about you all night,' she said after I kissed her about a dozen times or so. 'Had a miserable evening. Couple of bores.'

'You thought about me all night, huh?'

'Honestly, I did.' She kissed me again. 'I still have this awful feeling something's going to happen.'

'Every guy that ever went into battle has that feeling.'

'Is that what our marriage is going to be, a battle?'

'If it is, you'll win, baby. I'll surrender.'

'Wait'll I get you tonight,' she whispered. 'You'll surrender all right.'

'That green dress is gorgeous.'

'But you still like hot colours better?'

'Of course.'

'After we get married I'll wear nothing but reds and oranges and yellows....'

'You ready to talk?'

'Sure, what is it?'

'Cruz gave me a talking-to – about you.'

'Oh?'

'He thinks you're the greatest thing that ever happened to me.'

'Go on,' she smiled.

'Well ...'

'Yes?'

'Damn it, I can't go on. Not in broad daylight with no drink in me....'

'What did you talk about, silly?'

'About you. No, it was more about me. About things I need and things I'm afraid of. Twenty years he's my friend and suddenly I find out he's a damned intellectual.'

'What do you need? What're you afraid of? I can't believe you've ever been afraid of anything.'

'He knows me better than you know me.'

'That makes me sad. I don't want anyone knowing you better than I do. Tell me what you talked about.'

'I don't have time right now,' I said, feeling a gas bubble forming. Then I lied and said, 'I'm on the way to a call. I just had to stop for a minute. I'll tell you all about it tonight. I'll be at your pad at seven-thirty. We're going out to dinner, okay?'

'Okay.'

'Then we'll curl up on your couch with a good bottle of wine.'

'Sounds wonderful,' she smiled, that clean, hot, female smile that made me kiss her.

'See you tonight,' I whispered.

'Tonight,' she gasped, and I realized I was crushing her. She stood in the doorway and watched me all the way down the stairs.

I got back in the car and dropped two of each kind of pill and grabbed a handful from the glove compartment and shoved them in my pants pocket for later.

As I drove back on the familiar streets of the beat I wondered why I couldn't talk to Cassie like I wanted. If you're going to marry someone you should be able to tell her almost anything about yourself that she has a right to know.

I pulled over at a phone booth then and called Cruz at the station. Lieutenant Hilliard answered and in a couple seconds I heard Cruz's soft voice, 'Sergeant Segovia?' He said it like a question.

'Hello, Sergeant Segovia, this is future former Officer Morgan, what the hell you doing besides pushing a pencil and shuffling paper?'

'What're you doing besides ignoring your radio calls?'

'I'm just cruising around this miserable beat thinking how great it'll be not to have to do it any more. You decided where you want me to take you for lunch?'

'You don't have to take me anywhere.'

'Look, goddamnit, we're going to some nice place, so if you won't pick it, I will.'

'Okay, take me to Seymour's.'

'On my beat? Oh, for chrissake. Look, you just meet me at Seymour's at eleven-thirty. Have a cup of coffee but don't eat a damn thing because we're going to a place I know in Beverly Hills.'

'That's a long way from your beat, all right.'

'I'll pick you up at Seymour's.'

732

Okay, *'mano, ahí te huacho.'*

I chuckled after I hung up at that Mexican slang, because *watching* for me is exactly what Cruz always did when you stop and think about it. Most people say, 'I'll be seeing you,' because that's what they do, but Cruz he always watched for me. It felt good to have old sad-eye watching for me.

SIXTEEN

I got back in my car and cruised down Main Street, by the parking lot at the rear of the Pink Dragon. I was so sick of pushing this pile of iron around that I stopped to watch some guys in the parking lot.

There were three of them and they were up to something. I parked the car and backed up until the building hid me. I got out and walked to the corner of the building, took my hat off, and peeked around the corner and across the lot.

A skinny hype in a long-sleeved blue shirt was talking to another brown-shirted one. There was a third one with them, a little T-shirt who stood a few steps away. Suddenly Blue-shirt nodded to Brown-shirt, who walked up and gave something to little T-shirt, who gave Brown-shirt something back, and they all hustled off in different directions. Little T-shirt was walking towards me. He was looking back over his shoulder for cops, and walking right into one. I didn't feel like messing around with a narco bust but this was too easy. I stepped in the hotel doorway and when T-shirt walked past, squinting into the sun, I reached out, grabbed him by the arm, and jerked him inside. He was just a boy, scared as hell. I shoved him face forward into the wall, and grabbed the hip pocket of his denims.

'What've you got, boy? Bennies or reds? Or maybe you're an acid freak?'

'Hey, lemme go,' he yelled.

I took the bennies out of his pocket. There were six rolls, five in a roll, held together by a rubber band. The day of ten-benny rolls was killed by inflation.

'How much did they make you pay, kid?' I asked, keeping a good grip on his arm. He didn't look so short up close, but he was skinny, with lots of brown hair, and young, too young to be downtown scoring pills in the middle of the morning.

'I paid seven dollars. But I won't ever do it again if you'll lemme go. Please lemme go.'

'Put your hands behind you, kid,' I said, unsnapping my handcuff case.

'What're you doing? Please don't put those on me. I won't hurt you or anything.'

'I'm not afraid of you hurting me,' I laughed, chewing on a wet cigar stump that I finally threw away. 'It's just that my wheels are gone and my ass is too big to be chasing you all over these streets.' I snapped on one cuff and brought his palms together behind his back and clicked on the other, taking them up snug.

'How much you say you paid for the pills?'

'Seven dollars. I won't never do it again if you'll lemme go, I swear.' He was dancing around, nervous and scared, and he stepped on my right toe, scuffing up the shine.

'Careful, damn it.'

'Oh, I'm sorry. Please lemme go. I didn't mean to step on you.'

'Those cats charged you way too much for the pills,' I said, as I led him to the radio car.

'I know you won't believe me but it's the first time I ever bought them. I don't know *what* the hell they cost.'

'Sure it is.'

'See, I knew you wouldn't believe me. You cops don't believe nobody.'

'You know all about cops, do you?'

'I been arrested before. I know you cops. You all act the same.'

'You must be a hell of a heavyweight desperado. Got a ten-page rap sheet. What've you been busted for?'

'Running away. Twice. And you don't have to put me down.'

'How old are you?'

'Fourteen.'

'In the car,' I said, opening the front door. 'And don't lean back on the cuffs or they'll tighten.'

'You don't have to worry, I won't jump out,' he said as I fastened the seat belt over his lap.

'I ain't worrying, kid.'

'I got a name. It's Tilden,' he said, his square chin jutting way out.

'Mine's Morgan.'

'My first name's Tom.'

'Mine's Bumper.'

'Where're you taking me?'

'To Juvenile Narcotics.'

'You gonna book me?'

'Of course.'

'What could I expect,' he said, nodding his head disgustedly. 'How could I ever expect a cop to act like a human being.'

'You shouldn't even expect a human being to act like a human being. You'll just get disappointed.'

I turned the key and heard the click–click of a dead battery. Stone-cold dead, without warning.

'Hang loose, kid,' I said, getting out of the car.

'Where could *I* go?' he yelled, as I lifted the hood to see if someone had
torn the wires out. That happens once in a while when you leave your
black-and-white somewhere that you can't keep an eye on it. It looked okay
though. I wondered if something was wrong with the alternator. A call
box was less than fifty feet down the sidewalk so I moseyed to it, turning
around several times to keep an eye on my little prisoner. I called in and
asked for a garage man with a set of booster cables and was told to stand by
for about twenty minutes and somebody'd get out to me. I thought about
calling a sergeant since they carry booster cables in their cars, but I decided
not to. What the hell, why be in a rush today? What was there to prove
now? To anyone? To myself?

Then I started getting a little hungry because there was a small diner
across the street and I could smell bacon and ham. The odour was blowing
through the duct in the front of the place over the cooking stoves. The
more I sniffed the hungrier I got, and I looked at my watch and thought,
what the hell. I went back and unstrapped the kid.

'What's up? Where we going?'

'Across the street.'

'What for? We taking a bus to your station or something?'

'No, we gotta wait for the garage man. We're going across the street so
I can eat.'

'You can't take me in there looking like this,' said the kid, as I led him
across the street. His naturally rosy cheeks were lobster-red now. 'Take the
handcuffs off.'

'Not a chance. I could never catch a young antelope like you.'

'I swear I won't run.'

'I know you won't, with your hands cuffed behind you and me holding
the chain.'

'I'll die if you take me in there like a dog on a leash in front of all those
people.'

'Ain't nobody in there, you know, kid. And anybody that might be
in there's been in chains himself, probably. Nothing to be embarrassed
about.'

'I could sue you for this.'

'Oh *could* you?' I said, holding the door and shoving him inside.

There were only three counter customers, two con guys, and a wino
drinking coffee. They glanced up for a second and nobody even noticed the
kid was cuffed. I pointed towards a table at the rear.

'Got no waitress this early, Bumper,' said T-Bone, the proprietor, a
huge Frenchman who wore a white chef's hat and a T-shirt, and white
pants. I'd never seen him in anything else.

'We need a table, T-Bone,' I said, pointing to the kid's handcuffs.

'Okay,' said T-Bone. 'What'll you have?'

'I'm not too hungry. Maybe a couple over-easy eggs and some bacon, and a few pieces of toast. And oh, maybe some hash browns. Glass of tomato juice. Some coffee. And whatever the kid wants.'

'What'll you have, boy?' asked T-Bone, resting his huge hairy hands on the counter and grinning at the boy, with one gold and one silver front tooth. I wondered for the first time where in the hell he got a silver crown like that. Funny I never thought of that before. T-Bone wasn't a man you talked to. He only used his voice when it was necessary. He just fed people with as few words as possible.

'How can I eat anything?' said the kid. 'All chained up like a convict or something.' His eyes were filling up and he looked awful young just then.

'I'm gonna unlock them,' I said. 'Now what the hell you want? T-Bone ain't got all day.'

'I don't know what I want.'

'Give him a couple fried eggs straight up, some bacon, and a glass of milk. You want hash browns, kid?'

'I guess so.'

'Give him some orange juice too, and an order of toast. Make it a double order of toast. And some jam.'

T-Bone nodded and scooped a handful of eggs from a bowl by the stove. He held four eggs in that big hand and cracked all four eggs at a time without using the other hand. The kid was watching it.

'He's got some talent, hey, kid?'

'Yeah. You said you were taking these off.'

'Get up and turn around,' I said, and when he did I unlocked the right cuff and fastened it around the chrome leg of the table so he could sit there with one hand free.

'Is this what you call taking them off?' he said. 'Now I'm like an organ grinder's monkey on a chain!'

'Where'd you ever see an organ grinder? There ain't been any grinders around here for years.'

'I saw them on old TV movies. And that's what I look like.'

'Okay, okay, quit chipping your teeth. You complain more than any kid I ever saw. You oughtta be glad to be getting some breakfast. I bet you didn't eat a thing at home this morning.'

'I wasn't even *at* home this morning.'

'Where'd you spend the night?'

He brushed back several locks of hair from his eyes with a dirty right hand. 'I spent part of the night sleeping in one of those all-night movies till some creepy guy woke me up with his cruddy hand on my knee. Then I got the hell outta there. I slept for a little while in a chair in some hotel that was open just down the street.'

'You run away from home?'

'No, I just didn't feel like sleeping at the pad last night. My sis wasn't home and I just didn't feel like sitting around by myself.'

'You live with your sister?'

'Yeah.'

'Where's your parents?'

'Ain't got none.'

'How old's your sister?'

'Twenty-two.'

'Just you and her, huh?'

'Naw, there's always somebody around. Right now it's a stud named Slim. Big Blue always got somebody around.'

'That's what you call your sister? Big Blue?'

'She used to be a dancer, kind of. In a bar. Topless. She went by that name. Now she's getting too fat in the ass so she's hustling drinks at the Chinese Garden over on Western. You know the joint?'

'Yeah, I know it.'

'Anyway, she always says soon as she loses thirty pounds she's going back to dancing which is a laugh because her ass is getting wider by the day. She likes to be called Big Blue so even *I* started calling her that. She got this phony dyed-black hair, see. It's almost blue.'

'She oughtta wash your clothes for you once in a while. That shirt looks like a grease rag.'

'That's 'cause I was working on a car with my next door neighbour yesterday. I didn't get a chance to change it.' He looked offended by that crack. 'I wear clothes clean as anybody. And I even wash them and iron them myself.'

'That's the best way to be,' I said, reaching over and unlocking the left cuff.

'You're taking them off?'

'Yeah. Go in the bathroom and wash your face and hands and arms. And your neck.'

'You sure I won't go out the window?'

'Ain't no window in that john,' I said. 'And comb that mop outta your face so somebody can see what the hell you look like.'

'Ain't got no comb.'

'Here's mine,' I said, giving him the pocket comb.

T-Bone handed me the glasses of juice, the coffee, and the milk while the kid was gone, and the bacon smell was all over the place now. I was wishing I'd asked for a double order of bacon even though I knew T-Bone would give me an extra big helping.

I was sipping the coffee when the kid came back in. He was looking a hundred per cent better even though his neck was still dirty. At least his hair was slicked back and his face and arms up to the elbows were nice and clean. He wasn't a handsome kid, his face was too tough and craggy, but he had fine eyes, full of life, and he looked you right in your eye when he talked to you. That's what I liked best about him.

'There's your orange juice,' I said.

'Here's your comb.'

'Keep it. I don't even know why I carry it. I can't do anything with this patch of wire I got. I'll be glad when I get bald.'

'Yeah, you couldn't look no worse if you was bald,' he said, examining my hair.

'Drink your orange juice, kid.'

We both drank our juice and T-Bone said, 'Here, Bumper,' and handed a tray across the counter, but before I could get up the kid was on his feet and grabbed the tray and laid everything out on the table like he knew what he was doing.

'Hey, you even know what side to put the knife and fork on,' I said.

'Sure. I been a busboy. I done all kinds of work in my time.'

'How old you say you are?'

'Fourteen. Well, almost fourteen. I'll be fourteen next October.'

When he'd finished he sat down and started putting away the chow like he was as hungry as I thought he was. I threw one of my eggs on his plate when I saw two weren't going to do him, and I gave him a slice of my toast. He was a first class eater. That was something else I liked about him.

While he was finishing the last of the toast and jam, I went to the door and looked across the street. A garage attendant was replacing my battery. He saw me and waved that it was okay. I waved back and went back inside to finish my coffee.

'You get enough to eat?' I asked.

'Yeah, thanks.'

'You sure you don't want another side of bacon and a loaf or two of bread?'

'I don't get breakfasts like that too often,' he grinned.

When we were getting ready to leave I tried to pay T-Bone.

'From you? No, Bumper.'

'Well, for the kid's chow, then.' I tried to make him take a few bucks.

'No, Bumper. You don't pay nothin'.'

'Thanks, T-Bone. Be seeing you,' I said, and he raised a huge hand covered with black hair, and smiled gold and silver. And I almost wanted to ask him about the silver crown because it was the last time I'd have a chance.

'You gonna put the bracelets back on?' asked the boy, as I lit a cigar and patted my stomach and took a deep sniff of morning smog.

'You promise you won't run?'

'I swear. I hate those damn things on my wrists. You feel so helpless, like a little baby.'

'Okay, let's get in the car,' I said, trotting across the street with him to get out of the way of the traffic.

'How many times you come downtown to score?' I asked before starting the car.

'I never been downtown alone before. I swear. And I didn't even hitch-hike. I took a bus. I was even gonna take a bus back to Echo Park. I didn't wanna run into cops with the pills in my pocket.'

'How long you been dropping bennies?'

'About three months. And I only tried them a couple times. A kid I know told me I could come down here and almost any guy hanging around could get them for me. I don't know why I did it.'

'How many tubes you sniff a day?'

'I ain't a gluehead. It makes guys crazy. And I never sniffed paint, neither.'

Then I started looking at this kid, really looking at him. Usually my brain records only necessary things about arrestees, but now I found myself looking really close and listening for lies. That's something else you can't tell the judge, that you'd bet your instinct against a polygraph. I *knew* this boy wasn't lying. But then, I seemed to be wrong about everything lately.

'I'm gonna book you and release you to your sister. That okay with you?'

'You ain't gonna send me to Juvenile Hall?'

'No. You wanna go there?'

'Christ, no. I gotta be free. I was scared you was gonna lock me up. Thanks. Thanks a lot. I just gotta be free. I couldn't stand being inside a place like that with everybody telling you what to do.'

'If I ever see you downtown scoring pills again, I'll make sure you go to the Hall.'

The kid took a deep breath. 'You'll never see me again, I swear. Unless you come out around Echo Park.'

'As a matter of fact, I don't live too far from there.'

'Yeah? I got customers in Silverlake and all around Echo Park. Where do you live?'

'Not far from Bobby's drive-in. You know where that is? All the kids hang around there.'

'Sure I do. I work with this old guy who's got this pickup truck and equipment. Why don't you let us do your yard? We do front and back, rake, trim, weed and everything for eight bucks.'

'That's not too bad. How much you get yourself?'

'Four bucks. I do all the work. The old guy just flops in the shade some-where till I'm through. But I need him because of the truck and stuff.'

This kid had me so interested I suddenly realized we were just sitting there. I put the cigar in my teeth and turned the key. She fired right up and I pulled out in the traffic. But I couldn't get my mind off this boy.

'Whadda you do for fun? You play ball or anything?'

'No, I like swimming. I'm the best swimmer in my class, but I don't go out for the team.'

'Why not?'

'I'm too busy with girls. Look.' The boy took out his wallet and showed me his pictures. I glanced at them while turning on Pico, three shiny little faces that all looked the same to me.

'Pretty nice,' I said, handing the pictures back.

'*Real* nice,' said the kid with a wink.

'You look pretty athletic. Why don't you play baseball? That used to be my game.'

'I like sports I can do by myself.'

'Don't you have any buddies?'

'No, I'm more of a ladies' man.'

'I know what you mean, but you can't go through this world by yourself. You should have some friends.'

'I don't need nobody.'

'What grade you in?'

'Eighth. I'll sure be glad to get the hell out of junior high. It's a ghoul school.'

'How you gonna pass if you cut classes like this?'

'I don't ditch too often, and I'm pretty smart in school, believe it or not. I just felt rotten last night. Sometimes when you're alone a lot you get feeling rotten and you just wanna go out where there's some people. I figured, where am I gonna find lots of people? Downtown, right? So I came downtown. Then this morning I felt more rotten from sleeping in the creepy movie so I looked around and saw these two guys and asked them where I would get some bennies and they sold them to me. I really wanted to get high, but swear to God, I only dropped bennies a couple times before. And one lousy time I dropped a red devil and a rainbow with some guys at school, and that's all the dope I ever took. I don't really dig it, Officer. Sometimes I drink a little beer.'

'I'm a beer man myself, and you can call me Bumper.'

'Listen, Bumper, I meant it about doing your yard work. I'm a hell of a good worker. The old man ain't no good, but I just stick him away in a corner somewheres and you should see me go. You won't be sorry if you hire us.'

'Well, I don't really have a yard myself. I live in this apartment building, but I kind of assist the manager and he's always letting the damn place go to hell. It's mostly planted in ivy and ice plant and junipers that he lets get pretty seedy-looking. Not too much lawn except little squares of grass in front of the downstairs apartments.'

'You should see me pull weeds, Bumper. I'd have that ice plant looking alive and green in no time. And I know how to take care of junipers. You gotta trim them a little, kind of shape them. I can make a juniper look soft and trim as a virgin's puss. How about getting us the account? I could maybe give you a couple bucks kickback.'

'Maybe I'll do that.'

'Sure. When we get to the police station, I'll write out the old man's name and phone number for you. You just call him when you want us to come. One of these days I'm getting some business cards printed up. It impresses hell out of people when you drop a business card on them. I figure we'll double our business with a little advertising and some business cards.'

'I wouldn't be surprised.'

'This the place?' The kid looked up at the old brown brick station. I parked in the back.

'This is the place,' I said. 'Pretty damned dreary, huh?'

'It gives me the creepies.'

'The office is upstairs,' I said, leading him up and inside, where I found one of the Juvenile Narcotics officers eating lunch.

'Hi, Bumper,' he said.

'What's happening, man,' I answered, not able to think of his name. 'Got a kid with some bennies. No big thing. I'll book him and pencil out a quick arrest report.'

'Worthwhile for me talking to him?'

'Naw, just a little score. First time, he claims. I'll take care of it. When should I cite him back in?'

'Make it Tuesday. We're pretty well up to the ass in cite-ins.'

'Okay,' I said, and nodded to another plain-clothes officer who came in and started talking to the first one.

'Stay put, kid,' I said to the boy and went to the head. After I came out, I went to the soft drink machine and got myself a Coke and one for the boy. When I came back in he was looking at me kind of funny.

'Here's a Coke,' I said, and we went in another office which was empty. I got a booking form and an arrest report and got ready to start writing.

He was still looking at me with a little smile on his face.

'What's wrong?' I said.

'Nothing.'

'What're you grinning at?'

'Oh, was I grinning? I was just thinking about what those two cops out there said when you went to the john.'

'What'd they say?'

'Oh, how you was some kind of cop.'

'Yeah,' I mumbled as I put my initial on a couple of the bennies so I could recognize them if the case went to court. I knew it wouldn't though. I was going to request that the investigator just counsel and release him.

'You and your sister're gonna have to come in Tuesday morning and talk to an investigator.'

'What for?'

'So he can decide if he ought to C-and-R you, or send you to court.'

'What's C and R? Crush and rupture?'

'Hey, that's pretty good,' I chuckled. He was a spunky little bastard. I was starting to feel kind of proud of him. 'C and R means counsel and release. They almost always counsel and release a kid the first time he's busted instead of sending him to juvenile court.'

'I told you I been busted twice for running away. This ain't my first fall.'

'Don't worry about it. They're not gonna send you to court.'

'How do you know?'

'They'll do what I ask.'

'Those juvies said you was really some kind of cop. No wonder I got nailed so fast.'

'You were no challenge,' I said, putting the bennies in an evidence envelope and sealing it.

'I guess not. Don't forget to lemme give you the old guy's name and phone number for the yard work. Who you live with? Wife and kids?'

'I live alone.'

'Yeah?'

'Yeah.'

'I might be able to give you a special price on the yard-work. You know, you being a cop and all.'

'Thanks, but you should charge your full price, son.'

'You said baseball was your game, Bumper?'

'Yeah, that's right.' I stopped writing for a minute because the boy seemed excited and was talking so much.

'You like the Dodgers?'

'Yeah, sure.'

'I always wanted to learn about baseball. Maury Wills is a Dodger, ain't he?'

'Yeah.'

'I'd like to go to a Dodger game sometime and see Maury Wills.'

'You never been to a big league game?'

'Never been. Know what? There's this guy down the street. Old fat fart, maybe even older than you, and fatter even. He takes his kid to the school yard across the street all day Saturday and Sunday and hits fly balls to him. They go to a game practically every week during baseball season.'

'Yeah?'

'Yeah, and know what the best part of it is?'

'What?'

'All that exercise is really good for the old man. That kid's doing him a favour by playing ball with him.'

'I better call your sister,' I said, suddenly getting a gas bubble and a burning pain at the same time. I was also getting a little light-headed from the heat and because there were ideas trying to break through the front of my skull, but I thought it was better to leave them lay right now. The boy gave me the number and I dialled it.

743

'No answer, kid,' I said, hanging up the phone.

'Christ, you gotta put me in Juvenile Hall if you don't find her?'

'Yeah, I do.'

'You can't just drop me at the pad?'

'I can't.'

'Damn. Call Ruby's Playhouse on Normandie. That joint opens early and Slim likes to hang out there sometimes. Damn, not the Hall!'

I got Ruby's Playhouse on the phone and asked for Sarah Tilden, which he said was her name.

'Big Blue,' said the boy. 'Ask for Big Blue.'

'I wanna talk to Big Blue,' I said, and then the bartender knew who I was talking about.

A slurred young voice said, 'Yeah, who's this?'

'This is Officer Morgan, Los Angeles Police, Miss Tilden. I've arrested your brother downtown for possession of dangerous drugs. He had some pills on him. I'd like you to drive down to thirteen-thirty Georgia Street and pick him up. That's just south of Pico Boulevard and west of Figueroa.' After I finished there was a silence on the line for a minute and then she said, 'Well, that does it. Tell the little son of a bitch to get himself a lawyer. I'm through.'

I let her go on with the griping a little longer and then I said, 'Look, Miss Tilden, you'll have to come pick him up and then you'll have to come back here Tuesday morning and talk to an investigator. Maybe they can give you some advice.'

'What happens if I don't pick him up?' she said.

'I'd have to put him in Juvenile Hall and I don't think you'd want that. I don't think it would be good for him.'

'Look, Officer,' she said. 'I wanna do what's right. But maybe you people could help me somehow. I'm a young woman, too goddamn young to be saddled with a kid his age. I can't raise a kid. It's too hard for me. I got a lousy job. Nobody should expect me to raise a kid brother. I been turned down for welfare, even, how do you like that? If I was some nigger they'd gimme all the goddamn welfare I wanted. Look, maybe it would be best if you *did* put him in Juvenile Hall. Maybe it would be best for him. It's *him* I'm thinking of, you see. Or maybe you could put him in one of those foster homes. Not like a criminal, but someplace where somebody with lots of time can watch over him and see that he goes to school.'

'Lady, I'm just the arresting officer and my job is to get him home right now. You can talk about all this crap to the juvenile investigator Tuesday morning, but I want you down here in fifteen minutes to take him home. You understand me?'

'Okay, okay, I understand you,' she said. 'Is it all right if I send a family friend?'

'Who is it?'

'It's Tommy's uncle. His name's Jake Pauley. He'll bring Tommy home.'

'I guess it'll be okay.'

After I hung up, the kid was looking at me with a lopsided smile. 'How'd you like Big Blue?'

'Fine,' I said, filling in the boxes on the arrest report. I was sorry I had called her in front of the kid, but I wasn't expecting all that bitching about coming to get him.

'She don't *want* me, does she?'

'She's sending your uncle to pick you up.'

'I ain't got no uncle.'

'Somebody named Jake Pauley.'

'Hah! Old Jake baby? Hah! He's some uncle.'

'Who's he? One of her friends?'

'They're friendly all right. She was shacked up with him before he moved in with Slim. I guess she's going back to Jake. Jesus, Slim'll cut Jake wide, deep, and often.'

'You move around a lot, do you?'

'*Do* we? I been in seven different schools. Seven! But, I guess it's the same old story. You probably hear it all the time.'

'Yeah, I hear it all the time.'

I tried to get going on the report again and he let me write for a while but before I could finish he said, 'Yeah, I been meaning to go to a Dodger game. I'd be willing to pay the way if I could get somebody with a little baseball savvy to go with me.'

Now in addition to the gas and the indigestion, I had a headache, and I sat back with the booking slip finished and looked at him and let the thoughts come to the front of my skull, and of course it was clear as water that the gods conspire against men, because here was this boy. On my last day. Two days after Cassie brought up the thing that's caused me a dozen indigestion attacks. And for a minute I was excited as hell and had to stand up and pace across the room and look out the window.

Here it is, I thought. Here's the thing that puts it all away for good. I fought an impulse to call Cassie and tell her about him, and another impulse to call his sister back and tell her not to bother sending Jake baby, and then I felt dizzy on top of the headache. I looked down at my shield and without willing it I reached down and touched it and my sweaty finger left a mark on the brass part which this morning had been polished to the lustre of gold. The finger mark turned a tarnished orange before my eyes, and I thought about trading my gold and silver shield for a little tinny retirement badge that you can show to old men in bars to prove what you used to be, and which could never be polished to a lustre that would reflect sunlight like a mirror.

Then the excitement I'd felt for a moment began to fade and was replaced with a kind of fear that grew and almost smothered me until I got hold of myself. This was too much. This was all *much* too much. Cassie was one terrible responsibility, but I needed her. Cruz told me. Socorro told me. The elevator boy in the death room of the hotel told me. The old blubbering drunks in Harry's bar told me. I needed her. Yes, maybe, but I didn't need this other kind of responsibility. I didn't need *this* kind of cross. Not me. I walked into the other room where the juvenile officer was sitting.

'Listen, pal,' I said. 'This kid in here is waiting for his uncle. I explained the arrest to his sister and cited her back. I gotta meet a guy downtown and I'm late. How about taking care of him for me and I'll finish my reports later.'

'Sure, Bumper. I'll take care of it,' he said, and I wondered how calm I looked.

'Okay, kid, be seeing you,' I said, passing through the room where the boy sat. 'Hang in there, now.'

'Where you going, Bumper?'

'Gotta hit the streets, kid,' I said, trying to grin. 'There's crime to crush.'

'Yeah? Here's the phone number. I wrote it down on a piece of paper for you. Don't forget to call us.'

'Yeah, well, I was thinking, my landlord is a cheap bastard. I don't think he'd ever go for eight bucks. I think you'd be better off not doing his place anyway. He probably wouldn't pay you on time or anything.'

'That's okay. Give me your address, we'll come by and give you a special price. Remember, I can kick back a couple bucks.'

'No, it wouldn't work out. See you around, huh?'

'How 'bout us getting together for a ball game, Bumper? I'll buy us a couple of box seats.'

'I don't think so. I'm kind of giving up on the Dodgers.'

'Wait a minute,' he said, jumping to his feet. 'We'll do your gardening for four dollars, Bumper. Imagine that! Four dollars! We'll work maybe three hours. You can't beat that.'

'Sorry, kid,' I said, scuttling for the door like a fat crab.

'Why did you ever mention it then? Why did you ever say "maybe"?'

I can't help you, boy, I thought. I don't have what you need.

'Goddamn you!' he yelled after me, and his voice broke. 'You're just a cop! Nothing but a goddamn cop!'

I got back in the car feeling like someone kicked me in the belly and I headed back downtown. I looked at my watch and groaned, wondering when this day would end.

At the corner of Pico and Figueroa I saw a blind man with a red-tipped cane getting ready to board a bus. Some do-gooder in a mod suit was grabbing the blind man's elbow and aiming him, and finally the blind man said something to the meddler and made his own way.

'That's telling him, Blinky,' I said under my breath. 'You got to do for yourself in this world or they'll beat you down. The gods are strong, lonesome bastards and *you* got to be too.'

SEVENTEEN

At eleven-fifteen I was parking in front of Seymour's to meet Cruz. His car was there but I looked in the window and he wasn't at the counter. I wondered where he could be. Then I looked down the block and saw three black-and-whites, two detective cars, and an ambulance.

Being off the air with the kid I hadn't heard a call come out, and I walked down there and made my way through a crowd of people that was forming on the sidewalk around the drugstore. Just like everybody else, I was curious.

'What's happening, Clarence?' I said to Evans, who was standing in front of the door.

'Didn't you hear, Bumper?' said Evans, and he was sweating and looked sick, his coffee-brown face working nervously every-which way, and he kept looking around everywhere but at me.

'Hear what?'

'There was a holdup. A cop walked in and got shot,' said a humpbacked shine man in a sailor's hat, looking up at me with an idiotic smile.

My heart dropped and I felt the sick feeling all policemen get when you hear that another policeman was shot.

'Who?' I asked, worrying that it might've been that young bookworm, Wilson.

'It was a sergeant,' said the hunchback.

I looked towards Seymour's then and I felt the blood rush to my head.

'Let me in there, Clarence,' I said.

'Now, Bumper. No one's allowed in there and you can't do any-thing. ...'

I shoved Evans aside and pushed on the swinging aluminium doors which were bolted.

'Bumper, please,' said Evans, but I pulled away from him and slammed my foot against the centre of the two doors, driving the bolt out of the aluminium casing.

The doors flew open with a crash and I was inside and running through the checkstand towards the rear of the big drugstore. It seemed like the store was a mile long and I ran blind and lightheaded, knocking a dozen

748

hair spray cans off a shelf when I barrelled around a row of display counters towards the popping flashbulbs and the dozen plain-clothesmen who were huddled in groups at the back of the store.

The only uniformed officer was Lieutenant Hilliard and it seemed like I ran for fifteen minutes to cover the eighty feet to the pharmacy counter where Cruz Segovia lay dead.

'What the hell ...' said a red-faced detective I could barely see through a watery mist as I knelt beside Cruz, who looked like a very young boy sprawled there on his back, his hat and gun on the floor beside him and a frothy blood puddle like a scarlet halo fanning out around him from a through-and-through head shot. There was one red glistening bullet hole to the left of his nose and one in his chest which was surrounded by wine-purple bloodstains on the blue uniform. His eyes were open and he was looking right at me. The corneas were not yet dull or cloudy and the eyes were turned down at the corners, those large eyes more serious and sad than ever I'd seen them, and I knelt beside him in his blood and whispered, *''Mano! 'Mano! 'Mano!* Oh, Cruz!'

'Bumper, get the hell out of there,' said the bald detective grabbing my arm, and I looked up at him, seeing a very familiar face, but still I couldn't recognize him.

'Let him go, Leecher. We got enough pictures,' said another plain-clothesman, older, who was talking to Lieutenant Hilliard. He was one I should know too, I thought. It was so strange. I couldn't remember any of their names, except my lieutenant, who was in uniform.

Cruz looked at me so serious I couldn't bear it. And I reached in his pocket for the little leather pouch with the beads.

'You mustn't take anything from him,' Lieutenant Hilliard said in my ear with his hand on my shoulder. 'Only the coroner can do that, Bumper.'

'His beads,' I muttered. 'He won them because he was the only one who could spell English words. I don't want them to know he carried beads like a nun.'

'Okay, Bumper, okay,' said Lieutenant Hilliard, patting my shoulder, and I took the pouch. Then I saw the box of cheap cigars spilled on the floor by his hand. And there was a ten-dollar bill on the floor.

'Give me that blanket,' I said to a young ambulance attendant who was standing there beside his stretcher, white in the face, smoking a cigarette.

He looked at me and then at the detectives.

'Give me that goddamn blanket,' I said, and he handed the folded-up blanket to me, which I covered Cruz with after I closed his eyes so he couldn't look at me like that. '*Ahí te huacho,*' I whispered. 'I'll be watching for you, *'mano.*' Then I was on my feet and heading towards the door, gulping for breath.

'Bumper,' Lieutenant Hilliard called, running painfully on his bad right leg and holding his hip.

I stopped before I got to the door.

'Will you go tell his wife?'

'He came in here to buy me a going-away present,' I said, feeling a suffocating pressure in my chest.

'You were his best friend. You should tell her.'

'He wanted to buy me a box of cigars,' I said, grabbing him by the bony shoulder. 'Damn him, I'd never smoke those cheap cigars. Damn him!'

'All right, Bumper. Go to the station. Don't try to work any more today. You go on home. We'll take care of the notification. You take care of yourself.'

I nodded and hurried out the door, looking at Clarence Evans but not understanding what he said to me. I got in the car and drove up Main Street, tearing my collar open to breathe, and thought about Cruz lying frail and naked and unprotected there in the morgue and thinking how they'd desecrate him, how they'd stick that turkey skewer in him for the liver temperature, and how they'd put a metal rod in the hole in his face for the bullet angle and I was so damned glad I'd closed his eyes so he wouldn't be watching all that.

'You see, Cruz,' I said, driving over Fourth Street with no idea where I was going. 'You see? You almost had me convinced, but you were all wrong. I was right.'

'You shouldn't be afraid to love, *'mano*,' Cruz answered, and I slammed on my brakes when I heard him and I almost slid through the red light. Someone leaned on his horn and yelled at me.

'You're safe, Bumper, in one way,' said Cruz in his gentle voice, 'but in the way that counts, you're in danger. Your soul is in danger if you don't love.'

I started when the light was green but I could hardly see.

'Did you believe that when Esteban was killed? Did you?'

'Yes, I knew it was the God's truth,' he said, and his sad eyes turned down at the corners and this time I *did* blow a red light and I heard tyres squeal and I turned right going the wrong way on Main Street and everyone was honking horns at me but I kept going to the next block and then turned left with the flow of traffic.

'Don't look at me with those goddamn turned-down eyes!' I yelled, my heart thudding like the pigeon's wing. 'You're wrong, you foolish little man. Look at Socorro. Look at your children. Don't you see now, you're wrong? Damn those eyes!'

Then I pulled into an alley west of Broadway and got out of the car because I suddenly couldn't see at all now and I began to vomit. I threw it all up, all of it. Someone in a delivery truck stopped and said something but I waved him off and heaved and heaved it all away.

Then I got back in the car and the shock was wearing off. I drove to a pay phone and called Cassie before she left her office. I crowded in that phone booth doubled over by stomach cramps and I don't really know everything I said to her except that Cruz was dead and I wouldn't be going with her. Not now, not ever. And then there was lots of crying on the other end of the line and talking back and forth that didn't make any sense, and finally I heard myself say, 'Yes, yes, Cassie. You go on. Yes, maybe I'll feel different later. Yes. Yes. Yes. Yes. You go on. Maybe I'll see you there in San Francisco. Maybe someday I'll feel different. Yes.'

I was back in my car driving, and I knew I'd have to go to Socorro tonight and help her. I wanted to bury Cruz as soon as possible and I hoped she would want to. And now, gradually at first, and then more quickly, I felt as though a tremendous weight was lifted from my shoulders and there was no sense analysing it, but there it was. I felt somehow light and free like when I first started on my beat. 'There's nothing left now but the *puta*. But she's not a *puta*, *'mano*, she's not!' I said, lying to both of us for the last time. 'You couldn't tell a whore from a bewitching lady. I'll keep her as long as I can, Cruz, and when I can't keep her any more she'll go to somebody that can. You can blame her for that. That's the way the world is made.' And Cruz didn't answer my lie and I didn't see his eyes. He was gone. He was like Herky now, nothing more.

I began thinking of all the wandering people: Indians, Gypsies, Armenians, the Bedouin on that cliff where I'd never go, and now I knew the Bedouin saw nothing more than sand out there in that valley.

And as I thought these things I turned to my left and I was staring into the mouth of the Pink Dragon. I passed the Dragon by and drove on towards the station, but the further I drove, the more the anger welled up in me, and the anger mixed with the freedom I felt, so that for a while I felt like the most vigorous and powerful man on earth, a real *macho*, Cruz would've said. I turned around and headed back to the Dragon. This was the day for the Dragon to die, I thought. I could make Marvin fight me, and the others would help him. But no one could stand up to me and at last I'd destroy the Dragon.

Then I glanced down at my shield and saw that the smog had made the badge hideous. It was tarnished, and smeared with a drop of Cruz's blood. I stopped in front of Rollo's and went inside.

'Give it a fast buff, Rollo. I'm in a hurry.'

'You know there ain't a single blemish on this badge,' Rollo sighed.

'Just shine the goddamn badge.'

He glanced up with his faded eyes, then at my trousers, at my wet bloody knees, and he bent silently over the wheel.

'There you are, Bumper,' he said when he finished it.

I held the badge by the pin and hurried outside.

'Be careful, Bumper,' he called. 'Please be careful.'

Passing by Rollo's front store I saw the distorted reflection in the folds of the plastic sun covering. I watched the reflection and had to laugh at the grotesque fat policeman who held the four-inch glittering shield in front of him as he lumbered to his car. The dark blue uniform was dripping sweat and the fat policeman opened the burning white door and squeezed his big stomach behind the wheel.

He settled in his saddle seat and jammed the nightstick under the seat cushion next to him, pointed forward.

Then he fastened his shield to his chest and urged the machine westward. The sun reflecting off the hood blinded him for a moment, but he flipped down the visor and drove west to the Pink Dragon.

'Now I'll kill the Dragon and drink its blood,' said the comic blue policeman. 'In the *front* door, down the Dragon's throat.'

I laughed out loud at him because he was good for no more than this. He was disgusting and pathetic and he couldn't help himself. He needed no one. He sickened me. He only needed glory.